Kâlidâsa, Monier Williams

Sakuntala

A Sanskrit Drama, in seven Acts. Second Edition

Kâlidâsa, Monier Williams

Sakuntala
A Sanskrit Drama, in seven Acts. Second Edition

ISBN/EAN: 9783337186791

Printed in Europe, USA, Canada, Australia, Japan

Cover: Foto ©Andreas Hilbeck / pixelio.de

More available books at **www.hansebooks.com**

SAKUNTALĀ.

MONIER WILLIAMS.

London

HENRY FROWDE

OXFORD UNIVERSITY PRESS WAREHOUSE

7 PATERNOSTER ROW

॥ श्रीकालिदासविरचितमभिज्ञानशकुन्तलं नाम नाटकम् ॥

ŚAKUNTALĀ

A SANSKṚIT DRAMA, IN SEVEN ACTS,

BY

KĀLIDĀSA.

THE DEVA-NĀGARĪ RECENSION OF THE TEXT,

EDITED WITH LITERAL ENGLISH TRANSLATIONS OF ALL THE METRICAL
PASSAGES, SCHEMES OF THE METRES, AND

NOTES, CRITICAL AND EXPLANATORY,

BY

MONIER WILLIAMS, M.A., D.C.L.,

Hon. Doctor in Law of the University of Calcutta;
Hon. Member of the Bombay Asiatic Society;
Member of the Royal Asiatic Society of Great Britain and Ireland, and of the Oriental Society of Germany;
Boden Professor of Sanskṛit in the University of Oxford.

SECOND EDITION.

Oxford:
AT THE CLARENDON PRESS.
M.DCCC.LXXVI.

PREFACE.

THE following pages are the result of an endeavour to furnish English students of Sanskrit with a correct edition of the most celebrated drama of India's greatest dramatist. About a century has elapsed since Sir W. Jones discovered that there existed in India a number of Nâṭakas or Sanskrit dramas, many of them of great antiquity; some abounding in poetry of undoubted merit, and all of them containing valuable pictures of Hindū life and manners. Eager to apply the means thus gained of filling what was before an empty niche in the Temple of Sanskrit Literature, Sir W. Jones addressed himself at once to translate into English the Śakuntalā, which he was told was the most admired of all the extant plays.

This work is by the illustrious Kālidāsa, who is supposed by some native authorities (though on insufficient grounds) to have lived in Ujjayinī, the capital of king Vikramāditya, whose reign is the starting-point of the Hindū era called Saṃvat, beginning 57 years B.C. Kālidāsa is described as one of the 'nine gems' of that monarch's splendid court. It seems, however, more probable that Kālidāsa flourished in the third century of the Christian era (see p. 474 of *Indian Wisdom,* published by W. H. Allen & Co., 13, Waterloo Place, London). The Śakuntalā is acknowledged on all hands to be the masterpiece of the great Indian poet. Indeed, no composition of Kālidāsa displays more the richness and fertility of his poetical genius, the exuberance of his imagination, the warmth and play of his fancy, his profound knowledge of the human heart, his delicate appreciation of its most refined and tender emotions, his familiarity with the workings and counter-workings of its conflicting feelings,—in short, more entitles him to rank as 'the Shakespeare of India.' On the Continent such men as Goethe,

Schlegel, and Humboldt have all expressed their admiration of the
Hindū poet's greatest work.   Goethe's four well-known lines,
written in 1792, are—

> 'Willst du die Blüthe des frühen, die Früchte des späteren Jahres,
> Willst du was reizt und entzückt, willst du was sättigt und nährt,
> Willst du den Himmel, die Erde, mit einem Namen begreifen:
> Nenn' ich Sakontalá dich, und so ist Alles gesagt[1].'

Unfortunately the Paṇḍits omitted to inform Sir W. Jones that
the multiplication of manuscripts of this play, consequent upon
its popularity, had led to a perplexing result,—not, however,
unexampled, as has since been proved by what has happened to
the Rāmāyaṇa,—namely, that the numerous manuscripts separated
themselves into two classes: the one, embracing all those in Deva-
nāgarī writing, which, without being uniform, had still a community
of character; the other, all those in Bengālī.

These two classes of MSS. are usually distinguished by the
names 'Deva-nāgarī recension' and 'Bengālī recension,' which
terms may conveniently be adopted.   The Deva-nāgarī recension

---

[1] Thus translated by Mr. E. B. Eastwick :—

> 'Wouldst thou the young year's blossoms and the fruits of its decline,
> And all by which the soul is charmed, enraptured, feasted, fed,
> Wouldst thou the earth, and heaven itself in one sole name combine?
> I name thee, O Śakuntalā! and all at once is said.'

Augustus William von Schlegel, in his first Lecture on Dramatic Literature, says:
'Among the Indians, the people from whom perhaps all the cultivation of the human
race has been derived, plays were known long before they could have experienced any
foreign influence.   It has lately been made known in Europe that they have a rich
dramatic literature, which ascends back for more than two thousand years.   The only
specimen of their plays (Nāṭaka) hitherto known to us is the delightful Śakontalá,
which, notwithstanding the colouring of a foreign climate, bears in its general structure
a striking resemblance to our romantic drama.'

Alexander von Humboldt, in treating of Indian poetry, observes: 'The name of
Kālidāsa has been frequently and early celebrated among the western nations.   This
great poet flourished at the splendid court of Vikramāditya, and was, therefore,
contemporary with Virgil and Horace.   The English and German translations of the
Śakuntalā have excited the feeling of admiration which has been so amply bestowed
upon Kālidāsa.   Tenderness in the expression of feelings, and richness of creative
fancy, have assigned to him his lofty place among the poets of all nations.'   In another
place he says: 'Kālidāsa is a masterly describer of the influence which Nature
exercises upon the minds of lovers.   The scene in the forest, which he introduced in
the drama of Vikrama and Urvaśī, is one of the most beautiful and poetical produc-
tions which has appeared in any time.'

is thought by most scholars to be the older and purer. Many of the readings of the Bengālī, however, have been defended by Dr. R. Pischel and others; and this recension has been followed by the Sāhitya-darpaṇa, one MS. of which bears the date 1504 of our era. The MSS. of the Deva-nāgarī class are chiefly found in the Upper Provinces of India, where the great demand has produced copyists without scholarship, who have faithfully transcribed what they did not understand, and, therefore, could not designedly alter. On the other hand, the copyists in Bengal have been Paṇḍits whose *cacoëthes* for amplifying and interpolating has led to much repetition and amplification. Many examples might here be adduced; but I will only refer to the third Act of the Bengālī recension, where the love-scene between the King and Śakuntalā has been expanded to four or five times the length it occupies in the MSS. of the Deva-nāgarī recension. Even the names of the dramatis personæ have been altered: Dushyanta is changed into Dushmanta; Anasūyā into Anusūyā; Vātāyana into Pārvatāyana; Sānumatī into Miśrakeśī; Taralikā into Pingalikā; Dhanamitra into Dhanavṛiddhi; Mārkaṇḍeya into San-koćana.

Unhappily it was a MS. of this recension, and not a very good specimen of its class, that Sir W. Jones used for his translation. From him, therefore, was gained, about a century ago, the earliest incorrect knowledge of this, the first Sanskṛit play known to Europeans. No edition of the text appeared till about forty years afterwards, when one was produced in 1830, after immense labour, at Paris, by M. Chézy. He deserved great credit for the difficulties he surmounted; but his edition was also from a MS. of the Bengālī recension. It abounded also in typographical and other more serious errors. An edition of the Śakuntalā was subsequently printed in Calcutta, also from Bengālī MSS. and in Bengālī character, by Prema-ćandra, dated Śāka 1761 (A.D. 1839). Several editions of the Bengālī recension have been printed at Calcutta in the Deva-nāgarī character; one in 1860 by Prema-ćandra (under the superintendence of Professor E. B. Cowell), for European scholars; others in 1864 and 1870.

It was reserved for Dr. Boehtlingk to be the first to edit the Deva-nāgarī recension of this play at Bonn in the year 1842. No other edition of the text of this recension was published until my first edition in 1853. An edition of the same recension was published at Bombay in 1861, and one at Breslau in 1872 by

Dr. Burkhard, Professor in the University of Bonn, to which is added a glossary.

The translations which have been published since that of Sir W. Jones and the German version of his translation by Forster, in 1791, are—first, the French of M. Chézy; subsequently the German of Hirzel, Rückert, and Boehtlingk; a Danish translation by Hammerich; and more recently, another German translation in prose and verse by Meier; not to speak of Danish and Italian versions of Sir W. Jones' English; and my own English translation, the fourth edition of which was published (by W. H. Allen & Co., 13, Waterloo Place, London) in 1872.

The great Indian dramatist only wrote two other dramas. Of the Vikramorvaśi, the twin play of the Śakuntalā, two editions have appeared on the Continent; one at Bonn, by Lenz, and a more perfect one at St. Petersburg, by Bollensen: an edition of this play was also printed at the Education press in Calcutta in 1830, and one by myself in 1849, and another at Calcutta in 1869. Translations by Hoefer and Hirzel have been published in Germany, and in England by Wilson in prose and verse, and a literal translation in English prose by Professor Cowell. The third play, called Mālavikāgnimitra, was edited at Bonn, by Tullberg; and a more correct edition, with English notes, by Shankar P. Paṇḍit, was published at Bombay in 1869. This drama has been ably translated into German by Professor Weber.

I am bound to acknowledge that I made free use of Dr. Boehtlingk's edition of the text of the Śakuntalā in preparing the first edition for the press. The merit of his work can hardly be overrated; but I may, without presumption, say that I discovered many better readings, corrected a few errors, and introduced much original matter in the shape of annotations. It is no disparagement of Dr. Boehtlingk's labours to say that his edition does not adapt itself to the exigencies of an English student. The notes are in German; they are printed at the end of the volume— a practical obstacle to their utility; and they frequently contain corrections of the text. My experience has led me to prefer a system of synopsis, both in respect of the notes and metres.

In regard to the text of the present volume, if I have succeeded in producing a more correct edition of the Deva-nāgarī recension, than those of Dr. Boehtlingk and Dr. Burkhard, the merit is due to the more ample materials which have been placed at my command. In preparing the first edition I took care to avail myself of Dr. Boehtlingk's corrections of himself, and his after-thoughts at the end of his work, as well as of such critical remarks as coincided with my own views. Often working independently of him, I arrived at similar results, because I had access to all the materials whence his *Apparatus Criticus* was composed. Dr. Boehtlingk's edition was not prepared (as he has himself explained) from original MSS. Professors Brockhaus and Westergaard, having more or less carefully collated certain MSS. in the East India House Library and in the Bodleian at Oxford, and made partial extracts from three native Commentaries, handed over the results of their labours to him. All these MSS. and Commentaries were placed at my disposal, and most of them left in my possession until the completion of my work. Not a passage was printed without a careful collation of all of them, and the three Commentaries were consulted from beginning to end.

The MSS. which I principally used, were—

1. A MS. from the Colebrooke Collection, and therefore from the Eastern side of India, numbered 1718.

2. A MS. from the Mackenzie Collection, and therefore from Southern India, numbered 2696.

3. A MS. from the Taylor Collection, and therefore from Western India, numbered 1858, dated Śāka 1734.

All these belong to the India Office Library, and represent the three Indian Presidencies respectively.

4. A copy of a very good MS. at Bombay, presented to me by Mr. Shaw of the Bombay Civil Service.

5. An old Bengālī MS. belonging to the India Office Library, numbered 1060.

6. A very old Bengālī MS. from the Wilson Collection in the Bodleian.

I consulted other Bengālī MSS., but rarely admitted readings from them, unless supported by some one of the Deva-nāgarī. Thus the verses which I inserted at the beginning of the third Act are supported throughout by my own and the Taylor MS., and partially by that of the Mackenzie Collection.

The following are the three Indian Commentators—

1. Kāṭavema, whose commentary, from the Mackenzie Collection at the India Office, is the only one in the Nāgarī character. He was the son of Kāṭa Bhūpa, minister of Vasanta (himself the author

of a dramatic work called Vasanta-rājīya), king of Kumāra-giri,
a place on the frontiers of the Nizām's dominions. He must
have lived after the commencement of the sixteenth century,
as he quotes Halāyudha, the author of the Kavi-rahasya (see
Westergaard's preface to the Radices Linguæ Sanskritæ). This
commentary is very corrupt, but where it is intelligible, is of
great use in throwing light on the more difficult passages of this
play.

2. Śan-kara, whose commentary, from the Wilson Collection in
the Bodleian Library, is on the Bengālī recension, and written in
the Bengālī character. In many places it agrees with the readings
of the Deva-nāgarī recension, or at least notices them.

3. Ćandra-śekhara, whose commentary, belonging to the India
Office, is also on the Bengālī recension, and generally only repeats
the words of Śan-kara. If this Ćandra-śekhara is the same person
as the father of Viśva-nātha,—author of the Sāhitya-darpaṇa,—
he probably lived in the fifteenth century.

I never failed to consult the three commentaries before deciding
on the reading of my text, and made their interpretations the basis
of the literal translations of the metrical part of the play given in
the notes.

In this second edition, I have constantly consulted Dr. Burkhard's
text and glossary, and where better readings have been discovered,
they are generally mentioned in my notes.

On comparing the present edition with the previous one, it will
be observed that the red type has been dispensed with, and the
Sanskṛit interpretation of the Prākṛit passages has been given in
small type below.

In the Hindū drama, as is well known, the women and
inferior characters speak in Prākṛit—the name given to the collo-
quial Sanskṛit, prevalent throughout a great part of India in
early times. This spoken form of Sanskṛit, which was really the
precursor of the present vernacular tongues, must have varied
greatly, and particular dialects must have belonged to particular
districts and classes of men. There is, however, but one principal
Prākṛit, peculiar to the plays, viz. the Mahārāshṭrī, although
specimens of some varieties occasionally occur, and two of them
may be found in the interlude between the fifth and sixth Acts
of this play (see p. 217, note 2, and see Indian Wisdom, p. xxix,
note 2).

Other improvements and alterations will be noticed. For example, the rules of Sandhi have generally been carried out, even in the Sanskrit interpretation of the Prākṛit; the text and renderings in the notes have been carefully revised, and reference has been constantly made to Dr. Burkhard's edition; the stage-directions and names of the speakers have been printed in small type.

Mr. E. L. Hogarth, M.A., of Brasenose College, who has acted as Deputy Professor of Sanskrit at Oxford during my absence in India, has superintended the progress of this second edition of the Śakuntalā through the press, and has added a useful index.

My grateful acknowledgments are due to the Delegates of the Clarendon Press for the encouragement they are giving to the study of Sanskrit and Oriental literature generally, by undertaking the publication of standard works like the Śakuntalā.

M. W.

Cairo, March 1876.

ABBREVIATIONS.

[The commonest abbreviations are not given.]

Amara-k. = Amara-kosha.
B. and R. = Boehtlingk and Roth.
Beng. = Bengālī (MSS.) or Bengālī recension.
Bhartṛi-b. = Bhartṛi-harī (Bohlen's ed.)
Bhaṭṭi-k. = Bhaṭṭi-kāvya.
C. = the commentator C'andra-śekhara.
chap. = chapter.
cl. = class of verbs.
Deva-n. = Deva-nāgarī (MSS.) or Deva-nāgarī recension.
Dict. = my Sanskṛit-English Dictionary.
Draupadī-h. = Draupadī-haraṇa in Johnson's Selections from the Mahā-bhārata.
ed. = edition.
Gita-g. = Gīta-govinda (Lassen's ed.)
Gram. = my Sanskṛit Grammar, 4th ed.
Hari-v. = Hari-vaṇśa, the last Book of the Mahā-bhārata.
Hitop. = Hitopadeśa (Johnson's 1st ed.)
I. O. = India Office.
K. = the commentator Kāṭavema.
Kumāra-s. = Kumāra-sambhava.
l. = line.
Laghu-k. = Laghu-kaumudī.

Mahā-bh. Sel. = Johnson's Selections from the Mahā-bhārata.
Mālatī-m. = Mālatī-mādhava (the Calcutta ed. 1830).
Mālavik. = Mālavikāgnimitra (Tullberg's ed.)
Megha-d. = Megha-dūta.
Mṛiććh. or Mṛiććhak. = Mṛiććhakaṭika (Calcutta ed.)
Mudrā-r. = Mudrā-rākshasa (Calcutta ed. 1831).
Nalod. = Nalodaya.
Pāṇ. = Pāṇini (Boehtlingk's ed.)
Prāk. = Prākṛit.
Raghu-v. = Raghu-vaṇśa.
Rāmāy. = Rāmāyaṇa (Schlegel's ed.)
Ratn. = Ratnāvalī (Calcutta ed. 1832).
rt. = root.
S. = the commentator S'aṇkara.
Sāhit.-d. = Sāhitya-darpaṇa (Calcutta ed. 1828).
Sk. = Sanskṛit.
Vikram. = Vikramorvaśī.
Vishṇu-p. = Vishṇu-purāṇa (Wilson's translation, large ed.)

या सृष्टि: स्रष्टुराद्या वहति विधिहुतं या हविर्या च होत्री
ये द्वे कालं विधत्त: श्रुतिविषयगुणा या स्थिता व्याप्य विश्वम् ।
यामाहु: सर्वभूतप्रकृतिरिति यया प्राणिन: प्राणवन्त:
प्रत्यक्षाभि: प्रपन्नस्तनुभिरवतु वस्ताभिरष्टाभिरीशः ॥१॥

---

[1] '(That visible form, viz. water) which (was) the first creation of the Creator; (that, viz. fire) which bears the oblation offered-according-to-rule; and (that visible form, viz. the priest) which (is) the offerer-of-the-oblation; (those) two (visible forms, viz. the Sun and Moon) which regulate time; (that, viz. ether) which perpetually pervades all space, having the quality (sound) perceptible by the ear; (that, viz. the earth) which they call the originator of all created-things; (that, viz. the air) by which living beings are furnished with breath—may Īśa [the supreme Lord], endowed with [manifested in] these eight visible forms, preserve you!' The play begins and ends with a prayer to S'iva (see the last note in this play). After every relative pronoun some case of *pratyakshā tanuḥ* must be supplied. *Srishṭir ādyā:* see Manu i. 8–10, *apa eva sasarja ādau,* '(the Creator) first created the waters.' *Vidhi-hutam = veda-vidhānena agnau kshiptam,* C. *Hotrī = dīkshita-mayī tanuḥ,* K., *yajamāna-rūpā tanuḥ,* C., 'the Brāhman who is qualified by initiation to offer the oblation.' *Kālam vidhattaḥ = samayam kurutaḥ,* C.; *= srijataḥ,* S'. Hence the Sun is called *divā-kara,* 'maker of the day;' and the Moon, *niśā-kara,* 'maker of the night.' *Sruti-vi°:* the Hindūs reckon five elements, viz. water, fire, ether, earth, and air. Ether (*ākāśa*) is held to be the vehicle of sound, or of that quality which is the object of perception to the ear (see Manu i. 75). *Vyāpya sthitā,* i. e. 'keeps pervading.' Compare

---

Verse 1. The metre is SRAGDHARĀ (a variety of PRAKRITI), in which there are twenty-one syllables to the Pāda or quarter-verse, each Pāda being alike.

– – – – ∪ – – | ∪ ∪ ∪ ∪ ∪ ∪ – | – ∪ – – ∪ – – ‖

नान्द्यन्ते

सूत्रधारः ॥ नेपथ्याभिमुखमवलोक्यं ॥

आर्ये । यदि नेपथ्यविधानमवसितम् । तर्हीतस्तावदागम्य-
ताम् ।

---

vyāpya sthitaṃ rodasī in the opening of Vikramorvaśī. *Sthā* is joined
with an indecl. part. to express continuity of action. *Viśvam=prapañćam*,
'the whole visible universe,' K. *Sarva-bhūta-prakṛitiḥ*, so reads Kāṭavema, followed by my own MS., and supported by Manu ix. 37, *Iyam
bhūmir bhūtānāṃ śāśvatī yonir ućyate*, 'this earth is called the primeval
womb [*yoniḥ=kāraṇam*, Kul.] of all created things.' The other MSS.
have *sarva-vīja-prakṛitiḥ. Prakṛitiḥ = upādāna-kāraṇam*, K.; = *utpatti-
sthānam*, Ć.; = *nidānam*, S'. *Prapannaḥ=upetaḥ*, K. The Bengālī MSS.
have *prasannaḥ*. The worshippers of S'iva, who were Pantheists in the
sense of believing that S'iva was himself all that exists as well as the
cause of all that is, held that there were eight different manifestations
of their god, called Rudras (viz. Rudra, Bhava, Sarva, Īśāna, Paśu-pati,
Bhīma, Ugra, Mahā-deva), and that these had their types or representatives
in the eight visible forms enumerated here. So the Vishṇu-purāṇa (Wilson,
p. 58, large ed.), 'Brahmā assigned to them their respective stations:
water, the sun, earth, fire, air, ether, the officiating Brāhman [*dīkshito
brāhmaṇaḥ*], and the moon; these are termed their visible forms [*tana-
vaḥ*].' In the opening of Mālavik. mention is made of S'iva upholding
the universe by means of these forms, *ashṭābhis tanubhir bibhrataḥ
kṛitsnaṃ jagad api*. See also Kumāra-s. iv. 76. S'aṅkara, with far-
fetched subtilty, points out how each of these types of S'iva is intended
by the poet to correspond with circumstances in the life of S'akuntalā.
Thus, *yā sṛishṭiḥ*, &c., is compared with the sentiment in verse 43; and
ye dve, &c., with the two female friends.

[1] 'At the end of the Nāndī, the Sūtra-dhāra (speaks).' In the Hindū
drama every piece commences with a prologue, which is preceded by the
Nāndī or opening benediction, invoking the favour of some deity. It is
called Nāndī because it rejoices the hearts of the gods; *nandanty asyāṃ
surā yasmāt tena nāndī prakīrtitā*, S'. The Sāhitya-darpaṇa (p. 135)
says, 'What is recited in praise of a deity, a Brāhman, a king, or the like,
combined with a benediction, is called Nāndī.' It is said to be employed
vighnopaśāntaye, 'for the removal of obstacles.' The Sūtra-dhāra was
the principal manager who regulated the thread or rules of the drama;

नटी ॥ प्रविश्य ॥

[a] अज्ज। इअम्हि। आणवेदु अज्जो। को णिओओ अणु-चिट्ठीअदुत्ति।

[a] आर्ये। इयमस्मि। आज्ञापयत्वार्यः। को नियोगोऽनुष्ठीयतामिति।

---

yena nartanīya-kathā-sūtram prathamaṃ sūćyate, S. He is otherwise, especially when not a Brāhman, called the Sthāpaka, 'he who fixes or establishes the action of the play;' *kāvyārtha-sthāpanāt,* Ć. *Sthāpakaḥ sūtradhāra-sadṛiśa-guṇākāraḥ,* 'the Sthāpaka has qualities and an appearance like those of the Sūtra-dhāra,' Sāhit.-d. p. 137, l. 6. *Sūtra-dhāra-padena atra sthāpako 'bhimataḥ sūtradhāra-samānākārutvāt,* S. Bharata says, *Sūtradhāraḥ paṭhen nāndīm madhyamaṃ [prathamaṃ, Ć.] svaram āśritaḥ,* 'the Sūtra-dhāra should recite the Nāndī, employing a tone neither high nor low.' He was generally a Brāhman, and therefore qualified to recite the Nāndī in his own person. He did so, however, as a Brāhman, and not in his character of manager, which he did not assume till he had concluded the Nāndī. *Nāndy-ante sūtradhāraḥ* is therefore equivalent to 'at the end of the Nāndī, or after reciting the Nāndī, the Sūtra-dhāra continues speaking.' So Ćandra-śekhara, *Nāndī, etad-ante sūtradhāro vadati, nāndīm paṭhitvā anyad vadati ity arthaḥ.* Hence the word *praviśya,* 'entering,' is not required; the reciter of the Nāndī remaining on the stage in the character of manager. [*Iti nayena nāndy-ante sūtradhāra-praveśo 'pāstaḥ,* Ć.] If the manager happened not to be a Brāhman, he seems to have had no right to the title *Sūtra-dhāra,* nor could he recite the Nāndī, but in that case some Brāhman pronounced the blessing, and the manager was called Sthāpaka. Such, at least, seems to be the meaning of Bharata's aphorism [*ranga-pūjāṃ vidhāya ādau sūtradhāre vinirgate sthāpakaḥ praviśet paśćāt sūtradhāra-guṇākṛitiḥ*], though all the extant plays make the Sūtra-dhāra first recite the benediction, and then carry on the dialogue. The Sāhit.-d., p. 137, has the following: *Idānīm pūrva-rangasya samyak-prayogābhāvād eka eva sūtradhāraḥ sarvam proyojayati iti vyavahāraḥ sa sthāpakaḥ,* 'in these days, from the want of a complete performance of the Pūrva-ranga, the custom is that the Sūtra-dhāra alone does all, and he is the Sthāpaka.' The blessing is usually followed by some mention of the author of the piece, an appeal to the favour of the audience, and a short dialogue between the manager and an attendant actor (*pāripārśvika*). In the present play, an actress sings a song for the amusement of the audience.

[2] 'Looking towards the tiring-room,' which was behind the stage,

सूत्रधारः ।

आर्ये । अभिरूपभूयिष्ठा परिषदियम् । अद्य खलु कालि-
दासग्रथितवस्तुना नवेनाभिज्ञानशकुन्तलाख्येन नाटके-
नोपस्थातव्यमस्माभिः । तत्प्रतिपात्रमाधीयतां यत्नः ।

'looking behind the scenes.' *Nepathyam=vyatiriktaṃ yavanikāntaritaṃ
varṇikā-grahaṇādi-yogyaṃ naṭa-varga-sthānam*, K.;=*bhūshana-sthānaṃ
raṅgād vahiḥ-stham*, Ć., S'. In a Hindū theatre, a curtain [*apaṭī, paṭa,
yavanikā*] suspended across the stage, answered the purposes of scenes.
Behind it there was the space called *nepathya*, where the decorations were
kept, and where the actors attired themselves and remained in readiness
before entering the stage; whither also they withdrew on leaving it.
When an actor was to come ou hurriedly, the stage-direction is *paṭākshepeṇa* or *apaṭī-kshepeṇa*, 'with a hurried toss of the curtain.' When he
was to say something whilst hidden from the audience iu this space
behind the curtain, the direction is *nepathye*, '(a voice) in the postscenium.'
As to *nepathya-vidhānam* in the next line [=*prasādhana-kriyā*, S'.], it may
be translated, 'the act of decoration,' 'making the toilet,' or perhaps, 'the
arrangements of the tiring-room.' *Nepathye yad vidhīyate tan nepathya-
vidhānam*. Kāṭavema has *naipathya*. *Nepathyaṃ vidhā=nepathyaṃ raĆ*
or *nepathyaṃ kri*. Compare Ratnāvalī, p. 2, l. 16.

¹ 'For the most part (composed of) learned [educated] men.' The
audience consisted chiefly of good judges [*abhirūpa = vidvas, paṇḍita*,
K., Ć.] So *rāshṭraṃ śūdra-bhūyishṭham*, Manu viii. 22.

² 'With the new drama called "Token-S'akuntalā," or "Ring-(recognized) S'akuntalā."' *Abhijñāna-śakuntalā* is an anomalous compound
(Gram. 775); not one iu which the terms are inverted, but one in which
there is *uttara-pada-lopa* or *madhyama-pada-lopa*, 'elision of the second
member.' On the authority of Ćandra-śekhara, the second member to be
supplied is *smritā*, 'recognized;' and *abhijñāna* is 'the token of recognition—the ring.' The compound will thus be equivalent to *abhijñāna-
smritā Śakuntalā*, 'S'akuntalā recognized by the token.' So *śāka-pārthiva*,
'the king of the era,' is equivalent to *śāka-priya-pārthiva*, 'the king
beloved by the era.'

³ 'Therefore let care be applied by each to his own part [or character],'
'let pains be taken by all in their several parts.' *Pratipātram=pātre
pātre*, K. *Tat=tasmāt*, K. So *sveshu sthāneshv avahitair bhavitavyam*,
Vikram., Act I.

नटी ।

[a] सुविहिदप्पओअदाए अज्जस्स ण किम्पि परिहाइस्सदि ।

सूत्रधारः ।

आर्ये । कथयामि ते भूतार्थम् ।

आ परितोषाद्विदुषां न साधु मन्ये प्रयोगविज्ञानम् ।
बलवदपि शिक्षितानामात्मन्यप्रत्ययं चेतः ॥२॥

नटी ॥ सविनयम् ॥

[b] एव्वं णेदं । अणन्तरकरणिज्जं दाव अज्जो आणवेदु ।

<hr>

[a] सुविहितप्रयोगतया आर्यस्य न किमपि परिहास्यते ।   [b] एवं न्विदम् ।
अनन्तरकरणीयं तावदार्यं आज्ञापयतु ।

<hr>

1 'By reason of your honour's good assignment of the parts of the play
(to the several actors), nothing will be wanting;' i. e. 'by reason of your
skill in casting the characters, nothing is likely to go amiss in the acting;'
or, 'by reason of (our) good acting, nothing will be wanting to your
honour;' or, 'by reason of your honour's (skill in the) management of
the play,' &c. Such are the various interpretations of Kāṭavema, Candra-
śekhara, and S'aṅkara: the first seems preferable. So *yaḥ prayogo
bhavatīshu nibaddhaḥ*, Vikram., Act II. [*prayogaṃ nibandh = prayogaṃ
virać*].

2 *Bhūtārtham = satyam*, S'.; = *satyārtham*, K., 'the real truth,' 'the true
state of the case.'

3 'I do not consider skill-in-the-representation-of-plays to be good
[perfect] until (it cause) the satisfaction of the learned (audience); the
mind of those even who are very well instructed has no confidence in
itself.' *Balavad = sushṭhu*, C. *A-pratyaya*, 'distrustful of,' (with loc.)

<hr>

Verse 2. ĀRYĀ or GĀTHĀ, in which there are thirty Mātrās or measures (a short
syllable containing one, and a long, two) in the first half-verse, and twenty-seven in
the second. Each foot must contain four measures, except the sixth of the second
half-verse, which contains one; and the half-verse must be divided by a pause at the
end of the third foot.

```
– ∪ ∪ | – – | ∪ ∪ – ‖ ∪ – ∪ | – – | ∪ – ∪ | – – | –
∪ ∪ ∪ ∪ | ∪ – – | – – ‖ – – | – ∪ – | ∪ ∪ | – – | –
```

सूत्रधारः ।

किमन्यदस्याः परिषदः श्रुतिप्रसादनतः[1] ।

नटी ।

[a] अध कदमं उण उदुं अधिकरिस्स गाइस्सं ।

सूत्रधारः ।

नन्विममेव तावदचिरप्रवृत्तमुपभोगक्षमं ग्रीष्मसमयमधि-
कृत्य गीयताम् । सम्प्रति हि

सुभगसलिलावगाहाः पाटलसंसर्गसुरभिवनवाताः ।
प्रच्छायसुलभनिद्रा दिवसाः परिणामरमणीयाः ॥३॥

नटी ।

[b] तह । ।। इति गायति ॥

[a] अप कतमं पुनर्ऋतुमधिकृत्य गास्यामि ।   [b] तथा ।

---

[1] *Śruti-prasādana-taḥ = śravaṇendriya-tarpaṇāt*, K. Some MSS. insert
saṅgītāt karaṇīyam.

[2] Lit. 'having placed over,' 'having made the prominent subject.'
Hence, *adhikritya = krite*, 'about,' 'concerning,' 'with reference to,' Pāṇ.
iv. 3, 87. So, in the next sentence: 'Assuredly let a song be sung
concerning this very summer season, (so) suited to enjoyment [*upabhoga-
kshama*], that has not long set in.' As to *nanu*, see Pāṇ. viii. 1, 43.

[3] 'For now (are) the days on-which-there-are-grateful-bathings-in-the-
water (and) on-which-silvan-breezes-are-fragrant-from-contact-with-the-
trumpet-flower: (now are the days) on-which-sleep-is-easily-induced-in-
very-shady-spots (and) which-are-delightful-at-their-close.' *Pratchāya*°
= *prakrishṭa-chāyā yatra tat sthānam pratchāyam tasmin sulabhā nidrā
yeshu te tathoktāḥ*, K.; see p. 37, note 1 of this book. A short vowel
is the substitute for the long final of a fem. noun, when compounded
with such prepositions as *pra, ati*, &c.; thus *pragrīva* from *grīvā*;
atimālā from *mālā*; see Laghu-k. 1003. *Pariṇāma = virāma = sāyan-
kāla*, 'the evening,' K.

Verse 3. ĀRYĀ or GĀTHĀ. See verse 2.

⏑⏑⏑⏑ | ⏑–⏑ | – – ‖ – ⏑⏑ | – – | ⏑⏑⏑⏑ | ⏑⏑ – | –
– – | ⏑⏑⏑⏑ | – – ‖ ⏑⏑ – | ⏑⏑ – | ⏑ | ⏑⏑ – | –

[a] ईसीसिचुम्बिआइं भमरेहिं सुउमारकेसरसिहाइं ।
ओदंसअन्ति दअमाणा पमदाओ सिरीसकुसुमाइं ॥४॥

सूत्रधारः ।

आर्ये । साधु गीतम् । अहो रागबद्धचित्तवृत्तिरालिखित
इव सर्वतो रङ्गः । तदिदानीं कतमत्प्रकरणमाश्रित्यैनमा-
राधयामः ।

नटी ।

[b] णं अज्जमिस्सेहिं पढमं एव्व आसत्तं अहिण्णाणसउन्दलं

ūnam

[a] ईषदीषच्चुम्बितानि भ्रमरैः सुकुमारकेशरशिखानि ।
अवतंसयन्ति दयमानाः प्रमदाः शिरीषकुसुमानि ॥

[b] नन्वार्यमिश्रैः प्रथममेवाग्रमभिज्ञानशकुन्तलं

---

[1] 'Loving [amorous] fair-ones make ear-rings of the S'irīsha-blossoms
that-are-very-gently-kissed by bees (and) the points-of-whose-filaments-
are-very-delicate.' According to S'aṅkara, *keśara* = *kiñjalka*, and the
whole compound is a Bahuvrīhi, agreeing with *śirīsha-kusumāni*. There
is an allusion to the blossoms of the S'irīsha being thus used in Megha-
dūta 67, *čārukarṇe śirīsham;* and Raghu-v. xvi. 48, 61. Compare also
karṇa-śirīsha-rodhi, at the end of Act I. of this play; and Ritu-s. ii. 18,
kritāvatansaih kusumaih, &c. *Avatansayanti* is a nominal verb from
avatansa.

[2] 'On every side, the audience, having all the feelings of its soul fixed
on the melody, is as if formed into a picture,' i. e. motionless or riveted
with attention. *Ālikhita* = *niščala*, K.; *ranga* applies to the audience as
well as to the stage. *Prakarana*, 'a subject,' 'story,' 'poem.'

[3] 'By your reverence;' *ārya-miśraih* is here an epithet of the manager,
the respectful plural being used. In Vikramorvaśī, Act I, *ārya-vidagdha-*

Verse 4. A variety of ĀRYĀ called UDGĀTHĀ or GĪTI, used in Prākṛit. It consists
properly of four quarter-verses, containing eighteen measures in the fourth quarter as
well as in the second (see verse 69). But in this example the line is divided irregu-
larly.

$$\cup - \cup \mid \cup \cup - \mid - \cup \cup \mid \; - - \; \parallel \cup \cup - \mid \cup - \cup \mid \cup \cup - \mid$$
$$- - \mid \cup - \cup \mid \cup \cup - \mid - \cup \cup \mid \; - - \; \parallel \cup - \cup \mid \cup \cup - \mid$$

The first syllable of the second foot [*čumbiā*] is short by a license peculiar to Prākṛit
prosody. (See Colebrooke's Essays, new ed., vol. ii. p. 65, note.)

^aणाम अपुव्वं णाडञ्अं पञ्ओएण अधिकरीअदुन्ति ।

सूत्रधारः ।

आर्ये । सम्यगनुबोधितोऽस्मि । अस्मिन्स्थाने विस्मृतं खलु
मया । कुतः ।

तवास्मि गीतरागेण हारिणा प्रसभं हृतः ।
एष राजेव दुष्यन्तः सारङ्गेणातिरंहसा ‖ ५ ‖

‖ इति निष्क्रान्तौ ‖

‖ प्रस्तावना ‖

^a नाम अपूर्वं नाटकं प्रयोगेणाधिक्रियतामिति ।

---

miśrāḥ, 'respectable and intelligent persons,' occurs as an epithet of the
audience. *Miśra,* 'mixed,' in a compound of this kind has the force of
'gentleman.' *Ā-jñapta,* 'ordered,' 'arranged,' 'announced.'

[1] *Adhikriyatām = prakaṭī-kriyatām,* K., i. e. 'let it be made the subject
of exhibition,' 'let it be brought prominently forward;' see p. 6, note 2.
Some read *prayoge;* compare in Ratnāvalī, p. 2, l. 15, *nāṭikā prayogeṇa
nāṭayitavyā.*

[2] The rule is, that the conclusion of the prelude should prepare the
audience for the entrance of one of the dramatis personæ. Hence, the
manager exclaims, 'I was forcibly carried away by the ravishing melody
of thy song, like king Dushyanta here by the very fleet antelope.' *Pra-
sabham,* a kind of adverbial indeclinable participle from an old form *sabh*
(= rt. *sah*) with *pra,* and meaning 'forcibly,' 'violently;' (see Gram.
567.)

Verse 5. ŚLOKA or ANUSHṬUBH, consisting of four Pādas of eight syllables.

The first four syllables and the last syllable of each Pāda may be either long or short.

॥ अथ प्रथमोऽङ्कः ॥

॥ ततः प्रविशति मृगानुसारी सशरचापहस्तो राजा रथेन सूतश्च ॥

सूतः ॥ राजानं मृगं चावलोक्य ॥

आयुष्मन्[1] ।

कृष्णसारे ददच्चक्षुस्त्वयि चाधिज्यकार्मुके ।
मृगानुसारिणं साक्षात्पश्यामीव पिनाकिनम्[2] ॥ ६ ॥

राजा ।

सूत दूरममुना सारङ्गेण वयमाकृष्टाः । अयं पुनरिदानीमपि
ग्रीवाभङ्गाभिरामं मुहुरनुपतति स्यन्दने बद्धदृष्टिः
पश्चार्धेन प्रविष्टः शरपतनभयाद्भूयसा पूर्वकायम् ।

---

[1] 'O long-lived one!' a respectful mode of addressing kings. Ćandra-
śekhara quotes a verse of Bharata, *Vaded rājñīm ća ćetīm ća bhavatīti vidū-
shakaḥ, āyushman rathinam sūto vriddham tāteti ćetaraḥ.* Cf. Manu ii. 125.

[2] 'Casting (my) eye on the black-antelope and on thee with-thy-strung-
bow I behold, as it were, S'iva visibly present chasing the deer.' *Adhi-jya,*
'having the string [*jyā*] up;' at the end of the chase the bow would be
śithila-jya: see verse 40. *Sa-jya* is used like *adhi-jya.* *Pinākin* is
S'iva, armed with his bow called *Pināka.* [So the bow of Vishṇu has a
name *Śārn-ga,* and that of Arjuna, *Gāṇḍīva,* Megha-d. 48, 50.] In illustration, Kāṭavema refers to Raghu-v. xi. 44, *Dhanuḥ, yena vṛisha-dhvajo
vāṇam aṣṛijad vidruta-kratu-mṛigānusāriṇam.* S'iva, not having been
invited to Daksha's celebrated horse-sacrifice, was so indignant, that with
his wife he suddenly presented himself, confounded the sacrifice, dispersed
and mutilated the gods, and chasing Yajña, 'the lord of sacrifice,' who
fled in the form of a fleet deer, overtook and decapitated him. The
Vāyu-purāṇa makes S'iva create a manifestation of himself as a monstrous
being named Vīra-bhadra, who pursues Yajña in the form of a deer: see
Vishṇu-purāṇa, p. 65.

Verse 6. ŚLOKA or ANUSHTUBH. See verse 5.

दर्भैरर्धावलीढैः श्रमविवृतमुखभ्रंशिभिः कीर्णवर्त्मा
पश्योदग्रप्लुतत्वाद्वियति बहुतरं स्तोकमुर्व्यां प्रयाति ॥७॥

॥ सविस्मयम् ॥

कथमनुपतत एव मे प्रयत्नप्रेक्षणीयः संवृत्तोऽयं मृगः ।

सूतः ।

आयुष्मन् । उत्खातिनी भूमिरिति मया रश्मिसंयमनाद्-
यस्य मन्दीकृतो वेगः । तेन मृग एष विप्रकृष्टान्तरः संवृत्तः ।
सम्प्रति हि समदेशवर्तिनस्ते न दुरासदो भविष्यति ।

राजा ।

तेन हि मुच्यन्तामभीशवः ।

सूतः ।

यथाज्ञापयत्यायुष्मान् । ॥ रथवेगं निरूप्य ॥ आयुष्मन् । पश्य
पश्य ।

---

[1] 'There he is now, gracefully by the bending of his neck fixing a glance ever and anon at the chariot which pursues him, by (the contraction of) the hinder half (of his body) repeatedly drawing himself into the fore-(part of his) body through fear of the descent of the arrow; strewing the road with grass half-chewed which drops from his mouth kept open from exhaustion. See! by reason of his lofty boundings he springs forward chiefly in the air, little on the ground.' For *baddha-drishṭi*, compare Raghu-v. i. 40, *syandanābaddha-drishṭishu. Pravishṭaḥ pūrva-kāyam* is equivalent to *pravishṭa-pūrva-kāyaḥ*, lit. 'entering the fore-part of his body,' a Bahuvrīhi compound analogous to *baddha-drishṭiḥ* and *kīrṇa-vartmā*. In regard to Darbha or Kuśa grass, see note to verse 15.

[2] '[With surprise.] How now! the deer has become visible with difficulty [lit. with effort] to me pursuing (him).' Dr. Burkhard reads this line thus: *Sa esha katham anupadam eva prayatna-prekshanīyaḥ samvrittaḥ.*

[3] 'Because the ground is full of hollows, I have slackened the speed of the chariot by drawing in the reins.' *Utkhātinī*, lit. 'full of excavations.'

[4] 'Separated by a longer interval or distance.'

[5] The expressions *nirūpya* and *nāṭayitvā*, which occur so frequently in

Verse 7. SRAGDHARĀ. See verse 1.

‒ ‒ ‒ ‒ ‒ ◡ ‒ ‒ | ◡ ◡ ◡ ◡ ◡ ◡ ‒ | ‒ ◡ ‒ ‒ ◡ ‒ ‒

मुक्तेषु रश्मिषु निरायतपूर्वकाया
निष्कम्पचामरशिखा निभृतोर्ध्वकर्णाः।
आत्मोद्धतैरपि रजोभिरलङ्घनीया
धावन्त्यमी मृगजवाक्षममयेव रथ्याः॥८॥

the stage-directions, are synonymous, and may both be translated by 'acting,' 'gesticulating,' 'exhibiting by gesticulation.' The properties and paraphernalia of the Hindū stage were as limited as the scenery; and though seats, thrones, weapons, and cars were introduced, yet much had to be supplied by the imaginations of the spectators, assisted by the gesticulations of the actors. Thus, though the car of Dushyanta might have been represented on the stage, the horses would be left to the imagination, and the speed of the chariot would only be indicated by the gesticulations of the charioteer.

[1] 'The reins being loosed, these chariot-horses gallop along as if with impatience of the speed of the deer [i. e. impatient or emulous of its speed], having the fore-part of their bodies well stretched out, having the chowrie which forms their crest motionless, having the ears erect yet firmly fixed [or bent backwards], not to be overtaken even by the dust raised by themselves.'—The *ćamarī* or chowrie, formed of the white bushy tail of the Yak or Bos Grunniens, served for whisking off flies; and was used as an emblem of princely rank. It was placed as an ornament between the ears of horses, like the plume of the war-horse of chivalry. The velocity of the chariot caused it to lose its play and appear fixed in one direction, like a flag borne rapidly against the wind. A similar idea occurs in Act I. of the Vikramorvaśī, *ćitrārambha-viniśćalam hayaśirasi ćāmaram*. There is some difficulty in *nibhṛitordhva-karṇāḥ*. The commentator explains *nibhṛita* by *niśćala*, 'motionless.' The most usual sense of *nibhṛita* is 'secret,' 'modest,' 'depressed,' 'low' (Gīta-g. ii. 11, ii. 21; Hitop. passim). In Raghu-v. viii. 15 the sky is described as *nibhṛitendu*, 'having its moon nearly set' (=*astamayāsannaćandra*). Hence might flow the acceptation 'bent backwards.' The ears of a horse while running at full speed would be not only erect, but probably bent backwards so as to present the least resistance to the

राजा ॥ सहर्षम् ॥

सत्यमतीत्य हरितो हरींश्च वर्तन्ते वाजिनः । तथा हि
यदालोके सूक्ष्मं व्रजति सहसा तद्विपुलतां
यदर्धे विच्छिन्नं भवति कृतसन्धानमिव तत् ।
प्रकृत्या यद्वक्रं तदपि समरेखं नयनयो-
र्ने मे दूरे किञ्चित्क्षणमपि न पार्श्वे रथजवात् ॥ ९ ॥

---

wind. This interpretation is confirmed by the reading of the Bengálí
MSS., *cyuta-karna-bhanga;* but if the sense *niścala* be insisted on,
translate—'having the ears erect and immovable.'

[1] 'Truly, the horses are [or appear as if] outstripping the horses of the
Sun, and the horses of Indra,' i. e. the speed of the chariot seems like that
of the Sun or the Wind. *Harito* is taken by some commentators as
gen. case of *harit*, 'the Sun,' and *harīn* as acc. case plural of *hari*,
'a horse.' But *ća* after *harīn* indicates that both *harito* and *harīn* are
acc. cases after *atītya*. In the Rig-veda we find *harī* (dual) and *harayaḥ*
and *haribhiḥ* (I. 16, 1; 101, 10; 16, 4; 52, 8) for 'the horses of Indra;'
and *haritaḥ* for 'the seven horses of Súrya or the Sun' (I. 50, 8; 115, 4).
In Nirukta i. 15 the different vehicles of the gods are given, and among
them *harī Indrasya, haritaḥ ādityasya.* Hence Indra is called *hari-haya*
or *hari-váhana* (Vikram., Act III), and in Rig-veda, *hari-yojana;* and
the Sun is called *harid-aśva.* One name of the Sun is *saptáśva*, 'having
seven horses.' The Bengálí MSS. read *katham atītya harinam harayo,*
&c., but *harito harīnśća* is supported by all the Deva-nágarí MSS., and by
a parallel passage in Vikram., Act I, *anena ratha-vegena vainateyam api
āsādayeyam.*

[2] 'That which in my sight (appeared) minute suddenly attains magni-
tude; that which was divided in half becomes as if united; that also
which is by nature [really] crooked (appears) even-lined [straight] to my
eyes. Nothing (seems) at a distance from me nor at my side even for a
moment, by reason of the velocity of the chariot.' This is a method of
describing great velocity of motion, which may be well appreciated by
any one, in these days, who may have taken notice of the effect produced
upon adjacent objects by an express railway speed of a mile a minute.

Verse 9. ŚIKHARIṆÍ (a variety of the ATYASHṬI), containing seventeen syllables to
the Páda or quarter-verse, each Páda being alike.

∪ – – – – – | ∪ ∪ ∪ ∪ ∪ – – ∪ ∪ ∪ – – ||

सूत । पश्यैनं व्यापाद्यमानम् ।   ॥ इति शरसन्धानं नाटयति ॥

नेपथ्ये ।

भो भो राजन् । आश्रममृगोऽयं न हन्तव्यो न हन्तव्यः ।

सूतः   ॥ आकर्ण्यावलोक्य च ॥

आयुष्मन् । अस्य खलु ते वाणपथवर्तिनः कृष्णसारस्यान्तरे
तपस्विन उपस्थिताः ।

राजा   ॥ ससम्भ्रमम् ॥

तेन हि प्रगृह्यन्तां वाजिनः ।

सूतः ।

तथा ।   ॥ इति रथं स्थापयति ॥

॥ ततः प्रविशत्यात्मनातृतीयो वैखानसः ॥

वैखानसः   ॥ हस्तमुद्यम्य ॥

राजन् । आश्रममृगोऽयं न हन्तव्यो न हन्तव्यः ।
न खलु न खलु वाणः सन्निपात्योऽयमस्मि-
न्मृदुनि मृगशरीरे पुष्पराशाविवाग्निः ।

---

¹ 'With himself as the third,' or 'with himself making the third,'
i.e. himself and two others. This is a not unusual compound. Compare the expression, *Pāṇḍavā mātṛi-shashṭāḥ*, 'the Pāṇḍavas with
their mother as the sixth,' i.e. five persons, or six counting their
mother. Again, *chāyā-dvitīyo Nalaḥ*, 'Nala made two by his shadow,'
'umbra geminatus' (Nala v. 25). Also, *adhīte chaturo vedān ākhyāna-
pañchamān*, 'he reads the four Vedas with the Ākhyānas as a fifth' (Nala
vi. 9). A similar idiom prevails in Greek, αὐτός being used after ordinal
numbers: thus, πέμπτος αὐτός, 'himself with four others,' Thucydides
I. xlvi. Similarly, τρίτον ἡμιτάλαντον, 'two talents and a half,' and
ἕβδομον ἡμιτάλαντον, 'six talents and a half,' Herodotus I. 15, 50.

Verse 10. MĀLINĪ or MĀNINĪ (a variety of ATI-ŚAKVARĪ or ATI-ŚAKKARĪ), containing fifteen syllables to the Pāda or quarter-verse, each Pāda being alike.

∪ ∪ ∪ ∪ ∪ ∪ − − | − ∪ − − ∪ − − ||

क्व वत हरिणकानां जीवितं चातिलोलं
क्व च निशितनिपाताः वज्रसाराः शरास्ते ॥१०॥[1]
तत्साधु कृतसन्धानं प्रतिसंहर सायकम् ।
आर्तत्राणाय वः शस्त्रं न प्रहर्तुमनागंसि ॥११॥[2]

राजा ।

एष प्रतिसंहृतः । ॥ इति यथोक्तं करोति ॥

---

[1] 'Not indeed, not indeed must this arrow (of thine) be allowed to descend upon this tender body of the deer, like fire upon a heap of flowers. Where, forsooth, on the one hand (*ća*), is the very frail existence of fawns? and where, on the other (*ća*), are thy sharp-falling adamantine shafts?' i. e. Where is the suitability or congruity between the one and the other? What has the one to do with the other? How great a contrast or difference is there between the one and the other! Let not your shafts waste their strength upon an object so frail and tender, but let them be directed towards a mark more fitted to prove their adamantine qualities. This repetition of *kva* to express great contrast or unsuitability between two things is not uncommon. It is used by Kālidāsa again at the end of the Second Act of this play, *kva vayam*, &c.; also in Megha-dūta 5, thus, 'Where is a cloud which is a collection of vapour, fire, water, and wind? and where the meaning of messages to be received by intelligent mortals?' i. e. Why deliver a message intended for intelligent human beings to a cloud? What possible connection can there be between objects whose nature is so different? See also Raghu-v. i. 2, 'Where is the race sprung from the sun? and where my scanty powers of mind?' The majority of MSS. read *pushpa-rāśau*, some *tūla-rāśau*, 'on a heap of cotton.'

[2] 'Therefore withhold your well-aimed [lit. well fitted to the bow] arrow. Your weapon is for the deliverance of the distressed, not to inflict a wound on the innocent.' *Sandhā* is properly 'to unite or fix an arrow to a bow,' hence 'to take aim' (Draupadī-h. 149); and *sandhā-nam*, 'the act of taking aim.' *Prahartum* is here used where *praharaṇāya* might be expected, but the infinitive is interchangeable with the dative, and frequently has the force of that case.

Verse 11. ŚLOKA or ANUSHṬUBH. See verse 5.

वैखानसः ।

सदृशमेतत्पुरुवंशप्रदीपस्य भवंतः ।
जन्म यस्य पुरोर्वंशे युक्तरूपमिदं तव ।
पुचमेवङ्गुणोपेतं चक्रवर्त्तिनमाप्नुहि ॥१२॥

---

[1] 'This is worthy of your honour, who art the light of the race of Puru,' i. e. an illustrious descendant of Puru. Compare in Vikramorvaśī, Act I, *sadriśam idam soma-vaṇśa-sambhavasya*. In English we have the same idiom, 'this is just like [i. e. worthy of] one born in the Lunar race.' The two great lines or dynasties of kings according to Hindū mythology were the Solar and the Lunar. The Solar begins with Ikshvāku the son of Vaivasvata, the son of Vivasvat, or the Sun, and is carried on through Kakutstha, Dilīpa, Raghu, Aja, and Daśaratha, to his son, the great Rāma-ćandra, hero of the Rāmāyaṇa. Under the Lunar come Puru, Dushyanta, Krishna, and the heroes of the Mahā-bhārata, as, 1. Soma; 2. his son, Budha; 3. his son, Purūravas; 4. his son, Āyus; 5. his son, Nahusha; 6. his son, Yayāti; 7. his sons, Puru and Yadu. From Puru were descended Taṇsu, Anila, Dushyanta, and Bharata. From his brother Yadu came Sātvata, S'ūra, Vasu-deva, and his sons Bala-rāma and Krishṇa. From Bharata the son of Dushyanta and descendant of Puru came, after a time, Ajamīdha, Samvaraṇa, Kuru, S'āntanu, Bhīshma, and Krishṇa-dvaipāyana or Vyāsa. The latter was the father of Dhrita-rāshṭra and Pāṇḍu. The quarrels of the hundred sons of Dhrita-rāshṭra with their cousins, the five sons of Pāṇḍu (all of them being thus descended from Kuru and Puru), form the subject of the Mahā-bhārata. These two separate Solar and Lunar lines were occasionally intermixed by marriage, and a cross occurs at the very beginning, by the marriage of Ilā (Iḍā), daughter of Vaivasvata, with Budha. Paraśu-rāma, as a Brāhman, belonged to neither dynasty, but was connected with the Solar on his mother's side (see note to verse 22).

[2] 'This well becomes you, whose family belongs to the line of Puru, (therefore) be rewarded with a son gifted with all virtues, (and who shall become) a universal emperor.' A *ćakravartin* is one who reigns over a *ćakra*, or country reaching from sea to sea. According to the Vishṇu-purāṇa, a *ćakravartin* is one in whose hand the *ćakra*, or discus of Vishṇu, is delineated. There have been twelve of these emperors, commencing with Bharata, the son of Dushyanta.

Verse 12. S'LOKA or ANUSHTUBH. See verse 5.

इतरौ ॥ बाहू उद्यम्य ॥

सर्वथा चक्रवर्तिनं पुत्रमाप्नुहि ।

राजा ॥ सप्रणामम् ॥

प्रतिगृहीतम् ।

वैखानसः ।

राजन् । समिदाहरणाय प्रस्थिता वयम् । एष खलु कण्वस्य महर्षेरुपमालिनीतीरमाश्रमो दृश्यते । न चेदन्यकार्यातिपातः । तत्प्रविश्य प्रतिगृह्यतामातिथेयः सत्कारः । अपि च रम्यास्तपोधनानां प्रतिहतविघ्नाः क्रियाः समवलोक्य । ज्ञास्यसि कियद्भुजो मे रक्षति मौर्वीकिणाङ्क इति ॥१३॥

राजा ।

अपि सन्निहितोऽत्र कुलपतिः ।

---

[1] This exclamation usually serves to ratify any auspicious prayer or prophecy uttered by a Brāhman. *Brāhmaṇa-vaćas* may be supplied, 'the word of a Brāhman is accepted.' See the same phrase in Vikram., Act II.

[2] Compare Raghu-vaṇśa xiv. 70, i. 49.

[3] *Upa-mālinī-tīram*, 'near the banks of the Mālinī;' see Gram. 760. *b*.

[4] 'If it be not (the cause of) the neglect of any other duty,' or 'if it does not interfere with the discharge of any other duty.'

[5] 'Beholding the pleasing rites of the hermits, all the hindrances to which are warded off (by you), you will think to yourself, how much this arm of mine, marked with the scar of the bow-string, defends!' *Tapodhana*, 'a devotee,' or 'one rich in devotion.' A parallel passage occurs in Raghu-v. xviii. 47, 'The earth was preserved by his arm, though without the mark of the scar formed by the bow-string' (*abaddha-maurvi-kiṇa-lāñćhanena*). The ancient Hindūs extracted from the leaves of the Mūrvā plant (Aletris) very tough, elastic threads, with which they made their bow-strings (*maurvi*), and which, for that reason, were ordained by Manu to form the girdle or zone of the military or Kshatriya class. Manu ii. 42.

Verse 13. ĀRYĀ or GĀTHĀ. See verse 2.

```
– –  | ᴗ – ᴗ | – – ‖ ᴗ ᴗ ᴗ ᴗ | – – | ᴗ – ᴗ | ᴗ ᴗ – | –
– ᴗ ᴗ | ᴗ – ᴗ | – – ‖ – ᴗ ᴗ | – – |   ᴗ   | – ᴗ ᴗ | ᴗ
```

वैखानसः ।

इदानीमेव दुहितरं शकुन्तलामतिथिसत्काराय नियुज्य
दैवमस्याः प्रतिकूलं शमयितुं सोमतीर्थं गतः ।

राजा ।

भवतु । तां द्रक्ष्यामि । सा खलु विदितभक्तिर्मां महर्षेः
कथयिष्यति ।

वैखानसः ।

साधयामस्तावत् । ॥ इति सशिष्यो निष्क्रान्तः ॥

राजा ।

सूत । चोदयाश्वान् । पुण्याश्रमदर्शनेन तावदात्मानं पुनीमहे ।

सूतः ।

यदाज्ञापयत्यायुष्मान् । ॥ इति भूयो रथवेगं निरूपयति ॥

राजा ॥ समन्तादवलोक्य ॥

सूत । अकथितोऽपि ज्ञायत एव यथायमाभोगस्तपोव-
नस्येति ।

---

¹ *Soma-tīrtha* is a place of pilgrimage in the West of India, on the
coast of Gujarāt, near the temple of Somanāth. It is also called Prabhāsa.
The fable is that Soma, or the Moon, was here cured of the consumption
brought upon him by the imprecation of Daksha, his father-in-law
(Mahā-bh., S'alya-p. 2011; Vishṇu-p. p. 561). A *tīrtha* is a place of
pilgrimage, generally on the bank of some sacred stream, or near some
holy spring. The word is derived from *tṛī*, 'to cross over,' implying that
the stream has to be passed through, either for the washing away of sin,
or for extrication from some difficulty or adverse destiny. Thousands of
devotees still flock to the most celebrated Tīrthas, Benares, Haridwār, &c.

² *Ātmānam*, 'ourselves.' The sing. is used for du. and pl., Gram. 232.

³ *Ābhoga* = *vistāra*, 'extension,' 'amplitude;' *paripūrṇa-tā*, 'fulness.'
S'., in explaining *pariṇāha* in the sense of 'circumference,' gives *ābhoga*
as a synonym. In Megha-d. 90, *gaṇḍābhoga* is explained by *kapola-*
maṇḍala, 'the orb of the cheek;' and by *gaṇḍa-sthala*, 'the region of the
cheek;' and *stanābhoga* is said to mean 'fulness of breast.' Translate,
'Even without being told, it may be known indeed that here (we are
within) the expanse [or exuberant fulness] of the sacred grove.'

सूतः ।

कथमिव ।

राजा ।

किं न पश्यति भवान् । इह हि

नीवाराः शुकगर्भकोटरमुखभ्रष्टास्तरूणामधः
प्रस्निग्धाः क्वचिदिङ्गुदीफलभिदः सूच्यन्त एवोपलाः ।
विश्वासोपगमादभिन्नगतयः शब्दं सहन्ते मृगा-
स्तोयाधारपथाश्च वल्कलशिखानिष्यन्दरेखाङ्किताः ॥१४॥

---

[1] 'For here are the (grains of) wild-rice beneath the trees, fallen from the mouths [openings] of the hollow-trunks (*koṭara*) filled with parrots; in other places the polished stones (used) for crushing the fruit of the In-gudī are plainly observed; the fawns too, with undeviating step [i. e. not starting aside] from having acquired confidence, bear the sound (of the voice); and the paths of the reservoirs are marked with lines by the drippings from the ends of the bark-clothes.' *Mukha* is used for any opening. *Garbha*, as the last member of a compound, often denotes 'filled with,' as *ćūrṇa-garbhā nāḍiḥ*, 'a tube filled with powder.' The *Iṅgudī*, commonly called *Ingua* or *Jiyaputa*, is a tree from the fruit of which necklaces were made of a supposed prolific efficacy; whence the botanical name Nagelia Putran-jīva or Jīva-putraka. In Raghu-v. xiv. 81 there is an allusion to the fruit being used by hermits to supply oil for lamps, and in Act II. to its furnishing them with ointment. The synonym for the tree in the Amara-kosha is *tāpasa-taru*, 'the anchorite's tree.' S'. calls it *muni-pādapa*. *Abhinna-gati* may perhaps be translated 'not running away.' K. explains it by *avihata-gati*, 'not stopping in their walk.' So *abhinna-svara*, 'one who does not hesitate in speaking.' The sense of the last line is determined by a passage at the end of this Act, where the dust is described as falling 'on the bark dresses, moist with water, hung up (to dry) on the branches of trees' (*viṭapa-vishakta-jalārdra-valkaleshu*, verse 32). In carrying these dresses from the tank (*toyādhāra*) to the trees, a line would be formed by the drippings from the edges [*śikhā* = *añćala*, Schol.]

Verse 14. ŚĀRDŪLA-VIKRĪḌITA (a variety of ATIDHṚITI), containing nineteen sylla-bles to the quarter-verse, each quarter-verse being alike.

‒ ‒ ‒ ∪ ∪ ‒ ∪ ‒ ∪ ∪ ∪ ‒ | ‒ ‒ ‒ ∪ ‒ ‒ ∪ ‒ ‖

अपि च ।

कुल्याम्भोभिः पवनचपलैः शाखिनो धौतमूला
भिन्नो रागः किसलयरुचामाज्यधूमोद्गमेन ।
एते चार्वागुपवनभुवि छिन्नदर्भाङ्कुरायां
नष्टाशङ्का हरिणशिशवो मन्दमन्दं चरन्ति[1] ॥१५॥

सूतः ।

सर्वमुपपन्नम् ।

राजा ॥ स्तोकमन्तरं गत्वा ॥

तपोवनवासिनामुपरोधो मा भूत् । अत्रैव तावद्रथं स्थापय । यावदवतरामि ।

---

[1] 'The trees have their roots washed by the waters of canals [trenches], tremulous in the wind; the tint of (those trees which are) bright with fresh-sprouts is diversified [partially obscured] by the rising of the smoke of the clarified butter (burnt in oblations); and in front, these young fawns, free from timidity, leisurely graze on the lawn of the garden, where the stalks of Darbha grass have been mown.' The commentators explain *bhinna* by *anyathā-bhūta*, 'altered,' 'made different;' but it may also mean 'broken,' 'interrupted,' 'partially obscured.' *Arvāk* = *agrataḥ*, 'in front,' 'near.' *Darbha* is another name for *Kuśa* or sacrificial grass (Poa Cynosuroides). This was the plant held sacred by the Hindūs, as verbena was by the Romans. Ground prepared for a sacrifice was strewn with the blades of this grass. The officiating Brāhmans were purified by sitting on it, and by rubbing it between their hands. Its sanctifying qualities were various, see Manu ii. 43, 75, 182; iii. 208, 223, 255, 256; iv. 36; v. 115; xi. 149; and Vishṇu-p. p. 106. Its leaves are very long, with tapering points of which the extreme acuteness is proverbial; whence the expression *kuśāgra-buddhi* (Raghu-v. v. 4), 'one whose intellect is as sharp as the point of a Kuśa leaf.' In Atharva-v. xix. 28 this grass is addressed as a god. According to the commentators this verse and the last afford examples of *anumānālan·kāra*, or figure called 'Inference.'

Verse 15. MANDĀKRĀNTĀ (a variety of ATYASHṬI), containing seventeen syllables to the quarter-verse, each quarter-verse being alike. This is the metre of the Megha-dūta.

– – – – | ⏑ ⏑ ⏑ ⏑ ⏑ – | – ⏑ – – ⏑ – ⏓ ||

सूतः ।

धृताः प्रग्रहाः । अवतरत्वायुष्मान् ।

राजा ॥ अवतीर्य ॥

सूत । विनीतंवेषेण प्रवेष्टव्यानि तपोवनानि नाम । इदं तावद्गृह्यताम् । ॥ इति सूतस्याभरणानि धनुश्चोपनीयं ॥ सूत । याव-दहमाश्रमवासिनः प्रत्यवेक्ष्योपावर्ते । तावदार्द्रपृष्ठाः क्रि-यन्तां वाजिनः ।

सूतः ।

तथा । ॥ इति निष्क्रान्तः ॥

राजा ॥ परिक्रम्यावलोक्य च ॥

इदमाश्रमद्वारम् । यावत्प्रविशामि । ॥ प्रविश्य निमित्तं सूचयन् ॥

शान्तमिदमाश्रमपदं स्फुरति च बाहुः कुतः फलमिहास्य ।
अथवा भवितव्यानां द्वाराणि भवन्ति सर्वत्र ॥१६॥

---

[1] Compare Manu viii. 2.   Dr. Burkhard has *vinīta-vesha-praveśyāni.*

[2] 'Giving over his ornaments and bow (to the care) of the charioteer.' Observe the use of the gen. after *upanīya;* see Gram. 858.

[3] Lit. 'let the horses be made wet-backed,' i. e. let them be watered and refreshed.   'Let their fatigue be removed by giving them water and by rubbing their backs,' S'.

[4] 'Acting an omen,' or 'acting as if he observed an omen,' lit. 'mani-festing a sign.' *Nimitta* is any omen or sign, such as the throbbing of the arm or eyelid.   If this was felt on the right side it was a good omen in men; if on the left, a bad omen.   The reverse was true of women.

[5] 'This hermitage is tranquil [i. e. a peaceful spot, undisturbed by passion or emotion], and yet my arm throbs; whence can there be any result of this in such a place?   But yet the gates of destiny are every-where.'   A quivering sensation in the right arm was supposed to prognosticate union with a beautiful woman.   See Raghu-v. xii. 90; Bhaṭṭi-k. i. 27; Vikram., Act II.

Verse 16.   ĀRYĀ or GĀTHĀ.   See verse 2.

$$- \cup \cup \mid \cup - \cup \mid \cup \cup - \parallel \cup \cup \cup \cup \mid \;-\;-\; \mid \cup - \cup \mid \cup \cup - \mid \cup$$
$$\cup \cup - \mid \cup \cup - \mid \;-\;-\; \parallel \;-\;-\; \mid \cup \cup - \mid \;\cup\; \mid \;-\;-\; \mid \cup$$

नेपथ्ये ।

[a] इदो इदो सहीओ ।

राजा ।। कर्णं दत्त्वा ।।

अये । दक्षिणेन वृक्षवाटिकामालाप इव श्रूयते । यावदच
गच्छामि । ।। परिक्रम्यावलोक्य च ।। अये । एतास्तपस्विकन्यकाः
स्वप्रमाणानुरूपैः सेचनघटैर्बालपादपेभ्यः पयो दातुमित
एवाभिवर्त्तन्ते । ।। निरूप्य ।। अहो मधुरमासां दर्शनम् ।
शुद्धान्तदुर्लभमिदं वपुराश्रमवासिनो यदि जनस्य ।
दूरीकृताः खलु गुणैरुद्यानलता वनलताभिः ।।१७।।
यावदिमां छायामाश्रित्य प्रतिपालयामि । ।। इति विलोक-
यन्स्यितः ।।

।। ततः प्रविशति यथोक्तव्यापारा सह सखीभ्यां शकुन्तला ।।

[a] इत इतः सख्यौ ।

---

[1] 'To the right of the grove of trees.' *Dakshiṇena* governs the acc.
case as well as the gen. See Pāṇ. ii. 3, 31; v. 3, 35.

[2] 'With watering-pots (of a size) proportioned to their strength,' or
'with watering-pots suited to their size,' i. e. not too large for a woman
to carry.

[3] 'If this (beautiful) figure, rarely met with [or difficult to be found]
in the inner apartments of palaces [i. e. in harams], belongs to people
living in a hermitage, then indeed the shrubs of the garden are distanced
[surpassed] in excellencies by the (wild) shrubs of the forest.' Sir W. Jones
translates, 'the garden-flowers must make room for the blossoms of the
forest, which excel them in colour and fragrance.' The *suddhānta* is the
antaḥ-pura or 'inner suite of apartments, appropriated to women;' called
also the *avarodha* or 'private quarter,' shut out from the rest of the house
and strictly guarded. *Haram* is the equivalent Arabic word.

[4] 'Occupied in the manner described.' A noticeable Bahuvrīhi compound.

Verse 17. ĀRYĀ or GĀTHĀ. See verse 2.

$$- - | \cup - \cup | \cup \cup - || \cup \cup - | \cup \cup - | \cup - \cup | \cup \cup - | \cup$$
$$- - | \cup - \cup | \cup \cup - || - - | \cup \cup - | \quad \cup \quad | \cup \cup - | -$$

शकुन्तला ।

[a] इदो इदो सहीओ ।

अनसूया ।

[b] हला सउन्दले । तुवन्तोबि तादकस्सवस्स अस्समरुक्खआ पिञ्अदरेत्ति तक्केमि । जेण णोमालिं[1] आकुसुमपेलवाबि तुमं एदाणं आलं[2]वालपूरणे णिउत्ता ।

शकुन्तला ।

[c] हला अणसूए । ण केवलं तादणिओओ एव्व । अत्यि मे सोदरसिणेहोबि एदेसु । ॥ इति वृक्षसेचनं निरूपयति ॥

राजा ।

कथमियं सा कण्वदुहिता । असाधुदर्शी खलु तत्रभवान्का- श्यपः । य इमामाश्रमधर्मे नियुंक्ते[3] ।

---

[a] इत इतः सख्यौ ।   [b] हला शकुन्तले । त्वत्तोऽपि तातकाश्यपस्याश्रमवृक्षाः प्रि- यतरा इति तर्कयामि । येन नवमालिकाकुसुमपेलवापि त्वमेतेषामालवालपूरणे नियुक्ता । [c] हला अनसूये । न केवलं तातनियोग एव । अस्ति मे सोदरस्नेहोऽप्येतेषु ।

---

[1] *Mālikā* or *mallikā* is a kind of double jasmine with large flowers, sometimes called 'Arabian jasmine;' from its delicious perfume, and abundant nectar, much frequented by bees. See Raghu-v. xvi. 47.

[2] *Ālavāla*, 'the trench for water round the root of a tree.' See Raghu-v. i. 51; also Vikram., end of Act II. (*taror mūlālavālam*).

[3] 'Truly his reverence Kāśyapa is (a man) of little discrimination, inasmuch as he appoints her to the duties [manner of life] of the her- mitage [i. e. imposes upon her a hermitage-life; a mode of life such as is usual in a hermitage].' The sage Kaṇva is here called 'a descendant of Kaśyapa.' As a sage and Brāhman he might especially claim this celebrated personage as his progenitor; but Kaśyapa, who was the son of Marīci [who was the son of Brahmā, and one of the seven Prajāpatis], was a progenitor on a magnificent scale, as he is considered to have been the father of the gods, demons, man, fish, reptiles, and all animals, by Aditi, and twelve other daughters of Daksha. He is supposed by some to be a personification of the race who took refuge in the central Asiatic

इदं किलाव्याजमनोहरं वपु-
स्तपःक्षमं साधयितुं य इच्छति ।
ध्रुवं स नीलोत्पलपत्त्रधारया
शमीलतां छेत्तुमृषिर्व्यवस्यति ॥१८॥

भवतु । पादपान्तरित एव विश्वस्तां तावदेनां पश्यामि ।
॥ इति तथा करोति ॥

शकुन्तला ।

[a] सहि अणसूए । अदिपिणड्डेण वक्कलेण पिअंवदाए णि-
अन्तिदम्हि । सिढिलेहि दाव णं ।

अनसूया ।

[b] तह । ॥ इति शिथिलयति ॥

[a] सखि अनसूये । अतिपिनद्धेन वल्कलेन प्रियंवदया नियन्त्रितास्मि । शिथिलय
तावदेनम् ।   [b] तथा ।

---

chain, in which traces of his name may be found, as Koh-kas (or
Caucasus), the Caspian, Kaśmīra, &c. (Wilson's Hindū Theatre, vol. ii.
p. 12.)

[1] 'The sage who expects to make this artlessly-charming form capable
of (enduring) penance, certainly attempts to cut a branch of the hard
S'amī wood with the edge of the blue lotus-leaf.' *Avyāja-manoharam,*
'that which captivates without art or ornament,' 'naturally beautiful.'
For an account of the different orders of Ṛishis or sages, see *ṛishi* in my
Sanskṛit-English Dictionary. The S'amī tree is a kind of acacia (Acacia
Suma), the wood of which is very hard, and supposed by the Hindūs to
contain fire. [*S'amī abhyantara-līna-pāvakā,* Raghu-v. iii. 9. See also
Manu viii. 247.] Sacred fire is kindled by rubbing two dried pieces
together. The legend is that Purūravas generated primeval fire by
rubbing together two branches of the S'amī and Aśvattha tree. Other
kinds of wood are also held sacred by the Hindūs, such as the Vilva (Bel),
and only Brāhmans are allowed to use them as fuel.

Verse 18. VANŚA-STHAVILA (a variety of JAGATĪ), containing twelve syllables to the
quarter-verse, each quarter-verse being alike.

◡ – ◡ – – ◡◡ – ◡ – ◡ – ||

प्रियंवदा ।। सहासम् ।।

[a] एत्थ पओहरवित्थारइत्तअं अत्तणो जोव्वणं उवालह। मं किं उवालम्भेसि।

राजा।

सम्यगियमाह।

इदमुपहितसूक्ष्मयन्थिना स्कन्धदेशे
    स्तनयुगपरिणाहाच्छादिना वल्कलेन।
वपुरभिनवमस्याः पुष्यति स्वां न शोभां
    कुसुममिव पिनद्धं पाण्डुपत्त्रोदरेण ॥१९॥

अथवा काममनननुरूपमस्या वपुषो वल्कलम्। न पुन-
रलङ्कारश्रियं न पुष्यति। कुतः।

[a] अत्र पयोधरविस्तारयितृकम् आत्मनो यौवनमुपालभस्व। मां किमुपालभसे।

---

[1] 'This blooming [or youthful] body of hers, by (reason of) the bark dress fastened with delicate knots upon her shoulder (and) covering the orbs of her two breasts, does not exhibit (the fulness of) its own charms, like a flower enveloped by a calyx of pale leaves.' The first meaning of *push*, like *bhri*, is 'to nourish' or 'be nourished.' Thence, like *bhri*, it passes into the sense of 'maintain,' 'support,' 'bear;' and thence into that of 'possess,' 'enjoy,' 'exhibit,' 'make to appear.' In these last senses it may be used actively, though conjugated in cl. 4. (See Manu ix. 37; Rāmāy. ii. 94, 10; Raghu-v. xvi. 58; Mahā-bh. vol. ii. p. 186, l. 2607.) It is curious that our English word *exhibition* may have the sense of 'maintenance' (cf. Lat. *exhibeo*). Two Bombay MSS. read *svām abhikhyām* instead of *svām na śobhām:* the meaning would then be, 'maintains its own beauty' [*abhikhyā* is so used, Raghu-v. i. 46]; and this reading would be more consistent with what follows, but by the next word *athavā*, as the commentators observe, *svoktam ākshipati*, he corrects his previous remark. *Pi-naddha = api-naddha* from *api-nah*.

[2] 'Or rather, granted that the bark dress be ill suited to her figure, yet it really does [lit. it does not not] possess the charm of an embellish-

---

Verse 19. MĀLINĪ or MĀNINĪ (a variety of ATI-ŚAKVARĪ). See verse 10.

सरसिजमनुविद्धं शैवलेनापि रम्यं
मलिनमपि हिमांशोर्लक्ष्म लक्ष्मीं तनोति ।
इयमधिकमनोज्ञा वल्कलेनापि तन्वी
किमिव हि मधुराणां मण्डनं नाकृतीनाम् ॥ २० ॥

ment;' or less literally, 'it really does act as an embellishment to set off the beauty of her person.' Other instances are found in Kālidāsa of two negatives employed to strengthen an affirmative. See Megha-d. 106.

[1] 'The lotus, though intertwined [or overspread] with the S'aivala, is charming; the speck, though dark, heightens [lit. extends] the beauty of the moon; this graceful one even with her bark-dress is more lovely; for what is not an embellishment of sweet forms?' i. e. everything serves as an ornament to heighten the beauty of a figure which is naturally beautiful. *Sarasi-jam,* lit. 'that which is born in a pool,' a name applicable to any aquatic plant, but especially to the different kinds of lotus (Nelumbium or Nymphæa). This beautiful plant—the varieties of which, blue, white, and red, are numerous—bears some resemblance to our water-lily. It is as favourite a subject of allusion and comparison with the Hindū poets as the rose with the Persian. It is often figuratively used to express beauty, as 'lotus-face' or 'the lotus of the face,' 'lotus-hands,' 'lotus-feet' (Gīta-g. passim). It is also used by women as an ornament (Act III. of this play), and as a cooling remedy (Ratn., Act II). The S'aivala (Vallisneria) is an aquatic plant which spreads itself over ponds, and interweaves itself with the lotus. The interlacing of its stalks is compared in the S'ṛiṅgāra-tilaka (verse 1) to braided hair (*dhammilla*). See Sir W. Jones' Works, vol. iv. p. 113. The spots on the moon were thought to resemble those on an antelope, and hence one of the moon's names, *hariṇa-kalaṅka,* 'deer-spotted.'

The following verse, which is found in the Beng. MSS. immediately after verse 20, and has been adopted by the Calcutta edition, is omitted in all the Deva-n. MSS., and in the commentaries of S'. and K. It is probably spurious, as it repeats the same sentiment less poetically and with some harshness of expression :—

कठिनमपि मृगाक्ष्या वल्कलं कान्तरूपं
न मनसि रुचिभङ्गं स्वल्पमप्यादधाति ।

Verse 20. MĀLINĪ or MĀNINĪ (a variety of ATI-S'AKVARĪ). See verse 10.

शकुन्तला ॥ अग्रतोऽवलोक्य ॥

[a] एसो वादेरिदपल्लवङ्गुलीहिं तुवरेदि विञ्र मं केसर-रुक्खअो । जाव णं सम्भावेमि । ॥ इति परिक्रामति ॥

प्रियंवदा ।

[b] हला सउन्दले । एत्थ एव्व दाव मुहुत्तअं चिट्ठु ।

शकुन्तला ।

[c] किंणिमिंत्तं ।

प्रियंवदा ।

[d] जाव तुए उवगदाए लदासंणाहो विञ्र अञ्रं केसर-रुक्खअो पडिभादि ।

---

[a] एष वातेरितपल्लवाङ्गुलीभिस्त्वरयतीव मां केशरवृक्षक: । यावदेनं सम्भावयामि । [b] हला शकुन्तले । अत्रैव तावन्मुहूर्तं तिष्ठ । [c] किन्निमित्तम् । [d] यावत्त्वयोपगतया लतासनाथ इवायं केशरवृक्षक: प्रतिभाति ।

विकचसरसिजायाः स्तोकनिर्मुक्तकरठं
निजमिव कमलिन्याः कर्कशं वृन्तजालम् ॥

'The bark-dress, though rough, is beautiful on this fawn-eyed one. It does not in one's mind cause the slightest impairment of her beauty [or, of my liking for her]; just as its own rough tissue of stalks on the lotus-bed whose lotuses have expanded, so as slightly to release the neck-of-the-flower,' i. e. the pedicle, or that part of the stalk immediately under the flower.

[1] 'This Keśara tree, with its fingers of young shoots set in motion by the wind, bids me hasten as it were (towards it). I will just go and pay my respects to it.' The Keśara (Mimusops Elengi) is the same as the Bakula or Vakula, frequent mention of which is made in some of the Purāṇas, and in Ratn., Act III. It bears a strong-smelling flower, which is even placed among the flowers of the Hindū paradise. The tree is very ornamental in pleasure-grounds. The caus. of *sam-bhū* often means 'to honour, or pay one's respects to another in person.' Motion towards the object seems usually, though not always, implied. Thus, *sambhāvayāmo rājarshim*, Vikram., Act I; cf. Raghu-v. v. 2, x. 56.

[2] 'What for!' Dr. Burkhard omits this.

[3] 'Possessed of a creeper.' *Sa-nātha*, lit. 'having a lord or master;'

शकुन्तला ।

[a] अदोक्खु पिअंवदासि तुंमं ।

राजा ।

प्रियमपि तथ्यमाह शकुन्तलां प्रियंवदा । अस्याः खलु
अधरः किसलयरागः कोमलविटपानुकारिणौ बाहू ।
कुसुममिव लोभनीयं यौवनमङ्गेषु सन्नंद्धम् ॥२१॥

[a] अतः खलु प्रियंवदासि त्वम् ।

---

it is so used towards the end of this Act, where the devotees are said
to be *sa-nāthāḥ*, 'possessed of a guardian' in Dushyanta. A compound
verb *sanāthī-kṛi*, 'to cause to be possessed of a master,' occurs in Act II.
of this play, and in Hitop. l. 797. But here *sa-nātha = sahita, dvitīya,
yukta*, 'accompanied,' 'joined,' 'furnished with.' The transition into
this meaning may be understood from Act VI. of this play, and from
Vikram., Act II, where an arbour (*maṇḍapa*) is said to be *maṇi-śilā-
paṭṭa-sanātha*, 'having a slab of marble as its master,' i. e. in which the
most prominent object is a marble seat; or in plain words, 'an arbour
furnished with a marble seat.' Similarly in Act II. of this play the
surface of a stone seat (*śilā-tala*) is said to be *vitāna-sanātha*, 'furnished
with a canopy' by the shade of a tree. Cf. also *Lakshmī-sanātha*, 'possessed of Fortune,' and *kusuma-sanātha*, 'decked with flowers,' Vikram.,
Act IV. See also Mālatī-m. p. 58, l. 2; Megha-d. ver. 97; Mālavik.
p. 5, l. 9.

[1] 'Hence most truly art thou (named) Priyaṃ-vadā' (i. e. *priyam*,
'what is agreeable,' and *vada*, 'one who speaks;' cf. μελίφθογγος).

[2] 'Though agreeable (still it is) the truth (that) Priyaṃvadā says to
S'akuntalā. Truly her lip has the colour of a young bud, her two arms
resemble flexile stalks. Attractive youth, like the blossom, pervades her
limbs.' *Adhara*, properly 'the lower lip,' as distinguished from *oshṭha*
(i. e. *ava-stha*), 'the upper lip.' *San-naddham = sarvato vyāpakam*,
Schol.

Verse 21. ĀRYĀ or GĀTHĀ. See verse 2.

$$\cup\cup- \mid \cup\cup\cup\cup \mid --\parallel -\cup\cup \mid \cup\cup- \mid \cup-\cup \mid -- \mid -$$
$$\cup\cup\cup\cup \mid \cup-\cup \mid --\parallel -\cup\cup \mid -- \mid \cup \mid --\mid -$$

E 2

अनसूया ।

[a] हला सउन्दले । इअं सअंवरवहू सहआरस्स तुए किदणा-
महेआ वणजोसिणित्ति णोमालिआ । एं विसुमरिदासि ।

शकुन्तला ।

[b] तदा अत्ताणम्पि विसुमरिस्सं । ॥ लतामुपेत्यावलोक्य च ॥ [c] हला ।
रमणीएक्खु काले इमस्स लदापाअवमिहुणस्स वइअरी

[a] हला शकुन्तले । इयं स्वयंवरवधूः सहकारस्य त्वया कृतनामधेया वनज्योत्स्नेति
नवमालिका । एनां विस्मृतासि ।   [b] तदात्मानमपि विस्मरिष्यामि ।   [c] हला ।
रमणीये खलु कालेऽस्य लतापादपमिथुनस्य व्यतिकरः

---

[1] 'Here is the young Mālikā [a kind of double jasmine, see p. 22, n. 1]
named by you the Light of the Grove, the self-elected wife of the Sahakāra. Have you forgotten it ?' The Sahakāra is a sort of fragrant
Mango tree. Its union with other plants seems a favourite idea with
Kālidāsa; for in Raghu-v. viii. 60, allusion is made to its marriage with
the Phalinī or Priyangu. It is said to be a great favourite with bees
(Raghu-v. vi. 69). In Ratn. p. 11, l. 7, it is spoken of as *mandalā-
yamāna*, 'forming a circle.' *Svayaṃvara-vadhū*, 'a wife by self-election.'
The *Svayaṃvara*, or 'selection for one's self,' was a form of marriage in
which a princess made a free public choice of a husband from a number
of assembled suitors. In very early times the princesses of India seem
to have enjoyed this singular privilege. It is not mentioned amongst the
forms of marriage in Manu iii. 21, &c.; but the provision which is made
in Manu ix. 90, proves that a similar custom prevailed at that period.
When marriageable, she is there told to wait for three years; and after
that time, if she fail to obtain a suitable husband, she is to choose for
herself; [*samāna-jāti-guṇaṃ varaṃ svayaṃ vriṇīta*, Schol.] She is then
called *Svayaṃvarā*. In the Mahā-bh. we have a beautiful account of the
Svayaṃvara of Damayantī (who chooses Nala), and of Draupadī (who
chooses Arjuna); and in Raghu-v. vi. of the *Svayaṃvara* of Indumatī,
sister of Bhoja, king of Vidarbha (who chooses Aja, the son of Raghu).
See also Nalod. i. 30. Even the goddess Lakshmī is said to have exercised
this privilege. See the allusion to the *Lakshmī-svayaṃvara* at the beginning of Act III. of Vikram. *Vi-smṛita* is also used transitively between
verses 129 and 130 of this play. In Raghu-v. xix. 2, *vi-smṛita* has an
acc. after it. See Gram. 896; Pāṇ. iii. 4, 72.

ᵃसंवुत्तो । णवकुसुमजोव्वणा वणजोसिणी । बद्धपल्लवदाए
उवभोअक्खमो सहआरो । ॥ इति पश्यन्ती तिष्ठति ॥

प्रियंवदा ॥ सस्मितम् ॥

ᵇअणसूए । जाणासि किस्सिमित्तं सउन्दला वणजोसिणिं
अदिमेत्तं पेक्खदित्ति ।

अनसूया ।

ᶜणक्खु विभावेमि । कहेहि ।

प्रियंवदा ।

ᵈजह वणजोसिणी अणुरूवेण पाअवेण सङ्गदा । अवि

ᵃ संवृत्तः । नवकुसुमयौवना वनज्योत्स्ना । बद्धपल्लवतयोपभोगक्षमः सहकारः ।
ᵇ अनसूये । जानासि किन्निमित्तं शकुन्तला वनज्योत्स्नामतिमात्रं प्रेक्षत इति ।
ᶜ न खलु विभावयामि । कथय ।   ᵈ यथा वनज्योत्स्नानुरूपेण पादपेन
सङ्गता । अपि

---

[1] 'At a charming season, indeed, has the union between this pair, the
(Mālikā or jasmine) creeper and the (Sahakāra) tree, taken place. The
Light of the Grove (has) youthfulness by (its) fresh blossoms [i. e. its
fresh blossoms give it all the bloom of a young bride], and the Sahakāra
is capable of enjoyment by reason of (its) young shoots (just) formed.'
Vyatikara is properly 'mutual action,' 'co-operation;' hence 'union,'
'blending,' 'intertwining,' 'intermingling.' See Megha-d. 15. So also
vyatikara-sukham, 'mutual enjoyment.' The prepositions *vi* and *ati* in
composition imply both reciprocity and contrariety: hence, in Hitop.
l. 2319, *vyatikara* signifies 'reverse,' 'turn in affairs.' *Baddha-pallavatayā*,
'by the state of young shoots formed on it.' This is an idiomatic use of
the instr. case of the abstract noun in *tā*, to denote 'by reason of,' 'on
account of.' *Bandh* often means 'to form,' 'produce;' thus, *badhnanti
phalam* (Raghu-v. xii. 69); *drumeshu svayam phalam baddham* (Kumāra-s. v. 60). *Upabhoga-kshama* occurs in connection with *grīshma-
samaya* in p. 6, n. 2, and in Vikram., Act III, with *avakāśa*. The first
meaning of *kshama* is 'patient,' 'enduring.' Here and elsewhere it=
yogya, 'capable,' 'suitable;' so *drishṭi-kshama*, 'capable of being seen,'
'visible.' So in verse 22, *kshatra-parigraha-kshamā*, 'capable of marriage
with a Kshatriya.'

[a]णामं एव्वं अहम्पि अत्तणो अणुरूवं वरं लहेअंति ।

शकुन्तला ।

[b]एसो णूणं तुह अत्तगदो मणोरहो ।   ॥ इति कलशमायर्जैयति ॥

राजा ।

अपि नाम कुलपतेरियमसवर्णक्षेत्रसम्भवा स्यात्[2] । अथवा
कृतं सन्देहेन[3] ।

असंशयं क्षत्रपरिग्रहक्षमा
यदार्यमस्यामभिलाषि मे मनः ।

[a] नाम एवमहमपि आत्मनोऽनुरूपं वरं लभेयेति ।   [b] एष नूनं तवात्मगतो
मनोरथः ।

---

[1] *Api nāma,* 'would that!'   In this sense it occurs also in Vikram.,
Act III, *api nāma Purūravā bhaveyam,* 'would that I were Purūravas!'

[2] 'Can this (lady) possibly be sprung from a wife dissimilar in class
(to that) of the father of the family!' *Api nāma* here = 'may be,' 'can it
possibly be,' 'I wonder whether,' expressive of some doubt [*evaṃ sambhāvyate,* Schol.]   *Kshetra = kalatra,* 'a wife;' *a-savarṇa = asamāna-jātīya,*
'of a different (and inferior) tribe or caste.'   A Brāhman might marry a
Kshatriyā, i. e. a woman of the military or kingly class next below him
(Manu iii. 13), and the female offspring of such a marriage would belong
to the mixed class called *mūrdhābhishikta* or *mūrdhāvasikta,* 'head-
anointed' (Manu x. 6), and would be a suitable object of affection for a
Kshatriya, who in his kingly character was a *mūrdhābhishikta* also.   But
if S'akuntalā were a pure Brāhmaṇī woman, both on the mother's and
father's side, she would be ineligible as the wife of a Kshatriya (Manu
iii. 13).

[3] 'But, have done with [away with] doubt.'   *Athavā* is used to correct
a previous thought [*pakshāntare*].   *Kṛitam* used adverbially (like *alam*)
requires the instr. case.

Verse 22. VAṆŚA-STHAVILA (a variety of JAGATĪ).   See verse 18.

सतां हि सन्देहपदेषु वस्तुषु
प्रमाणमन्तःकरणप्रवृत्तयः ॥२२॥

---

[1] 'Without any doubt she is capable of marriage with a Kshatriya, since my honourable soul has a longing towards her: for in matters that are subjects of doubt, the tendencies [inclinations, promptings] of the hearts of good men are an authoritative guide (to the truth).' The meaning is, 'If this damsel be the daughter of a Brāhman by a Brāhmaṇī [or woman of the same caste], then why should I be conscious of a sudden liking for one whom I could never hope to marry? This feeling of sympathy could only arise towards a legitimate object: for in such matters, the secret prompting [inner voice] of the heart is decisive.' He therefore concludes that she must have been of mixed origin, with some Kshatriya or regal blood in her veins; and discovers afterwards that she was, in fact, the daughter of the Rājarshi Viśvāmitra (originally of the Kshatriya or regal tribe) by an Apsaras. Dushyanta, as a king, belonged of course to the Kshatriya caste. This caste came next to the Brāhmanical, and according to Manu (i. 87) sprang from the arm of Brahmā. They wore a girdle of *mūrvā* and a sacrificial cord of hemp (Manu ii. 42, 44), and were properly soldiers. They were said to have been exterminated by Paraśu-rāma, the representative of the Brāhmanical tribe, in revenge for the murder of his father, the sage Jamadagni, by the sons of Kārtavīrya. This fable is founded on the historical fact that, at some period or other, struggles, arising out of mutual jealousy of each other's encroachments, took place between the military and sacerdotal classes; and that the former did in the end succumb to the superior power and intelligence of the Brāhmans. The example of Viśvāmitra proves that it was possible for a Kshatriya, by the practice of religious austerities, to raise himself to the rank of a Brāhman. Other anomalies of caste occur. A number of men, half warriors, half priests, Kshatriyas by birth, and Brāhmans by profession, called *Angirasas* or 'descendants of Angiras,' were said to have sprung from Nabhāga (Vishṇu-p. p. 359; Mahā-bh. Sel. p. 23). Kings were never chosen from the Brāhmanical class, but were properly Kshatriyas (Manu vii. 2); though there was no positive law against their belonging to the two inferior classes of Vaiśyas and S'ūdras, or even to three mixed classes (*sankara*) formed by inter-marriage with the others, viz. Mūrdhābhishiktas, Māhishyas, and Karaṇas (Manu x. 6). One dynasty of kings of the line of Nanda were actually S'ūdras, and kept the Kshatriyas in subjection (Vishṇu-p. p. 467). In

तथापि तस्मात एवैनामुपलप्स्ये ।

शकुन्तला ॥ ससम्भ्रमम् ॥

[a]अम्मो सलिलसेचसम्भममुग्गदो णोमालिंश्रं उज्झिञ्ञ
वश्ररां मे महुञ्ररो अहिवंट्टइ । ॥ इति धमरबाधां नाटयति ॥

राजा ॥ सस्पृहं विलोक्य ॥

साधु बाधनमपि रमणीयमस्याः ।

यतो यतः षट्चरणोऽभिवर्त्तते

ततस्ततः प्रेरितलोललोचना ।

विवर्त्तितभूरियमद्य शिक्षते

भयादकामापि हि दृष्टिविभ्रमम् ॥ २३ ॥

[a] अहो सलिलसेकसम्भ्रमोन्नतो नवमालिकामुज्झित्वा वदनं मे मधुकरोऽभिवर्त्तते ।

---

fact, the king was but a high officer appointed to train the army, instruct in military exercises, administer justice, and execute the laws. These onerous duties were sufficient to deter the Bráhmans from desiring a rank inconsistent with their love of dignified repose. *Áryam*=*sa-maryádam*, 'correct,' 'upright' (Schol.) *Pramáṇam*, 'that by which anything is measured;' hence, 'a criterion or standard of truth,' 'a sure guide,' 'an authority' [*pramá-káraṇam*, 'a cause of true knowledge,' Schol.] In this sense it is usually found in the singular number, neuter gender, though in apposition to a masculine or feminine noun, or even to a plural noun, as here. Thus also, *Vedáḥ pramáṇam*, 'the Vedas are an authority.' See also Hitop. ll. 169, 1465. *Pravṛitti*, 'onward course;' hence, 'a course of action,' 'tendency,' 'inclination.'

[1] 'Nevertheless [however the suggestions of my heart are to be relied upon] I will accurately ascertain about her.' *Upalapsye*=*jñásye*, 'I will inform myself.'

[2] *Nava-máliká*, see p. 22, n. 1.

[3] *Madhu-kara*, 'a honey-maker,' 'a bee;' cf. Lat. *mellificus*, *mellifer*.

[4] Literally, 'turns towards,' 'attacks,' 'assaults.'

[5] 'Good! even her repulse is charming.'

[6] 'In whichever direction the bee turns towards (her), in that direction

---

Verse 23. VAṆŚA-STHAVILA (a variety of JAGATÍ). See verses 18, 22.

अपि च । ॥ सासूयमिव ॥

चलापाङ्गां दृष्टिं स्पृशसि बहुशो वेपथुमतीं
रहस्याख्यायीव खनसि मृदु कर्णान्तिकचरः ।
करं व्याधुन्वत्याः पिवसि रतिसर्वस्वमधरं
वयं तत्त्वान्वेषान्मधुकर हतास्त्वं खलु कृती ॥ २४ ॥

---

her rolling eye is darted; bending her brows through fear, she is already learning coquettish-movements of the eye even though (as yet) uninfluenced-by-love.' *Yataḥ* and *tataḥ* are properly 'whence' and 'thence;' *tataḥ=tasmāt sthānāt*, 'from that place,' S'. *Shaṭ-ćaraṇa*, 'a six-footed insect,' 'a bee.' *Dṛishṭi-vibhrama*, 'coquettish play of the eye,' 'amorous or sidelong glances,' 'rolling motion of the eyes, indicative of amorous feelings' (=*dṛishṭi-vilāsa*, S'.)

[1] 'Thou touchest repeatedly her quivering eye, whose outer-corner moves (playfully); going close to her ear, thou art softly humming as if whispering a secret (of love); thou art drinking the lip, containing all the treasures of delight, of her waving her hand; (whilst) we, O bee! through (the necessity for) inquiring into the truth (of her origin), are disappointed (of immediate fruition), thou indeed art in the full enjoyment (of thy desire).' In other words, 'Whilst I am kept in suspense by the necessity of ascertaining whether she be a Brāhmaṇī or a Kshatriyā woman, thou art in the act of enjoying her charms.' *Vyādhunvatyāḥ*, gen. case of the pres. part. fem. agreeing with *asyāḥ* understood. *Dhū* with *vi* and *ā*, 'to shake about.' Verbs of cl. 5 reject the nasal in the fem. of this participle, see Gram. 141. *c*, Pāṇ. vii. 1, 80. *Rati-sarvasvam = rati-nidhānam*, 'entirely made up of delight,' 'whose whole essence is delight.' So *khaḍga-sarvasvaḥ*, 'one whose whole property consists of a sword.' *Adhara*, properly 'the lower lip,' in contradistinction to *oshṭha* (i. e. *ava-stha*), 'the upper lip,' but here simply 'the lip.' *Adharam pivasi*, 'thou art drinking (the moisture of) the lip.' Cf. *adharam pātum pravṛittā* (Vikram., Act IV), and *adhara-madhu* ('the nectar of the lip') *pivanti* (Bhartṛi-h. i. 26). *Hata* here=*mano-hata*, 'disappointed,' or rather 'kept in anxious suspense.' *Kṛitī=kṛitārthaḥ* or *kṛita-kṛityaḥ*, 'one who has gained the object of his desire, and is in full enjoyment of it.'

Verse 24. ŚIKHARIṆĪ (a variety of ATYASHṬI). See verse 9.

शकुन्तला ।

[a] ण एसो धिट्ठो विरमदि । अक्खदो गमिस्सं । ॥ पदान्तरे स्थित्वा सदृष्टिक्षेपम् ॥ [b] कहं इदोवि आअच्छदि । हला परित्ताअध परित्ताअध मं इमिणा दुव्विणीदेण दुट्ठमहुअरेण अहि- हूअमाणं ।

उभे ॥ सस्मितम् ॥

[c] काओ वअं परित्ताळुं । दुस्सन्दं अक्कन्द । राळ रक्खिदाइं तवोवणाइं णाम ।

राजा ।

अवसरोऽयमात्मानं प्रकाशयितुम् । न भेतव्यम् । ॥ इत्यर्धोक्ते स्वगतम् ॥ राजभावस्त्वभिज्ञातो भवेत् । भवतु । एवं तावद्- भिधास्ये ।

शकुन्तला ॥ पदान्तरे स्थित्वा ॥

[d] कहं इदोवि मं अणुसरदि ।

[a] न एष भृष्टो विरमति । अन्यतो गमिष्यामि । [b] कथमितोऽप्यागच्छति । हला परित्रायध्वं परित्रायध्वं मामनेन दुर्विनीतेन दुष्टमधुकरेणाभिभूयमानाम् । [c] के आवां परित्रातुम् । दुष्यन्तमाक्रन्द । राजरक्षितानि तपोवनानि नाम । [d] कथमि- तोऽपि मामनुसरति ।

---

[1] Literally, 'ill-trained;' hence, 'ill-behaved,' 'ill-mannered.'

[2] 'Who (are) we to rescue (you)?' i. e. 'who are we that we should be able to rescue you? what power have we to rescue you?' [*āvayoḥ ko 'dhikāraḥ*, S'.] In a passage further on (*kā tvam visrashṭavyasya*, &c.) K. explains *ka* by *na prabhu, avaśa*, 'powerless.' All the Deva-n. MSS. read *parittādum* (Sk. *paritrātum*), but the Beng. read *parittāṇe* (Sk. *paritrāṇe*), and the Calcutta *kā satī amhe parittāṇe*. The infinitive may well stand for the dative *paritrāṇāya* (see p. 14, n. 2), especially in Prākṛit, which has no dative. A precisely similar construction occurs in the Mālavik. p. 55, l. 13, *kā vayaṃ jetum;* and again, p. 40, l. 16, *ke āvām parigrahāya* (Prāk. *pariggahassa*, the gen. being put for Sanskrit dative).

राजा ॥ सत्वरमुपसृत्य ॥

कः पौरवे वसुमतीं शासति शासितरि दुर्विनीतानाम् ।
अयमाचरत्यविनयं मुग्धासु तपस्विकन्यासु ॥ २५ ॥

॥ सर्वा राजानं दृष्ट्वा किञ्चिदिव सम्भ्रान्ताः ॥

अनसूया ।

[1] अज्ज । एक्खु किम्पि अच्चाहिदं । इअं णो पिअसही
महुअरेण अहिळुम्रमाणा कादरीभूदा । ॥ इति शकुन्तलां दर्शयति ॥

राजा ॥ शकुन्तलाभिमुखो भूत्वा ॥

[2] अपि तपो वर्धते ।

॥ शकुन्तला साध्वसादवचना तिष्ठति ॥

[a] आर्ये । न खलु किमप्यत्याहितम् । इयं नौ प्रियसखी मधुकरेणाभिभूयमाना
कातरीभूता ।

---

[1] 'Who is this that is practising rudeness towards the gentle maidens
of the hermits, (and that too) whilst a descendant of Puru [see p. 15,
n. 1], a chastiser of the ill-behaved, is governing the earth?' *Sāsati*, loc.
of the pres. part., used here absolutely, and liable in this root and in
roots of cl. 3 to be confounded with the 3rd pers. pl. present tense.
Mugdhāsu = apraudhāsu, apragalbhāsu, 'gentle,' 'timid,' 'modest,' 'innocent,' Schol.

[2] *Aty-āhita = mahā-bhīti*, 'great danger.' According to some, 'great
outrage,' 'great crime.' The same word occurs in the beginning of Acts
IV. and V. of Vikram. Cf. also Mālavik. 55, 19; 56, 4.

[3] 'I trust your devotion prospers,' 'does your piety thrive?' 'is all
well with your acts of devotion?' This was the regular salutation on
meeting a Brāhman. According to Manu, *kuśalam* implies an inquiry
respecting the well-being of a Brāhman's acts of penance, at all times
liable to be obstructed by evil spirits and demons. Manu ii. 127. See
also Rāmāy. i. 52, 4.

Verse 25. ĀRYĀ or GĀTHĀ. See verse 2.

– – | ◡ – ◡ | ◡ ◡ – ‖ – ◡ ◡ | – ◡ ◡ | ◡ – ◡ | – – | –
◡ ◡ – | ◡ – ◡ | ◡ ◡ – ‖ – – | ◡ ◡ – | ◡ – ◡ | – – | ◡

अनसूया ।

^aदाणिं अदिधिविसेसलाहेण । हला सउन्दले । गच्छ उडञ्झं । फलमिस्सं अग्घं उवहर । इदं पादोदञ्झं भविस्संदि ।

राजा ।

भवतीनां सूनृतयैव गिरा कृतमातिथ्यम् ।

^a इदानीमतिथिविशेषलाभेन । हला शकुन्तले । गच्छोटजम् । फलमिश्रमर्घमुपहर । इदं पादोदकं भविष्यति ।

---

[1] 'Now (indeed it does prosper) by the acquisition of a distinguished guest.' The rites of hospitality were enforced amongst the Hindūs by very stringent regulations. The observance of them ranked as one of the five great sacraments (*mahā-yajña*), under the title of *nṛi-yajña* or *manushya-yajña*, 'the man-sacrament.' Brahmā, Prajāpati, Indra, Fire, the Vasus, and the Sun were supposed to be present in the person of a guest, and to partake of the food that was given to him (Vishṇu-p. p. 306). No wonder then that reverence of him was said to be conducive to wealth, to fame, to life, and to a heavenly reward (Manu iii. 106). On the other hand, no punishment was thought too severe for one who violated these rites. If a guest departed disappointed from any house, his sins were to be transferred to the householder, and all the merits of the householder were to be transferred to him (Vishṇu-p. p. 305; Hitop. l. 361). Some of the things which were to be offered to a guest by even the poorest man were food, vegetables, water for the feet, and if more could not be given, ground on which to lie (Manu iii. 101; Vishṇu-p. p. 308).

[2] The *argha* or *arghya* was a respectful offering to Brāhmans of rice, Dūrvā grass, flowers, fruit, &c., with water in a small boat-shaped vessel. Cf. Rāmāy. i. 20, 9. 10; Wilson's note, Megha-d. 5. *Upahara=ānīya prayaćha*, 'having fetched, present.'

[3] 'This (which we have brought with us for watering our plants) will serve as water for the feet.' Water for the feet was one of the first things invariably presented to a guest in all Eastern countries. Should a guest arrive, a seat is to be offered to him, and his feet are to be washed and food is to be given him (Vishṇu-p. p. 305. Cf. also Luke vii. 44). *Idam*, i. e. *vṛikshārtham ānītam udakam*, Schol.

[4] *Sūnṛitā gīr*, 'kind yet sincere language,' 'complimentary and friendly words without flattery' (*priyaṃ satyaṃ ća vaćanam*). This is one of

प्रियंवदा ।

[a] तेण हि इमस्सिं पच्छाअसीअलाए सत्तवण्णवेदिआए
मुहुत्तअं उवविसिअ परिस्समविणोदं करेदु अज्जो ।

राजा ।

नूनं यूयमप्यनेन कर्मणा परिश्रान्ताः ।

[a] तेन ह्यस्यां प्रच्छायशीतलायां सप्तपर्णवेदिकायां मुहूर्तमुपविश्य परिश्रमविनोदं
करोत्वार्यः ।

---

the four things with which even the poorest man was to greet a guest.
'Grass and earth to sit on, water to wash the feet, and fourthly,
friendly yet sincere speech (*vāk sūnṛitā*) are never refused in the
houses of the good, even though they be poor.' Manu iii. 101;
Hitop. l. 301.

[1] 'On the raised-seat under the Saptaparṇa tree, cool with much
shade, having sat down for a short time, let your honour cause removal
of fatigue.' According to S. *praććhāya=prakṛishṭā yā ćhāyā*, 'excessive
shade.' The other commentators explain it by *prakṛishṭā ćhāyā yatra
deśaḥ*, 'a place where there is excessive shade,' and by *prakṛishṭā ćhāyā
yasyāḥ*, 'having excessive shade.' A parallel passage occurs in the
Mālavik. p. 3, l. 20, *praććhāya-śītale śilāpaṭṭake nishaṇṇā*, &c. It
seems clear that *pra* in this word gives intensity to the original idea.
It is needless to regard it either as a Tatpurusha or Karmadhāraya compound, although it is in such compounds especially that *ćhāyā* becomes
ćhaya. (See p. 6, n. 3, and Raghu-v. iv. 20, xii. 50; Megha-d. 103; Pāṇ.
ii. 4, 22. 25.) *Sapta-parṇa*, 'a tree having seven leaves on a stalk,'
called also *vishama-ććhada*, 'having an odd number of leaves,' and
viśāla-tvaċ, 'having a broad bark' (Raghu-v. iv. 23). *Vedikā=viśrāma-
sthānam*, 'place of repose or rest.' It was probably a quadrangular
raised-seat, something in the form of an altar, and covered with a roof
supported by pillars, used as a kind of arbour for sitting or standing
under. In this case it seems to have been erected under a Sapta-
parṇa tree. *Saptaparṇa-nāmno vṛikshasya tale nirmitā yā vedikā*, S.
According to Sir W. Jones this tree, when full-grown, is very large;
when young, light and elegant. *Muhūrta* is properly an Indian hour
of forty-eight minutes or two Daṇḍas, but is used for any short space
of time.

अनसूया ।

[a] हला सउन्दले । उइदं णो पज्जुवासणं अदिधीणं । एत्थ उवविसम्ह ।   ॥ इति सर्वे उपविशन्ति ॥

शकुन्तला ॥ आत्मंगतम् ॥[1]

[b] किं णु क्खु इमं जणं पेक्खिञ तवोवणविरोहिणो विआरस्स गमणीअम्हि संवुत्ता ।

राजा   ॥ सर्वा विलोक्य ॥

अहो समवयोरूपरमणीयं भवतीनां सौहार्दम् ।[3]

प्रियंवदा   ॥ जनान्तिकम् ॥[4]

[c] अणसूए । को णु क्खु एसो । चउरगम्भीराकिदी महुरं आ-

<hr>

[a] हला शकुन्तले । उचितं नः पर्युपासनमतिथीनाम् । अत्रोपविशामः ।   [b] किं नु खल्विमं जनं प्रेक्ष्य तपोवनविरोधिनो विकारस्य गमनीयास्मि संवृत्ता ।   [c] अन-सूये । को नु खल्वेषः । चतुरगम्भीराकृतिर्मधुरमा-

---

[1] *Ātma-gatam* and *sva-gatam* (lit. 'gone to one's self') used in theatrical language, like 'aside,' to denote that the words which follow are spoken privately, as if to the speaker's self, and not in the hearing of any one but the audience (=*ananya-prakāśam*). *Gata*, 'gone,' is used loosely at the end of a compound to express relationship and connexion without necessary implication of motion. It may mean simply 'in connexion with,' 'in relation to;' or, as here, 'with exclusive reference to,' 'addressed exclusively to.'

[2] 'How now! can it really be that, having looked upon this man, I am become susceptible of [lit. accessible to] an emotion inconsistent with a grove devoted to penance?' *Vikāra* is any alteration or transition from the natural and quiescent state of the soul; hence any emotion, whether of joy, grief, anger, &c. *Kim* is used *kutsāyām*, 'disdainfully,' and=*katham eva jātam*, 'how can it have happened?' The use of the gen. after *gamanīyā* is noticeable.

[3] *Sauhārda*, 'friendship,' an abstract noun from *su-hṛid*. Observe that both *su* and *hṛid* are vriddhied (see Gram. page 63, Prelim. Obs. *c*).

[4] *Janāntikam*, 'aside to a person standing near.' This is a theatrical direction similar to *ātma-gatam*, but the speech which follows is supposed to be audible by one other person, to whom a private signal is

ᵃलबन्ती पहाववन्दो विञ्च लक्खीअदि।

अनसूया।

ᵇसहि। ममवि अत्थि कोदूहलं। पुच्छिस्सं दाव णं।

॥प्रकाशम्॥ ᶜअज्जस्स महुरालाबजणिदो विस्सासो मं मन्तावेदि। कदमो अज्जेण राएसिवंसो अलङ्करीअदि। कदमो वा विरहपज्जुस्सुअजणो किदो देसो। किस्सिमित्तं

ᵃ लपन्प्रभाववानिव लक्ष्यते। ᵇ सखि। ममाप्यस्ति कौतूहलम्। प्रक्ष्यामि तावदेनम्। ᶜ आर्यस्य मधुरालापजनितो विश्वासो मां मन्त्रयति। कतम आर्येण राजर्षिवंशोऽलङ्क्रियते। कतमो वा विरहपर्युत्सुकजनः कृतो देशः। किन्निमित्तं

---

made. 'That which is spoken apart from the rest, with a signal, such as holding up three fingers of the hand (*tripatāka*), being a mutual speech (between two), is called *janāntikam*,' S'. and Sāhit.-d. p. 177.

[1] 'Who can this be (who being) lively (yet) dignified in mien, appears as if endowed with majesty (while) speaking to us sweetly.' *Ćatura*, 'lively,' 'sprightly,' 'animated,' may perhaps mean here, 'polite,' 'courteous,' in relation to *madhuram ālapan*. *Gambhīra*, 'profound,' is used metaphorically for one whose thoughts and feelings are deep or suppressed, 'reserved,' 'dignified,' 'not betraying emotion.' The oldest MS. reads *mahuram;* the others *mahuram piam;* but *piam* belongs properly to the margin.

[2] *Prakāśam*, 'aloud,' another theatrical direction denoting that the words which follow are to be made audible to all, those which precede having been spoken aside.

[3] 'Which race of royal-sages is adorned by your honour?' *Ka-tama*, 'which out of many?' A Rājarshi is a king or man of the Kshatriya and military class who has attained to the rank of a Rishi or saint by the practice of religious austerities. Such were Ikshvāku, Purūravas, Dushyanta, &c. There are six other classes of Rishis. The Rājarshi is inferior to the Brahmarshi or 'Brāhman-saint,' but it was possible for a Rājarshi to raise himself to the rank of the latter, and therefore to the state of a Brāhman, by very severe penance, as exemplified in the story of the celebrated Viśvāmitra, son of Gādhi, and father of S'akuntalā. See p. 43, n. 1; also Rāmāy. i. 20, 20; 65, 18; Astra-śiksha, 118.

[4] 'With its people pining by separation,' i. e. by your absence.

[a] वा सुउमारद्दरोवि तवोवणगमणपरिस्समस्स अत्ता पदं उबंणीदो ।

शकुन्तला ॥ आत्मगतम् ॥

[b] हिअश्र । मा उत्तम्म । एसा तुए चिन्दिदं अणसूश्रा मन्नेदि[2] ।

राजा ॥ आत्मगतम् ॥

कथमिदानीमात्मानं निवेदयामि । कथं वात्मापहारं करो-मिं[3] । भवतु । एवं तावदेनां वक्ष्ये । ॥ प्रकाशम् ॥ भवंति[4] । यः पौरवेण राज्ञा धर्माधिकारे नियुक्तः सोऽहमविघ्नक्रि-योपलभ्भाय धर्मारण्यमिदमायातः[5] ।

[a] वा सुकुमारतरोऽपि तपोवनगमनपरिश्रमस्यात्मा पदमुपनीतः । [b] हृदय । मा उत्ताम्य । एषा त्वया चिन्तितमनसूया मन्त्रयते ।

---

[1] 'Or on what account has your person, so very delicate [unaccustomed to hardships] as it (evidently) is, been brought to the point of (undergoing) the fatigue of visiting a grove of penance ?'

[2] 'O (my) heart! be not uneasy, this Anasūyā is giving utterance to all thy thoughts,' i.e. is making inquiry about all those points about which thou art anxious (such as, who this stranger is, whence he has come, &c.)

[3] 'Or how shall I make concealment of myself?' i.e. how shall I hide my real character? how shall I dissemble? *Apa-hāra = vañćana*, 'deception,' K., or = *ni-hnava* or *sangopana*, 'concealment,' 'dissimulation.' This is a very unusual sense of the word, but all the Deva-n. MSS. agree in reading *apahāra*. The Beng. have *parihāra*, which is also explained by *sangopana*. The oldest Beng. MS. (India Office, 1060) omits the words from *katham vā* to *karomi*.

[4] 'O lady!' voc. of *bhavatī*. A Brāhman is to be accosted with the respectful pronoun *bhavat*, and to any woman not related by blood, the address *bhavati*, 'Madam,' or *subhage bhagini*, 'amiable sister,' is to be used (Manu ii. 128, 129).

[5] 'I, that very person appointed by his majesty, the descendant of Puru, for the supervision of religion, have arrived at this sacred grove, for the purpose of ascertaining whether the (religious) rites are free from obstruction.' The sacrifices of holy men were liable to be disturbed by evil

अनसूया ।

a सणाहा दाणिं धम्मचारिणी ।

॥ शकुन्तला शृङ्गारलज्ज्ञां निरूपयति ॥

सख्यौ ॥ उभयोराकारं विदित्वा मनालितकम् ॥

b हला सउन्दले । जइ एत्थ अज्ज तादो सन्निहिदो भवे ।

शकुन्तला ॥ सरोषम् ॥

c तदो किं भवे ।

सख्यौ ।

d इमं जीविदसव्वसेणवि अदिधिविसेसं किदत्थं करिस्संदि ।

---

a सनाथा इदानीं धर्मचारिणः । सन्निहितो भवेत् । c ततः किं भवेत् ।
b हला शकुन्तले । यद्यवाद्य तातः d इमं जीवितसर्वखेनाप्यति-
पिविशेषं कृतार्थं करिप्यति ।

---

spirits called Rākshasas—the determined enemies of piety. No great
religious ceremony was ever carried on without these demons attempting
to impede its celebration; and the most renowned saints were obliged on
such occasions to acknowledge their dependence on the strong arm of the
military class for protection. The idea that holy men, who had attained
the utmost spiritual power, were unable to cope with the spirits of evil,
and the superiority of physical force in this respect is remarkable. (See
Rāmāy. bk. i. chaps. 20, 21, 32; and end of Act III. of this play.) In
point of fact the Rākshasas were poetical representations of the wild
aborigines of the woods.

[1] *Sa-nāthāḥ*, 'possessed of a guardian;' see p. 26, n. 3.

[2] 'Understanding the gestures of both,' i.e. of S'akuntalā and Dushyanta. *Ākāra*=*ćeshṭā* or *ingita*, 'a gesture,' 'sign,' or rather the state
of mind as evidenced by gestures and outward appearances, such as
change of colour, &c.

[3] 'What would then happen?' i.e. if he were near at hand, what would
he do? Schol.

[4] 'He would make this distinguished guest happy [possessed of the
object of his desire] with all the substance of his life,' i.e. he would do
worthy honour to his guest by offering him the best of his substance and
property. *Sarva-sva*, see p. 33, n. 1. S'. explains *sarva-svam* by *phala-
mūlādikam*, 'fruits, roots, and other necessaries of life.' Fruits and roots

शकुन्तला ।

[a] तुम्हे अवेध । किम्पि हिअए करिअ मन्तेध । ण वो वअणं सुणिस्सं ।

राजा ।

वयमपि तावद्भवत्यौ सखीगतं किमपि पृच्छामः ।

सख्यौ ।

[b] अज्ज । अणुग्गहो विअ इअं अब्भत्थणा ।

राजा ।

भगवान्काश्यपः शाश्वते ब्रह्मणि वर्तते । इयं च वः सखी तदात्मजेति कथमेतत् ।

[a] युवामपेतम् । किमपि हृदये कृत्वा मन्त्रयेथे । न वां वचनं श्रोष्यामि ।
[b] आर्ये । अनुग्रह इवेयमभ्यर्थना ।

---

were the chief food of anchorites, and constituted their whole substance. With an offering of these they were commanded to honour every one who came to their hermitage (Rāmāy. i. 52, 16; 61, 4; Manu vi. 7). The allusion, however, evidently is to S'akuntalā, who might be regarded as the holy father's most valuable possession.

[1] 'Get off with you! having formed some (idea) in your heart, you are speaking.' *Hridaye* or *manasi kri* is not an unusual idiom for 'to turn or cogitate in the mind' (see Rāmāy. ii. 64, 8). *Apetam* is the 2nd du. impv. of *i*, 'to go,' with *apa*.

[2] *Sakhī-gatam*, 'relating to your friend.' (*Śakuntalā-vishayakam*, Schol.) This use of *gata* is noticeable, see note on *ātma-gatam*, p. 38, n. 1. Only one Deva-n. MS. reads *bhavatyau;* but this is supported by the oldest Bengālī, which also adds *kimapi*.

[3] 'His reverence Kaśyapa [see p. 22, n. 1] lives in the constant practice-of-devotion [or in perpetual celibacy].' *Brahman* is properly the Supreme Spirit from which all created things are supposed to emanate and into which they are absorbed. It may also mean the Veda, or holy knowledge. S'. explains *brahman* by *tapas*, i.e. bodily mortification and penance; K. by *brahma-charya*, 'the practice of continence.'

अनसूया ।

[a]सुणादु अज्जी । अत्थि कोवि कोसिओ त्ति गोत्तणामहेओ महप्पहावो राएंसी[1] ।

[a] श्रूयोत्वार्यः । अस्ति कोऽपि कौशिक इति गोत्रनामधेयो महाप्रभावो राजर्षिः ।

---

[1] 'There is a certain Rājarshi [see p. 39, n. 3] of great majesty, whose family name is Kauśika,' i. e. the celebrated Viśvāmitra (descendant of Kuśa or Kuśika), whose story is told in Rāmāy. bk. i. chaps. 35 and 51–65. He is there described as the son of Gādhi (a prince of the Lunar dynasty, king of Gādhi-pur, or the ancient Kanouj), who is the son of Kuśa-nātha, who is the son of Kuśa or Kuśika. According to Vishṇu-p. the following is the pedigree of Viśvāmitra. One of the sons of Purūravas, a prince of the Lunar dynasty (see Vikramorvaśī), was Amāvasu. Thence in direct succession came Bhīma, Kāñcana, Jahnu, Sumantu, Ajaka, Valā-kāśva, and Kuśa. The latter had two sons, Kuśāmba and Kuśa-nātha; but Gādhi was son of Kuśāmba, and was said to be an incarnation of Indra (hence sometimes called Kauśika); for Kuśāmba had engaged in great penance, to obtain a son who should be equal to Indra; and the latter becoming alarmed, took upon himself the character of Kuśāmba's son. Gādhi had a daughter, Satyavatī, who married a Brāhman named Ŗićīka, son of Bhṛigu. This Ŗićīka—with the view of securing to himself a son who should be an illustrious Brāhman, and to his father-in-law a son of great prowess—made two messes of food, one for his own wife, and the other for the wife of Gādhi; infusing into one the qualities suited to a Brāhman, and into the other the properties of power and heroism. The two wives exchanged messes, and so it happened that the wife of Gādhi had a son, Viśvāmitra, who, though a Kshatriya, was born with the inclinations of a Brāhman; and the wife of Ŗićīka had a son, the sage Jamad-agni, who was the father of the warrior-priest Paraśu-rāma, she having by her entreaties induced her husband to transfer the effects of the exchange of food from her son to her grandson. There is something like anachronism in the history of Viśvāmitra. Satyavatī, his sister, was the grandmother of Paraśu-rāma, and it was not till the close of the latter's career that Rāma-ćandra appeared on the field and became the pupil of Viśvāmitra. At any rate the Rishi must have been very old. Indeed, in the Rāmāyaṇa he is stated to have mortified himself for two thousand years before he attained the rank of a Rishi; for many years more before his cohabitation with Menakā, which led to the birth of Śakuntalā;

राजा ।

अस्ति । श्रूयते ।

अनसूया ।

[a] तं णो पिअसहीए पहवं अवगच्छ । उज्झिआए सरीर-संवड्ढणादीहिं तादकस्सबो से पिदा ।

राजा ।

उज्झितशब्देन जनितं मे कौतूहलम् । आ मूलाच्छ्रोतु-मिच्छामि ।

अनसूया ।

[b] सुणादु अज्जो । गोदमीतीरे पुरा किल तस्स राएसिणो उग्गे तवसि वट्टमाणस्स किम्पि जादसङ्केहिं देवेहिं मेणआ णाम अच्छरा पेसिदा णिअमविग्घकारिणी ।

---

[a] तं नौ प्रियसख्याः प्रभवमवगच्छ । उज्झितायाः शरीरसंवर्धनादिभिस्तातकाश्यपोऽस्याः पिता । [b] शृणोत्वार्यः । गौतमीतीरे पुरा किल तस्य राजर्षेरग्रे तपसि वर्तमानस्य किमपि जातशङ्कैर्देवैर्मेनका नामाप्सराः प्रेषिता नियमविघ्नकारिणी ।

and for many thousand years more before he became a Brāhman. It was not till after this period that he became the preceptor of Rāma-ćandra. No chronological inconsistency is too monstrous for Hindū mythology.

[1] 'Know him (to be) the father of our dear friend; but father Kaṇva is the (reputed) father of her, through the fostering of her body, &c., when deserted.' *Prabhava*=*janma-hetu*, 'the operative cause of being,' i.e. a father.

[2] The story of Viśvāmitra, as told in the Rāmāyaṇa, is briefly this. On his accession to the throne in the room of his father Gādhi, in the course of a tour through his dominions, he visited the hermitage of the sage Vaśishṭha (one of the ten Brahmādikas or Prajāpatis, sons of Brahmā). There the cow of plenty, which granted its owner all desires, and was the property of Vaśishṭha, excited the king's cupidity. He offered the Muni untold treasures in exchange for the cow, but being refused, prepared to take it by force. A long war ensued between the King and the Muni (symbolical of the struggles between the Kshatriya and Brāh-

राजा ।

अस्त्येतदन्यसमाधिभीरुत्वं देवानाम् ।[1]

---

manical classes) which ended in the defeat of Viśvāmitra, whose vexation was such, that he devoted himself to tremendous austerities, hoping to force the gods to make him a Brāhman that he might fight with the saint Vaśishṭha on equal terms. The Rāmāyaṇa goes on to recount how, by gradually increasing the rigour of his bodily mortification through thousands of years, he successively earned the title of Rājarshi (i. 57, 5), Rishi (63, 2), Maharshi (63, 19), and finally, Brahmarshi (65, 18). Not till he had gained this last title did Vaśishṭha consent to acknowledge his equality with himself, and ratify his admission into the Brāhmanical state. It was at the time of Viśvāmitra's advancement to the rank of a Rishi, and whilst he was still a Kshatriya, that Indra and the gods, jealous of his increasing power—exhibited in his transporting king Triśanku to the region of the stars, and in saving S'unāḥśepa, the son of his own brother-in-law Ṛićīka, out of the hands of Indra, to whom he had been promised by king Ambarīsha as a victim in a sacrifice—sent the nymph Menakā, to seduce him from his life of continence. The Rāmāyaṇa records his surrender to this temptation, and relates that the nymph was his companion in the hermitage for ten years, but does not allude to the birth of S'akuntalā during that period. It only informs us that at the end of ten years the Rishi extricated himself from this hindrance (*niyama-vighna*), and abandoning the nymph, departed into another region. See Indian Wisdom, p. 363.

[1] 'Such is the dread which the (inferior) gods have of the devotion of others!' Indra and all the deities below Brahman are really, according to the Hindū system, finite beings, whose existence as separate deities will one day terminate, and whose sovereignty in Svarga, or 'heaven,' is by no means inalienable. They viewed with jealousy and alarm any persistency by a human being in acts of penance which might raise him to a level with themselves; and if carried beyond a certain point, might enable him to dispossess them of paradise. Indra was therefore the enemy of excessive devotion, and had in his service numerous nymphs (*apsaras*), such as Menakā, Rambhā, and Urvaśī, who were called his 'weapons' (*Indrasya praharaṇāni*, Vikram., Act I), and who were constantly sent by him to impede by their seductions the devotions of holy men.

अनसूया ।

[a] तदो वसन्तोदारसमए से उम्मादइत्तश्रं रूवं पेक्खिश्रश्र ।

॥ इत्यर्धोक्ते लज्जया विरमति ॥

राजा ।

परस्तादवगम्यत एवं । सर्वथाप्सरःसम्भवैषा ।

अनसूया ।

[b] अहइं ।

राजा ।

उपपद्यते ।

मानुषीषु कथं वा स्यादस्य रूपस्य सम्भवः ।
न प्रभातरलं ज्योतिरुदेति वसुधातलात् ॥ २६॥

[a] ततो वसन्तावतारसमयेऽस्या उन्मादयितृकं रूपं प्रेक्ष्य ।   [b] अथ किम् ।

---

[1] 'Then at the season of the descent of Spring, having looked upon the intoxicating beauty [form] of that (nymph).' Some commentators consider *vasantodāra* to be a compound of *vasanta* and *udāra;* but *odāra* is a legitimate Prākṛit contraction for *avatāra*, although *avadāra* would be equally correct. Cf. *odansayanti* for *avataṇsayanti* (p. 7, n. 1), *hodi* for *havadi* or *bhavati*, *jedi* for *jayadi* or *jayati*, &c. *Avatāra* is from *ava-tṛī*, 'to descend,' and applies especially to the descent of a god from heaven. *Vasanta*, 'the Spring,' is often personified as a deity. See Vikram., Act II, *Pekkhadu bhavaṃ vasantāvadārasūidam assa ahirāmattaṇam pamadavaṇassa*, 'let your honour observe the delightfulness of this pleasure-garden manifested by the descent of Spring.' *Unmādayitrikam* is for the neut. *unmādayitri*, 'that which causes to go mad or be intoxicated' (=*adhairya-janakam*, 'causing unsteadiness ').

[2] 'What (happened) afterwards is quite understood [or guessed by me].' The suffix *tāt*, in words like *parastāt*, *adhastāt*, may stand for the nominative case, as well as for abl. and loc. (Pāṇ. v. 3, 27). Hence *parastāt = para-vṛittāntaḥ*, 'the rest of the story,' 'the subsequent particulars.'

[3] 'Exactly so,' 'how can it be otherwise?' *Athakim* is a particle of assent.

[4] 'It is fitting (that she should be the daughter of an Apsaras). How

---

Verse 26. Śloka or Anushṭubh. See verses 5, 6, 11.

॥ शकुन्तलाधोमुखी भूत्वा तिष्ठति ॥

राजा ॥ स्वात्मगतम् ॥

लब्धावकाशो मे मनोरथः[1] । किन्तु सख्याः परिहासोदा-
हृतां वरप्रार्थनां श्रुत्वा धृतद्वैधीभावकातरं मे मनः[2] ।

प्रियंवदा ॥ सस्मितं शकुन्तलां विलोक्य नायकाभिमुखी भूत्वा[3] ॥

[a] पुणोबि वत्तुकामो विस्स अज्जो ।

[a] पुनरपि वक्तुकाम इवार्यः ।

---

otherwise could there be the birth of this beautiful-form amongst mortal females ? the tremulously-radiant flash does not rise from the surface of the earth (but descends from the skies).' *Apsaraḥ-sambhavatvam* is to be supplied before *upapadyate*. According to K., *prabhā-taralam* (i. e. *prabhayā ćañćalam*) *jyotis* = *vidyut*, 'lightning ;' but S'. applies it also to the beams of the sun and moon. The comparison of the unearthly beauty of a nymph to the radiance of lightning is common. Cf. Megha-d. 40.

[1] 'My desire has found (free) scope,' i. e. since it is certain that she is not a Brāhmaṇī woman (*asavarṇatva-niśćayāt*, 'from the certainty of her not being of the same class with the holy father'), it is clear that my desire is directed towards an attainable object. *Avakāśu* means 'free course,' 'range,' 'power of expatiating.' Cf. p. 55, l. 3, *labdhāvakāśā me prārthanā* ; K. there explains it by *labdhāśrayaḥ* or *sārtho me manorathaḥ*.

[2] 'Nevertheless, having heard her friend's prayer for a husband uttered in joke [see p. 30, l. 1], my heart is held in suspense and anxious,' i. e. anxious to know the truth, as to whether she is really destined for marriage, or for an ascetic life ; and fearful lest at some former time her husband may have been decided upon (*pūrvam asyā varo nirṇīto na vā*, K.) S'. interprets *vara-prārthanā* by *svāmy-abhilāsha*, 'wish for a husband.' *Dhrita-dvaidhībhāva-kātaram* is a complex Dvandva compound. *Dvaidhī-bhāva*, 'a state of difference, distraction, doubt.'

[3] 'Looking with a smile at S'akuntalā, (and then) turning her face towards the hero-of-the-poem ;' lit. 'having become with her face turned,' &c. All the Deva-n. MSS. have this latter clause. *Nāyaka*, in dramatic poetry, is the leading character or hero of the poem, and *nāyikā*, the heroine. Romeo, in Shakespeare, would be the *nāyaka*, and Juliet the *nāyikā*. In every Hindū play there is also a *prati-nāyaka*, or 'anti-hero,' and an *upa-nāyaka*, or 'sub-hero.' See Indian Wisdom, p. 467.

॥ शकुन्तला सखीमङ्गुल्या तर्जयति ॥

राजा ।

सम्यगुपलक्षितं भवत्या । अस्ति नः सच्चरित्रश्रवणलो-
भादन्यदपि प्रष्टव्यम् ।

प्रियंवदा ।

[a] अलं विचारिञ । अणिञन्तणाणुओओ तवस्सिञणो
णामं ।

राजा ।

सखीं ते ज्ञातुमिच्छामि ।
वैखानसं किमनया व्रतमा प्रदाना-
व्यापाररोधि मदनस्य निषेवितव्यम् ।

[a] अलं विचारयै । अनियन्त्रणानुयोगस्तपस्विजनो नाम ।

---

[1] 'S'akuntalā threatens [reproves] her friend with her finger,' i. e.
makes a threatening or chiding gesture, as if she were angry with her
friend for leading Dushyanta to pursue his interrogatories, and were
ashamed at the revelation of the particulars of her history (*ātmano
vrīḍā-janaka-svavṛittāntodghātanam*, K.) According to S'. this is an
example of the coquettish gesture called *lalita*, i. e. though she was really
eager to hear all that her lover had to say, yet by her outward gestures
she appeared to be the reverse (*priyajana-kathā-śuśrūshur api vahis
tad-anyathā*).

[2] 'Rightly judged by your ladyship; from an eagerness to hear (all
the particulars of) the history of pious people, there is still something
(that remains) to be asked by us.'

[3] 'Enough of deliberating; ascetic people may surely be questioned
unreservedly [freely].' *Aniyantraṇānuyoga*=*aniyama-praśna*, 'one to
whom a question may be put without any restraint or ceremony,' K.
Alam, in the sense of prohibiting or forbidding, is more usually found
with instr. case of a noun, but, like *khalu*, it may sometimes be used in
this sense with an indeclinable participle in *tvā* and *ya*, thus *alaṃ
dattvā*, 'enough of giving,' or 'having given, it is enough;' so *khalu
pītvā*, 'having drunk, hold!' See Gram. 918. *a*. The Beng. MSS. read
alam vicāritena.

अत्यन्तमात्मसदृशेक्षणवल्लभाभि-
राहो निवत्स्यति समं हरिणाङ्गनाभिः ॥ २७ ॥

प्रियंवदा ।

[1]अज्ज । धम्मचरणेवि परवसो अञ्जं जणो । गुरूणो उण
से अणुरूववरप्पदाणे सङ्कप्पो ।

[a] आर्ये । धर्मचरणेऽपि परवशोऽयं जनः । गुरोः पुनरस्या अनुरूपवरप्रदाने
सङ्कल्पः ।

---

[1] ‘I wish to ascertain (respecting) your friend—Is this monastic vow,
(so) opposed to the ways of love, to be observed by her (merely) until
her gift-in-marriage ; or else (*āho*), will she dwell to the end (of her
life) along with the female deer, her favourites (from) having eyes like
her own?’ Dr. Boehtlingk remarks that *sakhīṃ te jñātum iććhāmi kim
anayā*, &c., is equivalent to *jñātum iććhāmi kiṃ sakhyā te*, &c., ‘I wish
to know whether this vow is to be observed by thy friend,’ &c. He
gives instances of a similar construction in Draupadī-h. iv. 5 ; Mahā-bh.
iii. 269. *Vaikhānasa*, ‘relating to a *vikhānasa* or hermit ;’ *tena kṛitam
proktaṃ vā vrataṃ vaikhānasam, tat tu niyatāraṇya-vāsa-rūpam*, ‘the
vow which is performed by him or enjoined on him is called *vaikhānasa*,
and that consists in always living in the woods,’ S̒. *Ā pradānāt=pra-
dāna-paryantam*, or *ā vivāhāt*, ‘up to the period of her marriage.’ In
the time of Manu every Hindū girl was given away in marriage before
the season of maturity (*ṛitoḥ prāk pradāna-kālaḥ*), and that father incurred great disgrace who did not so give her away. It was deemed
highly reprehensible if the betrothed husband did not take her to his
own house, when the marriageable period of life arrived ; (see Manu ix. 4,
with commentary.) *Vyāpāra-rodhi madanasya=kāma-kriyā-nivārakam,*
‘hindering amatory actions.’ According to K. *ātma-sadṛiśekshaṇa-valla-
bhābhir* may be optionally resolved into *ātma-sadṛiśekshaṇa-vallabhā ābhir.*
Āho, a particle of doubt, is used *pakshāntare* or *vikalpe*, i. e. antithetically,
in stating an opposite alternative.

[2] ‘Even in the practice of religious duties this person [S̒akuntalā] is
subject to (the will of) another [viz. Kaṇva] ; nevertheless, it is the
settled purpose of the Guru to give her away to a husband suited to her.’
Ayaṃ janaḥ may possibly mean ‘we.’ The same expression occurs in

---

राजा ॥ आत्मगतम् ॥

न दुरवापेयं खलु प्रार्थनॆना ।
भव हृदय साभिलाषं सम्प्रति सन्देहनिर्णयो जातः ।
आशङ्क्से यदग्निं तदिदं स्पर्शेक्षमं रत्नम् ॥२८॥

Act IV. Manu (ix. 2, 3) declares that women were never to be deemed
fit for independence. Day and night they were to be held by their
protectors in subjection. But in certain matters, such as lawful recrea-
tions, and if they chose to enter upon a religious life, they were to be
left at their own disposal. It seems that even in those matters S'akuntalā
was not her own mistress. The holy father had enjoined a life of
penance upon her, but had settled that it should not be perpetual. *Api
sabdena dharmācaranasya sva-cchanda-karanīyatvam sūcitam*, 'by the
word "even" it is indicated that the duties of religion are generally to
be performed as a voluntary act,' K. Amara-sinha explains *sankalpaḥ* by
mānasam karma, 'a mental act or resolution.' Vararuci's rule (i. 22)
by which the Sanskrit *guru* becomes *garua* in Prākrit only applies to the
adjective.

¹ 'This prayer is not difficult of realization,' i. e. a suitable husband,
about whom there is this wish, is not difficult to be obtained; *prārthanā-
sabdena tad-vishayo varo lakshyate*, K., i. e. *prārthanā* is the prayer
supposed to have been made by Kanva, that he might find a suitable
husband for his foster-child.

² 'O (my) heart! become hopeful [possessed of desire]; now the
certainty (of what was a matter) of doubt has come to pass. That which
thou suspectedst (to be) fire, the same (is) a gem capable of being
touched.' *Sandeha-nirnaya*, 'arriving at positive certainty on a doubtful
point.' This was the doubt mentioned just before verse 22, see note to
verse 22. *Antaḥ-karana* is there used for *hridaya*. *Yad* [*Sakuntalā-
rūpam vastu*] *agnim tarkayasi*, 'the thing [viz. S'akuntalā] which thou
imaginedst fire,' S'. The power of a Brāhman, especially if exhibited
in anger, is compared to fire (verse 41 of this play; Bhatti-k. i. 23;
Mahā-bh. i. 3010). There may be some allusion to this here, or it may

---

Verse 28. ĀRYĀ or GĀTHĀ. See verse 2.

⏑⏑⏑⏑ | ⏑ − ⏑ | − − ‖ − ⏑⏑ | − − | ⏑ − ⏑ | − − | −
− − | ⏑ − ⏑ | − − ‖ ⏑⏑ − | − − | ⏑ | − − | −

शकुन्तला ॥ सरोषमिव ॥

[a] अणसूए । अहं गमिस्सं ।

अनसूया ।

[b] किस्सिमित्तं ।

शकुन्तला ।

[c] इमं असम्बंद्धप्पलाविणिं पिअंवदं अज्जाए गोदमीए णिवेदइस्सं ।

अनसूया ।

[d] सहि । ण जुत्तं ते अकिदसक्कारं अदिहिविसेसं विसज्जिअ सच्छन्ददो गमणं । ॥ शकुन्तला न किञ्चिदुक्त्वा प्रस्थितैव ॥

राजा ॥ ग्रहीतुमिच्छन्निगृह्णात्मानम् । आत्मगतम् ॥

अहो चेष्टाप्रतिरूपिका कामिनो मनोवृत्तिः । अहं हि

---

[a] अनसूये । अहं गमिष्यामि ।　　[b] किन्निमित्तम् ।　　[c] इमामसम्बद्धप्रलापिनीं प्रियंवदामार्यायै गौतम्यै निवेदयिष्यामि ।　　[d] सखि । न युक्तं तेऽकृतसत्कारम-तिथिविशेषं विसृज्य स्वच्छन्दतो गमनम् ।

---

simply mean that, supposing S'akuntalā to have been a Brāhmaṇī woman, she would have been as inapproachable to a Kshatriya as a flame of fire. *Sparśa-kshama = samparka-yogya*, see p. 29, n. 1, at end.

[1] *A-sambaddha*, properly 'unconnected;' hence, 'absurd,' 'nonsensical.' *A-baddha* is used with the same acceptation.

[2] Cf. p. 36, n. 1. S'. quotes an aphorism of Bhṛigu, 'Whosoever does not reverently honour an unknown guest, weary with travelling, and hungry and thirsty, him they call (equal in guilt to) the slayer of a Brāhman.'

[3] 'Wishing [making a movement] to arrest (her departure, but) checking himself.' So read all the Deva-n. MSS. The Beng. have, *utthāya jighṛikshur iva icchām nigṛihya*, 'rising up as if desirous of holding her (and then) restraining his intention.' It appears from p. 38, l. 3, that the whole party were seated. The Bengālī reading supposes that, with the idea of arresting her departure, he started up and then checked himself.

H 2

अनुयास्यन्मुनितनयां सहसा विनयेन वारितप्रसरः ।
स्थानादनुच्चलन्नपि गत इव पुनः प्रतिनिवृत्तः ॥२९॥

प्रियंवदा ॥ शकुन्तलां निरुध्य ॥

[a] हला ण दे जुत्तं गन्तुं ।

शकुन्तला ॥ सभ्रूभङ्गम् ॥

[b] किण्णिमित्तं ।

प्रियंवदा ।

[c] रुक्खसेअणाइं दुवे धारेसिं मे । एहि दाव । अत्ताणं
मोचिअ तदो गमिस्ससि । ॥ इति बलादेनां निवर्तयति ॥

राजा ।

भद्रे । वृक्षसेचनादेव परिश्रान्तामचभवतीं लक्ष्ये । तथा
ह्यस्याः

---

[a] हला न ते युक्तं गन्तुम् ।   [b] किन्निमित्तम् ।   [c] वृक्षसेचने द्वे धारयसि
मे । एहि तावत् । आत्मानं मोचयित्वा ततो गमिष्यसि ।

---

[1] 'Ah! what passes in the mind [the state of mind] of a lover has
not a counterpart in his gestures: for, being about to follow the hermit's
daughter, all at once I have been restrained from advancing by decorum;
although not (really) moving from my place, as if having gone, I have
turned back again,' i. e. I feel just as if I had gone and turned back.
Vinayena=kula-maryādayā, S. ;=*sauśilyena*, K., 'by family honour,' 'by
honourable, gentlemanly feeling.' *Vārita-prasara=niruddha-gamana.*

[2] 'With a frown.' *Bhrū-bhanga*, 'bending of the brow,' was one of
the acts of feminine coquetry called *su-kumāra*, 'very delicate.' Under
this head are included all coquettish glances of the eye, S. See p. 32, n. 6;
Megha-d. 73.

[3] 'Thou owest me two waterings of trees,' or according to Sir W.
Jones, 'You owe me the labour, according to our agreement, of watering
two more shrubs.' *Me=mahyam.* *Dhri* in the causal, in the sense of
'to owe,' requires a dative of the person.

Verse 29. ĀRYĀ or GĀTHĀ. See verse 2.

∪∪∪−|−∪∪|∪∪−‖∪∪−|∪∪−|∪−∪|−∪∪|−
−−|∪−∪|−∪∪‖−−|∪∪−|∪−|∪∪−|−

स्रस्तांसावनतिमाचलोहिततलौ बाहू घटोत्क्षेपणा-
द्द्यापि स्तनवेपथुं जनयति श्वासः प्रमाणाधिकः ।
बद्धं कर्णशिरीषरोधि वदने घर्माम्भसां जालकं
बन्धे स्रंसिनि चैकहस्तयमिताः पर्याकुला मूर्धजाः ॥३०॥
तदहमेनामनृणां करोमि । ॥ इत्यङ्गुलीयं दातुमिच्छति ॥
॥ उभे नाममुद्राक्षराण्यनुवाच्य परस्परमवलोकयतः ॥

---

[1] 'For her arms have the shoulders drooping, and the lower part [fore-arm] excessively red through tossing the watering-pot. Even now her unnaturally-strong breathing causes a heaving of her breast; a collection of drops of perspiration, impeding (the play of) the S'irīsha in her ears, has formed upon her face; her dishevelled locks, the fillet (that confined them) having given way [fallen], are held together with one hand.' *Bāhu* is the arm from the shoulder-joint (*aṇsa*) to the wrist, and does not include the *karabha*, or part from the wrist to the fingers. It is divided into two parts, the upper arm, *pragaṇḍa*, or that part of the arm from the elbow to the shoulder; and the lower arm, *prakoshṭha*, commonly called the fore-arm, extending from the elbow to the wrist. *Atilohita-talau* is a Bahuvrīhi comp., in agreement with *bāhū;* *talau* cannot, therefore, be translated by 'the palms of the hands.' One meaning of *tala* is 'fore-arm,' and S'. explains it by *bhujodara*. It may possibly mean the under-surface of the arms, which would be reddened by chafing against the bark-vesture in lifting the watering-pot. *Pramāṇādhikaḥ = svā-bhāvika-mānād adhikaḥ*, 'more than natural,' 'undue.' *Baddham*, 'formed' (see p. 29, n. 1). *Jālaka*, 'a net-work;' hence, 'a collection' (=*samūha*). S'. observes that her face was spotted with drops of perspiration resembling net-work. So *svedam ānana-vilagna-jālakam*, Raghu-v. ix. 68. *Karṇa-śirīsha-rodhi*, see p. 7, n. 1. The drops of perspiration would prevent the play of the pendent flower by causing it to adhere to her cheek (*sthirī-karaṇāt*, S'.; *saṃślesha-kāritvāt*, K.) A similar idea occurs in Megha-d. 28, where the lotus of the ears is described as faded by the act of removing the perspiration from the cheeks in hot weather. The lotus-flower, or one of its petals, furnished as common an ornament for the ear as the *śirīsha* (Megha-d. 69, 46). *Paryākulāḥ = vikīrṇāḥ*, 'scattered.'

[2] This is probably the ring which was afterwards given to S'akuntalā, and served as the *abhijñāna* or 'token of recognition.'

[3] 'Both, reading the letters of the seal with the name (of Dushyanta

राजा ।

अलमस्मानन्यथा सम्भाव्य राज्ञः प्रतिग्रहोऽयमिति रा-
जपुरुषं मामवगच्छथ[1] ।

प्रियंवदा ।

[a] तेण हि णार्हदि एदं अङ्गुलीअश्रं अङ्गुलीविश्रोअं । अज्जस्स वअणेण अणिरिणा दाणिं एसा । ॥ किञ्चिद्विहस्य ॥

[b] हला सउन्दले मोइदासि अणुअम्पिणा अज्जेण अहवा महारायेण । गच्छ दाणिं ।

शकुन्तला ॥ आत्मगतम् ॥

[c] जइ अत्तणो पहविस्सं । ॥ प्रकाशम् ॥ [d] का तुमं विसज्जि-द्व्वस्स रुन्धिद्व्वस्स वा[2] ।

[a] तेन हि नार्हत्येतदङ्गुलीयकमङ्गुलीवियोगम् । आर्यस्य वचनेनानृणेदानीमेषा ।
[b] हला शकुन्तले मोचितास्यनुकम्पिनार्येण अथवा महाराजेन । गच्छेदानीम् ।
[c] यद्यात्मनः प्रभविष्यामि ।   [d] का त्वं विस्रष्टव्यस्य रोद्धव्यस्य वा ।

---

stamped on it), look at each other;' [*asau rājā iti kritvā*, 'thinking to themselves, This is the king,' K.] All the Deva-n. MSS. read *nāma-mudrāksharāni*. *Mudrā* is here, not a 'seal-ring,' but 'the seal or engraved stone on the ring;' *nāma-mudrā*, lit. 'name-seal,' is a seal with a name engraved on it, a signet-seal. So in Mālavik. p. 5, l. 9, and 48, 4, *nāga-mudrā-sanātham anguliyakam*, and *sarpa-mudrakam angu-liyakam*, 'a ring possessed of a snake-seal,' or 'snake-stone seal.' *Anu-vāćya=paṭhitvā*, 'having read,' 'having deciphered.' *Vać* and *anuvać* in the causal have generally this sense in dramatic composition.

[1] 'Enough of considering me to be different (from what I am); (observing) that this (ring) is a present from the king, know me (to be) the king's officer,' i. e. do not imagine me to be the king himself; I am only the king's servant, and this is his ring, which he has given me to serve as my credentials. *Alam anyathā sambhāvya = alam anyathā sambhāvanayā* (see p. 48, n. 3). *Pratigraho 'yam*, i. e. *idam anguri-yakam mayi dattam*, S. *Pratigrah*, especially 'to receive a gift,' with gen., e. g. *na rājñaḥ* (or *nripasya*) *pratigrihnīyāt*, 'let him not receive any gift from the king,' Manu iv. 84. *Pratigraha* is 'that which is received' (*pratigrihyate*); hence, 'any gift.'

[2] 'Who art thou (in respect) of what is to be allowed to go and what

राजा ॥ शकुन्तलां विलोक्य । आत्मगतम् ॥

किं नु खलु यथा वयमस्यामेवमियमप्यस्मान्प्रति स्यात् ।
अथवा लब्धावकाशा मे प्रार्थना । कुतः ।

वाचं न मिश्रयति यद्यपि मे वचोभिः
कर्णं ददात्यभिमुखं मयि भाषमाणे ।
कामं न तिष्ठति मदाननसम्मुखी सा
भूयिष्ठमन्यविषया न तु दृष्टिरस्याः ॥३१॥

नेपथ्ये ।

भो भोस्तपस्विनः । सन्निहितास्तपोवनसत्त्वरक्षायै भवत ।
प्रत्यासन्नः किल मृगयाविहारी पार्थिवो दुष्यन्तः ।

तुरगखुरहतस्तथा हि रेणु-
र्विटपविषक्तजलार्द्रवल्कलेषु ।

---

it is to be held back?' i. e. what power have you to send me away or keep me back? *Kā=na prabhuḥ, avaśā*, K., i. e. you have no right or power (see p. 34, n. 2). This use of gen. for dat., and of the fut. pass. part. for the verbal noun, is peculiar to Prākṛit. The idiom of Sanskrit would require *visarjanāya rodhanāya vā*, 'for loosing or binding.'

[1] 'My wish has found (free) scope,' i. e. I am at liberty to indulge it. *Prārthanā=manoratha*, K.; see p. 47, n. 1.

[2] *Kutaḥ*, 'whence?' 'why so?' often used where a reason is about to be given in verse for some previous statement. Translateable by 'because.'

[3] 'Although she mingles not her speech with my words, (nevertheless) she places her ear directly opposite to me speaking [when I speak]. Granted that she does not stand with her face towards my face, (still) her eye for the most part is not fixed on any other object.' Thus he was free to indulge his hopes, without being actually certain of their realization. *Dadāti* [*nikshipati*, K.] *karṇam*, i. e. *avahitā, tatparā asti*, 'she is very attentive,' S. *Kāmam*, 'well!' 'granted!' see p. 24, l. 10.

[4] 'Be ye near at hand for the protection of the animals of the penance-grove.' *Sattva=jantu*, 'an animal,' S. Boehtlingk translates it by *Wesen*, 'being,' 'existence,' 'weal,' which is a legitimate acceptation of the word.

Verse 31. VASANTA-TILAKĀ (a variety of ŚAKVARĪ). See verses 8, 27.

पतति परिणतारुणप्रकाशः
शलभसमूह इवाश्रमंद्रुमेषु ॥३२॥

अपि च ।

तीव्राघातप्रतिहततरुस्कन्धलग्नैकदन्तः
पादाकृष्टव्रततिवलयासङ्गसञ्जातपाशः ।
मूर्तो विघ्नस्तपस इव नो भिन्नसारङ्गयूथो
धर्मारण्यं प्रविशति गजः स्यन्दनालोकभीतः ॥३३॥

॥ सर्वाः कर्णौ दत्त्वा किञ्चिदिव सम्भ्रान्ताः ॥

---

[1] 'For the dust, raised by the hoofs of the horses, like a swarm of locusts shining in the fading glow of sunset, falls on the trees of the hermitage, having bark-garments, moist with water, suspended (to dry) on the branches.' For *valkaleshu*, see p. 18, n. 1. *Aruṇa* is the glow either of sunrise or sunset, more usually the former. *Pariṇatāruṇa*, as explained by K., is the evening (*sāyantana*) redness of the sun, in contra-distinction to the *aruṇodaya* or ruddiness of dawn. *Śalabha-samūha* = *patanga-nivaha*, 'a multitude of grasshoppers.'

[2] 'An elephant, terrified at the sight of the (king's) chariot, enters the sacred grove, scaring the herd of deer, a corporeal interruption, as it were, of our penance; having a (kind of) tether, caused by the clinging of a coil of creepers dragged along by his feet; having one of his tusks fixed in the trunk of a tree, struck back with a violent blow.' Such is the reading of all the Deva-n. MSS. The Bengálí have *tivrāghātād abhi-mukha-taru-skandha-bhagnaika-danta*, 'with a violent blow having broken one tusk against the trunk of a tree standing in his way.' For *pāda* K. reads *kroḍa*, 'the breast.' *Valaya* = *veshṭana*, 'anything that encircles.' *Pāśa* = *bandhana-rajju*, 'a binding-rope.' *Mūrta* = *mūrti-mat*, 'possessed of a body,' 'corporeal,' as opposed to the spiritual obstruction caused by evil spirits, &c. *Bhinna-saranga-yūthaḥ* is a Bahuvríhi comp. agreeing with *gajaḥ*, 'an elephant by which (*yena*) the herd of deer (*saranga-yūtham*) has been scattered (*bhinnam = vikīrṇam*).' This was probably a wild elephant (*vanya-gaja*), from its being frightened at the sight of the chariot (*syandana*), K. Cf. a scene in Ratn. (Calcutta ed., p. 27).

Verse 32. PUSHPITĀGRĀ, containing twenty-five syllables to the half-verse, each half-verse being alike, the first and third quarter-verses ending at the twelfth syllable.

∪ ∪ ∪ ∪ ∪ – ∪ – ∪ – – ‖ ∪ ∪ ∪ ∪ – ∪ ∪ – ∪ – ∪ – ᴗ

Verse 33. MANDĀKRĀNTĀ (a variety of ATYASHṬI). See verse 15.

राजा ॥ आत्मगतम् ॥

अहो धिक् पौरा अस्मदन्वेषिणस्तपोवनमुपरुन्धन्ति । भवतु । प्रतिगमिष्यामस्तावत् ।

सख्यौ ।

[a] अज्ज । इमिणा आरण्णवुत्तन्तेणं पज्जाउलम्ह । अणुजाणाहि णो उडअगमणस्स ।

राजा ॥ ससम्भ्रमम् ॥

गच्छन्तु भवत्यः । वयमप्याश्रमपीडा यथा न भविष्यति तथा प्रयतिष्यामहे । ॥ सर्वे उत्तिष्ठन्ति ॥

सख्यौ ।

[b] अज्ज । असम्भाविदादिहिसक्कारं भूओवि पेक्खणणिमित्तं लज्जेमो अज्जं विण्णविदुं ।

राजा ।

मा मैवम् । दर्शनेनैव भवतीनां पुरस्कृतोऽस्मि ।

शकुन्तला ।

[c] अणसूए । अहिणवकुससूईएं परिक्खदं मे चलणं ।

[a] आर्ये । अनेनारण्यकवृत्तान्तेन पर्याकुलाः स्मः । अनुजानीहि न उटजगमनाय ।
[b] आर्ये । असम्भावितातिथिसत्कारं भूयोऽपि प्रेक्षणनिमित्तं लज्जामहे आर्यं विज्ञापयितुम् । [c] अनसूये । अभिनवकुशसूच्या परिक्षतं मे चरणम् ।

---

[1] 'By this forest-incident.' *Vrittānta* often means 'incident,' 'event.'

[2] There is no dative case in Prākrit, the genitive supplying its place.

[3] *Vijñāpayitum*, 'to represent respectfully' to a superior (with two accusatives). The phrase *sambhāvitātithi-satkāro bhūyo prekshaṇa-nimittam*, 'adequate hospitality to a guest is a cause of seeing (him) again,' was probably a proverb. The two friends were ashamed to represent this as an argument for a second visit from Dushyanta, as the hospitality they had shewn him had been *a-sambhāvita*, 'inadequate.'

[4] 'Nay, not so ; I have received all the honours (of a guest) by the mere sight of your ladyships.' *Puraskrita* = *satkrita*, 'hospitably entertained.'

[5] 'By the point of a young Kuśa (leaf).' *Sūci*, 'a needle,' here used for the long tapering point of the leaf of the Kuśa grass (see p. 19, n. 1).

I

[a]कुरवञ्झसाहापरिलग्गं च वक्कलं । दाव परिपालेध मं ।
जाव णं मोञ्चावेमि । ॥ इति राजानमेवावलोकयन्ती सव्याजं विलम्ब्य[2]
सह सखीभ्यां निष्क्रान्ता ॥

राजा ।

मन्दौत्सुक्योऽस्मि नगरगमनं प्रति । यावदनुयाचिकान्त-
मेत्य नातिदूरे तपोवनस्य निवेशयामि । न खलु शक्नोमि
शकुन्तलाव्यापारादात्मानं निवर्तयितुम् । मम हि
गच्छति पुरः शरीरं धावति पश्चादसंस्तुतं चेतः ।
चीनांशुकमिव केतोः प्रतिवातं नीयमानस्य ॥३४॥

॥ इति निष्क्रान्ताः सर्वे ॥

॥ प्रथमोऽङ्कः ॥

[a] कुरवकशाखापरिलग्नं च वल्कलम् । तावत्परिपालयतां माम् । यावदेनम्मोचयामि ।

---

[1] A kind of Barleria, with purple flowers and covered with sharp prickles.

[2] 'Pretendedly delaying,' i. e. making some pretext for lingering.

[3] 'I am become indifferent [slackened in my anxiety] about returning
to the city. Meanwhile having joined my followers, I will make (them)
encamp at no great distance from the penance-grove.' *Ni-viś*, 'to enter,'
'take up a station,' 'encamp' as an army (Manu vii. 188; Raghu-v. v. 42).

[4] 'From occupying myself about S'akuntalā.' *Śakuntalā-goćara-pra-
vartanāt*, K. *Śakuntalā-vividha-ćeshṭitatvāt*, S'.

[5] '(My) body goes forward (towards my retinue); (my) heart, not being
in harmony (with my body), runs back (towards S'akuntalā), like the silken
flag of a banner borne against the wind.' *Puraḥ*, i. e. *agrataḥ senām
prati*, 'forward towards (my) army.' *Paśćāt*, i. e. *prishṭhataḥ Śakunta-
lām prati*, K. *Asaṃstuta = aparićita, avaśa*, 'unacquainted,' 'unrelated,'
'not under control (of the body).' *Saṃ-stu*, properly 'to sing or praise
in chorus.' Hence *asaṃstuta* probably means, 'not harmonizing,' 'not in
concert.' The Beng. MSS. read *asaṃsthitam* (=*avyavastham*), 'restless,'
'unstable,' 'ill-regulated.' *Ćīnāṃśukam = ćīna-deśa-bhava-vastra-viśeshaḥ*,
'a kind of cloth produced in the land of China,' 'silk,' 'muslin.'

Verse 34. ĀRYĀ or GĀTHĀ. See verse 2.

॥ अथ द्वितीयोऽङ्कः ॥

॥ ततः प्रविशति विषण्णो विदूषकः ॥

विदूषकः[1] ॥ निःश्वस्य ॥

[a] भो दिट्ठं । एदस्स मिस्स्रआसीलस्स रञ्ञो वअस्सभावेण णिव्विण्णोम्हि । अञ्ञं मिस्रो । अञ्ञं वराहो । अञ्ञं सद्दूलो-

---

[a] भो दिष्टम् । एतस्य मृगयाशीलस्य राज्ञो वयस्यभावेन निर्विण्णोऽस्मि । अयं मृगः। अयं वराहः । अयं शार्दूल

---

[1] *Vidūshaka*, ‘merry,’ ‘facetious,’ ‘good-natured,’ is the title given to the jocose companion and confidential friend of the *nāyaka*, or hero of the piece. This character is to the hero, what the female companion and confidante is to the heroine (*nāyikā*) of the play. He is his constant attendant, and, by a curious regulation, is to be a Brāhman, that is to say, of a caste higher than that of the king himself; yet his business is to excite mirth by being ridiculous in person, age, and attire. S'. says he is grey-haired (*palita*), hump-backed (*kubja*), lame (*khañja*), and with distorted features (*vikritānana*); that the chief part of all that he says is humorous and nonsensical; and that he is allowed access to the female apartments (*antaḥpura-čara*). In fact, he is a kind of buffoon. His attempts at wit, which are never very successful, and his allusions to the pleasures of the table, of which he is a confessed votary, are absurdly contrasted with the sententious solemnity of the despairing hero, crossed in the prosecution of his love-suit. The shrewdness of the heroine's confidantes never seems to fail them under the most trying circumstances; but the clumsy interference of the Vidūshaka in the intrigues of his friend, only serves to augment his difficulties, and occasions many an awkward dilemma. As he is the universal butt, and is allowed in return full liberty of speech, he fills a character very necessary for the enlivenment of the otherwise dull monotony of a Hindū drama. He is called by S'. the *upa-nāyaka* of the piece, or the *nāyakasya upa-nāyakaḥ*, a kind of assistant to the hero (see p. 47, n. 3). K. says, ‘The

[a]त्ति मज्झह्णेवि गिम्हविरलपाअवच्छाआसु वणराईसु आहिअडीअदि अडवीदो अडविं । पत्तसङ्करकसाआणि कडुआणि गिरिणईजलाणि पीअन्ति । अणिअदवेलं सुल्लमंसभूइट्ठो आहारो अएहीअंदि । तुरगाणुधावण-कविडदसन्धिणो रत्तिम्मिवि णिकामं सइदव्वं णेंत्थि । तदो

[a] इति मध्याह्नेऽपि ग्रीष्मविरलपादपच्छायासु वनयजिष्वाहिण्ड्यतेऽटव्या अटवीम् । पत्रसङ्करकषायाणि कटूनि गिरिनदीजलानि पीयन्ते । अनियतवेलं शूल्यमांसभूयिष्ठ आहारोऽश्यते । तुरगानुधावनकष्ठिदसन्धे रात्रावपि निकामं शयितव्यं नास्ति । ततो

Vidūshaka is the name for a ridiculous, childish man (*māṇavaka*), who is always at the side of the hero (*nāyaka-pārśva-parivartin*). He is the companion of his sports and promoter of his amusement (*hāsya-kāri-narma-suhṛid*, or *narma-saćiva*). In effecting the three objects of human life, viz. religious merit, wealth, and pleasure, the family priests assist the king in the first; the heir-apparent (*yuva-rāja*) and the army in the second; the Vidūshaka, the parasite (*pīṭha-marda*), and the pimp (*viṭa*) in the third.' For *viṭa*, see Sanskṛit-English Dictionary.

[1] 'Oh (my evil) destiny! I am worn out by being the associate of this king, who is so addicted to the chase. "Here's a deer," "there's a boar," "yonder's a tiger;" (in the midst of) such (cries and shouts), even at mid-day, is it wandered about from forest to forest, in the paths of the woods, where the shade of the trees is scanty in the hot season.' *Vayasya* is properly 'an associate or companion of about the same age' (*vayas*). *Iti*, 'so saying,' here rather, 'so crying out.' *Vana-rāji*, 'a row of trees,' 'a long tract of forest.' *Āhiṇḍyate*, pres. pass. of rt. *hiṇḍ*, with prep. *ā*, 'to wander about' (an uncommon root); understand *asmābhiḥ*, 'by us.' The Prākṛit is answerable for the collocation of words in this sentence.

[2] 'The bad-smelling [pungent] waters of mountain-streams, astringent from the mixture of leaves, are drunk. At irregular hours a meal, consisting chiefly of meat roasted on spits, is eaten.' *Kaṭu*, 'pungent,' 'ill-scented.' *Śūlya-māṇsa*, 'roast-meat,' 'meat cooked on a spit.' *Bhūyishṭha*, see p. 4, l. 1, with note.

[3] 'Even in the night I cannot lie down comfortably (in my bed) through the dislocation of my joints by the galloping of the horse [or by my horse's pursuit of the game];' see p. 67, l. 6, and note 1. The above is the reading of all the Deva-nāgarī MSS. The Bengālī

॥ ततः प्रविशति यथानिर्दिष्टपरिवारो राजा ॥

राजा ।

कामं प्रिया न सुलभा मनस्तु तद्भावदर्शनाश्वासि ।
अकृतार्थेऽपि मनसिजे रतिमुभयप्रार्थना कुरुते ॥ ३५ ॥

---

tion.' *Yavanī*, properly a Muhammadan woman, a native of *Yavana* or Arabia, but applied also to a native of Greece. Wilson in the Vikramorvaśī (Act V, p. 261), where the same word occurs, remarks that Tartarian or Bactrian women may be intended. The business of these attendants was to act as the bearers of the king's bow and arrows. At the end of Act VI. a Yavanī enters again, *śārnga-hastā*, 'carrying a bow.' A commentator remarks, *Yavanī yuddha-kāle rājño 'straṃ dadāti*, 'the Yavanī in the time of war gives weapons to the king.' K. says, *Yavanī śastra-dhāriṇī*, 'the Yavanī is the weapon-bearer.' *Anga-bhanga*, properly 'palsy or paralysis of the limbs.' K. observes that the Vidūshaka here acts the *vishkambha*, which he defines as an *adhama-praveśakaḥ*, or inferior introductory scene, coming between two acts (*ankayor madhya-vartī*), and performed by inferior actors (*nīća-pātra-prayojitaḥ*). Its object is to connect or bind together the story of the drama and the subdivisions of the plot (*kathā-sanghaṭṭanārtham*), by concisely alluding to what has happened in the intervals of the acts, or what is likely to happen at the end (*bhūtānām bhāvinām api sankshepeṇa sūćanāt*). In the following stage-direction, *daṇḍa-kāshṭha* = *yashṭi*, 'a stick,' 'staff of wood.' Translate, 'he stands leaning on a staff.'

[1] 'Granted my beloved is not easy to gain, still my heart encourages (itself) by observing her gestures (of love). Even though love has not accomplished its object, the desire of both (of us) gives [causes] enjoyment.' *Kāmam*, see p. 55, n. 3. *Na sulabhā*, i. e. from her relationship to the Ṛishi, K. *Tad-bhāva-darśanāśvāsi* is the reading of all the Beng. MSS. and of S'. The Deva-n. read *tad-bhāva-darśanāyāsi*, where *āyāsi* means 'active,' 'kept in activity.' But K., though the MS. gives *āyāsi*, explains it by *santushyati*, 'is cheered,' and by *āśvāsitam*, 'consoled.'

Verse 35. ĀRYĀ or GĀTHĀ. See verse 2.

$$-\ -\ |\ \cup-\cup\ |\ \cup\cup-\ \|\ \cup-\cup\ |\ --\ |\ \cup-\cup\ |\ --\ |\ \cup$$
$$\cup\cup-\ |\ -\cup\cup\ |\ \cup\cup-\ \|\ \cup\cup\cup\cup\ |\ --\ |\ \cup\ |\ -\cup\cup\ |\ -$$

॥ स्मितं कृत्वा ॥ एवमात्माभिप्रायसम्भावितेष्टजनचित्तवृत्तिः
प्रार्थयिता विडम्ब्यते । तद्यथा
स्निग्धं वीक्षितमन्यतोऽपि नयने यत्प्रेरयन्त्या तया
यातं यच्च नितम्बयोर्गुरुतया मन्दं विलासादिव ।
मा गा इत्यवरुद्धया यदपि सा सासूयमुक्ता सखी
सर्वं तत्किल मत्परायणमहो कामी स्वतां पश्यति ॥३६॥

Bhāva=*śṛiṅgāra-ćeshṭā*, 'the expression of amorous sentiments by gestures.' The gestures here referred to are described in the next verse, 36. *Darśana* is either 'seeing,' 'looking at' (=*avalokana*, S.), or 'exhibiting,' 'shewing' (=*sākshāt-karaṇa*, K.) In the latter case, translate, 'by her exhibition of amorous gestures.' *Ubhaya* = *nāyaka-nāyikayoḥ* or *strī-purushayoḥ*. *Prārthanā*=*abhilāsha*, 'longing.'

[1] This is a long Bahuvrīhi comp., agreeing with *prārthayitā*. Translate, 'thus the suitor, who judges of the state of feeling of his beloved one by his own desires, is deluded.' *Evam*=*vakshyamāna-prakāreṇa*, 'in the following manner,' 'in the way about to be mentioned,' K. *Abhiprāya*=*abhilāsha*. *Sambhāvita*=*kalpita*, 'imagined,' or *śaṅkita*, 'suspected.' *Ishṭa-jana*=*manogata-vyakti*, 'the individual in one's thoughts.' *Prārthayitā*=*kāmukaḥ* or *yāćakaḥ*. *Viḍambyate*=*apahāsyate*, 'is mocked,' 'is made a fool of;' supply *kāmena*, 'by love.' The stage-direction *smitam kṛitvā* implies that he is to smile at his own folly in supposing that she was as fond of him as he was of her, merely because her gestures were coquettish.

[2] 'Whereas by her, even though casting her eyes in another direction, a tender glance was given [lit. it was looked tenderly]; and whereas by the weight of (her) hips she moved [lit. it was moved by her] slowly, as if from dalliance; and whereas by (her) detained in these (words), "Do not go" [see p. 52, l. 4], that friend was addressed with disdain; all that certainly had reference to me [or was directed at me]. Ah! (how) a lover discovers (what is) his own!' *Vīkshitam* is here the past pass. part., and *snigdham* an adverb, S. *Avaruddhayā* or, according to some MSS., *uparuddhayā*=*kṛita-gamana-bādhayā* or *kṛita-gati-vyāghātayā*. *Mat-parāyaṇam*=*mad-vishayakam*, 'relating to me.' *Aho* here denotes wonder

---

Verse 36. ŚĀRDŪLA-VIKRĪDITA (a variety of ATIDHṚITI). See verses 14, 30.

विदूषकः ।। तथा स्यात् एव ।।[1]

[a]भो वञस्स । ण मे हत्था पसरन्ति । ता वाञामेत्तेण जञ्ञाबीञसि[2] ।

राजा ।

कुतोऽयं गाचोपघातः ।

विदूषकः ।

[b]कुदो किल सञ्ञं अच्छी आउलीकरिञ असुकारणं पुंच्छेसि[3] ।

[a] भो वयस्य । न मे हस्तौ प्रसरतः । तद्वाचामात्रेण ज्ञाप्यसे । [b] कुतः किल स्वयमच्छिणी आकुलीकृत्याश्रुकारणं पृच्छसि ।

(*āścarye*, K.) *Svatām*=*ātmīyatām* or *svakīyatām*, i.e. *mat-kṛitaṃ sarvam idam*, 'all that was done on my account.' Although her gestures appeared to be unfavourable, yet it was easy to refer them to myself (*ātma-vishayatvāropa iti mantavyam*, K.)

[1] 'Still in the same position,' i. e. leaning on his stick, as if *anga-bhanga-vikala*, 'crippled by paralysis of his limbs.' See p. 62, l. 5.

[2] 'My hands are not capable of extension [lit. do not go forward], therefore by words merely are you wished victory [lit. you are made to be victorious],' i. e. I cannot greet you with the usual *añjali* or salutation made by joining the hands and applying them to the forehead; you must therefore be contented with the salutation *Jayatu !* or *Vijayī bhava !* This is the reading of two old MSS. [India Office, 1060; Bodleian, 233]. The Calcutta ed., without the support of these MSS., adds *jayatu, jayatu bhavān*, 'let your Majesty be victorious.' This is sufficiently implied in *jāpyase*, which is not derived from *jap*, 'to repeat,' 'mutter,' but rather from the causal of *ji*, 'to conquer.' If from *jap* it could only mean 'you are caused to mutter,' whereas the sense of *jāpyase*, as the 2nd pers. sing. pres. pass. of the causal of *ji*, is quite suitable, and, moreover, conforms to the interpretation of K. (*vijayī bhava*), and to that of the Calcutta ed. (*jayārho 'si*). Lassen considers Sanskṛit *jāpyase*=Prakṛit *jaābiasi*, although, with Chézy, he refers it to *jap* (Instit. Ling. Prāk. p. 361). Most of the Deva-n. MSS. read *jīābaissam* for *jīvayishyāmi*, 'I will cause to live,' 'I will wish life,' i. e. I will salute you with *ćiraṃ jīva*, 'long life to you !' Cf. p. 68, l. 9.

[3] 'Why indeed, having yourself troubled (my) eyes, do you inquire the

राजा ।

न खल्ववगच्छामि । भिन्नार्थमभिधीयताम् ।

विदूषकः ।

[a] भो वयस्स । जं वेदसो खुज्जलीलं विडम्बेदि । तं किं
अत्तणो पहावेण । णं णईवेअस्स ।

राजा ।

नदीवेगस्तच्च कारणम् ।

विदूषकः ।

[b] ममवि भवं ।

[a] भो वयस्य । यद्वेतसः कुञ्जलीलां विडम्बयति । तत्किमात्मनः प्रभावेण । ननु नदी-
वेगस्य ।   [b] ममापि भवान् ।

---

cause of (my) tears!' Thus explained by S'. *yathā ko'pi kasyaćin netrayor anguly-ādikam praveśya priććhati bhavataś ćakshushor aśru katham āyāti tathā tvam api,* 'you are like a person who, after thrusting a finger, &c., into the eyes of any one, asks, How does a tear come into your eyes?' The Vidūshaka probably here quotes some proverb, and the king observes in the next line that he does not understand its application in the present case.

[1] *Bhinnārtham = sphutārtham,* 'clearly,' 'distinctly,' Ć.

[2] 'When the reed imitates the character [gait] of the Kubja (plant), is that by its own power; (or) is it not (by the force) of the current of the river?' *Vetasa,* a large reed or cane (Calamus Rotang) growing in Indian rivers. *Kubja* or *kubjaka,* properly 'hump-backed,' but also the name for a crooked aquatic plant (Trapa Bispinosa), called also *vāri-kubja* and *jala-kubja.* S'. says it is sometimes called *kuvalaya,* but this is usually applied to a species of water-lily. He also mentions a reading *kuñja,* 'an arbour,' instead of *kubja.* Possibly this is the reading to which the *kujja* of the Deva-n. MSS. is to be referred, as (according to Vararući ii. 33) *khujja* is Prākṛit for *kubja.* There is doubtless a double meaning in the word, but the first allusion is to the Kubja plant. To appreciate the Vidūshaka's pleasantry in comparing himself to an upright reed, accidentally transformed into a crooked plant, we must bear in mind that his natural form was that of a lame, hump-backed man (see p. 59, n. 1).

राजा ।

कथमिव ।

विदूषकः ।

[a]एवं रज्झकज्जाणि उज्झित्र एआरिसे अमाणुससञ्चारे आउलप्पदेसे वणचरवुत्तिणा तुए होदव्वं । जं सच्चं पच्चहं साबदाणुसरणेहिं सङ्क्षोहिअसन्धिबन्धाणं मम गत्ताणं अणीसोम्हि संवुत्तो । ता पसाद्इस्सं विसज्जिदुं मं एक्का- हम्मि दाव विस्समिदुं ।

राजा ॥ स्वगतम् ॥

अयं चैवमाह । ममापि काश्यपसुतामनुस्मृत्य मृगया- विक्लवं[2] चेतः । कुतः ।

न नमयितुमधिज्यमस्मि शक्तो
धनुरिदमाहितसायकं मृगेषु ।

[a]एवं राजकार्याण्युज्झित्वैतादृशेऽमानुपसञ्चार आकुलप्रदेशे वनचरवृत्तिना त्वया भवितव्यम् । यत्सत्यं प्रत्यहं श्वापदानुसरणैः सङ्क्षोभितसन्धिबन्धानां मम गात्राणामनी- शोऽस्मि संवृत्तः । तत्प्रसादयिप्ये विस्रष्टुं मामेकाहमपि तावद्विश्रमितुम् ।

---

[1] 'By you, having thus relinquished the affairs of the kingdom, it is to be lived as a forester [lit. it is to be existed by you having the manner of life of a forester], in a wild unfrequented region like this. Since (then) I truly am become no (longer) master of my own limbs, whose joints are shaken about by daily chases after wild beasts, therefore I will beg you as a favour to let me go just for one day to rest myself' (cf. p. 60, l. 5, with note 3). *A-mānusha-saṅćāre*, lit. 'untrodden by man,' Taylor MS. *Sandhi-bandha* or *sandhi-bandhana*, properly 'the ligament or tendon which binds the joints together.' *Pra-sad* in causal Ātm. is 'to beg a favour (*prasāda*) from any one.'

[2] *Vi-klava*, according to K. = *vi-hvala*, *parān-mukha*, 'distracted,' 'averse,' 'turning from,' 'disinclined.' Some read *nir-utsuka*, 'in-different.'

सहवसतिमुपेत्य यैः प्रियायाः
कृत इव मुग्धविलोकितोपदेशः ॥३७॥

विदूषकः ॥ राज्ञो मुखं विलोक्य ॥

[a] अत्तभवं किम्पि हिअए करिस्स मंन्तेदि । अरखे मए
रुदिअं आसिं ।

राजा ॥ सस्मितम् ॥

किमन्यत् । अनतिक्रमणीयं मे सुहृद्वाक्यमिति स्थितोऽस्मिं ।

विदूषकः ।

[b] चिरं जीव । ॥ इति गन्तुमिच्छति ॥

राजा ।

वयस्य । तिष्ठ । शृणु सावशेषं मे वचः ।

विदूषकः ।

[c] आणवेदु भवं ।

[a] अत्रभवान्किमपि हृदये कृत्वा मन्त्रयते । अरण्ये मया रुदितमासीत् । [b] चिरं जीव । [c] आज्ञापयतु भवान् ।

---

[1] 'I am not able to bend this strung bow, having-the-arrow-fixed-on-it, against the deer, by whom, possessing (the privilege of) dwelling in the society of (my) beloved, instruction in beautiful glances is as it were given (to her).' *Adhi-jya*, see p. 9, n. 2. *Āhita-sāyaka=arpita-sāyaka*, S'. *Upetya*, lit. 'having undergone' (=*prāpya*, S'.); hence *upeta*, 'possessed of.'

[2] Compare the same expression, p. 42, l. 2, with note.

[3] 'By me a cry has been made in the wilderness,' i. e. I have spoken in vain, no one listens (*ko 'pi na śṛiṇoti*, C.) A kind of proverbial phrase; cf. *aham idaṃ śūnye raumi, kiṃ na śṛiṇoshi me*, Mahā-bh. i. 3022; also Amaru-śataka, 76.

[4] 'What else (ought I to have in my mind)! The words of a friend ought not to be disregarded by me; so (thinking to myself) I stand here.' Understand *hṛidaye kartavyam* after *kim anyat*; and *hṛidaye kṛitvā* after *iti*.

Verse 37. PUSHPITĀGRĀ, in which each half-verse is alike. See verse 32.

FIRST AND THIRD QUARTER-VERSE.   SECOND AND FOURTH QUARTER-VERSE.

⏑⏑⏑⏑⏑⏑‒⏑‒⏑‒‒ ‖ ⏑⏑⏑⏑⏑‒⏑⏑‒⏑‒⏑‒‒

राजा ।

विश्रान्तेन भवता ममाप्येकस्मिन्ननायासे कर्मणि सहायेन
भवितव्यम् ।

विदूषकः ।

[a] किं मोदअखज्जिआए ।

राजा ।

यच्च वक्ष्यामि ।

विदूषकः ।

[b] गहीदो खणो ।

कः कोऽच भोः ।

दौवारिकः ॥ प्रविश्य ॥

[c] आणवेदु भट्टा ।

राजा ।

रेवतक । सेनापतिस्तावदाहूयताम् ।

<hr>

[a] किं मोदकखादिकायाम् ।   [b] गृहीतः खणः ।   [c] आज्ञापयतु भर्ता ।

[1] 'Is it in eating sweetmeats (that you require my assistance)?' The
Calcutta ed. and my own Bombay MS. read *khañjiāe*, which might
equally stand for the Sanskrit *khādikāyām*, but the above is the reading
of the oldest MSS. *Khādikāyām* is given on the authority of Ć. and the
Bodleian MS. (233). According to Pāṇ. iii. 3, 108, Vārt. i. *khādikā* is
an admissible form.

[2] Lit. 'the opportunity is taken,' i.e. now is a good opportunity;
now is the time; I am all attention (*avadhānaṃ kṛitam*, Ć.); I have
nothing else to do but to listen. *Kshaṇa* may mean *nirvyāpāra-sthiti*
or *vyāpārāntara-rahita-sthiti*, 'the state of having no other occupation,'
i.e. leisure, opportunity (see Amara-kośa). The above is the reading
of the oldest MS. and of Kāṭavema. S. has *gṛihītaḥ praṇayaḥ*, and the
Deva-n. MSS. *sugṛihīta ayaṃ janaḥ*.

[3] Cf. the Hindūstānī كري مي.

[4] S'ankara quotes an aphorism of Bharata, as follows: 'A universal
monarch is to be addressed by his attendants with the title of *bhaṭṭa*
(=*bhartā*).' See Sāhit.-d. p. 178. K. remarks that only inferior attendants
ought to use this title; the others, *svāmin* or *deva*.

दौवारिकः ।

[a] तह । ॥ इति निष्क्रम्य सेनापतिना सह पुनः प्रविश्य ॥ [b] एसो अक्षा-
बणुक्कण्ठो भट्टा इदो दिष्ठदिट्ठी एव्व चिट्ठंदि । उवसप्पदु
अज्जो ।

सेनापतिः ॥ राजानमवलोक्य ॥

दृष्टदोषापि स्वामिनि मृगया केवलं गुण एव संवृत्ता ।
तथा हि देवः

अनवरतधनुर्ज्यास्फालनक्रूरपूर्वं
रविकिरणसहिष्णु क्लेशलेशैरभिन्नम् ।
अपचितमपि गात्रं व्यायतत्वादलक्ष्यं
गिरिचर इव नागः प्राणसारं बिभर्ति ॥३८॥

[a] तथा । [b] एस आज्ञापनोत्कण्ठो भर्त्तेषो दत्तदृष्टिरेव तिष्ठति । उपसर्पत्वार्यः ।

---

[1] 'There stands his Majesty eager to give (some) order, casting a look
in this direction.' *Utkaṇṭha*=*udgrīva*, 'having the neck erect with
expectation,' K. Here *utkaṇṭha*=*udyata*, 'ready,' 'on the point of.'

[2] 'Though observed to have evil effects [or regarded as a vice], the
chase has proved only an advantage [or is only a merit] in our master.'
See p. 71, n. 5 at end. One MS. reads *adrishta-doshāpi*, 'certainly hunting
shews no ill effects in our master.'

[3] 'For truly his Majesty, like a mountain-roving elephant, exhibits
[bears, possesses] a body, whose fore-part is hardened by the incessant
friction of the bow-string, patient of the rays of the sun, not affected
by the slightest fatigue [or not weakened one atom by the toils of the
chase], though losing flesh [reduced in bulk] not (in a manner) to be
observed, by reason of (increased) muscular development, (and) all life
and energy.' *Ā-sphālana*=*karshaṇa*, 'rubbing,' 'drawing;' the idea
generally implied is that of moving or flapping backwards and forwards.
Pūrva=*pūrva-bhāga*. *Kleśa-leśair*, so read S. and the India Office MS.
1060. K. passes it over. The others read *sveda-leśair*, but *sveda* was probably accidentally written for *kheda*, the synonym for *kleśa*. *Vyāyatatvāt*
=*kṛita-vyāyāmatvāt* (Ć.) and *dṛiḍhatvāt* (K.) It is the state produced

---

Verse 38. MĀLINĪ or MĀNINĪ (a variety of ATI-ŚAKVARĪ). See verses 10, 19, 20.

॥ उपेत्य ॥ जयतु स्वामी । गृहीतश्चापदमरण्यम् । किमिति
स्थीयते ।

राजा ।

मन्दोत्साहः कृतोऽस्मि मृगयापवादिना माठव्येन ।

सेनापतिः ॥ जनान्तिकम् ॥

सखे । स्थिरप्रतिबन्धो भव । अहं तावत्स्वामिनश्चित्तवृत्ति-
मनुवर्तिष्ये । ॥ प्रकाशम् ॥ प्रलपत्येष वैधेयः । ननु प्रभुरेव
निदर्शनम् । पश्यतु देवः ।

मेदश्छेदकृशोदरं लघु भवत्युत्थानयोग्यं वपुः
सत्त्वानामपि लक्ष्यते विकृतिमच्चित्तं भयक्रोधयोः ।
उत्कर्षः स च धन्विनां यदिषवः सिध्यन्ति लक्ष्ये चले
मिथ्यैव व्यसनं वदन्ति मृगयामीदृग्विनोदः कुतः ॥३९॥

---

by *vyāyāma*, 'athletic and manly exercise of the muscles of the body.'
A-lakshya = na vibhāvya, 'imperceptible.' Compare Act VI. ver. 138,
kshīno 'pi nālakshyate, and Act VII. ver. 174, *avatīrṇo 'pi na lakshyate*;
also Hitop. l. 2631, *kāyaḥ kshīyamāṇo na lakshyate*. *Prāṇa-sāra*, 'whose
whole essence or substance consists of life and spirit' (cf. *vajra-sāra*,
ver. 10). *Bibharti*, see p. 24, n. 1.

[1] 'The forest has its beasts of prey tracked, why then is it stayed?'
i. e. why do you delay? The first clause is the reading of the Deva-n.
MSS.; the second is that of the oldest MS. (I. O. 1060), supported by K.
Kimiti, cf. Hitop. l. 2618; Gīta-g. ix. 7. *Grihīta = jñāta*, 'found out,'
'discovered.' The Beng. MSS. insert *pracāra-sūcita*, 'indicated by their
tracks,' after *grihīta*.

[2] *Māṭhavya* (in the Beng. MSS. *Mādhavya*) is the Vidūshaka's name.

[3] 'Be firm in your opposition,' 'persevere in throwing obstacles in
his way.'

[4] *Pra-lap = yadvā tadvā bhāsh*, 'to talk nonsense,' 'to talk idly.'
Vaidheya = mūrkha, 'a fool,' 'blockhead.'

[5] 'The body (of the hunter) having the waist attenuated by the removal of fat becomes light (and) fit for exertion; moreover the spirit of

Verse 39. ŚĀRDŪLA-VIKRĪDITA (a variety of ATIDHRITI). See verses 14, 30, 36.

विदूषकः ॥ सरोषम् ॥

[a] अवेहि रे उच्छाहहेतुअं । अन्तभवं पकिदिं आपण्णो । तुमं दाव अडवीदो अडविं आहिण्डन्तो णरणासिआलोलु-बस्स जिण्णरिच्छस्स कस्सवि मुहे पडिस्संसि ।

राजा ।

भद्र सेनापते । आश्रमसन्निकृष्टस्थिताः स्मः । अतस्ते वचो नाभिनन्दामि । अद्य तावत्

[a] अपेहि रे उत्साहहेतुक । अन्नभवान्प्रकृतिमापन्नः । त्वं तावदटव्या अटवीमाहिण्डन्न-र्नासिकालोलुपस्य जीर्णर्क्षस्य कस्यापि मुखे पतिष्यसि ।

---

living creatures is observed (to be) affected with various emotions, through fear and anger; and that is the glory of the archers when the arrows fall true on the moving mark. Falsely indeed do they call hunting a vice; where (is) there such a recreation as this?' *Medas*, 'adeps or fat,'=*sthaulya-janaka-dhātu*, 'a secretion causing fatness,' K. It performs the same functions to the flesh that the marrow does to the bones; its proper seat is in the belly (*udara*); hence the flesh is called *medas-kṛit*, 'the maker of adeps.' *Ćheda*=*nāśa*, 'destruction,' 'removal,' 'reduction' (cf. *gharma-ććheda*, 'the cessation of the heat,' Vikram., Act IV). *Utthāna-yogyam*, the Beng. MSS. read *utsāha-yogyam*, but *utsāha* is merely a synonym for *utthāna*, which is applied to any kind of manly exertion. K. says it here refers especially to the act of mounting on horse-back. *Sattvānām*, i. e. *jantūnām siṅhādīnām*, 'of animals such as lions, &c.' *Sattva* may include both the hunters and the hunted. *Vikṛiti-mat*, 'affected with *vikṛiti* or *vikāra*,' i. e. any emotion which causes a change from the *prakṛiti*, or 'natural and quiescent state of the mind' (*parityakta-prakṛitikam*, K.); see p. 38, n. 2. *Bhaya-krodhayoḥ (satoḥ)*= *bhaye krodhe ća*. *Utkarsha*=*pratishṭhā*, 'fame,' 'honour,' S. *Vyasanam*, see Manu vii. 47, 50, where hunting is designated as one of the ten vices (*vyasanāni*) of kings, and is, moreover, included amongst the four most pernicious (*kashṭatama*).

[1] *Utsāha-hetuka*, 'one who encourages or incites to exertion;' opposed to *utsāha-bhaṅga-kara*, 'one who damps another's zeal,' Hitop. l. 1987.

[2] 'His Majesty has returned to his natural state [i.e. is no longer eager after the excitement of hunting]; but thou, wandering from forest to forest, wilt probably fall into the jaws of some old bear, greedy after a human nose.' *Prakṛiti*, 'the natural, quiescent state of the soul,' as

गाहन्तां महिषा निपानसलिलं शृङ्गैर्मुहुस्ताडितं
छायाबद्धकदम्बकं मृगकुलं रोमन्थमभ्यस्यतु ।
विस्रब्धं क्रियतां वराहततिभिर्मुस्ताक्षतिः पल्वले
विश्रामं लभतामिदं च शिथिलज्याबन्धमस्मद्धनुः ॥४०॥

opposed to *vikriti;* see above. *Āhiṇḍan,* see p. 60, l. 2 ; Daśa-kumāra-charita, p. 151, l. 6, says, *bhallūkā manushyāṇām nāsikām gṛihṇanti,* 'bears seize the human nose.' The Beng. read *śṛigāla-mṛiga-lolupasya,* 'eager after a jackal or deer.' *Ṛiććhassa* is Prākṛit for *ṛikshasya,* Vararući iii. 30.

[1] 'Let the buffaloes agitate-by-their-plunges the water of the tanks, repeatedly struck with their horns; let the herd of deer, forming groups under the shade, busy themselves in rumination ; let the bruising of the Mustā grass be made in (undisturbed) confidence by the lines [herds] of boars in the pool ; and let this my bow, having-the-fastening-of-its-string-loose, get repose.' *Gāhantām=lolayantu,* 'let them agitate, stir,' K., hence *lulāpa* is one of the names for a buffalo. *Gāh,* properly, 'to plunge into,' 'plunge about in.' *Nipāna=āhāra,* 'a reservoir or trough near a well' (*upakūpa*). *Romantha=adhara-ćalana,* 'the moving of the lower lip or lower jaw,' K., and *bhuktasya punar ākṛishya* or *udgīrya ćarvaṇam,* 'the chewing of what has been eaten after drawing or vomiting it up again,' i. e. 'chewing the cud,' S., Ć. *Abhyasyatu=paunaḥpunyena karotu,* 'perform again and again,' Ć. *Tatibhiḥ=yūthaiḥ,* 'by herds.' The Beng. read *varāha-patibhir,* 'by the chiefs of the boars.' There is no difficulty in *tatibhir;* many herds of animals form lines or tracks in moving from one place to another, or in grazing. *Mustā,* a sort of fragrant grass (Cyperus Rotundus) eaten by swine, which are hence called *mustāda. Kshati=vidāraṇa,* 'tearing,' 'uprooting,' K. ; =*luṇṭhana,* 'rolling,' S. The grass would probably be bruised by their trampling and rolling on it, as well as by their eating it. *Śithila-jyā-bandha=avaropita-guṇa.* S. and Ć. observe that the above verse furnishes an example of the figure called *Jāti* or *Svabhāvokti,* i. e. a description of living objects by circumstances or acts suited to their character. They also notice the change of construction from the nom. to the instr. in the third line, and its resumption in the fourth.

Verse 40. ŚĀRDŪLA-VIKRĪḌITA (a variety of ATIDHṚITI). See verses 14, 30, 36, 39.

सेनापतिः ।

यत्प्रभविष्णवे रोचते ।

राजा ।

तेन हि निवर्तय पूर्वंगतान्वनग्राहिणः । यथा न मे सैनि-
कास्तपोवनमुपरुन्धन्ति । तथा निषेद्धव्याः । पश्य ।

शमप्रधानेषु तपोधनेषु
गूढं हि दाहात्मकमस्ति तेजः ।
स्पर्शानुकूला इव सूर्यकान्ता-
स्तदन्यतेजोऽभिभवाद्वमन्ति ॥ ४१ ॥

सेनापतिः ।

यदाज्ञापयति स्वामी ।

---

[1] *Prabhavishṇu,* 'the mighty one,' equivalent to our expression 'your Majesty.'

[2] *Vana-grāhiṇaḥ* = *vanāvarodhakān,* see p. 61, n. 1.

[3] 'In ascetics with whom quietism [a passionless state] is predominant (over all other qualities), there lies concealed a consuming energy [fire]. That (energy), like sun-crystals, (which are) grateful [cool] to the touch, they put forth, from (being acted upon by) the opposing-influence of other forces,' i. e. the inhabitants of this hermitage, however passionless they may be, and however kind when unprovoked, contain within themselves a latent energy, which, when roused by opposing influences, will be put forth to the destruction of those who molest them; as a crystal lens, however cool to the touch in its natural state, will emit a burning heat when acted upon by the rays of the sun. *Sama-pradhāneshu,* 'in whom stoicism or self-control is everything;' who regard exemption from all passion and feeling as the *summum bonum.* *Sūrya-kānta,* lit. 'beloved by the sun;' also called *sūrya-maṇi,* 'the sun-gem,' and *dīptopala,* 'shining stone,' a stone resembling crystal. Wilson calls it a fabulous stone with fabulous properties, and mentions a fellow-stone called *candra-kānta,*

Verse 41. Upajāti or Ākhyānakī (a variety of Trishṭubh), each quarter-verse being either *Upendra-vajrā* or *Indra-vajrā,* the former only differing from the latter in the first syllable.

⏑ – ⏑ – – ⏑ ⏑ – ⏑ – – ‖

विदूषकः ।

[a] गच्छ भो दासीएंपुत्त । धंसिदो दे उच्छाहवुत्तंन्तो ।

॥ निष्क्रान्तः सेनापतिः ॥

राजा ॥ परिजनं विलोक्य ॥

अपनयन्तु भवंत्यो मृगयावेषम् । रैवतक । त्वमपि स्वं नियोगमशून्यं कुरु ।

परिजनः ।

[b] जं देवो आणवेदि । ॥ इति निष्क्रान्तः ॥

[a] गच्छ भो दास्याःपुत्र । ध्वंसितस्त उत्साहवृत्तान्तः ।   [b] यदेष आज्ञापयति ।

'moon-beloved,' or *candra-maṇi*, 'moon-gem.' It may be gathered from this passage that its properties resembled those of a glass lens, which instrument may possibly have been known to the Hindūs at the time when this play was written. The following parallel sentiment is from Bhartṛi-h. ii. 30: *Yad aćetano 'pi pādaiḥ sprishṭaḥ prajvalati savitur atikāntaḥ, tat tejasvī purushaḥ para-kṛita-nikṛitam katham sahate*, 'since even the lifeless (stone) beloved of the sun, when touched by its rays, burns; how then can the man of spirit put up with an injury inflicted by another?' *Abhi-bhava = tiras-kāra*, 'insult,' K. The sun's rays, disturbing the natural state of the stone, are compared to the hunter's disturbing the hermitage and provoking its inhabitants. *Vamanti*, so read all the Deva-n. MSS. and K. The Beng. have *sparśānukūlā api sūrya-kāntās, te hy anya-tejo-'bhibhavād dahanti*, 'although the sun-crystals be grateful to the touch, yet, from the influence of other heat, they burn.'

[1] This is inserted on the authority of Kāṭavema and one MS. (India Office, 2696). The Beng. read *bho utsāha-hetuka nishkrama*.

[2] 'Your arguments for exertion (in the chase) have fallen (to the ground),' i. e. all that you have alleged in praise of hunting, with the view of rousing the king's ardour, has been in vain.

[3] Some read *bhavanto;* but the fem. *bhavatyo* (supported by K.) seems more correct, as the female attendants, called Yavanī, are intended. See p. 62, n. 2, in the middle.

[4] 'Fulfil your office (of door-keeper),' i. e. *dvāra-stho bhava*, 'stand at the door,' Ć.

विदूषकः ।

[a] किदं भवदा दाणिं णिम्मच्छिअं । सम्पदं इमस्सिं पा-
दवच्छाआविरइदविदाणसणाहे सिलाअले उवविसदु
भवं । जाव अहम्पि सुहासीणो होमि ।

राजा ।

गच्छायतः ।

विदूषकः ।

[b] एदु भवं । ॥ उभौ परिक्रम्योपविष्टौ ॥

राजा ।

माठव्य । अनवाप्तचक्षुःफलोऽसि । येन त्वया द्रष्टव्यानां
परं न दृष्टम् ।

विदूषकः ।

[c] णं भवं अग्गदो मे वट्टदि ।

[a] कृतं भवतेदानीं निर्मक्षिकम् । साम्प्रतमस्मिन्पादपच्छायाविरचितवितानसनाथे
शिलातल उपविशतु भवान् । यावदहमपि सुखासीनो भवामि ।   [b] एतु भवान् ।
[c] ननु भवानग्रतो मे वर्तते ।

---

[1] '(The place) has now been made clear of flies by your Majesty,' i. e.
we are now left alone, and no one can interrupt us. *Nir-makshikam*=
nir-janam, 'free from people,' S'., C'. According to Pāṇ. ii. 1, 6, *nirmakshikam* is an Avyayībhāva compound, but it is here used adjectively.
The Prākṛit conforms to Vararući iii. 30. The phrase occurs again in the
beginning of Act VI. Has *makshika* here at all the sense of the French
mouchard, 'a spy,' which is derived from *mouche*, 'a fly 1'

[2] 'On this stone-seat, furnished with a canopy,' &c. See p. 26, n. 3.

[3] Lit. 'thou hast not obtained the fruit [benefit] of thy eyes, since
the best of things worthy to be seen has not been seen by thee,' i. e.
until you have seen S'akuntalā, you may consider your eyes as barren,
and created in vain; when they have fallen upon this object, they may
then be said to have yielded some fruit. So in Vikram., Act I, the king,
speaking of Urvaśī, says, *yasya netrayor abandhyayoḥ* (not barren)
pathi sthitā tvam. Cf. also Gīta-g. ix. 6, *Harim avalokaya saphalaya
nayane*, 'look upon Hari (and) make thy eyes fruitful.'

राजा ।

सर्वैः कान्तमात्मीयं पश्यति । अहं तु तामेवाश्रमलल^1-
मभूतां शकुन्तलामधिकृत्य ब्रवीमि ।

विदूषकः ॥ सगतम् ॥

^a होदु । से अवसरं ण दाइंस्सं ।^2 ॥ प्रकाशम् ॥ ^b भो वअस्स ।
जइ सा तवस्सिकण्णआ अणब्भत्थयणीआ । ता किं ताए
दिट्ठआए ।^3

राजा ।

सखे । न परिहार्यं वस्तुनि पौरवाणां मनः प्रवर्तते ।^4

^a भवतु । अस्यावसरं न दास्यामि ।
कानभ्यर्थनीया । तदा किं तया दृष्टया ।

^b भो वयस्य । यदि सा तपस्विकन्य-

---

1 'Every one regards his own as beautiful; but I speak in reference
to that same S'akuntalā who is the ornament of the hermitage.' *Ātmīyam*
is given in one Bombay MS. (India Office, 1858), and is supported by
K. *Lalāma=alankāra*. *Adhikritya*, see p. 6, n. 2. Cf. *mudrām adhikritya bravīmi*, Mālavik. p. 49, l. 11; also Raghu-v. xi. 62; Kumāra-s.
iv. 38.

2 'I will not give him an opportunity (of speaking about her).' *Se
=asya* or *asyāḥ*; K. here interprets it by the former. *Avasara=
vāg-avasara*. 'I will not hold a conversation with him respecting
S'akuntalā,' S'.

3 'If she be a hermit's daughter, she is not (fit) to be wooed (by you);
what (good) then (is to be got) by her seen?' This reading is adopted
from the Beng. MSS.

4 'The heart of the descendants of Puru does not engage in (the pursuit
of) a forbidden object;' see p. 31, n. 1. The Beng. and two Deva-n. MSS.
(India Office, 2696, and my own) insert the following curious verse before
the above sentence: *Mūrkha, Nirākrita-nimeshūbhir netra-panktibhir
unmukhaḥ Navām indu-kalām lokaḥ kena bhāvena paśyati*, 'O fool!
with what feeling [or sentiment] do people look at a new digit of
the moon, turning up their faces with a row of eyes free from
winking?'

सुरयुवतिसम्भवं किल मुनेरपत्यं तदुज्झिताधिगतम् ।
अर्कस्योपरि शिथिलं च्युतमिव नवमल्लिकाकुसुमम् ॥४२॥

विदूषकः ॥ विहस्य ॥

[a] जह कस्सवि पिण्डखज्जूरेहिं उव्वेजिदस्स तिन्तिडिआए
अहिलासो भवे । तह अन्तेउरइत्थिआरअणपरिभाविनो
भवदो इअं अब्भत्थणा ।

[a] यथा कस्यापि पिण्डखर्जूरैरुद्वेजितस्य तिन्तिडिकायामभिलापो भवेत् । तथान्तःपुर-
स्त्रीरत्नपरिभाविनो भवत इयमभ्यर्थना ।

---

[1] '(Although the reputed) offspring of the sage, she is really sprung
from a celestial nymph, (and was) found (by him when) deserted by her;
like a severed flower of the Nava-mallikā fallen on the sun-plant.' The
Nava-mallikā (p. 22, n. 1) is a delicate and tender plant (*atikomala-
pushpa-bheda*, Ć.) which, as a creeper, depends on some other tree for
support; the *arka*, Asclepias, or Calotropis Gigantea, is a large and
vigorous one (see Sir W. Jones, vol. v. p. 102); hence the former is
compared to S'akuntalā, the latter to the sage Kaṇva. S'. explains
arkopari by *raver upari*, 'upon the sun;' but hints that some interpret
arka by *arka-pushpa*. *Sura-yuvati*, see p. 44, n. 2. According to K.,
kila is used *vārtāyām*, 'it is reported;' but S'. interprets it by *niśćitam*,
'certainly.' *S'ithilam=vrintāć ćyutam*, 'fallen from the stalk,' Ć. The
correspondence of the words in the first line with those in the second
is noticeable; *sura-yuvati* with *nava-mallikā*, *muni* with *arka*, *apatya*
with *kusuma*, *ujjhita* with *śithila*, *adhigata* with *ćyuta*.

[2] 'Just as to any one [lit. of any one] having lost his relish for dates,
there may be a great desire for the tamarind; so is this desire of your
Majesty (for S'akuntalā), slighting the jewels of women in (your own)
inner apartments.' *Piṇḍa-kharjūra*, 'a kind of Kharjūra, or date tree,'
here probably used for the fruit, and therefore in the neuter. *Tintiḍikā*
or *tintiḍī*, 'the tamarind tree.' *Udvejitaḥ=vaimanasyam prāpitaḥ*,
'brought to a change of mind or feeling.' *Itthiā, itthikā*, and *itthī* are
Prākṛit equivalents for *strī*. See Lassen's Instit. Prāk. p. 182, note.

Verse 42. ĀRYĀ or GĀTHĀ. See verse 2.

⏑⏑⏑⏑ | ⏑–⏑ | –⏑⏑ ‖ ⏑–⏑ | –– | ⏑–⏑ | –⏑⏑ | –

–– | –⏑⏑ | ⏑⏑– ‖ ⏑⏑⏑⏑ | ⏑⏑– | ⏑ | –⏑⏑ | –

राजा ।

न तावदेनां पश्यसि । येनैवमवादीः ।

विदूषकः ।

[a]तं क्खु रमणिज्जं । जं भवदोबि विम्हञ्रं उप्पादेदि ।

राजा ।

वयस्य । किं बहुना ।

चित्रे निवेश्य परिकल्पितसत्त्वयोगा
रूपोच्चयेन मनसा विधिना कृता नु ।
स्त्रीरत्नसृष्टिरपरा प्रतिभाति सा मे
धातुर्विभुत्वमनुचिन्त्य वपुश्च तस्याः ॥४३॥

[a] तत्खलु रमणीयम् । यद्भवतोऽपि विस्मयमुत्पादयति ।

---

[1] 'Was she endowed with the properties of life by the Creator after
delineating her [placing her] in a picture, or was she rather formed by
the mind by a concentration [assemblage, selection] of lovely forms? She
appears to me like a matchless [the last] creation of the loveliest of women
[or like another creation of the goddess of beauty], when I recollect
[recollecting] the omnipotence of the Creator, and her (graceful) person,'
i. e. whatever was the method of her creation, whether she was formed
by the divine power of Brahmā by first painting a faultless figure and
then breathing into it the principle of life, or by the mind by collecting
into one ideal model a combination of various exquisite forms, it is clear
that she is an unequalled beauty (or, she appears to me as another creation
of the goddess Lakshmī). *Strī-ratna* is explained by S'. and C. to mean
Lakshmī; but it may be referred to the *antaḥpura-strī-ratna* mentioned
before, as *aparā*=*apūrvā*, 'matchless,' 'peerless,' 'without a fellow;' *na
vidyate parā*, K. and S'. *Citre*=*ālekhye*. *Niveśya*=*vinyasya*, 'having
placed, fixed, committed.' *Parikalpita*=*sampādita* or *sampanna*, 'endowed with,' 'provided with,' K. *Yoga*, at the end of a compound, is
often used in a vague manner; *sattva-yoga* may mean 'a combination of
the various properties of being and life.' K. refers to verse 146, beginning
Yad yat sādhu na citre syāt, which asserts that the figure of S'akuntalā

Verse 43. VASANTA-TILAKĀ (a variety of S'AKVARĪ). See verses 8, 27, 31.

विदूषकः ।

[a]जइ एव्वं । पच्चादेसो दाणिं रूववदीणं ।

राजा ।

इदं च मे मनसि वर्त्तते ।

अनाघ्रातं पुष्पं किसलयमलूनं करहहे-
रनाविद्धं रत्नं मधु नवमनास्वादितरसम् ।
अखण्डं पुण्यानां फलमिव च तद्रूपमनघं
न जाने भोक्तारं कमिह समुपस्थास्यति विधिः ॥ ४४ ॥

[a] यद्येवम् । प्रत्यादेश इदानीं रूपवतीनाम् ।

---

was faultless. *Rūpoččaya* = *čandrādy - upamāna - vastu - samuččaya,* i. e. collecting together such models of beauty as the moon, &c., for the purpose of forming one ideal perfect form, by a selection from each, K. *Manasā kṛi,* or *klṛip,* 'to form by means of the mind;' hence often simply, 'to imagine;' and hence, *mano-kalpitam,* 'an idea.' There may be an allusion here to the mind-born sons of Brahmā. *Vidhinā* = *vidhātrā.* K. observes that, being dissatisfied with the thought contained in the first line, he asserts in the second that her limbs were too delicate to have been fashioned by the hand in a picture; they must, therefore, have been formed in the mind. *Strī-ratna* = *strī-śreshṭha,* Ć. *Jātau jātau yad utkṛishṭam taddhi ratnam praćakshate,* 'whatever is best of its kind that indeed they call *ratna* (a gem),' Ć. The connection of *anučintya* with the dative case *me* is unusual, but not without precedent. The Beng. MSS. read *čitte* for *čitre.*

[1] 'The supplanter.' The verb *praty-ā-diś* = *nir-ā-kṛi,* 'to reject,' 're-move,' 'set aside,' and *pratyādeśa,* 'rejection,' is here used for 'the cause of rejection,' i. e. anything which, by its superiority, supplants and brings into contempt what was before highly prized. *Tayā nija-saundarya-mahimnā 'nya-rūpavatī-rūpam khaṇḍitam,* S. So also, in the beginning of Vikram., Urvaśī is called *pratyādeśo rūpa-garvitāyāḥ śrī-gauryāḥ.*

[2] 'That faultless form (is) a flower not (yet) smelt, a tender-shoot un-plucked [uncut, unhurt] by the nails, an unperforated jewel, fresh honey whose flavour (is yet) untasted, and the full [complete] reward of meri-

---

Verse 44. ŚIKHARIṆĪ (a variety of ATYASHṬI). See verses 9, 24.

विदूषकः ।

^a तेण हि लहु परित्ताअदु णं भवं । मा कस्सवि तवस्सि-
णो इङ्गुदीतेल्लचिक्कणसीसस्स हत्थे पडिस्संदि ।

राजा ।

परवती खलु तत्रभवती । न च सन्निहितोऽत्र गुरुजनः ।

विदूषकः ।

^b अध भवन्तां अन्तरेण कीदिसो से दिट्ठिरांओ ।

^a तेन हि लघु परित्रायतामेनां भवान् । मा कस्यापि तपस्विन इङ्गुदीतैलचिक्कण-
शीर्षस्य हस्ते पतिष्यति ।   ^b अथ भवन्तमन्तरेण कीदृशोऽस्या दृष्टिरागः ।

---

torious deeds. I know not to what possessor [enjoyer] here [of this
form] Destiny will resort;' i. e. I know not whom Destiny intends to
be the enjoyer of her beauty. *A-lūna*=*śākhāvasthita*, 'still remaining
on the branch.' *An-āviddha*=*a-samutkīrṇa*, 'unperforated,' K. (cf.
Raghu-v. i. 4, *maṇau vajra-samutkīrṇe sūtrasya gatiḥ*, 'the entrance of
a thread into a gem perforated by the adamant'). The Beng. MSS. read
an-āmuktam=*a-parihitam*, *ākarād ānīta-mātram*, 'not yet put on,' 'only
just drawn from the mine,' S'. *Phalam puṇyānām*, i. e. the fruit of
many virtuous acts in various former births come to its maturity (*pari-
ṇatī-bhūtam*), S'. *A-khaṇḍa*=*sam-pūrṇa*, 'unimpaired,' 'entire.' The
consequences of good deeds performed in former births are sometimes
not fully enjoyed; but sometimes they are perfected. Similarly the form
of S'akuntalā is *an-agha*, 'faultless' (=*pratyavāya-hetu-rahita*, K.) *Iha*,
i. e. *asmin rūpa-vishaye*, 'with reference to this form,' K. *Samupasthāsyati*
=*samprāpsyati*, 'will attain,' 'arrive at.' This verse is an example of
the figure called Rūpaka, see Indian Wisdom, p. 455.

[1] 'Therefore let your Highness quickly rescue her, lest she fall into
the hands of some wretched rustic, whose head is greasy with oil of
Ingudī.' *Ingudī*, see p. 18, n. 1. *Mā*=*yathā na*, K.

[2] 'Towards your Highness what kind of feeling (was displayed) by her
eyes?' *Atha* is used in asking a question, S'. *Bhavantam antareṇa*=
bhavan-nimittam, C.;=*bhavan-madhye*, S'. The same expression occurs
in Vikram., Act III, where the interpretation given is *bhavantam uddiśya*,
i. e. 'with regard to you.' *Antareṇa* (similarly used in Mālavik. p. 5, l. 3)
governs an acc. case, by Pāṇ. ii. 3, 4. *Dṛishṭi-rāga*=*ćakshuḥ-prīti*, 'the
love of the eyes,' K. So read the Deva-n. MSS., supported by K. and S'.;
but the Beng. read *ćitta-rāga*.

राजा ।

निसर्गादेवाप्रगल्भस्तपस्विकन्याजनः । तथापि तु
अभिमुखे मयि संहृतमीक्षितं
हसितमन्यनिमित्तकृतोदयम् ।
विनयवारितवृत्तिरतस्तया
न विवृतो मदनो न च संवृतः ॥४५॥

चिटूपकः ।

ᵃ णंक्खु दिट्ठमेत्तस्स तुह अङ्कं आरोहंदि ।

राजा ।

मिथःप्रस्थाने पुनः शालीनतयापि ममाविष्कृतो भाव-
स्तच्चभवत्या । तथा हि

दर्भाङ्कुरेण चरणः क्षत इत्यकाण्डे
तन्वी स्थिता कतिचिदेव पदानि गत्वा ।

ᵃ ननु खलु दृष्टमात्रस्य तवाङ्कमारोहति ।

---

¹ 'When I stood facing her, her glance was withdrawn, a smile was
(feigned to be) raised from some other cause (than love); hence love,
whose course was checked by modesty, was not (fully) displayed by her,
nor (yet) concealed.' *Anya-nimitta,* i. e. some other cause than love,
which was the true one (*abhilāsha-vyatirikta,* K.) 'By this her love was
concealed,' K. The Beng. have *kathodayam. Vinaya-vārita-vṛittir* is to
be taken with *madano,* K. Cf. p. 52, n. 1.

² 'Is it really (to be expected) that she will seat herself on the lap of
you, barely seen?' i. e. do you expect to gain her all at once, without
some effort?

³ 'Again, at our mutual departure, her feeling towards me was betrayed
by her ladyship, although with modesty.' *Sakhībhyām* before *mithaḥ* is
not supported by the commentators or best MSS.

Verse 45.   DRUTA-VILAMBITA (a variety of JAGATĪ), containing twelve syllables to
the Pāda or quarter-verse, each Pāda being alike.

⏑ ⏑ ⏑ – ⏑ ⏑ – ⏑ ⏑ – ⏑ – ‖

आसीद्विवृत्तवदना च विमोचयन्ती
शाखासु वल्कलमसक्तमपि द्रुमाणाम् ॥४६॥
विदूषकः ।

[a] तेण हि गहीदपाहेञ्ो होहि । किदं तुए उववणं तवो-
वणंत्ति पेक्खामि [2] ।

राजा ।

सखे । तपस्विभिः कैश्चित्परिज्ञातोऽस्मि । चिन्तय तावत्
केनापदेशेन पुनराश्रमपदं गच्छामः ।

विदूषकः ।

[b] की अवरो अबदेसो । एं भवं रात्रा ।

राजा ।

ततः किम् [3] ।

[a] तेन हि गृहीतपाथेयो भव । कृतं त्वयोपवनं तपोवनमिति प्रेक्षे ।   [b] कोऽय-
रोऽपदेशः । ननु भवानाज्ञा ।

---

[1] 'For, having proceeded only a few steps, (that) slim one stopped without any (real) occasion, saying, "My foot is hurt by a blade of Kuśa-grass" [p. 57, l. 16]; and remained with her face turned back (towards me), whilst (pretending to be employed in) releasing her bark-dress, although not (really) entangled in the branches of the shrubs.' *Darbhānkureṇa*, see p. 57, n. 5; p. 19, n. 1. *Akāṇḍe=akasmāt*, K.; *=animittam*, S'.; *=anavasaram*, C̓. One sense of *kāṇḍa* is 'occasion,' 'opportunity.' *Vivṛitta-vadanā*, i.e. *mad-avalokanāya*, 'for a look at me,' S'. This verse is an example of the Samādhi Alankāra, S'.

[2] 'Therefore be provided with a stock of provender; I perceive that you have made the penance-grove a pleasure-grove [pleasure-garden].' *Grihīta-pātheya*, 'one who has provided himself with provender or the necessaries for a lengthened stay from home.' According to K.=*san-naddha*, 'equipped,' 'prepared,' i.e. for rambling in the precints of the hermitage. The Vidūshaka is characteristically anxious about the provisions.

[3] 'And what of that?'

Verse 46. VASANTA-TILAKĀ (a variety of ŚAKVARĪ). See verses 8, 27, 31, 43.

विदूषकः ।

"नीवाराच्छेदुर्भाग्रं अम्हाणं उबहरन्तुत्ति ।

राजा ।

मूर्ख । अन्यमेव भागधेयमेते तपस्विनो निर्वपन्ति । यो
रत्नराशीनपि विहायाभिनन्द्यते । पश्य ।

यदुत्तिष्ठति वर्णेभ्यो नृपाणां क्षयि तत्फलम् ।
तपःषड्भागमक्षय्यं ददत्यारण्यका हि नः ॥४७॥

नेपथ्ये ।

हन्त सिद्धार्थौ स्वः ।

राजा ॥ कर्णं दत्त्वा ॥

अये धीरप्रशान्तस्वरैस्तपस्विभिर्भवितव्यम् ।

a नीवारपष्ठभागमस्माकमुपहरन्तीवति ।

---

[1] A king might take a sixth part of liquids, flowers, roots, fruit, grass,
&c.; but, even though dying with want, he was not to receive any tax
from a Brāhman learned in the Vedas (Manu vii. 131-133). See Indian
Wisdom, pp. 264, 265.

[2] 'These hermits pay another (kind of) tribute, which, leaving behind
heaps of jewels, is welcomed [rejoiced in],' i. e. which is welcomed more
than heaps of jewels. This reading of the oldest Beng. MSS. seems
preferable to that of the Deva-n. *anyad bhāgadheyam eteshām rakshaṇe
nipatati*, 'another tribute accrues (to me) for their protection.' *Bhāga-
dheya* in this sense is masculine, according to Amara-k. S'. and some
of the Beng. have *puṇya* for *anya*.

[3] 'That tribute which arises to kings from the (four) classes is perish-
able; but hermits [inhabitants of the woods] offer us a sixth part of (the
merit of their) penance, (which is) imperishable.' *Varṇebhyaḥ*, i.e. the four
classes of Brāhmans, Kshatriyas, Vaiśyas, and S'ūdras, according to K.,
S'., and Ć. Hence it would appear that the Brāhmans were liable to
some kind of tribute as well as the other classes, though Manu exempts
them. The Beng. have *dhanam* for *phalam*. *Dadati*, third person plural
(see Gram. 331. Obs.)

[4] 'We have accomplished our object,' i. e. in gaining an audience of the
king, S'. *Hanta*, an exclamation of pleasure, S'.

[5] 'Oh! it is to be by the hermits, [it must surely be the hermits] who

---

Verse 47. ŚLOKA or ANUSHṬUBH. See verses 5, 6, 11, 26.

दौवारिकः ॥ प्रविश्य ॥

[a] जेदु जेदु भट्टा । एदे दुवे इसिकुमारआ पडिहारभूमिं[1] उबट्ठिदा ।

राजा ।

तेन ह्यविलम्बितं प्रवेशय तौ ।

दौवारिकः ।

[b] एसो पवेसेमि[2] । ॥ इति निष्क्रम्य । ऋषिकुमाराभ्यां सह प्रविश्य ॥

[c] इदो इदो भवन्ता ।

॥ उभौ राजानं विलोकयतः ॥

प्रथमः ।

अहो दीप्तिमतोऽपि विश्वसनीयतास्य वपुषः । अथवा उपपन्नमेतदस्मिन्नृषिकल्पे[3] राजनि । कुतः ।

अध्याक्रान्ता वसतिरमुनाप्याश्रमे सर्वभोग्ये
रक्षायोगादयमपि तपः प्रत्यहं सञ्चिनोति ।

---

[a] जयतु जयतु भर्ता । एतौ द्वावृषिकुमारकौ प्रतिहारभूमिमुपस्थितौ । [b] एष प्रवेशयामि । [c] इत इतो भवन्तौ ।

---

have deep, calm voices,' i. e. to judge by the tone of the voices which I hear, some of the hermits must have arrived.

[1] Properly 'the ground near the gate of the palace' (*rāja-dvāra-pradeśa*, S'.), but here simply the station of the porter (*dvāra*, Ć.)

[2] The present for the future.

[3] 'Oh! the confidence (inspired by the sight) of his person, majestic though (it be)! But this is quite natural in this king very little inferior to a Rishi.' *Dīptimat=tejasvin*, 'splendid,' 'majestic.' *Viśvasanīyatā*, 'the state of being confided in.' *Upapanna*, 'fit,' 'proper,' 'reasonable,' 'to be expected.' Cf. Vikram., Act II, *upapannam viseshanam asya vāyoh*. *Rishi-kalpe*, 'resembling a Rishi, but with a degree of inferiority;' see *kalpa* in Dict. and Gram. p. 65. LVII. Dushyanta was a Rājarshi, and therefore one degree below a Rishi, see p. 44, n. 2, in the middle; and p. 39, n. 3. The Deva-n. reading is *rishibhyo nātibhinne rājani*, but the Beng. is here preferable.

अस्यापि द्यां स्पृशति वशिनश्चारणद्वन्द्वगीतः
पुएयः शब्दो मुनिरिति मुहुः केवलं राजंपूर्वः ॥४८॥
द्वितीयः ।
गौतम । अयं स बलभित्संखो दुष्यन्तः ।

---

[1] 'Although he abides in the Āśrama [order] of a royal householder where everything is to be enjoyed, yet he also day by day accumulates the-merit-of-penance through the act of protecting (his subjects). Of him also having-his-passions-in-subjection, the (same) sacred title of Muni [or Rishi], but (with this difference that it is) preceded by Rāja [i. e. Rājarshi], repeatedly ascends to heaven, being chanted by pairs of (celestial) minstrels.' *Adhyākrānta* = *svī-krita*, 'appropriated,' 'taken possession of,' K. *Āśrame* = *dharmāćaraṇa-sthāne*, K.; = *gārhasthye*, 'the order of a householder,' S'. and Ć. *Rakshā-yogāt*, see p. 79, l. 7; *yogāt*, 'in consequence of,' 'by reason of,' 'through' (at the end of comps.); cf. Manu vii. 144, 'The highest virtue of a king is the protection of his subjects.' *Ćāraṇa-dvandva* = *gandharva-mithuna*, 'pair of Gandharvas, or celestial choristers.' These beings were the musicians or minstrels of Indra's heaven, just as the Apsarases were the dancers and actresses; and their business was to amuse the inhabitants of Svarga by singing the praises of gods, saints, and heroes. *Ćāraṇa*, 'a bard,' 'herald.' *Kevalam* = *eva*, 'certainly,' K. This verse is an example of Vyatireka, i. e. a description of the difference of two things compared in some respects to each other, S'.

[2] 'The friend of Indra.' *Bala-bhid*, 'Indra,' who crushes armies with his thunderbolt. *Sakhi* at the end of some comps. (like *rātri*, *akshi*, &c.) changes its final to *a*, and becomes a noun of the first class (see Gram. 778; Pāṇ. v. 4, 87. 91. 98. 102). Indra is the chief of the Suras or secondary gods, being inferior to the gods of the Triad; and corresponds to the Jove or Jupiter Tonans of classical mythology. In his lordship over Svarga, or paradise, he might be supplanted by any one who could perform a hundred Aśva-medhas or horse-sacrifices (see p. 45, n. 1). He and the other Suras were for ever engaged in hostilities with their half-brothers, the demons called Asuras or Daityas, the giants or Titans of Hindū mythology, who were the children of Kaśyapa by Diti, as the Suras were by Aditi (see p. 22, n. 3). On such occasions the gods seem to have depended much upon the assistance they received from the heroes of the earth, such as Dushyanta, Purūravas, &c.

Verse 48. MANDĀKRĀNTĀ (a variety of ATYASHṬI). See verses 15, 33.

प्रथमः ।

अथ किम् ।

द्वितीयः ।

तेन हि

नैतच्चित्रं यदयमुदधिश्यामसीमां धरित्री-
मेकः कृत्स्नां नगरपरिघप्रांशुबाहुर्भुनक्ति ।
आशंसन्ते समितिषु सुराः सक्तवैरा हि दैत्ये-
रस्याधिज्ये धनुषि विजयं पौरुहूते च वज्रे ॥४९॥

उभौ ॥ उपगम्य ॥

विजयस्व राजन् ।

---

[1] 'This is not wonderful, that he whose arm is as long as the bar of a city (gate), should alone govern the entire earth, having the ocean as its dark [green] boundary [i. e. as far as the very ocean]. For the gods, constant in enmity, in their battles with the demons, expect victory through [in] his strung bow and the thunderbolt of Indra.' *Parigha*=*argala*, 'the bar or bolt which fastens a gate.' In a city-gate it was both massive and long (*styāna, dīrgha*, Ć.), and therefore an object of comparison highly significant of muscular strength. It should be borne in mind that length and vigour of arm were prime requisites in the ancient hero, whose fame depended on his skill and power in managing a bow. Hence the appositeness of such epithets as *mahā-bāhu* and *prānṡu-bāhu*, 'long-armed.' *Bhunakti* =*pālayati*, Ć.; *bhuj* is often applied to a king in the sense of ruling and protecting the earth; cf. *kritsnām prithivīm bhunkte*, Manu vii. 148; also Raghu-v. viii. 7, iii. 4. *Āṡansante*=*iććhanti*, 'wish for,' 'hope for,' 'aspire after.' *Samitishu surāḥ*, &c., this is the Beng. reading; the Deva-n. have *sura-yuvatayo baddha-vairā*, &c. *Daityaiḥ*, see last note. *Adhi-jye*, see p. 9, n. 2. The loc. has sometimes the force of the instr. *Pauruhūta*=*Aindra*, 'belonging to Indra;' *Puru-hūta*, 'much-worshipped,' is one of Indra's thousand names. This verse is an example of the figure called Dīpaka or 'illustration,' Ś.; its use is to throw light, as it were, upon an idea by some apposite illustration. See Indian Wisdom, p. 455.

[2] *Vi-ji*, 'to conquer,' is rightly conjugated in Ātm. (Pāṇ. i. 3, 19).

Verse 49. MANDĀKRĀNTĀ (a variety of ATYASHṬI). See verses 15, 33, 48.

राजा ॥ आसनादुत्थाय ॥

अभिवादये भवन्तौ ।

उभौ ।

स्वस्ति भवते । ॥ इति फलान्युपहरतः ॥

राजा ॥ सप्रणामं परिगृह्य ॥

आज्ञामिच्छामि ।

उभौ ।

विदितो भवानाश्रमसदामिहस्थः ।[1] तेन भवन्तं प्रार्थयन्ते ।

राजा ।

किमाज्ञापयन्ति ।

उभौ ।

तत्रभवतः कण्वस्य महर्षेरसान्निध्याद्रक्षांसि[2] न इष्टिविघ्न-मुत्पादयन्ति । तत्कतिपयरात्रं[3] सारथिद्वितीयेन[3] भवता सनाथीक्रियतामाश्रम[4] इति ।

राजा ।

अनुगृहीतोऽस्मि ।

विदूषकः ॥ अपवार्य ॥

ªएसा दाणिं अनुजला दे अब्भत्थणा ।

राजा ॥ स्मितं कृत्वा ॥

रैवतक । मद्वचनादुच्यतां सारथिः । सवाणासनं रथमुप-स्थापयेति ।

ª एषा इदानीमनुकूला तेऽभ्यर्थना ।

---

[1] 'Your Highness is known to the inhabitants of the hermitage (to be) staying here.' *Aśrama-sad*=*āśrama-vāsin*, 'a dweller in a hermitage,' 'a hermit;' so *nāka-sad*, 'a dweller in paradise,' 'a god;' hence *sadana*, 'a house.' *Vidita*, in construction with the gen., is noticeable; see Pāṇ. iii. 2, 188, ii. 3, 67; also Raghu-v. x. 40, *viditaṃ tapyamānaṃ tena me bhuvana-trayam*, 'the three worlds are known to me (as) being harassed by him.'

[2] *Rakshas*=*rākshasa*, see p. 40, n. 5.

[3] *Rātram*, see p. 86, n. 2. *Dvitīyena*, see p. 13, n. 1.

[4] *Sanāthī-kriyatām*, see p. 26, n. 3.

दौवारिकः ।

a जं देवी आणवेदि । ॥ इति निष्क्रान्तः ॥

उभौ ॥ सहर्षम् ॥

अनुकारिणि पूर्वेषां युक्तरूपमिदं त्वयि ।
आपन्नाभयसत्त्रेषु दीक्षिताः खलु पौरवाः ॥ ५० ॥[1]

राजा ॥ सप्रणामम् ॥

गच्छतां पुरो भवन्तौ । अहमप्यनुपदमागत एव ।

उभौ ।

विजयस्व । ॥ इति निष्क्रान्तौ ॥

राजा ।

माठव्य । अप्यस्ति[2] शकुन्तलादर्शने कुतूहलम् ।

विदूषकः ।

b पढमं सपरिवाहं आसि । दाणिं रक्खसवुत्तन्तेण विन्दूवि
णावसेसिंदो ।[3]

---

a यदेव आज्ञापयति ।   b प्रथमं सपरिवाहमासीत् । इदानीं राक्षसवृत्तान्तेन
विन्दुरपि नावशेषितः ।

---

[1] 'This is a becoming trait in you, an emulator of (your) ancestors.
Truly the descendants of Puru are ordained (to officiate) in the sacrifices
of (giving) exemption-from-fear to the distressed ;' i. e. whilst we Brāhmans
are consecrated to officiate in real sacrifices, the highest duty of kings is
the protection of their afflicted subjects (see p. 86, n. 1). So read all the
Deva-n. and some of the Beng. MSS. The Beng. (Bodleian, 234) has
satrena, and some begin the verse with *upakāriṇi sarveshām*, 'the helper
of all.' *Yukta-rūpam*, cf. p. 15, l. 3. *Āpannābhaya-sattreshu*=*āpad-
gatānām bhaya-trāṇe*, S'. *Dīkshitāḥ*=*kṛita-pratishṭhāḥ*, 'consecrated.'

[2] *Api* may be used *praśne*, 'in asking a question' (cf. p. 35, l. 9).

[3] 'At first it was overflowing; (but) now, by the account of the
Rākshasas, not even a drop is left.' *Parivāha* is either 'an inundation,'
or 'a channel for carrying off an excess of water;' the Beng. MSS. have
aparibādham, 'unchecked.' *Vṛittāntena*=*nāma-grahaṇena*, 'by the
mention.'

Verse 50. SLOKA or ANUSHTUBH. See verses 5, 6, 11, 12, 26, 47.

राजा ।

मा भैषीः । ननु मत्समीपे वर्तिष्यसे ।

विदूषकः ।

a एस तव चक्करक्खीभूदोम्हि ।

दौवारिकः ॥ प्रविश्य ॥

b सज्जो रधो भट्टिणो विजअप्पत्थाणं अवेक्खदि । एस उण णअरादो देवीणं आणत्तिहरो करभओ आअंदो ।

राजा ॥ सादरम् ॥

किमम्बाभिः प्रेषितः ।

दौवारिकः ।

c अहइं ।

राजा ।

ननु प्रवेश्यताम् ।

दौवारिकः ।

d तह । ॥ इति निष्क्रम्य । करभकेण सह प्रविश्य ॥ e एसो भट्टा । उबसप्प ।

करभकः ।

f जेदु जेदु भट्टा । देवी आणवेदि । आगामिणि चउत्थ-दिअहे पुत्तपिंडपालणो णाम उबवासो भविस्सदि ।

---

a एष तव चक्ररक्षीभूतोऽस्मि ।   b सज्जो रथो भर्तुर्विजयप्रस्थानमपेक्षते । एष पुनर्नगराद्देवीनामाज्ञप्तिहरः करभक आगतः ।   c अप किम् ।   d तथा ।
e एष भर्ता । उपसर्प ।   f जयतु जयतु भर्ता । देव्याज्ञापयति । आगामिनि चतुर्थ-दिवसे पुत्रपिंडपालनो नामोपवासो भविष्यति ।

---

1 'I will guard the wheel of your chariot.' There seems to be a humorous double meaning in *ćakra-raksha*, which may also be translated, 'the commander of the wing of your army;' the Deva-n. have *esa rakkhasādo rakkhidomhi*, 'I am protected from the Rākshasa.'

2 'The equipped chariot awaits your Majesty's advance to victory; but here is Karabhaka just arrived from the city, bearing a message from the queen-mother.' *Devīnām* is here in the respectful plural; so *ambābhiḥ* two lines below.

3 *Atha kim* (=*vāḍham*, 'yes') is used *aṅgīkritau*, see p. 46, n. 3.

[a] तहिं दीहाउणा अवसं अम्हे सम्भावइद्व्वत्ति ।

राजा ।

इतस्तपस्विकार्यम् । इतो गुरुजनाज्ञा । द्वयमप्यनतिक्रम-
णीयम् । किमत्र प्रतिविधेयम् ।

विदूषकः ।

[b] तिसङ्कू विञ्च अन्तरा चिट्ठ ।

[a] तच्च दीर्घायुषावश्यं वयं सम्भावयितव्या इति ।   [b] त्रिशङ्कुरिवान्तरा तिष्ठ ।

---

[1] 'On the fourth day, (which is now) coming [i. e. on the fourth day after to-day], the ceremony [fast] named Putra-piṇḍa-pālana [i. e. cherishing of the body of a son] will take place; thereat [on that occasion] certainly we ought to be honoured-with-a-visit by the long-lived-one [by your Majesty, long may you live!].' Most of the Beng. MSS. read *putra-piṇḍa-pāraṇa;* but Ć. substitutes *pālana,* and interprets the phrase by *pura-deha-pushṭi-prada.* S'. gives the same interpretation, but reads *paryupāsana* for *pālana. Piṇḍa, deha-mātre iti Medinī,* 'according to Medinī, *piṇḍa* has the sense of body,' S'. and Ć. *Putra* refers to the king in his relation to the queen-mother. The Deva-n. reading (*pravṛitta-pāraṇa upavāsaḥ,* 'a fast which has come to an end') is not very satisfactory. *Upa-vāsa=vrata,* 'a religious ceremonial accompanied with fasting, but not necessarily a fast.' K. and Ć. observe that one name for this ceremonial was *putra-rāja,* and that it consisted in offering various presents to the young king of sweetmeats, clothes, &c., just as might be done in the present day on the occasion of a birth-day. *Dīrghāyus,* see p. 9, n. 1. *Vayam* is used in plural like *devīnām* above. *Sambhāvayitavyāḥ,* see p. 26, n. 1.

[2] 'In this direction the business of the hermits, in the other the command of a venerable parent (calls me). Both are not to be neglected. How, in such a case, can an arrangement be effected?' *Dvayam api,* 'both the one and the other;' *api* is often affixed to *dvi* in this sense; see Amara-k. ii. 1, 5; Mālavik. p. 16, l. 22. In Hitop., l. 2048, *dvayam* without *api* has the sense of 'both.'

[3] 'Stand between, like Triśaṅku.' The story of this monarch is told at length in Rāmāy. i. 57-60 (see also p. 43, n. 1). He is there described as a just and pious prince of the Solar race, who aspired to celebrate a great sacrifice, hoping thereby to ascend to heaven in his mortal body. He first requested the sage Vaśishṭha to officiate for him; but, being

राजा ।

सत्यमाकुलीभूतोऽस्मि ।

कृत्ययोर्भिन्नदेशत्वाद्‌द्वैधीभवति मे मनः ।
पुरः प्रतिहतं शैलैः स्रोतः स्रोतोवहो यथा ॥५१॥

॥ विचिन्त्य ॥ सखे । त्वमम्बया पुत्र इति प्रतिगृहीतः । अतो
भवानितः प्रतिनिवृत्य मां तपस्विकार्यव्यग्रमानसमावेद्य

---

refused, he then applied to the sage's hundred sons, by whom he was
cursed and degraded to the condition of a Ćaṇḍāla. In this pitiable state
he had recourse to Viśvāmitra, who undertook to conduct the sacrifice,
and invited all the gods to be present ; they, however, refused to attend.
Upon this the enraged Viśvāmitra, by his own power, transported Triśanku to the skies, whither he had no sooner arrived than he was hurled
down again, head foremost, by Indra and the gods ; but, being arrested in
his downward course by Viśvāmitra, remained suspended *between heaven
and earth*, forming a constellation in the southern hemisphere. The story
is differently told in some of the Purāṇas (Wilson's Vishṇu-p. p. 371, note).
They and the Hari-v. describe Triśanku as a wicked prince, guilty of
three heinous sins (*śanku*). S. adopts this view of his character, and
calls him *kṛita-bahutara-malina-karmā rājā*. *Antarā* = *tapovana-sva-
nagarayor madhye*, 'between the hermitage and the city.' The facetious
allusion to Triśanku is quite characteristic of the Vidūshaka, and affords
an example of the Vyāhāra Alaṅkāra, S. and Ć.

[1] 'Verily I am embarrassed. From the difference of the places of the
two duties [i. e. on account of the distance between the place where the
two duties have to be performed] my mind is divided in two, as the stream
of a river driven back [made to recoil] by rocks (lying) before it' (cf. the
sentiment at verse 34). *Puraḥ* = *agre*, 'in front,' 'ahead.' Although
pratihataṃ śaile, 'which has struck on a rock,' is the reading of the Beng.
MS. (Bodleian, 233) and most of the Deva-n., yet the other Bengālī and
S. read *śailaiḥ*, which I prefer. The Deva-n. read *srotovaho*, gen. case
of *sroto-vah*, f. 'a river.' Some MSS. have *srotovaham* = *nadī-sambandhi*,
'belonging to a river' (K., S., and Ć.), an adjective agreeing with *srotaḥ*.
This verse is an example of the Yathopamā Alaṅkāra, or 'comparison by
the use of the conjunction *yathā*.'

Verse 51. Śloka or Anushṭubh. See verses 5, 6, 11, 12, 26, 47, 50.

तत्रभवतीनां पुत्रकृत्यमनुष्ठातुमर्हति ।[1]

विदूषकः ।

[a]सां खलु मं रक्खोभीरुअं गणेसि ।[2]

राजा ॥ सस्मितम् ॥

भो महाब्राह्मण । कथमेतद्भवति सम्भाव्यते ।[3]

विदूषकः ।

[b]जह राआणुएण गन्तव्वं । तह गमिस्सं ।

राजा ।

ननु तपोवनोपरोधः परिहरणीय इति सर्वाननुयाचि-
कांस्त्वयैव सह प्रस्थापयामि ।

विदूषकः ॥ सगर्वम् ॥

[c]तेण हि जुवराआओम्हि दाणिं संवुत्तो ।

राजा ॥ आत्मगतम् ॥

चपलोऽयं वटुः ।[6] कदाचिदसत्प्रार्थनामन्तःपुरेभ्यः कथ-[7]

<hr>

[a] ननु खलु मां रक्षोभीरुकं गणयसि ।   [b] यथा राजानुजेन गन्तव्यम् । तथा
गमिष्यामि ।   [c] तेन हि युवराजोऽस्मि इदानीं संवृत्तः ।

<hr>

[1] 'You have been received by the queen-mother as a son; therefore let your honour, having returned from hence and having announced that my mind is intent on [zealous for] the business of the hermits, have the goodness to discharge the office of a son towards her Majesty.' *Putra iti pratigrihītaḥ*, i. e. *tvam poshita-putro bhavasi*, 'you are an adopted son,' S'. Some MSS. have *putratvam* for *putra-kṛityam*.

[2] 'Surely you do not suppose me to be afraid of the Rākshasas.'

[3] 'How is this possible in your honour?' or, 'how could such a thing be thought of in your honour?' *Bhavati*, loc. sing. of *bhavat*. *Sambhāvyate* may mean, 'is fitting,' 'is consistent.' *Mahā-brāhmaṇa* is generally used ironically.

[4] 'I will go, as it should be gone by the younger brother of a king.'

[5] *Yuva-rāja*, 'the young prince,' who was the heir-apparent and generally associated with the reigning monarch in the throne.

[6] *Vaṭu*, 'a youth,' 'a lad;' here it is equivalent to 'follow,' 'chap.'

[7] *Kadācid*, 'perchance.' *Prārthanā=abhilāshita*, 'desire,' 'pursuit,'

येत् । भवतु । एनमेवं वक्ष्ये । ॥ विदूषकं हस्ते गृहीत्वा । प्रकाशम् ॥

वयस्य । ऋषिगौरवादाश्रमं गच्छामि । न खलु सत्यमेव
तापसकन्यकायां शकुन्तलायां ममाभिलाषः । पश्य ।

क्व वयं क्व परोक्षमन्मथो मृगशावैः सममेधितो जनः ।
परिहासविजल्पितं सखे परमार्थेन न गृह्यतां वचः ॥५२॥

विदूषकः ।

[a] अहइं ।

॥ इति निष्क्रान्ताः सर्वे ॥

॥ द्वितीयोऽङ्कः ॥

[a] अथ किम् ।

'suit;' i. e. *Śakuntalā-vishayānusandhāna-rūpa-kathā*, 'the story of my pursuit of S'akuntalā,' S'.

[1] 'From reverence for the Ṛishis,' lit. 'from the venerableness of the Ṛishis.'

[2] 'Where are we, (and) where a person brought up with fawns out of sight of love? O friend! let not a word uttered heedlessly in jest be taken in earnest.' *Kva-dvayam atyantāsambhāvanāyām*, 'two *kva's* are expressive of excessive incompatibility,' S'. (see p. 14, n. 1). *Nāgarikāraṇya-janayoḥ sambandho nopapadyate iti bhāvaḥ*, 'the meaning is that a connection between a town-bred person and a forester is not possible,' K. *Paroksha-manmatha = apratyaksha-manmatha* or *ajñāta-manmatha* or *agoćara-kāma*, 'one who has had no perception or experience of love,' 'one who is out of the reach of its influence.' *Parihāsa-vijalpita = hāsya-bhāshita*, K.; *= kautuka-bhāshita*, S'.; cf. *parihāsa-vijalpa* in Act VI. The Beng. MSS. read *vikalpita*, 'invented.' *Paramārthena = tattvena*.

Verse 52. VAITĀLĪYA, containing twenty-one syllables to the half-verse, each half-verse being alike, the first and third quarter-verses ending at the tenth syllable.

◡◡−◡◡−◡−◡− ‖ ◡◡−−◡◡−◡−◡−

॥ अथ तृतीयाङ्कादौ विष्कम्भः ॥

॥ ततः प्रविशति कुशानादाय यजमानशिष्यः ॥

शिष्यः ।

अहो महाप्रभावो राजा दुष्यन्तः । येन प्रविष्टमात्र एवा-
श्रमं तत्रभवति निरुपप्लवानि नः कर्माणि संवृत्तानि ।
का कथा वाणसन्धाने ज्याशब्देनैव दूरतः ।
हुङ्कारेणेव धनुषः स हि विघ्नानपोहति ॥५३॥

---

[1] 'A pupil of the sacrificing-(Brāhman) bearing Kuśa grass.' *Yajamāna*=*yajvan*, 'a sacrificer,' 'priest' (see Raghu-vaṇśa xviii. 11). In
Telugu it has acquired the sense of 'master.' Cf. *tataḥ praviśato Bharata-
śishyau*, Vikram., Act III. Some read *yajamānaḥ śishyaḥ*. The translation would then be, 'a pupil occupied about a sacrifice.' The pupil, or
religious student, certainly, did not officiate himself. *Śishya*, in fact,
denotes a Brahmaćārin, or young Brāhman in that state of pupilage
through which every Brāhman had to pass, living in the house of his
preceptor, who, in return for instruction given, required his assistance
in various menial offices, in collecting materials for sacrifice, and in asking
alms. 'Let the student carry water-pots, flowers, cow-dung, fresh earth,
and Kuśa grass, as much as may be useful to his preceptor; let him bring
wood for the oblation to fire; let him go begging through the whole
district,' &c. (Manu ii. 176, &c.) *Kuśa*, see p. 19, n. 1.

[2] 'Since on his Highness having merely entered the hermitage, our rites
have become free from molestation.' So read the oldest MSS. supported
by K.; others *pravishṭa evāśramaṃ tatra-bhavati*, &c.

[3] 'What mention of fitting the arrow (to the bow)? for by the mere
sound of the bow-string from afar, as if by the roar of the bow, he dispels
the obstacles.' *Kā kathā*, 'what account?' i. e. what necessity for fitting

---

Verse 53. ŚLOKA or ANUSHṬUBH. See verses 5, 6, 11, 12, 26, 47, 50, 51.

यावदिमान्वेदिसंस्तरणार्थं दर्भानृत्विंग्भ्य उपहरामि ।
॥ परिक्रम्यावलोक्य च । आकाशे ॥ प्रियंवदे । कस्येदमुशीरानुलेपनं
मृणालवन्ति च नलिनीपत्त्राणि नीयन्ते । ॥ श्रुतिमभिनीय ॥
किं ब्रवीषि । आतपलङ्घनाद्बलवदस्वस्था शकुन्तला ।

the arrow? the expulsion of the demons who impede our rites is effected by the mere twanging of the bow, without the use of the arrow (*sara-san-dhānam antarena*, S'.), in the same manner as a threatening roar often suffices to scare those who hear it. Cf. *pratisabdo hi harer hinasti nāgān*, Vikram., Act I. *Hunkāra* is the roar of any fierce animal. The use of *iva* shews that the figure by which the sound of the bow is thus designated is Utprekshā, see Indian Wisdom, p. 454. So Bhatti-k. (x. 44), in giving an example of this figure, describes a mountain as stretching out, as it were, a huge *body* between heaven and earth to protect the land from the inroads of the sea.

[1] 'For strewing on the altar,' or 'on the ground near it,' see p. 19, n. 1.

[2] *Ritvij*, 'a priest,' especially 'an officiating priest,' lit. 'one who sacrifices at the prescribed time,' from *ritu*, 'a season,' and *ij=yaj*, 'to sacrifice.' *An-ritvig yajñam na gacchet*, 'one ought not to go to (perform) a sacrifice unattended by an officiating Brāhman.' See Manu iv. 57, ii. 143.

[3] 'In the air,' i. e. speaking in the air. This is an example of *ākāsa-bhāshitam* or *ākāsa-vākyam*, which is defined by S'. to be *dūra-stha-bhāshanam*, 'speech at a distance,' or *asarīram nivedanam*, 'bodiless statement;' and by K. as *apravishtaih saha ālāpah*, 'conversation with (characters) not on the stage.' It is, in fact, a speech addressed to some person outside or off the stage, the actor at the same time fixing his eyes in the air, or on some object only visible to himself. Hence in K. *ākāse* is followed by the words *laksham* or *lakshyam baddhvā*, 'fixing his gaze.' Cf. *ākāsa-baddha-lakshah*, Vikram., Act IV; Mudrā-r. p. 6, l. 19; p. 31, l. 3. The answer which is supposed to be given is also *ākāsa-bhāshitam*, and is not heard by the audience. The actor on the stage pretending to listen (*srutim abhinīya*) repeats the imaginary reply, always introducing it with the words *kim bravīshi*, Sāhit.-d. p. 177.

[4] 'For whom are brought this Usīra-ointment and lotus-leaves, with fibres attached?' *Usīra=vīrana-kanda*, 'the root of Vīrana,' a fragrant grass (Andropogon Muricatum) with which a cooling ointment was made. *Mrināla=visa*, 'the fibres of the stalk of the lotus.'

तस्याः शरीरनिर्वापणायेति । प्रियंवदे यत्नादुपचर्यताम् ।
सा हि तत्रभवतः कुलपतेरुच्छ्वसितम् । अहमपि तावदै-
तानिकं शान्त्युदकमस्यै गौतमीहस्ते विसर्जयिष्यामि ।

|| इति निष्क्रान्तः ||

|| विष्कम्भः ||

---

¹ 'S'akuntalā is excessively indisposed, from injury inflicted by the heat [from a sun-stroke]; is it for the cooling of her body that you say (they are brought)?' *Langhanāt=āghātāt*, K. ;=*abhibhavāt*, S'. ;= *paribhavāt*, C'. Root *langh* means 'to leap over,' 'overstep,' 'transgress,' 'to inflict an injury,' 'insult.' *Nirvāpaṇa*, 'a refrigerant remedy,' from the causal of *nir-vā*, 'to refresh,' 'cool;' cf. *nirvāpayitā*, ver. 65.

² 'Let her be nursed with care; for she is the (very) breath of his reverence (Kaṇva), the head of (our) society. I also will just deliver into the hands of Gautamī for her the soothing water consecrated in the sacrifice.' *Upaćar*, 'to attend on a patient,' 'administer remedies,' &c. *Ućhvasitam=prāṇāḥ*, 'breath;'=*jīvanam*, 'life,' i. e. as precious as his own life. Cf. Lam. iv. 20, 'The breath of our nostrils, the anointed of the Lord, was taken,' &c.; also Kumāra-s. vii. 4. *Vaitānika=vitānākhya-yāya-sambandhin*, 'belonging to the sacrifice called *vitāna*,' 'sacred,' 'holy.' See Indian Wisdom, p. 197. *Vitāna* is also 'the sacrificial hearth on which the sacred fire was kept.' The *śānty-udaka* may have been a kind of holy water, like the 'eau bénite' of the Roman Catholics. *Gautamī*, the name of the sister of Kaṇva, K.

³ The Vishkambha or Vishkambhaka, according to the Sāhitya-darpaṇa and Kātavema's commentary on the opening speech of Act II. of this play, is an introductory monologue or dialogue, so called from its concisely compressing (*vi-shkambh*) into a short space an account of those subordinate parts of the plot not enacted before the audience, a knowledge of which is essential to the comprehending of the action of the remainder of the play (*vṛitta-vartishyamānānāṃ kathānśānāṃ nidarśakaḥ, sankship-tārthas tu vishkambhaḥ*, Sāhit-d. p. 146; see also p. 62, n. 2 of this play). The Vishkambha may occur at the beginning of any of the Acts, even of the First, immediately after the Prastāvanā (*ādāv ankasya darśitaḥ*). It may be spoken by two out of the three sets of characters into which the dramatis personæ of an Indian play are divided, viz. the inferior (*nīća*), who speak Prākrit *anudāttoktyā*, 'in the low tone;' and the middling

O

॥ अथ तृतीयोऽङ्कः ॥

॥ ततः प्रविशति समदनावस्थो राजा ॥

राजा ॥ सखिन्नां निःश्वस्य ॥

जाने तपसो वीर्यं सा बाला परवतीति मे विदितम् ।
न च निम्नादिव सलिलं निवर्तते मे ततो हृदयम् ॥५४॥

(*madhya, madhyama*), who speak Sanskṛit *udāttoktyā*, 'in the high tone;'
but not by the chief (*pradhāna*), such as the hero, &c.   Agaiu, it may be
spoken by one character iu the form of a soliloquy, or by two in the form
of a dialogue; and either by characters of the middle class only, when it
is called *śuddha*, 'pure;' or by those of the middle aud lower combined,
when it is called *miśra* or *sankīrṇa*, 'mixed' (*madhyena madhyamā-
bhyāṃ vā pātrābhyāṃ samprayojitaḥ śuddhaḥ syāt tu sankīrṇo nīća-
madhyama-kalpitaḥ*).   Sometimes the characters are exclusively those of
the inferior class, who speak Prākṛit; sometimes more than two appear
on the stage at once, in which cases it is properly called Praveśaka,
though these terms are regarded as identical by the MSS. and commentators (*vishkambha eva suvyaktaiḥ praveśaka iti smṛitaḥ*, K.; *praveśaka eva vishkambhakaḥ*, S'.)   The Sāhit.-d. restricts the former title still
further by applying it to an interlude only (*praveśako 'nudāttoktyā nīća-
pātra-prayojitaḥ, anka-dvayāntar vijñeyāḥ śeshaṃ vishkambhake yathā*).
In Vikram., Act V, the opeuing soliloquy is styled Praveśaka both in
the MSS. and in the Calcutta edition.   According to the Sāhit-d. the
present monologue is a S'uddha-vishkambha.   In the Beng. MSS. it is
termed a Praveśaka.

¹ 'I know the potency of penance; it is (also) known to me that that
maiden is subject to another [is in a state of tutelage].   But as water
does not turn back from the valley, (neither) does my heart from that
(S'akuntalā);' i.e. I know that if I attempt to carry her off by force or by
stealth, the power acquired by penance is such, that the Ṛishi will effect
my destruction by a curse, &c. (*śāpādinā nāśam vidhāsyati*, S'.)   *Nimnād,*

Verse 54.   ĀRYĀ or GĀTHĀ.   See verse 2.

भगवन्कुसुमायुध । त्वया चन्द्रमसा च विश्वसनीयाभ्याम-
तिसन्धीयते कामिजनसार्थः । कुतः ।
तव कुसुमशरत्वं शीतरश्मित्वमिन्दो-
र्द्वयमिदमयथार्थं दृश्यते मद्विधेषु ।
विसृजति हिमगर्भैरग्निमिन्दुर्मयूखै-
स्त्वमपि कुसुमबाणान्वज्रसारीकरोषि ॥ ५५ ॥

---

scil. *deśāt*, 'from low land,' see Hitop. l. 2651. The Deva-n. MSS., unsupported by the commentators, substitute the following for the second
line of the above verse, *Alam asmi tato hridayaṃ tathāpi nedaṃ nivarta-
yitum*, 'nevertheless, I am not able to turn back this heart from that
(damsel).'

[1] 'O divine flower-armed (god), by thee and by the moon, who (seem)
to be worthy of confidence, the whole company of lovers is deceived.
Why so? [because] of thee, (there is said to be) the property of having
flowers for arrows, of the moon the property of having cold beams;
both these (properties) are observed to be untrue in such as me; (for)
the moon emits fire with rays charged with cold; thou also makest (thy)
flower-arrows hard as adamant.' The Hindū Cupid or Kāma-deva, 'god
of love,' is the son of Vishṇu or Krishṇa by Lakshmī, who is then called
Māyā or Rukmiṇī. He is armed with a bow made of sugar-cane, the
string consisting of bees, and with five flower-tipped arrows (whence his
name Pańća-vāṇa) which pierce the heart through the five senses. The
names of the five arrows (according to Bharata, cited by Ś.) are—1.
Harshaṇa, 'Gladdener;' 2. *Prahasana*, 'Exhilarator;' 3. *Mohana*,
'Fascinator;' 4. *Mūrćhana*, 'Sense-destroyer;' 5. *Vikarshaṇa*, 'Distractor.'
According to K. the names of the five flowers which point these arrows,
and may be supposed to possess properties similar to those implied in the
names of the arrows themselves, are—1. *Aravinda*, a kind of lotus;
2. *Aśoka*; 3. *Sirīsha*; 4. *Ćūta* or *Āmra*, i. e. the mango; 5. *Utpala* or
blue lotus. But according to Sir W. Jones [Hymn to Kāma-deva] they
are—1. *Ćampaka*; 2. *Ćūta* or *Āmra*; 3. *Keśara* or *Nāga-keśara*; 4.
Ketaka; 5. *Vilva* or *Bilva*. In both lists the Ćūta occurs. This is
certainly the favourite flower of the god (cf. the frequent allusions to it

---

Verse 55. MĀLINĪ or MĀNINĪ (a variety of ATI-ŚAKVARĪ). See verses 10, 19, 20, 38.

भगवन्कामदेव। न ते मय्यनुक्रोशः। ॥ मदनबाधां निरूप्य ॥ कुतस्ते कुसुमायुधस्य सतस्त्वैदृश्यमेतत्। आं ज्ञातम्।

अद्यापि नूनं हरकोपवह्नि-
स्त्वयि ज्वलत्यौर्व इवाम्बुराशौ।
त्वमन्यथा मन्मथ मद्विधानां
भस्मावशेषः कथमित्यमुष्ण: ॥५६॥

---

in Gīta-g. iii. 12, iv. 6, &c.); but in verse 135 the epithet *pañćābhyadhika* is applied to this flower, and is explained by S'. to mean 'a sixth arrow, in addition to the five' (cf. Vikram., Act II, *kimuta upavana-sahakāraiḥ,* &c.) It is clear that some authorities do not include the mango in the list. The Gīta-g. (x. 14) mentions five other flowers as occasionally employed by the god, viz. the *bandhūka, madhūka, nīla-nalina* or blue lotus, *tila,* and *kunḍa.* Another account includes the Mallikā or jasmine amongst the five. In Hindū erotic poetry, cooling properties are attributed to the rays of the moon, said to distil nectar; hence some of his names—*śīta-mayūkha, hima-raśmi, hima-kara, amrita-sū, sudhā-nidhi,* &c. On the other hand, the heating effect of these rays on the lover is often alluded to, e. g. *śītānśus tapanaḥ,* Gīta-g. ix. 10, iv. 7, v. 3; cf. *nandana-vana-vātāḥ śikhina iva* (Vikram., Act II), and *pādās te śaśinaḥ sukhayanti,* &c. (end of Act III). *Sārtha* = *samūha,* properly 'a caravan,' Hitop. l. 2574. *Kutaḥ,* p. 55, n. 2. *A-yathārtham* = *viparīta-kriyam,* 'having a contrary effect.' *Dvayam,* see p. 91, n. 2. *Garbhaiḥ,* see p. 18, l. 5. *Vajrasārī-karoshi,* see p. 14, l. 2.

[1] 'Verily, e'en now the fire of S'iva's wrath burns in thee like the submarine fire in the ocean; otherwise how couldst thou, O agitator of the soul, with nothing left but ashes, be so scorching towards such as me?' The story of the incineration of Kāma-deva by a beam of fire darted from the central eye of S'iva is thus told in the Rāmāyana (i. 25, 10): 'Kandarpa, whom the wise call Kāma (Cupid), had formerly a body. He once approached S'iva, the husband of Umā (Parvatī), soon after his marriage, that he might influence him with love for his wife. S'iva

---

Verse 56. UPAJĀTI or ĀKHYĀNAKĪ (a variety of TRISHṬUBH), each Pāda or quarter-verse being either *Indra-vajrā* or *Upendra-vajrā,* the former only differing from the latter in the length of the first syllable. See verse 41.

अथवा ।
अनिशमपि मकरकेतुर्मनसीरुजमावहन्नभिमतो मे ।
यदि मदिरायतनयनां तामधिकृत्य प्रहरंतीति ॥ ५७ ॥

happened then to be practising austerities, and intent on a vow of chastity. He therefore cursed the god of love in a terrible voice, and at the same time a flash from his terrific eye caused all the limbs of his body to shrivel into ashes. Thus Kāma was made incorporeal [whence, as some say, is his power over the minds of men] by the anger of the great god, and from that time has been called "the bodiless one" (*An-anga*).' *Aurva,* 'submarine fire,' called *badava* or *bādava,* and personified as the son of the saint Urva. The fable is told in Hari-v. (ch. xlv), and is noticed in Troyer's Rāja-taran-gịnī (iii. 170). The Rishi Urva, who had gained great power by his austerities, was pressed by the gods and others to beget children that he might perpetuate his race. He consented, but warned them that his offspring would consume the world. Accordingly, he created from his thigh a devouring fire, which, when produced, demanded nourishment, and would have destroyed the whole earth, had not Brahmā appeared and assigned the ocean as its habitation, and the waves as its food. The spot where it entered the sea was called *Badavā-mukha,* 'the mare's mouth.' Doubtless the story was invented to suit the phenomenon of a marine *jvālā-mukhī* or 'volcano,' which exhaled bitumenous inflammable gas, and which occasionally shewed itself above the sea, perhaps in the form of a horse's mouth. Langlois places the position of it on the coast north of Malabar.

[1] 'Nevertheless, the fish-bannered (god), even though incessantly bringing mental anguish, (will be) acceptable to me, if employing (as the subject about which he inflicts pain) that (maiden) with long intoxicating eyes he so strike (me).' *Makara-ketu,* a name of Kāma-deva, is derived from the *makara,* or marine monster, subdued by him, which was painted on his banner (*ketu*). 'By the mention of this title, his invincibleness is indicated,' S. *Adhikritya=uddiśya,* 'with reference to,' S. and Ć.; see p. 6, n. 2, and p. 77, n. 1; also Raghu-v. xi. 62, *śāntim adhikritya anvayunkta.*

Verse 57. ĀRYĀ or GĀTHĀ. See verse 2.

भगवन्कन्दर्प । एवमुपालब्धस्य ते न मां प्रत्यनुक्रोश: ।

वृथैव सङ्कल्पशतैरजस्र-
मनङ्ग नीतोऽसि मया विवृद्धिम् ।
आकृष्य चापं श्रवणोपकण्ठे
मय्येव युक्तस्तव वाणमोक्ष: ॥५८॥

॥ सखेदं परिक्रम्य ॥ क्क नु खलु संस्थिते कर्मणि सदस्यैरनुज्ञात:
श्रमक्लान्तमात्मानं विनोदयामि । ॥ नि:श्वस्य ॥ किं नु खलु
मे प्रियादर्शनादृते शरणमन्यत् । यावदेनामन्विष्यामि ।
॥ सूर्यमवलोक्य ॥ इमामुप्रातपां वेलां प्रायेण लतावलयवत्सु
मालिनीतीरिषु ससखीजना शकुन्तला गमयन्ति । तथैव

---

[1] 'In vain, truly, O bodiless (god), hast thou perpetually been brought
by me to growth by hundreds of desires. Is it becoming of you, drawing
your bow to your very ear, (to) discharge (your) arrows even upon me
(your votary)?' *Sankalpa=iććhā*, 'wish.' *Śravaṇopakaṇṭhe ākṛishya=
karṇāntikam āniya*, 'drawing the string of the bow back as far as the
ear.' *Upakaṇṭha*, 'near,' lit. 'near the neck;' cf. Raghu-v. ix. 57, *ākarṇa-
kṛishṭam vāṇam*. *Yukta=uḍita*. The passage from *Bhagavan Kāmadeva*
(p. 100) to *vāṇamokshaḥ* is given on the authority of the Taylor and my
own Bombay Deva-n. MS., supported by S'. and Ć. and all the Beng.
MSS. The Mackenzie MS. has part of the passage, but Colebrooke's omits
it altogether.

[2] 'Where, indeed, at the conclusion of the rite being permitted to
depart by those who were present at the sacrifice, shall I refresh myself
weary with fatigue?' *Sadasya*, 'any assistant or by-stander at a sacrifice.'
The Beng. have *nirasta-vighnais tapasvibhiḥ*, 'by the hermits whose
obstacles have been removed.'

[3] 'S'akuntalā along with her female friends is passing [lit. causing to
go] this intensely hot time of the day probably on the banks of the
Mālinī, possessed of inclosures of creepers.' *Valaya*, properly 'an encir-
cling hedge;' here it may mean 'a bower.'

Verse 58. UPAJĀTI or ĀKHYĀNAKI (a variety of TRISHṬUBH). See verses 41, 56.

तावद्गच्छामि । ॥ परिक्रम्यावलोक्य च ॥ अनया बालपादप-
वीथ्या सुतनुरचिरं गतेति तर्कयामि । कुतः ।

सम्मीलन्ति न तावद्बन्धनकोषास्तयावचितपुष्पाः ।
क्षीरस्निग्धाश्चामी दृश्यन्ते किशलयच्छेदाः ॥५९॥

॥ स्पर्शं रूपयित्वा ॥ अहो प्रवातसुभगोऽयमुद्देशः ।

शक्यमरविन्दसुरभिः कणवाही मालिनीतरङ्गाणाम् ।
अङ्गैरनङ्गतप्तैरविरलमालिङ्गितुं पवनः ॥६०॥

---

[1] 'I conjecture that the very delicate one has not long since passed by
this avenue of young trees, because the cavities of the flower-stalks whose
flowers have been plucked off by her, do not yet close up, and these
fragments of tender-shoots are seen (still) unctuous with milky-juice.'
Vīthi = pankti. Sammīlanti = sankućanti, 'contract.' *Bandhana = prasava-bandhana = vṛinta,* 'a flower-stalk,' S. *Bandhana-koshās = vṛintā-
bhyantarāṇi,* S.; = *vṛinta-garbhāṇi,* Ć. *Amī,* 'these,' i. e. *puro-vartinaḥ,*
'lying in front of us.' *Kiśalaya-ććhedāḥ = pallava-khaṇḍāḥ. Kshīra-
snigdhāḥ = dugdha-ćikkaṇāḥ.* When a stalk has been some time broken
off, it contracts and the milk dries up. 'The duty of gathering flowers
and cutting stalks for sacrificial purposes might have been entrusted by
the hermits to S'akuntalā; hence it would be inferred that she had
passed that way. This is an example of the Anumāna Alan-kāra,' S'. and
Ć. Some of the Deva-n. MSS. omit the above couplet.

[2] 'Oh! how delightful is this spot by (reason of) the fresh breeze!'
Aho, an exclamation implying approbation (*praśansāyām*), S'. *Pra-
vāta = prakṛishṭa-vāta,* K.; = *praśasta-vāta,* 'a good breeze,' S'. (see
p. 37, n. 1).

[3] 'The breeze, fragrant with the lotuses (and) wafting the spray
[particles] of the waves of the Mālinī, is able to be closely embraced by

---

Verse 59. ĀRYĀ or GĀTHĀ. See verse 2.

<pre>
  ̄ ̄ | ̄ ⏑⏑ | ̄ ̄ ‖ ̄ ⏑⏑ | ̄ ̄ | ⏑ ̄ ⏑ | ⏑⏑ ̄ | ̄
  ̄ ̄ | ̄ ̄ | ̄ ̄ ‖ ̄ ̄ | ̄ ⏑⏑ | ⏑ | ̄ ̄ | ̄
</pre>

Verse 60. ĀRYĀ or GĀTHĀ. See verse 2.

<pre>
 ̄ ⏑⏑ | ⏑ ̄ ⏑ | ⏑⏑ ̄ ‖ ⏑⏑ ̄ | ̄ ̄ | ⏑ ̄ ⏑ | ̄ ̄ | ̄
  ̄ ̄ | ⏑ ̄ ⏑ | ̄ ̄ ‖ ⏑⏑⏑⏑ | ̄ ̄ | ⏑ | ̄ ⏑⏑ | ̄
</pre>

।। परिक्रम्यावलोक्य च ।। अस्मिन्नेतस्मिन्परिक्षिप्ते लतामण्डपे सन्नि-
हितया तया भवितव्यम् । तथा हि । ।। अधो विलोक्य ।।

अभ्युन्नता पुरस्तादवगाढा जघनगौरवात्पश्चात् ।
द्वारेऽस्य पाण्डुसिकते पदपङ्क्तिर्दृश्यतेऽभिनवा ।।६१।।

यावद्वटिपान्तरेणावलोकयामि । ।। परिक्रम्य । तथा कृत्वा । सहर्षम् ।।

अये लब्धं नेत्रनिर्वाणम् । एषा मे मनोरथप्रियतमा

(my) limbs inflamed by the bodiless one.' *Śakya* (like *yogya* and sometimes *yukta*) gives a passive sense to the infinitive. The Beng. MSS. and
the Calcutta ed. read *śakyo* in the nom. case agreeing with *pavanaḥ*,
which would appear at first sight to be the better reading. But K.
expressly states that *śakyam* is here used adverbially, and quotes a
parallel passage from Rāmāyaṇa, *śakyam añjalibhiḥ pātum vātāḥ*, 'the
breezes are able to be drunk by the hollowed palms.' A passage may be
added from the Hitop., *vibhūtayaḥ śakyam avāptum*, 'great successes are
able to be obtained;' and another from Mālavik. verse 58, *na śakyam
upekshitum kupitā* (see also Maha-bh. i. 769). *Aravinda*, a kind of
lotus, see p. 25, n. 1. *Kaṇa-vāhin=śīkara-vāhaka*, 'wafting cool spray,'
S. *An-anga*, 'the bodiless god,' see p. 100, n. 1. *A-virala*, lit. 'having
no interstices,' 'close.' The Beng. read *nirdayam=dṛiḍham*.

[1] 'At the entrance of it where-there-is-white-sand, a fresh line of footsteps is seen, raised in front, depressed behind through the weight of her
hips.' *Avagāḍhā=nimnā*. *Pāṇḍu-sikate* (=*dhavala-bāluke*) is a Bahuvrīhi comp. agreeing with *dvāre*. The weight of the hips of a beautiful
female is a favourite subject of allusion (cf. *paśćād-natā guru-nitam-
batayā asyāḥ pada-panktiḥ*, Vikram., Act IV; *śroṇī-bhārād alasa-
gamanā*, Megha-d. 81). Hence one of the names of a lovely woman is
nitambinī, 'having large and handsome hips and loins.' Compare the
epithet 'Callipyge' applied to a celebrated statue of Venus.

[2] 'Through the branches.' The Calcutta ed. has *viṭapāntarito*, 'concealed by the branches.'

[3] 'The highest object of my eye-sight,' 'the full bliss of my eyes' (=*netrā-*

Verse 61. ĀRYĀ or GĀTHĀ. See verse 2.

– – | ∪ – ∪ | – – ‖ ∪ ∪ – | – ∪ ∪ | ∪ – ∪ | – – | –
– – | ∪ – ∪ | ∪ ∪ – ‖ ∪ ∪ – | – – | ∪ | – ∪ ∪ | –

सकुसुमास्तरणं शिलापट्टमधिशयाना सखीभ्यामन्वास्यते।
भवतु। श्रोष्याम्यासां विश्रम्भकथितानि। ॥ इति विलोकयन्तिष्ठतः ॥

॥ ततः प्रविशति यथोक्तव्यापारा सह सखीभ्यां शकुन्तला ॥

॥ सख्यावुपवीजयतः ॥

सख्यौ ॥ उपवीज्य। सस्नेहम् ॥

[a] हला सउन्दले। अवि सुहाअदि दे णलिणीपत्तवादो।

शकुन्तला।

[b] किं वीजयन्ति मं सहीओ।

॥ सख्यौ विषादं नाटयित्वा परस्परमवलोकयतः ॥

राजा।

बलवदस्वस्थशरीरा शकुन्तला दृश्यते। ॥ सचिन्तकम् ॥ तत्कि-
मयमातपदोषः स्यात्। उत यथा मे मनसि वर्तते।
॥ साभिलाषं निर्वर्ण्य ॥ अथवा कृतं सन्देहेन।

[a] हला शकुन्तले। अपि सुखायते ते नलिनीपत्त्रवातः।   [b] किं वीजयतो
मां सख्यौ।

---

nanda, K.; *nayana-nirvṛiti, ćakshuḥ-sukha,* S.) *Nirvāṇa* or *apavarga*
is properly 'final beatitude, consisting in emancipation from further
transmigration.'

[1] 'Yonder the best-beloved object of my wishes, reclining on a stone-
seat strewed with flowers, is attended by her two friends.' *Manoratha-
priyatamā,* 'most dear by desire,' i. e. not by actual possession or by any
other method, K. *Śilā-paṭṭa=pāshāna-khaṇḍa,* see p. 76, n. 2. *Anvās,*
'to sit near' (*anu, ās*).

[2] 'Are in the act of fanning her.' *Upa-vīj,* 'to fan;' cf. *vy-ajana,* 'a fan.'

[3] 'Is this wind from the (fan of) lotus-leaves agreeable to thee?' see p. 25,
n. 1, in the middle. *Api,* see p. 89, n. 2. Some Deva-n. MSS. read *suhaadi*
for *sukhayati,* but the above is supported by K. and the oldest MSS.

[4] 'Can this be the fault of the heat? or, as is passing in my mind (is it
owing to love)?' i. e. or is love, as I conjecture, the true cause?

[5] *Kṛitaṃ sandehena,* see p. 30, l. 6, with note.

स्तनन्यस्तोशीरं प्रशिथिलमृणालैकवलयं
प्रियायाः साबाधं तदपि कमनीयं वपुरिदम् ।
समस्तापः कामं मनसिजनिदाघप्रसरयो-
—ने तु यौषस्यैवं सुभगमपराङ्गं युवतिषु ॥ ६२ ॥

प्रियंवदा ॥ जनान्तिकम् ॥

[a] अणसूए । तस्स राएसिणो पढमदंसणादो आरहिअ
पज्जुस्सुआ विञ्च सउन्दला । किं णुक्खु से तस्सिमिन्तो
अञ्चं आतङ्की भवे ।

[a] अनसूये । तस्य राजर्षेः प्रथमदर्शीनादारभ्य पर्युत्सुकेव शकुन्तला । किं नु खल-
स्यास्तन्निमित्तोऽयमातङ्को भवेत् ।

---

[1] 'This form of my beloved, having the Uśīra applied to the bosom,
and having only one armlet (and that formed) of lotus-fibres hanging-
loose, (is certainly) disordered, but even so is lovely. Granted that the
heat of the two influences of love and the hot season [or the heat induced
by the prevalence either of love or of the sultry weather] be equal, still
disorder is not inflicted on maidens by the hot weather in such a charming
manner,' i. e. since the disorder apparent in the person of S'akuntalā only
contributes to her beauty, it is clearly not caused by the hot weather, but
by love. *Uśīra,* see p. 96, n. 4. Two other names for this plant are
jalāśaya, 'growing in water,' and *avadāha,* 'allaying fever;' the slender
fibres of it are now known by the name of Khaskhas, and are used in
India in trellises for cooling the air. *Praśithila=adridha,* S'. ;=*komala,*
'withered,' C'. 'Her body was so enfeebled that she could not bear the
weight of two armlets or bracelets; she therefore had only one, and that
made, not of gold, but of lotus-fibres (*mrināla-ghatita*) tied loosely round
the arm,' S'. *Sābādha=sa-pīda,* C'. ;=*sa-vyadha,* K. 'diseased,' 'deranged.'
Tadapi, 'even so;' even in this manner or under these disadvantages; *tad*
is here used adverbially. This reading is supported by the oldest MSS.
and by K.; but some of the Deva-n. have *kimapi ramanīyam,* 'somewhat
pleasing.' *Kāmam,* see p. 55, n. 3. *Prasarayoh,* lit. ' of the two preva-
lences;' *prasara=prasanga,* 'attachment,' 'connection,' S'.; but the simple
meaning is 'spreading,' 'prevalence.'

[2] *Tan-nimitta,* 'resulting from it,' i. e. arising from love.

Verse 62. S'IKHARINĪ (a variety of ATYASHTI). See verses 9, 24, 44.

अनसूया ।

[a] सहि । ममवि ईदिसी आसङ्का हिअअस्स । होदु । पुच्छिस्सं दाव एं । ॥ प्रकाशम् ॥ [b] सहि । पुच्छिदव्वासि किम्पि । बलिअंक्खु दे सन्दाबो ।

शकुन्तला ॥ पूर्वार्धेन शयनादुत्थाय ॥

[c] हला । किं वत्तुकामासि ।

अनसूया ।

[d] हला सउन्दले । अणब्भन्तरा खु अम्हे मदणगदस्स वुत्तन्तस्स । किन्तु । जादिसी इदिहासणिबन्धेसु कामअमाणाणं अवत्था सुणीअदि । तादिसिं दे पेक्खामि । कहेहि । किस्सिमित्तं दे सन्दाबो । विआरंक्खु परमत्थदो अजाणिअ अणारम्भी पडिआरस्स ।

राजा ।

अनसूययापि मदीयस्तर्कोऽवगतः ।[1]

---

[a] सखि । ममापीदृश्याशङ्का हृदयस्य । भवतु । प्रक्ष्यामि तावदेनाम् । [b] सखि । प्रक्ष्यासि किमपि । बलीयान्खलु ते सन्तापः । [c] हला । किं वक्तुकामासि । [d] हला शकुन्तले । अनभ्यन्तरे खल्वावां मदनगतस्य वृत्तान्तस्य । किन्तु । यादृशीतिहासनिबन्धेषु कामयमानानामवस्था श्रूयते । तादृशीं ते प्रेक्षे । कथय । किंनिमित्तं ते सन्तापः । विकारं खलु परमार्थतोऽज्ञात्वानारम्भः प्रतिकारस्य ।

---

1 'We are not indeed intimately conversant with matters relating to love; but as the condition of lovers is heard of (by us) in legendary tales, of such a kind I perceive is thy (condition). Say, from what cause (is) thy disorder? (for) indeed without being accurately acquainted with the disease, (there) can be no application of the remedy.' *An-abhyantare*, nom. du. fem. of a Bahuvrīhi or compound adjective formed from the substantive *abhyantara*, 'interior,' 'inside,' by prefixing the privative *an*, in the same manner as in *an-antara*, 'uninterrupted.' *An-abhyantara*, lit. 'one not admitted to the inside.' Cf. *gaṇābhyantara*, 'one who is a member of a religious association.' *Madana-gatasya*, see p. 38, n. 1. *Itihāsa*=*purā-vritta*, S. *Ni-bandha*, 'a composition,' 'narrative.'

शकुन्तला ॥ आत्मगतम् ॥

[a]बलिअंक्खु मे अहिणिवेसो[1] दाणिंपि । सहसा एदाणं
ण सक्कणेमि णिवेदिदुं ।

प्रियंवदा ।

[b]सहि सउन्दले । सुट्ठु एसा भणादि । किं अत्तणो आतङ्कं
उवेक्खसि । अणुदिअहंक्खु परिहीअसि अङ्गेहिं । केवलं
लावण्णमई छाआ तुमं ण मुञ्चदि[2] ।

राजा ।

अवितथमाह प्रियंवदा । तथा हि

क्षामक्षामकपोलमाननमुरः काठिन्यमुक्तस्तनं
मध्यः क्लान्ततरः प्रकामविनता वंसौ छविः पाण्डुरा ।
शोच्या च प्रियदर्शना च मदनक्लिष्टेयमालक्ष्यते
पत्त्राणामिव शोषणेन मरुता स्पृष्टा लता माधवी[3] ॥६३॥

[a] बलीयान्खलु मेऽभिनिवेश इदानीमपि । सहसैतयोर्नँ शक्नोमि निवेदितुम् ।
[b] सखि शकुन्तले । सुष्ठ्वेषा भणति । किमात्मन आतङ्कमुपेक्षसे । अनुदिवसं खलु परि-
हीयसेऽङ्गैः । केवलं लावण्यमयी छाया त्वां न मुञ्चति ।

---

[1] 'My attachment [affection] even now is strong.' *Abhi-niveśa* implies
'firm attachment to' or 'intense pursuit of' any object (here=*abhilāsha*).

[2] 'Thy limbs are wasting away [lit. thou art abandoned by thy limbs].
Thy lovely complexion alone deserts thee not.'

[3] 'For, indeed, her face has its cheeks excessively emaciated, her bosom
has its breasts destitute of firmness, her waist is more slender, her shoulders
are quite drooping, her complexion is pale; she being tormented by love
appears both deplorable and (yet) lovely, like a Mādhavī-creeper touched
by the wind, the scorcher of (its) leaves.' *Kshāma-kshāma-kapola*=
atikṛiśa-gaṇḍa, S. The repetition of *kshāma* may imply 'becoming
gradually every day more and more emaciated,' as Priyaṃvadā had said
anu-divasam parihīyase aṅgaiḥ. *Kāṭhinya-mukta*, the Beng. have *yukta*,

---

Verse 63. ŚĀRDŪLA-VIKRĪDITA (a variety of ATIDHRITI). See verses 14, 30, 36,
39, 40.

शकुन्तला ।

[a]सहि । कस्स वा अण्णस्स कहइस्सं । किन्दु आस्सासइत्तित्रा
दाणिं वो भविस्सं ।

उभे ।

[b]अदो एव्वक्खु णिब्बन्धो । सिणिद्धजणसंविभत्तं हि दुक्खं
सज्झवेदणं होदि ।

राजा ।

पृष्टा जनेन समदुःखसुखेन बाला
नेयं न वक्ष्यति मनोगतमाधिहेतुम् ।
दृष्टो विवृत्य बहुशोऽप्यनया सतृष्ण-
मन्तरे श्रवणकातरतां गतोऽस्मि ॥६४॥

[a] सखि । कस्य वान्यस्य कथयिष्यामि । किन्न्वायासयित्रीदानीं वां भविष्यामि ।
[b] अत एव खलु निर्बन्धः । स्निग्धजनसंविभक्तं हि दुःखं सह्यवेदनं भवति ।

---

but the loss of firmness in the breasts would rather be a sign of debility.
Prakāma=atyartham, 'excessively,' S'. So the commentator on Gīta-g.
iv. 17, vii. 40, explains *nikāmam* by *atiśayena.* Similarly *kāmam* has
the sense of *niśćitam,* 'certainly.' May the meaning not be 'stoop of
their own accord,' i. e. 'languidly,' 'listlessly,' from their being allowed to
fall without any effort being made to raise them? *Śoshaṇena=śoshakena,*
i. e. by the wind that dries up the leaves and causes them to fall (*pattra-
pātaka-vāyunā*), K., S'. *Mādhavī,* a large and beautiful creeper bearing
white fragrant flowers, constantly alluded to in the plays (see p. 112, n. 3).

[1] 'To whom else shall I relate it (if not to you, my two friends)?' *Yadi
kathanīyam tadā bhavatībhyām,* S'.

[2] 'Our importunity is on this very account. Grief shared with affec-
tionate friends becomes supportable suffering.' *Nir-bandha,* 'urgency,'
'pressing solicitation.'

[3] 'This maiden being questioned by the persons who are the partners of
her sorrows and joys, will most certainly declare the cause of her anguish
(now) concealed in her breast. Although (I was) looked upon longingly
by her repeatedly turning round, I (nevertheless) at the present moment

---

Verse 64. VASANTA-TILAKĀ (a variety of ŚAKVARĪ). See verses 8, 27, 31, 43, 46.

शकुन्तला ।

[a] सहि । जदो पहुदि मम दंसणपहं आअदो सो तवोवण-
रक्खिदा राएसी । ॥ इत्यर्धोक्तिन लज्जां नाटयति ॥

उभे ।

[b] कधेदु पिअसही ।

शकुन्तला ।

[c] तदो पहुदि तग्गदेण अहिलासेण एतदवत्थम्हि संवुत्ता ।

राजा ॥ सहर्षम् ॥

श्रुतं श्रोतव्यम् ।

स्मर एव तापहेतुर्निर्वापयिता स एव मे जातः ।
दिवस इवाभ्रश्यामस्तपात्यये जीवलोकस्य ॥ ६५ ॥

[a] सखि । यातः प्रभृति मम दर्शनपथमागतः स तपोवनरक्षिता राजर्षिः । [b] कध-
यतु प्रियसखी । [c] ततः प्रभृति तद्गतेनाभिलाषेणैतदवस्थास्मि संवृत्ता ।

experience an uneasy-anxiety for hearing (her reply).' *Jana=sakhī-
jana;* though used in sing., it may have a plural signification. *Sama-
duḥkha-sukha,* 'one who has the same joys and sorrows' (cf. *sama-duḥkha-
sukhaḥ pīyate loćanābhyām,* Vikram., Act I). *Bālā,* properly 'a girl
sixteen years of age,' S'. *Na na vakshyati=vakshyati eva,* S'.; two
negatives give intensity to the affirmative (*dvau nishedhau prakritam
artham gamayataḥ,* S'.); see p. 24, n. 2. *Mano-gatam=hridaya-stham,*
see p. 38, n. 1. *Atrāntare=asminn avasare,* K. *Sravaṇa-kātaratām=
Śakuntalā-prativaćana-śravaṇa-bhīrutām.* According to Bharata the four
ways by which a maiden encouraged the advances of her lover were *lekha-
prasthāpana,* 'sending a letter;' *snigdha-vīkshita,* 'a loving glance;' *mridu-
bhāshita,* 'soft speech;' and *dūtī-sampreshaṇa,* 'sending a messenger,' S'.
Although S'akuntalā had favoured her lover with one of these tokens, yet
he was fearful that, when about to reply to her friends, she might through
carelessness (*pramādatas*) confess to an affection for some other person, S'.

[1] 'Met my eye,' 'crossed my sight,' lit. 'came across the path [range]
of my sight.' Cf. *yasya netrayoḥ pathi sthitā tvam,* Vikram., Act I.

[2] 'Love, indeed, the cause of my fever, has himself become the cooler of

Verse 65. ĀRYĀ or GĀTHĀ. See verse 2.

```
∪ ∪ − | ∪ − ∪ | − − ‖ − − | ∪ ∪ − | ∪ − ∪ | − − | −
∪ ∪ ∪ ∪ | − − | − − ‖ ∪ − ∪ | − − | ∪ | − − |
```

शकुन्तला ।

[a] तं जइ वो अणुमदं । तह वट्टह । जह तस्स राएसिणो अणुकम्पणिज्जा होमि । अण्णहा अवस्सं सिञ्चह मे तिलोदंअं ।

[a] तद्यदि वामनुमतम् । तथा वर्तेंघाम् । यथा तस्य राजर्षेरनुकम्पनीया भवामि । अन्यथावश्यं सिञ्चतं मे तिलोदकम् ।

---

it; as, on the passing off of the heat, a day dark with clouds (which was at first hot, becomes afterwards the cooler) of living creatures.' This refers to the clouds which rise and disperse at the end of the hot season, making the air fearfully close and stifling; until at last a downpour comes and with it cool weather. *Smara*, 'the ideal one,' is one of the names of Kāma-deva, from *smṛi*, 'to recollect;' see p. 100, n. 1. *Nirvāpayitā*, 'the extinguisher,' 'refresher,' 'cooler' (see p. 97, n. 1);=*sukha-hetuḥ*, 'the cause of pleasure,' S'. *Tapātyaye*=*grīshmānte*, 'at the end of the hot season,' K.; K. and S'. quote a parallel passage from the Ratnāvali (p. 64), *tapati prā-vrishi nitarām abhyarṇa-jalāgamo divasaḥ*, 'in the rainy season when the rain is near at hand the day is especially hot.' Some of the Deva-n. MSS. read *ardha-śyāma*, 'half-obscured,' which is not supported by any of the commentators, nor by the oldest MSS.

[1] 'Then if (it be) approved by you, so act, that I may be commiserated by the royal sage. Otherwise most certainly (it will happen that you will have to) pour out for me water with sesamum-seed;' i.e. you will have to celebrate my funeral obsequies. Oblations to the spirits of deceased relatives, called S'rāddha, generally consisted in offering a cake made of rice and milk (*piṇḍa-nirvāpaṇa*), or in pouring out water (*udaka-dāna, udaka-kriyā*), or water and sesamum seed mixed. In the latter case it was called *tilodaka-dāna, tila-tarpaṇa*, &c. The ceremony as performed by Brāhmans is described in Manu iii. 203, &c.; see especially iii. 223. *Dattvā sapavitraṃ tilodakam*, 'having poured out water with sesamum seed and Kuśa grass.' See Indian Wisdom, pp. 208, 253, &c. K. refers in illustration to a verse towards the end of Act VI. of this play, where Dushyanta says, *Nūnam prasūti-vikalena mayā prasiktaṃ dhautāśru-śesham udakam pitaraḥ pivanti*, 'in all probability my (deceased) ancestors are (now) drinking the only offering-of-water that is left to them, (consisting of) glistening tears poured forth by me destitute of posterity.' *Siñćatam*=*nirvapatam*, K. *Vartethām*, sometimes *vṛit* has the sense of 'to behave,' 'to act.'

राजा ।

संशयच्छेदि वचनम् ।

प्रियंवदा ॥ जनान्तिकम् ॥

[a] अणसूए । दूरगअवम्महा अक्खमा इअं कालहरणस्स । जस्सिं बद्धभावा एसा । सो ललामभूदो पोरवाणं । ता जुत्तं से अहिलासो अहिणन्दिदुं ।

अनसूया ।

[b] तह । जह भणासि ।

प्रियंवदा ॥ प्रकाशम् ॥

[c] सहि । दिट्ठिआ । अणुरूबो से अहिणिवेसो । साअरं वज्जिअ कहिं वा महाणई ओदरइ । को दाणिं सहआरं अन्तरेण अदिमुत्तलदं पल्लविदं सहेदि ।

<hr>

[a] अनसूये । दूरगतमन्मथाक्षमेयं कालहरणस्य । यस्मिन्बद्धभावैषा । स ललामभूतः पौरवाणाम् । तद्युक्तमस्या अभिलापोऽभिनन्दितुम् ।   [b] तथा । यथा भणसि ।
[c] सखि । दिष्टया । अनुरूपोऽस्या अभिनिवेशः । सागरं वर्जयित्वा कुत्र वा महानद्यव-तरति । क इदानीं सहकारमन्तरेणातिमुक्तलतां पल्लवितां सहते ।

<hr>

[1] 'She is far gone in love, and unable to bear loss of time,' i. e. her love has reached that point which brooks no delay. Cf. *durārūḍho 'syāḥ praṇayaḥ*, Vikram., beginning of Act IV. *Vammaha* or *bammaha* is the proper Prākṛit equivalent for *manmatha*, according to Vararući ii. 38, iii. 43. Lassen, Instit. Prāk. p. 245, although the MSS. give *mammaha*.

[2] 'He on whom she has fixed her affections is the ornament of the Pauravas [p. 15, n. 1], therefore her love is fit to be approved,' or 'it is proper that her love should meet with our approval.' *Yuktam* is here used like *śakyam*, see p. 103, n. 3. *Baddha-bhāvā*, cf. *yasmin baddha-bhāvā asi tvam*, Vikram., beginning of Act III.

[3] 'Where should a great river end its course excepting at the ocean? What (tree) excepting the Sahakāra [mango] can support the Atimukta [Mādhavī creeper] with (its) new sprouts?' *Ava-tṛī* (properly 'to descend' or 'alight') is here applied to the disemboguing of a river into the ocean. *Yathā mahā-nadī samudram praviśati, tathā rūpavatī tvam Dushyante*

राजा।

किमच चिचम्। यदि विशाखे शशाङ्कलेखामनुवर्तते[1]।

अनसूया।

[a] को उण उवाओ भवे। जेण अविलम्बिअं णिहुअं अ सहीए मणोरहं सम्पादेम्ह।

[a] कः पुनरुपायो भवेत्। येनाविलम्बितं निभृतं च सख्या मनोरथं सम्पादयाव:।

---

evānuraktā, S'. The Sahakāra is described p. 28, n. 1. The Atimukta is the same as the Mādhavī or vernal creeper, called also Vāsantī and Puṇḍraka (see p. 108, n. 3). 'The beauty and fragrance of the flower of this creeper give them a title to all the praises which Kālidāsa and Jayadeva bestow on them. It is a gigantic and luxuriant climber; but when it meets with nothing to grasp, it assumes the form of a sturdy tree, the highest branches of which display, however, in the air, their natural flexibility and inclination to climb,' Sir W. Jones, vol. v. p. 124.

[1] 'Why need we wonder at this, since the constellation Viśākhā courts [goes after] the young-moon?' i. e. if the constellation Viśākhā (or the sixteenth lunar asterism, which is frequently written in the dual Viśākhe, as containing two stars) is eager for a union with the Moon, why need we wonder at S'akuntalā's desire to be united with a prince of the Lunar race? *Śaśāṅka-lekhā* is properly 'a digit of the moon,' or the moon in its most beautiful form when quite young. A complete revolution of the moon, with respect to the stars, being made in twenty-seven days, odd hours, the Hindūs divide the heavens into twenty-seven constellations [asterisms] or lunar stations, one of which receives the moon for one day in each of his monthly journeys. As the Moon [Ćandra] is considered to be a masculine deity, the Hindūs fable these twenty-seven constellations as his wives, and personify them as the daughters of Daksha. Of these twenty-seven wives (twelve of whom give names to the twelve months) Ćandra is supposed to shew the greatest affection for the fourth (Rohiṇī), but each of the others, and amongst them Viśākhā, is represented as jealous of this partiality, and eager to secure the Moon's favour for herself. Dushyanta probably means to compare himself to the Moon (he being of the Lunar race, p. 15, n. 1), and S'akuntalā to Viśākhā. The selection of Viśākhā, rather than Rohiṇī, may perhaps be explained by a reference to p. 6, l. 6, where we learn that the summer-season had barely set in at the period when the events of the drama were supposed to be taking place. If

प्रियंवदा ।

^a णिहुस्संति चिन्तणिज्जं भवे । सिग्घंति सुञ्जरं ।

अनसूया ।

^b कहं विञ ।

प्रियंवदा ।

^c यं सो राएसी इमस्सिं सिणिङ्दिट्ठीए सूइदाहिलासो इमाइं दिअहाइं पज्जाञरकिसो लक्खीअदि ।

राजा ॥ आत्मानमवलोक्य ॥

सत्यमित्थम्भूत एवास्मि । तथा हि

इदमंशिशिरैरन्तस्तापाद्विवर्णमणीकृतं
निशि निशि भुजन्यस्तापाङ्गप्रवर्तिभिरस्रुभिः ।
अनतिलुलितज्याघाताङ्कं मुहुर्मणिबन्धना-
त्कनकवलयं स्रस्तं स्रस्तं मया प्रतिसार्यते ॥ ६६ ॥

^a निभृतमिति चिन्तनीयं भवेत् । शीघ्रमिति सुकरम् ।   ^b कथमिव ।   ^c ननु स राजर्षिरस्यां स्निग्धदृष्ट्या सूचिताभिलाष इमानि दिवसानि प्रजागरकृशो लक्ष्यते ।

---

therefore the season corresponded to the middle of May, the month would probably be Vaiśākha, and Viśākhā would, therefore, be appropriately chosen before Rohiṇī. This passage may also be interpreted, but not so consistently with the fable, by referring *viśākhe* to the two female friends, and *śaśānka-lekhā* to Śakuntalā. The meaning would then be, 'It is not to be wondered at that these two friends should follow Śakuntalā and assist in carrying out her schemes, any more than that the two stars of Viśākhā should go after the young moon.' *Anuvartete=anusaratah,* K. Cf. in Vikram., Act I, *Ćitralekhā-dvitīyām priya-sakhīm Urvaśīm grihītvā Viśākhā-sahita iva bhagavān Soma upasthitah sa rājarshih.*

[1] '(Your) "unobservedly" will require thought, (your) "quickly" (is) easy.' This use of *iti* in quoting previous words is noticeable.

[2] 'For this golden bracelet, having its jewels sullied by the tears

---

Verse 66. HARIṆĪ (a variety of ATYASHṬI), containing seventeen syllables to the Pāda or quarter-verse, each Pāda being alike.

◡◡◡◡◡– | – – – – | ◡–◡◡–◡–‖

प्रियंवदा ॥ विचिन्त्य ॥

[a] हला । मञ्चणलेही से करीत्रदु । इमं देवदासेत्ताबदेसेण सुमणोगोबिदं करित्र से हत्थत्रं पाबइंसं ।

[a] हला । मदनलेखोऽस्य क्रियताम् । इमं देवताशेषापदेशेन सुमनोगोषितां कृत्वास्स हस्तं प्रापयिष्यामि ।

(rendered) scorching from internal fever night after night flowing from the outer-corner-of-my-eye which rests on my arm, slipping, slipping down [i.e. as it constantly slips down] from the wrist, without pressing on [catching on, hitching on] the scars (that are caused) by the friction of the bow-string, is repeatedly pushed back by me.' *Vivarṇa-maṇī-kṛita*, lit. 'made into a colourless gem,' 'made so that its jewels are devoid of colour.' *Apāṅga*=*netra-prānta*. *Pravartibhiḥ*=*skhaladbhiḥ*. *An-atilulita*=*an-atisakta*, 'not closely adhering,' K.;=*nābhilupta*, S'. and C'. The same word occurs at the end of this Act, where allusion is made to the flowery couch of S'akuntalā, *śarīra-lulitā*, 'which her body had pressed.' One sense of root *lul* is certainly to 'adhere,' 'stick,' 'cleave.' The Deva-n. MSS. all have *an-abhilulita* with the same meaning, unsupported by K. and the other scholiasts, and the oldest Beng. MSS. Through emaciation and disuse of the bow (cf. p. 70, l. 8, with p. 67, l. 12) the callosities on the fore-arm, usually caused by the bow-string, were not sufficiently prominent to prevent the bracelet from slipping down from the wrist to the elbow, when the arm was raised to support the head. This is a favourite idea with Kālidāsa to express the attenuation caused by love (cf. Megha-d. 2, *kanaka-valaya-bhraṇśa-rikta-prakoshṭhaḥ*, 'having the fore-arm bare by the falling of the golden bracelet).' The Beng. have *an-atilulita-jyā-ghātāṅkād*, agreeing with *maṇi-bandhanāt*, which would appear at first sight to be the better reading. I have followed K. and the Deva-n. MSS. in making this compound agree with *valayam*. It may, however, as K. observes, be taken adverbially. *Maṇi-bandhana*, 'the place for binding on jewels,' 'the wrist.'

[1] 'Let a love-letter be composed for him. Having hidden it [made it hid] in a flower, I will deliver it into [cause it to reach] his hand under the pretext of [as if it were] the remains (of an offering presented) to an idol.' *Madana-lekhaḥ*=*ananga-lekhaḥ*, C'.;=*smara-bhāva-sūćakaṁ lekhaṁ*, S'. *Sumano-gopita*=*kusuma-saṅgupta*, S'. *Devatā-śeshāpadeśena*, the Beng., supported by S'., read *devatā-sevāpadeśena*, 'under pretext of honouring a divinity.' K. reads *devatā-vyapadeśena*, with the word *prasāda* inserted in the margin. *Devatā-śesha* is supported by C'., and

अनसूया ।

[a] रोच्चइ मे सुउमारो पञ्ओञो । किं वा सउन्दला भणादि ।

शकुन्तला ।

[b] सहीणिओओवि विकप्पीअदि ।

प्रियंवदा ।

[c] तेण हि अत्तणो उवण्णासपुव्वं चिन्तेहि दाव किम्पि ललिअपदबन्धयं ।

शकुन्तला ।

[d] हला । चिन्तेमि अहं । अवहीरणभीरुअं पुणो वेवइ मे हिअञं ।

राजा ॥ सहर्षम् ॥

अयं स ते तिष्ठति सङ्गमोत्सुकी
विशङ्कसे भीरु यतोऽवधीरणाम् ।

---

[a] रोचते मे सुकुमारः प्रयोगः । किं वा शकुन्तला भणति । [b] सखी-नियोगोऽपि विकल्प्यते । [c] तेन ह्यात्मन उपन्यासपूर्वं चिन्तय तावत्किमपि ललितपदबन्धनम् । [d] हला । चिन्तयाम्यहम् । अवधीरणभीरुकं पुनर्वेपते मे हृदयम् ।

---

explained by him as *nirmālya*, 'the remains of an offering of flowers presented to an idol.' Garlands of flowers were so offered. A love-letter was one of the four recognized modes of encouraging a lover (see p. 109, n. 3).

[1] 'This very injunction [suggestion] of my friend is weighed (in my mind),' i. e. I must consider before I can consent to it. This is the reading of the two oldest MSS. One, however, has *sahi* or *sahī*.

[2] 'Therefore just think of some pretty composition in verse, accompanied by an allusion to yourself.' *Upanyāsa-pūrva*, lit. 'preceded [headed] by an allusion.' *Lalita-pada-bandhana*, cf. *lalitārtha-bandham*, Vikram., Act. II; *pada-bandhana*, lit. 'the connection or composition of quarter-verses,' cf. *padāni*, ver. 68 of this play.

लभेत वा प्रार्थयिता न वा श्रियं
श्रिया दुरापः कथमीप्सितो भवेत् ॥ ६७ ॥

सख्यौ ।

[a] अयि अत्तगुणावमानिणि । को दाणिं सरीरणिव्वाव-
इत्तिं सारदिश्रं जोसिणिं पडन्तेण वारेदि ।

शकुन्तला ॥ सस्मितम् ॥

[b] णिओइदा दाणिंम्हिं । ॥ इत्युपविष्टा चिन्तयति ॥

[a] अयि आत्मगुणावमानिनि । को इदानीं शरीरनिर्वापयित्रीं शारदीं ज्योत्स्नां
पटान्तेन वारयति ।   [b] नियोजितेदानीमस्मि ।

---

[1] 'That very one, O timid one, from whom thou apprehendest a refusal, stands pining for a union with thee. The lover may or may not win Fortune, (but) how, being beloved (by her), should he be difficult-to-be-won by Fortune?' *Śrī* = *Lakshmī*, 'the goddess of beauty and fortune,' here identified with S'akuntalā or with the object of the lover's hopes and aspirations. The commentators throw no light on this passage. The meaning seems to be, 'There is always a doubt whether the suitor will gain favour with Fortune, or with the beautiful maiden who may be the object of his love, but when it is certain that he is beloved by her, how can *she* have any difficulty in gaining *him?* for there surely will be no doubt of his being willing to accept her favours, however uncertain may be her encouragement of his advances.' The verse which follows this in the Beng. MSS. is probably spurious.

[2] 'O thou undervaluer of thine own excellences, who now would ward off with the skirt of a garment the autumnal moonlight, the cooler of his body?' i. e. (according to S'.) this prince is too sensible to be averse to a union with one so beautiful as thou art. *Nirvāpayitrīm*, cf. *nirvāpayitā*, ver. 65, and see p. 97, n. 1. *Paṭāntena*, cf. in Act V. *paṭāntena mukham āvṛitya roditi*.

[3] 'I am now (acting) under (your) directions,' i. e. it is by your orders that I do this; *niyojitāsmi bhavatībhyāṃ gīti-karaṇe*, 'I am directed by you to compose verses,' S'.; 'I am only following your directions, therefore you are responsible if I meet with a repulse,' S'.

Verse 67. VANŚA-STHAVILA (a variety of JAGATĪ). See verses 18, 22, 23.

राजा ।

स्थाने खलु विस्मृतनिमेषेण चक्षुषा प्रियामवलोक-
यामि । यतः

उन्नमितैकभ्रूलतमाननमस्याः पदानि रचयन्त्याः ।
कण्टकितेन प्रथयति मय्यनुरागं कपोलेन ॥६८॥

शकुन्तला ।

ᵃ हला । चिन्तिदा मए गीदिआ । ण क्ख सन्निहिदाणि
उण लेहणसाहणाणि ।

प्रियंवदा ।

ᵇ इमस्सिं सुओदरसुउमारे एलिणीपत्ते णहेहिं णिक्खित्त-
वण्णं करेहि ।

ᵃ हला । चिन्तिता मया गीतिका । न खलु सन्निहितानि पुनर्लेखनसाधनानि ।
ᵇ अस्मिन्शुकोदरसुकुमारे नलिनीपत्रे नखैर्निक्षिप्तवर्णं कुरु ।

---

[1] 'Fitly, indeed, do I gaze on my beloved with an eye that forgets to wink, because the countenance of her composing [whilst she is in the act of composing] verses has one eyebrow raised; (and) by her thrilling cheek she discloses her affection for me.' *Vismṛita-nimeshena* is very expressive of a fixed, earnest gaze. Chézy translates, 'O spectacle enchanteur! dont je serais jaloux que le moindre clignement d'œil me privât un instant!' *Kaṇṭakita*, lit. 'having the downy hair of the cheek erect like thorns' (= *pulakāñćita*). The erection of the hair of the body (*pulaka, roma-kaṇṭaka, romāñćana*) indicates exquisite delight, according to the notions of the Hindūs. Cf. Vikram., Act I, *mama angaṃ sa-roma-kaṇṭakam aṅkuritam.*

[2] 'But the writing-materials indeed are not at hand.' Most of the MSS. have *hu* for Sanskrit *khalu*. Lassen (Instit. Prāk. p. 192) shews that *kkhu* is the proper form after a short vowel.

[3] 'Engrave the letters [make engraving of the letters] with your nails

---

Verse 68. ÁRYÁ or GÁTHÁ. See verse 2.

− ∪ ∪ | − − | − ∪ ∪ ‖ − ∪ ∪ | − − | ∪ − ∪ | ∪ ∪ − | −
− ∪ ∪ | − − | ∪ ∪ ∪ ∪ ‖ − ∪ ∪ | − − | ∪ | − − | ∪

शकुन्तला ॥ यथोक्तं रूपयित्वा ॥

[a] हला । सुणुह दाणिं सङ्गदत्थं ण वेत्ति ।

उभे ।

[b] अवहिदम्ह ।

शकुन्तला ॥ वाचयति ॥

[c] तुज्झ ण आणे हिअअं मम उण कामो दिवावि रत्तिम्मि ।
णिग्घिण तवेइ बलिअं तुइ वुत्तमणोरहाइ अङ्गाइं ॥६९॥

[a] हला । शृणुतमिदानीं सङ्गतार्थं न वेति ।   [b] अवहिते खः ।

[c] तव न जाने हृदयं मम पुनः कामो दिवापि रात्रिमपि ।
निष्पृण तपति बलीयस्त्वयि वृत्तमनोरथाया अङ्गानि ॥६९॥

---

on this lotus-leaf smooth as a parrot's breast.' *Śukodara*, 'a parrot's breast,' it also means 'a leaf of the Tālīśa tree' (=*tālīśa-pattra*); in Vikram., Act IV, the colour of a scarf is compared to the same thing (*śukodara-śyāmaṃ stanānśukam*), and in Mahā-bh. ii. 1035, the colour of horses (*śukodara-samān hayān*). The Prākṛit is answerable for *nikshipta-varṇaṃ kuru*. This is the reading of all the Deva-n. MSS.; the Beng. have *padaccheda-bhaktyā nakhair ālikhyatām*.

[1] 'Thy heart I know not, but day and night, O cruel one, Love vehemently inflames the limbs of me, whose desires are centred in thee.' Such is the reading of the Taylor MS. and my own.. The other Deva-n. agree, but give *maṇorahāim* for *manorathāni*, in concord with *awgāni*. *Maṇorahāi* and *maṇorahae* may both stand for the Sanskrit gen. fem. *manorathāyāḥ* (in concord with *mama*), and both are equally admissible into the metre (Lassen's Instit. Prāk. pp. 304, 305, 147). The interpretation of Ćandra-śekhara supports this reading (*nishkṛipa tapayati balīyas tvad-abhimukha-manorathāyā angāni*). This verse is called by Kāṭavema the *upanyāsa* or 'allusion,' see p. 116, n. 2; see also the next note on verse 70.

Verse 69. UDGĀTHĀ or GĪTI. See verse 4.

‒ ∪ ∪ | ‒ ‒ | ∪ ∪ ‒ ‖ ∪ ∪ ∪ ∪ | ‒ ‒ | ∪ ‒ ∪ | ‒ ‒ | ‒

‒ ∪ ∪ | ∪ ‒ ∪ | ∪ ∪ ‒ ‖ ∪ ∪ ‒ | ∪ ∪ ‒ | ∪ ‒ ∪ | ‒ ‒ |

राजा ॥ सहसोपसृत्य ॥

तपति तनुगाचि मदनस्त्वामनिशं मां पुनर्दहत्येव ।
ग्लपयति यथा शशाङ्कं न तथा हि कुमुद्वतीं दिवसः ॥७०॥

सख्यौ ॥ विलोक्य सहर्षमुत्थाय ॥

[a] स्वागदं अविलम्बिनो मनोरहंस [2] ।

॥ शकुन्तलाभ्युत्थातुमिच्छति ॥

राजा ।

अलमलमायासेन ।

संदष्टकुसुमशयनान्याशुक्लान्तविसभङ्गसुरभीणि ।
गुरुपरितापानि न ते गात्राण्युपचारमर्हन्ति [3] ॥७१॥

[a] स्वागतमविलम्बिनो मनोरथस्य ।

---

[1] 'Thee, O slender-limbed one, Love inflames; but me he actually consumes incessantly; for the Day does not so cause the lotus to fade as it does the moon.' *Kumuda* or *kumudvatī* is a kind of lotus, which blossoms in the night and fades by day (*kumudvatī čandra-virahena santaptā bhavati*, S'.), here compared to S'akuntalā. *Kumudvatī* is usually 'a group of lotuses.' *S'as'ānka*, 'hare-marked,' i. e. the moon. Dushyanta again compares himself to the moon (cf. p. 113, n. 1). This with the preceding verse, according to S'. and Č., is an example of the figure called Uttarottara.

[2] 'Welcome to the speedy (fulfilment of thy) desire!' or 'welcome to the object of thy desire which does not delay (its appearance).' The Beng. insert *samīhita-phalasya* or *čintita-phalasya*.

[3] 'Thy limbs, which closely press the couch of flowers, (and are) fragrant by the crushing of the quickly-faded lotus-fibres, being grievously

---

Verse 70. ĀRYĀ or GĀTHĀ. See verse 2.

```
∪ ∪ ∪ ∪ | ∪ – ∪ | ∪ ∪ – || – ∪ ∪ | – – | ∪ – ∪ | – – | ∪
∪ ∪ ∪ ∪ | ∪ – ∪ | – – || ∪ ∪ – | ∪ ∪ – | ∪ | – ∪ ∪ | –
```

Verse 71. ĀRYĀ or GĀTHĀ. See verse 2.

```
– – | ∪ ∪ ∪ ∪ | ∪ ∪ – || – – | – ∪ ∪ | ∪ – ∪ | ∪ ∪ – | ∪
∪ ∪ ∪ ∪ | – – | ∪ ∪ – || – – | ∪ ∪ – | ∪ | ∪ – – | ∪
```

अनसूया ।

^a इदो सिलातलेक्कदेसं अणुगेएहदु वअस्सो ।

॥ राजोपविशति । शकुन्तला सलज्जा तिष्ठति ॥

प्रियंवदा ।

^b दुवेएम्पि वो अखोखाणुरात्तो पच्चक्खो । सहीसिणेहो उण मं पुणरुत्तवादिणिं करेदि ।

^a इतः शिलातलैकदेशमनुगृह्णातु वयस्यः ।   ^b द्वयोरपि युवयोरन्योन्यानुरागः प्रत्यक्षः । सखीस्नेहः पुनर्मां पुनरुक्तवादिनीं करोति ।

---

inflamed, do not deserve (to perform) obeisance;' i. e. are excused the usual salutation. In consideration of the state of your bodily frame, you are privileged to keep your recumbent posture even before me. *Upaćāram,* i. e. *mat-kṛite vinayādi-rūpam. San-dan̄ś,* lit. 'to press the teeth closely together;' hence *sandashṭa,* 'coming in close contact with.' Cf. Raghu-v. xvi. 65, *sandashṭa-vastreshu nitambeshu,* 'on (their) hips to which garments were closely fitted.' Our English word 'bite' has the same acceptation. *Āśu-klānta,* &c. The Beng. have *āśu-vimardita-mṛiṇāla-valayāni* or *āśu-vivarṇita* (= *mlānī-bhūta,* Ć.), &c., 'having bracelets of lotus-fibres that have quickly faded (from the heat of her limbs).' Cf. p. 106, n. 1.

¹ 'Will our friend deign to take a seat here on the stone ?' cf. p. 76, l. 3. The stone-seat served also for the couch of S'akuntalā, S'. *Anugṛihṇātu,* 'let him favour,' is the reading of K. For *anugeṇhadu* Dr. Burkhard reads *alankaredu* (= Sanskrit *alan-karotu*).

² 'But affection for my friend prompts me to be the speaker of something superfluous,' i. e. of what has been so often repeated as to be already sufficiently well-known. *Punar-ukta,* which properly means 'said again,' 'repeated,' has, in dramatic composition, acquired the acceptation of 'superfluous,' and sometimes simply 'additional.' Thus in the Vikram., Act III, the torches are said to be *punar-uktāś ćandrikāyām,* 'rendered superfluous in the moonlight;' and in Act V. of that play, tears dropping from the eyes on the breast are said to cause *muktāvalī-viraćanam punar-uktam,* 'the formation of an additional necklace of pearls.' Cf. also *kim punar-uktena,* Mālavik. p. 63, l. 5. *Sakhī-snehaḥ = sakhī-vishayaka-praṇayaḥ.*

राजा ।

भद्रे । नैतत्परिहार्यम् । विवक्षितं ह्यनुक्तमनुतापं जनयति ।[1]

प्रियंवदा ।

[a] आवण्णस्स विसअवासिणो जणस्स अत्तिहरेण रक्खा होदव्वन्ति एसो वो धम्मो ।[2]

राजा ।

नास्मात्परम् ।[3]

प्रियंवदा ।

[b] तेण हि इअं णो पिअसही तुमं उद्दिसिअ इमं अवत्थन्तरं भअवदा मअणेण आरोविदा । ता अरहसि अब्भुववत्तीए जीविदं से अवलम्बिदुं ।[4][5]

राजा ।

भद्रे । साधारणोऽयं प्रणयः । सर्वथानुगृहीतोऽस्मि ।[6]

[a] आपन्नस्य विषयवासिनो जनस्यार्तिहरेण राज्ञा भवितव्यमित्येष वो धर्मः ।
[b] तेन हीयमावयोः प्रियसखी त्वामुद्दिश्येदमवस्थान्तरं भगवता मदनेनारोपिता । तदर्हस्यभ्युपपत्त्या जीवितमस्या अवलम्बितुम् ।

---

[1] 'That (which you have to say) ought not to be suppressed [omitted], for that-which-was-intended-to-be-spoken and is not spoken produces subsequent regret.' *Anu-tāpa*, 'after-pain,' i. e. repentance. *Vivakshita*, from the desid. of root *vać*.

[2] 'It is to be become by the king [the king ought to be] the remover of the suffering of one dwelling in his kingdom (who has) fallen into trouble; such is your duty.' The Beng. have *āśrama-vāsino* for *vishaya-vāsino*. The latter reading is supported by K.

[3] 'No other than this,' i. e. nothing short of this; this is exactly my duty.

[4] 'Therefore (know that) this our dear friend has been reduced to this altered condition by the divinity Love on thy account.' *Ud-diśya*, 'aiming at,' 'regarding,' see p. 101, n. 1. *Avasthāntara*, 'another state,' i. e. an alteration from the natural and healthy state. *Āropitā=prāpitā*, S.

[5] *Avalambitum*, properly 'to cling to,' 'depend upon;' here used transitively, 'to sustain,' 'support.'

[6] Cf. Vikram., Act II, *sādhārano 'yam ubhayoḥ praṇayaḥ.*

शकुन्तला ॥ प्रियंवदामवलोक्य ॥

[a] हला । किं अन्तेउरविरहपज्जुसुञ्अस्स राएसिणो उवरोहेण ।

राजा ।

सुन्दरि ।

इदमनन्यपरायणमन्यथा
हृदयसन्निहिते हृदयं मम ।
यदि समर्थयसे मदिरेक्षणे
मदनवाणहतोऽस्मि हतः पुनः ॥७२॥

अनसूया ।

[b] वअस्स । बहुवल्लहा राञ्आणो सुणीअन्ति । जह णे पिञ्असही बन्धुञअणसोञणिज्जा ण होइ । तह णिव्वा-हेहि ।

<hr>

[a] हला । किमन्तःपुरविरहपर्युत्सुकस्य राजर्षेरुपरोधेन । [b] वयस्य । बहुवल्लभा राजानः श्रूयन्ते । यथा नौ प्रियसखी बन्धुजनशोचनीया न भवति । तथा निर्वाहय ।

[1] 'What (can you mean) by detaining the Rājarshi, who is pining (by reason of) separation from his royal-consorts?' *Antaḥ-pura*, 'the inner part of the palace,' 'the female apartments,' here put for the occupants thereof.

[2] 'O thou that art near my heart, if this heart of mine which is devoted to no other, thou judgest to be otherwise, (then) O lovely-eyed one, being (already) slain by Love's shafts, I am slain again,' i. e. I suffer a second death. Cf. Bhartṛi-h. i. 63, *hatam api nihanty eva madanaḥ*. *Hridaya-sannihite*=*man-mano-'vasthāyini*, 'O thou that abidest in my heart,' S'.; =*ćittārūḍhe*, Ć. *Madirā*, 'wine,' as applied to *īkshaṇa*, 'the eye,' is said by S'. to be equivalent to *sundara*, 'beautiful;' or to *īshad-ghūrṇana-sīla*, 'slightly inclined to roll about.' 'Wine-eyed' may mean 'one whose eyes intoxicate like wine.'

<hr>

Verse 72. DRUTA-VILAMBITA (a variety of JAGATI). See verse 45.

राजा ।

भद्रे । किं बहुना ।

परिग्रहबहुत्वेऽपि द्वे प्रतिष्ठे कुलस्य मे ।
समुद्ररसना चोर्वी सखी च युवयोरियम् ॥ ७३ ॥

उभे ।

[a] णिव्वुदम्ह[2] ।

प्रियंवदा ॥ सदृष्टिक्षेपम् ॥

[b] अणसूए । जह एसो इदो दिष्टदिट्ठी उस्सुओ मिअपो-
दओ मादरं अखेसदि । एहि । सञ्जोएम णं[3] । ॥ इत्युभे प्रस्थिते ॥

शकुन्तला ।

[c] हला । असरणम्हि । अखदरा वो आसञ्छदु ।

---

[a] निर्वृते खः ।   [b] अनसूये । यचैष इतो दत्तदृष्टिरुत्सुको मृगपोतको मा-
तरमन्विष्यति । एहि । संयोजयाव एनम् ।   [c] हला । अशरणास्मि । अन्यतरा
युवयोरागच्छतु ।

---

[1] 'Even in the multitude of (my) wives [however numerous may be my wives] there (will be) but two chief-glories of my race, the sea-girt earth on the one hand (*ća*), and on the other (*ća*) this friend of yours,' i. e. there will be but two sources of glory to my race, viz. the sea-girt earth and S'akuntalā. *Prati-shṭhā*=*utkarsha-hetu*, 'a cause of renown,' 'a distinguished ornament,' S'.; properly 'a cause of stability,' 'a support.' *Parigraha-bahutve*=*kalatra-bāhulye*. The Deva-n. MSS. read *samudra-vasanā*, 'clothed in the ocean,' 'having the ocean for its garments' (*samudra eva vastrāṇi yasyāḥ*, S'.) The Beng. all have *samudra-rasanā*, which is literally 'sea-girt' (*rasanā*=*mekhalā*), and seems to be the better reading. Cf. Hitop. l. 2542. Confusion between *rasanā* and *vasanā* may easily have arisen. *Ća ća*, see p. 14, n. 1.

[2] In the Beng. MSS. the dialogue which follows these words has several interpolations.

[3] Lit. 'let us cause it to join (its mother),' 'let us lead it to its mother.' *Mātrā saha iti anushanga*, S'. Some word like *paśya*, 'See!' may be supplied before *yathā* in the sentence preceding.

उभे ।

[a] पुहवीए जो सरणं । सो तुह समीबे वट्टइ । ॥ इति निष्क्रान्ते ॥

शकुन्तला ।

[b] कहं गदाग्रो एव्व ।

राजा ।

अलमावेगेन । नन्वयमाराधयिता जनस्तव समीपे वर्त्तते ।

किं शीतलैः क्लमविनोदिभिरार्द्रवाता-
न्सञ्चारयामि नलिनीदलतालवृन्तैः ।
अङ्कं निधाय करभोरु यथासुखं ते
संवाहयामि चरणावुत पद्मताम्रौ ॥७४॥

[a] पृथिव्या यः शरणम् । स तव समीपे वर्त्तते ।   [b] कथं गते एव ।

---

[1] 'Does not this person, thy humble-servant [thy adorer], remain near thee?' i. e. am not I here to wait upon thee, in place of thy friends? The Beng. add *sakhī-bhūmau*. *Ārādhayitā=paricārakaḥ*, 'an attendant,' S., but it is also 'the worshipper of a deity,' and therefore implies adoration as well as service. There is designedly a 'double-entendre.'

[2] 'Shall I set in motion moist breezes by (means of) cool lotus-leaf-fans which-remove langour? or placing thy feet, brown as the lotus, O round-thighed (maiden), in (my) lap shall I rub them soothingly?' *Karabhoru*, voc. case of *karabhorū*; according to Pāṇ. iv. 1, 69, *ūru*, 'a thigh or hip,' at the end of this and some other compounds becomes *ūrū*, and is declined like *vadhū*; and *karabhorūḥ* is said to be equivalent to *vṛittorūḥ strī*, 'a woman with round thighs.' *Karabha* is 'the thick part of the hand,' 'the part between the wrist and the fingers;' it is also 'a young elephant.' Dr. Boehtlingk considers that the comparison is taken from the first of these senses. It may with more reason be taken from the other; for from the following gloss of Ć. it seems probable that as *kara* stands for both the human hand and the trunk of an elephant, and *karabha* for the upper

---

Verse 74. VASANTA-TILAKĀ (a variety of ŚAKVARĪ). See verses 8, 27, 31, 43, 46, 64.

शकुन्तला ।

[a] ए माणणीएसु अत्ताणं अवराहइस्सं ।[1] ॥ इत्युत्थाय गन्तुमिच्छति ॥

राजा ।

सुन्दरि । अपरिनिर्वाणो दिवसः ।[2] इयं च ते शरीरावस्था ।
उत्सृज्य कुसुमशयनं नलिनीदलकल्पितस्तनावरणम् ।
कथमातपे गमिष्यसि परिबाधापेलवैरङ्गैः ॥७५॥

॥ इति बलादेनां निवर्तयति ॥

[a] न माननीयेष्वात्मानमपराधयिष्यामि ।

---

part of the hand, so the latter word may be taken for the same part of an
elephant's trunk. *Karabhaḥ prāny-angam* ('is part of an animal') *tadiva
ūrur yasyāḥ śubha-lakshaṇam idaṃ tad uktam, hasti-hasta-nibhair* ('like
an elephant's trunk') *vrittair* ('round') *asthābhaiḥ karabhopamaiḥ prāpnu-
vantyūrūbhiḥ śaśvat striyaḥ sukham anangajam.* The epithet may therefore mean 'having thighs gracefully tapering like the trunk of an
elephant.' Cf. *karabhopamorūḥ*, Raghu-v. vi. 83, and *dvirada-nāsorūḥ*,
Bhaṭṭi-k. iv. 17. *Saṃvāhayāmi = mardayāmi;* *saṃ-vāh* (or more
correctly *saṃ-vah* in the causal) is applied especially to the rubbing or
shampooing of the limbs. *Padma-tāmrau,* Chézy observes that the
Hindū women extracted a rosy-coloured dye from a plant called Law-
sonia Inermis, with which they were in the habit of dyeing their nails
and fingers, as well as their feet. Cf. *strī-nakha-pāṭalaṃ kuruvakam,*
Vikram., Act II.

[1] 'I will not make myself in fault with those whom I am bound to
respect [towards those who are worthy of respect],' i. e. with my foster-
father and others.

[2] 'The day is not (yet) cool.' *A-parinirvāṇa=an-apagata-tīvrātapa,*
'having its great heat not yet passed off;' 'it was still noon,' S'. Some
MSS. have *a-nirvāṇa,* and others *apa-nirvāṇa* (=*a-nirvāṇa, nirvāṇa-
rahita*).

[3] 'Having left the couch of flowers (and) the covering of thy bosom

---

Verse 75. ĀRYĀ or GĀTHĀ. See verse 2.

    − − | ∪ ∪ ∪ ∪ | ∪ ∪ − ‖ ∪ ∪ − | ∪ ∪ − | ∪ − ∪ | − ∪ ∪ | −
    ∪ ∪ − | ∪ − ∪ | − ∪ ∪ ‖ ∪ ∪ − | − − | ∪ | − − | −

शकुन्तला ।

[a]पोरव । एक्ख विणञ्चं । मञ्अणसन्तत्ताबि ए हु अत्तणो पहवामि ।[1]

राजा ।

भीरु । अलं गुरुजनभयेन । दृष्ट्वा ते विदितधर्मा तच्-
भवान्नाच दोषं महीष्यति कुलपतिः ।[2] अपि च
गान्धर्वेण विवाहेन बह्यो राजर्षिकन्यकाः ।
श्रूयन्ते परिणीतास्ताः पितृभिश्चाभिनन्दिताः ॥७६॥[3]

[a] पोरव । रक्ख विनयम् । मदनसन्तप्तमपि न खल्वात्मनः प्रभवामि ।

---

formed of lotus leaves, how wilt thou go in the heat, with thy limbs (too)
delicate for hardships?' *Paribādhā-pelava*=*duḥkhāsahishṇu*, 'incapable
of bearing hardship.' The Beng. have *komala* for *pelava*.

[1] 'Even though inflamed by Love, I have not the power (of disposing)
of myself,' i. e. *yena tvam-manoratha-pūraṇam kriyate*, 'so that your
wishes may be fulfilled,' S'.

[2] 'Having seen it, his reverence the head-of-your-society who knows-
the-law will not take (it as a) fault in you,' i. e. will not attribute blame
to you in this matter. *Drishṭvā te* is supported by the concurrent
authority of the Taylor, Mackenzie, and Colebrooke MSS. *Vidita-dharmā*,
see Pān. v. 4, 124; *dharma* at the end of a Bahuvrīhi comp. becomes
dharman (cf. *yuvām kshatriya-dharmāṇau*, Hitop. l. 2473).

[3] 'Many daughters of Rājarshis [p. 44, notes 1 and 2] are heard to have
been married by the marriage (called) Gāndharva, and (even) they have
received the approval of their fathers [been approved by their fathers].'
The Gāndharva marriage is one of the forms of marriage described in
Manu iii. 22, &c. It is a marriage proceeding entirely from love (*kāma-
sambhava*) or the mutual inclination (*anyonyecchā*) of a youth and maiden,
and concluded without any ceremonies and without consulting relatives,
see Manu iii. 32; Indian Wisdom, p. 199. *Gāndharvaḥ = paraspara-
bhāshayā kṛito vivāhaḥ*, K. The long scene which follows this verse in
the Beng. MSS. is omitted in all the Deva-n., and must be regarded as
an interpolation.

Verse 76. ŚLOKA or ANUSHTUBH. See verses 5, 6, 11, 12, 26, 47, 50, 51, 53, 73.

शकुन्तला ।

[a] मुञ्च दाव मं । भूओबि सहीजणं अणुमाणइस्सं ।

राजा ।

भवतु । मोक्ष्यामि ।

शकुन्तला ।

[b] कदा ।

राजा ।

अपरिक्षतकोमलस्य ताव-
त्कुसुमस्येव नवस्य षट्पदेन ।
अधरस्य पिपासता मया ते
सदयं सुन्दरि गृह्यते रसोऽस्य[2] ॥७७॥

॥ इति मुखमस्याः समुन्नमयितुमिच्छति । शकुन्तला परिहरति नाट्येन ॥

नेपथ्ये ।

[c] चक्कवाकवहुए । आमन्तेहि सहअरं । उवट्ठिदा रअंणी ।

[a] मुञ्च तावन्माम् । भूयोऽपि सखीजनमनुमानयिष्यामि ।   [b] कदा ।
[c] चक्रवाकवधुके । आमन्त्रयस्व सहचरम् । उपस्थिता रजनी ।

---

[1] 'I will again take counsel with my female friends.' *Anu-man* in the causal may mean 'to ask the consent of,' 'to cause or to induce to assent.'

[2] '(As) by the bee (the honey) of the fresh, untouched tender blossom, (so) now by me eager-to-allay-my-thirst must the nectar of this under-lip of thine be gently stolen, O fair one, (ere I can let thee go).' *A-parikshata*, lit. 'unhurt,' 'uninjured,' applied to a virgin. *Adhara*, compare p. 33, n. 1.

[3] '[*Behind the scenes.*] O female-Ćakravāka, bid farewell to thy mate; the night is at hand [arrived].' *Ćakravāka-vadhukā* (Pāṇ. vii. 4, 13), i. e.

Verse 77. AUPAĆĆHANDASIKA, containing eleven syllables to the first Pāda or quarter-verse, and twelve to the second, each half-verse being alike.

◡◡−◡◡−◡−◡−− ‖ ◡◡−−◡◡−◡−◡−−

शकुन्तला ॥ ससम्भ्रमम् ॥

[a] पोरव । असंसत्तं मम सरीरवुत्तन्तोवलम्भस्स[1] अज्जा गोदमी इदो एव्व आच्छदि । दाव विडबन्तरिदो[2] होहि ।

राजा ।

तथा । ॥ इत्यात्मानमावृत्य तिष्ठति ॥

॥ ततः प्रविशति पात्रहस्ता[3] गौतमी सख्यौ च ॥

सख्यौ ।

[b] इदो इदो अज्जा गोदमी ।

गौतमी ॥ शकुन्तलामुपेत्य ॥

[c] जादे । अवि लहुसन्दावाइं दे अङ्गाइं ।

[a] पौरव । असंशयं मम शरीरवृत्तान्तोपलम्भायायाौ गौतमीत एवागच्छति । ताव-द्विटपान्तरितो भव । [b] इत इत आर्या गौतमी । [c] जाते । अपि लघुसन्तापानि तेऽङ्गानि ।

---

the Ćakravākī or female of the Ruddy goose, commonly called the Brāhmanī duck (Anas Casarca). The male and female of these birds keep together during the day (whence one of their names, *dvandva-ćara*, 'going in pairs') and are, like turtle-doves, patterns of constancy and connubial affection ; but the legend is that they are doomed to pass the night apart (whence the name *rātri-viślesha-gāmin*) in consequence of a curse pronounced upon them by some saint whom they had offended. Accordingly, as soon as night commences, they take up their station on opposite banks of a river, and call to each other in piteous cries. The name *rathānga* or *ratha-pāda*, 'chariot-footed,' sometimes given to them, indicates some peculiar formation of the feet. Constant allusion is made to their habits ; thus in Vikram., Act IV, *sahaćarīṃ dūre matvā viraushi samutsukaḥ;* cf. also Megha-d. 82, and Raghu-v. viii. 55.

[1] 'To ascertain the state of my bodily health.' Prākṛit has no dative, but gives the force of that case to the genitive.

[2] 'Concealed by the branches ;' see p. 104, n. 2.

[3] 'With a vessel in her hand.' One MS. has *udaka-pātra-hastā*, 'with a vessel of water in her hand.'

शकुन्तला ।

[a] अज्जे । अत्थि मे विसेसो ।

गौतमी ।

[b] इमिणा दब्भोदॅएण णिराबाधं एव्व दे सरीरं भविस्सदि ।

॥ शिरसि शकुन्तलामभ्युक्ष्य ॥ [c] वच्छे । परिणदो दिअहो । एहि । उडजं एव्व गच्छम्ह । ॥ इति प्रस्थिताः ॥

शकुन्तला ॥ आत्मगतम् ॥

[d] हिअअ । पढमं एव्व सुहोवणदे मणोरहे कादरभावं ण मुञ्चसि । साणुसअविहडिअस्स कहं दे सम्पदं सन्दावो ।

॥ पदान्तरे स्थित्वा । प्रकाशम् ॥ [e] लदावलअ सन्दावहारअ । आमन्तेमि तुमं भूओवि परिभोञ्जस्सं ।

॥ दुःखेन निष्क्रान्ता शकुन्तला सहेतराभिः ॥

---

[a] आर्ये । अस्ति मे विशेषः ।   [b] अनेन दर्भोदकेन निराबाधमेव ते शरीरं भविष्यति ।   [c] वत्से । परिणतो दिवसः । एहि । उटजमेव गच्छामः ।   [d] हृदय । प्रथममेव सुखोपनते मनोरथे कातरभावं न मुञ्चसि । सानुशयविघटितस्य कथं ते साम्प्रतं सन्तापः ।   [e] लतावलय सन्तापहारक । आमन्त्रये त्वां भूयोऽपि परिभोगाय ।

---

¹ 'O venerable mother! there is a change for the better in me.' *Nairujyaṃ kiñcid idānīṃ vṛittam*, 'there is now some freedom from pain,' S'. *Ajje* is the reading of the oldest MSS., supported by S'. and Ć. *Viśesha* is 'a change for the better,' in contradistinction to *vikāra*, 'a change for the worse.' The very same expression occurs in Mālavik. p. 46, l. 9.

² 'With this Darbha-water,' i. e. water and Kuśa grass, mixed and used for the *śānty-udaka*, mentioned at p. 97, l. 3; see also p. 19, n. 1, in the middle.

³ 'O heart, even before, when the object-of-thy-desire readily presented itself, thou didst not abandon (thy) anxiety. How (great) now (will be) the anguish of thee regretful (and) dispirited! [*After advancing a step, standing still again, aloud*] O bower of creepers, remover of my suffering,

राजा ॥ पूर्वस्थानमुपेत्य । सनिःश्वासम् ॥

अहो विघ्नवत्यः प्रार्थितार्थसिद्धयः । मया हि
मुहुरङ्गुलिसंवृताधरोष्ठं
प्रतिषेधाक्षरविक्लवाभिरामम् ।
मुखमंशविवर्ति पक्ष्मलाक्ष्याः
कथमप्यनुन्नमितं न चुम्बितं तु ॥७८॥

I bid thee adieu, (hoping) to occupy (thee) again [to have enjoyment of
thee again].' *Prathamam eva*, &c., see p. 120, l. 5. *Sukhopanate*, compare
yad upanatam duḥkham sukham tat, Vikram., end of Act III. *Vi-ghaṭita*
'broken,' 'distracted with grief.' *Paribhoassa*, the genitive in Prākṛit
used for the Sanskrit dative, see p. 129, n. 1. *Paribhogāya*, cf. *pari-
bhukta*, p. 132, l. 1.

¹ 'Alas! the fulfilment of desired objects has hindrances [there are
many obstacles in the way of the accomplishment of one's wishes]; for
by me the face of the lovely-eyelashed-eyed (maiden), having its upper
and lower lip repeatedly protected by (her) fingers, beautiful in stammering
out the syllables of denial, turning (away from me) towards the shoulder,
was with some difficulty raised but not kissed.' *Anguli-saṃvṛita* =
angulibhyām pihita, S. *Adharoshṭha*, see p. 33, n. 1, in the middle.
Pratishedhākshara, i.e. *na mamādharam ćumbanīyam [unnamanīyam]*,
'my lips must not be kissed,' S. and Ć. *Alam alam mā iti prabhṛitibhiḥ*,
by such expressions as 'enough,' 'enough,' 'don't,' K. Some of the Deva-n.
MSS. read *pratishedhāntara*. *Akshara* is 'a syllable,' as well as 'a letter.'
Aṇśa-vivarti = *tiryak-kṛitam*, 'turned on one side,' Ć. It may, however,
also mean 'revolving on the shoulders' (*aṇśayor vivarti*). S. mentions
another reading, *aṇga-vivarti* = *kroḍa-ghūrṇamānam*. *Pakshmalākshī* =
ćāru-bahu-pakshma-yuktam, or *praśasta-pakshma-yuktam akshi yasyāḥ*,
'who has eyes with beautiful eye-lashes,' S. and Ć., i.e. whose eye-lashes
are brown like the leaf of a lotus, Ć. The Hindū women used collyrium
to darken the eye-lashes and eye-brows. *Pakshmala* is properly 'possessed
of eye-lashes' (*pakshma-vat*), an adjective formed from *pakshman* as *sidh-
mala* from *sidhman*, Pāṇ. v. 2, 97; Gram. 80. LXXX. *Ut-pakshmala*,

---

Verse 78. AUPAĆĆHANDASIKA. See verse 77.

क्व नु खलु सम्प्रति गच्छामि । अथवा । इहैव प्रियापरि-
भुक्तमुक्ते लतावलये मुहूर्तं स्यास्यामि ।[1] ॥ सर्वतोऽवलोक्य ॥

तस्याः पुष्पमयी शरीरलुलिता शय्या शिलायामियं
क्लान्तो मन्मथलेख एष नलिनीपत्रे नखैरर्पितः ।
हस्ताद्भ्रष्टमिदं विसाभरणमित्यासज्यमानेक्षणो
निर्गन्तुं सहसा न वेतसगृहाच्छक्तोऽस्मि शून्यादपि ॥७९॥[2]

आकाशे ।

राजन् ।

सायन्तने सवनकर्मणि सम्प्रवृत्ते
वेदीं हुताशनवतीं परितः प्रकीर्णाः ।

'having upturned eye-lashes,' occurs about the middle of the Second Act of Vikram. *Katham-api*, 'somehow or other,' 'hardly,' compare p. 128, l. 12. *Na ćumbitaṃ tu* is the reading of the Calcutta ed. and of the Sāhit.-d. p. 116, supported by Ć.

[1] 'Or rather, I will remain for a brief space in this bower of creepers (once) occupied, (but now) abandoned by my beloved.' *Athavā*, see p. 30, n. 3, and p. 24, n. 1, at the end. *Paribhukta*, compare *paribhogāya*, p. 130, n. 3, at the end. *Muhūrtam*, see p. 37, n. 1, at the end.

[2] 'Here on the stone-seat is her flowery couch impressed by her form; here is the faded love-letter committed to the lotus-leaf with her nails; here is the lotus-fibre bracelet slipped from her hand—having my eyes fixed on such (objects as these) I am not able to tear myself away [go out hastily] from the Vetasa-arbour, even though deserted (by her).' *Śarīra-lulitā*＝*deha-sanghrishṭā*, 'rubbed by the body;' see *anatilulita*, p. 114, n. 2. *Śilāyām*, see p. 105, n. 1, and p. 121, n. 1. *Klānta*, Ś. and the Beng. MSS. read *kānta*, 'charming,' 'dear.' *Visābharaṇa*＝*mrināla-valaya*, see p. 106, n. 1. *Āsajyamānekshaṇa*＝*āropyamānekshaṇa*. *Vetasa-grihāt*＝*latā-maṇḍapāt*, 'from the arbour of creepers,' see p. 104, l. 1.

Verse 79. ŚĀRDŪLA-VIKRĪḌITA (a variety of ATIDHRITI). See verses 14, 30, 36, 39, 40, 63.

छायाश्चरन्ति बहुधा भयमादधानाः
सन्ध्यापयोदकपिशाः पिशिताशनानाम् ॥८०॥

राजा ।

अयमयमागच्छामि ।   ॥ इति निष्क्रान्तः ॥

॥ तृतीयोऽङ्कः ॥

---

[1] '[*In the air.*] The evening sacrificial rite being commenced, the shadows of the Rākshasas, brown as evening clouds, scattered around the altar which bears the consecrated fire, are flitting about in great numbers, producing consternation.' *Ākāśe*, see p. 96, n. 3. *Savana-karmaṇi = homa-karmaṇi*. *Sampravṛitte = upakrānte*. *Pari-tas*, 'on all sides of,' 'around,' here governing an accusative. *Prakīrṇāḥ* is the reading of the oldest MSS.; S. reads *vistīrṇāḥ*; the Deva-n. *prayastāḥ*, 'striving,' 'using effort.' *Hutāśanavatīm = āhitāgnim*. *Bhayam ādadhānāḥ = trāsam utpādayantyaḥ*. *Kapiśa*, properly 'ape-coloured,' generally 'brown,' 'dark-brown.' *Piśitāśanānām = rākshasānām*. The Rākshasas (see p. 40, n. 5) were remarkable for their appetite for raw flesh (*piśita*).

[2] Observe the use of *ayam*, 'this one,' with the first person of the verb. Dr. Burkhard reads *ayam aham* for *ayam ayam*; cf. p. 136, l. 7, *ayam aham bhoḥ*.

Verse 80. VASANTA-TILAKĀ (a variety of ŚAKVARĪ). See verses 8, 27, 31, 43, 46, 64, 74.

॥ अथ चतुर्थाङ्कादौ विष्कम्भः[1] ॥

॥ ततः प्रविशतः कुसुमावचयमभिनयन्त्यौ सख्यौ ॥

अनसूया ।

[a] हला पिअंवदे । जइवि गन्धव्वेण विवाहविहिणा णिव्वुत्त-
कल्लाणा सउन्दला अणुरूवभत्तुगामिणी संवुत्तेत्ति णिव्वुदं
मे हिअअं । तहवि एत्तिअं चिन्तणिज्जं ।

प्रियंवदा ।

[b] कहं विअ ।

अनसूया ।

[c] अज्ज सो राएसी इट्टिं परिसमाविअ इसीहिं विसज्जिओ
अन्तणी णअरं पविसिअ अन्तेउरसमागदो इदोगदं वुत्तन्तं
सुमरदि वा ण वेत्ति ।

---

[a] हला प्रियंवदे । यद्यपि गान्धर्वेण विवाहविधिना निर्वृत्तकल्याणा शकुन्तलानु-
रूपभर्तृगामिनी संवृत्तेति निर्वृतं मे हृदयम् । तथापीयच्चिन्तनीयम् ।   [b] कथमिव ।
[c] सद्य स राजर्षिरिष्टिं परिसमाप्यर्षिभिर्विसर्जित आत्मनो नगरं प्रविश्यान्तःपुरसमागत
इतोगतं वृत्तान्तं स्मरति वा न वेति ।

---

[1] See the note on the term Vishkambha, p. 97, n. 3.

[2] 'Although my heart is comforted by the thought that S'akuntalā has
become completely happy in being united to a husband worthy of her by
a Gāndharva marriage ; nevertheless, there is still some cause for anxiety
[there is still something to be thought about].' *Gāndharvena*, see p. 127,
n. 3. *Anurūpa-bhartṛi-gāminī*, the Beng. have *anurūpa-bhartṛi-bhāginī*.
Iti may often be translated by 'so thinking,' see p. 140, n. 2.

प्रियंवदा ।

[a] वीसद्धा होहि । ण तादिसा आकिदिविसेसा गुणवि-रोहिणो होन्ति । किन्तु तादो दाणिं इमं वुत्तन्तं सुणिऋ ण आणे किं पडिवज्जिस्सदि त्ति ।

अनसूया ।

[b] जह अहं देक्खामि । तह तस्स अणुमदं भवे ।

प्रियंवदा ।

[c] कहं विअ ।

अनसूया ।

[d] गुणवदे कण्णआ पडिबादणिज्जेत्ति अऋं दाव पढमो सङ्कप्पो । तं जइ देव्वं एव्व सम्पादेदि । णं अप्पाआसेण किदत्थो गुरुअणो ।

प्रियंवदा ॥ पुष्पभाजनं विलोक्य ॥

[e] सहि । अवइदाइं बलिकम्मपज्जत्ताइं कुसुमाइं ।

___

[a] विस्रब्धा भव । न तादृशा आकृतिविशेषा गुणविरोधिनो भवन्ति । किन्तु तात इदानीमिमं वृत्तान्तं श्रुत्वा न जाने किं प्रतिपत्स्यत इति ।   [b] यथाहं पश्यामि । तथा तस्यानुमतं भवेत् ।   [c] कथमिव ।   [d] गुणवते कन्या प्रतिपादनीयेत्ययं तावत्प्रथमः सङ्कल्पः । तं यदि दैवमेव सम्पादयति । नन्वस्वायासेन कृतार्थो गुरुजनः ।   [e] सखि । अवचितानि बलिकर्मपर्याप्तानि कुसुमानि ।

---

[1] 'Such distinguished characters as these do not become opposite in their qualities (to what they formerly were). But I know not now what reply the father will make when he has heard this intelligence.' *Ákṛiti*, properly 'form,' 'figure.' *Kintu* is inserted by the Mackenzie MS., supported by K. *Pratipatsyate*=*abhidhāsyati*, S.; =*prativakti*, K.; Westergaard gives 'respondere' as one sense of *pratipad* (cf. *taċ ċhrutvā tatheti pratyapadyata*, Rāmāy. i. 10, 15). It might be translated, 'what he will think of the matter,' 'what he will do,' 'whether he will ratify it.'

[2] 'The maiden is to be given to a worthy (husband), such was the first purpose-of-his-heart.' *Sankalpa*=*mano-ratha*, S.; properly 'a resolve,' 'mental determination' (see p. 49, l. 5, with note 2 at the end).

अनसूया ।

a गं पिअसहीए सउन्दलाए सोहग्गदेवआ अच्च-णीआ ।

प्रियंवदा ।

b जुज्जदि । || इति तदेव कर्मारभेते ||

नेपथ्ये ।

अयमहं भोः[2] ।

अनसूया || कर्णे दत्त्वा ||

c सहि । अदिधिणा विअ णिवेदिदं[3] ।

प्रियंवदा ।

d गं उडजसणिहिदा सउन्दला । || आत्मगतम् || e अज्ज उण हिअएण असणिहिदा[4] ।

a ननु प्रियसख्याः शकुन्तलायाः सौभाग्यदेवतार्चनीया ।   b युज्यते ।
c सखि । अतिथिनेव निवेदितम् ।   d ननूटजसन्निहिता शकुन्तला ।   e अद्य पुनर्हृदयेनासन्निहिता ।

---

[1] 'Is not the guardian-deity of our dear friend S'akuntalā to be honoured (with an offering)?' *Saubhāgya-devatā*, 'the tutelary deity,' 'the deity who watches over the welfare of any one.' The Beng. read *devatāḥ*, 'deities,' and S'. adds *shashṭikā-gaurī-prabhṛitayaḥ*, 'such as Shashṭikā [Durgā], Gaurī, &c.'

[2] '[*Behind the scenes.*] It is I, ho there!' *Nepathye*, see p. 3, n. 2. *Ayam aham āgato 'smi iti arthaḥ*, S'. See Manu ii. 122, &c., 'After salutation, a Brāhman must address an elder, saying, "I am such a one" (*asau nāmāham*), pronouncing his own name. If any persons (through ignorance of Sanskṛit) do not understand the form of salutation (in which mention is made) of the name, to them should a learned man say, "It is I" (*aham iti*), and in that manner should he address all women. In the salutation he should utter the word *bhoḥ* (*bhoḥ-śabda*), for the particle *bhoḥ* is held by sages to have the same property with names (fully expressed).'

[3] '(It seems) as if an announcement were made by a guest [as if a guest were announcing himself].' So read the Beng. MSS., the Deva-n. have *atithīnām*.

[4] 'With her heart she is not near,' i. e. her heart is absent with Dushyanta.

अनसूया ।

[a] होदु । अलं एत्तिएहिं कुसुमेहिं ।   ॥ इति प्रस्थिते ॥

नेपथ्ये ।

आ अतिथिपरिभाविनि ।

विचिन्तयन्ती यमनन्यमानसा
तपोधनं वेत्सि न मामुपस्थितम् ।
स्मरिष्यति त्वां न स बोधितोऽपि स-
न्कथां प्रमत्तः प्रथमं कृतामिव ॥ ८१ ॥

प्रियंवदा ।

[b] हद्दी हद्दी । अप्पिअं एव्व संवुत्तं । कस्सिंपि पूआरुहे
अवरद्धा सुसहिअआ सउन्दला ।   ॥ पुरोऽवलोक्य ॥   [c] ण हु
जस्सिं कस्सिंपि । एसो दुव्वासो सुलहकोवो महेसी ।
तह सविअ वेअचहुलुप्फुल्लदुव्वाराए गईए पडिणिवुत्तो ।

---

[a] भवतु । अलमियद्भिः कुसुमैः ।   [b] हाधिक् हाधिक् । अप्रियमेव संवृत्तम् ।
कस्मिन्नपि पूजार्हेऽपराद्धा शून्यहृदया शकुन्तला ।   [c] न खलु यस्मिन्कस्मिन्नपि ।
एष दुर्वासाः सुलभकोपो महर्षिः । तथा शप्त्वा वेगचटुलोत्फुलदुर्वारया गत्वा प्रतिनिवृत्तः ।

---

[1] 'Woe! thou that art disrespectful to a guest! that (man) of whom
(thou art) thinking to-the-exclusion-of-every-other-object-from-thy-mind,
(so that) thou perceivest not me, rich in penance, to have approached,
shall not recall thee to his memory, even being reminded; as a drunken-
man (does not recall) the talk [speech] previously made (by himself).'
Atithi-paribhāvini, see p. 36, n. 1; the Beng. have *katham atithim pari-
bhavasi*. *Vetsi = vibhāvayasi*, S'. *Bodhitaḥ = smāritaḥ*, S'. *Kritām*, i. e.
ātmanaiva, S'.; *kathām kri = root kath*, 'to speak,' 'tell,' 'say;' and
kathām kritām = kathitām, 'what is spoken,' 'said.'

[2] 'A very unpleasant thing has occurred. S'akuntalā, in her absence of
mind, has committed an offence against some person deserving of respect.

Verse 81. VANS'A-STHAVILA (a variety of JAGATĪ). See verses 18, 22, 23, 67.

[a] को अक्खो हुदवहादो दहिदुं पहविस्सदि[1] ।

अनसूया ।

[b] गच्छ । पादेसु पणमित्र .णिवत्तेहि णं । जाव अहं अग्घोदअं उबकप्पेमि[2] ।

[a] कोऽन्यो हुतवहाद्वग्धुं प्रभविष्यति ।   [b] गच्छ । पादयोः प्रणम्य निवर्तयैनम् ।
यावदहमर्घ्योदकमुपकल्पयामि ।

[*Looking on in front.*] Not, indeed, against some (mere ordinary) person ; (for I see that) it is the great Ṛishi Durvāsas, easily-provoked to anger. After uttering such a curse, he has turned back with a step tremulous, bounding, and difficult to be checked through its impetuosity.' *Śūnya-hṛidayā*, lit. 'empty-hearted,' one whose heart is engrossed with some other object. *Vega-ćaṭula*, &c. This is the reading of the Mackenzie MS., and seems to have been that of K. All the Deva-n. have *upphulla* for the Sanskrit *utphula*, from root *sphul*, 'to leap,' allied to *sphur*. As to the Prākṛit *upphulla*, it may be observed that many consonants in Prākṛit are too weak to sustain themselves singly, and that if elision does not take place, the consonant is sometimes doubled. Thus *sukkha* or *suha* may be written for the Sanskrit *sukha*, and *nīhitta* or *nīhia* for *nīhita*, Lassen's Instit. Prāk. p. 276, 3. The oldest Beng. MS. has *avirala-pādoddhārayā*, and the Calcutta ed. *avirala-pāda-tvarayā gatyā*. Durvāsas is a saint or Muni, represented by the Hindū poets as excessively choleric, and inexorably severe. The Purāṇas and other poems contain frequent accounts of the terrible effects of his imprecations on various occasions, the slightest offence being in his eyes deserving of the most fearful punishment. On one occasion he cursed Indra, merely because his elephant let fall a garland which he had given to this god; and in consequence of this imprecation all plants withered, men ceased to sacrifice, and the gods were overcome in their wars with the demons (see Vishṇu-p. p. 70). For Maharshi, see p. 39, n. 3, and p. 44, n. 2.

[1] 'Who beside Fire will have (such) power to consume ?' S'. alone has *tathā* (*taha*) at the end of this sentence. The wrath of a Brāhman is frequently compared to fire (see p. 74, n. 3, and p. 50, n. 2).

[2] 'Therefore, bowing down at his feet, persuade him to return, whilst I prepare a propitiatory offering and water.' The Beng. have *patitvā*, 'having fallen,' for *praṇamya*. *Arghyodaka*, see p. 36, notes 2 and 3.

प्रियंवदा ।

[a] तह । ॥ इति निष्क्रान्ता ॥

अनसूया ॥ पदान्तरे स्खलितं निरूप्य ॥

[b] अम्मो । आवेअक्खलिदाए गईए पब्भटुं मे हत्थादो पुप्फभाअणं । ॥ इति पुष्पोच्चयं रूपयति ॥[1]

प्रियंवदा ॥ प्रविश्य ॥

[c] सहि । पकिदिवक्को सो कस्स अणुणअं पडिगेण्हदि । किम्पि उण साणुक्कोसो किंदो ।[2]

अनसूया ॥ सस्मितम् ॥

[d] तस्सिं बहु एदम्पि । कहेहिं ।[3]

प्रियंवदा ।

[e] जदा णिवत्तिदुं ण इच्छदि । तदा विण्णविदो मए । भअवं । पढमंत्ति पेक्खिअ अविण्णादतवप्पहावस्स दुहिदुजणस्स भअवदा एक्को अवराहो मरिसिदव्वोत्ति ।[4]

---

[a] तथा । [b] सखो । आवेगस्खलितया गता भ्रष्टं मे हस्तात्पुष्पभाजनम् ।
[c] सखि । प्रकृतिवक्रः स कस्यानुनयं प्रतिगृह्णाति । किमपि पुनः सानुक्रोशः कृतः ।
[d] तस्मिन्बह्वेतदपि । कथय ।   [e] यदा निवर्तितुं नेच्छति । तदा विज्ञापितो मया ।
भगवन् । प्रथममिति प्रेक्ष्याविज्ञाततपःप्रभावस्य दुहितृजनस्य भगवतैकोऽपराधो मर्षयि-
तव्य इति ।

---

[1] 'She acts the gathering up of the flowers.' *Uččaya* has the same sense as *samuččaya*, 'collecting together in a heap,' see p. 79, l. 8.

[2] 'Whose friendly-persuasion will this crooked-tempered (person) accept? however, he was somewhat softened [he was made a little merciful].' *Prakṛiti-vakra*, 'one whose disposition is crooked or harsh,' 'ill-tempered,' 'cross-grained.'

[3] 'Even this (somewhat) was much for him; say on.'

[4] 'Considering (it is) the first-time, this one offence of the daughter, who is unaware of the potency of penance, is to be pardoned by your

अनसूया ।

[a] तदो तदो ।

प्रियंवदा ।

[b] तदो मे वअणं अण्णहाभविदुं णारिहदि । किन्तु अहिण्णा-णाभरणदंसणेण साओ णिअत्तिस्सदिति मन्तअन्तो सअं अन्तरिहिदो ।

अनसूया ।

[c] सक्कं दाणिं अस्ससिदुं अत्थि । तेण राएसिणा सम्पत्थिदेण सणामहेअङ्किअं अङ्गुलीअअं सुमरणी-अन्ति सअं पिणद्धं । तस्सिं साहीणोवाआ सउन्दला भविस्सदि ।

प्रियंवदा ।

[d] सहि । एहि । देवकज्जं दाव णिव्वत्तेम्ह ।

॥ इति परिक्रामतः ॥

[a] ततस्तत: ।   [b] ततो मे वचनमन्यथाभवितुं नार्हति । किन्त्वभिज्ञानाभरण-दर्शनेन शापो निवर्तिष्यत इति मन्वयमाण: स्वयमन्तर्हित: ।   [c] शक्यमिदानीमा-श्वसितुमस्ति । तेन राजर्षिणा सम्प्रस्थितेन स्वनामधेयाङ्कितमङ्गुलीयकं स्मरणीयमिति स्वयं पिनद्धम् । तस्मिन्स्वाधीनोपाया शकुन्तला भविष्यति ।   [d] सखि । एहि । देवकार्यं तावन्निर्वर्तयाव: ।

---

reverence.' *Prathamam iti*, the Beng., supported by K., have *prathama-bhaktim avekshya*, 'in consideration of her former devotion.'

[1] '"My word must not be falsified; but at the sight of the jewel-of-recognition, the curse shall cease:" so speaking, he withdrew himself from sight [vanished].' *Abhijñānābharaṇa*, lit. 'the recognition-ornament,' 'the token-ring,' see p. 4, n. 2. *Ṇārihadi* (=Sanskrit *na arhati*) is correct, according to Lassen's Instit. Prāk. p. 193, 10. The MSS. frequently read *ṇāruhadi*, as on p. 54, l. 5. *Svayam antarhitaḥ*, lit. 'he became self-hidden.'

[2] 'A ring stamped with his name was by that Rājarshi himself, at his departure, fastened on (her finger) as a souvenir. In that [with that],

प्रियंवदा ॥ अवलोक्य ॥

[a] अणसूए । पेक्ख दाव । वामहत्थोवहिदवअणा आलि-
हिदा विञ पिअसही । भत्तुगदाए चिन्ताए अत्ताणम्पि
ण एसा विभावेदि । किं उण आअन्तुअं ।

अनसूया ।

[b] पिअंवदे । दुवेणं एव्व णो मुहे एसो वुत्तन्तो चिट्ठदु ।
रक्खणीआ खु पकिदिपेलवा पिअसही ।

प्रियंवदा ।

[c] की दाणिं उण्होदएण णोमालिअं सिञ्चेदि ।

॥ इत्युभे निष्क्रान्ते ॥

॥ विष्कम्भः ॥

[a] अनसूये । प्रेक्षस्व तावत् । वामहस्तोपहितवदनालिखितेव प्रियसखी । भर्तृगतया
चिन्तयात्मानमपि नैषा विभावयति । किं पुनरागन्तुकम् ।   [b] प्रियंवदे । द्वयोरेव
नौ मुख एव वृत्तान्तस्तिष्ठतु । रक्षणीया खलु प्रकृतिपेलवा प्रियसखी ।   [c] क इदा-
नीमुष्णोदकेन नवमालिकां सिञ्चति ।

S'akuntalā will be possessed-of-a-resource-in-her-own-power.' *Sva-nāma-
dheyānkitam*, see p. 53, notes 2 and 3. *Smaraṇīyam iti*, properly
'saying, "It is a remembrance."' *Iti* often involves the sense of 'saying,'
'thinking,' &c., see p. 60, n. 1. The Beng. MSS. add *S'akuntalā-haste*, but
not the Deva-n. nor K. For *tasmin*, S'. has *tasmāt*.

[1] 'Our dear friend, her face resting on her left hand, (is motionless) as
if in a picture,' see p. 7, n. 2.

[2] *Bhartṛi-gata*, 'relating to her husband,' see p. 42, n. 2.

[3] 'Let this circumstance remain in the mouth of us two only. Our
dear friend being of a delicate nature must be spared [preserved],' i. e.
she must not be told about this imprecation, lest her feelings be so
hurt, that her delicate constitution be injured. *Vṛittāntaḥ*, i. e. *s'āpa-
vṛittāntaḥ*, S'.

॥ अथ चतुर्थोऽङ्कः ॥

॥ ततः प्रविशति सुप्तोत्थितः[1] शिष्यः ॥

शिष्यः ।

वेलोपलक्षणार्थमादिष्टोऽस्मि तत्रभवता प्रवासादुपावृत्तेन काश्यपेन । प्रकाशं निर्गतस्तावदवलोकयामि कियद्वशिष्टं रजन्या इति ।[2] ॥ परिक्रम्यावलोक्य च ॥ हन्त प्रभातम् । तथा हि

यात्येकतोऽस्तशिखरं पतिरोषधीना-
माविष्कृतारुणपुरःसर एकतोऽर्कः ।
तेजोद्वयस्य युगपद्व्यसनोदयाभ्यां
लोको नियम्यत इवात्मदशान्तरेषु ॥८२॥[3]

[1] 'Arisen from sleep,' = *suptānantaram utthitaḥ*, 'just arisen after sleep,' S'.

[2] 'I am commissioned by his reverence Kāśyapa, (who has just) returned from his pilgrimage [residence abroad], to observe the time of day. Having gone out into the open air, I will just see how much of the night remains.' *Pravāsāt*, i. e. *soma-tīrthāt*, see p. 17, n. 1. *Prakāśa = vivrita-pradeśa*, 'an open spot,' K. ; = *ćatvara*, 'a court-yard,' S'.

[3] 'On the one side the lord of the plants [the Moon] descends to the summit of the western mountain ; on the other side (rises) the Sun, whose forerunner Aruṇa [the Dawn] has just become visible. By the contemporaneous setting and rising of the two luminaries, human beings are warned, as it were, in their different states,' i. e. by the alternations of these luminaries, the vicissitudes of human life are indicated. The Moon is called *Oshadhī-pati*, 'lord of medicinal plants,' being supposed to exercise some influence over the growth of such plants. Cf. Deut. xxxiii. 14, 'The precious fruits brought forth by the sun, and the precious things put forth by the moon.' *Oshadhī* is described as 'dying (*phala-pākāntā*, Manu i. 46) after the ripening of its fruit.' *Asta* is the name for the mountain in the West, behind which, in Hindū poetry, the sun and moon are supposed to set, as *Udaya* is the name of that over which they are supposed to rise. *Arka* is a name of Sūrya, 'the Sun.' He is represented as seated in a chariot drawn by seven green horses, or by one horse with seven heads (whence his name *Saptāśva*), and before him is a lovely youth

Verse 82. VASANTA-TILAKĀ. See verses 8, 27, 31, 43, 46, 64, 74, 80.

अपि च। अन्तर्हिते शशिनि सैव कुमुद्वती मे
टृष्टिं न नन्दयति संस्मरणीयशोभा ।
इष्टप्रवासजनितान्यबलाजनस्य
दुःखानि नूनमतिमात्रसुदुःसहानि ॥ ८३ ॥

without legs, who acts as his charioteer, and who is called Aruṇa, or Dawn personified. Aruṇa is the son of Kaśyapa and Vinatā, and elder brother of Garuḍa. His imperfect form may be allusive to his gradual or partial appearance, his legs being supposed to be lost, either in the darkness of the departing night, or in the blaze of the coming day. With this verse cf. Mṛicchak. p. 321, l. 4, thus translated by Wilson, 'In heaven itself the sun and moon are not free from change (*vipattiṃ labhete*); how should we poor weak mortals hope to escape it in this lower world? One man rises but to fall, another falls to rise again,' &c.

[1] 'The moon having disappeared, even the lotus no longer gladdens my sight, its beauty being now only a matter of remembrance. The sorrows produced by the absence of a lover are beyond measure hard to be supported by a tender-girl.' Some species of the lotus open their petals during the night, and close them during the day, whence the Moon is often called the Friend, Lover, or Lord of the lotuses (*kumuda-bāndhava, kumudinī-nāyaka, kumudeśa*). For *abalā-janasya*, the Beng. have *abalā-janena;* the genitive is equally admissible. Cf. *svabhāvas tasya durati-kramaḥ,* Hitop. l. 1945.

The following are given after verse 83 in the Beng. MSS. and in the Calcutta and French editions, supported by S'., but not in the Deva-n. nor in K. :

अपि च। कर्कन्धूनामुपरि तुहिनं रञ्जयत्यग्रसन्ध्या
दार्भं मुञ्चत्युटजपटलं वीतनिद्रो मयूरः ।
वेदिप्रान्तात्खुरविलिखितादुत्थितश्चैव सद्यः
पश्चादुच्चैर्भवति हरिणः स्वाङ्गमायच्छमानः ॥

अपि च। पादन्यासं क्षितिधरगुरोर्मूर्ध्नि कृत्वा सुमेरोः
क्रान्तं येन क्षयिततमसा मध्यमं धाम विष्णोः ।
सोऽयं चन्द्रः पतति गगणादल्पशेषैर्मयूखै-
स्त्याज्यारूढिर्भवति महतामप्यपभ्रंशनिष्ठा ॥

'Moreover, the early dawn impurples the dew-drops upon the jujubes ;

अनसूया || प्रविश्य पटाक्षेपेण¹ ||

ᵃ एव्वं णाम विसअपरम्मुहस्सवि इमस्स जणस्स ण
एदं ण विदिश्रं । तेण रण्णा सउन्दलाए अणज्जं आ-
अरिदं्तिं² ।

ᵃ एवं नाम विषयपराङ्मुखस्याप्यस्य जनस्य नैतद्व विदितम् । तेन राज्ञा शकुन्तला-
यामनार्यमाचरितमिति ।

---

the peacock, shaking off sleep, quits the Darbha-grass thatch of the cottage;
and yonder the antelope, rising hastily from the border of the altar impressed by his hoofs, afterwards raises himself on high, stretching his
limbs.   Moreover, after planting his foot on the head of Sumeru, lord of
mountains, the Moon, by whom, dispersing the darkness, the central
palace of Vishṇu has been invaded, even he, descends from the sky
with diminished beams.   The highest ascent of the great terminates in
a fall.'

¹ 'With a hurried toss of the curtain.' *Paṭākshepeṇa* (so read all the
Deva-n. MSS. and K.) is from *paṭa*, with the same sense as *apaṭī*, i. e. the
curtain separating the stage from the *nepathya* (see p. 3, n. 2) and *ākshepa*,
'tossing aside.'   The Beng. reading is *apaṭī-kshepeṇa*.   *Paṭākshepeṇa* =
yavanikāpanodanena, K.; = *akasmāt*, 'suddenly,' S'.   According to K.,
the entrance of an actor under the influence of flurry caused by joy,
sorrow, or any other emotion (*harsha-śokādi-janita-sambhrama-yuktasya*)
is made with a toss of the curtain.

² 'It is not unknown to this person [myself], however withdrawn (she
may be) from worldly concerns, that an indignity has been wrought
towards S'akuntalā by that king.' *Evaṃ nāma* is the reading of the
Mackenzie MS., supported by K. *Na etat na viditam* is given on the
authority of K. *Imassa* is inserted from the old MS. (India Office, 1060);
S'. has *amushya janasya*.   The other Deva-n. MSS. read *yady api nāma
vishaya-parān-mukhasyāpi janasya etan na viditaṃ tathāpi tena*, &c.
The margin of the Beng. MS., as well as that of Chézy, has a note referring
vishaya-parān-mukhasya janasya to Kaṇva; but a comparison of other
passages shews that by *ayaṃ janaḥ* the person or persons speaking
are commonly intended (cf. p. 125, l. 6, and p. 156, l. 12). *An-āryam*,
lit. 'anything unworthy or dishonourable,' 'ungentlemanly conduct,' i. e.
according to S'. and Ć., *S'akuntalā-vismaraṇa-rūpam*, 'consisting of the
forgetting of S'akuntalā.'

शिष्यः ।

यावदुपस्थितां होमवेलां गुरवे निवेदयामि । ॥ इति
निष्क्रान्तः ॥

अनसूया ।

[a]पडिबुद्धावि किं करिस्सं । ण मे उद्देसुवि णिञ्जकर-
णिज्जेसु हत्थपाआ पसरन्ति । कामो दाणिं सकामो होदु ।
जेण असच्चसन्धे जणे सुद्धहिअआ सही पदं कारिदा ।
अहवा दुव्वाससाबो एसो विआरेदि । अण्णहा कहं सो
राएसी तारिसाणि मन्तिअ एत्तिअस्स कालस्स लेह-
मत्तम्पि ण विसज्जेदि । ता इदो अहिणाणं अङ्गुलीअअं से

---

[a] प्रतिबुद्धापि किं करिष्यामि । न म उचितेष्वपि निजकरणीयेषु हस्तपादाः
प्रसरन्ति । काम इदानीं सकामो भवतु । येनासत्यसन्धे जने शुद्धहृदया सखी पदं
कारिता । अथवा दुर्वासःशाप एष विकारयति । अन्यथा कथं स राजर्षिस्तादृशानि
मन्त्रयित्वैतावतः कालस्य लेखमात्रमपि न विसर्जयति । तस्मादितोऽभिज्ञानमङ्गुलीयकमस्य

---

[1] 'The time for (making) the burnt-offering;' see p. 148, n. 1.

[2] 'Although wide-awake, what shall I do? My hands and feet do not
move-freely in their own usual occupations.   Let Love now be possessed
of his wish [enjoy his triumph], by whom our innocent-minded friend has
been made to place confidence in that perfidious man.'   *Uĉiteshu karaṇī-*
yeshu, such as 'gathering flowers,' &c., S.   *Sa-kāmaḥ=kṛitārthī,* 'one who
has attained his end,' S. (cf. *bhavatu panĉa-vāṇaḥ kṛitī,* Vikram., Act II).
Asatya-sandha, lit. 'one who is not true to his contract (*sandhā*) ;'=*asatya-*
pratijña, S. ;=*mithyā-pratijña,* Ĉ.   *Suddha-hṛidayā* is the reading of two
Deva-nāgarī MSS. and of the Bengālī.   *Pada=sthāna,* 'a place,' S. ;
=*vyavasāya* or *vyavasiti,* 'industry,' 'application,' 'business,' Ĉ. and
Amara-k.   Hence *padaṃ kṛi* in the causal must mean 'to cause to have
dealings or transactions with,' 'to cause to apply one's self,' 'to cause to
take up a station ;' whence may easily flow the interpretation, 'made to
trust.'   Cf. a similar phrase in Kumāra-s. vi. 14, where also the commentators explain *pada* by *vyavasāya.*

[3] 'Or rather, it is the curse of Durvāsas that has caused the change.'
Athavā, see p. 24, l. 10; p. 30, n. 3. *Vikārayati,* see p. 130, n. 1.

[a] विसज्जेम । दुक्खसीले तवस्सिजणे को अब्भत्थी-
अदु । णं सहीगामी दोसोत्ति ववसिदाबि ण पारेमि
पवासपडिणिउत्तस्स तादकस्सवस्स दुस्सन्दपरिणीदं आ-
बण्णसत्तं सउन्दलं णिवेदिदुं । इत्थंगए अम्हेहिं किं
करणिज्जं ।

प्रियंवदा ॥ प्रविश्य । सहर्षम् ॥

[b] सहि । तुवर तुवर सउन्दलाए पत्थाणकोदुअं
णिव्वत्तिदुं ।

अनसूया ।

[c] सहि । कहं एदं ।

[a] विसर्जयावः । दुःखशीले तपस्विजने कोऽभ्यर्थ्येताम् । ननु सखीगामी दोष इति
व्यवसितापि न पारयामि प्रवासप्रतिनिवृत्तस्य तातकाश्यपस्य दुष्यन्तपरिणीतामापन्न-
सत्त्वां शकुन्तलां निवेदयितुम् । इत्थंगतेऽस्माभिः किं करणीयम् । [b] सखि ।
त्वरय त्वरय शकुन्तलायाः प्रस्थानकौतुकं निर्वर्तयितुम् । [c] सखि ।
कथमेतत् ।

---

[1] 'Among ascetics inured-to-hardships, who is to be solicited (to carry
the ring to the king)? Assuredly, even though I were convinced that
blame was attributable to S'akuntalā, I should not have the power to
make known to father Kaśyapa, (just) returned from his pilgrimage, that
S'akuntalā is married to Dushyanta, and is pregnant. Such being the
case, what is to be done by us?' *Duḥkha-śīle*, so read all the Deva-n.;
the oldest Bengālī, supported by Ć., has *nirduḥkha-śītale*. *Sakhī-gāmin*,
see p. 42, n. 2. *Vyavasitā*, past pass. part. of *vy-ava-so*, 'to determine,'
'resolve,' 'strive;' also 'to be persuaded,' 'convinced,' as in Rāmāy. ii.
12, 61, *satīṃ tvāṃ vyavasyāmi*. *Pārayāmi* is either the causal form of
pri, meaning 'to conduct across,' 'bring over,' 'accomplish,' 'fulfil,' and
thence 'to be able,' or is a nominal from *pāra*, 'the opposite bank
(of a river),' 'the other side,' 'the end.' *Ittham-gate*, i. e. *evam-prāpte
karmaṇi*.

[2] 'Hasten to celebrate [complete] the festivities at the departure of
S'akuntalā.' *Prasthāna-kautuka*=*prayāna-mangala*, 'festive solemnities
which take place at the departure of a member of the family.'

प्रियंवदा ।

ᵃसुणाहि दाणिं । सुहसइदं पुच्छिदुं[1] सउन्दलासआसं गदम्हि ।

अनसूया ।

ᵇतदो तदो ।

प्रियंवदा ।

ᶜदाव एणं लज्जावणदमुहिं परिस्सजिअ सअं तादकस्सबेण एव्वं अहिणन्दिदं । दिट्ठिआ । धूमाउलिदददिट्ठिणोबि जञ्ञमाणस्स पाअए एव्व आहुदी पडिदा[2] । वच्छे । सुसिस्सपरिदिस्सा विअ विज्जा असोअणिज्जा संवुत्ता । अज्ज एव्व इसिपडिरक्खिदं तुमं भत्तुणो सआसं विसज्जेमिन्ति[3] ।

ᵃ शृणिष्विदानीम् । सुखशयितां प्रष्टुं शकुन्तलासकाशं गतास्मि ।   ᵇ ततस्ततः ।
ᶜ तावदेनां लज्जावनतमुखीं परिष्वज्य स्वयं तातकाश्यपेनैवमभिनन्दितम् । दिष्ट्या ।
धूमाकुलितदृष्टेरपि यजमानस्य पावक एवाहुतिः पतिता । वत्से । सुशिष्यपरिदत्तेव
विद्याशोचनीया संवृत्ता । अद्यैव ऋषिप्रतिरक्षितां त्वां भर्तुः सकाशं विसर्जयामीति ।

---

¹ 'To inquire (whether she had had) a comfortable sleep.' *Puččhidum*
for *prashṭum*, so reads my own Bombay MS., supported by a parallel
passage in Mālavik. 44, 7, *suham puččhidum āgatā*. The other Deva-n.
have *suha-saida-puččhiā* for *sukha-śayita-praččhikā*, which is given as
another reading in Mālavik. Dr. Boehtlingk remarks that the agent may
be used with the sense of a fut. part. active, and refers to Pāṇ. iii. 3, 10.

² 'By father Kaṇva [see p. 22, n. 3] having of his own accord embraced her whilst her face was bowed down with shame, she was thus
congratulated [congratulation was made], "Hail (to thee)! the oblation of
the sacrificing priest, although his sight was obscured by the smoke, fell
directly into the fire;"' see n. 3 below. *Dhūmākulita*, cf. p. 65, l. 7.
Yajamāna, see p. 95, n. 1.

³ 'My child, as knowledge delivered over to a good student (is not to
be deplored, so has it) come to pass that thou art not to be sorrowed for.
This very day I dismiss thee protected by [under the escort of some]

अनसूया ।

a अह केण सूइदो ताद्कस्सवस्स वुत्तन्तो ।

प्रियंवदा ।

b अग्गिसरणं पविट्ठस्स सरीरं विणा छन्दोमईए वाआए ।

a अथ केन सूचितस्तातकाश्यपस्य वृत्तान्तः ।   b अग्निशरणं प्रविष्टस्य शरीरं विना छन्दोमय्या वाचया ।

Ṛishis to the presence of (thy) husband.' Compare Manu ii. 114, 'Learning having approached a Brāhman said to him, "I am thy divine treasure, deliver me not to a scorner, but communicate me to that student who will be a careful guardian of the treasure."' The Beng. and K. insert *me* before *aśoćanīyā*, and read *parigṛihītām* for *pratirakshitām*.

[1] 'By an incorporeal [without body, without visible speaker] metrical speech (addressed to him from heaven), when he had entered the fire-sanctuary.' *Śarīraṃ vinā*, i. e. *ākāśe Sarasvatyā niveditaḥ*, 'he was informed by Sarasvatī (by a voice) in the sky,' S'.; see p. 96, n. 3. *Agni-śarana=agny-āgāra*, 'the place where the sacred fire was kept;'=*yajña-śālā*, 'hall of sacrifice.' Fire is an important object of veneration with the Hindūs, almost as much so as with the ancient Persians. Perhaps the chief worship recommended in the Vedas is that of Fire and the Sun. According to Manu, Brāhmans when they married and became householders, were to kindle with two pieces of the hard S'amī, Araṇi, or Khadira wood, or with a piece of the S'amī and Aśvattha wood (see p. 23, n. 1), a sacred fire (*homāgni, gṛihyāgni, hutāgni*), which they were to deposit in a cavity or hearth called *agni-kuṇḍa* or *vitāna* (Indian Wisdom, p. 197), in some hallowed part of the house (or, like the Persians, in some sacred building proper for the purpose) called *aynyʹ-āgāra* (Manu iv. 58), *homa-śālā, agni-gṛiha*, and which they were to keep lighted throughout their lives, using it first for their nuptial ceremony (Manu ii. 231, iii. 171); and for the regular morning and evening oblations to Agni (*homa, hotra*), performed by dropping clarified butter &c. into the flame, with prayers and invocations (Manu xi. 41, iii. 81, 84, 85; see also p. 133, n. 1 of this play); for the performance of solemn sacrifices (Manu ii. 143); for the S'rāddha or obsequies to departed parents and ancestors (Manu iii. 212 sqq.; see also p. 111, n. 1 of this play); and, finally, for the funeral pile. The perpetual maintenance of this sacred fire was called *agni-hotra, agny-ādhāna, agni-rakshaṇa;* and the consecration of it, *agny-ādheya*

अनसूया ॥ सविस्मयम् ॥

[a] कहेहि ।

प्रियंवदा ॥ संस्कृतमाश्रित्य ॥

दुष्यन्तेनाहितं तेजो दधानां भूतये भुवः ।
अवेहि तनयां ब्रह्मन्नग्निगर्भां शमीमिव ॥८४॥

[a] कथय ।

(Manu ii. 143); and the Brāhman or householder who maintained it, *agni-
hotrin, āhitāgni, agny-āhita, sāgnika*. At Benares even to this day many
Agni-hotras are kept burning. Sometimes the householder did not himself attend to the sacred fire, but engaged an officiating priest (*ritvij,
yajamāna, agnīdhra*, see p. 95, n. 1; p. 96, n. 2). The Brāhman who did
not maintain a fire was called *an-āhitāgni* (Manu xi. 38). According to
Manu iii. 212 (with commentary) there were three periods when he was
necessarily without it, viz. just before his investiture, before his marriage
after the completion of his studentship, and at the death of his wife ; but
the usual daily oblation was then to be placed in the hand of a holy
Brāhman, who is said to be one form of fire (see p. 74, n. 3; p. 50, n. 2).
Sacred fire is sometimes considered to be of three kinds (*tretā*, 'the triad of
fires'): 1. *Gārhapatya*, 'nuptial or household ;' 2. *Āhavanīya*, 'sacrificial,'
taken from the preceding; 3. *Dakshiṇa*, 'that placed towards the south,'
taken from either of the former; see Manu ii. 231. The man who
maintained all these three was called *tretāgni*. See Indian Wisdom,
p. 198, n. 1.

¹ ' [*Having recourse to Sanskrit.*] Know that (thy adopted) daughter,
O Brāhman, has conceived a glorious-germ [seed] implanted [lodged,
deposited] by Dushyanta for the welfare of the earth, as the S'amī-tree is
pregnant with fire.' *Samī*, 'a kind of thorny acacia' (see the last note,
and p. 23, n. 1). The legend is that the goddess Pārvatī, being one day
under the influence of strong passion, reposed on a trunk of this tree,
whereby an intense heat was generated in the pith or interior of the
wood, which ever after broke into a sacred flame on the slightest attrition.
Āhita=arpita. Tejaḥ=śukra, Ć. (cf. Raghu-v. ii. 75; Megha-d. 45.)
'By this it was indicated that S'akuntalā would have a son in glory equal
to Agni,' S'.

Verse 84. S'LOKA or ANUSHṬUBH. See verses 5, 6, 11, 12, 26, 47, 50, 51, 53,
73, 76.

अनसूया ॥ प्रियंवदामाश्लिष्य ॥

ᵃसहि । पिअं मे । पिअं मे । किन्तु अज्ज एव्व सउन्दला णीअदित्ति उक्कण्ठासाहारणं परितोसं अणुहोमि ।

प्रियंवदा ।

ᵇसहि । वअं दाव उक्कण्ठं विणोदइस्सामो । सा तवस्सिणी णिव्वुदा होदु ।

अनसूया ।

ᶜतेण हि एदस्सिं चूदसाहावलम्बिदे णारिएरसमुग्गए एतस्सिमित्तं एव्व कालन्तरक्खमा णिक्खित्ता मए केसर-मालिआ । ता इमं हत्थसन्निहिदं करेहिं । जाव अहम्पि से

ᵃ सखि । प्रियं मे । प्रियं मे । किन्त्वद्यैव शकुन्तला नीयत इत्युत्कण्ठासाधारणं परितोषमनुभवामि ।   ᵇ सखि । आवां तावदुत्कण्ठां विनोदयिष्यावः । सा तपस्विनी निर्वृता भवतु ।   ᶜ तेन हि एतस्मिंश्चूतशाखावलम्बिते नारिकेरसमुद्गक एतन्निमित्तमेव कालान्तरक्षमा निक्षिप्ता मया केशरमालिका । तदिमां हस्तसन्निहितां कुरु । यावदहमप्यस्या

---

[1] ‘O friend, how pleased I am! but when I think that this very day S'akuntalā is being conveyed away (to her husband's house), I feel a satisfaction mingled with regret.’ *Iti*, ‘so thinking,’ see p. 140, n. 2. *Utkaṇṭhā-sādhāraṇa*, lit. ‘in common with regret' or sorrow.’ ‘I am partly glad, partly sorry,’ S'.

[2] ‘(Only) let this (our) poor-sister be made happy.’ *Tapasvin*, ‘a devotee,’ also denotes ‘a person in a pitiable state,’ ‘a poor wretch.’ *Nir-vṛitā=susthita-ćittā*, S'.

[3] ‘Therefore in this cocoa-nut box, suspended on a bough of the mango, a Keśara-garland, capable of (keeping fresh for) the intervening period, was with this very object deposited by me. Therefore make it rest on (my) hand [take it down and give it to me].’ *Nārikera* or *nārikela*, ‘the cocoa-nut,’ ‘the fruit of the cocoa-nut tree.’ *Ćūta* or *āmra*, ‘the mango tree.’ *Kālāntara-kshamā=virala-kāla-sthāyinī*, S'. *Keśara-mālikā*, ‘a wreath made of the flowers of the Bakula,’ see p. 26, n. 1. This was

[a] मिश्रलोअणं णित्यमित्तिअं दुव्वाकिसलआणिति मङ्ग-
लसमालम्भणाणि विरएमि।

प्रियंवदा।

[b] तह करीअदु।

|| अनसूया निष्क्रान्ता। प्रियंवदा नाख्येन सुमनसो गृह्णाति ||

नेपथ्ये।

गौतमि। आदिश्यन्तां शार्ङ्गरवमिश्राः शकुन्तलानयनाय।

[a] मृगरोचनां तीर्थमृत्तिकां दूर्वाकिसलयानीति मङ्गलसमालम्भनानि विरचयामि।
[b] तथा क्रियताम्।

---

probably a *mangala-pushpa-mayī srak*, or 'garland made of auspicious
flowers,' to be suspended round the neck of S'akuntalā, such as that
described in Raghu-v. vi. 84. S'. and the Beng. read *kesara-guṇḍāḥ* or
kesara-ćūrṇāḥ, and S'. observes that the fragrant dust of this plant is
much used by women in making unguents (*udvartanāni*).

[1] 'Whilst I also will compound auspicious unguents composed of
Mṛiga-roćanā, holy earth, (and) Dūrbā sprouts.' *Mṛiga-roćanā* is said to
be either the concrete bile of a deer or an exudation from his head, used
as a medicine, a yellow dye or a perfume (see *go-roćanā* in Dict.) The
latter word is the reading of the Beng. MSS. *Tīrtha-mṛittikā* is earth
brought from Tīrthas or holy bathing-places (see p. 17, n. 1). *Dūrbā* or
dūrvā, 'bent-grass,' a kind of sacred grass, not quite so sacred as *darbha*,
but possessing many virtues, and used for the *argha* (see p. 36, n. 2). Sir
W. Jones says of it, 'Its flowers, in their perfect state, are among the
loveliest objects in the vegetable world, and appear, through a lens, like
minute rubies and emeralds. It is the sweetest and most nutritious
pasture for cattle, and its usefulness, added to its beauty, induced the
Hindūs to believe that it was the mansion of a benevolent nymph.' *Samā-
lambhana* is the act of smearing the body with coloured perfumes, such
as saffron, sandal, &c.; the plural is here used for the unguents themselves, which are said to be *mangala*, 'conducive to good fortune.' The
Beng. have *samālambhanam*.

[2] 'S'ārn-garava and the (other) good-people;' see p. 7, n. 3. The Beng.
have *Sārn-garava-śāradvata-miśrāḥ*. According to S'. and Ć. these were
the names of two *sishyāḥ*, 'religious students,' pupils of Kaṇva.

प्रियंवदा ॥ कर्णं दत्ता ॥

[a] अणसूए । तुवर तुवर । एदे खु हत्थिणाउरगामिणो इसीओ सद्दाबीअन्ति ।

अनसूया ॥ प्रविश्य समालम्भनहस्ता ॥

[b] सहि । एहि । गच्छम्ह । ॥ इति परिक्रामतः ॥

प्रियंवदा ॥ विलोक्य ॥

[c] एसा सुज्जोदए एव्व सिहामज्जिदा पडिच्छिदणीवार-हत्याहिं सोत्तियवाअणकाहिं तावसीहिं अहिणन्दीअमाणा सउन्दला चिट्टइ । उवसप्पम्ह णं । ॥ इत्युपसर्पतः ॥

[a] अनसूये । त्वरय त्वरय । एते खलु हस्तिनापुरगामिन ऋषयः शब्दाय्यन्ते ।
[b] सखि । एहि । गच्छावः ।   [c] एषा सूर्योदय एव शिखामार्जिता प्रतिच्छितनी-वारहस्ताभिः स्वस्तिवाचनिकाभिस्तापसीभिरभिनन्द्यमाना शकुन्तला तिष्ठति । उपसर्पाव एनाम् ।

---

[1] 'Truly these Ṛishis who are to go to Hastināpur are being called.' *Śabdāyyante*=*āhūyante*, S. and Ć. It is the passive form of the nominal *śabdāyate;* S. has *śabdāyante*, which would properly mean 'they sound,' 'make a noise,' Pāṇ. iii. 1, 17. *Hastināpura*, 'city of elephants,' was the ancient Delhi, situated on the Ganges, and the residence of Dushyanta.

[2] 'There stands S'akuntalā at earliest sunrise, with her locks combed-and-washed, in the act of being congratulated by the holy-women, (having) consecrated wild-rice in their hands, (and) invoking-blessings-with-their-offerings.' *Śikhā-mārjitā*, lit. 'having her top-knot combed and cleansed,' a compound similar to *śiraḥ-snāta*, 'having the head bathed.' The Beng. MSS. have *kṛita-majjanā*. *Svasti-vāćanikābhiḥ* is here an epithet of the women who make the *svasti-vāćana*, i. e. according to K. 'a gift of flowers, sweetmeats (*prahelaka*), fruit, or any eatables presented with good wishes and prayers for the blessing of some deity.' It is especially the blessing which is coupled with the gift. In the present case the hallowed rice which they held in their hands, might have constituted the offering which accompanied the *svasti-vāćana*. In Vikram. the Vidūshaka is propitiated by a *svasti-vāćana* (or *-naka*), consisting of a *modaka-śarava*, 'dish of sweetmeats.' Birthday-gifts, wedding-presents, Christmas-boxes,

|| ततः प्रविशति यथोद्दिष्टव्यापारासनस्था शकुन्तला ||

तापसीनामन्यतमा || शकुन्तलां प्रति ||

[a] जादे । भत्तुणो बहुमाणसूअञ्झं महादेईसद्दं लहेहिं ।

द्वितीया ।

[b] वच्छे । वीरप्पसविणी होहि ।

तृतीया ।

[c] वच्छे । भत्तुणो बहुमदा होहि ।

|| इत्याशिषो दत्त्वा गौतमीवर्जं निष्क्रान्ताः ||

सख्यौ || उपसृत्य ||

[d] सहि । सुहमज्जणं दे होदु ।

शकुन्तला ।

[e] साअदं मे सहीणं । इदो णिसीदह ।

उभे || मङ्गलपात्राण्यादाय । उपविश्य ||

[f] हला । सज्जा होहि । जाव मङ्गलसमालभ्भणं विरएम ।

---

[a] जाते । भर्तुर्बहुमानसूचकं महादेवीशब्दं लभस्व ।   [b] वत्से । वीरप्रसविनी भव ।
[c] वत्से । भर्तुर्बहुमता भव ।   [d] सखि । सुखमार्जनं ते भवतु ।   [e] स्वागतं मे
सखीभ्याम् । इतो निषीदतम् ।   [f] हला । सज्जा भव । यावन्मङ्गलसमालम्भनं
विरचयावः ।

&c., with their accompanying compliments, are the *svasti-vácanaka* of our day. The words *váyana* and *váyanaka* seem to have a similar signification, though without any necessary implication of *good-wishes*. *Nívára*, 'wild-rice,' Manu vi. 16.

[1] 'My child, take the title of "Great Queen," indicative of the high esteem of (thy) husband.' *Játá*, 'a child,' is used affectionately in addressing any young female. *Mahá-deví*, 'chief queen ;' cf. p. 124, n. 1.

[2] 'May it be to thee an auspicious ablution!' i. e. may it bring thee good fortune! May it be an omen of happiness to thee !

[3] 'Taking up the propitiatory-vessels,' i. e. the vessels containing the flowers, unguents, &c., intended to propitiate Fortune in favour of S'akuntalá. So read all the Deva-n. MSS., excepting one (Colebrooke's), which has *patráni*.

शकुन्तला ।

[a] एदम्पि बहुमन्तव्वं । दुल्लहं दाणिं मे सहीमराडणं भविस्सदि । ॥ इति बाष्पं विसृजति[1] ॥

उभे ।

[b] सहि । उइदं ण दे मङ्गलकाले रोइदुं । ॥ इत्यश्रूणि प्रमृज्य नाट्येन प्रसाधयतः ।

प्रियंवदा ।

[c] आहरणोइदं रूवं अम्हसुलहेहिं पसाहणेहिं विप्पआरीअदि[2] ।

॥ प्रविश्योपायनहस्तावृषिकुमारकौ ॥

उभौ ।

इदमलङ्करणम् । अलङ्क्रियतामत्रभवती ।

॥ सर्वा विलोक्य विस्मिताः ॥

गौतमी ।

[d] वच्छ णारअ । कुदो एदं ।

प्रथमः ।

तातकाश्यपप्रभावात् ।

---

[a] एतदपि बहुमन्तव्यम् । दुर्लभमिदानीं मे सखीमण्डनं भविष्यति ।   [b] सखि । उचितं न ते मङ्गलकाले रोदितुम् ।   [c] आभरणोचितं रूपमाश्रमसुलभैः प्रसाधनैर्विप्रकार्यते ।   [d] वत्स नारद । कुत एतत् ।

---

[1] 'This (friendly service of yours) too ought to be highly valued (by me). The being attired by (you) my friends, will now be a rare occurrence. [*So she sheds tears.*]' *Visrijati* is the reading of my own Deva-n. MS.; the others have *viharati*.

[2] '(Thy) person worthy of (the costliest) ornaments is slighted [or disfigured] by decorations easily procured in a hermitage,' i. e. thy beauty, which deserves to be set off by golden ornaments, &c., is impaired by such decorations as sprouts of Dūrvā grass, &c., S. *Viprakāryate*, K. has *vikāryate*, the Beng. *vipralabhyate* and *vipratāryate*.

गौतमी ।

[a] किं माणसी सिड्डी[1] ।

द्वितीयः ।

न खलु । श्रूयताम् । तच्चभवता वयमाज्ञप्ताः । शकुन्तला-
हेतोर्वनस्पतिभ्यः कुसुमान्याहँरतेति[2] । तत इदानीं
क्षौमं केनचिदिन्दुपाण्डु तरुणा माङ्गल्यमाविष्कृतं
निष्ठ्यूतश्वरणोपभोगसुलभो लाक्षारसः केनचित् ।
अन्येभ्यो वनदेवताकरतलैरापर्वभागोत्थितै-
र्दत्तान्याभरणानि तत्किसलयोद्भेदप्रतिद्वन्द्विभिः[3] ॥८५॥

[a] किं मानसी सिद्धिः ।

---

[1] 'Was it a mental creation?' i. e. were these ornaments created by the power of his mind? K. has *srishṭiḥ* for *siddhiḥ*. Cf. p. 79, n. 1.

[2] 'Bring hither flowers for S'akuntalā from the trees of the forest.'

[3] 'By a certain tree a fine-linen-robe white-as-the-moon indicative-of-good-fortune was made to appear [produced]; by another, juice-of-lac, ready for the use of [the dyeing of] the feet was distilled [exuded]; from others, ornaments were presented by the hands [palms] of wood-nymphs stretched out (so as to be visible) as far as the wrist, emulating the first sprouting of the young-shoots of those (trees).' *Kshauma=vālkala-vastra-bheda*, Ć. *Kshaumam mangalyam=dukūlam mangalārham*, S'. *Māngalya* may mean 'with words of good omen,' 'with blessings and prayers for good fortune (*kalyāṇa-vākyaiḥ*), such as, "May she be the beloved wife of her lord,"' &c., S'. *Indu-pāṇḍu=ćandra-dhavala*. *Āvish-kritam = ud-bhāvitam*, K.; *= dānāya prakāśitam*, S'. *Nishṭhyūtaḥ = udgīrṇaḥ*. *Ćaraṇopabhoga-sulabho*, some Beng. MSS. have *ćaraṇoparāga-subhago*; the oldest have *upabhoga*. Here *sulabha=kshama* or *yogya*, 'adapted' (cf. Kumāra-s. v. 69). *Lākshā=alakta* or *alaktaka*, 'lac,' 'a red dye,' prepared from an insect, analogous to the cochineal insect. This minute red insect is found in great numbers in the Palāśa, Indian fig tree, and some other trees. It punctures the bark, whence exudes a resinous

---

Verse 85. S'ĀRDŪLA-VIKRĪḌITA (a variety of ATIDHṚITI). See verses 14, 30, 36, 39, 40, 63, 79.

प्रियंवदा ॥ शकुन्तलां विलोक्य ॥

हला । इमाए अब्भुबबत्तीए सूइदा दे भत्तुणो गेहे अणुहोद्वा रायलच्छित्ति[1] ।

॥ शकुन्तला ब्रीडां रूपयति ॥

प्रथमः ।

गौतम । एह्येहि । अभिषेकोत्तीर्णायं[2] काश्यपाय वनस्प-तिसेवां निवेद्यावः ।

द्वितीयः ।

तथा ।

॥ इति निष्क्रान्तौ ॥

सख्यौ ।

अए । अणुबहुत्तभूसणो अम्हं जणो । चित्तकम्मपरिअरएण अङ्गेसु दे आहरणविणिओअं करेम्ह[3] ।

---

[a] हला । अनयाभ्युपपत्त्या सूचिता ते भर्तुगृहेऽनुभवितव्या राजलक्ष्मीः ।   [b] अये । अनुपभुक्तभूषणोऽयं जनः । चित्रकर्मपरिचयेनाङ्गेषु त आभरणविनियोगं कुर्वः ।

---

milky juice, with which it surrounds itself in a kind of nest, and which when dry may be broken off, and used for various purposes. This hardened and reddened substance is variously called gum-lac, shell-lac, stick-lac, &c. *Ā-parva*, &c.=*parva-bhāga-paryantam udgataiḥ*. *Parva-bhāga*=*maṇi-bandha*, 'the wrist,' K. *Ā*, 'as far as,' generally requires the abl. of a word not in composition; thus, *ā-maṇi-bandhāt pāṇiḥ*, 'the hand as far as [from] the wrist.' *Tat-kisalaya*, &c., the Beng. and S´. read *naḥ*, 'to us,' for *tat*, and *kisalaya-ććhāya-parispardhibhiḥ*, 'rivalling the hue of young shoots.' According to Kavikaṇṭha-hāra, quoted by S´., ornaments are divided into four kinds: 1. *Āvedhya*, as ear-rings, &c.; 2. *Bandhanīya*, as flowers, &c.; 3. *Kshepya* or *prakshepya*, as anklets, foot-ornaments, &c.; 4. *Āropya*, as necklaces, garlands, &c.

[1] 'By this favour, royal fortune is indicated as (ever) to be enjoyed by thee in the house of thy husband.' *Abhyupapattyā*=*vṛikshānugraheṇa*, 'by the favour of the sylvan deities.'

[2] 'Returned [come up] from bathing.' *Ut-tṛī* is 'to come out of the water,' 'to come to land.' So *jalād uttīrya*, Mahā-bh. iii. 211.

[3] 'We [these persons] are unused to ornaments. By our acquaintance

शकुन्तला ।

[a] जाणे वो णेउणं । ॥ उभे नान्द्येनालङ्कुरुतः ॥

॥ ततः प्रविशति ध्यानोत्तीर्णः काश्यपः ॥

काश्यपः ।

यास्यत्यद्य शकुन्तलेति हृदयं संस्पृष्टमुत्कण्ठया
कण्ठः स्तम्भितवाष्पवृत्तिकलुषश्चिन्ताजडं दर्शनम् ।
वैक्लव्यं मम तावदीदृशमपि स्नेहादरण्यौकसः
पीड्यन्ते गृहिणः कथं नु तनयाविश्लेषदुःखैर्नवैः ॥८६॥

॥ इति परिक्रामति ॥

[a] ज्ञाने वां नैपुणम् ।

---

with the art of painting we will make the arrangement of the ornaments
on thy limbs.' *Anubahutta* for *anupabhukta* is the reading of my own
MS. and the Mackenzie, supported by K. *Ćitra-karma*, &c., 'by our
knowledge of painting,' i. e. we will decorate thee in the manner we have
seen in paintings (*ćitra-likhane yathābharana-prayogo dṛishṭo 'sti tenaiva
prakāreṇa*, S'.)

[1] '"This very day will S'akuntalā depart," at such (a thought), my
heart is smitten with melancholy [grief for her loss]; my voice [throat] is
agitated by suppressing the flow of tears; my sight is paralysed by
anxious thought. So great indeed through affection (is) the mental-
agitation even of me a hermit. How (much more) then, are householders
afflicted by new pangs at separation from their daughters !' *Iti*, see p. 140,
n. 2. *Saṃsprishṭam*, &c., one MS. (India Office, 1060) reads *sprishṭaṃ
samutkanṭhayā*. *Kanṭhaḥ*, &c., the Beng. have *antar-vāshpa-bhāro-
parodhi gaditam*, 'my voice is obstructed by the weight (*ādhikyena*, S'.)
of suppressed tears.' *Vāshpa*, i. e. *aśruṇaḥ pūrvāvasthā*, 'the first stage
or state of a tear,' 'the hot moisture that overspreads the eye, before the
tear-drop is formed,' K. *Darśana*=*nayana*, 'eye-sight.' *Jaḍa*=*vishayā-
grāhaka*, 'having no perception of external objects ;' or =*kartavyāpari-
ćchedaka*, but in this case *darśana*=*jñāna*, S'. The effect of deep thought

---

Verse 86. ŚĀRDŪLA-VIKRĪḌITA (a variety of ATIDHṚITI). See verses 14, 30, 36,
39, 40, 63, 79, 85.

सख्यौ ।

(a) हला सउन्दले । अवसिदमराडणासि । परिधेहि सम्पदं खोमजुम्मलं ।

॥ शकुन्तलोत्याय परिधत्ते ॥

गौतमी ।

(b) जादे । एसो दे आणन्दपरिवाहिणा चक्खुणा परिस्स-जन्तो वित्र गुरू उवट्ठिदो । आश्रां दाव पडिबंज्जस्स ।

शकुन्तला ॥ सव्रीडम् ॥

(c) ताद् । वन्दामि ।

---

a हला शकुन्तले । अवसितमण्डनासि । परिधत्स्व साम्प्रतं क्षौमयुगलम् ।
b नाते । एष न आनन्दपरिवाहिणा चक्षुषा परिष्वजमान इव गुरुरुपस्थितः ।
आचारं तावत्प्रतिपद्यस्व ।   c तात । वन्दे ।

---

and abstraction of mind might be to paralyse for the moment the organs of vision. S'. quotes an aphorism of Bharata, *Nidrā-nāśaś ča čintā ča bhrāntiś čotsuka-četasām.* *Nu* is used *praśne,* 'in asking a question,' S'. *Araṇyaukas = vānaprastha* or *araṇya-vāsin,* 'one whose dwelling (*okas*) is in the woods,' 'a hermit,' see *vanaukas.* *Gṛihin = gṛihastha,* 'a householder,' 'the father of a family.' The Brāhman was required to divide his life into four orders (*āśrama*). In the first he was a *Brahmačārin,* or 'student of religion;' in the second, a *Gṛihastha,* or 'householder;' in the third, a *Vānaprastha* (*Vaikhānasa*), or 'anchorite;' in the fourth, a *Bhikshu,* or 'religious mendicant;' see Indian Wisdom, p. 245.

[1] 'Thy decoration [toilet] is completed. Now do thou put on the pair of linen vestments.' A Hindū woman's dress generally consisted of two pieces; one covered the breast and shoulders, the other was a long robe enveloping the person. *Avasita-maṇḍanā = nishpanna-prasādhanā.*

[2] 'Here close-at-hand-stands thy spiritual-father as if (already) embracing thee [about to embrace thee], with an eye overflowing with joy. Perform now the customary-salutation.' *Ānanda-parivāhiṇā,* the Beng. have *ānanda-vāshpa-parivāhiṇā,* cf. p. 89, l. 13. *Āčāra,* 'good manners,' 'the usual complimentary greeting.' *Paḍibajjassa* for *pratipadyasva* is the reading of my own MS. and the Mackenzie, cf. p. 135, l. 4. The same expression occurs in Vikram., Act II.

काश्यपः ।

वत्से ।

ययातेरिव शर्मिष्ठा भर्तुर्बहुमता भव ।
सुतं त्वमपि सम्राजं सेव पुरुमवाप्नुहि ॥८७॥

गौतमी ।

[a] भत्रवं । वरोक्खु एसो । एा आसिंसा ।

काश्यपः ।

वत्से । इतः सद्यो हुताग्नीन्प्रदक्षिणीकुरुष्व ।

॥ सर्वे परिक्रामन्ति ॥

[a] भगवन् । वरः खल्वेषः । नाशीः ।

---

[1] 'Daughter, be thou highly honoured of thy husband, as was S'ar-mishṭhā of Yayāti. Do thou also obtain a son, a sovereign monarch, as she (obtained) Puru.' S'armishṭhā, according to K., was the daughter of Vṛisha-parvan, king of the Asuras or demons, and wife of Yayāti, son of Nahusha, one of the princes of the Lunar race, and ancestor of Dush-yanta, see p. 15, n. 1. The Sāhitya-darpaṇa (p. 190) cites this verse as an example of *āśīr-vāda*, 'benediction,' but reads (as also do the Beng.) *patyur* for *bhartur*, and *putram* for *sutam*. *Samrāj* is a sovereign prince, who has performed a *Rājasūya* sacrifice, and exercises despotic sway over others.

[2] 'This is actually a boon (conferred), not a (mere) benediction.' *San-tushṭa-devādīnām avaśyam-bhāvi vaćanaṃ varaḥ, āśis tu kadāćit phala-dāyinī vāk*, 'a *vara* is the promise of a propitiated deity, &c., which must necessarily come to pass; an *āśis* is a benediction which occasionally bears fruit [comes true],' Ć. and S'.

[3] 'My child, this way! do thou at once circumambulate the sacrificial fires,' see p. 148, n. 1. *Sadyo-hutāgnīm=tatkshaṇa-kṛita-homāgnīm*, S'. The Taylor and my own MS. have *sadyohutān*. *Sadyo* may, however, be separated from the next word, and translated 'at once,' 'immediately.' The rite of circumambulation is performed by slowly walking round any object, keeping the right side towards it.

Verse 87. SLOKA or ANUSHTUBH. See verses 5, 6, 11, 12, 26, 47, 50, 51, 53, 73, 76, 84.

काश्यपः ॥ ऋक्छन्दसाशास्ते ॥

अमी वेदिं परितः क्लृप्तधिष्ण्याः
समिद्वन्तः प्रान्तसंस्तीर्णदर्भाः ।
अपघ्नन्तो दुरितं हव्यगन्धै-
र्वैतानास्त्वां वह्नयः पावयन्तु ॥८८॥

प्रतिष्ठस्वेदानीम् । ॥ सदृष्टिक्षेपम् ॥ क्व ते शार्ङ्गरवमिश्राः ।

---

¹ '[*Pronounces a blessing in the metre of the Ṛić*, i. e. according to the usual metre of the Ṛig-veda.] Let these fires, taken-from-the-sacred-hearth [*vaitānas*] whose places are fixed round the altar, fed with (consecrated) wood, having Darbha [Kuśa] grass strewed around the margin, destroying sin by the perfume of the oblations, purify thee.' Each stanza of the Sūktas or hymns of the Ṛig-veda is called a *ṛić*. *Asya vṛittasya vedoktāśīrvāda-sadṛiśatram agni-prayuktatvādi boddhavyam*, 'it is to be understood that there is a similarity between the metre of this verse and that of the benedictions uttered in the Vedas addressed to fire,' &c., K. The verse itself does not occur in the Ṛig-veda, but the metre is Vedic. Doubtless Kālidāsa intended it as an imitation of Vedic poetry. That it is addressed to Agni constitutes in itself a point of resemblance. *Vaitāna*, see Indian Wisdom, p. 197. *Klṛipta-dhishnyāḥ = raćitādhishṭhānāḥ*. *Prānta-saṃstīrṇa-darbhāḥ*, i. e. *pārśveshu ćatasṛishu dikshu sankīrṇā darbhā yeshām*. At a sacrifice, the fires, severally termed *Āhavanīya*, *Mārjālīya*, *Gārhápatya*, and *Āgnīdhrīya*, were lighted at the four cardinal points, east, west, north, and south, and Kuśa grass (see p. 19, n. 1) was scattered round each fire. See Indian Wisdom, p. 205; see also Sāyaṇa's commentary on Ṛig-v. i. 1, 4, and cf. Ṛig-v. i. 31, 13, 'thou, four-eyed

---

Verse 88. TRISHṬUP ĆATUSH-PĀDĀ, a form of Vedic metre, consisting of four times eleven syllables, the first and third Pādas resembling the VĀTORMĪ, and the second and fourth, the ŚĀLINĪ variety of TRISHṬUBH. In the second, however, the first syllable is short.

$$\cup - - - \cup \cup - - \cup - - \parallel \cup - - - - \cup - - \cup - -$$
$$\cup - - - \cup \cup - - \cup - - \parallel - - - - - \cup - - \cup - -$$

In Ṛig-veda i. 59, 5, the first Pāda is exactly like the first in the above scheme, but the other Pādas are arranged differently, as far at least as the seventh syllable. Kālidāsa, accustomed to the strictness of the later Sanskrit metres, seems here to have endeavoured to imitate the Vedic rhythm, in which greater liberty was allowed. Thus he produced a verse too irregular to come under any of the later metres, but rather too regular for a Vedic hymn.

शिष्यः ॥ प्रविश्य ॥

भगवन् । इमे स्मः ।

काश्यपः ।

भगिन्यास्ते मार्गमादेश्य ।

शाङ्गेरवः ।

इत इतो भवती । ॥ सर्वं परिक्रामन्ति ॥

काश्यपः ।

भो भोः सन्निहितास्तपोवनतरवः ।

पातुं न प्रथमं व्यवस्यति जलं युष्मास्वपीतेषु या
नादत्ते प्रियमण्डनापि भवतां स्नेहेन या पल्लवम् ।
आद्ये वः कुसुमप्रसूतिसमये यस्या भवत्युत्सवः
सेयं याति शकुन्तला पतिगृहं सर्वैरनुज्ञायंताम् ॥८९॥

Agni, blazest as the protector of the worshippers,' &c. *Pālayantu* (=*rakshantu*) is the reading of all the Beng. MSS., supported by K., S'., and Ć., but all the Deva-n. MSS. have *pāvayantu*.

[1] S'. quotes a verse of Bharata, *Devāś ća, munayaś ćaiva, liṅginaḥ, sādhanāś ća* [*sādhakāś ća,* Ć.] *ye, bhagavann iti te vāćyāḥ sarvaiḥ strī-pun-napunsakaiḥ,* 'both gods and also Munis, Liṅ-gins and Sādhanas (? *sādhavas,* "saints," see Vishṇu-p. p. 300) are to be addressed as "Bhagavan," by all women, men, and eunuchs.'

[2] Cf. Vikram., Act II, *bhavān pramada-vana-mārgam ādeśayatu.*

[3] 'Listen! listen! ye neighbouring trees of the penance-grove. She who never attempts to drink water first, when you have not drunk, and who, although fond of ornaments, never plucks a blossom, out of affection for you, whose greatest-holiday [highest-joy] is at the season of the first appearance of your bloom, even that same S'akuntalā now departs to the house of her husband. Let her be affectionately-dismissed by (you) all.' *Bhoḥ* is a vocative particle, often joined with *śrūyatām,* 'listen!' *Vyava-syati,* 'makes effort,' may also mean 'resolves upon,' 'makes up her mind;' (with *na*), 'it never enters into her head.' *A-pīteshu,* the Beng. have *a-sik-teshu,* i.e. 'as long as you remain unwatered.' The Deva-n. reading is supported by K., who includes *pīta* among the passive participles, like

---

Verse 89. ŚĀRDŪLA-VIKRĪDITA (a variety of ATIDHRITI). See verses 14, 30, 36, 39, 50, 63, 79, 85, 86.

॥ कोकिलत्वं सूचयित्वा[1] ॥

अनुमतगमना शकुन्तला
तरुभिरियं वनवासबन्धुभिः ।
प्रभृतविरुतं कलं यथा
प्रतिवचनीकृतमेभिरीटृंशम् ॥९०॥[2]

आकाशे ।

रम्यान्तरः कमलिनीहरितैः सरोभि-
र्च्छायाद्रुमैर्नियमिताकैमयूखतापः ।

gata, sthita, ārūdha, &c. (Pāṇ. iii. 4, 72), which may have an active signification. *Vismṛita* may be included in the same list, see p. 28, l. 3. *Priya*, in the sense 'fond of,' may stand at the beginning of a compound, cf. φιλοσοφία, φιλόξενος (*priyātithi*), &c.; sometimes at the end, e. g. *jala-priya*, 'fond of water.'

[1] 'Acting as if he heard the note of a cuckoo,' lit. 'shewing the note of a cuckoo.' Compare *nimittaṃ sūćayitvā*, Vikram., Act II.

[2] 'This S'akuntalā is permitted to depart by the trees, the foresters' kinsfolk; since a song to this effect, warbled by the cuckoo, was employed as an answer by them.' *Vana-vāsa-bandhubhiḥ = araṇya-vāsa-snigdhaiḥ*, 'beloved by foresters.' It may be translated 'her sylvan relatives.' *Para-bhṛita (=pika)*, lit. 'nourished by a stranger.' The Indian Koïl or cuckoo is supposed to leave her eggs in the nest of the crow to be hatched, but has little resemblance to the bird known as the cuckoo in Europe. One of its names is *vasanta-dūta*, 'messenger of spring.' Its song is said to be sweet (*madhura*, Ṛitu-s.), but cannot be compared to that of the nightingale. 'The beauty of cuckoos is their song,' Hitop. l. 839. 'On a journey (*yātrāyām*) the note of a cuckoo is indicative of good-fortune (*śubha-sūćakaḥ*). The answer of the trees was effected by the song of the cuckoo (*pika-ravenaiva sampannam*). Next the answer of the sylvan deities is given (by a voice in the air),' S'. *Kala* as an adj. means 'soft,' 'sweet,' and *parabhṛita-virutam kalam* may be 'the sweet notes of the cuckoo' (cf. Raghu-v. viii. 58).

Verse 90. APARA-VAKTRĀ, containing eleven syllables to the first Pāda or quarter-verse, and twelve to the second, each half-verse being alike.

∪ ∪ ∪ ∪ ∪ ∪ – ∪ – ∪ – ‖ ∪ ∪ ∪ ∪ – ∪ ∪ – ∪ – ∪ –

भूयात्कुशेशयरजोमृदुरेणुरस्याः
शान्तानुकूलपवनश्च शिवश्च पन्थाः ॥ ९१ ॥

॥ सर्वे सविस्मयमाकर्ण्ययन्ति ॥

गौतमी ।

[a]जादे । णादिजणसिणिद्धाहिं अणुणादगमणासि तवो-
वणदेवदाहिं । पणम भअवंदीणं ।

[a] ज्ञाते । ज्ञातिजनस्निग्धाभिरनुज्ञातगमनासि तपोवनदेवताभिः । प्रणम भगवतीभ्यः ।

---

[1] 'May her path be pleasantly-diversified [pleasant at intervals] by lakes (that are) verdant with-lotus-beds, (may it have) the heat of the sun's rays moderated by shady trees, (may) its dust be soft with the [as the] pollen from the lotuses, and (may it be cheered by) gentle favourable breezes and (be altogether) prosperous.' *Ramyāntaraḥ=manohara-madhyaḥ*, S'. ; = *manojña-madhyaḥ*, C'., 'having its middle space delightful,' 'pleasant throughout the intervening distance,' an epithet of *panthāḥ*. *Chāyā-drumaiḥ* = *chāyā-pradhānair-vṛikshaiḥ*, 'trees chiefly abounding in shade,' K. ;=*chāyā-lakshita-drumaiḥ*, 'trees characterized by shade,' C'. It is a compound similar to *śāka-pārthiva* and *abhijñāna-śakuntalā*, see p. 4, n. 2. 'That is called a *chāyā-taru*, 'shade-tree,' whose under-part (*talam*) excessively cool shade (*atyanta-śītala-chhāyā*) does not quit either in the forenoon or afternoon,' S'. and C'. *Niyamita* = *apanīta*. *Kuśe-śaya*, lit. 'lying in water ;'=*śata-pattra*, 'a lotus.' *Śānta* =*śānta-vega, manda*, K. ;=*pāṭachcharādi-śunya*, 'free from robbers,' &c., S'. and C'. The compound may therefore be translated 'free from molestation and having favourable breezes.' *Śivaś cha bhūyāt panthāḥ*, this seems to have been a phrase commonly used as a parting benediction, like 'A pleasant journey to you !' Cf. *panthānas te santu śivāḥ*, Hitop. l. 1442, Sāhit.-d. p. 344, Mudrā-r. p. 30, l. 17, and p. 179, l. 4 of this play.

[2] 'Dear to thee as (thy own) kinsfolk.' Cf. *vana-vāsa-bandhubhiḥ* in verse 90. My own Bombay MS. has *ṇṇādi* (supported by the Calcutta edition), the others all *ṇādi* for *jñāti*. There is no doubt about the doubling of the *ṇ* when not initial, as Vararuchi, iii. 44, gives *viṇṇāṇa* for *vijñāna*.

[3] *Bhaavadīṇam*, a Prākṛit gen. for Sanskrit dat., see p. 129, n. 1.

Verse 91. VASANTA-TILAKĀ (a variety of ŚAKVARĪ). See verses 8, 27, 31, 43, 46, 64, 74, 80, 82, 83.

शकुन्तला ॥ सप्रणामं परिक्रम्य। जनान्तिकम् ॥

a हला पिअंवदे। एं अज्जउत्तदंसणुस्सुआएवि अस्सं
परिच्चन्तीए दुक्खेणं मे चलणा पुरदो पवट्टन्ति।

प्रियंवदा।

b णा केवलं तवोवणविरहकादरा सही एव्व। तुए उव्वट्टि-
दविओस्रस्स तवोवणस्सवि दाव समवत्था दीसइ।

उग्गलिअदब्भकवला मिआ परिच्चत्तणच्चणा मोरा।

ओसरिअपराडुपत्ता मुञ्चन्ति अंसू विअ लदाओ॥९२॥

a हला प्रियंवदे। नन्वार्यपुत्रदर्शनोत्सुकाया अभ्याश्रमं परित्यजन्त्या दुःखेन मे
चरणौ पुरतः प्रवर्तेति।   b न केवलं तपोवनविरहकातरा सख्येव। त्वयोपस्थि-
तवियोगस्य तपोवनस्यापि तावत्समवस्था दृश्यते।

उद्गलितदर्भकवला मृगाः परित्यक्तनर्तना मयूराः।
अपसृतपाण्डुपत्रा मुञ्चन्त्यश्रूणीव लताः॥९२॥

---

[1] My own MS., supported by K., has *duḥkhena*, the others *duḥkha-duḥkhena*.

[2] 'One may observe the same (troubled) condition [the same condition is observed] of the penance-grove, as the (time of) separation from thee approaches.' *Samavasthā=samāvasthā*, as in Raghu-v. viii. 41. The Taylor MS. reads *samāvatthā*.

[3] 'The deer let fall the mouthfuls of Darbha-grass, the peacocks cease (their) dancing, the creepers, as they cast [in casting] their pale leaves, appear to shed tears [as it were shed tears].' *Udgalita*, from *ud-gal*, lit. 'to trickle out,' 'drop from.' The Beng. MSS. read *ugginna* (=*udgīrna*), 'ejected from the throat or mouth.' *Mṛigāḥ*, all the Deva-n. read *mio* for *mrigyaḥ*, and in the next line *assūni* for *aśrūni*, apparently in violation of the metre. Dr. Boehtlingk has suggested *miā* and *aṇsū*, the latter is a legitimate acc. pl. from *aṇsu*, the masc. Prākṛit equivalent of the neuter *aśru*; see Vararući iv. 15. *Parityakta-nartanā*, the dancing of

---

Verse 92. ĀRYĀ or GĀTHĀ. See verse 2.

    — ∪ ∪ | ∪ — ∪ | ∪ ∪ — ‖ ∪ — ∪ | — — | ∪ — ∪ | — — | —
    — ∪ ∪ | ∪ — ∪ | — — ‖ ∪ — ∪ | — — | ∪ | ∪ ∪ — | —

शकुन्तला ॥ स्मृत्वा ॥

[a] ताद्‍। लदाबहिणिं वणजोसिणिं दाव आमन्तइस्सं।

काश्यपः।

अवैमि ते तस्यां सोदर्यस्नेहम्। इयं तावद्दक्षिणेन।

शकुन्तला ॥ लतामुपेत्य ॥

[b] वणजोसिणि। चूदसङ्गदादि मं पल्लालिङ्ग इदोगदाहिं साहाबाहाहिं। अज्जप्पहुदि दूरपरिवत्तिणी दे खु भविस्सं।

काश्यपः।

सङ्कल्पितं प्रथममेव मया तवार्थे
भर्त्तारमात्मसदृशं सुकृतैर्गता त्वम्।

<hr>

[a] तात्‍। लताभगिनीं वनज्योत्स्नां तावदामन्त्रयिष्ये। [b] वनज्योत्स्ने। चूतसङ्गतापि मां मत्प्यालिङ्गेतोगताभिः शाखाबाहाभिः। अद्यप्रभृति दूरपरिवर्तिनी ते खलु भविष्यामि।

<hr>

the Indian peacock, especially at the approach of rain, in which it is said to take especial delight, is frequently alluded to in Hindū poetry. Cf. Megha-d. 46, 78; Ṛitu-s. ii. 6; Bhartṛi-h. i. 43. *Osaria* for *apasṛita*, see Lassen's Instit. Prāk. p. 363. Raghu-v. xiv. 69 contains a sentiment precisely parallel to the above, *Nṛityam mayūrāḥ, kusumāni vṛikshā, darbhān upāttān vijahur harinyaḥ,* &c.

[1] 'Father, I will just bid farewell to (my) tendril-sister, the Light of the Grove,' i. e. the Nava-mālikā, or young jasmine-creeper, mentioned at p. 28, l. 3.

[2] 'I know thy sisterly affection for it. Here it is now to the right.' *Sodarya,* 'of whole blood,' 'born from the same womb' (*udara*); compare p. 22, l. 9.

[3] 'O Light of the Grove, though united with the mango-tree, embrace me with (thy) arms-of-branches turned in this direction.' *Ćūta-saṅgatā,* see p. 28, n. 1. *Ito-gatābhiḥ,* &c., is the reading of all the Deva-n. MSS. (supported by K.) excepting one, which has *idogadehiṃ sāhā-bāhūhiṃ* for *ito-gataiḥ śākhā-bāhubhiḥ.* The feminine noun *bāhā* is more appropriately joined with *śākhā,* but *bāhu* is admissible, compare p. 26, l. 2. The Beng. have *śākhāmayair bāhubhiḥ,* 'with arms consisting of branches.'

चूतेन संश्रितवती नवमालिकेय-
मस्यामहं त्वयि च सम्प्रति वीतचिन्तः ॥ ९३ ॥

इतः पन्थानं प्रतिपंद्यस्व ।

शकुन्तला ॥ सख्यौ प्रति ॥

[a] हला । एसा दुवेणं वो हत्थे णिक्खेबो ।

सख्यौ ।

[b] अम्हं जणो कस्स हत्थे समप्पिंदो । ॥ इति बाष्पं विहरतः ॥

काश्यपः ।

अनसूये । अलं रुदित्वा । ननु भवतीभ्यामेव स्थिरीकर्तव्या
शकुन्तला ।

॥ सर्वे परिक्रामन्ति ॥

[a] हला । एषा द्वयोर्वां हस्ते निक्षेपः ।   [b] अयं जनः कस्य हस्ते समर्पितः ।

---

[1] 'Thou by (thy) merits hast obtained [hast gone to] a husband suited-to-thyself, just as originally determined upon by me on thy account : this young Mālikā (creeper) has united itself with the mango-tree; now (therefore) I am free from solicitude about it and about thee.' *Saṅkalpitam, &c.,* see p. 49, l. 5; and p. 135, l. 10 with note 2. *Tavārthe* = *tava kṛite,* K. *Ātma-sadṛiśam* = *tvat-samam,* K.; *rūpa-kulādinā sva-sadṛiśam,* 're-sembling thyself in beauty, family,' &c., S'.; see p. 31, n. 1. *Gatā* = *prāptā,* K.; see p. 161, n. 3 at the end. *Saṃśritavatī* = *saṅgatavatī,* K. My own MS. has *sanskṛitavatī,* and the Colebrooke *sammitavatī. Vīta-ćinta* = *tyakta-varānusandhāna,* 'ceased from searching after a husband,' S'.

[2] 'Set out on thy journey hence.' *Pratipadyasva,* see p. 135, n. 1.

[3] 'This (creeper) is (entrusted) as a pledge into the hand of you two.' *Nikshepa* = *sthāpya,* S'. *Yathā sthāpyo rakshyate tatheyam.*

[4] 'Into whose hands are we committed (by thee)?' *Ayaṃ janah,* i. e. *asmad-rūpaḥ,* S'. and C'.

[5] *Vi-hṛi* seems here used in the sense of 'to wipe away.'

[6] 'Enough of weeping! Surely S'akuntalā should be cheered [rendered

---

Verse 93. VASANTA-TILAKĀ (a variety of S'AKVARĪ). See verses 8, 27, 31, 43, 46, 64, 74, 80, 82, 83, 91.

शकुन्तला ।

[a] ताद् । एसा उडजपज्जन्तचारिणी गब्भमन्थरा मिस्सबहू जदा अणघप्पसवा होइ । तदा मे कम्पि पिअणिवेदइत्तअं विसज्जइस्संह ।

काश्यपः ।

नेदं विस्मरिष्यामः ।

शकुन्तला ॥ गतिभङ्गं रूपयित्वा ॥

[b] की णुक्खु एसो णिवसणे मे सज्जइ । ॥ इति परावर्तते ॥

काश्यपः ।

वत्से ।

यस्य त्वया व्रणविरोपणमिङ्गुदीनां
  तैलं न्यषिच्यत मुखे कुशसूचिविद्धे ।
श्यामाकमुष्टिपरिवर्धितको जहाति
  सोऽयं न पुत्रकृतकः पदवीं मृगस्ते ॥९४॥

[a] तात । एषोटजपर्यन्तचारिणी गर्भमन्थरा मृगवधूर्यदानघप्रसवा भवति । तदा मे कमपि प्रियनिवेदयितारं विसर्जयिष्यथ ।   [b] को नु खल्वेष निवसने मे सज्जति ।

firm, supported] by you indeed ?' i. e. you are the very persons who should rather support and comfort your friend. *Alam ruditvā*, see p. 48, n. 3. *Sthirī-kartavyā = tapovana-viraha-kheda-rahitā vidheyā*, S'.

[1] 'When this doe [female deer] grazing in the neighbourhood of the hut, slow by (the weight of) her young, has happily brought forth; then you will send some one to announce [as an announcer of] the agreeable news to me.' *Anagha-prasavā = vyasana-rahita-prasūtiḥ*, 'bringing forth without any mishap,' K. *Priya*, i. e. *priya-vārtā*, S'.

[2] 'That same fawn, thy adopted child, tenderly reared with handfuls of S'yāmāka-grains, on whose mouth, when pricked by the sharp-points of the Kuśa-grass, sore-healing oil of In-gudī-plants was sprinkled by thee,

Verse 94. VASANTA-TILAKĀ (a variety of S'AKVARĪ). See verses 8, 27, 31, 43, 46, 64, 74, 80, 82, 83, 91, 93.

शकुन्तला ।

[a] वच्छ । किं सहवासपरिच्चाइणिं मं अणुसरसि ।
अचिरप्पसूदाए जणणीए विणा विवड्ढिदो एव्व ।
दाणिम्मि मए विरहिदं तुमं तादो चिन्तइस्सदि ।
णिवत्तेहि दाव । ॥ इति रुदती प्रस्थिता ॥

काश्यपः ।

उत्पक्ष्मणोर्नयनयोरुपरुद्धवृत्तिं
वाष्पं कुरु स्थिरतया विरतानुबन्धम् ।

[a] वत्स । किं सहवासपरित्यागिनीं मामनुसरसि । अचिरप्रसूतया जनन्या विना
विवर्धित एव । इदानीमपि मया विरहितं त्वां तातश्चिन्तयिष्यति । निवर्तस्व
तावत् ।

---

will not forsake thy footsteps [path].' *Vraṇa-viropaṇa=kshata-praro-
haka*, S'., lit. 'that which causes a scar to cicatrize.' See *ropaṇa* in Dict.
Ingudīnām, see p. 18, n. 1. *Kuśa-sūci*, see p. 57, n. 5. *Parivardhitaka=
anukampayā vardhitaḥ*, 'compassionately reared,' K.;=*atiśayena poshitaḥ*,
'excessively nourished,' S'. and Ć. The suffix *ka* sometimes gives the
sense of compassionating (*anukampāyām*). So *putrakaḥ=anukampitaḥ
putraḥ* according to Pāṇ. v. 3, 76. The preposition *pari* may give the
sense of *atiśayena* noticed by the other commentators. *Syāmāka=vrīhi-
viśesha*, 'a kind of rice,' S'. It is rather the grain of a kind of Panic
grass, eaten by the Hindūs. *Mushṭi*, 'a handful,' is the first measure of
capacity, equivalent to $\frac{1}{8}$th of a *kuñji*, $\frac{1}{12}$th of a *kuḍava*, $\frac{1}{18}$th of a *prastha*.
Putra-kritaka=kritrima-putra, 'a factitious or adopted son,' S'. and Ć.
K. explains this compound by referring to Pāṇ. ii. 1, 59, so that *putra-
krita*, 'made into a son' (i. e. *a-putra*, 'not really a son'), is like *śreṇi-krita*,
'made into a line,' and *pūga-krita*, 'made into a heap.'
[1] 'Why dost thou follow me, an abandoner of (my) companions ? Thou
indeed wast reared (by me) without (thy) mother [when deprived of thy
mother] shortly after she had brought thee forth.' *Saha-vāsa*, lit. 'one
who lives with another.' The Beng. have *aćira-prasūtoparatayā=pra-
savāvyavahita-kāla-mritayā*, 'that died directly after bringing thee
forth.'

अस्मिन्नलक्षितनतोन्नतभूमिभागे
मार्गे पदानि खलु ते विषमीभवन्ति ॥ ९५ ॥

शार्ङ्गरवः ।

भगवन् । आोदकान्तात्स्निग्धो जनोऽनुगन्तव्य इति श्रूयते ।
तदिदं सरस्तीरम् । अत्र सन्दिश्य प्रतिगन्तुमर्हसि ।

---

[1] 'By-a-vigorous-effort [by firmness] make the tears cease to hang [cling] in (thy) upturned-eyelashed eyes, obstructing (their) free-action [impeding our business]. In this path in which the undulations of ground [the depressed and elevated portions of ground] are not discernible, thy footsteps must certainly be uneven.' *Utpakshmaṇoḥ*, see p. 131, n. 1 in the middle. *Uparuddha-vṛittim = pratiruddha-vyāpāram*, 'impeding the functions or proper action of the organs of vision,' C. *Uparuddhā antaritā vṛittir vyāpāro yena*, K. In p. 157, l. 6, *vṛitti* is applied to the course of a tear; but if so translated here, the other epithet, *viratānubandham*, would be superfluous. It is not necessary, however, to connect it with *nayanayoḥ*, as the passage might be rendered 'make the tears that impede our business cease to cling in (thy) upturned-eyelashed-eyes.' *Vāshpa* is 'the hot moisture that precedes the formation of tears,' see p. 157, n. 1. It is used in the singular. Cf. *muñċato vāshpam ushṇam*, Megha-d. 12. *Viratānubandha*, my own MS. has *vihatānubandha*; *anubandha*, lit. 'binding after,' 'following after;' hence 'cleaving,' 'adhering.' The Beng. MSS. have *śithilānubandham = sāntārambham* (sic?), S. *Vishamī-bhavanti = skhalitāni syuḥ*, 'are liable to trip or stumble,' S. and C. Cf. p. 139, l. 3.

[2] '"A friend is [or friends are] to be escorted as far as the water's brink"—such is the sacred precept. This, then, is the margin of a lake. Here having given (us) directions, be pleased to return.' *Odakāntāt*, i.e. *ā + udakāntāt = ā jalāntāt* (see p. 155, n. 3 near the end). *Odakāntād* is found in all the Deva-n. MSS.; my own has *odakāntam*. *Snigdho janaḥ* may be either 'a friend' or 'friends,' cf. *sakhī-jana*, p. 128, l. 2, with note 1. *Srūyate*, lit. 'it is heard,' i.e. it is enjoined in *śruti*, 'scripture,' 'holy writ.'

Verse 95. VASANTA-TILAKĀ (a variety of ŚAKVARĪ). See verses 8, 27, 31, 43, 46, 64, 74, 80, 82, 83, 91, 93, 94.

काश्यपः ।

तेन हीमां क्षीरवृक्षच्छायामाश्रयामः ।

॥ सर्वं परिक्रम्य स्थिताः ॥

काश्यपः ॥ आत्मगतम् ॥

किं नु खलु तत्रभवतो दुष्यन्तस्य युक्तरूपमस्माभिः सन्देष्टव्यम् । ॥ इति चिन्तयति ॥

शकुन्तला ॥ जनान्तिकम् ॥

[a] हला । पेक्ख । एलिणीपत्तन्तरिदं पिअसहस्सरं अदेक्खन्ती आदुरा चक्कवाई आरडदि । दुक्करं अहं करेमिन्ति ।

---

[a] हला । प्रेक्षस्व । नलिनीपत्त्रान्तरितं प्रियसहचरमपश्यन्त्यातुरा चक्रवाक्यारटति । दुष्करमहं करोमीति ।

---

[1] *Kshíra-vṛiksha*, lit. 'milk-tree,' a kind of fig tree, not the Vaṭa or Banyan tree (Ficus Indica), nor the Pippala (Ficus Religiosa), but the glomerous fig tree (Ficus Glomerata), which yields a resinous milky juice from its bark (see p. 155, n. 3 in the middle) and is large enough to afford abundant shade.

[2] 'What message is to be sent by us (that will be) most appropriate for his majesty Dushyanta?' *Yukta-rūpa*, cf. p. 89, n. 1; and p. 15, l. 3.

[3] 'Friend, see! the poor female-Cakravāka, not perceiving her dear mate hidden by the lotus-leaves, calls to (him) thus, "Hard (is the lot) I suffer;"' see p. 128, n. 3, and cf. in Vikram., Act IV, *Sarasi nalinī-pattreṇāpi tvam āvṛita-vigrahāṁ nanu sahacarīṁ dūre matvā viraushi samutsukaḥ*, 'thou indeed (i. e. the male Cakravāka) art sorrowfully crying to thy mate thinking her to be far away, although her body is only concealed from thee by a lotus-leaf in the lake.' A few lines before this passage, the cry is compared to the sound *ka ka*. Possibly this may account for the somewhat peculiar phrase *dukkaram karemi*, here employed as the cry of the bird. K. has *dushkaram khalu ahaṁ tarkayāmi*. It is true that *kṛi* sometimes has the sense of *tark*, 'think,' 'imagine' (cf. p. 42, n. 1), but *dushkaram kṛi* is not more harsh than *śokam kṛi*, 'to make or suffer sorrow.' S. has *dushkaram ayaṁ cakravākaḥ karoti*. Instead of *pia*

अनसूया ।

[a] सहि । मा एव्वं मन्तेहि ।

एसा वि पिएण विणा गमेइ रञणिं विसाञ्चदीहञरं ।
गरुञम्मि विरहदुक्खं आसाबन्धो सहाबेदि ॥९६॥

काश्यपः ।

शार्ङ्गरव । त्वया मद्वचनात्स राजा शकुन्तलां पुरस्कृत्य[2]
वक्तव्यः ।

शार्ङ्गरवः ।

आज्ञापयतु भवान् ।

---

[a] सखि । मैवं मन्त्रयस्व ।

एषापि प्रियेण विना गमयति रजनीं विषाददीर्घतराम् ।
गुर्व्यपि विरहदुःखमाशाबन्धः साहयति ॥९६॥

---

three of the MSS. have *bi* for *api*. 'This verse indicates that S'akuntalā foresees she is about to experience similar sorrow, in having to endure separation from Dushyanta in consequence of the curse' (*śāpa-tirohita-Dushyantam a-lapsyamānā*), K.

[1] 'Speak not so. Even she [the female C'akravāka], without her beloved, passes away the night made too long by sorrow. Expectation (of meeting again) makes the pain of separation, however severe, supportable.' *Gamayati*, lit. 'causes to go,' i.e. brings to an end. The Prākṛit *visāa* =*vishāda*, 'melancholy.' S'. explains the phrase by *visūranā-dīrghām, kheda-dīrghām, duḥkha-dustarām*. *Āśā-bandha*, 'hope,' i.e. *prātar mām sangamayishyati*, 'in the morning he will be united to me.' S'. makes this verse an example of the Āśvāsa Alan-kāra. K. refers to a parallel passage in the Megha-d. 10, *Āśā-bandhaḥ kusuma-sadriśaḥ* [sic] *prāyaśo hy anganānāṃ sadyaḥ-pāti pranayi hṛidayaṃ viprayoge ruṇaddhi.*

[2] 'Having placed in front,' i.e. 'having introduced,' 'having presented.'

Verse 96. ĀRYĀ or GĀTHĀ. See verse 2.

-- | ⌣⌣- | ⌣⌣-‖⌣-⌣ | ⌣⌣- | ⌣-⌣ | -⌣⌣ | -
⌣⌣- | ⌣⌣⌣⌣ | --‖ -- | -- | ⌣ | -- | ⌣

काश्यपः ।

अस्मान्साधु विचिन्त्य संयमधनानुच्चैःकुलं चात्मन-
स्त्वय्यस्याः कथमप्यबान्धवकृतां स्नेहप्रवृत्तिं च ताम् ।
सामान्यप्रतिपत्तिपूर्वकमियं दारेषु दृश्या त्वया
भाग्यायत्तमतःपरं न खलु तद्वाच्यं वधूबन्धुभिः ॥९७॥

शाङ्गरवः ।

गृहीतः सन्देशः ।

---

[1] 'Having well considered us as rich in devotion, and the exalted family of thyself, and that (free) flow of affection of this (maiden) towards thee [or the spontaneous flow of affection springing up in you for her] not in any manner brought about by relatives; she is to be regarded by thee, as (one) amongst (thy) wives, after raising her to an equality of rank [or with equal respect]. Beyond this is dependent on destiny, nor indeed ought that to be called in question by a wife's relations.' *Samyama-dhanān*, 'this implies that they were worthy of respect,' K. *Uććaiḥ-kulam*, &c., 'this implies that he would act with justice,' K.; see p. 15, n. 1. *Kathamapi* = *dur-graheṇa*, S. and C. Cf. p. 131, l. 6. *A-bāndhava-kritām*, see p. 127, n. 3. *Sneha-pravrittim* = *prema-ćeshṭām*, C. *Sāmā-nya-pratipatti-pūrvakam* = *sādhāraṇa-gaurava-puraḥsaram*, 'preceded by equal respect;' *yādriśena gauraveṇa aparā vadhūr ālokyate tādriśena 'iyam*, &c., S. *Pratipatti* is either 'the act of preferring to rank,' or 'the respect paid to rank.' *Pūrva* or *pūrvaka* at the end of a compound often simply denotes the manner in which anything is done, translateable by 'with' or 'after' (cf. *sa bhavantam anāmaya-praśna-pūrvakam idam āha*, p. 198, l. 2; also p. 116, n. 2). *Dāreshu*, S. explains thus, *dāra-śabdaḥ puṃ-liṅgaḥ kalatra-vāćako nitya-bahuraćanāntaḥ*, 'the word *dāra*, mean-ing a wife, is of the masculine gender, and always has a plural termination.' *Dārāḥ* therefore may be either wives or wife. *Ataḥ-param*, &c., 'here he tells the reason why he does not demand higher rank or greater honour for S'akuntalā,' S. In the first line, my own MS. reads *asmān sādhu samīkshya samyama-parān*. All marriages in the East are arranged by the relatives of the parties.

Verse 97. S'ĀRDŪLA-VIKRĪDITA (a variety of ATIDHRITI). See verses 14, 30, 36, 39, 40, 63, 79, 85, 86, 89.

काश्यपः ।

वत्से । त्वमिदानीमनुशासनीयासि । वनौकसोऽपि सन्तो
लौकिकज्ञा वयम् ।[1]

शाङ्गरवः ।

न खलु धीमतां कश्चिदविषयो नाम ।[2]

काश्यपः ।

सा त्वमितः पतिकुलं प्राप्य

शुश्रूषस्व गुरून्कुरु प्रियसखीवृत्तिं सपत्नीजने
भर्तुर्विप्रकृतापि रोषणतया मा स्म प्रतीपं गमः ।
भूयिष्ठं भव दक्षिणा परिजने भाग्येष्वनुत्सेकिनी
यान्त्येवं गृहिणीपदं युवतयो वामाः कुलस्याधयः ॥९८॥[3]

कथं वा गौतमी मन्यते ।

---

[1] 'We (are) acquainted with worldly affairs,' 'we know the ways of the world' (=*loka-vyavahāra-jñāḥ*, S'.)

[2] 'There is no subject out of the reach [*agočaraḥ*, S'.] of the intelligent,' i. e. wise men are conversant with all subjects.

[3] 'Pay respectful attention to (thy) superiors. Act the part of a dear friend towards (thy) fellow-wives [rival wives]. Even though wronged [treated harshly] by thy husband, do not out of anger shew [go to] a refractory-spirit. Be ever courteous towards (thy) attendants; not puffed up [arrogant] in prosperity—in this manner young-women attain the station [title] of housewife [matron]. Those of an opposite character are house-banes [banes of the family].' The Sāhit.-d. p. 185 adduces this as an example of the figure Upadishṭa, which is defined as *manohāri vākyam śāstrānusārataḥ*. S'. quotes the following aphorism, *Parisangṛihya śā-strārtham yad vākyam abhidhīyate vidvan manoharam jñeyam upa-dishṭam tad eva tu. Gurūn=svasurādīn*, 'father-in-law,' &c., C'. A Guru is not only a father or a father-in-law, but also a preceptor, and in fact any male relation entitled to *gaurava*, 'respect.' *Śuśrūshasva=ārādhaya. Vṛittim*, some of the Beng. and the Sāhit.-d., supported by S'., read *vṛittam*

Verse 98. ŚĀRDŪLA-VIKRĪḌITA (a variety of ATIDHṚITI). See verses 14, 30, 36, 39, 40, 63, 79, 85, 86, 89, 97.

गौतमी ।

[a]एत्तिओ वहूजणस्स उवदेसो । जादे । एदंक्खु सव्वं
ओधारेहि[1] ।

काश्यपः ।

वत्से । परिष्वजस्व मां सखीजनं च ।

शकुन्तला ।

[b]ताद । इदो एव्व किं पिअंवदामिस्सांओ सहीओ
णिवत्तिस्सन्ति ।

काश्यपः ।

वत्से । इमे अपि प्रदेये[3] । न युक्तमनयोस्तत्र गन्तुम् ।
त्वया सह गौतमी यास्यति ।

शकुन्तला ॥ पितरमाश्लिष्य ॥

[c]कहं दाणिं तादस्स अङ्कादो परिब्भट्टा मलअतटुम्मूलिआ

<hr>

[a] एतावान्वधूजनस्योपदेशः । जाते । एतत्खलु सर्वमवधारय ।   [b] तात ।
इत एव किं प्रियंवदामिश्राः सख्यो निवर्तिष्यन्ते ।   [c] कथमिदानीं तातस्याङ्कात्प-
रिभ्रष्टा मलयतटोन्मूलिता

=*caritram*, 'action,' 'deed,' 'behaviour,' 'demeanour.' *Viprakṛitā*=
pīḍitā, C.;=*kṛita-vipriyā*, 'offended,' S. *Pratīpam*=*prātikūlyam*. *Bhū-
yishṭham*=*atiśayena*. *Dakshiṇā*=*sa-snehā*. *Bhāgyeshu*, the Beng. and
S. have *bhogeshu*=*sukheshu*, 'in enjoyments,' 'in pleasures,' in which case
anutsekinī will mean 'not given to excess.' The latter word is literally
'spouting up' like a fountain. Compare *anutseko lakshmyām*, Bhartṛi-h.
ii. 54. *Padam*=*śabdam*, 'a title,' S.;=*vyavasāyam* or *pratishṭhām*, C.
Vāmāḥ=*tad-viparīta-kāriṇyaḥ*, S. ;=*tad-viruddhāḥ*, C.

[1] 'Lay to heart,' 'treasure up in thy heart,' 'ponder well.'

[2] 'Priyaṃvadā and my other dear friends;' cf. *Śārngarava-miśrāḥ*,
p. 151, l. 7, with note. My own MS. and two others insert *kim*.

[3] 'Are to be given away in marriage.' Cf. p. 48, l. 10, with note
thereon. *Ime api*; the dual terminations ī, ū, e do not coalesce with
following vowels, see Gram. 38; Pāṇ. i. 1, 11.

ᵃ चन्दणलदा विञ्व देसन्तरे जीविञ्चं धारइस्सं ।

काश्यपः ।

वत्से । किमेवं कातरासि ।

अभिजनवतो भर्तुः श्लाघ्ये स्थिता गृहिणीपदे
विभवगुरुभिः कृत्यैस्तस्य प्रतिक्षणमाकुला ।
तनयमचिरात्प्राचीवार्कं प्रसूय च पावनं
मम विरहजां न त्वं वत्से शुचं गणयिष्यसि ॥९९॥

‖ शकुन्तला पितुः पादयोः पतति ‖

ᵃ चन्दनलतेव देशान्तरे जीवितं धारयिष्यामि ।

---

¹ 'How now, removed from my foster-father's side, like a tendril of the
sandal-tree uprooted from the slopes of Malaya, shall I support life in a
strange place ?' The Candana or sandal tree (σάνταλον), Sirium Myrti-
folium, is 'a large kind of myrtle with pointed leaves,' the wood of which
affords many highly esteemed perfumes, unguents, &c., and is celebrated
for its delicious scent. It is found chiefly on the slopes [*tata, upatyakā,*
Raghu-v. iv. 46, 48] of the Malaya mountains, which are thence called
candanāčala, the tree being sometimes called *Malaya-ja,* 'Malaya-born.'
Frequent allusion is made to this tree being infested by snakes (see
Raghu-v. iv. 48; Hitop. l. 1582). *Tara,* of which the Sanskrit equivalent
is probably *tata,* is the reading of all the Deva-n. MSS. It is synonymous
with *utsanga,* 'the slope of a hill,' so that *Malayasya utsangāt* exactly
answers to *tātasya-ankāt* [*anka=utsanga,* Amara-k. iv. 1, 4]. *D* and *r*
are certainly interchangeable in Sanskrit and Prākrit, and the substitution
of *ḍ* for *ṭ* is usual. *L,* however, is the more common substitute, and it
might be supposed that *Malaya-tara* was for *Malaya-tala=Malayasya
upatyakā,* Raghu-v. iv. 46.

² 'Stationed in the honourable post of wife to a nobly-born husband ;
(and) incessantly [every moment] distracted with his affairs important
from his dignity ; having very shortly given birth to a pure son, like as
the Eastern-quarter (gives birth to) the Sun, thou wilt not take account,
O daughter, of the sorrow produced by separation from me.' *Abhijana-*

Verse 99. HARIṆĪ (a variety of ATYASHṬI). See verse 66.

काश्यपः ।

यदिच्छामि ते तदस्तु ।

शकुन्तला ॥ सख्यावुपेत्य ॥

[a] हला । दुवेबि मं समं एव्व परिस्सजह ।

सख्यौ ॥ तथा कृत्वा ॥

[b] सहि । जइ णाम सो राआ पच्चहिषाणमन्थरो भवे । तदो से इमं अत्तणोमहेअङ्किअं अङ्गुलीअअं दंसेहि ।

शकुन्तला ।

[c] इमिणा सन्देहेण वो आकम्पिदम्हि ।

सख्यौ ।

[d] मा भाआहि । अदिसिणेहो[2] पावसङ्की ।

शार्ङ्गरवः ।

युगान्तरमाारूढः सविता । त्वरतामत्रभवती ।

---

[a] हला । द्वे अपि मां सममेव परिष्वजेयाम् । [b] सखि । यदि नाम स राजा प्रत्यभिज्ञानमन्थरो भवेत् । ततोऽस्मायिदमात्मनामधेयाङ्कितमङ्गुलीयकं दर्शय ।
[c] अनेन सन्देहेन वामाकम्पितासि । [d] मा विभीहि । अतिस्नेहः पापशङ्की ।

---

vato = kulīnasya, see p. 15, n. 1. *Ākulā = vyagrā*, 'perplexed,' 'intently occupied,' S.; *= sasambhramā*, 'bewildered,' K. *Aćirāt = gamanāvyavahita-samaye*, 'immediately on thy arrival.' *Prāćī iva*, &c. *= yathā pūrva-dik pavitra-janakaṃ sūryam*, S.

[1] *Ātmanāmadheyāṅkita*, see p. 53, notes 2 and 3, and p. 140, l. 9, with note 2.

[2] 'Excessive affection is apt to suspect evil.' *Ati-snehaḥ*, so reads the Taylor MS. as well as my own, supported by K. S. observes, *tathā ćoktaṃ kirāte, prema paśyati bhayāni apade 'pi*, 'and so it is said in the Kirā-tārjunīya, "Affection sees causes of alarm [or dangers], even without foun-dation."' (See Kirāt. ix. 70.)

[3] 'The sun has ascended to another division (of the sky).' The Mackenzie MS. has *yugāntam adhirūḍhaḥ*; the Calcutta edition, *dūram adhirūḍhaḥ*; Chézy, *gagaṇāntaram adhirūḍhaḥ*. According to C., *yuga*

शकुन्तला ॥ आश्रमाभिमुखी स्थित्वा ॥

[a] ताद। कदा णु भूत्रो तवोवणं पेक्खिस्सं।

काश्यपः।

श्रूयताम्।

भूत्वा चिराय चतुरन्तमहीसपत्नी
दौष्यन्तिमप्रतिरथं तनयं निवेश्य।
भर्त्रा तदर्पितकुटुम्बभरेण सार्धं
शान्ते करिष्यसि पदं पुनराश्रमेऽस्मिन् ॥१००॥

[a] तात। कदा नु भूयस्तपोवनं प्रेक्षिष्ये।

---

is by some considered equivalent to *prahara*, 'a division of the day, comprising one-eighth of the sun's diurnal revolution, or three hours;' by others, to *hasta-ćatushṭaya*, 'a space of four cubits.' Dr. Boehtlingk translates, 'The sun has already entered the afternoon-quarter of the heavens.'

[1] 'Having become for a long time the fellow-wife of the Earth bounded by the four cardinal-points, having settled-in-marriage thy matchless-warrior son Daushyanti, in-company-with thy husband (Dushyanta), who shall have (first) transferred the cares of government [the burthen of family-cares] to him, thou shalt again set foot in this tranquil hermitage.' *Ćatur-anta-mahī* seems to be equivalent to *ćatur-dig-anta-mahī*, i. e. 'the earth as far as the four quarters,' 'the entire earth.' The Beng. have a parallel phrase *sa-dig-anta-mahī*. K. explains it by *ćatvāraḥ antāḥ yasyāḥ sā*. Cf. p. 124, l. 4. *Daushyanti* is a regular patronymic, from Dushyanta, as Dākshi, 'a descendant of Daksha,' from Daksha; Aindri from Indra, &c. (see Gram. 81. X). *A-pratiratham* = *asat-paripanthinam*, 'having no antagonist,' = *a-pratirathikam*, K.; *ratha* being put for *rathika* or *rathin*, 'a warrior who fights from a chariot.' *Niveśya* = *vivāhya*, 'having caused to marry,' K.; *niviś* has this sense in Mahā-bh. i. 7138. *Tad* refers to *Daushyanti*. *Arpita*, &c., cf. *aham api sūnau vinyasya rājyam*, Vikram., Act V; also

---

Verse 100. VASANTA-TILAKĀ (a variety of ŚAKVARI). See verses 8, 27, 31, 43, 46, 64, 74, 80, 82, 83, 91, 93, 94, 95.

गौतमी ।

a जादे । परिहीञ्चदि गमणवेला । णिवत्तेहि पिदरं । अहवा चिरेणबि पुणो पुणो एसा एव्वं मन्तइस्सदि । णिवत्तदु भंवं ।

काश्यपः ।

वत्से । उपरुध्यते तपोऽनुष्ठानम् ।

शकुन्तला ॥ भूयः पितरमालिङ्ग्य ॥

b तवच्चरणपीडिदं तादसरीरं । ता मा अदिमेत्तं मम किदे उक्कण्ठथ ।

a जाते । परिहीयते गमनवेला । निवर्तय पितरम् । अथवा चिरेणापि पुनः पुनरेवैवं मन्तयिष्यते । निवर्ततां भवान् । b तपश्चरणपीडितं तातशरीरम् । तस्मातिमात्रं मम कृते उत्कण्ठस्व ।

Manu vi. 2, 3, 'When the father of a family perceives his own wrinkles and grey hair, committing the care of his wife to his sons, or accompanied by her, let him repair to the woods,' i. e. let him enter upon the third quarter of his life, that of a hermit (see p. 157, n. 1 at the end). *Śānte,* cf. p. 20, l. 12. *Karishyasi padam,* cf. p. 145, n. 2 at the end.

[1] 'Allow the father to return; or rather, (since) even for a long time she will go on talking again and again in this manner, let your reverence return,' i. e. return at once yourself, without asking her permission. To depart without asking leave, is contrary to all Hindū ideas of politeness. *Athavā,* see p. 30, n. 3.

[2] 'The prosecution of (my) devotions is interrupted (by this detention).' Compare in Vikram., Act V, *uparudhyate me āśrama-vāsa-dharmaḥ.*

[3] 'Therefore do not beyond measure sorrow on my account.' *Ukkaṇṭha* for Sanskṛit *utkaṇṭha* or *utkaṇṭhasva* is the reading of my own MS. *Mā ukkaṇṭhidum* seems questionable. K. has *Bhūyo 'pi tapaś-caraṇa-pīḍitam tātasya śarīram atimātram mama kṛite utkaṇṭhitam bhavishyati.*

काश्यपः ॥ सनिःश्वासम् ॥

शममेष्यति मम शोकः कथं नु वत्से त्वया चरितपूर्वम् ।
उटजद्वारविरूढं नीवारबलिं विलोकयतः ॥१०१॥

गच्छ । शिवास्ते पन्थानः सन्तु ।

॥ निष्क्रान्ता शकुन्तला सहयायिनश्च ॥

---

[1] 'How, my child, will the grief of me, looking at the oblation of rice-grains formerly offered by thee, germinating at the door of the cottage, ever be assuaged [ever go to assuagement]?' *Carita*, so reads the Colebrooke MS.; the others have *racita-pūrvam = purā-vihitam*, S. *Carita* is supported by *caru*, 'an oblation of rice.' The *bali*, or *griha-bali*, is a particular kind of offering, identical with the *bhūta-yajña*, i.e. a sacrifice for all creatures, but especially in honour of those demigods and spiritual beings called *griha-devatāḥ*, 'household deities,' which are supposed to hover round and protect households (Manu iii. 80), or to whom some particular part of the house is sacred. This offering was made by throwing up into the air (Manu iii. 90), in some part of the house, generally at the door (Manu iii. 88), the remains of the morning and evening meal of rice or grain; uttering at the same time a *mantra* or prayer to some of the inferior deities, according to the place in which it was made (Manu iii. 87, &c.), whether to Indra with his followers the Maruts, or to Kuvera with his followers the Guhyakas, Kinnaras, Yakshas, &c., or to the spirits of trees, waters, &c. (Manu iii. 88, 89). According to Colebrooke it might be presented with the following Paurāṇik prayer, 'May gods, men, cattle, birds, demigods, benevolent genii, serpents, demons, departed spirits, blood-thirsty savages, trees, and all who desire food given by me—may reptiles, insects, flies, and all hungry beings or spirits concerned in this rite, obtain contentment from this food left them by me!' It was sometimes offered by the women of the house, who might assist in any sacrifice, provided they abstained from repeating the Mantras (Manu iii. 121), and as the offering was intended for all creatures, even the animals were supposed to have their share in it (Manu iii. 92). In point of fact the crows, dogs, insects, &c. in the neighbourhood of the house were the real consumers of it (whence *bali-pushṭa, bali-bhuj, griha-bali-bhuj*, as names

---

Verse 101. ĀRYĀ or GĀTHĀ. See verse 2.

⏑⏑− | ⏑⏑⏑⏑ | −− ‖ ⏑−⏑ | −− | ⏑−⏑ | ⏑⏑− | −
⏑⏑− | −⏑⏑ | −−‖ −− | ⏑⏑− | ⏑ | −⏑⏑ | −

सख्यौ ॥ शकुन्तलां विलोक्य ॥

[a] हद्दी हद्दी । अन्तलिहिदा[1] सउन्दला वणराईए ।

काश्यपः ॥ सनिःश्वासम् ॥

अनसूये । गतवती वां सहधर्मचारिणी । निगृह्य
शोकमनुगच्छतं मां प्रस्थितम् ।

उभे ।

[b] ताद । सउन्दलाविरहिदं सुष्षं विच्च तवोवणं कहं
पविसामो ।

काश्यपः ।

स्नेहप्रवृत्तिरेवंदर्शिनी[2] । ॥ सविमर्शं परिक्रम्य ॥ हन्तं[3] भोः । शकुन्त-

[a] हा धिक् हा धिक् । अन्तर्हिता शकुन्तला वनराज्या ।   [b] तात ।
शकुन्तलाविरहितं शून्यमिव तपोवनं कथं प्रविशावः ।

---

of a crow, crane, sparrow, &c., compare Hitop. l. 1076), and such of the
grains as escaped being devoured by them would be likely to germinate
about the threshold. This *bali* formed one of the five great religious rites,
sometimes called sacraments, which the householder who maintained a
perpetual fire (see p. 148, n. 1) had daily to perform (Manu iii. 67, iv. 21).
See Indian Wisdom, pp. 203, 251. It was in honour of all creatures of
every description, but particularly of those not provided for by the other
four sacrifices. It might have reference, however, to the deities and beings
honoured in the other sacraments. That it had especial reference to the
Griha-devatāh is indicated in Manu iii. 117, with commentary; and in the
Mṛicchakaṭikā, where Ćārudatta, after fulfilling the Deva-kārya, or second
of the five rites (cf. p. 140, l. 17), is described as offering the *bali* to the
household gods around the threshold. His speech, as he offers it, corresponds remarkably with that of Kāśyapa, *Yāsām balih sapadi mad-
griha-dehalīnām, hansaiś ća sārasa-ganaiś ća vilupta-pūrvah, tāsv eva samprati virūdha-triṇānkurāsu, vījānjalih patati kīṭa-mukhāvalīḍhah.* See
Mṛicch., Act I, verse 1. For *śivās te panthānah santu,* in the next line,
see p. 163, n. 1 at the end.

[1] So read all the Deva-n. for *antarihidā,* cf. p. 140, l. 6.

[2] 'The course of affection views it thus.' The Beng. MSS. have *sneha-
vrittir,* and one (I. O. 1050) *evaṃ śansinī* for *evaṃ darśinī. Yasmin
vishaye sneho bhavati tad-asānnidhyād etādṛiśa eva kramo bhavati,* S'.

[3] *Hanta,* here an exclamation of joy (*harshe,* S'.)

लां पतिकुलं विसृज्य लब्धमिदानीं स्वास्थ्यम्¹ । कुतः ।
अर्थो हि कन्या परकीय एव
तामद्य सम्प्रेष्य परिग्रहीतुः ।
जातो ममायं विशदः प्रकामं
प्रत्यर्पितन्यास इवान्तरात्मा² ॥ १०२ ॥

॥ इति निष्क्रान्ताः सर्वे ॥

॥ चतुर्थोऽङ्कः ॥

---

¹ 'My natural serenity of mind,' 'my natural good spirits.'   A load of
anxiety is taken off my mind.

² 'Verily a girl is another's property.   Having to-day sent her to her
husband, this my conscience has become quite clear, as if (after) restoring a
deposit.' *Kanyā-rūpo 'rthaḥ*, &c., ' the property consisting of a girl belongs
to another,' S'. and C̓.   *Parigrahītuḥ=pariṇetuḥ*.   Hence *parigraha*, ' a
wife,' see p. 124, l. 3.   The ceremonies of marriage are described by Colebrooke in the Asiatic Researches, vol. vii. pp. 288–311, thus :—The bridegroom goes in procession to the house of the bride's father.   The bride is
given to him by her father, and their hands, on which turmeric has been
previously rubbed, are bound together with Kuśa grass.   The bridegroom
next makes oblations to the sacred household fire, and the bridegroom
drops rice into it.   The bridegroom solemnly takes her hand in marriage
(whence he is called *pāṇi-grahītri*, and marriage *pāṇi-grahaṇa*), and leads
her round the sacred fire (whence he is called *pariṇetri*).   The bride steps
seven times, and the marriage is then irrevocable.   *Viśadaḥ=prasannaḥ*,
' serene,' ' tranquil,' K. ;=*susthaḥ*, S'.   Cf. *manasaḥ prasādaḥ*, Vikram.,
Act V.   *Prakāmam=atyartham*, see p. 108, n. 3.   The Beng. reading is
jāto 'smi samyag viṣadāntarātmā, ćirasya nikshepam ivārpayitvā.

Verse 102.   INDRA-VAJRĀ (a variety of TRISHṬUBH), containing eleven syllables to
the Pāda or quarter-verse, each Pāda being alike.

− − ◡ − − ◡◡ − ◡ − − ‖

॥ अथ पञ्चमोऽङ्कः ॥

॥ ततः प्रविशत्यासनस्थो राजा विदूषकश्च ॥

विदूषकः ॥ कर्णं दत्त्वा ॥

[1]भो भो वअस्स । सङ्गीदसालन्तरे अवधाणं देहि । कलविसुद्धाए गीदीए सरसञ्ञोओ सुणीअदि । जाणे । तत्तहोदी हंसवदिआ वण्णपरिञ्चअं करेदि[3]त्ति ।

राजा ।

तूष्णीं भव । यावदाकर्णयामि ।

[a] भो भो वयस्य । सङ्गीतशालान्तरेऽवधानं देहि । कलविशुद्धायां गीतां स्वरसंयोगः श्रूयते । जाने । तच्चभवती हंसपदिका वर्णपरिचयं करोतीति ।

---

[1] In the Beng. MSS. the speech of the Chamberlain at p. 186 commences the Act.

[2] 'Turn (thy) attention to the interior of the music-hall. In a soft and clear song harmonious sounds are heard [the union of notes is heard].' *Īśvarāṇāṃ yatra nṛityādikam bhavati sā saṅgīta-śālā,* 'a music-saloon is a place where dancing &c. is performed before princes,' S. *Avadhānam,* K. has *avadhāraṇam. Gītyām=dhruvāyām,* K. Prākṛit *gīdie* may stand for instr., gen., or loc. cases. *Svara-saṃyoga,* K. has *svara-yoga.* Both expressions occur in Mṛicch. (p. 33, l. 2; p. 94, l. 1; p. 222, l. 5; p. 339, l. 9), and in the Mālavik. (p. 67, l. 6, with note).

[3] 'Is practising singing,' lit. 'is making acquaintance with the Varṇas.' *Paricaya=abhyāsa,* C. *Varṇa,* 'the order or arrangement of a song.' It may also mean 'a musical mode.' These modes are numerous, personified either as male (Rāga) or female (Rāgiṇī). According to S. and C., the Varṇas intended here are of four kinds, the first two corresponding with the division of the Bhāvas, or 'affections.' *Gītishu ćatvāra varṇā bhavanti yad āha Bharataḥ, Sthāyī tathaiva Sanćārī tathā Rohāvarohiṇau. Varṇāś ćatvāra evaite kathitāḥ sarva-gītishu.*

|| आकाशे गीयते ||

[a]अहिणवमहुलोलुबो तुमं
तह परिचुम्बिञ्च चूअमञ्जरिं।
कमलवसइमेत्तणिव्वुदो
महुअर विम्हरिदोसि णं कहं ॥१०३॥

राजा।

अहो रागपरिवाहिणी गीतिः[2]।

[a] अभिनवमधुलोलुपस्त्वं तथा परिचुम्ब्य चूतमञ्जरीम्।
कमलवसतिमात्रनिर्वृतो मधुकर विस्मृतोऽस्येनां कथम् ॥

---

[1] 'O Bee, how (can it be) that thou, eagerly-longing for fresh honey, after having so kissed the mango-blossom, shouldst (now) be forgetful of it, being altogether satisfied with (thy) dwelling in the lotus!' *Ćūta-mañjarī=āmra-kalikā*, S'. Cf. in Vikram., Act II, *Īshad-baddha-rajaḥ-kaṇāgra-kapiśā ćūte navā mañjarī*. *Kamala-vasati=kamalāvasthiti*, C. The fondness of the bee (which in Sanskrit is masculine) for the lotus is so great that he will remain for a long time in the interior of the flower. Cf. *na pankajam tad yad alīna-shaṭpadam*, 'that is not a lotus which has no bee clinging to it,' Bhaṭṭi-k. ii. 19; also *guñjad-dvirepho 'yam ambuja-sthaḥ*, 'the murmuring bee remaining in the lotus,' Ṛitu-s. vi. 15; and *idam ruṇaddhi mām padmam antaḥ-kvaṇita-shaṭpadam*, Vikram., Act IV. *Madhu-kara*, see p. 33, n. 1. *Vismṛita*, see p. 161, n. 3. In Prākṛit, two forms *mar* and *sumar* are used for *smṛi;* the first becomes *mhar* after a preposition (as in *vimhao* for *vismayaḥ*, Vararući iii. 32); but *vimarido* would be equally correct according to Vararući iii. 56. K. observes that, under the figure of a bee, Haṇsapadikā covertly reproves the king for having forgotten her. S'. and C. call this verse a *Praććhādaka*, and the following from Kavi-kaṇṭhahāra is quoted, *anyāsaktam patim matvā prema-viććheda-manyunā vīṇā-purahsaram gānam striyāḥ praććhādako mataḥ.*

[2] 'Oh, what an impassioned strain!' lit. a song overflowing with affection or passion. *Rāga-parivāhiṇī=anurāga-nishyandinī*, S'.;=*kāma-sampūrṇā*, K. Cf. p. 89, n. 3.

Verse 103. APARA-VAKTRĀ. See verse 90.

विदूषकः ।

[a] किं दाव गीदीए अवगदो अक्खरत्थो ।

राजा ॥ स्मितं कृत्वा ॥

सकृत्कृतप्रणयोऽयं जनः । तदस्या देवीं वसुमतीमन्तरेण महदुपालम्भनं गतोऽस्मि । सखे माठव्य । मङ्गचनादुच्यतां हंसपदिका । निपुणमुपालब्धोऽस्मीति ।

विदूषकः ।

[b] जं भवं आणवेदि । ॥ उत्थाय ॥ [c] भो वअस्स । गहीदस्स ताए परकीएहिं हत्थेहिं सिहरडए ताडीअमाणस्स अच्छराए वीदरागस्स विअ एत्थिय दाणिं मे मोक्खो ।

---

[a] किं तावद्गीत्या अवगतोऽक्षरार्थः ।   [b] यद्भवानाज्ञापयति ।   [c] भो वयस्य । गृहीतस्य तया परकीयैर्हस्तैः शिखण्डके ताड्यमानस्याप्सरसा वीतरागस्येव नास्तीदानीं मे मोक्षः ।

---

[1] 'The meaning of the words,' lit. 'of the letters or syllables.'

[2] 'This person [*i. e.* I] once made love (to her); therefore I am incurring her severe censure on account of the queen Vasumatī.' *Krita-praṇayaḥ* = *kṛita-premā. Ayaṃ janaḥ,* i. e. *mad-rūpaḥ,* 'consisting of me,' S'. Cf. p. 144, n. 2. *Vasumatī* is a name for the earth, cf. p. 124, n. 1. *Anta-reṇa,* with accusative, see p. 81, n. 2. After *kṛita-praṇayo 'yaṃ janaḥ,* the Calcutta edition adds *ity aksharārthaḥ,* 'such is the meaning of the words.'

[3] 'There is not now any liberation for me (suffered to be) seized by her with the hands of others by-the-hair-on-the-crown-of-my-head (and) beaten, any more than for a sage-with-suppressed-passions (if taken un-awares) by a lovely-nymph.' *S'ikhaṇḍaka* is 'the lock of hair left on the crown of the head at tonsure.' This was the only portion of hair suffered to remain on the head of a Brāhman; but in the case of the military class, three or five locks, called *kāka-pakshāḥ,* were left on each side. The two ceremonies of tonsure are included by Manu among the twelve S'aṇskāras or rites which every Brāhman had to undergo. The first, or *chūḍā-karaṇa,* took place from one to three years old, generally after teething (Manu ii. 35); the second, or final tonsure *kes'ānta,* in the sixteenth year from con-ception (ii. 65). *Moksha* has here a double sense, 'liberation of the body

राजा ।

गच्छ । नागरिकवृत्त्या सञ्ज्ञापयैनाम् ।

विटूषकः ।

[a] का गई । ॥ इति निष्क्रान्तः ॥

राजा ॥ आत्मगतम् ॥

किं नु खलु गीतार्थमाकर्ण्येष्टजनविरहादृते ऽपि बल-
वदुत्कण्ठितो ऽस्मि । अथवा ।

रम्याणि वीक्ष्य मधुरांश्च निशम्य शब्दा-
न्पर्युत्सुकीभवति यत्सुखितो ऽपि जन्तुः ।
तच्चेतसा स्मरति नूनमबोधपूर्वं
भावस्थिराणि जननान्तरसौहृदानि ॥१०४॥

॥ इति पर्याकुलस्तिष्ठति ॥

[a] का गतिः ।

---

from danger,' and 'liberation of the soul from further transmigration;'
see n. 3 below. The last was the great object of sages and devotees in
their bodily mortifications, but was often obstructed by the seductive
artifices of Indra's nymphs (see p. 45, n. 1).

[1] 'In the courtly [fashionable] style.' *Praviṇasya ṛityā*, K. *Nāgarika*
here means more than 'polite.' It implies 'insincerity,' as when a man
shews exaggerated attention to his first mistress, while he is courting some
one else.

[2] *Kā gatiḥ*, see p. 62, l. 2, with note 2.

[3] 'When a being (in other respects) happy becomes conscious-of-an
ardent-longing on seeing charming objects and hearing sweet sounds, then
in all probability, without being aware of it, he remembers with his mind
the friendships of former births, firmly-rooted in his heart.' *Ramyāṇi*, i. e.
vastūni, S. For *ramyāṇi* K. has *rūpāṇi* and *sthitāni* for *sthirāṇi*. *A-bodha-
pūrvam*, 'without any previous intimation or suggestion,' 'unconsciously.'
Compare the similar expressions, *a-mati-pūrvam, a-buddhi-pūrvam*, 'without
any previous idea.' The doctrine of transmigration is an essential dogma

---

Verse 104. VASANTA-TILAKĀ (a variety of ŚAKVARĪ). See verses 8, 27, 31, 43, 46,
64, 74, 80, 82, 83, 91, 93, 94, 95, 100.

॥ ततः प्रविशति कञ्चुकी ॥

कञ्चुकी ।

अहो नु खल्वीदृशीमवस्यां प्रतिपन्नोऽस्मि ।

आचार इत्यवहितेन मया गृहीता

या वेत्रयष्टिरवरोधगृहेषु राज्ञः ।

काले गते बहुतिथे मम सैव जाता

प्रस्थानविक्लवगतेरवलम्बनार्थम् ॥१०५॥

---

of the Hindū religion; see Indian Wisdom, p. 67. Dim recollections of occurrences in a former life are supposed occasionally to cross the mind, and the present condition of every person is supposed to derive its character of happiness or misery, elevation or degradation, from the virtues or vices of a previous state of being. The consequences of actions in a former birth are called *vipāka*.

[1] The Kañćukin or Chamberlain was the attendant on the women's apartments. S'. and C'. quote the following from Bharata: *Antaḥpura-ćaro vriddho vipro guṇa-gaṇānvitaḥ sarva-kāryārtha-kuśalaḥ kañćukīti abhidhīyate. Jarā-vaiklavya-yuktena viśed gātreṇa kañćukī*, 'the character styled Kañćukin is an attendant in the inner apartments, an old man, a Brāhman, endowed with numerous good qualities, and a clever man of business. The Kañćukin should enter with a body decrepit and tottering from age.' Compare this scene, and the speeches of the Chamberlain, with the opening scene of Act III. of Vikram.

[2] 'The wand [staff of office] which was assumed by me, having to watch over the royal female apartments, thinking, "It is a matter of form," much time having elapsed since then, that same (wand) has become (indispensable, or a useful crutch) for the support of me whose step falters in walking.' *Vetra-yashṭi*, properly 'a cane-stick,' used as a badge of office, like the gold stick or black rod in European courts. *Avahitena*, lit. 'attentive,' 'careful,' 'watchful,' i. e. appointed to a careful superintendence or watch. So read all the Deva-n.; the Beng., with S'., have *adhikṛitena*, i. e. 'by me set over,' &c. *Avarodha-griheshu*, see p. 21, n. 3. *Bahutithe* = *bahu-saṅkhye*, Chézy. K. observes that *bahu* is here treated as a numeral, *titha* being a kind of ordinal suffix (Gram. p. 66. LXIII).

Verse 105. VASANTA-TILAKĀ (a variety of S'AKVARĪ). See verses 8, 27, 31, 43, 46, 64, 74, 80, 82, 83, 91, 93, 94, 95, 100, 104.

भोः । कामं धर्मकार्यमनतिपात्यं देवस्य । तथापीदानीमेव
धर्मासनादुत्थितस्य पुनरुपरोधकारि कखशिष्यागमन-
मस्मै नोत्सहे निवेदयितुम् । अथवा । अविश्रामोऽयं
लोकतन्त्राधिकारः । कुतः ।

भानुः सकृद्युक्ततुरङ्ग एव
राचिन्दिवं गन्धवहः प्रयाति ।
शेषः सदैवाहितभूमिभारः
षष्ठांशवृत्तेरपि धर्म एषः ॥१०६॥

यावन्नियोगमनुतिष्ठामि । ॥ परिक्रम्यावलोक्य च ॥ एष देवः ।

प्रजाः प्रजाः स्वा इव तन्त्रयित्वा
निषेवते श्रान्तमना विविक्तम् ।

---

¹ 'But (why should I hesitate?) this office of supporting the world
does not (admit of) repose.' *Athavā*, see p. 30, n. 3. *Loka-tantra*, one
meaning of *tantra* is 'supporting a family.'

² 'Because the Sun having but once (and once) only yoked his steeds
travels onwards; night and day the wind (also travels); S'esha has the
burden of the earth always resting (on his head). This also is the duty
of him whose subsistence is on the sixth part (of the produce of the soil).'
Kutah, see p. 55, n. 2. *Bhānu*, 'the Sun;' see p. 142, n. 3. 'In other
chariots the horses are yoked again after an interval of rest, but the horses
of the Sun are allowed no repose,' S'. *Sūrya evambhūtah san prayāti*, S'.
Gandha-vaha, lit. 'the scent-bearer,'=*vāyu*, S'. *S'esha*=*Ananta*, a mytho-
logical serpent, the personification of eternity (*ananta-tā*) and king of the
Nāgas or snakes who inhabit the lowermost of the seven Pātālas or infernal regions. His body formed the couch of Vishnu, reposing on the
waters of Chaos, whilst his thousand heads were the god's canopy. He is
also said to uphold the world on one of his heads. He has become incarnate at various times, especially in the god Bala-rāma, the elder brother of
Krishna. *Ahita*, see p. 149, n. 1. *Shashthānsa-vritter*, see p. 84, n. 1.

Verse 106. INDRA-VAJRĀ (a variety of TRISHṬUBH), containing eleven syllables to
the Pāda or quarter-verse, each Pāda being alike.

$$-- \cup -- \cup \cup - \cup -- \parallel$$

यूथानि सञ्चार्य रविप्रतप्तः
श्रीतं दिवा स्थानमिव द्विपेन्द्रः ॥१०७॥[1]

॥ उपगम्य ॥ जयतु जयतु देवः । एते खलु हिमवतो
गिरेरुपत्यकारण्यवासिनः काश्यपसन्देशमादाय सस्त्रीका-
स्तपस्विनः सम्प्राप्ताः । श्रुत्वा देवः प्रमाणम्[2] ।

राजा ॥ सादरम् ॥

किं काश्यपसन्देशहारिणः ।

कञ्चुकी ।

अथ किम्[3] ।

राजा ।

तेन हि मद्वचनाद्विज्ञाप्यतामुपाध्यायः सोमरातः ।
अमूनाश्रमवासिनः श्रौतेन विधिना[4] सत्कृत्य स्वयमेव
प्रवेशयितुमर्हतीति । अहमप्यत्र तपस्विदर्शनोचिते प्रदेशे
स्थितः प्रतिपालयामि ।

---

[1] 'Having supported his subjects as his own children, wearied in mind he seeks seclusion, as the chief of the elephants scorched by the sun, after conducting the herds to their pastures, in the (heat of the) day (seeks) a cool spot.' *Tantrayitvā*, from a nominal verb *tantraya* (see p. 187, n. 1), is the reading of all the Beng. MSS., supported by K.; two of the Deva-n., *sāntrayitvā*; the Mackenzie, *harshayitvā*. *Śrānta-manāḥ* is the reading of the Mackenzie, supported by K.; the other Deva-n., *śānta-manāḥ*, 'composed in mind.' *Sañcārya*, lit. 'having caused to move about or graze,'=*bhramayitvā*, S. *Vivikta*=*vijana-pradeśa*. *Divā*=*madhyāhne*, 'in the middle of the day.' *Dvipendraḥ* = *hasti-rājaḥ* = *yūtha-nāthaḥ*, 'a large elephant, the leader of a wild herd.'

[2] 'Having heard, your Majesty must decide (what is to be done).' K. supplies *yat kartavyam*. *Pramāṇam*, see p. 31, n. 1 at the end.

[3] *Atha kim* is used *svīkāre*, S. (see p. 46, n. 3).

[4] 'In the form enjoined by the scriptures' (=*śruti-bodhitena pra-kāreṇa*, S.)

Verse 107. Upajāti or Ākhyānakī (a variety of Trishṭubh). See verse 41.

कञ्चुकी ।

यदाज्ञापयति देवः । ॥ इति निष्क्रान्तः ॥

राजा ॥ उत्थाय ॥

वेत्रवति । अग्निशरणमार्गमादेशय[1] ।

प्रतीहारी ।

[a]इदो इदो देवी ।

राजा ॥ परिक्रामति । अधिकारखेदं निरूप्य ॥

सर्वः प्रार्थितमर्थमधिगम्य सुखी सम्पद्यते जन्तुः । राज्ञां
तु चरितार्थता दुःखोत्तरैव[2] ।

औत्सुक्यमात्रमवसादयति प्रतिष्ठा
क्लिश्नाति लब्धपरिपालनवृत्तिरेव ।
नातिश्रमापनयनाय न च श्रमाय
राज्यं स्वहस्तधृतदण्डमिवातपत्रम् ॥१०८॥[3]

[a] इत इतो देवः ।

---

[1] *Agni-śarana,* see p. 148, n. 1. *Mārga,* see p. 161, l. 4, with note.

[2] 'The attainment of the object (of their ambition) is followed by pain.' *Ćaritārthatā=rājya-prāptiḥ,* 'the attainment of the throne,' S. *Duḥkhottarā=kheda-samvalitā,* 'encompassed with trouble,' S.

[3] 'The-attainment-of-the-object-of-ambition satisfies anxious longing merely; the very business of guarding what has been obtained, harasses. Royalty [the office of king], like a parasol, the handle of which is held in the hand, is not for the removal of great fatigue without leading to fatigue.' *Autsukyam=utkaṇṭhā,* 'longing,' 'eager desire;' such as *kadā rājā bhavishyāmītyādi,* 'when shall I become king, &c.?' *tam eva duḥkha-dāyinī pratishṭhā avasādayati,* 'that (desire) certainly the harassing attainment-of-the-highest-rank allays,' Ć. S. reads *pratishṭhām,* and places it in opposition to *autsukya-mātram,* making *rājyam* nom. to *avasādayati.* The Beng. MS. [I. O. 1060] gives *pratishṭhām* in the margin, and this reading is certainly supported by a parallel passage (*sādayantī pratishṭhām,* &c.) in the beginning of Act III. of Vikram. Ć. also notices

---

Verse 108. VASANTA-TILAKĀ (a variety of ŚAKVARI). See verses 8, 27, 31, 43, 46, 64, 74, 80, 82, 83, 91, 93, 94, 95, 100, 104, 105.

॥ नेपथ्ये ॥

वैतालिकौ[1] ।

विजयतां देवः ।

प्रथमः ।

स्वसुखनिरभिलाषः खिद्यसे लोकहेतोः
प्रतिदिनमथवा ते वृत्तिरेवंविधैव ।

this reading, but adopts the one in the text and censures the interpretation of S'. *Pratishṭhā* may have the sense I have given, which agrees with the *prārthitārthādhigamaḥ* and *ćaritārthatā* of the preceding lines. *Atiśrama* may either refer to the trouble which the king has undergone in arriving at the object of his ambition, or to the troubles of his subjects which it is his office to remove. In the latter case *na ća śramāya* will mean 'without leading to personal trouble or weariness.' The Indian *ćhattra*, or parasol, from the shelter it affords has been chosen as one of the insignia of royalty. It is very heavy, and being fixed on a long pole greatly fatigues the person holding it. It is always borne by a servant; but here the king is figuratively made to bear it himself, so that he cannot give shelter to himself and others, without undergoing great personal fatigue. *Na ća śramāya* is found in all the Deva-n. MSS.; the Beng. have *yathā śramāya*, i.e. 'royalty does not so much lead to the removal of fatigue as to fatigue.' According to K., who repeats the first negative before *na ća śramāya*, the two negatives are here employed affirmatively, i.e. to affirm that royalty does lead to personal fatigue. 'It is not for the removal of great fatigue and not not for fatigue.' Cf. a similar use of two negatives on p. 24, l. 10, with note.

[1] *Vaitālika = vandin*, 'a herald,' Ć.; = *stuti-pāṭhaka*, 'a panegyrist,' S'. He was a kind of herald or crier, whose duty was to announce, in measured verse, the fixed periods into which the king's day was divided. The strain which he poured forth usually contained allusions to incidental circumstances. In Vikram. and Ratn., only one Vaitālika appears, but here and in the Mālavik. there are two. In Vikram., Act II, he announces the sixth hour or watch of the day, about two or three o'clock, at which period alone the king is allowed to amuse himself. From the Daśakumāra it appears that a king's day and night were supposed to be divided into eight portions of one hour and a half, reckoned from sunrise, for distributing which strict directions are given, thus: Day—1. The king being dressed, is to audit accounts; 2. He is to pronounce judgment in appeals; 3. He is to breakfast; 4. He is to receive and make presents;

अनुभवति हि मूर्ध्ना पादपस्तीव्रमुष्णं
शमयति परितापं छायया संश्रितानाम् ॥१०९॥

द्वितीयः ।

नियमयसि विमार्गप्रस्थितानात्तदण्डः
प्रशमयसि विवादं कल्पसे रक्षणाय ।
अतनुषु विभवेषु ज्ञातयः सन्तु नाम
त्वयि तु परिसमाप्तं बन्धुकृत्यं प्रजानाम् ॥११०॥

---

5. He is to discuss political questions with his ministers; 6. He is to amuse himself; 7. He is to review his troops; 8. He is to hold a military council. Night—1. He is to receive the reports of his spies and envoys; 2. He is to sup or dine; 3. He is to retire to rest, after the perusal of some sacred work; 4 and 5. He is to sleep; 6. He is to rise and purify himself; 7. He is to hold a private consultation with his ministers, and instruct his officers; 8. He is to attend upon the *Purohita*, or family priest, for the performance of religious ceremonies. See Wilson's Hindū Theatre, vol. i. p. 209.

[1] 'Indifferent to thine own ease, thou endurest toil every day for the sake of (thy) people. But thy regular-business is of this very kind. For the tree suffers intense heat with its head (while) it allays by (its) shade the heat of those seeking (its) shelter.' *Athavā*, see p. 30, n. 3. *Vṛittir,* some of the Beng., supported by K. and S'., have *sṛishṭir.*

[2] 'Having assumed the mace [sceptre] thou restrainest those who advance on the wrong road [set out on bad courses]; thou composest differences; thou art adequate to the protection (of thy people). Let kinsmen make their appearance forsooth in affluent circumstances [when there is abundant property], but in thee the whole duty of a kinsman is comprehended towards thy subjects.' *Átta-daṇḍa = gṛihīta-daṇḍa; daṇḍa,* 'a magistrate's staff,' taken as a symbol of punishment and justice; it is sometimes 'the sceptre of a king;' hence *daṇḍa-dhara, daṇḍin,* 'staff-bearer,' &c., are names for Yama, the god of justice and lord of punishment. *Vimārga,* some have *kumārga,* 'bad ways.' *Kalpase = sampadyase,* K. Manu furnishes several examples of *kḷrip* in the sense of 'to be sufficient,' 'to be fit' (see ii. 151, ii. 266, vi. 20; also Raghu-v. viii. 40).

Verses 109 and 110. MĀLINĪ or MĀNINĪ (a variety of ATI-ŚAKVARĪ). See verses 10, 19, 20, 38, 55.

राजा ।

एते क्लान्तमनसः पुनर्नवीकृताः स्मः । ॥ इति परिक्रामति ॥

प्रतीहारी ।

[1]अहिणवसम्मज्जणससिरीओ सन्निहिदहोमधेणू अग्गि-
सरणालिंदो । आरुहदु देवो ।

राजा ॥ आरुह्य परिजनांसावलम्बी तिष्ठति ॥

वेत्रवति । किमुद्दिश्य भगवता काश्यपेन मत्सकाशमृषयः
प्रेरिताः स्युः ।

किं तावद्व्रतिनामुपोढतपसां विघ्नैस्तपो दूषितं
धर्मारण्यचरेषु केनचिदुत प्राणिष्वसच्चेष्टितम् ।
आहो स्वित्प्रसवो ममापचरितैर्विष्टम्भितो वीरुधा-
मित्यारूढबहुप्रतर्कमपरिच्छेदाकुलं मे मनः ॥१११॥

[a] अभिनवसम्मार्जनसश्रीकः सन्निहितहोमधेनुरग्निशरणालिन्दः । आरोहतु देवः ।

___

Atanushu vibhaveshu=utsaveshu, ‘at times of festivity.’ *Kukshim-bhari-bhis taiḥ kim prayojanam,* ‘what is the use of these parasitical gluttons as relations?’ K. The Calcutta ed. and S'. have *samvibhaktāḥ* for *santu nāma.* The meaning may certainly be, ‘let kinsmen make their appearance (i. e. start up they will on all sides) when there is plenty of property to divide.’ K. refers to verse 155, towards the end of Act VI. of this play, *yena yena viyujyante prajāḥ,* &c., ‘let it be publicly announced that of whatever dear kinsman his subjects are deprived, Dushyanta will be (in the place of) that (kinsman) to them, the wicked excepted.’

[1] The use of *ete* with 1st pers. pl. of the verb is noticeable, see p. 133, n. 2.

[2] ‘The terrace of the fire-sanctuary, with the cow (that yields the ghee) for the oblations close by, is beautiful after its recent purification.’ *Sa-śrīka,* lit. ‘possessed of the goddess of beauty;’ a bold metaphor, used elsewhere by Kālidāsa. *Homa-dhenu, agni-śarana,* see p. 148, n. 1.

[3] ‘Has the devotion [penance] of the ascetics, who have collected a store of penitential merit, been frustrated by impediments? or else has any harm been inflicted by any one on the animals grazing in the sacred

___

Verse 111. ŚĀRDŪLA-VIKRĪḌITA (a variety of ATIDHṚITI). See verses 14, 30, 36, 39, 50, 63, 79, 85, 86, 89, 97, 98.

प्रतीहारी ।

ᵃसुञ्चरिदणन्दिणो इसीओ देवं सभाजइदुं आञ्चदेत्ति तक्केमि ।

॥ ततः प्रविशन्ति गौतमीसहिताः शकुन्तलां पुरस्कृत्य मुनयः । पुरस्त्वैषां कञ्चुकी पुरोहितश्च ॥

कञ्चुकी ।

इत इतो भवन्तः ।

शार्ङ्गरवः ।

शारद्वत ।

महाभागः कामं नरपतिरभिन्नस्थितिरसौ
न कश्चिद्वर्णानामपथमपकृष्टोऽपि भजते ।
तथापीदं शश्वत्परिचितविविक्तेन मनसा
जनाकीर्णं मन्ये हुतवहपरीतं गृहमिव ॥११२॥

ᵃ सुचरितनन्दिन ऋषयो देवं सभाजयितुमागता इति तर्कयामि ।

grove? Or is it that the flowering of the creeping plants has been checked [stopped, stunted] through my misdeeds? Thus my mind, in which so many doubtful-conjectures have arisen, is perplexed with an inability to decide.' *Upoḍha=samprāpta*, K. *Vighnais*, see p. 40, n. 5. *Dharmā-raṇya-ćareshu prāṇishu*, cf. p. 13, l. 3. *Āho svit*, used as particles of doubt, see Gram. 717. h. *Prasavaḥ*, i. e. *pushpa-phalādi*, 'the flower, fruit, &c.,' K. *Apa-ćaritaiḥ=dur-āćāraiḥ*.

[1] 'To pay homage to.' *Sabhāj* is one of the few dissyllabic roots.

[2] 'Granted that this king eminent-in-virtues [of high parts] swerves not from rectitude; (and that) not one of the classes, (not) even the lowest, addicts itself to evil courses; nevertheless with my mind perpetually familiarized to seclusion I regard this thronged (palace) as a house enveloped in flames.' *Kāmam* occurs frequently in this sense (cf. p. 24, l. 10; p. 55, n. 3). *Abhinna-sthitiḥ=avihata-maryādaḥ*, K.;=*sa-mar-yādaḥ*, S'. *Asau*, so read the Beng. and the Mackenzie MSS.; the others have *aho*. *Varṇānām*, i. e. *brāhmaṇādīnām*. *Apakṛishṭo 'pi*, 'even the lowest (class).' The castes were originally four in number : 1. Brāhmans or priests; 2. Kshatriyas or soldiers; 3. Vaiśyas or merchants and husband-men; 4. Sūdras or slaves; see p. 84, n. 3. *A-patha*, 'a wrong road,' 'a bad

Verse 112. ŚIKHARIṆĪ (a variety of ATYASHṬI). See verses 9, 24, 44, 62.

शार्ङ्गरवः ।

स्थाने भवान्पुरप्रवेशादित्थम्भूतः संवृत्तः । अहमपि
अभ्यक्तमिव स्नातः शुचिरशुचिमिव प्रबुद्ध इव सुप्तम् ।
बद्धमिव स्वैरगतिर्जनमिह सुखसङ्गिनमवैमि[1] ॥११३॥

शकुन्तला ॥ निमित्तं सूचयित्वा ॥

[a] अम्महे । किं मे वामेदरं[3] णञ्चणं[2] विप्फुरदि ।

गौतमी ।

[b] जादे । पडिहदं अमङ्गलं । सुहाइं दे भत्तुकुलदेवदाओ
वितरन्दु । ॥ इति परिक्रामति ॥

पुरोहितः ॥ राजानं निर्दिश्य ॥

भो भोस्तपस्विनः । असावत्रभवान्वर्णाश्रमाणां रक्षिता[4]
प्रागेव मुक्तासनो[5] वः प्रतिपालयति । पश्यतैनम् ।

[a] अहो । किं मे वामेतरं नयनं विस्फुरति ।   [b] जाते । प्रतिहतममङ्गलम् ।
शुभानि ते भर्तृकुलदेवता वितरन्तु ।

---

road ;' a common metaphor, like *a-mārga, un-mārga, vi-mārga*, to express
wicked courses. *Idaṃ janākīrṇam*, i. e. *idam puro-varti nṛipāṅgaṇam*,
'this royal court before my eyes,' S. ; *janākīrṇam* may perhaps be used,
as in Vikram., Act II, l. 2, for a substantive, meaning 'a crowded thorough-
fare.' *Hutavaha-parīta=lagnāgni*, S.

[1] 'I also regard (these) people here devoted to pleasure, as one-who-
has-performed-his-ablutions (regards) one-smeared (with dirt), as the pure
the impure, as the waking the sleeping, as he-whose-motion-is-free the
bound.'

[2] See p. 20, n. 4.   One MS. has *durnimittam*, 'a bad omen.'

[3] *Vāmetara*, 'other than left,' 'right.'

[4] 'The protector of the (four) classes and (four) orders;' see p. 193,
n. 2, and p. 157, n. 1 at the end.

[5] 'Having but just quitted the seat (of justice);' see p. 190, n. 1.

Verse 113.   ĀRYĀ or GĀTHĀ.   See verse 2.

$$- - \mid \cup \cup - \mid \; - - \; \|\, \cup \cup \cup \cup \mid \cup \cup - \mid \cup - \cup \mid \cup \cup - \mid -$$
$$- \cup \cup \mid \; - - \; \mid \cup \cup - \; \|\, \cup \cup \cup \cup \mid \cup \cup - \mid \; \cup \; \mid \cup \cup - \mid \cup$$

शार्ङ्गरवः ।

भो महाब्राह्मण । काममेतदभिनन्दनीयम् । तथापि
वयमत्र मध्यस्थाः । कुतः ।

भवन्ति नम्रास्तरवः फलागमै-
र्नवाम्बुभिर्भूरिविलम्बिनो घनाः ।
अनुद्धताः सत्पुरुषाः समृद्धिभिः
स्वभाव एवैष परोपकारिणाम् ॥७७४॥

प्रतीहारी ।

[a]देव । पसण्णमुहवण्णा दीसन्ति । जाणामि । विस्सद्धकज्जा
इसीओ ।

[a] देव । प्रसन्नमुखवर्णा दृश्यन्ते । जानामि । विस्रब्धकार्या ऋषयः ।

---

[1] 'This is certainly a subject of rejoicing [to be rejoiced at]; nevertheless
we here are indifferent parties [have nothing to do with it],' i. e. our
merits and interests have nothing to do with his conduct. This favour
and protection is only what might be expected from his benevolent nature.
It is possible that by *vayam madhyasthāḥ* may be meant, 'we are indifferent persons,' 'we have no suit to urge nor petition to present.'

[2] 'Because trees become bent down by the growing-weight of fruit;
clouds hang down the more (when charged) with fresh rain; good men
are not made arrogant by abundant riches; this is the very nature of
the benefactors of others.' *Kutaḥ*, see p. 55, n. 2. *Bhūri*, generally
found in composition, but not always; see Mahā-bh. xii. 1410. Most of
the Beng. MSS. have *dūra*. This verse occurs in Bhartṛi-h. (ii. 62, ed.
Bohlen), where *udgamaiḥ* is adopted for *āgamaiḥ*, and another reading
bhūmi for *bhūri* is noticed. Oriental poets are fond of adducing trees
and clouds as examples of disinterested liberality. 'The tree does not
remove its shade from him who cuts it down,' Hitop. l. 353.

[3] 'The Ṛishis appear to have serene complexions. (Hence) I conclude
they have some business that inspires confidence,' or 'some quiet and
easy business.' *Prasanna-mukha-varṇāḥ*, so read two of the Deva-n. MSS.,
supported by a similar compound in Mālavik. p. 55, l. 20. The Colebrooke MS. has *maṇḍana*, and my own *pankaā* for *vaṇṇā*.

Verse 114. VANṢA-STHAVILA (a variety of JAGATĪ). See verses 18, 22, 23, 67, 81.

C C 2

राजा ॥ शकुन्तलां दृष्ट्वा ॥

अथाचभवती ।

का स्विदवगुण्ठनवती नातिपरिस्फुटशरीरलावण्या ।
मध्ये तपोधनानां किसलयमिव पाण्डुपत्त्राणाम् ॥ ११५ ॥

प्रतीहारी ।

[a] देव । कुदूहलगब्भो पडिहिदो ण मे तक्को पसरँदि । णं
दंसणीत्रा उण से आकिदी लक्खीत्रदि ।

राजा ।

भवतु । अनिर्वर्णनीयं परकलत्रम् ।

शकुन्तला ॥ हस्तमुरसि कृत्वा । आत्मगतम् ॥

[b] हित्रत्र । किं एव्वं वेवसि । अज्जउत्तस्स भावं ओधारित्र
धीरं दाव होहिं ।

पुरोहितः ॥ पुरो गत्वा ॥

एते विधिवदर्चितास्तपस्विनः । कश्चिदेषामुपाध्यायसन्देशः ।

[a] देव । कुतूहलगर्भः प्रतिहितो न मे तर्कः प्रसरति । ननु दर्शनीया पुनरस्या
आकृतिर्लक्ष्यते ।   [b] हृदय । किमेवं वेपसे । आर्यपुत्रस्य भावमवधार्य धीरं तावद्भव ।

---

1 'Who is this veiled-one, the loveliness of whose person is not fully displayed?' *Svid* is a particle of question and doubt. *Avaguṇṭhana* =*mastakācchādana-vastra, C.* The second half of this verse is clear.

2 'My conjecture full of curiosity being hindered (by the veil) does not succeed.' The Mackenzie MS., supported by K., has *paḍihādi* for *prati-bhāti* (in place of *pasaradi* for *prasarati*, the reading of the other Deva-n.) and *paḍihado* for *pahido*, the reading of the others.

3 'Ought not to be gazed at.' *A-nirvarṇanīya=a-darśanīya.*

4 'Having reflected on [called to mind] the affection of thy lord, be firm.' *Bhāva=sneha* (cf. p. 112, n. 2). The Beng. have *smritvā* for *ava-dhārya. Ārya-putra,* 'son of a venerable parent,' is the regular dramatic mode of addressing a husband.

5 'They have some message from the preceptor.'

Verse 115. ĀRYĀ or GĀTHĀ. See verse 2.

    — ⏑ ⏑ | ⏑ — ⏑ | ⏑ ⏑ — ‖ — ⏑ ⏑ | — ⏑ ⏑ | ⏑ — ⏑ | — — | —
    — — | ⏑ — ⏑ | — — ‖ ⏑ ⏑ ⏑ ⏑ | ⏑ ⏑ — | ⏑ | — — | —

तं देवः श्रोतुमर्हति ।

राजा ।

अवहितोऽस्मि ।

ऋषयः ॥ हस्तानुद्यम्य ॥

विजयस्व राजन् ।

राजा ।

सर्वानभिवादये ।

ऋषयः ।

इष्टेन युज्यस्व ।

राजा ।

अपि निर्विघ्नतपसो[1] मुनयः ।

ऋषयः ।

कुतो धर्मक्रियाविघ्नः सतां रक्षितरि त्वयि ।
तमस्तपति घर्मांशौ कथमाविर्भविष्यति ॥ ७७६ ॥[2]

राजा ।

अर्थवान्खलु मे राजशब्दः[3] । अथ भगवाँल्लोकानुग्रहाय
कुशली काश्यपः[4] ।

---

[1] *Nirvighna-tapasaḥ*, cf. p. 35, n. 3. *Api*, see p. 89, n. 2.

[2] 'Whence (can there be) obstruction to the religious rites of the good, thou being (their) defender? How should darkness appear, the Sun emitting light [when the Sun shines]?' *Tapati*, loc. of the pres. part., here used absolutely. *Gharmānśau=sūrye*, S.

[3] 'My title of Rāja has indeed significancy.' The Rishis had, in the preceding verse, compared the king to the Sun, and *rājan* is derived from *rāj*, 'to shine.' It is, however, probable that the play is on the words *rājan* and *rakshitṛi*. Cf. Manu vii. 3, *rakshārtham asya sarvasya rājānam asrijat prabhuḥ*, 'the Supreme Being created a king for the protection of this universe.' Dr. Boehtlingk remarks that in these cases it little signifies whether the derivation be true or false. In Mahā-bh. xii. 1032, *rājan* is derived from *rañj*, 'to conciliate.'

[4] 'Is his reverence Kāśyapa prosperous for the welfare of the world?'

Verse 116. ŚLOKA or ANUSHṬUBH. See verses 5, 6, 11, 12, 26, 47, 50, 51, 53, 73, 76, 84, 87.

ऋषयः ।

स्वाधीनकुशलाः सिद्धिमन्तः । स भवन्तमनामयप्रश्न-
पूर्वकमिदमाह ।

राजा ।

किमाज्ञापयति भगवान् ।

शाङ्गरवः ।

यन्नियःसमयादिमां मदीयां दुहितरं भवानुपायंस्त ।
तन्मया प्रीतिमता युवयोरनुज्ञातम् । कुतः ।

त्वमर्हतां प्रायसरः स्मृतोऽसि नः
    शकुन्तला मूर्तिमिती च सत्क्रिया ।
समानयंस्तुल्यगुणं वधूवरं
    चिरस्य वाच्यं न गतः प्रजापतिः ॥११७॥

Kuśalin, see p. 35, n. 3. *Bhagavāl*, &c., when the letter *l* is preceded by *t*, *d*, or *n* dental, it requires the assimilation of the letters to itself, and in the case of dental *n*, the mark called C'andra-vindu is written over, to shew that the *l* substituted for it has a nasal sound, Laghu-k. No. 79, see Gram. 56.

[1] 'Saints have prosperity in their power. He with inquiries about your safety says this to your Highness.' It will be readily remarked that the character of these Ṛishis is evidently that of plain, honest, independent men. *Siddhimantaḥ*, lit. 'men endowed with or capable of perfection,' 'saints,' Vishṇu-p. p. 45. *Anāmaya*, see Manu ii. 127, 'Let a man ask a Brāhman, on meeting him, as to his *kuśala;* a Kshatriya, as to his *anāmaya;* a Vaiśya, as to his *kshema;* and a S'ūdra, as to his *ārogya*.' The king was of course a Kshatriya, see p. 31, n. 1.

[2] The third sing. aor. Ātm. of *upa-yam*, 'to marry,' is either *upāyata* or *upāyaṇsta*, Pāṇ. i. 2, 16. The Beng. have *upayeme*, perf.

[3] 'Thou art esteemed by us the chief of the worthy, and S'akuntalā, incarnate virtue. Brahmā [Fate], bringing together a bride and bridegroom of equal merit, has after a long time (now first) incurred no censure.' *Naḥ*, the Colebrooke MS. reads *yat*. *Vadhū-varam*, a Dvandva comp. in the neuter gender. *Vāćyaṃ na gataḥ*, probably this refers to the blame popularly laid on Fate for preventing the smooth course of true love.

Verse 117. VAṆŚA-STHAVILA (a variety of JAGATĪ). See verses 18, 22, 23, 67, 81, 114.

तदिदानीमापन्नसत्त्वा प्रतिगृह्यतां सहधर्मचरणायेति ।

गौतमी ।

a अज्ज । किम्पि वत्तुकामम्हि । ण मे वयणावसरो अत्थि । कहंति ।

णावेक्खिदो गुरुअणो इमिणा ण तुएवि पुच्छिदो बन्धू ।
एक्कक्कं एव्व चरिए किं भणदु एक्क एक्कस्स ॥११८॥

शकुन्तला ॥ आत्मगतम् ॥

b किं णुक्खु अज्जउत्ती भणादि ।

a आर्ये । किमपि वक्तुकामास्मि । न मे वचनावसरोऽस्ति । कथमिति ।
नापेक्षितो गुरुजनोऽनया न त्वयापि पृष्टो बन्धुः ।
एकैकमेवं चरिते किं भणत्वेक एकस्य ॥११८॥ *bhanāmi kim e'*

b किं नु खल्वार्यपुत्रो भणति ।

---

[1] 'Therefore now let her, being quick with child, be received, for the joint discharge of religious-rites,' i. e. those Saṇskāras or rites, which were performed for the child before and after birth, probably by the parents conjointly (*saha*); see Manu ii. 27, &c.

[2] 'Her elder-relatives were not referred to by her; nor by you was any kinsman asked; (the affair) having been transacted quite privately [lit. one with the other], what has each one to say to the other?' *Guru-jana*, see p. 173, n. 3 in the middle. The Deva-n. MSS. have *imāe* for *imiṇā*. The latter, which is the reading of the oldest Beng., I have retained on account of the metre. There is no reason why in Prākṛit *imiṇa* should not be used for the fem. instr., since *imassim* is admissible for the fem. loc.; see p. 37, l. 2. *Ekaikam=anyonyam*, 'mutually,' S. and C. *Bhaṇṇadu* is the reading of some of the Beng. MSS. followed by the Calcutta edition; I have written *bhaṇṇadu* for *bhaṇādu*, on account of the metre, and on the authority of Lassen's Instit. Prāk. p. 277. The Deva-n. have *kim bhaṇāmi*, which reading violates the metre and makes the construction of the sentence very obscure. They also read *ekkam ekkassa*. *Eka* may be for *eka-janaḥ*, applicable to either gender. The commentary of C. is in favour of the above interpretation.

Verse 118. ĀRYĀ or GĀTHĀ. See verse 2.

‒ ‒ | ⏑ ‒ ⏑ | ⏑ ⏑ ‒ ‖ ⏑ ⏑ ‒ | ⏑ ⏑ ‒ | ⏑ ‒ ⏑ | ‒ ‒ | ‒
‒ ‒ | ⏑ ‒ ⏑ | ⏑ ⏑ ‒ ‖ ‒ ‒ | ⏑ ⏑ ‒ | ⏑ | ‒ ‒ ⏑

राजा ।

किमिदमुपन्यस्तम् ।

शकुन्तला ॥ आत्मगतम् ॥

[a] पावओक्खु एसो वञ्चणोवंषासो ।[1]

शाङ्गंरवः ।

कथमिदं नाम । भवन्त एव सुतरां लोकवृत्तान्तनिष्णाताः ।[2]

सतीमपि ज्ञातिकुलैकसंश्रयां
जनोऽन्यथा भर्तृमतीं विशङ्कते ।
अतः समीपे परिणेतुरिष्यते
तदप्रियापि प्रमदा स्वबन्धुभिः ॥ ११९ ॥[3]

राजा ।

किं चाचभवती मया परिणीतपूर्वा ।

शकुन्तला ॥ सविषादम् । आत्मगतम् ॥

[b] हिअअ । सम्पदं दे आसङ्का ।

[a] पावकः खल्वेष वचनोपन्यासः ।   [b] हृदय । साम्प्रतं न आशङ्का ।

---

[1] 'Truly, the import of this speech [that which is proposed by this speech] is (like) fire.' The Mackenzie MS. inserts *eso* after *kkhu*.

[2] 'Such-persons-as-your-Majesty are certainly full well acquainted with the ways of the world.' *Loka-vrittānta-nishṇātāḥ = loka-vyavahāra-jñātāḥ*, S. *Ni-shṇāta* (=*abhijña*, C.), lit. 'bathed in ;' hence 'conversant with.' The Sāhit-d. (p. 193) reads *bhavān loka-vrittānte nishṇātaḥ*.

[3] 'People suspect a married woman [woman who has a husband] residing wholly in her kinsmen's family, although chaste, (to be) the reverse. Hence a young woman is preferred by her own relatives (to be) near her husband, even though she be disliked by him.' *Jñāti-ku°=nija-griha-vāsinīm*, S. *Anyathā*, i. e. *vyabhiċāriṇīm*, 'unchaste,' S. *Ishyate=ākān-kshyate*, S. *Tad-apriyāpi*, the Beng., my own MS., and the Sāhit.-d. read *priyāpriyā vā*, 'liked or disliked ;' but K. supports the other reading.

Verse 119. VAṆŚA-STHAVILA (a variety of JAGATĪ). See verses 18, 22, 23, 67, 81, 114, 117.

शार्ङ्गरवः ।

किं कृतकार्यद्वेषाद्धर्मं प्रति विमुखतोचिता राज्ञः[1] ।

राजा ।

कुतोऽयमसत्कल्पनाप्रश्नः[2] ।

शार्ङ्गरवः ।

मूर्छन्त्यमी विकाराः प्रायेणैश्वर्यमत्तेषु[3] ।

राजा ।

विशेषेणाधिक्षिप्तोऽस्मि[4] ।

गौतमी ।

[a] जादे । मुहुत्तअं मा लज्ज । अवणइस्सं दाव दे ओउण्ठणं । तदो तुमं भट्टा अहिजाणिस्सदि । ॥ इति यथोक्तं करोति ॥

राजा ॥ शकुन्तलां निर्वर्ण्य । आत्मगतम् ॥

इदमुपनतमेवं रूपमक्लिष्टकान्ति
प्रथमपरिगृहीतं स्यान्न वेत्यव्यवस्यन् ।

[a] जाते । मुहूर्तं मा लज्जस्व । अपनेष्यामि तावत्तेऽवगुण्ठनम् । ततस्त्वां भर्ताभिज्ञास्यति ।

---

[1] 'On account of dislike to a deed done, is opposition to justice becoming in a king?' This is the reading of the oldest Bengālī, and I have adopted it as preferable to that of the Deva-n., *kiṃ kṛita-kārya-dvesho dharmam prati vimukhatā kṛitāvajñā.* Dr. Boehtlingk suggests that *kṛitāvajñā* is probably an interpolation from the margin.

[2] 'Whence is this inquiry (accompanied) by the fabrication of a falsehood?' *Avidyamānārthasya kalpanayā kṛitaḥ praśnaḥ*, K. According to Dr. Burkhard, 'inquiry about a crime which has not been committed.'

[3] 'These changes-of-purpose [fickleness of disposition] mostly take effect [wax strong] in those who are intoxicated with sovereign-power.' *Mūrćhanti=vardhante*, S.; *=vyāpnuvanti*, K. (cf. Raghu-v. xii. 57, vi. 9, x. 80). Root *mūrćh* has generally the opposite sense, 'to lose strength,' 'faint away.' It is applied to the thickening of darkness, in Vikram., Act III, *tamasāṃ niśi mūrćhatām.*

[4] 'I am especially aimed-at-by-this censure,' i.e. I am the especial object of this censorious remark about 'persons intoxicated with power.'

भ्रमर इव विभाते कुन्दमन्तस्तुषारं
न खलु च परिभोक्तुं नैव शक्नोमि हातुम् ॥१२०॥
॥ इति विचारयन्निस्यतः ॥

प्रतीहारी ।

[a] अहो धम्मावेक्खिदा भट्टिणो । ईदिसं णाम सुहोवणदं रूवं देक्खिन्न को अण्णो विआरेदि ।

शाङ्गरवः ।

भो राजन् । किमिति जोषमास्यते ।

राजा ।

भोस्तपोधनाः । चिन्तयन्नपि न खलु स्वीकरणमभवत्याः स्मरामि । तत्कथमिमामभिव्यक्तसत्त्वलक्षणां प्रत्यात्मानं श्वेचिणमाशङ्कमानः प्रतिपत्स्ये ।

[a] अहो धर्मावेक्षिता भर्तुः । ईदृशं नाम सुखोपनतं रूपं दृष्ट्वा कोऽन्यो विचारयति ।

---

[1] 'Not settling-in-my-mind [not deciding or determining] whether this form of unblemished beauty thus presented (to me) [brought near to me] may or may not have been formerly married [by me]; verily I am neither able to enjoy nor to abandon (it), like a bee at the break of day, the jasmine-blossom filled with dew.' *Aklishṭa-kānti = anavadya-saundaryam*, K. *Parigṛihītam*, see p. 181, n. 2. *A-vyavasyan* (= *a-niśćinvan*), so reads K.; I have ventured to follow him, although nearly all the Deva-n. MSS. have *vyavasyan* (cf. p. 146, l. 2, n. 1; and p. 161, l. 9). If *vyavasyan* is retained, it must be translated 'deliberating,' 'striving to discover.' *Antas-tushāra*, lit. 'having dew in the interior.'

[2] 'Why do you sit [is it sat] so silent?' *Kimartham maunam kritam asti*, S. Cf. *kim tūshṇīm evāste*, Vikram., Act IV.

[3] *Svīkaraṇam* (= *vivāham*, S.), 'making one's own,' i.e. 'taking in marriage.'

[4] 'How, then, shall I act towards her, bearing evident signs of pregnancy, doubting myself to be her husband.' *Katham pratipatsye* may mean 'how shall I make any reply?' referring to *kim josham āsyate* in the previous speech; or, 'how shall I receive her?' see p. 135, n. 1.

Verse 120. MĀLINĪ or MĀNINĪ (a variety of ATI-ŚAKVARĪ). See verses 10, 19, 20, 38, 55, 109, 110.

शकुन्तला ॥ अपवार्य ॥

[a] अज्जस्स परिणए एव्व सन्देहो । कुदो दाणिं मे दूराहिरोहिणी आसा ।

शार्ङ्गरवः ।

मा तावत्

कृताभिमर्शामनुमन्यमानः
सुतां त्वया नाम मुनिर्विमान्यः ।
मुष्टं प्रतिग्राहयता स्वमर्थं
पात्रीकृतो दस्युरिवासि येन ॥१२१॥

शारद्वतः ।

शार्ङ्गरव । विरम त्वमिदानीम् । शकुन्तले । वक्तव्यमुक्त-
मस्माभिः । सोऽयमत्रभवानेवमाह । दीयतामस्मै प्रत्यय-
प्रतिवचनम् ।

[a] आर्यस्य परिणय एव सन्देहः । कुत इदानीं मे दूराधिरोहिण्याशा ।

---

[1] 'Is the sage after-consenting to his daughter, who had been seduced [carnally-embraced] by thee, to be (thus) insulted forsooth? (he) by whom allowing his stolen property [i. e. Sakuntalā] to be kept [taken], thou hast been made as it were a justified ravisher [robber].' *Kritābhi-marśām = krita-saṃsparśām = krita-saṅgrahaṇām*, K. The first sense of *abhi-mriś* is 'to touch,' 'to handle.' Here, as in *parā-mriś* (Bhaṭṭi-k. xvii. 38), there is an implication of carnal connexion. *Mushṭam*, the Taylor MS. has *ishṭam*, and the Beng. *dushṭam*. It must be borne in mind that Sakuntalā was married to Dushyanta, according to the Gāndharva form (p. 127, n. 3), during the absence of her foster-father (see pp. 134, 135, with notes). *Pratigrāhayatā*, the causal may sometimes give the sense of 'allowing' or 'permitting,' as in *nāśayati*, 'he suffers to perish.' *Pātrī-kṛita*, is a C'vi compound, formed from *pātra*, neut. 'a receptacle,' applied to express any deserving or worthy person (see Manu iv. 227).

Verse 121. Upajāti or Ākhyānakī (a variety of Trishṭubh). See verses 41, 107.

शकुन्तला ॥ अपवार्य ॥

[a] इमं अवत्थन्तरं गदे तारिसे अणुराए किं वा सुमराविदेण । अत्ता दाणिं मे सोअणीओत्ति ववसिदं ।

॥ प्रकाशम् ॥ [b] अज्जउत्त । ॥ इत्यर्धोक्ते ॥ [c] संसइदे दाणिं परिणए या एसो समुदाआरो । पोरव । ण जुत्तं णाम दे तह पुरा अस्समपदे सहावुत्ताणहिअअं इमं जणं समअपुव्वं पतारिअ ईदिसेहिं अक्खरेहिं पच्चाचक्खिदुं ।

राजा ॥ कर्णौ पिधाय ॥

शान्तम् । पापम् ।

[a] इदमवस्थान्तरं गते तादृशेऽनुरागे किं वा स्मारितेन । आत्मेदानीं मे शोचनीय इति व्यवसितम् । [b] आर्यपुत्र । [c] संशयित इदानीं परिणये नैष समुदाचारः । पौरव । न युक्तं नाम ते तथा पुराश्रमपदे स्वभावोन्नानहृदयमिमं जनं समयपूर्वं प्रतार्यै-दृशैरक्षरैः प्रत्याचष्टुम् ।

---

[1] K., S., and the old Beng. MS. interpret *soaṇio* by *śoćanīya*, 'to be sorrowed for;' but C. has *śodhanīya*, and is followed by Chézy and the Calcutta edition. The meaning will then be, 'I myself am now to be cleared [justified] by myself.' All the MSS., except one, insert *me*.

[2] 'Now that my marriage is called-in-question, this is not the (proper) form-of-address;' see p. 196, n. 4. All the MSS. agree in reading *samudāāro* for *samudāćāro;* otherwise it might be suspected that *samudāhāro* was the correct word, to which *samudāćāro* must be here equivalent.

[3] 'It is not becoming in thee, having awhile since in the hermitage so seduced, after-a-formal-agreement, this person [myself] naturally open-hearted, to repudiate her with such words.' *Uttāna*, 'shallow,' 'unreserved,' is the opposite of *gambhīra*, 'deep,' 'reserved;' see p. 39, n. 1. *Samaya-pūrvam*, cf. p. 198, l. 3; and p. 172, l. 4, with note.

[4] 'Peace! a sin!' i.e. Silence! let me not listen to such sinful words; or, if no stop is placed after *śāntam*, 'May the sin be palliated!' This seems to be the usual formula in the plays for averting the ill effects of blasphemous, malevolent, or lying words. Sometimes the stage-direction *karṇau pidhāya* is omitted, compare Acts vii. 57; Mṛiććhak. p. 36, l. 5; p. 230, l. 6; p. 306, l. 9; p. 329, l. 1; Mālavik. p. 69, l. 10; Mudrā-r. p. 24, l. 5.

व्यपदेशमाविलयितुं किमीहसे जनमिमं च पातयितुम् ।
कूलङ्कषेव सिन्धुः प्रसन्नमम्भस्तटतरुं चं ॥१२२॥

शकुन्तला ।

[a] होदु । जइ परमत्थदो परपरिग्गहसङ्किणा तुए एव्वं पउत्तं ।
ता अहिखाणेण इमिणा तुह आसङ्कं अवणइस्सं ।

राजा ।

उदारः कल्पः ।

शकुन्तला ॥ मुद्रास्थानं परामृश्य ॥

[b] हद्दी । हद्दी । अङ्गुलीअअसुखा मे अङ्गुली ।
॥ इति सविषादं गौतमीमवेक्षते ॥

गौतमी ।

[c] णूणं दे सक्कावदाऽब्भन्तरे सचीतित्थसलिलं वन्दमाणाए
पब्भट्ठं अङ्गुलीअअं ।

[a] भवतु । यदि परमार्थतः परपरिग्रहशङ्किना त्वयैवं प्रवृत्तम् । तदभिज्ञानेनानेन तवाशङ्कामपनेष्यामि ।   [b] हाधिक् । हाधिक् । अङ्गुलीयकशून्या मेऽङ्गुलिः ।
[c] नूनं ते शक्रावताराभ्यन्तरे शचीतीर्थसलिलं वन्दमानायाः भ्रष्टमङ्गुलीयकम् ।

---

[1] 'Why seekest thou to sully the royal-title [race, family] and to ruin this person [myself]; as a stream that-carries-away-its-own-banks (disturbs) the clear water (and overturns) the tree on its margin ?' *Vyapadeśam*, i. e. *kulaṃ nāma vā*, 'either family or name,' *C.*; *vyapadiśyate anena iti vyapadeśaḥ kulam*, S. *Āvilayitum*, infin. of a nom. verb from *āvila*, 'turbid.' *Sindhuḥ*, 'a river,' in classical Sanskrit is generally fem., in the older language generally masc.; when *Sindhu* means 'the district Scinde' it is usually masc.

[2] 'In all probability the ring slipped from (the finger of) thee as thou wert offering homage to the water at Śacī's holy-pool, within Śakrāvatāra.' Śakra is a name of Indra, and Śakrāvatāra some sacred place of pilgrimage where he descended upon earth. Śacī is his wife, to whom there was probably a Tīrtha, or holy bathing-place (see p. 17, n. 1), consecrated at this place, where Śakuntalā had performed her ablutions.

Verse 122. ĀRYĀ or GĀTHĀ. See verse 2.

⏑⏑–|⏑–⏑|⏑⏑–‖⏑–⏑|–⏑⏑|⏑–⏑|–⏑⏑|–
––|⏑–⏑|––‖⏑–⏑|––|⏑|⏑⏑–|⏑

राजा ॥ सस्मितम् ॥

इदं तत्प्रत्युत्पन्नमति स्त्रैणमिति यदुच्यते ।[1]

शकुन्तला ।

[a] एत्थ दाव विहिणा दंसिदं पहुत्तणं । अवरं दे कहिस्सं ।

राजा ।

श्रोतव्यमिदानीं संवृत्तम् ।[3]

शकुन्तला ।

[b] णं एक्कदिअहे णोमालिआमरण्डए णलिणीपत्तभा-
अणगअं उअअं तुह हत्थे सण्णिहिदं आसि ।

राजा ।

शृणुमस्तावत् ।

शकुन्तला ।

[c] तक्खणं सो मे पुत्तकिदओ दीहापंङ्गी णाम मिअपोदओ[6]

[a] अत्र तावद्विधिना दर्शितं प्रभुत्वम् । अपरं ते कथयिष्यामि ।   [b] नन्वेकदिवसे नवमालिकामण्डपे नलिनीपत्रभाजनगतमुदकं तव हस्ते सन्निहितमासीत् ।   [c] तत्क्षणं स मे पुत्रकृतको दीर्घापाङ्गो नाम मृगपोतक

---

[1] 'This is that which is said [thus is proved the truth of the proverb], "Woman-kind is ready-witted."' *Straiṇam* = *strī-jātiḥ*, 'the female sex,' K. The Beng. have *idaṃ tat pratyutpanna-matitvaṃ strīṇām;* cf. Hitop. l. 2320, where *pratyutpanna-matiḥ* is the name given to the ready-witted fish. See also Hitop. l. 2338, 'The food of women is said to be two-fold, their wit four-fold, their cunning six-fold, and their passion eight-fold.'

[2] 'Here, however, sovereignty has been shewn by destiny.' A similar sentiment occurs further on in this play, and at the beginning of Act IV. of Vikram., *bhavitavya-tā atra balavatī,* 'here destiny has shewn its power.'

[3] Dr. Boehtlingk considers that *śrotavyam* is here taken as a substantive, and construes, 'The moment-for-hearing (what else you have to say) has now arrived' (cf. p. 110, l. 9). As the pass. part. is often used substantively the translation may be, 'what took place is now to be heard.'

[4] 'Lying in a lotus-leaf-cup.' As to *gatam*, see p. 38, n. 1.

[5] *Sannihitam*, see p. 150, l. 10, with note 3.

[6] 'Having eyes with long outer corners.' This was the fawn mentioned in verse 94.

[a] उबट्टिदो। तुए अत्तं दाव पढमं पिअउत्ति अणुअम्पिणा
उबच्छन्दिदो उअएण। ण उण दे अपरिचिआदो हत्थब्भांसं
उबगदो। पच्छा तस्सिं एव्व मए गहिदे सलिले येण
किदो पणओ। तदा तुमं इत्थं पहसिदोसि। सव्वो सगन्धेसु
विस्ससदि। दुवेवि एत्थ आरण्णआ त्ति।

राजा।

एवमादिभिरात्मकार्यनिवर्तिनीनामनृतमयवाङ्मधुभिरा-
कृष्यन्ते विषयिणः।

गौतमी।

[b] महाभाअ। ण अरुहसि एव्वं मन्तिदुं। तवोवणसंवड्ढिदो
अणभिण्णो अत्तं जणो कइदवस्स।

[a] उपस्थितः। त्वयायं तावत्प्रथमं पिवन्त्वित्यनुकम्पिनोपच्छन्दित उदकेन। न
पुनस्तेऽपरिचयाद् हस्ताभ्यासमुपगतः। पश्चात्तस्मिन्नेव मया गृहीते सलिलेऽनेन कृतः
प्रणयः। तदा त्वमित्थं प्रहसितोऽसि। सर्वैः सगन्धेषु विश्वसिति। द्वावप्यत्रारण्यका-
विति। [b] महाभाग। नार्हस्येवं मन्तयितुम्। तपोवनसंवर्धितोऽनभिज्ञोऽयं जनः
कैतवस्य।

---

[1] *Upaćchanditaḥ*=*jala-pānāya preritaḥ*, 'was coaxed to drink the water,'
S.;=*pralobhitaḥ*, 'enticed,' 'coaxed,' Chézy.   According to Pān. i. 3, 47,
upa-ćchand means 'to conciliate privately by flattering or coaxing language.'
Cf. Raghu-v. v. 58, where Stenzler translates it by *obsecro*, 'supplicate,' 'beg.'

[2] *Hastābhyāsa*, lit. 'use of the hand,' i. e. 'stroking with the hand,'
'caressing;' with *upa-gam*, 'to approach for fondling,' 'to allow to be
caressed,' 'to entrust one's self into any one's hands' (cf. p. 209, l. 10).

[3] *Praṇayaḥ* here, 'trust,' 'confidence' (=*viśvāsaḥ*, S.) *Sagandheshu*, 'in
relatives.' *Sagandha*=*sadṛiśa*=*sannihita*.   *Gandha*=*sambandha*, S.

[4] So reads my own MS. K. has *āraṇṇaa* (Lassen's Instit. Prāk. p. 187),
and interprets it by *āraṇyakau*.   Some read *āraṇṇao*, which seems to be
an error for *araṇṇaāo* nom. pl. fem.   The feminine is admissible on the
principle of the superiority of the human species over animals.

[5] 'Voluptuaries are allured by such false honied words as these of
women turning (them) away from their own duty.'   The Taylor and my
own MS. have *nirvartinīnām*, which has been adopted in B. and R.'s
dictionary and by Dr. Burkhard; if this reading be preferred, translate

राजा ।

तापसवृद्धे[1] ।

स्त्रीणामशिक्षितपटुत्वममानुषीषु
सन्दृश्यते किमुत याः प्रतिबोधवत्यः ।
प्रागन्तरिक्षगमनात्स्वमपत्यजात-
मन्यैर्द्विजैः परभृताः खलु पोषयन्ति ॥१२३॥[2]

शकुन्तला ॥ सरोषम् ॥

[a]अणज्ज । अत्तणो हिअआणुमाणेण पेक्खसि । को
दाणिं अण्णो धम्मकञ्चुअप्पवेसिणो तिणच्छण्णकूवोवमस्स
तव अणुकिदं[3] पडिवज्जिस्संदि ।

राजा ॥ आत्मगतम् ॥

सन्दिग्धबुद्धिं मां कुर्वन्नकैतव इवास्याः कोपो लक्ष्यते ।
तथा ह्यनया

[a] अनार्य । आत्मनो हृदयानुमानेन प्रेक्षसे । क इदानीमन्यो धर्मकञ्चुकप्रवेशिनस्तृ-
णच्छन्नकूपोपमस्य तवानुकृतं प्रतिपत्स्यते ।

'of women seeking to accomplish their own ends.' The Mackenzie has
yoshitām madhura-gīrbhiḥ for *anṛitamaya-vān-madhubhiḥ*.

[1] According to Pāṇ. ii. 2, 38, *tāpasa-vṛiddhā* is a legitimate compound,
although *vṛiddha-tāpasī* would be more usual.

[2] 'The untaught cunning is observed of females (even) in-those-that-are-
not-of-the-human-race [i. e. even in animals]; how much more (of those)
who are endowed with reason [i. e. of women]! The female cuckoos, as-
is-well-known [*khalu*] allow their own offspring to be reared by other birds,
before soaring in the sky.' *A-mānushīshu*, i. e. *mānusha-jāti-vyatiriktāsu
tiryag-jātishu*, K. *Pratibodhavatyaḥ = jñāninyaḥ = čaitanya-bhājaḥ*, S.;
the most obvious sense, if the context would allow it, would be, 'those
women who have received instruction.' *Para-bhṛitāḥ*, see p. 162, n. 2.

[3] 'What other (person) now would act like [in imitation of] thee, that
putting on the garb of virtue resemblest a grass-concealed well?' *Pratipatsyate*, see p. 135, l. 4, with note 1.

Verse 123. VASANTA-TILAKĀ (a variety of ŚAKVARĪ). See next verse.

मय्येव विस्मरणदारुणचित्तवृत्तौ
वृत्तं रहःप्रणयमप्रतिपद्यमाने ।
भेदाद्भुवोः कुटिलयोरतिलोहिताक्ष्या
भग्नं शरासनमिवातिरुषा स्मरस्य ॥१२४॥[1]

॥ प्रकाशम् ॥ भद्रे । प्रथितं दुष्यन्तस्य चरितम् । तथापीदं न
लक्ष्ये ।

शकुन्तला ।

[a]सुट्ठु दाव अत्त सच्छन्दचारिणी[2] किदम्हि । जा अहं
इमस्स पुरुवंसप्पच्चएण मुहमहुणो हिअअट्टिअविसस्स
हत्थव्भासं उवगदा । ॥ इति पटान्तेन मुखमावृत्य रोदिति ॥

शाङ्गरवः ।

इत्यमात्मकृतमप्रतिहतं चापलं दहति ।

[a] सुष्ठु तावदत्र स्वच्छन्दचारिणी कृतास्मि । याहमस्य पुरुवंशमत्ययेन मुखमधोहृदय-
स्थतविषस्य हस्ताभ्यासमुपगता ।

---

[1] 'For (when) I, whose state of feeling was dreadfully-severe from the
absence of (all) recollection, (persisted in) not admitting that affection had
privately existed (between us); it (seemed) as if (the god) Smara's bow
was snapped asunder by that very-red-eyed one with excessive anger, on
the parting of her curved eyebrows.' The double-entendre in the word
Smara, which means 'recollection' as well as 'the god of Love,' is noticeable (see the notes on Kāma-deva, p. 99, n. 1, and p. 100, n. 1). The figure
by which the eyebrows of a beautiful woman are compared to Cupid's bow
is common, and the glances from the eye are by a similar metaphor often
likened to arrows discharged from it. Sakuntalā is said to break the bow
by the parting of her eyebrows, which were contracted in anger. Possibly
one effect of anger might be to wrinkle the brow, which would appear to
separate the eyebrows.

[2] Lit. 'a wilful, self-willed woman,' 'one who acts on the impulse of
the moment.' It may have this sense here, but S'. interprets it by *gaṇikā*,
'a wanton, unchaste woman.'

[3] 'Thus a self-committed hasty action, when not counteracted, leads-to-

---

Verse 124. VASANTA-TILAKĀ (a variety of S'AKVARĪ). See verses 8, 27, 31, 43, 46,
64, 74, 80, 82, 83, 91, 93, 94, 95, 100, 104, 105, 108, 123.

अतः परीक्ष्य कर्तव्यं विशेषात्सङ्गतं रहः ।
अज्ञातहृदयेष्वेवं वैरीभवति सौहृदम् ॥१२५॥

राजा ।

अयि भोः । किमचभवतीप्रत्ययादेवास्मान्सम्भृतदोषैरधि-
क्षिपथ ।

शार्ङ्गरवः ॥ सासूयम् ॥

श्रुतं भवद्भिरधरोत्तरम् ।

---

keen-remorse [burns].' Most of the Deva-n. MSS. have *parihatam* for *apratihatam;* the Mackenzie has *pratihatam;* the oldest Beng. *apratihatam.* *Câpalam* is 'any action proceeding from thoughtlessness or over-precipitation.' *Dahati,* the Hindūs connect a burning or smarting sensation with the idea of remorse of conscience (cf. *manas-tāpa, paśćāt-tāpa, anu-tāpa,* &c.)

[1] 'Therefore a union, especially (when) in private, ought to be formed with-great-circumspection [after having made proper inquiry or experiment, i. e. after investigating each other's character and circumstances]. Thus (is it that) between those who know not (each other's) hearts, friendship becomes enmity.' *Parīkshya,* the Beng. have *samīkshya. Sangatam rahaḥ=rahasi sangamaḥ,* K.

[2] 'Do you reproach us with accumulated accusations [faults]?' Most of the Deva-n. MSS. have *samyuta-doshākshareṇa kshinutha.* The above is the reading of the oldest Beng., supported by K., who has *sambhṛita-dosha-karshaṇena.*

[3] *Sāsūyam,* 'scornfully,' 'sarcastically;' lit. 'with detraction.'

[4] *Adharottaram = nikṛishṭa-prādhānyam,* 'ascendancy of the low,' 'placing that at the top which ought to be at the bottom,' C. In Manu viii. 53, the word occurs in the sense of 'confused and contradictory statement;' and again in vii. 21, it is applied to express the confusion of ranks [*adharam=śūdrādi; uttaram=pradhānam*] which would ensue, if justice were not duly administered by the king. It may be translated here 'confusion of principles,' 'inversion of the proper order of things,' and probably refers to the ironical statement in the succeeding verse. Hence the meaning may be, 'You have been taught upside down or backwards.' In other words, 'The usual definition of the fourth Pramāṇa (*śabda*) is *āpta-vākya,* you would make it *anāpta-vākya,* the words of an improper person.' See Indian Wisdom, pp. 72, 92. *Adharottara* may mean 'reply to a statement' or 'question and answer.'

Verse 125. Śloka or Anushtubh. See verses 5, 6, 11, 12, 26, 47, 50, &c., 87.

आ जन्मनः शाठ्यमशिक्षितो य-
स्तस्याप्रमाणं वचनं जनस्य ।
परातिसन्धानमधीयते यै-
र्विद्येति ते सन्तु किलाप्तवाचः ॥१२६॥

राजा ।

भोः सत्यवादिन् । अभ्युपगतं तावदस्माभिरेवम् । किं
पुनरिमामतिसन्धाय लभ्यते ।

शार्ङ्गरवः ।

विनिपातः ।

राजा ।

विनिपातः पौरवैः प्रार्थ्यत इति न श्रद्येयमेतत् ।

शारद्वतः ।

शार्ङ्गरव । किमुत्तरेण । अनुष्ठितो गुरोः सन्देशः ।
प्रतिनिवर्तामहे वयम् । ॥ राजानं प्रति ॥

तदेषा भवतः कान्ता त्यज वैनां गृहाण वा ।
उपपन्ना हि दारेषु प्रभुता सर्वतोमुखी ॥१२७॥

---

[1] 'The declaration of that person who from birth is untrained to guile
(is) without authority. Let those persons, forsooth, by whom the de-
ceiving of others is studied, calling it a science, be (alone considered)
worthy of belief.' *Ā janmanaḥ*, see p. 155, n. 3 at the end. *A-pramāṇam*
= *a-yathārtham*, S. *Ati-sandhānam*, cf. p. 99, l. 2. *Āpta-vācaḥ* = *ya-
thārtha-vacanāḥ*, S. ; = *pramāṇa-vācaḥ*, K.

[2] *Vinipāta*, 'ruin,' 'destruction,' = *pratyavāya*, K. ; = *naraka-ga-
mana*, S.

[3] 'She is, then, your wife; either abandon her or take her; for the
authority over wives is admitted to be unlimited [reaching everywhere,
unbounded].' *Kāntā*, the Beng. MSS. have *patnī*. *Sarvato-mukhī*, lit.
'looking or facing in every direction;'=*sarva-karaṇa-samarthā*, 'omni-
potent,' 'able to do everything,' C.;=*sarva-prakāreṇa*, 'of every kind,' S.

Verse 126. UPAJĀTI or ĀKHYĀNAKĪ (a variety of TRISHṬUBH). See verses 41, 107, 121.
Verse 127. SLOKA or ANUSHṬUBH. See verses 5, 6, 11, 12, 26, 47, 50, 51, &c., 125.

गौतमी ।

गच्छायतः । ॥ इति प्रस्थिताः ॥

शकुन्तला ।

[a] कहं इमिणा किदवेण विप्पलद्धम्हि । तुम्हेवि मं परिदेविणिं परिच्चअह । ॥ इत्यनुप्रतिष्ठते ॥

गौतमी ॥ स्थित्वा ॥

[b] वच्छ सङ्गरव । अणुगच्छदि इअंक्खु णो करुणपरि-देविणी सउन्दला । पच्चादेसपरुसे भत्तुणि किं वा मे पुत्तिआ करिस्सदि ।

शाङ्र्रव: ॥ सरोषं निवृत्य ॥

किं पुरोभागिनि स्वातन्च्यमवलम्बसे । ॥ शकुन्तला भीता वेपते ॥

शाङ्र्रव: ।

शकुन्तले ।

यदि यथा वदति क्षितिपस्तथा

त्वमसि किं पितुरुत्कुलया त्वया ।

अथ तु वेत्सि शुचि व्रतमात्मनः

पतिकुले तव दास्यमपि क्षमम् ॥१२८॥

[a] कथमनेन कितवेन विप्रलब्धास्मि । यूयमपि मां परिदेविनीं परित्यजथ । [b] वत्स शाङ्र्रव । अनुगच्छतीयं खलु नः करुणपरिदेविनी शकुन्तला । प्रत्यादेशपरुषे भर्तरि किं वा मे पुत्री करिष्यति ।

---

[1] 'O naughty one, dost thou affect independence [art thou determined to have thy own way]?' *Puro-bhāgini* = *dushṭe*, K.; = *doshaikadarśini*, *doshaika-dṛik*, S. and C. *Puro-bhāgin* first means 'one who takes the first share or more than his proper share,' i.e. 'a grasping character' (cf. Vikram., end of Act III, *mā mām puro-bhāginī iti samarthayasi*); then, 'malevolent,' 'censorious;' lastly, as here, 'a wilful, perverse person.' Most of the Deva-n., unsupported by the commentators, have *purobhāge*. *Svātantrya*, cf. Manu ix. 3, *na strī svātantryam arhati;* and see p. 49, n. 1.

[2] 'If thou art so, as the king asserts, what (connexion will remain) to

Verse 128. DRUTA-VILAMBITA (a variety of JAGATĪ). See verses 45, 72.

तिष्ठ । साधयामो वयम् ।

राजा ।

भोस्तपस्विन् । किमत्रभवतीं विप्रलभसे । कुतः ।

कुमुदान्येव शशाङ्कः सविता बोधयति पङ्कजान्येव ।

वशिनां हि परपरिग्रहसंश्लेषपराङ्मुखी वृत्तिः ॥१२९॥

शाङ्गरवः ।

यदा तु पूर्ववृत्तमन्यसङ्गाद्विस्मृतो भवान् । तदा कथम-
धर्मभीरुः ।

राजा ।

भवन्तमेवाच गुरुलाघवं पृच्छामि ।

---

the father with thee fallen from thy family [an outcast from thy family]?
but if thou art conscious that thy own marriage-vow [conduct] is free-from-
taint [pure], even slavery will be supportable in thy husband's household.'
Kim pitur, some Beng. MSS. have *kim punar utkulayā*, i. e. *kula-vyava-
hārātikrameṇa vidyamānayā*, S. *Vrata=ćaritra*, K.; =*pati-vrata*, S.

[1] 'We must set off on our return,' lit. 'we must finish our business.'

[2] 'The moon awakes [expands] the night-lotuses only, the sun the day-
lotuses only; for the character [feelings] of those who control their
passions recoils [turns away with abhorrence] from embracing the wife
of another.' *Kumuda* is a kind of lotus, which blossoms in the night
(see p. 120, n. 1); the *pawka-ja*, or mud-born lotus, opens its petals only
in the day. *Bodhayati=prakāśayati*. *Parigraha*, see p. 181, n. 4.

[3] *Anya-sawgāt*, i. e. *anyasyāḥ kāntāyāḥ sawgāt*, 'on account of union
with another wife.' *Vismṛita*, see p. 161, n. 3 at the end; Gram. 896.

[4] *Guru-lāghava* is properly a kind of abstract noun formed from the
Dvandva *guru-laghu*, the Vriddhi taking place in the second member of
the compound instead of the first. The sense will then be, 'I ask your
reverence as to the greater and the less [i. e. the heavier and the lighter]
sin.' This is addressed to the Brāhman who acts as the Purohita, whose
duty it would be to advise the king as to which was the more or less sinful
course. This sense of *guru-lāghava* is supported by several other passages
(Mahā-bh. xii. 1273, iii. 10572; Manu ix. 299). The more obvious sense
would be, 'the alleviation [solution] of a grave matter.'

Verse 129. ĀRYĀ or GĀTHĀ. See verse 2.

मूढः स्यामहमेषा वा वदेन्मिथ्येति संशये ।
दारत्यागी भवाम्याहो परस्त्रीस्पर्शपांशुलः[1] ॥१३०॥

पुरोहितः ॥ विचार्य ॥

यदि तावदेवं क्रियताम् ।

राजा ।

अनुशास्तु मां भवान् ।

पुरोहितः ।

अयमभवती तावदा प्रसवादस्मद्गृहे तिष्ठतु । कुत इदमुच्यत
इति चेत् । त्वं साधुभिरुद्दिष्टः । प्रथममेव चक्रवर्तिनं[2] पुत्रं
जनयिष्यसीति । स चेन्मुनिदौहित्रस्तल्लक्षणोपपन्नो[3] भवि-
ष्यति । अभिनन्द्य शुद्धान्तमेनां प्रवेशयिष्यसि । विपर्यये तु
पितुरस्याः समीपनयनमवस्थितमेव ।

राजा ।

यथा गुरुभ्यो रोचते ।

पुरोहितः ।

वत्से । अनुगच्छ माम् ।

शकुन्तला ।

[a]भअवदि वसुहे । देहि मे विवरं[4] ।

[a] भगवति वसुधे । देहि मे विवरम् ।

---

[1] 'In a doubt as to whether I may be infatuated or she may speak
falsely, shall I become a repudiator of my wife, or defiled by contact
with another's wife?' *Aho*, see p. 49, n. 1 at the end.

[2] 'A son who has the mark of the C'akra [or discus] in his hand.'
When the lines of the right hand formed themselves into a circle, this
was the mark of a future hero and emperor. *C'akra-vartin*, 'one whose
empire extends to the horizon (*c'akra*) or from sea to sea' (see p. 15, n. 2).

[3] 'If the Muni's daughter's-son shall be endowed with this mark, having
congratulated her thou shalt introduce her to the female-apartments.' *Dauhitra*, from *duhitṛi*, is like *pautra*, from *putra*. *Suddhānta*, see p. 21, n. 3.

[4] 'Grant me admission or entrance,' 'open to receive me,' i. e. let me

---

Verse 130. ŚLOKA or ANUSHṬUBH. See verses 5, 6, 11, 12, 26, 47, 50, 51, &c., 127.

॥ इति रुदन्ती प्रस्थिता । निष्क्रान्ता सह पुरोधसा सह तपस्विभिश्च । राजा
शापव्यवहितस्मृतिः शकुन्तलागतमेव चिन्तयति ॥

नेपथ्ये ।

आश्चर्यम् ।

राजा ॥ आकर्ण्य ॥

किं नु खलु स्यात् ।

पुरोहितः ॥ प्रविश्य । सविस्मयम् ॥

देव । अद्भुतं खलु संवृत्तम् ।

राजा ।

किमेवम् ।

पुरोहितः ।

देव । परावृत्तेषु कथञ्चिदृषिषु
सा निन्दन्ती स्वानि भाग्यानि बाला
बाहूत्क्षेपं क्रन्दितुं च प्रवृत्ता ।

राजा ।

किं च ।

पुरोहितः ।

स्त्रीसंस्थानं चाप्सरस्तीर्थमारा-
दुत्क्षिप्यैनां ज्योतिरेकं जगाम ॥ १३१ ॥

॥ सर्वे विस्मयं रूपयन्ति ॥

---

remain uo longer in the land of the living. *Mama praveśāya dvidhā
bhava,* S. The Beng. MSS. have *antaram = avakāśam* instead of *vivaram.*

[1] 'That young-creature upbraiding her own fortunes, throwing up her
arms, and beginning to weep,' or 'and beginning to weep with repeated
uplifting of her arms.' *Bāhūtkshepam* (so read all the MSS.) = *bāhū
utkshipya;* this is an instance of an adverbial indecl. part. of repetition
compounded with a noun (*bhujoċċālanaṃ yathā bhavati evaṃ kranditum
pravṛittā,* S.) Examples of this participle are numerous in Bhaṭṭi-k., as
in ii. 11, *Latānupātaṃ kusumāni agrihṇāt,* &c.; see Gram. 567.

[2] 'A single flash-of-light in female shape having snatched her up near

---

Verse 131. ŚĀLINĪ (a variety of TRISHṬUBH), consisting of eleven syllables to the
Pāda or quarter-verse, each Pāda being alike.

‒ ‒ ‒ ‒ | ‒ ‿ ‒ ‒ ‿ ‒ ‒ ॥

राजा ।

भगवन् । प्रागपि सोऽस्माभिरर्थः प्रत्यादिष्ट एव । किं
वृथा तर्केणान्विष्यते । विश्राम्यतु भवान् ।

पुरोहितः ॥ विलोक्य ॥

विजयस्व । ॥ इति निष्क्रान्तः ॥

राजा ।

वेचवति । पर्याकुलोऽस्मि । शयनभूमिमार्गमादेशय ।

प्रतीहारी ।

ᵃ इदो इदो देवो । ॥ इति प्रस्थिता ॥

राजा ।

कामं प्रत्यादिष्टां स्मरामि न परिग्रहं मुनेस्तनयाम् ।
बलवत्तु दूयमानं प्रत्याययतीव मां हृदयम् ॥१३२॥

॥ इति निष्क्रान्ताः सर्वे ॥

॥ पञ्चमोऽङ्कः ॥

ᵃ इत इतो देवः ॥

Apsaras-tīrtha went off (with her).' *Strī-saṃsthānam*, i. e. *striyā iva
ākṛtir yasya*, S. *Ārāt=antike, nikaṭe*, K. and S. *Jyotiḥ=tejaḥ. Jagāma*,
the Beng. and the Mackenzie MSS. have *tiro-'bhūt*, 'disappeared.'

[1] 'Granted, I remember not the repudiated Muni's daughter (to be my)
wife; nevertheless (my) heart being powerfully agitated forces me as it
were to believe (her).' *Kāmam=atyartham*, K. *Kāmaṃ kāmānumatau*,
S. (cf. p. 24, l. 10; p. 55, n. 3). *Pratyāyayati*, i. e. *tatparigrahe*, S.

Verse 132. ĀRYĀ or GĀTHĀ. See verse 2.

<pre>
 – – | – – | – – || ᴗ – ᴗ | ᴗ ᴗ – | ᴗ – ᴗ | – ᴗ ᴗ | –
 ᴗ ᴗ – | ᴗ – ᴗ | – – || – – | ᴗ ᴗ – | ᴗ | – ᴗ ᴗ | –
</pre>

॥ अथ पञ्चमषष्ठाङ्कमध्ये प्रवेशकः ॥

॥ ततः प्रविशति नागरिकः श्यालः पञ्चाङ्गपुरुषमादाय रक्षिणौ च ॥

रक्षिणौ ॥ ताडयित्वा ॥

अले कुम्भिलंआ । कहेहि । कहिं तुए एशे मणिबन्ध-णुक्किषर्णामहिए लाअकीए अङ्गुलीअए शमाशादिए ।

a अरे कुम्भिलक । कथय । कुत्र त्वयैतन्मणिबन्धनोत्कीर्णनामधेयं राजकीयमङ्गु-लीयकं समासादितम् ।

---

[1] *Praveśaka*, see p. 97, n. 3.

[2] 'Then enters the king's-brother-in-law (as) superintendent of the city-police, and two policemen [guards] bringing a man (with his hands) bound behind.' *Nāgarikaḥ = nagarādhikārī*, 'superintendent of the city,' S.; = *nagare niyuktaḥ*, 'one set over the city,' K.; here 'the chief of the police.' *Syāla* (also written *syāla*) = *rāshṭriya* or *rāshṭrīya* (Amara-k.) The king's brother-in-law, who here acts as superintendent of police, is a character not unfrequently introduced in the plays (cf. Mṛicchak. p. 224, l. 4; p. 227, l. 12; p. 230, l. 1, in which passages he is called *rāja-śyālaḥ* and *rāshṭriya-śyālaḥ*). K. observes that the policemen and the fishermen in this scene speak the Māgadhī form of Prākrit (see Lassen's Instit. Prāk. p. 391), but S. affirms that the fisherman speaks the Sakāra dialect (*ćaura-pātras tu śakāra-nāmadheyaḥ śakāra-prāya-bhāshaṇāt*), see Lassen's Instit. Prāk. p. 422. Both S. and K. have omitted to make mention of the dialect spoken by the Syāla or Nāgarika. According to Viśvanātha (Sāhit.-d. p. 180, l. 12) he ought to speak the Dākshiṇātyā form of Prākrit. In the Beng. MSS., and some of the Deva-n., he is certainly made to speak a dialect distinct from the other characters of this scene, but in the best MSS. pure Prākrit forms are found in the speeches attributed to him. Indeed, as brother-in-law of the king, he must have been a Kshatriya, or one of the military caste.

[3] 'O thief!' *Kumbhila* or *kumbhilaka* seems to be identical with *kumbhila, kumbhilaka, kumbhīra, kumbhīraka*, &c. Compare in the beginning of Act V. of Vikram., *maṇi-kumbhīraka*, 'gem-stealer' (applied to the bird who swallowed the crest-jewel); and at the end of Act II, *loptreṇa sūćitasya kumbhīrakasya;* and in Mālavik., *aho kumbhīlakaiḥ parihara-ṇīyā ćandrikā*.

[4] 'The setting of which is engraven with his name.' *Maṇi-bandhana*, which usually signifies 'the wrist,' is here the place of the setting

पुरुषः ॥ भीतिनाटितकेन[1] ॥

[a] पशीदन्तो भावमिश्शे । अहके ण ईदिशकम्मकाली ।

प्रथमः ।

[b] किं खु शोहणे बम्हणेत्ति कलिश्च लद्धा पडिग्गहे दिंन्ते ।

पुरुषः ।

[c] शुणुह दाणिं । अहके शक्कावदालब्भन्तलवाशी धीवले ।

द्वितीयः ।

[d] पाडच्चला । किं अम्हेहिं जादी पुच्छिदा ।

श्यालः ।

[e] सूञ्चअ[5] । कहेदु सव्वं अणुक्कमेण । मा णं अन्तरा पडिबन्धह ।

[a] प्रसीदन्तु भावमिश्राः । अहं नेदृशकर्मकारी । [b] किं खलु शोभनो ब्राह्मण इति कृत्वा राज्ञा प्रतिग्रहो दत्तः । [c] शृणुतेदानीम् । अहं शक्रावताराभ्यन्तरवासी धीवरः । [d] पाटच्चर । किमस्माभिर्ज्ञातिं पृष्टः । [e] सूचक । कथयतु सर्वम- नुक्रमेण । मैनमन्तरा प्रतिबभीतम् ।

[technically, the collet, داں نگين *nigīn dān*] of the jewel which formed the *mudrā* or seal of the ring, mentioned p. 53, n. 3. *Maṇiḥ khaćyate yasminn iti maṇi-bandhanaḥ*, K. The name might have been engraven on the stone itself, or on the gold in which it was set. *Utkṛī* is used in the sense of 'excavating,' in Mahā-bh. i. 5813; and *samutkīrṇa* with the meaning 'perforated,' in Raghu-v. i. 4.

[1] 'With a gesticulation of fear.' The *ka* added to *nāṭita* may possibly signify a poor, sorry, or ludicrous gesture. It is often pleonastic, but in the plays it will sometimes be found affixed to the past passive participle, to which it gives the sense of a verbal noun. Thus *udbhrāntaka* and *apavāritaka* (Mṛićchak. p. 171) for *udbhrānti* and *apavāraṇa*.

[2] 'Your honour.' *Bhāva* = *mānya*, S., 'venerable,' 'respectable,' to which *miśra* may be added (see p. 7, n. 3).

[3] 'Was it forsooth a present given by the king (to thee), imagining (thee to be) an illustrious Brāhman?' *Pratigraha* (see p. 54, l. 2, with note) is especially 'a donation to a Brāhman at suitable periods.' *Kṛitvā*, 'thinking,' see p. 170, n. 3 in the middle; and cf. Mālavik. p. 23, l. 9, *parakāryam iti kṛitvā;* also Mṛićchak. p. 147, l. 5.

[4] Verbs of 'asking' in Sanskrit govern a double accusative case, one of which is retained after the past passive participle.

[5] *Sūćaka*, 'informer,' is the name of one of the *rakshiṇaḥ*, or 'policemen.'

उभौ ।

a जं आबुत्ते आणबेदि । कहेहि ।

पुरुषः ।

b अहके जालुग्गालादीहिं मच्छबन्धणोबाएहिं कुडुम्बभ-
लणं कलेमि ।

श्यालः ॥ विहस्य ॥

c विसुद्धो दाणिं आजीवो ।

पुरुषः ।

d भट्टा । मा एव्वं भण ।

सहजे किल जे विणिन्दिए ण हु दे कम्म विवज्जणीअए ।
पशुमालणकम्मदालुणे अणुकम्पामिदु एव्व शोत्तिए ॥१३३॥

a यदावुत्त आज्ञापयति । कथय ।　　b अहं जालोद्धारादिभिर्मत्स्यबन्धनोपायैः
कुटुम्बभरणं करोमि ।　　c विशुद्ध इदानीमाजीवः ।　　d भर्तः । नैवं भण ।
सहजं किल यद्विनिन्दितं न खलु तत्कर्म विवर्जनीयम् ।
पशुमारणकर्मदारुणोऽनुकम्पामृदुरेव श्रोत्रियः ॥

---

[1] *Ābutta,* 'a sister's husband,' or 'brother-in-law,' according to Amara-k.
vii. 12. In Mṛicchak. p. 339, l. 12, this word is applied as a title of respect
by a son to his father; but Dr. Boehtlingk conjectures that this may be
an error for *āvuka,* the regular theatrical term for 'father.' According to
Dr. Burkhard, *ābutta*=Sanskrit *bhāva,* 'an honourable sir,' 'gentleman.'

[2] 'I make the support of my family by nets, hooks, and the other con-
trivances for catching fish.' *Udgāla* or *udgāra*=*valiśa* or *vaḍiśa,* 'a fish-
hook,' K. *Jāla-valiśa-ppahudihiṃ*=*jāla-vaḍiśa-prabhṛitibhiḥ* is the reading of the Bengālī Recension. *Jālodgāra* may mean 'the casting of nets.'

[3] This is spoken ironically, as, according to Manu (x. 46–48), the *nishāda,*
or fisherman caste, was one of the lowest. 'Those who are considered as
low-born shall subsist only by such employments as the twice-born despise.
Nishādas (must subsist) by catching fish,' &c. Any occupation which in-
volved the sin of slaughtering animals (excepting in the case of sacrificing
to the god S'iva) was considered despicable. Butchers and leather-sellers
were as great, or even greater, objects of scorn.

[4] 'That occupation in which one was born, as-the-saying-is (*kila*),

---

Verse 133. VAITĀLĪYA. See verse 52.

श्यालः ।

^a तदो तदो ।

पुरुषः ।

^b एक्कस्सिं दिअसे खरइशो लोहिअमच्छे¹ मए कप्पिदे जाव ।

^a ततस्ततः ।   ^b एकस्मिन्दिवसे खरइशो रोहितमत्स्यो मया कल्पितो यावत् ।

---

though in-bad-repute, verily must not be abandoned. The same Brāhman, who is savage in the act of slaughtering animals, may be (of a disposition) tender with compassion.' *Saha-ja* = *kula-kramānugata*, 'inherited from one's forefathers.' See Indian Wisdom, p. 140 and note. Manu is very peremptory in restricting special occupations to the different castes, especially to the mixed and lowest castes, formed by intermarriage with the others. 'A man of the lowest class, who, through covetousness, lives by the acts of the highest, let the king strip of all his wealth and banish. His own office, though badly performed, is preferable to that of another, though well performed; for he who lives by the duties of another class, immediately falls from his own' (Manu x. 96, 97). Hence we find the employments of fishing, slaughtering animals for food, leather-selling, basket-making, burning the dead, &c. &c., assigned to men born in certain impure castes, and confined perpetually to their descendants. To the higher and purer castes a greater variety of employment was allowed. S'. observes that the Brāhman is called *Shaṭ-karman*, from the precept of Manu (i. 88), which enjoins upon him six occupations, viz. reading, teaching, sacrificing, assisting others to sacrifice, giving, and receiving. See Indian Wisdom, p. 244. Under certain circumstances he was allowed by Manu to engage even in trade, and other employments. The sacrifice of animals was enjoined only on the priests of the god S'iva. The Brāhman, in the worship of this god, might have to kill animals; but this was as much a necessary part of his business, as killing fish, of the fisherman, and was no proof of any natural cruelty of disposition. S'. defines a S'rotriya Brāhman thus: *Janmanā Brāhmaṇo jñeyaḥ, sanskārair dvija ućyate, vidyayā yāti vipratvam, tribhiḥ śrotriya ućyate*, 'birth constitutes the title Brāhman; sacramental rites (especially that of investiture with the sacred thread), the title Dvija, or twice-born; knowledge, the title Vipra; and all three S'rotriya.' The usual definition of this word is, a Brāhman conversant with *śruti*, or scripture.

[1] The *Rohita* or *Rohi* fish (Cyprinus Rohita), lit. 'red-fish,' is a kind of carp, found in lakes and ponds in the neighbourhood of the Ganges. It grows to the length of three feet, is very voracious, and its flesh, though

ᵃ तश्श उदलब्भन्तले एदं लदणभाशुलं अङ्गुलीअं देक्खिअं। पच्छा अहके शे विक्कआअ दंशअन्ते गहिदे भाव-मिश्शेहिं। मालेह वा। मुञ्चेह वा। अअं शे आअमवुत्तन्ते।

श्यालः।

ᵇ जाणुअ। विस्सगन्धी गोहादी मच्छबन्धी एव्व णिस्संसअं[1]। अङ्गुलीअअदंसणं से विमरिसिदव्वं[2]। राउलं एव्व गच्छामो।

रक्खिणौ।

ᶜ तह। गच्छ अरे गण्ठिभेदअ[3]।   ॥ सर्वे परिक्रामन्ति ॥

श्यालः।

ᵈ सूअअ। इमं पुरदुवारे अप्पमत्ता पडिबालह। जाव इमं

ᵃ तस्योदराभ्यन्तर एतद्रत्नभासुरमङ्गुलीयकं दृष्टम्। पश्चादहमस्य विक्रयाय दर्शयन्गृहीतो भावमिश्रैः। मारयत वा। मुञ्चत वा। अयमस्यागमवृत्तान्तः।   ᵇ जानुक। विस्रगन्धिर्गोघाती मत्स्यबन्ध एव निःसंशयम्। अङ्गुलीयकदर्शनमस्य विमर्ष्टव्यम्। राजकुलमेव गच्छामः।   ᶜ तथा। गच्छ अरे ग्रन्थिभेदक।   ᵈ सूचक। इमं पुरद्वारेऽप्रमत्तौ प्रतिपालयतम्। यावदिदम्

---

coarse, is eaten. Its back is olive-coloured, its belly of a beautiful golden hue, its fins and eyes red.

[1] 'O Jānuka, the villain stinking (as he does) of raw flesh (is) doubtless a fisherman.' Jānuka is the name of the other policeman, who is supposed to have detected the thief (*jānuka iti ćora-jñātur apara-padāter nāma, S'.*) Some Beng. MSS. have *jālua* (=*jāluka*). *Visra-gandhi=āmisha-gandhi*, C'. *Go-ghātī*, the killing of a cow (*go-hatyā*), is reckoned by the Hindūs a most heinous crime (cf. Hitop. 1. 162). Hence *go-ghātin*, 'cow-killer,' is applied as a reproachful epithet to any rogue or low person. Thus in the Mṛićchak. p. 299, l. 4; p. 317, l. 2, the Ćāṇḍāla is called *go-ha* or *go-ghna*.

[2] '(But) the finding [seeing, shewing] of the ring by him must be (more closely) inquired into.' *Vimarshṭavyam=jijñāsitavyam*, S'. Root *mriś* with *vi* has usually the sense of 'to consider,' 'investigate;' but if the root be *mrij*, the sense would be 'must be pardoned,' 'overlooked.' K. has *vimārshṭavyam*, from *mrij*.

[3] *Granthi-bhedaka*, 'cut-purse,' lit. 'knot-breaker' or 'knot-cutter.' The Hindūs generally carry their money tied up in a knot in one end of a cloth, which is bound round the waist.

^a अङ्गुलीअञ्अं जहागमणं भट्टिणो णिवेदिअ तदो सासणं पडिच्छिअ णिक्कमामि ।

उभौ ।

^b पविशदु आउत्ते शामिपशादश्श ।

॥ निष्क्रान्तः श्यालः ॥

प्रथमः ।

^c जाणुअ । चिलाञ्अदि खु आउत्ते ।

द्वितीयः ।

^d यं अवशलोबशप्पणीञ्आ लाञ्आणो ।

प्रथमः ।

^e जाणुअ । फुलन्ति मे हत्था इमश्श बज्झकूश्श शुमणो पिअंडुं ।[1] ॥ इति मुहुअं निर्दिशति ॥

मुहुअः ।

^f ण अलुहदि भावे अकालणमालणे भविदुं ।

द्वितीयः   ॥ विलोक्य ॥

^g एशे अम्हाणं शामी पन्नहत्थे लाञ्अशाशणं पडिच्छिअ इदोमुहे देक्खीअदि । गिड्डवली भविश्शशि शुणो मुहं

^a अङ्गुलीयकं यथागमनं भर्तुर्निवेद्य ततः शासनं प्रतीष्य निष्क्रमामि ।   ^b प्रविशत्वावुत्तः स्वामिप्रसादाय ।   ^c जानुक । चिरायति खल्वावुत्तः ।   ^d नन्ववसरोपसर्पणीया राजानः ।   ^e जानुक । स्फुरतो मे हस्तावस्य बध्यस्य सुमनः पिनद्धुम् ।   ^f नार्हति भावोऽकारणमारणो भवितुम् ।   ^g हय नौ स्वामी पन्नहस्तो राजशासनं प्रतीष्येतोमुखो दृश्यते । गृध्रबलिर्भविष्यसि शुनो मुखं

---

[1] 'My hands tingle [my fingers itch] to bind a flower (about the head) of this victim [criminal about to be executed].'   All the Deva-n. MSS. have *sumanaḥ pinaddhum*, excepting the Mackenzie, which has *sumahaṇam* for *sumaṇo*.   The Beng. have got rid of the difficulty by substituting *vyāpādayitum*, 'to kill.'   It is clear from what follows that the two policemen expected that their master would return with the king's order for putting the fisherman to death.   From the Mālati-m. and other plays, it is evident that a person about to be offered as a victim to Śiva or Durgā had a wreath of flowers bound round the head.   This was also the case with common criminals, previous to their execution.

[a] वा देक्खिस्सशि[1] ।

श्यालः ॥ प्रविश्य ॥

[b] सूञ्चञ्च । मुञ्चेदु एसो जालोञ्अजीवी । उववञ्चो किल अञ्सं अङ्गुलीञ्अञ्सस आअमो ।

सूचकः ।

[c] जह आवुत्ते भणादि ।

द्वितीयः ।

[d] एंशे जमशदंशं पविशिञ्अ[2] पडिणिवुत्ते ।

॥ इति पुरुषं परिमुक्तबन्धनं करोति ॥

पुरुषः ॥ श्यालं प्रणम्य ॥

[e] भट्टा । अह कौलिशे[3] मे आजीवे ।

श्यालः ।

[f] एस भट्टिणा अङ्गुलीञ्अञ्अमुल्लसम्मिदो पसांदोबि[4] दाविदो ।

॥ इति पुरुषायार्घ्यं प्रयच्छति ॥

---

[a] वा द्रक्ष्यसि ।   [b] सूचक । मुच्यतामेष जालोपजीवी । उपपन्नः किलायमङ्गुलीय-कस्यागमः ।   [c] यथायुक्तो भणति ।   [d] एष यमसदनं प्रविश्य प्रतिनिवृत्तः ।   [e] भर्तः । अथ कीदृशो म आजीवः ।   [f] एष भर्त्राङ्गुलीयकमूल्यसम्मितः प्रसादोऽपि दापितः ।

---

[1] 'Thou wilt be food for [an offering to] the vultures, or wilt see the face of a dog.' *Gridhra-bali*, see p. 179, n. 1. *S'uno mukham*, so read all the Deva-n. MSS., excepting the Mackenzie, which omits the clause entirely. Dr. Boehtlingk has adopted as an emendation, *śiśuno muham*, i. e. *śiśor* [not *śiśuno*] *mukham*, and translated 'or thou wilt see the face of (thy) child (once more).' He has supported this interpretation by a reference to two other passages, one in Act VII. of this play (*putra-mukha-darśanena*), another in Mṛićchak. p. 303, l. 4. Doubtless *putra-mukham dṛiś* is a common phrase, but the whole point of this passage seems to me to lie in the ludicrous substitution of *śunaḥ* for *putrasya*.

[2] *Yama-sadana*, 'the abode of Yama,' i. e. the infernal city, Yama-pur, whither the Hindūs believe a departed soul immediately repairs, and receives a just sentence from Yama, the Hindū Pluto or Minos. The name Yama, i. e. Restrainer or Punisher (from *yam*, 'to restrain'), is given to him as judge of departed spirits and god of punishment.

[3] This is said ironically, in reference to p. 219, l. 7, n. 3.

[4] *Prasāda*, properly 'a favour,' here 'a present,' 'a gift.'

पुरुषः ॥ समग्घ्यां प्रतिगृह्य ॥

[a] भट्टकेण अणुग्गहिदम्हि ।

सूचकः ।

[b] एशे णाम अणुग्गहिदे जे शूलादो अवदालिञ हत्थिक्खन्धे पडिट्ठाबिदे ।

ज्ञानुकः ।

[c] आबुत्त । पालिदोशिञं कहेदि तेण अङ्गुलीअएण भट्टिणो शम्मदेण होदव्वं ।

श्यालः ।

[d] ण तस्सं महारुहं रदणं भट्टिणो बहुमदंति तक्केमि । तस्स दंसणेण भट्टिणो अभिमदो जणो सुमरिदो । मुहुत्तञं पकिदिगम्भीरोवि पज्जुस्सुअमणो आसिं ।

सूचकः ।

[e] शेविदं णाम आबुत्तेण ।

---

[a] भवतानुगृहीतोऽस्मि ।　　[b] एष नामानुगृहीतो यः शूलादवतार्य हस्तिस्कन्धे प्रतिष्ठापितः ।　　[c] आवुत्त । पारितोषिकं कथयति तेनाङ्गुलीयकेन भर्तुः सम्मतेन भवितव्यम् ।　　[d] न तस्मिन्महार्हं रत्नं भर्तुर्बहुमतमिति तर्कयामि । तस्य दर्शनेन भर्तुरभिमतो जनः स्मृतः । मुहूर्तं प्रकृतिगम्भीरोऽपि पर्युत्सुकमना आसीत् ।　　[e] सेवितं नामाबुत्तेन ।

---

[1] 'This (fellow) forsooth (may well say he) has been favoured, who, after being made to descend from the stake, has been mounted on the withers of an elephant.' *Śūla*, 'a stake for impaling criminals.' The act of impaling was called *śūlāropaṇa*, and one who deserved it *śūlya*. 'Mounting on an elephant' denotes elevation to high dignity, elephants being used in triumphal processions.

[2] This is the reading of K. Most of the Deva-n. have *palidośam kahehi* (=*paritoṣam kathaya*). Translate: 'The present proves [betokens, bespeaks] that this ring must be highly prized by the king.'

[3] 'Though naturally reserved [unruffled, deep, profound] he became for a moment agitated in mind.' *Gambhīra*, see p. 39, n. 1, and p. 204, n. 3. K. reads *pajjassu-ṇaaṇo* (=*paryaśru-nayanaḥ*). All Asiatics are skilful in concealing emotion.

ज्ञानुकः ।

[a] षं भणाहि । इमश्च कए मम्छिआभतुणोत्ति ।

॥ इति पुरुषमसूयया पश्यति ॥

पुरुषः ।

[b] भट्टालके । इदो अडं तुम्हाणं शुमणोमुल्लं होदु ।

ज्ञानुकः ।

[c] एत्तके जुज्जइ ।

श्यालः ।

[d] धीवर । महन्तरी तुमं पिञ्अवञअस्सको दाणिं मे संवुत्तो ।
कादम्बरीसक्खिञं अम्हाणं पढमसोहिदं इच्छीञदि । ता
सोणिडआपणं एव्व गच्छामो ।

सर्वे ।

[e] तह ।

॥ इति निष्क्रान्ताः सर्वे ॥

॥ प्रवेशकः ॥

[a] ननु भण । अस्य कृते मत्स्यिकाभर्तुरिति । [b] भट्टारकाः । इतोऽर्धं युष्माकं सुमनोमूल्यं
भवतु । [c] एतावच्छुज्यते । [d] धीवर । महत्तरत्त्वं प्रियवयस्यक इदानीं मे संवृत्तः ।
कादम्बरीसाक्षिकमस्माकं प्रथमसौहृदमिष्यते । तच्छौणिडकापणमेव गच्छामः । [e] तथा ।

---

[1] So read most of the Deva-n. MSS. *Matsyikā* is not given in the
Dictionary. Dr. Boehtlingk translates it by *Fisch-brut*, 'the fry of fish,'
and observes that it is also the name for a kind of fish called in German
Schaar. Had the word been *matsyika* or *mātsyika*, 'a fisherman,' there would
have been no difficulty. May it not mean 'a fish-woman,' and *matsyikā-
bhartṛi*, 'this husband of a fish-woman ?' K. and the Bengālī have *matsya-
śatroḥ*, 'enemy of fishes.' Burkhard follows this, and reads *maćcha-śattuṇotti*,
but in the Vocabulary prefers *maśćhiā=matsyikā*, 'a fish' (?).

[2] 'Let the half of this be the price of your flower (for binding about
my head).' The fisherman is again ironical. The allusion of course is to
the flower mentioned at p. 222, l. 11. There is probably a double-entendre
in *sumanaḥ*, which may signify 'good-will,' as well as 'flower.'

[3] 'Our first friendship requires to be attested over (some) wine,' i. e.
we must pledge ourselves over our cups or in drinking each other's health.
Kādumbarī, 'an intoxicating liquor distilled from the Kadamba flower.'
Sākshikam, compare Mālavik. p. 53, l. 7; Raghu-v. xi. 48; Hitop. l. 842.

॥ अथ षष्ठोऽङ्कः ॥

॥ ततः प्रविशत्याकाशयानेन सानुमती नामाप्सराः ॥

सानुमती ।

[a] णिव्वत्तिदं मए पज्जाअणिव्वत्तणिज्जं अच्छरातित्थ-
सण्णिज्झं । जाव साहुजणस्स अभिसेअकालोत्ति सम्पदं
इमस्स राएसिणो उदन्तं पच्चक्खीकरिस्सं । णं मेणआ-
सम्बन्धेण सरीरभूदा दाणिं मे सउन्दला । ताएअ

[a] निर्वर्तितं मया पर्यायनिर्वर्तनीयमप्सरस्तीर्थसान्निध्यम् । यावत्साधुजनस्याभिषेक-
काल इति साम्प्रतमस्य राजर्षेरुदन्तं प्रत्यक्षीकरिष्यामि । ननु मेनकासम्बन्धेन शरीर-
भूतेदानीं मे शकुन्तला । तया च

---

[1] 'Attendance at Apsaras-tīrtha (which is wont) to be performed (by us) in regular-rotation has been performed by me. Now, whilst (it is) the bathing-time of the good people [i. e. of Śakuntalā and the nymphs], I will with my own eyes ascertain the circumstances [news] of this Rājarshi.' *Sānnidhyam* (from *san-nidha*), lit. 'proximity;' here it denotes 'close attendance or waiting,' as in Hitop. l. 1112, *anujīvinā sānnidhyam avaśyaṃ karaṇīyam.* In the interlude before Act IV. of Vikram., *upasthāna* occurs with the same sense in a parallel passage : *Apsaro-vyāpāra-paryāyeṇa sūryasya upasthāne vartamānayā priya-sakhyā vinā vasanta-samaya āyata iti balavad utkaṇṭhitāsmi,* 'I am mightily troubled that the spring season has arrived during the absence of my dear friend, who is in attendance upon Sūrya, according to the regular cycle of nymph's duty.' *Ud-anta* (lit. 'reaching to the end'), 'telling to the end,' 'full tidings,' 'news.'

[2] 'Verily by (my) connexion with Menakā, Śakuntalā has now become part of myself,' lit. 'my own body,' i. e. 'part of my own flesh and blood,' 'identified with myself.' As to the nymph Menakā, the mother of Śakuntalā, see p. 44, l. 11 with n. 2, and p. 45, n. 1. *Śarīra-bhūtā,* this is the same sort of compound as *pūga-krita* or *pūga-bhūta;* see Pāṇ. ii. 1, 59, and p. 167, n. 2 at the end. Cf. *śarīram asi me,* 'thou art my body,' Mālavik. p. 33, l. 12.

ᵃदुहिदुणिमित्तं आदिट्टुपुव्वम्हि । ॥ समन्तादवलोक्ष्य ॥ ᵇकिं
णुक्खु उदुस्संवेबि णिरुस्सवारम्भं विच्त्र एदं रास्त्रउलं
दीसइ । अत्यि मे विहवो पणिधाणेण सव्वं परिस्सादुं ।
किन्दु सहीए आदरो मए माणइदव्वो । होदु । इमाणं एव्व
उज्जाणपालिआणं तिरक्खरिणीपरिच्छण्णा पस्सपरि-
वत्तिणी भविच्त्र उवलम्भिस्सं । ॥ इति नाट्येनावतीर्य स्थिता ॥

ᵃदुहितृनिमित्तमादिष्टपूर्वाऽस्मि । ᵇकिं नु खलु ऋतूत्सवेऽपि निरुत्सवारम्भमि-
वैतद्राजकुलं दृश्यते । अस्ति मे विभवः प्रणिधानेन सर्वं परिज्ञातुम् । किन्तु सख्या
आदरो मया मानयितव्यः । भवतु । अनयोरेवोद्यानपालिकयोस्तिरस्करिणीपरिच्छन्ना
पार्श्वपरिवर्तिनी भूत्वोपलप्स्ये ।

---

¹ *Ṛitūtsava*, lit. 'the festival of the season,' i. e. the *Vasantotsava*, or
'great vernal festival,' in celebration of the return of spring, and said to
be in honour of the god Kṛishṇa. Originally his son Kāma-deva, the god
of love, must have been the object of worship in this festival. It is
identified with the Holi or Dolā-yātra, the Saturnalia, or rather, Carnival
of the Hindūs, when people of all conditions take liberties with each other,
especially by scattering red powder and coloured water on the clothes of
persons passing in the street, as described in Ratnāvali, pp. 5, 6, 7, where
syringes and waterpipes are used by the crowd. Flowers, and especially
the opening blossoms of the mango, would naturally be much used for
decoration at this festival, and as offerings to the god of love. It was
formerly held on the full moon of the month Caitra, or about the beginning of April, but now on the full moon of Phālguna, or about the
beginning of March. The other great Hindū festival, held in the autumn,
about October, is called *Durgotsava* or *Durgā-pūjā*, being in honour of
the goddess Durgā.

² *Praṇidhāna*, 'profound meditation,' or that mental faculty by
which divine beings were supposed to be able to ascertain future
events. The verb *pra-ṇi-dhā* (sometimes with *manas*) is primarily 'to
fix in;' hence 'to fix the mind on,' 'be intent on.' Compare *mayā
praṇidhāna-sthitayā atyāhitam upalabdham*, Vikram. (interlude before
Act IV).

³ *Tiras-kariṇi*, a kind of magical veil, rendering the wearer invisible.

॥ ततः प्रविशति चूताङ्कुरमवलोकयन्ती चेटी । अपरा च पृष्ठतस्तस्याः ॥

प्रथमा ।

[a] आअबहरिअपण्डुर वसन्तमासस्स जीअसव्वस्स ।
दिट्ठोसि चूदकोरअ उंदुमङ्गलं तुमं पसाएमि ॥१३४॥

द्वितीया ।

[b] परहुदिए । किं एआइणी मन्तेसि ।

प्रथमा ।

[c] महुअरिए । चूदकलिअं देक्खिअ उम्मत्तिआ परहुदिआ होदि ।

<hr>

[a] आताम्रहरितपाण्डुर वसन्तमासस्य जीवसर्वस्व ।
दृष्टोऽसि चूतकोरक च्युतुमङ्गलं त्वां प्रसादयामि ॥१३४॥

[b] परभृतिके । किमेकाकिनी मन्त्रयसे ।   [c] मधुकरिके । चूतकलिकां दृष्टोन्मत्ता परभृतिका भवति ।

<hr>

[1] 'O reddish pale-green mango-blossom, the very essence of the life of the vernal month, thou art seen (by me, and) I bid thee hail, auspicious-harbinger of the season.' *Ā-tāmra-harita-pāṇḍura*, this kind of Dvandva Bahuvrīhi compound, expressing varieties of colour, is noticed by Pāṇ. ii. 1, 69 (cf. *kṛishṇa-śukla, lohita-śavala,* &c.) *Ā* prefixed, implies diminution, and is equivalent to *īshat*. So *ā-pāṇḍu*, 'yellowish,' or 'slightly yellow,' Vikram., Act II. *Jīva-sarvasva*, lit. 'whose whole substance is constituted of life,' see p. 33, n. 1 in the middle. Some MSS. have *jīva-sarvasvam*, agreeing with *tvām*. *Mangalam*, 'anything auspicious,' 'any symbol or sign of happiness;' in this latter sense it seems to be used here. The goddess Durgā is called in the same way *sarva-mangalā*, 'presiding over the happiness of the whole world.' *Ṛitu* is evidently here the season *par excellence*, the season of all others. *Prasādayāmi*, lit. 'I ask thee to be favourable,' 'I entreat thee to be propitious.'

[2] *Para-bhṛitikā*, 'the female of the Indian cuckoo,' see p. 162, n. 2.

<hr>

Verse 134. ĀRYĀ or GĀTHĀ. See verse 2.

```
— — | ∪ ∪ ∪ ∪ | — ∪ ∪ ‖ ∪ — ∪ | — — | ∪ — ∪ | — — | ∪
— — | ∪ — ∪ | — ∪ ∪ ‖ ∪ ∪ — | ∪ — ∪ | ∪ | ∪ — ∪ | —
```

In the last Pāda the syllables *mam* and *e* are considered short by a license peculiar to Prākṛit prosody.

द्वितीया ॥ सहर्षं त्वरयोपगम्य ॥

[a] कहं उवट्ठिदो महुमासो ।

प्रथमा ।

[b] महुञ्चरिए । तव दाणिं कालो एसो मदविब्भमगीदाणं ।

द्वितीया ।

[c] सहि । अवलम्ब मं । जाव अग्गपादट्ठिआ भविञ चूदकलिञं गेण्हिञ कामदेवच्चणं करेमि ।

प्रथमा ।

[d] जइ ममबिक्खु अडं अच्चणफलस्स ।

द्वितीया ।

[e] अकहिदेबि एदं सम्पज्जइ । जदो एक्कं एव्व णो जीविदं । दुधाठिदं सरीरं । ॥ सखीमवलम्ब्य स्थिता चूताङ्कुरं गृह्णाति ॥ [f] अए । अप्पडिबुडोबि चूदप्पसवो एत्थ बन्धण[1]भङ्गसुरभी होदि ।

॥ कपोतहस्तकं[2] कृत्वा ॥

[a] कथमुपस्थितो मधुमासः ।   [b] मधुकरिके । तवेदानीं काल एव मदविभ्रमगीतानाम् ।   [c] सखि । अवलम्बख माम् । यावदग्रपादस्थिता भूत्वा चूतकलिकां गृहीत्वा कामदेवार्चनं करोमि ।   [d] यदि ममापि खल्वर्धमर्चनफलस्य ।   [e] सक्थितेऽपि एतत्सम्पद्यते । यत एकमेव नौ जीवितम् । द्विधास्थितं शरीरम् ।   [f] अये । अप्रतिबुद्धोऽपि चूतप्रसवोऽत्र बन्धनभङ्गसुरभिर्भवति ।

---

[1] *Bandhana*, i. e. *prasava-bandhana*, 'the foot-stalk of the flower,' see p. 103, l. 3, n. 1.

[2] 'Having joined the hands together,' or 'having placed them one over another.' *Kapota* is properly 'a dove or pigeon;' but K. informs us that it is also the name for a mode of joining the hands. Probably the hands and fingers were brought into a position bearing some fancied resemblance to a pigeon. S'. and C. quote the following verse, which seems to intimate that this position was significant of humble entreaty, respectful representation, or fear : *Sarva-pārśva-samāśleshāt kapotaḥ sarva-śīrshakaḥ* [*sarpa-śīrshakaḥ, S'.*], *bhītau vijñāpane ćaiva vinaye ća prayujyate.*

[a] तुंसि मए चूदङ्कुर दिण्णो कामस्स गहिदधणुअस्स ।
पहिअजणजुवइलक्खो पञ्चब्भहिओ सरो होहि ॥१३५॥

॥ इति चूताङ्कुरं क्षिपति ॥

कञ्चुकी ॥ प्रविश्य पटाक्षेपेण[2] कुपितः ॥

मा तावदनात्मज्ञे[3] । देवेन प्रतिषिद्धे वसन्तोत्सवे त्वमाम्र-
कलिकाभङ्गं किमारभसे ।

उभे ॥ भीते ॥

[b] पसीददु अज्जो । अग्गहीदत्थाओ वअं ।

कञ्चुकी ।

न किल श्रुतं युवाभ्याम् । यद्वासन्निकैस्तरुभिरपि देवस्य
शासनं प्रमाणीकृतं तदाश्रयिभिः पत्त्रिभिश्च । तथा हि[4]

[a] त्वमसि मया चूताङ्कुर दत्तः कामस्य गृहीतधनोः ।
पथिकजनयुवतिलक्ष्यः पञ्चाभ्यधिकः शरो भव ॥१३५॥

[b] प्रसीदन्त्वार्यैः । अगृहीतार्थौ आवाम् ।

---

[1] 'O mango-sprout, thou art offered by me to Kāma-deva (now in the act of) taking-up-his-bow. Become the most excellent arrow of the five, having-for-thy-mark maidens whose lovers are journeying (to some distant land).' As to Kāma and the epithet *pañćābhyadhika* (=*śreshṭha*, K.; = *shashṭha*, S.), see p. 99, n. 1. *Pathika-jana-yuvati*, cf. Megha-d. ver. 8, *pathika-vanitāḥ*. With reference to the offering of flowers to Kāma-deva, cf. Ratn. pp. 14, 17.

[2] 'With a hurried toss of the curtain,' see p. 144, n. 1.

[3] 'Do not so, thou thoughtless woman!' *An-ātmajña* (=*ātma-parićaya-rahita*), lit. 'one who does not know his own nature.' It denotes here, 'one who is thoughtless about orders.' As to the Kańćukin or Chamberlain, see p. 186, n. 1.

[4] 'When even by the vernal shrubs, and by the feathered tribes [birds] their inhabitants, the commands of the king are made the rule [obeyed].' *Pramāṇa* is 'a rule or standard of action,' and *pramāṇī-kri*, 'to receive as a rule,' 'to admit as authority' (cf. p. 188, l. 5).

Verse 135. ĀRYĀ or GĀTHĀ. See verse 2.

चूतानां चिरनिर्गतापि कलिका बध्नाति न स्वं रजः
सन्नद्धं यदपि स्थितं कुरुवकं तत्कोरकावस्थया ।
कण्ठेषु स्खलितं गतेऽपि शिशिरे पुंस्कोकिलानां रुतं
शङ्के संहरति स्मरोऽपि चकितस्तूणार्धकृष्टं शरम् ॥१३६॥[1]

उभे ।

[a] णत्थि सन्देहो । महप्पहावो राएसी ।

प्रथमा ।

[b] अज्ज । कदि दिअहाइं अम्हाणं मित्तावसुणा रट्टिएण
भट्टिणो पाअमूलं पेसिदाणं[2] । इत्थं च णो पमदवणस्स

<hr>

[a] नास्ति सन्देहः । महाप्रभावो राजर्षिः ।   [b] आर्ये । कति दिवसान्यावयोर्मित्रा-
वसुना राष्ट्रियेण भर्तुः पादमूलं प्रेषितयोः । इत्थं च नौ प्रमदवनस्य

<hr>

[1] 'The bud of the mangoes, though long since protruded, does not form [gather] its own pollen [dust]. The Kuruvaka flower, though all ready to blossom, remains in its budding state. The note falters in the throats of the male-cuckoos, though the cold-dews are passed. I suspect even Smara, being daunted, arrests [replaces] the shaft half-drawn from (his) quiver.' *Badhnāti*, see p. 29, n. 1 in the middle; and compare *īshad-baddha-rajaḥ-kaṇāgra-kapiśā ćūte navā mañjarī*, Vikram., Act II. *Sannaddham* = *pushpitum udyatam*, S.; = *vikāsonmukham*, K. (cf. p. 27, l. 6, n. 2). *Sthitam*, cf. p. 1, l. 2. *Kuruvaka* is either the crimson amaranth, or a purple species of Barleria. *Tat-korakāvasthayā* = *kalikā-daśayā*, S.; i.e. *na vikāsitam*, C. *Skhalitam* = *gadgaditam*, K. *Śiśira*, properly 'the dewy season,' or 'season of hoar-frost.' The Hindūs divide the year into six seasons of two months each, viz. 1. Spring, *Vasanta*, beginning about the middle of March, or according to some, February; 2. Summer, *Grīshma;* 3. Rains, *Varshā;* 4. Autumn, *Śarad;* 5. Winter, *Hemanta;* 6. Dews, *Śiśira*. *Puṇs-kokilānāṃ rutam*, cf. *parabhṛita-virutam*, p. 162, l. 4, with note. *Saṃharati*, cf. p. 14, l. 3. It is clear that *saṃ-hṛi* and *prati-saṃ-hṛi* may have the sense of 'replace,' in reference to a quiver, as in Mahā-bh. iii. 772, we have *saṃharasva punar vāṇam*. See also Raghu-v. iii. 64. *Smara*, see p. 209, n. 1.

[2] '(But) few days (have elapsed) to us sent to the feet of his Majesty

<hr>

Verse 136. ŚĀRDŪLA-VIKRĪḌITA (a variety of ATIDHṚITI). See verses 14, 30, 36, 39, 40, 63, 79, 85, 86, 89, 97, 98, 111.

[a]पालणकम्म समप्पिदं । ता आअन्तुअदाए अस्सुदपुव्वो अम्हेहिं एसो वुत्तन्तो ।

कञ्चुकी ।

भवतु । न पुनरेवं प्रवर्तितव्यम् ।

उभे ।

[b]अज्ज । कोदूहलं णो । जइ इमिणा जणेण सोदव्वं । कहेदु भट्टं । किस्सिमित्तं भट्टिणा वसन्तूसवो पडिसिद्धो ।

सानुमती ।

[c]उस्सवप्पिआ खु मणुस्सा । गरुणा कारणेण होदव्वं ।

कञ्चुकी ।

बहुलीभूतंमेतत्किं न कथ्यते । किमचभवत्योः कर्णपथं नायातं शकुन्तलामत्यादेशकौलीनंम् ।

---

[a] पालनकर्म समर्पितम् । तदागन्तुकतयाश्रुतपूर्वं आवाभ्यामेव वृत्तान्तः ।   [b] आर्य । कौतूहलं नौ । यद्यनेन जनेन श्रोतव्यम् । कथयतु भवान् । किंनिमित्तं भर्त्रा वसन्तोत्सवः प्रतिषिद्धः ।   [c] उत्सवप्रियाः खलु मनुष्याः । गुरुणा कारणेन भवितव्यम् ।

---

by Mitrā-vasu, the king's brother-in-law.' *Kati*, like *kiyat*, may be either interrogative or indefinite. So *kati padāni galvā*, Ratn. p. 14, l. 6. After *divasāni*, K. supplies *gatāni*, 'have passed.' This construction of the genitive after *gata*, expressing the lapse of time, is not uncommon. Cf. *ashṭa-pañćāśatam rātryaḥ śayānasya adya me gatāḥ*, Mahā-bh. xiii. 7732; *adya daśamo māsas tātasya uparatasya*, Mudrā-r. p. 80, l. 11. *Māso jātasya*, Pāṇ. ii. 2, 5. *Pāda-mūlam*, lit. 'the root of the feet,' 'the heel.' The phrase *pādu-mūlam preshitaḥ*, expressive of the most humble servitude, occurs elsewhere; see Mudrā-r. p. 16, l. 8; and p. 64, l. 16. *Rāshṭriyeṇa*, see p. 217, n. 2; the king's brother-in-law probably acted as a kind of viceroy.

[1] *Āgantukatayā*, 'since we are but just arrived,' or 'by reason of our being strangers;' see note on *buddha-pallavatayā*, p. 29, l. 1.

[2] 'By us;' see note to *ayaṃ janaḥ*, p. 144, l. 2, and cf. p. 109, l. 8.

[3] *Utsava-priyāḥ*, 'fond of festivals,' see p. 161, n. 3 at the end.

[4] *Bahulī-bhūtam = sakala-viditam*, 'generally known,' 'notorious,' S.

[5] 'Has not the scandal about the repudiation of Śakuntalā reached your ladyships' ears?' *Karṇa-patha*, lit. 'the path or range of the ears,' cf.

उभे ।

[a] सुदं रट्टिणी मुहादो जाव अङ्गुलीअअदंसणं ।

कञ्चुकी ।

तेन ह्यल्पं कथयितव्यम् । यदेव खलु स्वाङ्गुलीयकदर्श-
नादनुस्मृतं देवेन सत्यमूढपूर्वा मया तत्रभवती रहसि
शकुन्तला मोहात्तत्यादिष्टेति । तदा प्रभृत्येव पश्चात्तापमु-
पगतो देवः । तथा हि

रम्यं द्वेष्टि यथा पुरा प्रकृतिभिर्न प्रत्यहं सेव्यते
शय्याप्रान्तविवर्तनैर्विगमयत्युन्निद्र एव क्षपाः ।
दाक्षिण्येन ददाति वाचमुचितामन्तःपुरेभ्यो यदा
गोत्रेषु स्खलितस्तदा भवति च व्रीडाविलक्षश्चिरम् ॥१३७॥

[a] श्रुतं राट्रियस्य मुखाद्यावदङ्गुलीयकदर्शीनम् ।

---

darśana-patha, p. 110, l. 2; and *loċana-pathaṃ yāntyā*, Ratn. l. 2.
Kaulīna=*loka-vāda*, 'report,' K.;=*parīvāda* or *apavāda*, 'evil report,' C.
It is derived from *kula*, 'a family,' and may signify 'report relating to
family or private matters,' 'family scandal.' It is so used in Vikram.,
Act II, *etat kaulīnaṃ vijṛimbhate*.

[1] This supposes a Sanskṛit stem *rāshṭṛi* or *rāshṭrin* instead of the
more usual *rāshṭriya*.

[2] 'He abhors (everything) pleasurable. He is not, as formerly, respect-
fully-waited-on every day by (his) courtiers [counsellors, ministers]. He
spends his nights, without even closing his eyes, in tossing [rolling] about
on the edge of his couch. When, out of politeness, he addresses the usual-
civil speeches to the women of the palace, then he blunders in (their)
names and becomes for a long while disconcerted [abashed] with shame.'
Ramyam, i. e. *srak-ċandana-vanitādi*, 'garlands, sandal, women, &c.,' K.;
in fact, 'the pleasures of sense.' *Prakṛitibhiḥ*=*saċivaiḥ*, C.;=*śishṭaiḥ*, S.
Uċitūm=*arhām*=*tatkāla-yogyām*, K.; see p. 145, l. 5. *Antaḥpurebhyo*,
see p. 123, n. 1. *Gotreshu*=*nāmasu*, S. and C.;=*nāmadheyeshu*, K.
Skhalitaḥ=*viparyastaḥ*, K., i. e. 'by mistake he utters the name of
Śakuntalā,' K. and S. To indicate a lover's absence of mind or rather

Verse 137. ŚĀRDŪLA-VIKRĪḌITA (a variety of ATIDHṚITI). See verse 136.

सानुमती ।

[a] पिअं मे ।

कञ्चुकी ।

अस्मात्प्रभवतो वैमनस्यादुत्सवः प्रत्याख्यातः ।

उभे ।

[b] जुज्जइ ।

नेपथ्ये ।

[c] एदु एदु भवं ।

कञ्चुकी ॥ कर्णं दत्त्वा ॥

अये । इत एवाभिवर्त्तते देवः । स्वकर्मानुष्ठीयताम् ।

उभे ।

[d] तह । ॥ इति निष्क्रान्ते ॥

॥ ततः प्रविशति पश्चात्तापसदृशवेशो राजा विदूषकः प्रतीहारी च ॥

कञ्चुकी ॥ राजानमवलोक्य ॥

अहो सर्वास्ववस्थासु रमणीयत्वमाकृतिविशेषाणाम् ।
एवमुत्सुकोऽपि प्रियदर्शनो देवः । तथा हि

[a] प्रियं मे ।   [b] युज्यते ।   [c] इतु इतु भवान् ।   [d] तथा ।

---

the one engrossing object of his thoughts, Hindū poets are fond of making
him fall into the trap of calling others by the name of his mistress (cf.
Kumāra-s. iv. 8; also Raghu-v. xix. 24, *nāma vallabha-janasya te mayā
prāpya bhāgyam api tasya kānkshyate iti tam gotra-viskhalitam ūćur
angunāḥ,* 'the women thus addressed him, making mistakes in their
names [calling them by the name of his beloved], since I have received
the name of thy beloved I desire also her lot ;' also Praveśaka to Act II.
of Vikram., *yan-nimittam bhartā utkanṭhitas tasyāḥ striyā nāmnā bhartrā
devī ālapitā;* and another passage in the Vishkambha at the opening of
the next Act, *tayā purushottama iti vaktavye purūravasīti nirgatā vāṇī*).

[1] 'In consequence of this mental derangement of his Majesty.' *Vaima-
nasya,* abstract noun from *vi-manas,* 'disordered or changed in mind,'
'absent in mind' (Gram. p. 67, LXXVII). *Prabhavato* (= *rājñaḥ,* Chézy;
= *prabhoḥ,* K.), gen. of *prabhavat,* 'ruling,' 'one who rules ;' it seems to
be used like *prabhu* and *prabhavishṇu* in addressing or speaking of kings
(cf. *nāsti prabhavato 'parādhaḥ,* Vikram., Act II. at the end).

प्रत्यादिष्टविशेषमण्डनविधिर्वामप्रकोष्ठार्पितं
बिभ्रत्काञ्चनमेकमेव वलयं श्वासापरक्ताधरः ।
चिन्ताजागरणप्रताम्रनयनस्तेजोगुणादात्मनः
संस्कारोल्लिखितो महामणिरिव क्षीणोऽपि नालक्ष्यते ॥१३८॥

सानुमती ॥ राजानं दृष्ट्वा ॥

[a] ठाणेक्खु पच्चादेसविमाणिदाबि इमस्स किदे सउन्दला
किलम्मदि ।

राजा ॥ ध्यानमन्दं परिक्रम्य ॥

प्रथमं सारङ्गाक्ष्या प्रियया प्रतिबोध्यमानमपि सुप्तम् ।
अनुशयदुःखायेदं हतहृदयं सम्प्रति विबुद्धम् ॥१३९॥

[a] स्थाने खलु प्रत्यादेशविमानितातापस्य कृते शकुन्तला क्लाम्यति ।

---

[1] 'Scorning distinguished [superior] forms of decoration; wearing but a single golden bracelet fastened [placed] on the left fore-arm; with lips bloodless from sighing; with eyes very red from sleeplessness (caused) by thought (upon S'akuntalā); through the excellence of his own (inherent) lustre, though he be attenuated he is not observed (to be so), like a magnificent gem (whose surface is) ground away by the polishing-stone.' *Pratyādishṭa-viśesha-maṇḍana-vidhiḥ* = *nirākṛita-viśishṭālankāra-vidhā-naḥ*, S. (cf. Megha-d. ver. 92, and *prasādhana-vidheḥ prasādhana-viśe-shaḥ*, Vikram., Act II). *Prakoshṭha* (see p. 53, n. 1) = *kūrpara-maṇi-ban-dhana-madhyabhāga*, K. (cf. p. 114, n. 2). *Bibhrat* = *dadhat*; in the pres. part. Par. of verbs of cl. 3, the nom. is identical with the stem (Gram. 141. *a*). *Apa-rakta* = *nī-rakta, rakta-hīna*, 'bloodless,' 'pale.' The effect of long and deep sighs would be to draw the blood away from the lips (cf. Megha-d. verses 83, 89). *Cintā-jāgaraṇa*, i. e. *S'akuntalā-vishayiṇyā cintayā*, S. *Guṇāt* = *utkarshāt*, K. *Sanskāra* = *śāna*, K.; = *prastara-viśesha*; (*sanskāra* has the sense 'polishing;' cf. Hitop. l. 15); *śānollikhitaḥ* = *śānodghṛishṭaḥ*, K. *Nālakshyate* (i. e. *na āl°*), see p. 70, n. 3 at the end.

[2] 'Previously this paralysed [blighted] heart slumbered even whilst-it-was-being-roused-from-sleep by my fawn-eyed beloved. Now it is broad-

---

Verse 138. SĀRDŪLA-VIKRĪḌITA (a variety of ATIDHṚITI). See verses 14, &c., 137.
Verse 139. ĀRYĀ or GĀTHĀ. See verse 2.

◡◡– | –– | –– ‖ ◡◡– | ◡◡– | ◡–◡ | ◡◡– | –
◡◡◡◡◡ | –– | –– ‖ ◡◡◡◡◡ | –– | ◡ | ◡◡– | –

सानुमती ।

[a]एं ईदिसाणि तवस्सिणीए भाग्गहेआणि ।

विदूषकः ॥ अपवार्य ॥

[b]लग्घिदो एसो भूत्रोबि सउन्दलावाहिणा । ए आणे । कहं चिकिच्छिदव्वो भविस्सदिति ।

कञ्चुकी ॥ उपगम्य ॥

जयतु जयतु देवः । महाराज । प्रत्यवेक्षिताः प्रमदवन-भूमयः । यथाकाममध्यास्तां विनोदस्थानानि महाराजः ।

राजा ।

वेच्चवति । मद्वचनादमात्यमार्यपिशुनं ब्रूहि । चिरप्रबोधान्न सम्भावितमस्माभिरद्य धर्मासनमध्यासितुम् । यत्प्रत्यवेक्षितं पौरकार्यमार्येण । तत्पत्त्रमारोप्य दीयतामिति ।

प्रतीहारी ।

[c]जं देवो आणबेदि । ॥ इति निष्क्रान्ता ॥

राजा ।

वातायन । त्वमपि स्वं नियोगमशून्यं कुरु ।

कञ्चुकी ।

यदाज्ञापयति देवः । ॥ इति निष्क्रान्तः ॥

[a] नन्वीदृशानि तपस्विन्या भाग्धेयानि ।   [b] लग्धित एष भूयोऽपि शकुन्तला-व्याधिना । न जाने । कथं चिकित्सितव्यो भविष्यतीति ।   [c] यदेव आज्ञापयति ।

awake to the anguish of remorse.' *Anuśaya-duḥkhāya*=*paśćāttāpa-khedāya*. *Samprati*, i. e. *tad-virahe*, S. *Vibuddham*=*jāgṛitam*, S.

[1] 'He is again attacked [seized, afflicted] by a Śakuntalā-fever,' i. e. he is again love-sick for Śakuntalā. *Langhita*, see p. 97, n. 1.

[2] 'Having committed that to writing [to a letter], let it be sent to me;' or, 'having written that in a letter, let it be given (to some messenger).' *Dīyatām*=*prahīyatām*, S.

[3] *Sva-niyogam antaḥpurāvekshā-rūpam*, 'thy stated business consisting of superintendence of the female apartments,' S. *Vātāyana*, this is the name of the Kańćukin, see p. 186, n. 1.

विदूषकः ।

ᵃ किदं भवदा णिम्मच्छिद्रं । सम्पदं सिसिरातवच्छेत्र-रमणीए इमस्सिं पमदवणुद्देसे अत्ताणं रमइस्ससि ।

राजा ।

वयस्य । रन्ध्रोपनिपातिनोऽनर्था इति यदुच्यते । तदव्य-भिचारि वचः । कुतः ।

मुनिसुतामप्रणयस्मृतिरोधिना
मम च मुक्तमिदं तमसा मनः ।
मनसिजेन सखे प्रहरिष्यता
धनुषि चूतशरश्च निवेशितः ॥१४०॥

ᵃ कृतं भवता निर्मक्षिकम् । साम्प्रतं शिशिरातपच्छेदरमणीयेऽस्मिन्प्रमदवनोद्देश आत्मानं रमयिष्यसि ।

---

¹ *Nirmakshikam,* see p. 76, l. 2, n. 1. *Makshikāyā apy abhāvān nirja-nam,* Ś.

² 'Misfortunes rush in through the (first) hole (they can find),' i. e. mis-fortunes are continually on the watch for an opening or vulnerable point -by which to assail us; they seize the first opportunity that offers for attacking us; they quickly succeed each other before we have time to stand on our guard. This must have been a common proverb, something like our 'Misfortunes never come alone.' The king observes that 'this which is a saying commonly current among men is quite consistent and true [*a-vyabhičāri*] in his own case,' and he then proceeds to explain why [*kutas,* see p. 55, n. 2] in the subsequent verse. *Randhra=čhidra,* K. *Upanipātino = samāpatanti,* K. *Anarthāḥ = āpadaḥ,* K. *Yad učyate,* i. e. *lokena,* K.; *avyabhičāri=aviparyāsi* (i. e. *nānyathā bhavati*), K.; *= avaśyam-bhāvi* or *yathārtham,* Ś. Dr. Boehtlingk translates, 'The un-fortunate fall into a hole [grave],' which seems supportable by a reading *randhroparipātino 'narthā,* noticed by K., although not adopted by him. Cf. Bhartṛi-h. ii. 86, *prāyo gaččhati yatra bhāgya-rahitas tatraiva yānty āpadaḥ.*

³ 'No sooner is this my soul freed from the darkness that obstructed the remembrance of my love for the sage's daughter, than a mango-blossom-shaft, O my friend, is fixed on (his) bow by the heart-born (god)

Verse 140. DRUTA-VILAMBITA (a variety of JAGATĪ). See verses 45, 72, 128.

विदूषकः ।

[a]चिट्ठ दाव । जाव इमिणा दण्डकट्ठेण कन्दप्पवाणं णासइस्सामि ।   ॥ इति दण्डकाष्ठमुद्यम्य भूताङ्कुरं पातयितुमिच्छति ॥

राजा   ॥ सस्मितम् ॥

भवतु । दृष्टं ब्रह्मवर्चसम् । सखे । कोपविष्टः प्रियायाः किञ्चिदनुकारिणीषु लतासु दृष्टिं विलोभयामि ।

विदूषकः ।

[b]णं आसण्णपरिञ्चारिआ चदुरिआ भवदा सन्दिट्ठा । माहवीमरण्डबे इमं वेलं अदिवाहिस्सं । तहिं मे चित्तफलअगदं सहत्थलिहिदं तब्भोदीए सउन्दलाए पडिकिदिं आणेहिन्ति ।

[a] तिष्ठ तावत् । यावदनेन दण्डकाष्ठेन कन्दर्पैवाणं नाशयिष्यामि ।   [b] नन्वा-सन्नपरिचारिका चतुरिका भवता सन्दिष्टा । माधवीमण्डप इमां वेलामतिवाहयिष्यामि । तस्मिन्मे चित्रफलकगतां सहस्तलिखितां तत्रभवत्याः शकुन्तलायाः प्रतिकृतिमानयेति ।

---

now-about-to-shoot-at-me.' The occurrence of *ća* in each clause denotes immediate connexion or succession, expressed in English by 'no sooner—than,' 'so soon as,' 'scarcely—when,' &c. (cf. verse 131 and Kumāra-s. iii. 58). *Manasi-ja*, 'born in the mind or heart,' a name of Kāma-deva (see p. 100, n. 1). *Praharishyat*, 'about to strike,' participle of the 2nd future. *Ćūta-śara*, see p. 99, n. 1 in the middle. The verse which follows this in the Beng. and Mackenzie MSS. is probably spurious.

[1] I have adopted *vānam* from the oldest Beng. MSS. S. and C. have *vānān*. The Deva-n. *vvāhim* (=*vyādhim*). K. reads *vvāham* (=*vyādham*), 'a hunter,' 'shooter.' May not *vyādhi*, like *vyādha*, signify 'hunting,' 'shooting,' 'sport?' in which case the Deva-n. reading might be retained.

[2] 'The mighty power of a Brāhman is seen (by me).' This is said ironically in reference to the Vidūshaka's ridiculous attempt to destroy the arrows of Kāma-deva.

[3] Lit. 'a near attendant,' i. e. an attendant about one's person.

[4] *Ati-vah*, in causal, has the sense 'to pass time.' Cf. Raghu-v. xix. 47, ix. 70.

[5] *Ćitra-phalaka*, 'a picture-tablet,' 'a tablet for painting.' The same expression occurs in Ratn. p. 21, l. 8, and p. 22, l. 1, and Vikram., Act II. As to *gatām*, here meaning 'committed to,' see p. 206, n. 4.

राजा ।

ईदृशं हृदयविनोदस्थानम् । तत्तमेव मार्गमादेशय ।

विदूषकः ।

"इदो इदो भवं ।   ॥ उभौ परिक्रामतः । सानुमत्यनुगच्छति ॥

विदूषकः ।

b एसो मणिसिलापट्टअसणाहो माहवीमअडवो उबहार-
रमणिज्जदाए णिस्संसअं सागदेण विअ णो पडिच्छदि ।
ता पविसिअ णिसीददु भवं ।

॥ उभौ प्रवेशं कृत्वोपविष्टौ ॥

सानुमती ।

c लदासंसिदा देक्खिस्सं दाव सहीए पडिकिदिं । तदो से
भत्तुणो बहुमुहं अणुराअं णिवेदइस्सं । ॥ इति तथा कृत्वा स्थिता ॥

राजा ।

सखे । सर्वमिदानीं स्मरामि शकुन्तलायाः प्रथमवृत्तान्तम् ।
कथितवानसि भवते । सं भवान्प्रत्यादेशवेलायां मत्तमी-
पमुपगतो नासीत् । पूर्वमपि न त्वया कदाचित्सङ्कीर्तितं
तत्रभवत्या नाम । कच्चिदहमिव विस्मृतवानसि त्वम् ।

a इत इतो भवान् ।   b एम मणिशिलापट्टकसनाथो माधवीमण्डप उपहाररमणीय-
तया निःसंशयं स्वागतेनेव नौ प्रतीच्छति । तत्प्रविश्य निषीदतु भवान् ।   c लतासंश्रिता
द्रष्ट्यामि तावत्सख्याः प्रतिकृतिम् । ततोऽस्या भर्तुर्बहुमुखमनुरागं निवेदयिष्यामि ।

---

[1] *Maṇi-śilāpaṭṭaka-sanātha*, 'furnished with a marble seat,' see p. 26, n. 3.

[2] 'With the agreeableness of its flowery offerings,' 'with its charming flowery gifts.' *Upahāra*, or according to the commentators *upacāra* = *kusumādi-vistāra*, S. Flowers were used as complimentary presents or offerings, especially to the god of love.

[3] *Bahu-mukha* (lit. 'having many faces'), 'manifold,' 'excessive.' *Bahu-madam* (= *bahu-matam*) is another reading.

[4] So read all the MSS. except my own, which omits *sa*. *Sa* may be used to emphasize other pronouns, and *sa bhavān* therefore = *ille tu*, i.e. 'your honour, that same person to whom alone I mentioned the circumstances.'

विदूषकः ।

a णं विसुमरामि । किन्दु सव्वं कहिञ्च अवसाणे उण तुए
परिहासविञ्झप्पञ्झो एसो णं भूदत्त्योत्ति आचक्खिदं ।
मएवि मिप्पिरंडबुद्धिणा तह एव्व गहीदं । अहवा भवि-
दव्वदा बलवदी ।

सानुमती ।

b एव्वं णोदं ।

राजा ॥ ध्यात्वा ॥

सखे । चायस्व माम् ।

विदूषकः ।

c भो । किं एदं । अणुबबखंखु ईदिसं तुइ । कदाचि सप्पुरिसा
सोऽपत्तप्पाणो ण होन्ति । णं पवादेवि णिक्कम्पा गिरीञ्झो ।

राजा ।

वयस्य । निराकरणविक्लवायाः प्रियायाः समवंस्थाम-
नुस्मृत्य बलवदशरणोऽस्मि । सा हि

---

a न विस्मरामि । किन्तु सर्वं कथयित्वावसाने पुनस्त्वया परिहासविजल्प इय न
भूतार्थ इत्याचक्षितम् । मयापि मृत्पिखडबुद्धिना तथैव गृहीतम् । अथवा भवितव्यता
बलवती ।   b एवं न्वेतत् ।   c भोः । किमेतत् । अनुपपन्नं खल्वीदृशं त्वयि ।
कदाचित्सत्पुरुषा शोकपात्रात्मानो न भवन्ति । ननु प्रवातेऽपि निष्कम्पा गिरयः ।

---

[1] *Parihāsa-vijalpa*, see p. 94, l. 5.   As to *bhūtārtha*, see p. 5, n. 2.

[2] 'Whose brains [intellect] are like a lump of clay,' 'whose understanding is dense as a clod of earth.'   (Cf. the expressions 'clod-pated,'
'clod-poll,' 'blockhead,' &c.)   Some MSS. have *manda-buddhinā*.   As to
bhavitavya-tā balavatī, see p. 206, n. 2.

[3] 'Have not hearts that give place to sorrow,' 'do not give themselves
up to uncontrolled grief.'   *Pātra*, 'a receptacle,' see p. 203, n. 1 at the
end.   I have followed Kāṭavema's reading.   That of the other Deva-n. MSS.,
soa-vattarvā, is hardly intelligible.

[4] *Sam-avasthā*, with the sense of *avasthā*, 'state,' 'condition,' occurs
not unfrequently in the plays.   Cf. Mālavik. p. 66, l. 1; p. 68, l. 15.   See
also p. 164, l. 6 of this play, where it has the sense of *samāvasthā*.

इतः प्रत्यादेशात्स्वजनमनुगन्तुं व्यवसिता
मुहुस्तिष्ठेत्युच्चैर्वदति गुरुशिष्ये गुरुसमे ।
पुनर्दृष्टिं वाष्पप्रकरकलुषामर्पितवती
मयि क्रूरे यत्तत्सविषमिव शल्यं दहति माम्[1] ॥१४१॥

सानुमती ।

[a] अम्महे । ईदिसी सकज्जपरदा । इमस्स सन्दावेण अहं रमामि ।

विदूषकः ।

[b] भो । अत्थि मे तक्को । केणवि तत्तहोदी आआसचारिणा णीदेत्ति ।

राजा ।

कः पतिदेवतामन्यः परिमार्ष्टुमुत्सहेतं । मेनका किल

[a] अहो । ईदृशी स्वकार्यपरता । अस्य सन्तापेनाहं रमे ।   [b] भोः । अस्ति मे
तर्कः । केनापि तत्रभवत्याकाशचारिणा नीतेति ।

---

[1] '(The thought) that after her repudiation from hence, (when) she
attempted to follow her attendants, the Guru's pupil, (who claimed
obedience) like-the-Guru-himself, repeatedly saying to her in a loud
voice, "Stay," she cast on me inexorable [cruel, hard-hearted] a second
look bedimmed with gushing tears; that (it is which) torments me like
an envenomed shaft.' *Itaḥ*, i. e. *mattaḥ*, 'by me,' S'. *Vyavasitā=yat-
nam kṛitavatī*, S'. *Muhus tishṭha*, &c., see p. 213, l. 1. *Guru-same*,
i. e. *alanghyādeśatayā.*

[2] 'Alas! such is the force of absorption in one's own object that I am
actually pleased by his distress (instead of compassionating it).' *Paratā*
means here 'the being addicted to.' Some Beng. MSS. have *a-kajja-paradā.*
Sva-kārya, i. e. 'relating to S'akuntalā,' S'.   Cf. p. 207, l. 7.

[3] 'Who else could presume [would have the power] to-lay-a-finger-on
[touch, bear off] the idol of (her) husband?' *Kaḥ anya*, cf. p. 208, ll. 8, 9.
Pati-devatā, 'the goddess of her husband,' or as we should say, 'a wife
idolized by her husband.'   This is probably the sense of this expression,
which is found in all the Deva-n. MSS.   The Beng. have *pati-vratām*,
'a wife devoted to her husband.' *Pari-mārshṭum* (so read all the Deva-n.)
must come from *pari-mṛij*, 'to wipe off,' 'remove.'   It may be used like

सख्यास्ते जन्मप्रतिष्ठेति श्रुतवानस्मि । तत्सहचारिणीभिः
सखी ते हतेति मे हृदयमाशङ्कते ।

मानुमती ।

[a] सम्मोहो क्खु विम्ह अणिज्जो ण पडिबोही ।

विदूषकः ।

[b] जइ एवं । अत्थिक्खु समागमो कालेण तब्भोदीए ।

राजा ।

कथमिव ।

विदूषकः ।

[c] णक्खु मादापिदरा भत्तुविश्रोअदुक्खिदं दुहिदरं देक्खिदुं
पारेन्ति ।

राजा ।

वयस्य ।

स्वप्नो नु माया नु मतिभ्रमो नु
क्लिष्टं नु तावत्फलमेव पुण्यम् ।

[a] सम्मोहः खलु विस्मयनीयो न प्रतिबोधः ।   [b] यद्येवम् । अस्ति खलु समागमः
कालेन तत्रभवत्या ।   [c] न खलु मातापितरौ भर्तृवियोगदुःखितां दुहितरं द्रष्टुं पारयतः ।

pari-mriś, 'to lay hold of;' cf. p. 203, n. 1.   One MS. (I. O. 1060) has
parā-marshṭum (from *parā-mriś*), 'to seize,' 'lay violent hands on,' and this
reading is adopted by the St. Petersburg dictionary and by Dr. Burkhard.

[1] *Jánma-pratishṭhā = janma-sthānam*, 'place of birth;' = *mātā*,
'mother,' Chézy.   *Janma-pratishṭhā=jananī*, S'.   Dushyanta speaks of
S'akuntalā to the Vidūshaka as, 'thy friend.'   So the Yaksha speaks of
his wife to the Cloud, in Megha-d. 87, 93.

[2] 'Truly the state-of-mental-delusion [delirium, hallucination] is to be
wondered at, not the recovery-from-it [the awakening from it].'   S'. explains *sammoha* by 'forgetfulness,' and *pratibodha* by 'recollection.'

[3] *Pārayataḥ*, 'are able,' from the causal of root *pri*, meaning properly
'to carry over,' 'conduct,' 'achieve,' &c.; cf. p. 146, l. 2.   In Prākṛit
and more modern Sanskrit (as also in Bengālī) it has, as here, the sense
'to be able.'   It may come from a nominal verb from *pāra*, 'the other
side.'   (Cf. πέρα, πέρας, πέραω, περαίνω.)

असन्निवृत्त्यै तदतीतमेव
मनोरथानामततटप्रपातः ॥१४२॥

विदूषकः ।

[a]मा एव्वं । यं अङ्गुलीअअं एव्व णिदंसणं । अवस्सम्भा-
विणो अचिन्तणिज्जो समाअमो होदित्ति ।

राजा ॥ अङ्गुलीयकं विलोक्य ॥

अये । इदं तावदसुलभस्थानभ्रंशि शोचनीयम् ।

[a] नैवम् । नन्वङ्गुलीयकमेव निदर्शनम् । अवश्यम्भाविनोऽचिन्तनीयः समागमो भवतीति ।

---

[1] 'Was it a dream? or an illusion-of-magic? or a mental-delusion? or (the result of my) good-works so far indeed rewarded (and then) marred? It has certainly passed away, never to return; (and so has become) the steep precipice of my heart's-fondest-hopes.' Such is the reading of all the Deva-n. MSS., and doubtless the true one. In the third and fourth Pādas I have adopted *eva* and *prapātaḥ* (in place of *ete* and *prapātāḥ*) from the Mackenzie, the former supported by K. *Māyā*, i. e. *indra-jālādi-kriyā*, S'. *Bhrama*, one so affected imagines that to be present which does not really exist (*asad api sākshāt-karoti*, S'. and C'.) *Puṇyam*, i. e. *svakīyaṃ sukṛitam*, K. *Tāvat-phalam eva*, i. e. *darśana-phalam eva*, K.; *darśana-mātra-phalam*, C'., 'fruitful so far only as the sight of S'akuntalā,' K. *Klishṭam* (cf. p. 201, l. 13); the best explanation of this idea will be found in p. 80, l. 7, with n. 2, and in n. 2 below. *Asannivrittyai*, cf. Raghu-v. viii. 48, *para-lokam asannivrittaye gatāsi*, 'thou art gone to the other world never to return.' S'. thus explains the second half of the verse, 'As a man after ascending the peak of a mountain falls headlong, so my hopes after ascending to the sight of S'akuntalā are precipitated.' As to *taṭa*, see p. 175, n. 1. Amara-k. (ii. 3, 4) gives *ataṭa* as a synonym of *prapāta* and *bhṛigu*, each of these words signifying 'a precipice,' but there is no reason why *ataṭa* should not be used as an epithet of *prapāta*, to denote a very precipitous declivity. The Beng. MSS. read *klṛiptaṃ nu tāvat phalam eva puṇyaiḥ, asannivrittau tad [asannivrittyai tad] atīva manye manorathūnām ataṭa-prapātam.*

[2] 'Is not the very ring a proof that there may be an unexpected meeting with that which must necessarily come?' *Nanu* often = Latin *nonne.*

Verse 142. UPAJĀTI or ĀKHYĀNAKĪ (a variety of TRISHṬUBH). See verses 41, 107, 121, 126.

तव सुचरितमङ्गुलीय नूनं
प्रतनु ममेव विभाव्यते फलेन ।
अरुणनखमनोरमासु तस्या-
श्च्युतमसि लब्धपदं यदङ्गुलीषु ॥ १४३ ॥[1]

सानुमती ।

[a] जइ अण्णहत्थगदं भवे । सच्चं एव्व सोअणिज्जं भवे ।

विदूषकः ।

[b] भो । इअं णाम मुद्दा केण उद्देसेण तत्तहोदीए हत्थसंसग्गं पाविदा ।

सानुमती ।

[c] ममवि कोदूहलेण आआरिदो एसो ।

राजा ।

श्रूयताम् । तदा स्वनगराय प्रस्थितं मां प्रिया सवाष्पमाह ।
कियच्चिरेणार्यपुत्रः प्रतिपत्तिं[3] दास्यतीति ।

विदूषकः ।

[d] तदो तदो ।

<hr>

[a] यद्यन्यहस्तगतं भवेत् । सत्यमेव शोचनीयं भवेत् । [b] भोः । इयं नाम मुद्रा केनोद्देशेन तत्रभवत्या हस्तसंसर्गं प्रापिता । [c] ममापि कौतूहलेनाकारित एषः । [d] ततस्ततः ।

<hr>

[1] 'Verily, O ring, the-merit-of-thy-good-works like mine is judged [proved] to be insignificant [slender] by the reward [result]; since after-gaining-a-station on the charming-rosy-nailed fingers of that-lady thou hast fallen (from it).' The doctrine of laying up a store of merit by good deeds performed in the present and former births is an essential part of the Hindū creed (see last verse, and cf. p. 185, n. 3). *Aruṇa-nakha*, see p. 125, n. 2 at the end. *Aruṇa* may imply 'ruddy as the dawn,' see p. 142, n. 3.

[2] 'By my curiosity also he (would be) incited (to tell the reason).' *Kautūhala* = *śravaṇotkaṇṭhā*, 'desire of hearing,' S'. *Ākārita* = *āhata, prerita*, K. Cf. *taṃ vara-dānāya ākārayāmāsa*, Rāmāy. ii. 13, 2. S'. reads *vādita*, 'made to speak,' for *ākārita*. The Beng. MSS. have *vyāpārita*.

[3] *Pratipatti*, cf. p. 172, l. 4, with note thereon.

Verse 143. PUSHPITĀGRĀ. See verses 32, 37.

राजा ।

पश्चादिमां मुद्रां तदङ्गुलौ निवेशयता मया प्रत्यभिहिता ।
एकैकमच दिवसे दिवसे मदीयं
नामाक्षरं गणय गच्छसि यावदन्तम् ।
तावन्निये मदवरोधगृहप्रवेशं
नेता जनस्तव समीपमुपैष्यंतीति ॥ १४४ ॥

तच्च दारुणात्मना मया मोहान्धानुष्ठितम् ।

सानुमती ।

[a] रमणीओक्खु अवही विहिणा विसंवादिंदो ।

विदूषकः ।

[b] कहं धीवलकप्पिञ्चस्स लोहिञमच्छस्स उदलब्भनले
आसि[3] ।

[a] रमणीयः खल्ववधिर्विधिना विसंवादितः ।   [b] कथं धीवरकल्पितस्य रोहित-
मत्स्यस्योदराभ्यन्तर आसीत् ।

---

[1] 'Count [spell] hereon [i. e. on this ring] one by one each day the
letters of my name until thou reachest the end. So soon, O loved one,
(as thou hast spelt the whole name) a messenger will come into thy
presence who-will-conduct thee to the entrance of my private-apartments.'
Nāmāksharam, cf. p. 53, l. 6. *Gaćchasi*, so reads the Taylor MS. as well
as my own, supported by the Calcutta ed. ; the others, *gaćchati*. *Netā*,
the noun of agency has sometimes the sense of a future participle, and
may govern the case of the verb. So *vaktā vākyam*, 'one who is about
to speak a speech,' Draupadī-h. 32. Indeed the nom. masc. of this form
of noun is identical with the 3rd pers. of the 1st future.

[2] 'Verily (this) charming period (of expectation) was by Destiny made
(to pass away) without-the-appointment-being-kept,' or 'Destiny caused
that the delightful appointment-of-a-period (for the reunion of these lovers)
should fail of being kept.' *Vi-saṃ-vad* is 'to fail in keeping a promise
or agreement.' Cf. *phale visaṃvadati*, Vikram., Act II.

[3] The Vidūshaka designedly uses the dialect of the fisherman ; see
p. 220, l. 4 sq.; p. 217, n. 2.

Verse 144. Vasanta-tilakā (a variety of Śakvarī). See verses 8, 27, 31, 43, 46,
64, 74, 80, 82, 83, 91, 93, 94, 95, 100, 104, 105, 108, 123, 124.

राजा ।

शचीतीर्थं वन्दमानायाः सख्यास्ते हस्तादङ्गात्स्रोतसि
परिभ्रष्टम् ।

विदूषकः ।

[a] जुज्जइ ।

सानुमती ।

[b] अदो एव्व तवस्सिणीए सउन्दलाए अधम्मभीरुणो
इमस्स राएसिणो परिणए सन्देहो आसि । अहवा ।
ईदिसी अणुराओ अहिसाणं अवेक्खदि । कहं विज्ञ एदं ।

राजा ।

उपालप्स्ये तावदिदमङ्गुलीयकम् ।

विदूषकः ॥ आत्मगतम् ॥

[c] गहीदो योण पन्था उम्मत्तआणं ।

राजा ।

कथं नु तं बन्धुरकोमलाङ्गुलिं
    करं विहायासि निमग्नमम्भसि ।
अथवा । अचेतनं नाम गुणं न लक्ष्ये-
    न्मयैव कस्मादवधीरिता प्रियाँ ॥१४५॥

[a] युज्यते । [b] अत एव तपस्विन्याः शकुन्तलायाः अधर्मभीरोरस्य राजर्षेः परिणये
सन्देह आसीत् । अथवा । ईदृशोऽनुरागोऽभिज्ञानमपेक्षते । कथमिवैतत् । [c] गृही-
तोऽनेन पन्था उन्मत्तानाम् ।

---

[1] Compare p. 205, ll. 12, 13, n. 2.

[2] 'How (couldest) thou (allow thyself) to be immersed in the water,
having abandoned that hand with (its) slender delicate fingers? But
(where is the wonder? for) an inanimate-object may well not distinguish
excellence.   How (was it that) even by me (my) beloved was rejected?'
Bandhura=unnatānata, 'undulating;'=*ramya*, 'beautiful,' C.   *Athavā*,
see p. 30, n. 3.

Verse 145.   VAṆŚA-STHAVILA (a variety of JAGATĪ).   See verses 18, 22, 23, 67, 81,
114, 117, 119.

विटूषकः ॥ आत्मगतम् ॥

[a] कहं बुभुक्खाए खादिदव्वोम्हि ।

राजा ।

अकारणपरित्यक्ते । अनुशयमहृदयस्तावदनुकम्प्यतामयं जनः पुनर्दर्शनेन ।

॥ प्रविश्य पटाक्षेपेण चित्रफलकहस्ता ॥

चतुरिका ।

[b] इञं चित्तगदा भट्टिणी । ॥ इति चित्रफलकं दर्शयति ॥

विटूषकः ।

[c] साहु वञ्रस्स । महुरावत्थाणदंसणिज्जो भावाणुप्पवेसो । खलदि विञ्र मे दिट्ठी णिखुस्स-अप्पदेसेसु ।

सानुमती ।

[d] अम्मो एसा राएसिणो णिउणदा । जाणे । सही अग्गदो मे वट्टदिन्ति ।

राजा ।

यद्यत्साधु न चिचे स्यात्क्रियते तत्तदन्यथा ।
तथापि तस्या लावण्यं रेखया किञ्चिदन्वितम् ॥१४६॥

[a] कथं बुभुक्षया खादितव्योऽसि । [b] इयं चित्रगता भर्त्री । [c] साधु वयस्य । मधुरावस्थानदर्शनीयो भावानुप्रवेशः । खलतीव मे दृष्टिर्निम्नोन्नतप्रदेशेषु । [d] अहो एषा राजर्षेर्निपुणता । जाने । सख्यग्रतो मे वर्तैत इति ।

---

[1] 'Why am I to be devoured by hunger (while he is apostrophizing his ring)?' A very characteristic remark, see p. 59, n. 1 in the middle.

[2] 'The presence of the prevailing sentiment (love, *rati*) is delightful by its sweet abiding in every part. My sight stumbles as it were amidst the depressions and prominences;' i. e. the relief or appearance of projection and depression in the picture is so well managed that my eye is deceived, and seems to follow the inequalities of surface. For *anu-praveśa*, cf. Raghu-v. iii. 22; and for *avasthāna*, Sāhit.-d. p. 75, l. 2. It may mean 'by the sweet position of the figures,' but *bhāva* means here *rati*.

[3] 'Whatever is not well (executed) in the picture [whatever falls short

Verse 146. Śloka or Anushtubh. See verses 5, 6, 11, 12, 26, 47, 50, 51, 53, 73, 76, 84, 87, 125, 127, 130.

सानुमती ।

[a] सरिसं एव्वं पच्छादावगरुणो सिणेहस्स अणवलेवस्स अ ।

विदूषकः ।

[b] भो । दाणिं तिस्सि तत्तहोदीओ दीसन्ति । सव्वाओ अ दंसणीआओ । कदमा एत्थ तत्तहोदी सउन्दला ।

सानुमती ।

[c] अणभिण्णोक्खु ईदिसस्स रूवस्स मोहंदिट्ठी अश्रं जणो ।

राजा ।

त्वं तावत्कतमां तर्कयसि ।

विदूषकः ।

[d] तक्केमि । जा एसा सिढिलकेसबन्धणुब्बन्तकुसुमेण केसन्तेण उब्भिण्णसेअविन्दुणा वअणेण विसेसदो ओसरिआहिं बाहाहिं अवसेअसिणिद्धतरुणपल्लवस्स चूअपाअवस्स पासे इसिपरिस्सन्ता विअ आलिहिदा । एसा सउन्दला । इदराओ सहीओत्ति ।

[a] सदृशमेवं पश्चात्तापगुरोः स्नेहस्यानवलेपस्य च ।   [b] भोः । इदानीं तिस्रस्तद्भवत्यो दृश्यन्ते । सर्वाश्च दर्शनीयाः । कतमात्र तद्भवती शकुन्तला ।   [c] अनभिज्ञः खल्वीदृशस्य रूपस्य मोघदृष्टिरयं जनः ।   [d] तर्कयामि । यैषा शिथिलकेशबन्धनोद्धान्तकुसुमेन केशान्तेनोद्भिन्नस्वेदबिन्दुना वदनेन विशेषतोऽपसृताभ्यां बाहुभ्यामवसेकस्निग्धतरुणपल्लवस्य चूतपादपस्य पार्श्वे ईयत्परिश्रान्तेवालिखिता । एषा शकुन्तला । इतरे सख्याविति ।

---

of perfect beauty], all that is wrongly (portrayed). Nevertheless her loveliness is in some measure possessed by the drawing;' i.e. the artist has to some extent made a likeness, though very inferior to the original. *Rekhā=lekhana*, 'a sketch,' 'delineation,' K. The Beng. have *lekhayā*.

[1] *Mogha-dṛṣṭi*, cf. p. 76, l. 10, n. 3; Bhaṭṭi-k. v. 19.

[2] 'I imagine that she who is delineated as if a little fatigued at the side of the mango-tree, the tender shoots of which are glistening after her watering (of them), with arms extended in a peculiar manner, with a face having drops of perspiration breaking out (upon it), with locks of hair the flowers of which have escaped through the slackened hair-band—this (I imagine) is Śakuntalā, the other two (are her) female friends.' *Udvānta*,

राजा ।

निपुणो भवान् । अस्त्यच मे भावचिह्नम् ।

स्विन्नाङ्गुलिविनिवेशो रेखाप्रान्तेषु दृश्यते मलिनः ।
अश्रु च कपोलपतितं दृश्यमिदं वर्णिकोच्छ्वासात् ॥१४७॥

चतुरिके । अर्धलिखितमेतद्विनोदस्थानम् । तस्मादागच्छ । वर्तिकां तावदानय ।

चतुरिका ।

[a] अज्जमाठव्व । अवलम्ब चित्तफलअं । जाव आअच्छामि ।

राजा ।

अहमेवैतदवलम्बे । ॥ इति यथोक्तं करोति ॥

॥ निष्क्रान्ता चेटी ॥

[a] आर्यमाठव्य । अवलम्बस्व चित्रफलकम् । यावदागच्छामि ।

---

lit. 'vomited up,' here 'dropped off,' 'fallen down.' *Udbhinna-sveda-vindunā*, cf. p. 70, n. 3; hence in line 9 of that page, *sveda-leśair abhinnam* is a better reading than *kleśa-leśair*. *Viśeshato 'pasritābhyām*, it appears from a subsequent passage that she is represented in the act of warding off the bee mentioned at p. 32, l. 4. *Itare*, nom. dual feminine.

[1] 'Here is a sign of my passion; the soiled impression of (my) perspiring fingers is observed on the edges of the picture, and a tear here [this tear] fallen from (my) cheek is perceptible from the coming out of the colour.' However offensive to our notions of good taste, it is certain that in Hindū erotic poetry, perspiration is considered to be one of the signs of passionate love. So in the Vikram., *anguli-svedena me lupyante aksharāṇi*; cf. also Raghu-v. vii. 19, *svinnānguliḥ saṃvavṛite kumārī*, &c. *Varṇikā* (=*varṇa*) is the reading of K., supported by most of the Beng. MSS., which have *varṇakā*. The other Deva-n. have *vartikā*, which may, like *varti*, mean 'collyrium,' 'pigment.' *Varṇikocchvāsāt* means 'from the brightness (i. e. coming out) of the pigment;' Prema-candra explains it by *rangasya utphullatvāt*. *Kapola-patita*, 'fallen from my cheek,' or perhaps 'fallen on the cheek' (of the portrait).

[2] Lit. 'pleasure-ground,' i. e. landscape; *lieu de la scène*, Chézy.

Verse 147. ĀRYĀ or GĀTHĀ. See verse 2.

$$-- \mid \cup\cup\cup\cup \mid -- \parallel -- \mid -- \mid \cup - \cup \mid - \cup\cup \mid -$$
$$- \cup\cup \mid \cup - \cup \mid \cup\cup - \parallel - \cup\cup \mid -- \mid \cup \mid -- \mid -$$

राजा ।

अहं हि

साक्षात्प्रियामुपगतामपहाय पूर्वं
चित्रार्पितां मुहुरिमां बहुमन्यमानः ।
स्रोतोवहां पथि निकामजलामतीत्य
जातः सखे प्रणयवान्मृगतृष्णिकायाम् ॥१४८॥[1]

विदूषकः ॥ आत्मगतम् ॥

[a] एसो अत्तभवं एदिं अदिक्कमिच्र मित्रतिपिहआए सङ्क्रन्तो । ॥ प्रकाशम् ॥ [b] भो । अवरं किं एत्थ लिहिदव्वं ।

सानुमती ।

[c] जो जो पदेसो सहीए मे अहिरूवो । तं तं आलिहिदुकामो भवे ।

राजा ।

श्रूयताम् ।

काार्या सैकतलीनहंसमिथुना स्रोतोवहा मालिनी
पादास्तामभितो निषण्णहरिणा गौरीगुरोः पावनाः ।

[a] एषोऽत्रभवान्नदीमतिक्रम्य मृगतृष्णाया संक्रान्तः । [b] भोः । अपरं किमत्र लिखितव्यम् ।   [c] यो यः प्रदेशः सख्या मेऽभिरूपः । तं तमालिखितुकामो भवेत् ।

---

[1] '(While) again and again making much of her (image) committed to a picture, having previously repudiated my beloved when she came into my presence, I have become, O friend, (as it were) possessed of a longing for the waters-of-the-mirage, after passing by a river in-my-road having-plenty-of-water;' i. e. I am like one who prefers the shadow to the substance, the semblance to the reality. *Citrārpitām*=*citra-gatām*, see p. 238, n. 5. *Sroto-vahā*, beautiful women are often compared by Hindū poets to rivers, which in Sanskṛit are generally feminine. *Nikāma-jalām*, 'yielding abundance of water, as much as can be desired;' as to *nikāma* in this sense, see p. 108, n. 3 in the middle. *Mṛiga-tṛishṇikā*, lit. 'thirst of deer,' 'a vapour floating over waste places, which appears at a distance like water, and deceives men and animals.'

Verse 148. VASANTA-TILAKĀ (a variety of ŚAKVARĪ). See verses 8, 27, 31, &c., 144.

शाखालम्बितवल्कलस्य च तरोर्निर्मातुमिच्छाम्यधः
शृङ्गे कृष्णमृगस्य वामनयनं कण्डूयमानां मृगीम्॥१४९॥

विदूषकः ॥ आत्मगतम् ॥

[a] जह अहं देक्खामि । पूरिदव्वं णेण चित्तफलअं लम्बकुच्चाणं[2] ताबसाणं कदम्बेहिं ।

राजा ।

वयस्य । अन्यच्च शकुन्तलायाः प्रसाधनमभिप्रेतमत्र[3] विस्मृतमस्माभिः ।

विदूषकः ।

[b] किं विअ ।

[a] यथाहं पश्यामि । पूरयितव्यमनेन चित्रफलकं लम्बकूर्चानां तापसानां कदम्बैः ।
[b] किमिव ।

---

[1] 'The river Mālinī ought to be drawn [made] with a pair of swans [flamingoes] resting on a sandbank ; (and) on both sides of it the sacred hills-contiguous to Himālaya [Gaurī's father], with-some-deer-reclining (on them); and I wish under a tree, on-whose-boughs-some-bark-garments-are-suspended, to form a doe rubbing (her) left eye on the horn of a black antelope.' *Hansa*, a kind of wild-goose of a white colour, with golden wings ; something between a swan and a flamingo. It serves the god Brahmā as a vehicle, and hence the *hansa-nāda* or 'cry' of this bird has a sacred character, just as the cry of the swan, with the Greeks ; the voice of a beautiful woman is even compared to it (Bhaṭṭi-k. v. 18). *Mālinī*, cf. p. 103, l. 6 ; p. 16, l. 7. *Pādāḥ=pratyanta-parvatāḥ*, S'.; =*paryanta-parvatāḥ*, K. *Gaurī-guroḥ=Himālayasya*, S'.; Himālaya, the god of the great snowy range, was the father of Gaurī, the wife of S'iva, whence she is called Pārvatī, Himavat-sutā, Hima-jā, &c. *S'ākhā-lambita-valkala*, cf. *viṭapa-vishakta-jalārdra-valkaleshu*, verse 32, and p. 18, n. 1 at the end.

[2] 'With multitudes of long-bearded monks.' *Lamba*, lit. 'hanging down ;' *kūrća=śmaśru*, S'. The Mackenzie reads *lamba-kuććhāṇam paḍi-kamma kuvvāṇeṇa tābasaṇim ṇiareṇa*.

[3] The meaning may be, 'there is another of S'akuntalā's ornaments intended (to be drawn) on this picture (but) forgotten by me.'

Verse 149. S'ĀRDŪLA-VIKRĪḌITA (a variety of ATIDHṚITI). See verses 14, 30, 36, 39, 40, 63, 79, 85, 86, 89, 97, 98, 111, 137, 138.

सानुमती ।

[a]वणवासस सोउमारस्सञ्ज जं सरिसं भविस्सदि ।

राजा ।

कृतं न कर्णार्पितबन्धनं सखे
शिरीषमागण्डविलम्बिकेशरम् ।
न वा शरच्चन्द्रमरीचिकोमलं
मृणालसूचं रचितं स्तनान्तरे ॥ १५० ॥

विदूषकः ।

[b]भो । किं णु तब्भहोदी रत्तकुवलअपल्लवसोहिणा
अग्गहत्येण मुहं आवारिअ चइदचइदा विअ ठिदा ।

॥ सावधानं निरूप्य । दृष्ट्वा ॥ [c]आ । एसो दासीएपुत्तो कुसुमरस-
पाडच्चरी तब्भहोदीए वअणं अहिलङ्घदि महुअरो ।

राजा ।

ननु वार्यतामेष धृष्टः ।

विदूषकः ।

[d]भवं एव्व अविणीदाणं सासिदा इमस्स वारणे पहविस्सदि ।

[a] वनवासस्य सौकुमार्यस्य च यत्सदृशं भविष्यति ।   [b] भोः । किं नु तत्रभवती रक्तकुवलयपल्लवशोभिनाग्रहस्तेन मुखमावार्य चकितचकितेव स्थिता ।   [c] आः । एष दास्याःपुत्रः कुसुमरसपाठच्चरस्तत्रभवत्या वदनमभिलङ्घति मधुकरः ।   [d] भवानेवा-
विनीतानां शासितास्य वारणे प्रभविष्यति ।

---

[1] 'A S'irīsha-blossom, with its stalk fastened in her ear, (and) its-fila-ments-hanging-down-to-her-cheek, has not been drawn [made], O friend. Nor has a necklace-of-lotus-fibres, soft-as-the-rays-of-the-autumnal-moon, been formed in the midst of her bosom.' *Bandhana*=*prasava-bandhana*=*vṛinta*, S'. and C. (cf. p. 103, n. 1, and p. 229, n. 1). *S'irīsha*, see p. 7, n. 1, and p. 53, n. 1. The blossom of a plant is neuter in Sanskṛit.

[2] With regard to this passage and what follows, compare pp. 32, 33, 34. As to *rakta-kuvalaya*, &c., see p. 25, n. 1. As to *dāsyāḥ-putra*, see p. 61, n. 1.

Verse 150. VAṆŚA-STHAVILA (a variety of JAGATĪ). See verses 18, 22, 23, 67, 81, 114, 117, 119, 145.

राजा ।

युज्यते । अयि भोः कुसुमलताप्रियातिथे । किमत्र परि-
पतनखेदमनुभवसि ।

एषा कुसुमनिषण्णा तृषितापि सती भवन्तमनुरक्ता ।
प्रतिपालयति मधुकरी न खलु मधु विना त्वया पिवति ॥१५१॥

सानुमती ।

[a] अज्ज अभिजादंक्खु एसो वारिदो । [^1]

विदूषकः ।

[b] पडिसिद्धाबि वामा एसा जादी ।

राजा ।

एवं भी न मे शासने तिष्ठसि । श्रूयतां तर्हि सम्प्रति ।

अक्लिष्टबालतरुपल्लवलोभनीयं
पीतं मया सदयमेव रतोत्सवेषु ।
बिम्बाधरं स्पृशसि चेद्भ्रमर प्रियाया-
स्त्वां कारयामि कमलोदरबन्धनस्थम् ॥१५२॥

[a] सद्याभिजातां खलेष वारितः ।   [b] प्रतिषिद्धापि वामैषा जातिः ।

---

[1] 'Wherefore dost thou undergo the fatigue of hovering round about? There [*eshā*] resting-on-a-flower the-devotedly-attached female-bee, although being thirsty, waits for thee; nor indeed without thee will she sip (its) nectar.' *Paripatana*, 'flying round about,' the first sense of *pat* is 'to fly.'

[2] 'For-once-now this (bee) is warned-off [kept off] quite in a courteous manner.' The meaning is somewhat obscure, but there seems to be a satirical allusion to the king's polite address to the bee, followed as it is by a threat.

[3] 'This race (of animals), however (it may be) driven off, is perverse.' The Beng. MSS. and K. have *pratishiddha-vāmā*. *Vāma*, properly 'left,' 'not right;' hence 'turned from the right,' 'reverse,' 'perverse,' 'refractory.'

[4] 'If, O bee, thou touchest the Bimba-lip of (my) beloved, charming as

Verse 151. ĀRYĀ or GĀTHĀ. See verse 2.

    – – | ᴜ ᴜ ᴜ ᴜ | – – ‖ ᴜ ᴜ – | ᴜ ᴜ – | ᴜ – ᴜ | ᴜ ᴜ – | –
    – ᴜ ᴜ | ᴜ – ᴜ | ᴜ ᴜ – ‖ ᴜ ᴜ ᴜ ᴜ | ᴜ ᴜ – | ᴜ | – ᴜ ᴜ | –

Verse 152. VASANTA-TILAKĀ (a variety of ŚAKVARĪ). See verses 8, 27, 31, &c., 148.

विदूषकः ।

[a] एव्वंतिएहदराइस्स किं ण भाइस्संदि । ॥ सहस्य । आत्मगतम् ॥
[b] एसो दाव उम्मत्तो । अहम्पि एदस्स सङ्गेण ईदिसवच्रणी
विच्च संवुत्तो । ॥ प्रकाशम् ॥ [c] भो । चित्तंक्खु एदं ।

राजा ।

कथं चिचम् ।

सानुमती ।

[d] अहम्पि दाणिं अणवगदत्था । किं उण जहलिहिदाणु-
भावी एंसो ।

राजा ।

वयस्य । किमिदमनुष्ठितं पौरोभाग्यम् ।

[a] एवंतीक्ष्णदराडस्य किं न भेष्यति । [b] एष तावदुन्मत्तः । अहमप्येतस्य सङ्गेने-
दूषवचन इव संवृत्तः । [c] भोः । चित्रं खल्वेतत् । [d] अहमपीदानीमनवग-
तार्था । किं पुनर्यथालिखितानुभाख्येष: ।

the uninjured blossom of a young tree, that very (lip which has been)
tenderly drunk by me in love's banquets, (then) I will make thee im-
prisoned in the hollow of a lotus' (cf. verse 77, with note). *Bimbādhara*,
'lip like the Bimba,' i. e. of a bright red colour, like the gourd of the
Bimba (Momordica Monadelpha), a cucurbitaceous plant. So *bimbādharā-
laktakaḥ*, Mālavik. p. 30, l. 1; Raghu-v. xiii. 16. Compare our expression,
'cherry-lip.' *Kamalodara-ba°*, see p. 183, n. 1. *Bandhana* seems here
to mean 'the place of imprisonment.'

[1] 'How should he not stand in awe of one who has (threatened him
with) so severe a punishment?' *Tīkshṇa-daṇḍa*, 'severe in punishing,' 'a
strict disciplinarian.' The Prākṛit equivalent of *tīkshṇa* is *tiṇha*, according to Vararuči iii. 33, although most of the MSS. have *tikkhaṇa*. Root *bhī*
in Sanskrit is usually joined with an abl., but the gen. is admissible (Gram.
855, 859); K., however, observes that this construction is peculiar to
Prākṛit (cf. *dākshiṇya-paścāttāpasya bibhemi*, Vikram., end of Act II).

[2] 'Even I now did not understand the thing; how much less should he
perceive that it was painted?' *An-avagatārthā*, so reads the Mackenzie
MS., supported by K.; the others, *avagatārthā*.

[3] 'Why has this ill-natured-act been perpetrated (by you)?' *Pauro-
bhāgya*, see p. 212, n. 1. K. observes, *purobhāgī = doshaika-darśī = dush-
ṭaḥ, tasya karma paurobhāgyam*, and refers to Pāṇ. v. 1, 124.

दर्शनसुखमनुभवतः साक्षादिव तन्मयेन हृदयेन ।
स्मृतिकारिणा त्वया मे पुनरपि चिच्नीकृता कान्ता ॥१५३॥
॥ इति बाष्पं विहरति ॥
सानुमती ।
पुव्वाबरविरोही अपुव्वो एसो विरहमग्गो ।
राजा ।
वयस्य । कथमेवमविश्रान्तदुःखमनुभवामि ।
प्रजागरात्खिलीभूतस्तस्याः स्वप्ने समागमः ।
वाष्पस्तु न ददात्येनां द्रष्टुं चिच्चगतामपि ॥१५४॥

a पूर्वापरविरोध्यपूर्व एव विरहमार्गः ।

---

[1] 'My beloved is once more transformed into a picture by thee reviving the recollection of me enjoying the bliss of beholding her just-as-if (she were) present before my eyes, having my (whole) soul wrapped-up-in-her.' *Tan-mayena=Śakuntalā-mayena*, Ś., lit. 'with a heart made of Śakuntalā,' i.e. wholly absorbed by her.

[2] *Viharati*, 'wipes away,' or 'sheds;' see p. 166, n. 5, and p. 154, n. 1.

[3] 'This demeanour of (one in a state of) separation, opposing first one thing and then another, is singular [unexampled, without a precedent].' *Pūrvāpara-virodhī* may mean 'setting itself against everything from first to last,' or 'from first to last untoward.' Lovers, when separated from each other, were supposed to find comfort and amusement in various trifling employments expressive of their passion (see Megha-d. 86); but here was the case of one whom nothing could divert.

[4] '(The hope of) meeting her in sleep is rendered vain through (my) wakefulness. Moreover the (blinding) tears (that fill my eyes) will not permit me to behold her even represented-in-a-picture.' *Vāshpa*, see p. 157, n. 1 in the middle. *Khilī-bhūta=dur-labha*, Ś. In Hindū poetry dreams and pictures are the regular standing artifices of lovers for tricking themselves into fictitious unions with their mistresses; just as sleeplessness and tears are the regular standing impediments to such devices. Cf.

Verse 153. ĀRYĀ or GĀTHĀ. See verse 2.

    — ᴗ ᴗ | ᴗ ᴗ ᴗ ᴗ | ᴗ ᴗ — ‖   — — | ᴗ ᴗ — | ᴗ — ᴗ | ᴗ ᴗ — | ᴗ
    ᴗ ᴗ — | ᴗ — ᴗ | — — ‖ ᴗ ᴗ ᴗ ᴗ | — — | ᴗ | — — | —

Verse 154. ŚLOKA or ANUSHTUBH. See verses 5, 6, 11, 12, 26, 47, 50, 51, 53, 73, 76, 84, 87, 125, 127, 146.

सानुमती ।

[a] सव्वहा पमंज्जिदं तुए पच्चादेसदुक्खं सउन्दलाए ।

चतुरिका ॥ प्रविश्य ॥

[b] जेदु जेदु भट्टा । वट्टिआकरंडअं गेण्हिअ इदोमुहं पन्थिदम्हि ।

राजा ।

किं च ।

चतुरिका ।

[c] सो मे हत्थादो अन्तरा तरलिआदुदिआए देवीए वसुम-दीए अहं एव्व अज्जउत्तस उवणइस्संति सबलक्कारं गहिदो ।

विदूषकः ।

[d] दिट्ठिआ तुमं मुक्का ।

चतुरिका ।

[e] जाव देवीए विडबलग्गं उत्तरीअं तरलिआ मोचेदि । ताव मए णिव्वाहिदो अत्ता ।

[a] सर्वथा प्रमार्जितं त्वया प्रत्यादेशदुःखं शकुन्तलायाः । [b] जयतु जयतु भर्ता । वर्तिकाकरण्डकं गृहीत्वेतोमुखं प्रस्थितास्मि । [c] स मे हस्तादन्तरा तरलिकाद्वि-तीयया देव्या वसुमत्या अहमेवार्यपुत्रस्योपनेष्यामीति सबलात्कारं गृहीतः । [d] दिष्ट्या त्वं मुक्ता । [e] यावद्देव्या विटपलग्नमुत्तरीयं तरलिका मोचयति । तावन्मया निर्वाहित आत्मा ।

Megha-d. 104, *Tvām ālikhya aśrais tāvan muhur upaćitair dṛishṭir ālupyate me krūras tasminn api na sahate sangamaṃ nau kṛitāntaḥ.* See also Megha-d. 89, and Vikram., Act II, *Katham upālabhe nidrāṃ svapne samāgama-kāriṇīm; na ća suvadanām ālekhye 'pi priyāṃ sama-vāpya tām mama nayanayor udvāshpatvaṃ sakhe na bhavishyati.*

[1] *Pramārjita*, 'atoned for,' lit. 'wiped clean,' 'wiped out.'

[2] *Vartikā-karaṇḍaka*, 'box of colours,' see p. 249, n. 1.

[3] *Antarā*, 'on the way,' 'midway.' The same expression occurs in p. 257, l. 14. See also Mālavik. p. 8, l. 18. As to Vasumatī, see p. 184, n. 2.

[4] 'I took myself off,' 'I made my escape,' lit. 'by me my own person was carried off.' The Prākṛit is responsible for this idiom and con-struction. *Nirvāhita* is the reading of most of the Deva-n. MSS., and

राजा ।

वयस्य । उपस्थिता देवी बहुमानगर्विता च । भवानिमां[1]
प्रतिकृतिं रक्षतु ।

विदूषकः ।

[a] अत्ताणंत्ति भणाहि । ॥ चित्रफलकमादायोत्थाय च ॥ [b] जइ भवं
अन्तेउरकालकूडादो मुञ्चीअदि । तदो मं मेहप्पडिच्छन्दे
पासादे सद्दावेहि । ॥ इति द्रुतपदं निष्क्रान्तः ॥

सानुमती ।

[c] अण्णसङ्कन्तहिअओबि पढमसम्भावणं अवेक्खदि ।
अदिसिढिलसोहदो दाणिं एसो ।

प्रतीहारी ॥ प्रविश्य पत्रहस्ता ॥

[d] जेदु जेदु देवो ।

राजा ।

वेत्रवति । न खल्वन्तरा दृष्टा त्वया देवी ।

[a] आत्मानमिति भण ।
मेघप्रतिच्छन्दे प्रासादे शब्दय ।
अतिशिथिलसौहृद इदानीमेघः ।

[b] यदि भवानन्तःपुरकालकूटादुच्यते । ततो मां
[c] अन्यसङ्क्रान्तहृदयोऽपि प्रथमसम्भावनामपेक्षते ।
[d] जयतु जयतु देवः ।

---

there seems no reason why it should not stand with the sense 'carried
away,' 'borne off.' K. has *nirvāsita*, 'expelled.' Some of the Bengālī,
nihṇavida for *nihnuta*, 'concealed.' S'. has *nirgata*.

[1] 'Rendered insolent by my great attention to her.'

[2] 'From the bane of the inner apartments.' *Kāla-kūṭa*, at the churning
of the ocean, after the deluge, by the gods and demons, for the recovery
or production of fourteen sacred things, a deadly poison called Kāla-kūṭa
or Halāhala was generated, so virulent that it would have destroyed the
world, had not the god S'iva swallowed it. Its only effect was to leave
a black mark on his throat, whence his name Nīla-kaṇṭha. K. has *kala-
hādo* (= *kalahāt*), 'from the strife,' and S'. *kūṭāt*, 'from the snare.'

[3] 'Call me in the palace (named) Megha-praticchanda.' *S'abda* may
form either a nominal or a verb of the 10th class; cf. p. 152, n. 1.

[4] 'Although his heart [affection] is transferred to another.' Cf. in
Vikram., Act III, *Anya-sankrānta-premāṇo nāgarā adhikaṃ dakshiṇā
bhavanti*.

L l

प्रतीहारी ।

[a] अहइं । पत्तहत्थं मं देक्खिद्ध पडिणिउत्ता ।

राजा ।

कार्यज्ञा कार्योपरोधं मे परिहरति ।

प्रतीहारी ।

[b] देव । अमच्चो विण्णवेदि । अत्थजादस्स गणणाबहुलदाए एक्कं एव्व पोरकज्जं अवेक्खिदं । तं देवो पत्ताऊढं पच्चक्खीकरेदु त्ति ।

राजा ।

इतः पत्त्रिकां दर्शय ।   ॥ प्रतीहार्युपनयति ॥

राजा   ॥ अनुवाच्य ॥

कथम् । समुद्रव्यवहारी सार्थवाहो धनमित्रो नाम नौव्यसने विपन्नः । अनपत्यश्च किल तरस्वी । राजगामी तस्यार्थ- सञ्चय इत्येतदमात्येन लिखितम् । कष्टं खल्वनपत्यता । बहुधनत्वाद्बहुपत्नीकेन तत्रभवता भवितव्यम् । विचार्य- ताम् । यदि काचिदापन्नसत्त्वा तस्य भार्यासु स्यात् ।

प्रतीहारी ।

[c] देव । दाणिं एव्व साकेदस्स सेट्ठिणो दुहिस्रा णिव्वुत्त- पुंसवणा जाआ से सुण्णीअदि[2] ।

<hr>

[a] अथ किं । पत्तहस्तां मां दृष्ट्वा प्रतिनिवृत्ता ।   [b] देव । अमात्यो विज्ञापयति । अर्थजातस्य गणनाबहुलतयैकमेव पौरकार्यमपेक्षितम् । तद्देवः पत्ताऊढं प्रत्यक्षीकरोत्विति । [c] देव । इदानीमेव साकेतकस्य श्रेष्ठिनो दुहिता निर्वृत्तपुंसवना जायास्य श्रूयते ।

<hr>

[1] 'By reason of the length of the calculation of the various-items-of-revenue, only one case among the citizens has been brought under consideration.' *Artha-jātasya*, &c., some of the Beng. have *rāja-kāryasya bahulatayā*. *Bahulatayā*, cf. *pallavatayā*, p. 29, n. 1.

[2] 'It is reported that his wife, the daughter of the foreman of a guild belonging to Ayodhyā, has even now just completed the ceremony (performed) at the quickening (of the unborn child).' *Sāketakasya*, Sāketa is a name of Ayodhyā, 'the invincible city,' the ancient capital of Rāma-

राजा ।

ननु गर्भः[1] पित्र्यं रिक्थमर्हति । गच्छ । एवममात्यं ब्रूहि ।

प्रतीहारी ।

[a] जं देवो आणबेदि । ॥ इति प्रस्थिता ॥

राजा ।

एहि तावत् ।

प्रतीहारी ।

[b] इअम्हि ।

राजा ।

किमनेन सन्ततिरस्ति नास्तीति ।

येन येन वियुज्यन्ते प्रजाः स्निग्धेन बन्धुना ।

स स पापाट्टूते तासां तुष्यन्त इति घुष्यताम्[2] ॥१५५॥

प्रतीहारी ।

[c] एव्वं णाम घोसइदव्वं । ॥ निष्क्रम्य । पुनः प्रविश्य ॥ [d] काले पवुट्टुं विञ्च अहिणंन्दिदं[3] देवस्स सासणं ।

राजा ॥ दीर्घमुष्णां च निःश्वस्य ॥

एवं भीः सन्ततिच्छेदनिरवलम्बानां कुलानां मूलपुरुषा-

[a] यदेव आज्ञापयति ।   [b] इयमस्मि ।   [c] एवं नाम घोषयितव्यम् ।
[d] काले प्रवृष्टमिवाभिनन्दितं देवस्य शासनम् ।

ćandra and founded by Ikshvāku, the first of the monarchs of the Solar dynasty (see p. 15, n. 1). It was situated on the river Sarayu in the North of India, and is now called Oude. *S'reshṭhin*, 'the head of a guild or corporation practising the same trade.' *Puṃ-savana*, 'the rite performed on the quickening of the fœtus,' is the second of the twelve purificatory ceremonies enjoined by Manu on the three superior classes (ii. 27, &c.) It comes next in order to the *garbhādhāna* or 'ceremony on conception;' cf. p. 199, l. 1, with note; see Indian Wisdom, p. 246.

[1] *Garbhaḥ=garbha-sthaḥ putraḥ*, 'the child in the womb,' K.

[2] See the translation of this verse, p. 191, n. 2 at the end.

[3] 'Like grateful-rain at the right season.' *Pravṛishṭam=prahṛishṭa-varshaṇam.* Some of the Beng. have *paviṭṭham* (=*pravishṭam*).

Verse 155. ŚLOKA or ANUSHṬUBH. See verses 5, 6, &c., 154.

वसाने सम्पदः परमुपतिष्ठन्ति । ममाप्यन्ते पुरुवंशश्रीर-
काल इवोप्तवीजा भूरेवंवृत्ता ।

प्रतीहारी ।

[a] पडिहदं अमङ्गलं ।

राजा ।

धिङ्मामुपस्थितश्रेयोऽवमानिनम् ।

सानुमती ।

[b] असंसञ्चं सहिं एव्व हिअए करिञ णिन्दिदो येण अप्पा ।

राजा ।

संरोपितेऽप्यात्मनि धर्मपत्नी
त्यक्ता मया नाम कुलप्रतिष्ठा ।
कल्पिष्यमाणा महते फलाय
वसुन्धरा काल इवोप्तवीजा ॥१५६॥

सानुमती ।

[c] अपरिच्छिन्ना दाणिं दे सन्ददी भविस्सदि ।

[a] प्रतिहतममङ्गलम् ।   [b] असंशयं सखीमेव हृदये कृत्वा निन्दितोऽनेनात्मा ।
[c] अपरिच्छिन्नेदानीं ते सन्ततिर्भविष्यति ।

---

[1] 'The goods of families who are bereft of support through the failure
of lineal descendants, pass over to a stranger at the decease of the re-
presentative-of-the-original-stock.' *Mūla-purusha*, 'the man who represents the original progenitor, from whom, in a direct line, the family is
descended,' 'the eldest surviving son,' lit. 'the stock-man.'

[2] 'The misfortune be averted!' compare p. 194, l. 8.

[3] 'Although myself was implanted (in her womb), verily (my) lawful
wife, the glory of (my) family, was repudiated by me, like the earth sown
with seed at the right-season, about to become adequate to the production
of mighty fruit.' *Saṃropite ātmani* = *svasmin upte sati*, K., lit. 'myself
being sown,' 'she being sown with myself,' i. e. 'she bearing my second
self in her womb.' According to the Hindū notion, a child is a repro-
duction of one's self. *Ātmaiva patnyā jāyate*, K. *Kula-pratishthā*, see
p. 124, n. 1. *Kalpishyamāṇā*, see p. 191, n. 2 in the middle. *Vasun-
dharā*, cf. p. 184, n. 2.

Verse 156. UPAJĀTI or ĀKHYĀNAKĪ (a variety of TRISHTUBH). See verses 41, &c., 142.

चतुरिका ॥ जनान्तिकम् ॥

[a] अए । इमिणा सत्थवाहवुत्तन्तेण विउणुव्वेओ भट्टा ।
णं अस्सासिदुं मेहप्पडिच्छन्दादो अज्जं माठव्वं गेण्हिअ
आअच्छेहि ।

प्रतीहारी ।

[b] सुदृतु भणासि ।   ॥ इति निष्क्रान्ता ॥

राजा ।

अहो दुष्यन्तस्य संशयमारूढाः पिण्डभाजः । कुतः ।

अस्मात्परं वत यथाश्रुति सम्भृतानि
       को नः कुले निवपनानि नियच्छतीति ।
नूनं प्रसूतिविकलेन मया प्रसिक्तं
       धौताश्रुशेषमुदकं पितरः पिवन्ति ॥१५७॥

॥ इति मोहमुपागतः ॥

[a] अये । अनेन सार्थवाहवृत्तान्तेन विगुणोद्वेगो भर्ता । एनमाश्वासयितुं मेघप्रति-
च्छन्दादायें माठव्यं गृहीत्वागच्छ ।   [b] सुष्ठु भणसि ।

---

[1] 'Woe is me! the ancestors of Dushyanta are brought to a critical situation; because—Thinking to themselves, Who, alas! after this (man), in our family, will offer (us) the oblations prepared according to scriptural-precept? in all probability,' &c. ; see p. 111, n. 1. *Piṇḍa-bhājaḥ=pitaraḥ*, S'., lit. 'partakers of oblations to the dead,' i. e. the Manes of deceased ancestors for whom the S'rāddha was performed. *Kutaḥ*, see p. 55, n. 2. *Asmāt*, i. e. *Dushyantāt*, S'. *Dhautāśru-śesha*, compare the analogous compounds *tvag-asthi-śesha*, 'having nothing left but skin and bone;' *nāma-śesha*, 'having nothing surviving but a name.' The Beng. MSS. read *dhautāśru-sekam*. The duty of performing the S'rāddha devolved on the eldest son or on the nearest surviving relative. If no one survived to celebrate this rite, the Manes of deceased progenitors sank from their celestial abode to the lower regions. Cf. Raghu-v. i. 66, 67 ; see Indian Wisdom, p. 253 sqq.

Verse 157. VASANTA-TILAKĀ (a variety of S'AKVARI). See verses 8, 27, 31, 43, 46, 64, 74, 80, 82, 83, 91, 93, 94, 95, 100, 104, 105, 108, 123, 124, 144, 148, 152.

चतुरिका   ॥ ससम्भ्रममवलोकम ॥

[a] समस्ससदु समस्ससदु भट्टा ।

सानुमती ।

[b] हड्डी हड्डी । सदिक्खु दीबे ववधाणदोसेण एसो अन्धआ-रदोसं अणुहोदि । अहं दाणिं एव्व णिव्वुदं करेमि । अहवा सुदं मए सउन्दलं समस्सासअन्तीए महेन्दजणणीए मुहादो । जण्णभाओसुआं देवा एव्व तह अणुचिट्टिस्सन्ति जह अइरेण धम्मपदिणिं भट्टा अहिणन्दिस्सदित्ति । ता जुत्तं एदं कालं पडिपालिदुं । जाव इमिणा वुत्तन्तेण

[a] समाश्वसितु समाश्वसितु भर्त्तौ ।   [b] हा धिक् हा धिक् । सति खलु दीपे व्यवधानदोषेणैषोऽन्धकारदोषमनुभवति । अहमिदानीमेव निर्वृतं करोमि । अथवा श्रुतं मया शकुन्तलां समाश्वासयन्त्या महेन्द्रजनन्या मुखात् । यज्ञभागोत्सुका देवा एव तथानुशास्यन्ति यथाचिरेण धर्मपत्नीं भर्त्ताभिनन्दिष्यतीति । तस्माद्युक्तमेतं कालं प्रतिपालयितुम् । यावदनेन वृत्तान्तेन

---

[1] 'A light being really (near at hand) this-man by reason [fault] of the screen (which covers it) experiences (all the) ill-effects of darkness.' Dr. Boehtlingk proposes to interpret *andhaāra-dosam* by *andhakāra-doshām*, 'dark night,' or 'the darkness of night,' but this seems hardly a legitimate compound, nor does the sense require it.

[2] 'Longing for their portions of the sacrifice.' *Janna* is the Prākṛit equivalent for *yajña* (Vararuči iii. 44). Great sacrifices were performed by kings in celebration of auspicious events, especially after marriage, in the hope of securing issue, and Indra as well as the inferior gods were invited to partake of portions set apart for them. These sacrifices were accompanied by largesses to the Brāhmans, and festivities, in which the gods were supposed to be eager to participate. Cf. Rāmāy. i. 13, 6. 8. The mother of Indra was Aditi, who was the wife of Kaśyapa (see p. 22, n. 3). It appears from Act VII. of this play that Śakuntalā was at this time enjoying an asylum with the illustrious pair Kaśyapa and Aditi in some sacred retreat, where they were engaged in acts of mortification and penance.

[3] 'Therefore it is proper to wait for this period.' This is the reading of K. Some of the Deva-n. have *tā na juttam kālam*, &c. (=*tasmān na yuktam kālam*, &c.)

ᵃ पिअसहिं समस्सासेमि ।   ॥ इत्युद्भ्रान्तकेन निष्क्रान्ता[1] ॥

नेपथ्ये ।

ᵇ अब्म्हसं अब्म्हसं[2] ।

राजा   ॥ प्रत्यागतप्राणः[3] । कर्णं दत्त्वा ॥

अये । माठव्यस्यैवार्तस्वरः । कः कोऽत्र भोः ।

प्रतीहारी   ॥ प्रविश्य ॥

ᶜ परित्ताअदु देवी संसअंगदं[4] वअस्सं ।

राजा ।

केनात्तगन्धी[5] माणवकः ।

प्रतीहारी ।

ᵈ अदिट्ठरूवेण केणवि सत्तेण अदिक्कमिअ मेहप्पडिच्छन्दस्स पासादस्स अग्गभूमिं आरोविंदो[6] ।

ᵃ प्रियसखीं समाश्वासयामि ।   ᵇ अब्रह्मण्यम् अब्रह्मण्यम् ।   ᶜ परित्रायतां देवः संशयगतं वयस्यम् ।   ᵈ अदृष्टरूपेण केनापि सत्त्वेनातिक्रम्य मेघप्रतिच्छन्दस्य प्रासादस्याग्रभूमिमारोपितः ।

---

[1] See p. 218, n. 1, i. e. *udbhramaṇena ākāśam pratyudgamena*, K.

[2] *Abrahmaṇyam* ('Help! to the rescue!'), according to Amara-k. i. 7, 14, is *abadhyoktau*, i. e. implies an assertion that the thing in question is not to be killed. *Abadhyo 'ham ity arthaḥ*, S., 'the meaning is that, as a Brāhman, my person is sacred and inviolable.' Cf. in the Uttara-Rāma-ćaritra, p. 30, 'Then by a Brāhman, having placed his dead son at the royal gate, a cry of "Abrahmaṇya" was set up, accompanied by a smiting on the breast.' *A-brahmaṇya*, lit. '(anything) unworthy of a Brāhman.'

[3] So reads my own MS. One Deva-n. has *pratyāgataḥ*, the others simply *karṇam dattvā*. The Beng. *pratyāgata-ćetanaḥ*.

[4] 'Fallen into danger,' 'placed in jeopardy.' As to *gata*, see p. 38, n. 1.

[5] *Atta-gandha*=*ātta-garva*, 'humbled,' 'having the pride taken down,' 'insulted.' Compare in the Mahā-bh. *rājyam ātta-lakshmi*, 'a kingdom stripped of its wealth.' According to some, *ātta-gandha*=*ārta-kaṇṭha*, 'throttled,' 'strangled.'

[6] 'By some demon of invisible form, having seized [overpowered] him, he has been mounted on a pinnacle of the palace (called) Megha-prati-ććhanda.' *Sattva*=*bhūta*, 'a goblin,' 'evil spirit.'

राजा ।। उत्थाय ।।

मा तावत् । ममापि सद्भैरभिभूयन्ते गृहाः[1] । अथवा ।

अहन्यहन्यात्मन एव ताव-
ज्ज्ञातुं प्रमादस्खलितं न शक्यम् ।
प्रजासु कः केन पथा प्रयाती-
त्यशेषतो वेदितुमस्ति शक्तिः ।।१५८।।[2]

नेपथ्ये ।

[a]भो वयस्स । अविहा अविहा ।[3]

राजा ।। गतिभेदेन परिक्रामन् ।।[4]

सखे । न भेतव्यं न भेतव्यम् ।

^a भो वयस्य । अविधा अविधा ।

---

¹ *Griha*, 'a house,' or 'a wife,' is masc. in the plural (Amara-k. ii. 5). The Sāhit.-d. (p. 190) inserts *nāma*, 'forsooth,' after *mamāpi*.

² 'Even one's own false-steps (proceeding from) heedlessness (occurring) day by day cannot be altogether ascertained. Is there (then) the power to know in every case by what road each of my subjects is walking?' lit. 'by what road who among my subjects,' &c. *Tāvat=sākalyena*, K. *Pramāda-skhalitam*, 'tripping from carelessness,' 'stumbling,' 'blundering.' *A-śeshataḥ=sākalyena*, K. According to K., this last clause presents an example of *kāku*, which is defined as 'a change in the tone of the voice,' 'giving emphasis.' Thus, 'Is there the power?' becomes equivalent to 'there certainly is not the power' (see Sāhit.-d. p. 24). *Kāku* is constantly used by Paṇḍits of a sentence spoken interrogatively, and so with a change of voice.

³ *Avidhā ity ākrośe*. The interjection *avidhā* is used in calling for assistance, K. Translate, 'Help! help!' Two of the MSS. have *aviha* for *avidha*; the Mackenzie, *aviddho*; my own, *avidū*. *Aviha* and *avihā* seem to be interchangeable. *Avihā* occurs in Mālavik. p. 12, l. 22; p. 24, l. 7; p. 56, l. 8. Dr. Boehtlingk suggests that *avida* in Mriċċhak. p. 213, l. 6; p. 312, l. 9, may be for *aviha* or *avihā*.

⁴ *Gati-bhedena*, 'with hurried broken steps;' *tvarita-gamanena ity arthaḥ*, K.

Verse 158. Upajāti or Ākhyānakī (a variety of Trishṭubh). See verse 41, 107, 121, 126, 142, 156.

नेपथ्ये ॥ पुनस्तदेव पठित्वा ॥

[a] कहं ण भाइस्सं । एस मं कोवि पच्चावणदसिरोहरं इक्खुं विअ तिरहभङ्गं करेदि ।[1]

राजा ॥ सदृष्टिक्षेपम् ॥

धनुस्तावत् ।

यवनी ॥ प्रविश्य शार्ङ्गहस्ता ॥[2]

[b] भट्टा । एदं हत्यावावसहिदं सरासणं ।[3]

॥ राजा सशरं धनुरादत्ते ॥

नेपथ्ये ।

एष त्वामभिनवकण्ठशोणितार्थी
शार्दूलः पशुमिव हन्मि चेष्टमानम् ।
आर्तानां भयमपनेतुमात्तधन्वा
दुष्यन्तस्तव शरणं भवत्विदानीम् ॥१५९॥

राजा ॥ सरोषम् ॥

कथं मामेवोद्दिशति । तिष्ठ कुणपाशन । त्वमिदानीं न भविष्यसि । ॥ शार्ङ्गमारोप्य ॥ वेचवति । सोपानमार्गमादेशय ।

[a] कथं न भेष्यामि । एष मां कोऽपि पश्चादवनतशिरोधरमिषुमिव तीक्ष्णभङ्गं करोति ।

[b] भर्तैः । एतद्धस्तावापसहितं शरासनम् ।

---

[1] *Paśćād-avanata-śirodharam*, a Bahuvrīhi compound agreeing with *mām.* Some MSS. have *praty-avanata.*

[2] As to *Yavanī* and *śārṅga-hastā*, see p. 62, n. 2.

[3] *Hastāvāpa*=*jyāghāta-vāraṇa*, K.;=*aṅguli-trāṇa*, 'a guard to protect the hand or fore-arm from the bow-string,' 'an arm-guard,' 'a finger-guard;' from *hasta*, 'a hand,' or 'the lower arm,' and *āvāpa*, 'a band' or 'bracelet;' cf. p. 114, n. 2. The Beng. have *hastāvāra.*

[4] 'Here, thirsting for (thy) fresh throat-blood, will I slay thee struggling, as a tiger (slays) a beast. Let Dushyanta now, who grasps his bow to remove the fear of the oppressed, be thy refuge [protector].' *Artānām*, &c., cf. p. 14, l. 4. *Atta-dhanvā*, cf. p. 230, l. 1.

Verse 159. PRAHARSHINĪ (a variety of ATIJAGATĪ), containing thirteen syllables to the Pāda or quarter-verse, each Pāda being alike.

— — — | ◡ ◡ ◡ ◡ — ◡ — ◡ — — ॥

प्रतीहारी ।

[a] इदो इदो देवो ।

॥ सर्वे सत्वरमुपसर्पन्ति ॥

राजा ॥ समन्ताद्विलोक्य ॥

शून्यं खल्विदम् ।

नेपथ्ये ।

[b] अविहा[1] अविहा । अहं अत्तभवन्तं पेक्खामि । तुमं मं
ण पेक्खसि । विडालग्गहिदो मूसओ विअ णिरासोम्हि
जीविदे संवुत्तो ।

राजा ।

भोस्तिरस्करिणीगर्विते[2] । मदीयमस्त्रं त्वां द्रक्ष्यति । एष
तमिषुं सन्धत्ते ।

यो हनिष्यति वध्यं त्वां रक्ष्यं रक्षति च द्विजम् ।
हंसो हि क्षीरमादत्ते तन्मिश्रा वर्जयत्यपः ॥१६०॥[3]

॥ इत्यस्त्रं सन्धत्ते ॥

[a] इत इतो देवः ।   [b] अविधा अविधा । अहमत्रभवन्तं प्रेक्षे । त्वं मां न प्रेक्षसे ।
विडालगृहीतो मूषक इव निराशोऽस्मि जीविते संवृत्तः ।

---

[1] *Avidhā*, see p. 264, n. 3.   My own MS. has *avihā* in this place.

[2] 'Priding thyself on the power of rendering thyself invisible.' *Tiras-
kariṇī* is properly a veil to cover the head, used by celestial beings to
render themselves invisible (cf. p. 227, l. 5).   It is here the science or art,
peculiar to such beings, of so concealing themselves.   This interpretation
is supported by the gloss of Ranganātha on *tiraskariṇī-pračchannā* in
Act II. of Vikram.; *tiraskarinī = antardhāna-vidyā*.   It answers to
the *śikhā-bandhanī vidyā*, 'art of tying [covering] the top-knot,' called
a-parājitā in a preceding page.

[3] 'He it is fits the arrow (to the bow) who will slay thee worthy-
of-death, and save a Brāhman worthy-of-preservation.   For the flamingo
extracts [takes] the milk (and) leaves behind the water that is mixed
with it.'   The Hindūs imagine that the Haṇsa or flamingo (see p. 251,
n. 1) has the power of separating milk from water.   Compare Mahā-bh.,

Verse 160.   ŚLOKA or ANUSHṬUBH.   See verses 5, 6, 11, 12, 26, 47, 50, 51, 53, 73,
76, 84, 87, 125, 127, 130, 146, 154, 155.

॥ ततः प्रविशति विदूषकमुत्सृज्य मातलिः ॥

मातलिः ।

कृताः शरव्यं हरिणा तवासुराः
शरासनं तेषु विकृष्यतामिदम् ।
प्रसादसौम्यानि सतां सुहृज्जने
पतन्ति चक्षूंषि न दारुणाः शराः ॥१६१॥

राजा ॥ अस्त्रमुपसंहरन् ॥

अये मातलिः । स्वागतं महेन्द्रसारथे ।

विदूषकः ॥ प्रविश्य ॥

[a] अहं जेण इट्ठिपसुमारं मारिदो । सो इमिणा साम्मदेण अहिणन्दीअदि ।

[a] अहं येनेष्टिपशुमारं मारितः । सोऽनेन स्वागतेनाभिनन्द्यते ।

S'akuntalopākhyāna, vii. 88, *Prājñas tu jalpatām puṇsāṃ śrutvā vāćaḥ śubhāśubhāḥ, guṇavad vākyam ādatte, haṇsaḥ kshīram ivāmbhasaḥ* (i. 3078). Bhartṛi-h. (ii. 15) has the following sentiment : 'Brahmā [whose vehicle is the flamingo] when very angry with this bird, can destroy his nest among the lotuses, but cannot deprive him of that celebrated and inestimable faculty which he possesses, of separating milk from water.' The reference is probably to the milky juice of the water-lily, which would be its natural food, and to which allusion is often made by the Hindū poets.   As to *rakshati*, see p. 85, n. 2.

[1] *Mātali* is the charioteer of Indra.   In the pictures which represent this god mounted on his other vehicle, an elephant (called Airāvata), Mātali is seen seated before him on the withers of the animal, acting as its driver.   In the drama, however (see p. 12, n. 1), Indra is generally borne in a chariot drawn by two horses (called Harī or Harayaḥ), which were guided by Mātali.

[2] 'The demons are made by Indra thy mark ; let this bow (of thine) be drawn against them.   Not on a friendly-person are dreadful arrows directed [fall] by the good, [but rather] eyes soft-with-(looks of)-favour.' *Asurāḥ*, &c., see p. 86, n. 2 ; p. 87, n. 1.

[3] 'He by whom I was being slaughtered like a sacrificial victim, is

Verse 161.   VAṆŚA-STHAVILA (a variety of JAGATĪ).   See verses 18, 22, 23, 67, 81, 114, 117, 119, 145, 150.

मातलिः ॥ सस्मितम् ॥

आयुष्मन् । श्रूयताम् । यदर्थमस्मि हरिणा भवत्सकाशं
प्रेषितः ।

राजा ।

अवहितोऽस्मि ।

मातलिः ।

अस्ति कालनेमिप्रसूतिर्दुर्जयो नाम दानवगणः ।

राजा ।

अस्ति श्रुतपूर्वं मया नारदात् ।

मातलिः ।

सख्युस्ते स किल शतक्रतोरजय्य-
स्तस्य त्वं रणशिरसि स्मृतो निहन्ता ।
उच्छेत्तुं प्रभवति यन्न सप्तसप्ति-
स्तन्नैशं तिमिरमपाकरोति चन्द्रः ॥१६२॥

---

greeted with a welcome by this man!' *Ishṭi-paśu-māram māritaḥ=ishṭi-
paśur iva māritaḥ,* K. This kind of adverbial compound is noticed in
Pāṇ. iii. 4, 45. 46. So *aja-nāśaṃ nashṭaḥ* is equivalent to *aja iva nashṭaḥ,* and *ghṛita-nidhāyaṃ nihitaḥ* to *ghṛita iva nihitaḥ.*

¹ The Mackenzie MS. has *yadartham,* supported by some of the Bengālī.

² *Kālanemi,* son of the demon Hiraṇya-kaśipu, was a Daitya or Asura
(see p. 86, n. 2) with a hundred arms and as many heads. These Daityas
were sometimes called Dānavas, from their mother Danu, who as well as
Diti was one of the wives of Kaśyapa and daughters of Daksha. The
Rākshasas, or cannibal demons who, for the sake of human flesh, waged
perpetual war with men, as the Daityas did with the gods, were related to
the Daityas.

³ *Nārada* is a celebrated divine sage or Ṛishi, usually reckoned among
the ten Prajāpatis or Brahmādikas first created by Brahmā, and called his
sons. He acts as a kind of messenger of the gods (see the end of Act V.
of the Vikramorvaśī).

⁴ 'Verily that (troop of demons) is not to be subdued by thy friend
Indra; thou, at the head of the fight, art appointed [termed, called] its
destroyer. That nocturnal darkness which the sun has no power to

---

Verse 162. PRAHARSHIṆĪ (a variety of ATIJAGATĪ). See verse 159.

स भवानान्तशस्त्र एवमिदानीं तमैन्द्ररथमारुह्य विजयाय
प्रतिष्ठताम् ।

राजा ।

अनुगृहीतोऽहमनया मघवतः सम्भावनया । अथ माठव्यं
प्रति भवता किमेवं प्रयुक्तम् ।

मातलिः ।

तदपि कथ्यते । किञ्चिन्निमित्तादपि मनःसन्तापादा-
युष्मान्मया विक्लवो दृष्टः । पश्चात्कोपयितुमायुष्मन्तं तथा
कृतवानस्मि । कुतः ।

ज्वलति चलितेन्धनोऽग्निर्विप्रकृतः पन्नगः फणां कुरुते ।
प्रायः स्वं महिमानं क्षोभात्प्रतिपद्यते हि जनः ॥१६३॥

राजा ॥ जनान्तिकम् ॥

वयस्य । अनतिक्रमणीया दिवस्पतेराज्ञा । तदच परिगतार्थं

---

remove, the moon dispels.' *Sata-kratu*, 'lord of a hundred sacrifices;'
another of Indra's thousand names. He is so called because the rank
which he occupies is unattainable excepting through a hundred Asva-
medhas, or 'horse-sacrifices' (see p. 86, n. 2). *Sapta-saptiḥ*, 'drawn by
seven steeds;' see p. 12, n. 1. *Candraḥ*, the appositeness of this comparison depends on the fact that Dushyanta's pedigree was traceable to
the moon (see p. 15, n. 2; p. 113, n. 1).

[1] *Atta-sastra*, cf. *ātta-daṇḍaḥ*, p. 191, l. 4, and *ātta-dhanvā*, p. 265, l. 12.

[2] 'Fire blazes up when the fuel is stirred; the snake when irritated
expands its hood; verily a man generally regains his own high-spirited-
ness [greatness, courage] through being roused-to-action [shaken, excited].'
Phaṇaṃ kurute, lit. 'makes a hood;' *phaṇa*, 'the expanded hood of the
cobra.' *Kshobhāt*, K. has *kopāt*. My own MS. and the Mackenzie have
jantuḥ for *hi janaḥ*. Most of the Bengālī MSS. read *tejasvī saṃkshobhāt
prāyaḥ pratipadyate tejaḥ*.

[3] Indra, as the Hindū Jove, is lord of the atmosphere and winds (see
p. 86, n. 2).

Verse 163. ĀRYĀ or GĀTHĀ. See verse 2.

ᴗᴗᴗᴗ | ᴗ–ᴗ | – – ‖ – ᴗᴗ | – – | ᴗ–ᴗ | – ᴗᴗ | –
– – | – ᴗᴗ | – – ‖ – – | ᴗᴗ– | ᴗ | – ᴗᴗ |

कृत्वा मद्वचनादमात्यपिशुनं ब्रूहि ।[1]
तन्मतिः केवला तावत्परिपालयितुं प्रजाः ।
अधिज्यमिदमन्यस्मिन्कर्मणि व्यापृतं धनुः ॥१६४॥[2]

इति ।

विदूषकः ।

[a]जं भवं आणबेदि । ॥ इति निष्क्रान्तः ॥

मातलिः ।

आयुष्मानन्यथमारोहतु ।

॥ राजा स्थारोहणं नाटयति ॥

॥ इति निष्क्रान्ताः सर्वे ॥

॥ षष्ठोऽङ्कः ॥

[a] यद्भवानाज्ञापयति ।

---

[1] 'Having made acquainted with the circumstance ;' Piśuna, 'informer,'
is the name of the minister (cf. p. 236, l. 10).

[2] 'Let the-powers-of-thy mind be wholly and solely (exerted) to protect-
by-good-government (my) subjects. This (my) braced [strung] bow is (for
a time) occupied in a different employment.' *Tāvat*, cf. p. 264, l. 3. The
root *pāl*, 'to protect,' in reference to a king or his officers, implies protection by a just administration of the laws. *Samyak pāl* occurs frequently
in the sense of 'to govern justly.' *Adhi-jyam*, see p. 9, n. 2 ; and cf. p. 67,
l. 12 ; p. 87, l. 8.

Verse 164. ŚLOKA or ANUSHṬUBH. See verses 5, 6, 11, 12, 26, 47, 50, 51, 53,
73, 76, 84, 87, 125, 127, 146, 154, 155, 160.

॥ अथ सप्तमोऽङ्कः ॥

॥ ततः प्रविशत्याकाशयानेन रथ्याधिरूढो राजा मातलिश्च ॥

राजा ।

मातले । अनुष्ठितनिदेशोऽपि मघवतः सत्क्रियाविशे-
षादनुपयुक्तमिवात्मानं समर्थये[1] ।

मातलिः ॥ सस्मितम् ॥

आयुष्मन्[2] । उभयमप्यपरितोषं समर्थये ।

प्रथमोपकृतं मह्वतः प्रतिपत्त्या लघु मन्यते भवान् ।
गणयत्यवदानतोषितो भवतः सोऽपि न सत्क्रियागुणान् ॥१६५[3]

राजा ।

मातले । मा मैवम् । स खलु मनोरथानामप्यभूमिर्विसर्जना-
वसरसत्कारः[4] । मम हि दिवौकसां समक्षमर्धासनोपवेशितस्य

---

[1] 'Although I have executed (his) commission, after-such-a-distinguished reception (on the part) of Indra, I consider myself as unworthy (of so much honour).' *Satkriyā-viseshāt*, cf. p. 41, l. 9; p. 134, l. 18. The ablative may imply 'in consequence of,' 'after.' *An-upayuktam*, i.e. *tādṛik-satkriyāyā ayogyam*, Chézy. *Samarthaye=avagacchāmi*.

[2] *Āyushman*, cf. p. 9, n. 1.

[3] 'Your Highness makes light of the prior benefit (conferred by you) on Indra, (compared) with the (subsequent) mark-of-distinction (conferred by him on you). He too (Indra) takes no account of the distinguished honours (bestowed) on your Highness, being-filled-with-admiration at your heroic-achievement.' *Prathamopakṛitam*, i.e. *rākshasa-jaya-rūpam pūrvo-pakāram*, K. *Pratipattyā=sambhāvanayā*. *Avadāna=paurusha*, 'a deed of heroism,' K. The Colebrooke MS. has *toshito* for *vismito*. *Satkriyā-guṇān=sambhāvanā-viseshān*, K. *Guṇa* is used at the end of a compound with the sense of *visesha* (cf. *sambhāvanā-guṇa*, verse 168). The Beng. reading is, *Upakṛitya hares tathā bhavān laghu satkāram avekshya manyate, gaṇayaty avadāna-sammitām bhavataḥ so 'pi na satkriyām imām*.

[4] 'That honorary-distinction on the occasion of (his) dismissing (me)

Verse 165. VAITĀLĪYA. See verses 52, 133.

अन्तर्गतप्रार्थनमन्तिकस्थं
जयन्तमुद्वीक्ष्य कृतस्मितेन ।
आमृष्टवक्षोहरिचन्दनाङ्का
मन्दारमाला हरिणा पिनद्धा ॥१६६॥

मातलिः ।

किमिव नामायुष्मानमरेश्वरान्नार्हतीति । पश्य ।
सुरसखस्य हरेरभयैः कृतं
चिदिवमुज्झृतदानवकण्टकम् ।
तव शरैरधुना नतपर्वभिः
पुरुषकेशरिणश्च पुरा नखैः ॥१६७॥

---

was certainly beyond the compass [reach, place] of my hopes,' i. e. exceeded all my expectation. *A-bhūmi*=*a-sthāna*, 'want of place;'=*a-vishaya*, 'beyond the reach,' K. Cf. p. 285, l. 7, and Mālavik. p. 35, l. 4, *abhūmir iyam mālavikāyāḥ*.

¹ 'For a garland of Mandāra (flowers), marked with yellow-sandal from (its) rubbing on (his) breast, was fastened (round the neck) of me, made to sit on half his throne, before the eyes of the gods, by Indra, smiling and looking up at (his son) Jayanta, (who was) standing by and inwardly longing (for the same honours).' *Āmṛishṭa*, the breast of Indra was dyed yellow with a fragrant sandal-wood called Hari-candana (cf. Kumāra-s. v. 69), and the garland, from coming in contact with it, became tinged with the same colour. Wreaths and garlands of flowers were much used by the Hindūs as marks of honorary distinction, as well as for ornaments on festive occasions, and to adorn sacrificial victims (cf. p. 222, l. 11, n. 1). They were suspended round the neck (see p. 150, n. 3), or placed on the head. Mandāra is one of the five ever-blooming trees of Svarga, or Indra's heaven. Another of these trees is said to be the Hari-candana mentioned above, and another the Santāna; but the two most celebrated are the Pārijāta and the Kalpa-druma, or tree granting all desires. Jayanta is the son of Indra by his favourite wife Paulomī or Saci.

² 'The heaven of Indra, friend of the gods, has been made free from the plague of the Dānavas by two (means); now by thy flat-jointed arrows,

---

Verse 166. UPAJĀTI or ĀKHYĀNAKĪ (a variety of TRISHṬUBH). See verses 41, &c., 158.
Verse 167. DRUTA-VILAMBITA (a variety of JAGATĪ). See verses 45, 72, 128, 140.

अच खलु शतक्रतोरेव महिमा स्तुत्यः ।
सिध्यन्ति कर्मसु महत्स्वपि यन्नियोज्याः
सम्भावनागुणमवेहि तमीश्वराणाम् ।
किं वाभविष्यदरुणस्तमसां विभेत्ता
तं चेत्सहस्रकिरणो धुरि नाकरिष्यत् ॥१६८॥

and formerly by the claws of the man-lion.' *Sura-sakha*, see p. 86, n. 2. *Tri-diva=svarga*, each of the superior Hindū gods has a heaven or paradise of his own. That of Brahmā is called Brahma-loka, situated on the summit of Mount Meru; that of Vishṇu, Vaikuṇṭha, on the Himālayas; that of S'iva and Kuvera, Kailāsa, also on the Himālayas; that of Indra, Svarga or Nandana. The latter, though properly on one of the points of Mount Meru, below Brahmā's paradise, is sometimes identified with the sphere of the sky or heaven in general. *Uddhṛita-dā°*, lit. 'having the thorns of Dānavas extracted.' *Kaṇṭaka*, 'a thorn,' is often used for a noxious person or thing. *Dānava*, see p. 268, n. 2. *Nata-parvabhiḥ = nimna-parvabhiḥ* (*natāni anunnatāni parvāṇi yesham*, K.) Cf. *nata-nāsika*, 'flat-nosed;' also Rāmāy. i. 1, 64, *śareṇānata-parvaṇā* [*bibheda sapta-tālān*], which should be resolved into *śareṇa ānata-parvaṇā*, not *anata*, &c. *Purusha-keśarin=nara-siṇha*, 'the man-lion,' i. e. Vishṇu; for in this monstrous shape of a creature half-man, half-lion, which was his fourth Avatāra or incarnation, Vishṇu delivered the three worlds, or earth, Pātāla, and heaven, from the tyranny of an insolent demon called Hiraṇya-kaśipu, who had usurped the sovereignty of Indra (see Vishṇu-p. p. 126; Indian Wisdom, p. 331).

[1] 'Verily, when servants [delegates] succeed in mighty enterprises, understand thou that (there has been) peculiar condescension [distinguished capacity] on-the-part-of (their) masters. How indeed could Aruṇa be the disperser of the-shades-of-night, if the thousand-rayed-one did not place him in front (of his car)?' *Niyojyāḥ=sevakāḥ*, S. *Sambhāvanā-guṇam =satkāra-viśesham*, K. (see p. 271, n. 1). *Sambhāvanā* may mean 'fitness,' 'capability,' as well as 'honour.' The condescension consisted in placing Dushyanta in front of the battle, just as the Sun places the Dawn in front of his chariot. *Sahasra-kiraṇa* is one of the innumerable names for the Sun. As to Aruṇa, 'the Dawn,' see p. 142, n. 3. *Dhuri=rathāgre*, S.;*=agre, puro-bhāge*, K.

Verse 168. Vasanta-tilakā (a variety of S'akvarī). See verses 8, 27, 31, &c., 157.

मातलिः ।

सदृशमेवैतत् । ॥ स्तोकमनल्पमतीत्य ॥ आयुष्मन् । इतः । पश्य
नाकपृष्ठगतस्य सौभाग्यमात्मयशसः ।
विच्छित्तिशेषैः सुरसुन्दरीणां
वर्णैरमी कल्पलतांशुकेषु ।
सञ्चिन्त्य गीतिक्षममर्थबन्धं
दिवौकसस्त्वच्चरितं लिखन्ति ॥१६९॥

राजा ।

मातले । असुरसम्प्रहारोत्सुकेन पूर्वेद्युर्दिवमधिरोहता न

---

[1] 'Behold the sublimity [beauty, auspiciousness] of (thy) own fame that
has reached to the vault of heaven. With the tints remaining from the
colours (used in the toilet) of the heavenly fair-ones, these inhabitants of
the sky are painting [tracing] thy exploits on vestments [tapestry, leaves]
of the Kalpa-tree, thinking of verses suitable for singing.' *Vicchitti =
ranga, rāga,* S. and C. *Vicchitti-śeshaih = viśishṭair varṇaih,* K., i.e.
kusuma-kasturikā-candanādibhih, 'with flowers, musk, sandal, and other
cosmetics.' The first sense of the word is 'excision,' 'cutting off;' it rarely
has the sense required here, of 'rouge,' 'paint.' Compare *bhakti-ccheda,*
'the coloured streak (marking Vaishṇava) devotion,' Megha-d. verse 20.
*Sura-sundarīṇām = divya-strīṇām. Kalpa-latānśukeshu = kalpa-latā-
vastreshu,* S. and C. The first sense of *anśuka* is 'cloth,' 'tapestry;' it is
said to bear the meaning 'leaf,' and may be so used here; in which case
the idea may be that the gods are writing Dushyanta's memoirs on the
leaves of the Kalpa tree. K.'s comment is not quite clear, *kalpa-latāsu
anśukābharaṇādi* [*na*] *vidyante iti prasiddha;* but it seems likely, especially
if reference is made to p. 155, n. 3 of this play, that he intends to imply
that the Kalpa tree, which was a tree yielding everything (see p. 272, n. 1),
produced the vestments or tapestry on which they might be supposed to
design the adventures of Dushyanta. *Gīti-kshamam = gāna-yogyam* is
the reading of K. and the Bengālī; most of the Deva-n. MSS. have *gīta-
kshamam* (cf. p. 29, n. 1 at the end). *Artha-bandham = padam,* 'a verse,'
'word;' *artho badhyate anena iti artha-bandhah padam,* K.; cf. *tulyānu-
rāga-piśunam lalitārtha-bandham pattre niveśitam udāharaṇam priyāyāh,*
&c., Vikram., Act II.

Verse 169. UPAJĀTI or ĀKHYĀNAKĪ. See verses 41, 107, 121, 126, 142, 156, 158, 166.

लक्षितः स्वर्गमार्गः । कतरस्मिन्महतां पथि वर्तामहे ।
मातलिः ।
चित्रस्रोतसं वहति यो गगनप्रतिष्ठां
ज्योतींषि वर्तयति च प्रविभक्तरश्मिः ।
तस्य द्वितीयहरिविक्रमनिस्तमस्कं
वायोरिमं परिवहस्य वदन्ति मार्गम् ॥१७०॥

---

[1] 'In which course [path, orbit] of the (seven) winds are we now moving?' The Hindūs divide the heavens into seven Mārgas or Pathas, i. e. paths, courses, orbits (like the stories of the Mussalmān creed), assigning a particular *vāyu* or wind to each. Cf. Vishnu-p. p. 212. The first of these seven, *vāyu-mārgāḥ* or *vāyu-pathas*, is identical with the *bhuvar-loka*, or atmospheric region, extending from the *bhūr-loka*, or terrestrial region [comprising the earth, and the *adho-loka*, called Pātāla], upwards to the sun. The wind assigned to this Mārga is called *āvaha*, and its office is to bear along the atmosphere, clouds, meteors, lightning, &c. The other six make up the *svar-loka* or heavenly region with which Svarga is often identified (cf. p. 272, n. 2) in the following order :—The 2nd Mārga is that of the sun, and its wind, called *pravaha* or *pravāha*, causes the sun to revolve; 3rd, that of the moon, its wind *samvaha* or *samvāha* impels the moon; 4th, that of the *nakshatra*, or lunar constellations, its wind *udvaha* causes the revolution of these asterisms; 5th, that of the *graha*, or planets, its wind *vivāha* bears along the seven planets; 6th, that of the *saptarshi*, or seven stars of the Great Bear, its wind *parivaha* bears along these luminaries, as well as the *svar-gangā*, or heavenly Ganges [*saptarshi-ćakram svar-gangām shashṭhaḥ parivahas tathā*]; it appears from the next verse that this was the Mārga in which Indra's car was at the moment moving; 7th, that of *dhruva*, or the polarstar, the pivot or axis of the whole planetary system, to which, according to the Vishnu-p. (pp. 230, 240), 'all the celestial luminaries are bound by aerial cords, and are made to travel in their proper orbits, being kept in their places by their respective bands of air.' According to the Brahmānḍa-p., from which, as quoted by K., the above account is taken, the wind of the seventh Mārga, causing the revolution of the polar-star, is *parāvāha* [? *parāvaha*]. All the Deva-n. MSS. read *katarasmin* for *katamasmin;* sometimes *katara* is used for *katama*.

[2] 'They call this road, freed-from-all-impurities-by-the-second-stride-of-

---

Verse 170. VASANTA-TILAKĀ (a variety of ŚAKVARĪ). See verses 8, 27, 31, &c., 168.

राजा ।

मातले । अतः खलु सबाह्यान्तःकरणो ममान्तरात्मा

Vishṇu, (the road) of that wind Parivaha, which bears along the triple-flowing-river [Ganges] located in heaven, and causes the stars [of the Great Bear] to revolve, duly-distributing-their-rays.' See the last note. *Tri-srotas = svar-gangā = mandākinī*, K. The Ganges was supposed to take its rise in the toe of Vishṇu [whence one of its names, *Vishṇu-padī*]; thence it flowed through the heavenly sphere, being borne along by the wind Parivaha and identified with the Mandākinī, or Milky way: its second course is through the earth; but the weight of its descent was borne by S'iva's head, whence after wandering among the tresses of his hair, it descended through a chasm in the Himālayas: its third course is through Pātāla, or the lower regions, the residence of the Daityas and Nāgas, and not to be confounded with Naraka, 'hell,' 'the place of punishment.' *Gagana-pratishṭhām = ākāsa-sthām*, S'. and C'.; were it not for this interpretation I should translate 'the glory of the skies;' cf. p. 260, l. 11. There is doubtless a double-entendre. *Jyotīnshi*, &c., i. e. *saptarshīṇām dhishṇyāni*, K. *Pravibhakta-rasmiḥ*, i. e. *asankīrṇa-rasmayas tejānsi yasmin karmaṇi tat tathoktam*, K. *Vartayati = sanćārayati*, K. *Dvitīya-hari°*, i. e. *dvitīyena harer vishṇor vikrameṇa pāda-nyāsena nirdosham*, K. *Tasya vāyor*, &c., i. e. *tasya parīvāhākhyasya vāyor mārgam panthānam imam gṛihṇanti āmananti. Parivāho* [sic] *nāma svar-gangām saptarshi-maṇḍalam pravartayati shashṭho vāyu-skandho yathoktam Brahmāṇḍa-purāṇe*, K. The story of Vishṇu's second stride was this—An Asura or Daitya (see p. 86, n. 2) named Bali or Mahābali, a descendant of Hiraṇya-kasipu had, by his devotions, gained the dominion of Heaven, Earth, and Pātāla. Vishṇu undertook to trick him out of his power, and assuming the form of a Vāmana, or dwarf (his fifth Avatāra), he appeared before the giant, and begged, as a boon, as much land as he could pace in three steps. This was granted, and the god immediately expanded himself till he filled the world, deprived Bali at the first step, of earth; at the second, of heaven; but, in consideration of some merit, left Pātāla still under his rule. Another account makes him comprehend earth in his first step, the region of the air in his second, and heaven in his third. Hence *tri-vikrama, tri-pāda*, as names of Vishṇu. See Indian Wisdom, p. 331, n. 1. The Beng. MSS. have, in place of *tasya dvitīya* &c., *tasya vyapeta-rajasaḥ pravahasya vāyor mārgo dvitīya-hari-vikrama-pūta eshaḥ*.

[1] ' Hence, indeed, do-I-feel-a-delightful-repose in all my senses [organs] external and internal,' lit. 'hence my inner soul along with my external

प्रसीदति । ॥ रथाङ्गमवलोक्य ॥ मेघपदवीमवतीर्णौ स्वः ।

मातलिः ।

कथमवगम्यते ।

राजा ।

अयमरविवरेभ्यश्चातकैर्निष्पतद्भि-
र्हरिभिरचिरभासां तेजसा चानुलिप्तैः ।
गतमुपरि घनानां वारिगर्भोदराणां
पिशुनयति रथस्ते शीकरक्लिन्ननेमिः ॥१७१॥

---

organs feels (a pleasurable) repose.' Cf. in Vikram. end of Act IV, *tvad-darśanena prasanno me savāhyāntarātmā*, i. e. 'body and soul,' 'my external and internal being,' 'my outer and inner man.' And again, *Urvaśī-gātra-sparśād iva nirvritam me sa-hridayam śarīram*. The organs of sense (*indriya*) according to the Sānkhya system are divided into two classes, external, *vāhyendriya;* and internal, *antar-indriya*. The external are of two kinds : the five 'organs of perception,' *jñānendriya*, viz. the ear, eye, skin, tongue, and nose ; and the five 'organs of action,' *karmendriya*, viz. the throat, hand, foot, organ of excretion, and that of generation. The internal organs are three, viz. *manas*, 'the mind,' or organ of thought; *buddhi*, 'the reason,' or organ of apprehension ; *ahankāra*, 'individuality,' or 'self-consciousness.' *Citta*, 'the heart,' or organ of feeling, is sometimes added. The Amara-k. (i. 4, 17) divides the Indriyas into two grand classes : 1. *karmendriyāṇi;* and 2. *buddhīndriyāṇi* or *dhīndriyāṇi*, 'intellectual organs;' the latter comprises the *jñānendriyāṇi* with *manas;* this seems to be the popular division. Cf. Vikram., Act III, *bhavitavya-tānuvidhayīni buddhīndriyāṇi*.

[1] 'We have descended to the path of the clouds,' i. e. to the atmospheric region between the sun and the earth, the Mārga of the clouds and of the Āvaha wind (see p. 275, n. 1). The chariot must, therefore, have traversed with the speed of lightning, the four intervening Mārgas of the planets, lunar constellations, moon, and sun. If the Beng. reading, *pravahasya*, be adopted in the last verse, the transition would merely be from one Mārga to the next.

[2] 'Here [*ayam*] by the Cātakas flying forth through the interstices of the spokes, and by the horses glistening with the flash of the lightnings, thy chariot, the rings [circumferences] of whose wheels are bedewed with

---

Verse 171. MĀLINĪ or MĀNINĪ. See verses 10, 19, 20, 38, 55, 109, 110, 120.

मातलिः ।

क्षणादायुष्मान्स्वाधिकारभूमौ वर्तिष्यते ।

राजा ॥ अधोऽवलोक्य ॥

वेगावतरणादाश्चर्यदर्शनः संलक्ष्यते मनुष्यलोकः । तथा हि
शैलानामवरोहतीव शिखरादुन्मज्जतां मेदिनी
पर्णाभ्यन्तरलीनतां विजहति स्कन्धोदयात्पादपाः ।
सन्तानात्तनुभावनष्टसलिला व्यक्तिं भजन्त्यापगाः
केनाप्युत्क्षिपतेव पश्य भुवनं मत्पार्श्वमानीयते ॥१७२॥

---

mist, betrays (our) progress over clouds whose bellies are pregnant with
rain.' *Ara=nemy-avashṭambha;* the Beng. MSS. and the Mackenzie
read *aga,* 'a mountain.' *Ara-vivarebhyaś ćakrāvayavānāṃ vivarebhyo
antarāla-pradeśebhyaḥ,* K. *Nishpatadbhiḥ=nirgaćchadbhiḥ,* K. (see p. 253,
n. 1 at the end). The Ćātaka is a kind of cuckoo. The Hindūs suppose
that it drinks only the water of the clouds, and their poets usually introduce allusions to this bird in connexion with cloudy or rainy weather
(see Megha-d. verses 9, 23, 113; Raghu-v. xvii. 60). So *trishākulaiś
ćātaka-pakshiṇāṃ kulaiḥ prayāćitā valāhakāḥ,* Ṛitu-s. ii. 3. *Haribhir=
aśvaiḥ,* especially Indra's horses (see p. 12, n. 1, and cf. Raghu-v. iii. 43).
Aćira-bhāsām = vidyutām, S. *Gatam, &c., teshām meghānām upari
ūrdhva-bhāge gatam gamanam,* K. *Piśunayati=sūćayati,* K.

[1] 'The earth descends as it were from the summit of the upward-rising
[emergent] mountains. The trees, from the elevation [coming-into-view,
rising, appearing] of (their) trunks, lose their state of being enveloped
[concealed, wrapped] in their foliage. The rivers whose-waters-were-lost-
in-narrowness, become visible [acquire manifestation] from the expansion
(of their waters). Behold! the earth is being brought up to my side
[near me], as if by some one flinging it upwards.' In the same way to a
voyager in a balloon at a very great height, the surface of the earth would
seem flat, the trees would be compressed within their foliage like mush-
rooms, and the rivers shrivel into threads or tiny rivulets; but, on
descending, the mountains would appear to stand out, and the earth to
recede from them, the trees would exhibit their elevation, and the rivers
their breadth of water. *Unmajjatām=udgaćchatām,* K. *Avarohati=adho-
gaćchati,* K. *Parṇābhyantara°.* The Colebrooke MS. and my own have

---

Verse 172. ŚĀRDŪLA-VIKRĪDITA. See verses 14, 30, 36, 39, 40, 63, 79, 85, &c., 149.

मातलिः ।

साधु दृष्टम् । ।। सबहुमानं विलोक्य ।। अहो उदाररमणीया पृथिवी ।

राजा ।

मातले । कतमोऽयं पूर्वापरसमुद्रावगाढः कनकरसनि-
स्यन्दी सान्ध्य इव मेघपरिघः सानुमानालोक्यते[1] ।

मातलिः ।

आयुष्मन् । एष खलु हेमंकूटो[2] नाम किम्पुरुषपर्वतस्तपसां
सिद्धिक्षेत्रम् । पश्य ।

स्वायम्भुवान्मरीचेर्यः प्रबभूव प्रजापतिः ।
सुरासुरगुरुः सोऽत्र सपत्नीकस्तपस्यति[3] ।। १७३ ।।

---

parṇa-svāntara; the Taylor, *parṇeshvantara;* the Mackenzie, *parṇa-pra-stara;* K., *parṇāntara-vilīnam. Skandhodayāt=kroḍāvirbhāvāt,* K. *San-tānat=jala-vistārāt,* K.; the other Deva-n. have *santānais. Tanubhāva°, tanubhāvena sūkshmatvena adrishṭam salilaṃ yāsām,* K. *Vyaktim bha-janti,* i.e. *vyaktā bhavanti,* K.

[1] 'What mountain yonder is seen, bathing itself in the eastern and western ocean, pouring down a golden stream like a bar [bank, gate] of evening clouds?' *Parigha* occurs in p. 87, l. 6, meaning 'the bar of a gate,' but it may also denote the gate itself. *Sānu-mat,* lit. 'possessed of table-land,' 'a mountain having extensive level ground on its summit.'

[2] *Hema-kūṭa,* 'golden-peaked,' a sacred range of mountains lying among the Himālaya chain, and apparently identical with, or immediately adjacent to Kailāsa, the paradise of Kuvera, the god of wealth, as it is here described as the mountain of the Kimpurushas, or servants of Kuvera. They are a dwarfish kind of monster, with the body of a man and the head of a horse, and are otherwise called Kinnara (*aśva-mukha, turanga-mukha*). This mountain is also here described as 'the scene [place, field] of the perfect fulfilment of penance.' The Mackenzie MS. has *tapasvinām* for *tapasām.*

[3] 'That Prajāpati [Kaśyapa], who sprang from Marīci, the Self-existent's-son [i.e. from Marīci, son of Brahmā], (and who is) the father of the gods and demons, practices penance here along with his wife (Aditi).' An account of Kaśyapa, who, as son of Marīci, is called Mārīca, is given

---

Verse 173. ŚLOKA or ANUSHṬUBH. See verses 5, 6, 11, 12, 26, 47, 50, 51, &c., 164.

राजा ।

तेन ह्यनतिक्रमणीयानि[1] श्रेयांसि । प्रदक्षिणीकृत्य[2] भगवन्तं गन्तुमिच्छामि ।

मातलिः ।

प्रथमः कल्पः[3] ।

॥ नाट्येनावतीर्णौ ॥

राजा ॥ सविस्मयम् ॥

उपोढशब्दा न रथाङ्गनेमयः
प्रवर्तमानं न च दृश्यते रजः ।
अभूतलस्पर्शतया निरुन्धत-
स्त्वावतीर्णोऽपि रथो न लक्ष्यते ॥ १७४ ॥

---

in p. 22, n. 3, and p. 86, n. 2. He is here said to be one of the Prajāpatis, or fathers of all created things, who were Brahmā's sons, created by him to supply the universe with inhabitants, and who, after fulfiling their mission, retired from the world to practise penance and prepare for death. The Vāyu-purāṇa certainly reckons Kaśyapa, with his father-in-law Daksha and other sages, among the Prajāpatis, but he does not belong to the seven original Prajāpatis of whom his father Marīći is one, nor to the ten enumerated by Manu (i. 35). Of the thirteen daughters of Daksha married to Kaśyapa, the eldest, and his favourite wife, was the Aditi introduced here, from whom were born the gods and particularly the twelve Ādityas, the several representatives of the sun in the twelve months of the year. From Diti, Danu, and others of the remaining twelve, came the Asuras or demons; and, from Vinatā, Aruṇa, 'the Dawn' (see p. 142, n. 3), and Garuḍa, 'the vehicle of Vishṇu and king of birds.' *Svāyambhuvāt = Brahma-sunoḥ*, K. *Surāsura-guruḥ*, as to *guru*, see p. 173, n. 3, and p. 91, l. 3. *Sa-patnīkas*, i. e. *patnyā Adityā saha* (cf. *sa-strīka, sa-śrīka*, &c.)

[1] *Anatikramaṇīya*, cf. p. 68, l. 7; p. 91, l. 3. *Sreyāṇsi = śubhāni, kaśyapa-darśana-namaskārādīni*, 'lucky occasions,' 'opportunities for obtaining blessings, such as visiting and paying homage to Kaśyapa.'

[2] *Pradakshiṇī-kritya*, see p. 159, l. 8.

[3] 'A noble resolve,' 'a prime idea,' = *mukhyaḥ pakshaḥ*, K.; cf. p. 205, l. 7.

[4] 'The circumferences of the chariot-wheels cause no sound, and no

Verse 174. VAṆŚA-STHAVILA (a variety of JAGATĪ). See verses 18, 22, 23, &c., 161.

मातलिः ।

एतावानेव शतक्रतोरायुष्मतश्च विशेषः ।

राजा ।

मातले । कतमस्मिन्प्रदेशे मारीचाश्रमः ।

मातलिः ॥ हस्तेन दर्शयन् ॥

वल्मीकार्धनिमग्नमूर्तिरुरसा सन्दष्टसर्पत्वचा
कण्ठे जीर्णलतामतानवलयेनात्यर्थसम्पीडितः ।
अंसव्यापि शकुन्तनीडनिचितं बिभ्रज्जटामण्डलं
यत्र स्थाणुरिवाचलो मुनिरसावभ्यर्कबिम्बं स्थितः ॥१७५॥

---

dust is seen rising-in-advance (of us); the chariot of thee reining-in (thy
steeds), although it has descended (to the earth), is not observed (to have
done so) by-reason-of-its-not-touching the surface of the ground.' *Upodha-
śabdāḥ=prāpta-dhvanayaḥ*, K. (cf. *upodha-rāga*, Vikram., Act II). *Pra-
vartamāna* may mean 'rising in front of us' (cf. p. 11, l. 3). *Nirundha-
taḥ=nigrihṇataḥ*, K. *Na lakshyate*, see p. 70, n. 3 at the end. In Vikram.,
Act I, when the car of Purūravas touches the ground, the direction is
rathāvatāra-kshobhaṃ nāṭayantī, 'acting the concussion (caused) by the
descent of the chariot.' Such, Mātali remarks, is the difference between
the car of Indra and that of mortal heroes.

[1] 'Where stands yon sage, towards [facing] the sun's orb, immovable
as the trunk-of-a-tree, (his) body half-buried in an ant-hill, with (his)
breast closely-encircled by a snake's-skin, round the throat excessively
pinched by a necklace (formed) of the tendril of a withered creeper, wearing a circular-mass-of-matted-hair enveloping (his) shoulders (and) filled
with bird's-nests.' *Valmīkārdha*, &c., so read K. and the Mackenzie MS.;
the other Deva-n., *valmīkāgra*. *Valmīka* (=*krimi-kṛita-mṛittikāćaya*) is
the mound of earth thrown up by the large ants of India. These hillocks
sometimes rise, in Bengal, to the height of eight or ten feet, and are held
sacred; (see Manu iv. 46. 238.) Such was the immovable impassiveness
of this ascetic, that the ants had thrown up their mound as high as his
waist, without being disturbed, and the birds had built their nests in his
hair. *Sandashṭa-s°=āślishṭa-nirmokena*, cf. p. 120, n. 3. The serpent's
skin was used by the ascetic in place of the regular Brahmanical cord,
called *yajñopavīta;* see Indian Wisdom, p. 201. *Latā-pratāna=latā-san-*

Verse 175. ŚĀRDŪLA-VIKRĪḌITA (a variety of ATIDHṚITI). See verses 14, &c., 172.

राजा ।

नमस्ते कष्टतंपसे ।

मातलिः ॥ संयतप्रग्रहं रथं कृत्वा ॥

महाराज । एतावदिति परिवर्धितमन्दारवृक्षं प्रजापतेराश्रमं प्रविष्टौ स्वः ।

राजा ।

स्वर्गादधिकतरं निर्वृत्तिस्थानम् । अमृतह्रदमिवावगा-
ढोऽस्मि ।

मातलिः ॥ रथं स्थापयित्वा ॥

अवतरत्वायुष्मान् ।

राजा ॥ अवतीर्य ॥

मातले । भवान्कथमिदानीम् ।

मातलिः ।

संयन्त्रितो मया रथः । वयमप्यवतरामः । ॥ तथा कृत्वा ॥ इत
आयुष्मन् । ॥ परिक्रम्य ॥ दृश्यन्तामनुभवतामृषीणां तपो-
वनभूमयः ।

---

tāna, 'the spreading part of a creeper.' *Jaṭā-maṇḍala* is the circle or bundle of matted entangled hair which ascetics allowed to grow on the crown of their heads, and which fell in long clotted tresses over the back and shoulders. *Jaṭā* is, especially, S'iva's hair so plaited and arranged, through which the Ganges meandered before its descent upon the earth. *Niċitam = pūritam*, K. *Sthāṇuḥ = śākhā-hīnas taru-skandhaḥ*. *Abhyarkavimbam = sūrya-maṇḍalābhimukham*, K. The Mackenzie MS. has *adhyarka*°.

[1] *Kashṭam kṛċċhram tapo yasya sa tathoktaḥ*, K.

[2] 'Possessed of the Mandāra-tree reared by Aditi.' This was one of the five trees of Svarga (see p. 272, n. 1), and is probably the tree intended here, as, in verse 176, the Kalpa tree also is said to have graced Kaśyapa's retreat, which the commentator thence infers to have been located in part of Svarga. *Mandāra*, 'the coral tree,' may also mean 'swallow-wort.'

[3] *Amṛita*, 'the beverage of immortality,' 'the nectar' of the Hindū gods, supposed to be a liquid substance distilled by the moon, who is thence called *amṛita-sū*, 'nectar-producer;' *amṛitādhāra*, 'nectar-repository.'

[4] *Avatarishyati iti śeshaḥ*, S'.; i. e. supply *avatarishyati*.

राजा ।

ननु विस्मयादवलोकयामि ।

प्राणानामनिलेन वृत्तिरुचिता सत्कल्पवृक्षे वने
तोये काञ्चनपद्मरेणुकपिशे धर्माभिषेकक्रिया ।
ध्यानं रत्नशिलातलेषु विबुधस्त्रीसन्निधौ संयमो
यत्काङ्क्षन्ति तपोभिरन्यमुनयस्तस्मिंस्तपस्यन्त्यमी[1] ॥ १७६ ॥

मातलिः ।

उत्सर्पिणी खलु महतां प्रार्थना[2] ।   ॥ परिक्रम्य । आकाशे[3] ॥   अये
वृद्धशाकल्य । किमनुतिष्ठति भगवान्मारीचः । किं ब्रवीषि[4] ।
दाक्षायण्या पतिव्रताधर्ममधिकृत्य पृष्टस्तस्यै महर्षि-
पत्नीसहितायै कथयंतीति ।

---

[1] ' (The place) to which other sages aspire by (their) penances, (where
there is) habitual [suitable, adequate] support of life by air in a grove in-
which-the-Kalpa-tree-is-found; (where there is) the performance of religious ablutions in water, brown with the dust of the golden lotus; (where
there is) meditation (while seated) on jewelled slabs of marble, (and) restraint (of the passions) in the presence of celestial nymphs; in (such a
place as) this these (sages) are performing penance.' *Prāṇānāṃ vrittiḥ=
jīvanam*, K. The Hindūs imagine that supporting life upon air is a proof
of the highest degree of spirituality to which a man can attain. *Sat-kalpa-
vrikshe=vidyamāna-kalpa-drume*, K.; =*vidyamāna-kalpa-tarau*, S. and C.
The Colebrooke MS. has *sankalpa-vrikshe;* this use of *sat* is noticeable.
Śilā-tala, 'the surface of a stone slab or seat;' cf. p. 76, l. 3. *Vibudha-strī
=divyāṅganā*, K. *Samyama=niyatendriyatva*, K. *Ebhiḥ sat-kalpa-vri-
kshatvādikair viśeshair ayam pradeśaḥ svarga iti pratīyate*, 'by these attri-
butes of the Kalpa tree, &c., it is inferred that this place was part of Svarga,'
K. As to the Kalpa tree, see p. 272, n. 1. *Yat*, &c., i. e. *yat sthānam
anye kānkshanti tasmin svarga-pradeśe amī munayas tāni phalāni pari-
hritya tapasyanti iti anena teshām mokshārthitvaṃ gamyate*, K.

[2] ' Verily the aspirations [desire] of the great soar upwards [are ever
mounting upwards].' *Utsarpinī=udgamana-śīlā=atiśayinī*, K.

[3] As to *ākāśe* and *kim bravīshi*, see p. 96, n. 3.

[4] ' Being questioned by Dākshāyaṇī [i. e. his wife Aditi] respecting the

---

Verse 176. ŚĀRDŪLA-VIKRĪḌITA. See verses 14, 30, 36, 39, 40, 63, 79, 85, &c., 175.

राजा ॥ कर्णे दत्त्वा ॥

अये । प्रतिपाल्यावसराः खलु मुनयः ।

मातलिः ॥ राजानमवलोक्य ॥

अस्मिन्नशोकवृक्षमूले तावदास्तामायुष्मान् । यावत्वा-
मिन्द्रगुरवे निवेदयितुमन्तरान्वेषी भवामि ।

राजा ।

यथा भवान्मन्यते । ॥ इति स्थितः ॥

मातलिः ।

आयुष्मन् । साधयाम्यहम् । ॥ इति निष्क्रान्तः ॥

---

duties [duty] of a wife devoted to her husband, he is recounting them [it]
to her, in company with the wives of the Maharshis.' *Dākshāyaṇī* is a
patronymic applicable to any of the daughters of Daksha (see p. 279, n. 3).
Pati-vratā, cf. p. 241, n. 3. *Adhikṛitya,* see p. 6, n. 2. *Maharshi,* 'a great
saint;' the Maharshi was one step in advance of the Ṛishi or simple 'saint.'
The classification of Ṛishis varies, but the following seems to be the usual
gradation : 1. Ṛishi; 2. Maharshi; 3. Paramarshi; 4. Devarshi; 5. Brahmarshi. Amara mentions two other orders, Kāṇḍarshis and S'rutarshis.
The Rājarshi was a mixed order (see p. 39, n. 3).

[1] 'We must await the leisure of saints.' So reads the Mackenzie MS.,
supported, apparently, by K. *Munayaḥ* is of course the nominative, but
such is the terseness of compounds like *pratipālyāvasarāḥ* that a literal
English translation is impossible. The other Deva-n. have *pratipālyā-
vasaraḥ khalu prastāvaḥ.*

[2] The Aśoka (Jonesia Asoka) is one of the most beautiful of Indian
trees. Sir W. Jones observes that 'the vegetable world scarce exhibits
a richer sight than an Aśoka tree in full bloom. It is about as high as
an ordinary cherry tree.' The flowers are very large, and 'beautifully
diversified with tints of orange-scarlet, of pale yellow, and of bright orange,
which form a variety of shades according to the age of the blossom.'

[3] 'Opportune time' is one of the meanings of *antara.* As to *gurave,*
cf. p. 173, n. 3 in the middle. Kaśyapa was the reputed father of
Indra.

[4] 'I go-to-do (what I proposed),' 'I will-do (as I said);' cf. p. 213,
l. 1, and p. 17, l. 8.

राजा ॥ निमित्तं सूचयित्वा ॥[1]

मनोरथाय नाशंसे किं बाहो स्पन्दसे वृथा ।
पूर्वावधीरितं श्रेयो दुःखं हि परिवर्त्तते ॥१७७॥

नेपथ्ये ।

[a]मा खु चावलं करेहि । कहं गदो एव्व अत्तणो पकिंदिं ।

राजा ॥ कर्णं दत्वा ॥

अभूमिरियमविनयस्य । को नु खल्वेष निषिध्यते ।
॥ शब्दानुसारेणावलोक्य । सस्मितम् ॥ अये । को नु खल्वयमनुबध्य-
मानस्तपस्विनीभ्यामबालसत्त्वो बालः ।

अर्धपीतस्तनं मातुरामर्दक्लिष्टकेशरम् ।
प्रक्रीडितुं सिंहशिशुं बलात्कारेण कर्षति ॥१७८॥

[a]मा खलु चापलं कुरु । कथं गत एवात्मनः प्रकृतिम् ।

---

[1] *Nimittaṃ sūčayitvā* (=*śakunaṃ nirūpya*, K.), see p. 20, n. 4.

[2] 'I expect not to (obtain my) desire; why, O arm, throbbest thou (thus) vainly? For happiness formerly scorned turns to misery.' K. observes that *manorathāya* here=*manoratham prāptum*, and refers to Pāṇ. ii. 3, 14; so *phalebhyo yāti*=*phalāny āhartuṃ yāti*. As to the throbbing of the arm, see p. 20, n. 5. *Sreyaḥ*=*śubham*, i. e. *Sakuntalā-rūpam*, 'consisting of Sakuntalā,' K. *Hi parivartate*, K. has *vipari-vartate* and *sat parivartate*.

[3] 'Act not so wildly [do not commit such a wild, wilful act]. What! has he gone already to his own nature?' Cf. Raghu-v. iii. 42. *Prakṛiti*, 'one's natural character;' cf. p. 72, n. 2. *Gata*, see p. 161, n. 3 at the end.

[4] 'This is no place for petulance [insolence];' cf. p. 271, l. 11.

[5] 'Who is this child with unchild-like disposition [nature], closely attended by two female ascetics?' *Anubadhyamāna*, the Mackenzie MS. has *anugamyamāna*. *Anubandha*, lit. 'tying after,' 'following at the heels,' 'sticking closely to,' very forcibly expresses the close attendance of a nurse upon a child.

[6] 'He forcibly drags to play (with him) a lion's cub that-has-but-half-sucked-its mother's dug, (and) whose-mane-is-disordered-by-rough-hand-ling,' or 'he forcibly drags from its mother,' &c.

Verses 177 and 178. SLOKA or ANUSHTUBH. See verses 5, 6, 11, 12, 26, 47, 50, 51, 53, 73, 76, 84, 87, 125, 127, 146, 154, 155, 160, 164.

॥ ततः प्रविशति यथानिर्दिष्टकर्मा तपस्विनीभ्यां बालः ॥

बालः ।

[a] जिम्भ सिङ्घ । दन्ताइं दे गणइस्सं ।

प्रथमा ।

[b] अविणीद । किं णो अपच्चणिब्बिसेसाणि सत्ताणि विप्प-
अरेसि । हन्त वड्ढइ दे संरम्भो । ठाणेक्खु इसिजणेण
सव्वदमणोत्ति किदणामहेओसि ।

राजा ।

किं नु खलु बालेऽस्मिन्नौरस इव पुत्रे स्निह्यति मे मनः ।
नूनमनपत्यता मां वत्सलयति ।

द्वितीया ।

[c] एसा खु केसरिणी तुमं लंङ्घेदि । जइ से पुत्तअं ण मुञ्चेसि ।

बालः ॥ सस्मितम् ॥

[d] अम्हहे । बलिअंक्खु भीदोम्हि । ॥ इत्यधरं दर्शयति ॥

---

[a] जृम्भस्व सिंह । दन्तांस्ते गणयिष्यामि । [b] अविनीत । किं नोऽपत्यनिर्वि-
शेषाणि सत्त्वानि विप्रकरोषि । हन्त वर्धते ते संरम्भः । स्थाने खलु ऋषिजनेन सर्वदमन
इति कृतनामधेयोऽसि । [c] एषा खलु केशरिणी त्वां लङ्घयति । यद्यस्याः पुत्रकं
न मुञ्चसि । [d] अहो । बलीयः खलु भीतोऽस्मि ।

---

[1] 'Why dost thou teaze the animals (cherished by us as if) not-differing-
from-our-offspring?' *Sattvāni*, cf. p. 55, n. 4. *Nir-viśeshāni*, cf. *suta-
nirviśeshaḥ nakulaḥ*, 'the ichneumon dear to him as a son,' Hitop. l. 2721,
and *mūshika-nirviśesha*, Hitop. l. 2395.

[2] 'It must certainly be my childlessness that causes me to yearn
(towards this child).' *Vatsala* or *vātsalya* is, properly, the yearning
affection of a cow for its calf, or a parent for its offspring.

[3] *Langhayati* = *ākramati*, K. Cf. p. 97, n. 1.

[4] K. quotes a passage from the Vasanta-rājīya to shew that different
movements of the lips, such as biting the lip, pouting the under-lip, &c.,
were significant of various emotions. The text is corrupt, but it appears
that *adhara-darśana* = *adhara-prasāraṇa* is [*an-ādare*] a gesture of contempt. Cf. Psalm xxii. 7, 'All they that see me laugh me to scorn; they
shoot out the lip.'

राजा ।

महत्तेजसो बीजं बालोऽयं प्रतिभाति मे ।
स्फुलिङ्गावस्थया वह्निरेधापेक्ष इव स्थितः ॥१७९॥[1]

प्रथमा ।

[a] वच्छ । एदं बालमिन्दं मुञ्च । अवरं दे कीलणअं दाइस्सं ।

बालः ।

[b] कहिं । देहि णं ।   ॥ इति हस्तं प्रसारयति ॥

राजा ।

कथं चक्रवर्त्तिलक्षणमप्यनेन धार्यते । तथा ह्यस्य
प्रलोभ्यवस्तुप्रणयप्रसारितो
विभाति जालग्रथिताङ्गुलिः करः ।
अलक्ष्यपत्त्रान्तरमिद्रागया
नवोषसा भिन्नमिवैकपङ्कजम् ॥१८०॥[2][3]

[a] वत्स । एतं बालमृगेन्द्रकं मुञ्च । अपरं ते क्रीडनकं दास्यामि ।   [b] कुत्र ।
देह्येनम् ।

---

¹ 'This child appears to me (to possess) the germ [rudiment] of mighty
energy [spirit, courage].   He stands like fire in a state of scintillation [in
a smouldering state], waiting (only) for fuel (that it may blaze up).'
Edhāpekshah = *indhanāni kānkshinī*, K.   The Bengālī MSS. have *edhaḥ-
kshayaḥ*.

² 'The mark of a universal emperor;' see p. 15, n. 2, and p. 214,
n. 2.

³ 'His hand stretched forth to beg for a coveted object, having the
fingers connected by a web, appears like [shines like] a single lotus-
blossom, the spaces between whose petals is imperceptible, expanded by
the early dawn, whose-glow-is-just-kindled.' *Pranaya* = *prārthana*, S.
Jāla, &c.; *jāleshu antareshu grathitāḥ samhatā angulayo yasya*, K.   For
grathitāngulih, S. has *samhatāngulih* = *samślishṭāngulih*, and remarks

---

द्वितीया ।

[a] सुव्वदे । ण सक्को एसो वाप्पामेत्तेण विरमाविदुं । गच्छ ।
मम केरए उडए मक्कण्डेअस्स इसिकुमारस्स वट्टचित्तिदो
मित्तिआमोरओ चिट्ठदि । तं से उवहर ।

प्रथमा ।

[b] तह । ॥ इति निष्क्रान्ता ॥

---

[a] सुव्रते । न शक्य एष वाष्पामात्रेण विरमयितुम् । गच्छ । मदीय उटजे मार्कण्डेयस्य
ऋषिकुमारस्य वर्त्यश्चित्रितो मृत्तिकामयूरकस्तिष्ठति । तमस्योपहर ।   [b] तथा ।

that a hand whose fingers were thus united was indicative of great valour
(*mahā-purushatva*). He adds *jāla-pāda-bhujāviti nara-nārāyaṇa-viśesha-
ṇam uktam*, 'webbed-feet and webbed-hands are said to be character-
istics of Nara and Nārāyaṇa.' Hindū poets reckon thirty-two marks of
greatness, and he who possessed them all was said to be *dvātriṅśal-laksha-
ṇopetaḥ*. The child's fingers, being drawn together by this membrane or
web, would bear some resemblance to an expanding lotus-flower, the
fingers answering to the long petals, which would be only separated
towards the top. This seems to be the sense : my first inclination was to
translate, 'having the fingers regularly marked with reticulated lines,' or
'having the fingers drawn together into (the form of) a bud.' *Alakshya*
(=*adriśya*, K.), so read all the Deva-n. MSS. excepting my own, which
has *ālakshya*, with the Beng.; Ś., however, has *alakshya*. *Pattrāntaram*
=*dala-vivaram*, K. and Ś. *Iddha-rāgayā navoshasā*, &c.; *ushas*, 'the
dawn,' is usually neuter in classical Sanskṛit. In the Vedas, as here, it
is feminine. Thus in Ṛig-v. i. 46, 1, *Esho ushā apūrvyā vyućchati priyā
divaḥ;* see also Ṛig-v. i. 48, 3. 5. 7. 8. 13; i. 62, 8; i. 92, 4; and i. 113,
4, &c. It is possible that the feminine noun *ushā* may form its vowel
cases from *ushas*, as *jarā* from *jaras ;* nom. *jarā, jarasau, jarasaḥ;* instr.
jarasā, jarābhyām, jarābhiḥ, &c. (see Gram. 171). The following is the
corrupt gloss of Ś. : *ushaḥ-pratyushasi klīvam pihaprasvāntu yoshatīti
koshaḥ*. K. explains *navoshasā* as a Bahuvrīhi, 'by the early-dawned
one,' *navam usho yasyāḥ sā navoshā prātaḥsandhyā tayā bhinnaṃ
vikasitam*. As to *pankaja*, see p. 213, n. 2.

[1] This pleonastic word, according to Lassen (Instit. Prāk. p. 118), is
derived from the Sanskṛit *kṛite*, and is equivalent to *pertinens ad*, 'in the
cottage belonging to me,' &c. Some MSS. omit the word.

बालः ।

^aइमिणा एव्व दाव कीलिस्सं ।   ॥ इति तापसीं विलोक्य हसति ॥

राजा ।

स्पृहयामि खलु दुर्ललितायास्मै[1] ।

आलक्ष्यदन्तमुकुलाननिमित्तहासै-
र्व्यक्तवर्णैरमणीयवचःप्रवृत्तीन् ।
अङ्काश्रयप्रणयिनस्तनयान्वहन्तो
धन्यास्तदङ्गरजसा मलिनीभवन्ति ॥१८१॥

^a अनेनैव तावत्क्रीडिष्यामि ।

---

[1] 'I have a great fancy for this unmanageable (child).' *Durlalita*, i. e. *durlabham īpsitaṃ yasya* (S'.), 'difficult to be coaxed or pleased,' 'way-ward,' 'naughty.' K. reads *durlasitāya* and interprets by *dhūrtāya*, 'roguish,' 'mischievous.' The causal sense of the root *lal* is 'to coax,' though *dur-lālita* might then be expected. The primitive idea is certainly that of 'sporting,' 'toying,' 'taking pleasure,' as in the root *las*. So in Vikram., Act II, the king complains that his eye-sight has become *durlali-tam*, i. e. 'difficult to be pleased,' 'fastidious,' by looking on Urvaśī, and that the beauties of Nature have no longer any charms for him ; *upavana-latāsu ćakshur na badhnāti dhṛitiṃ tad-anganāloka-durlalitam*. The commentator there explains the word by *dur-āgrastam*. In Sāhit.-d. p. 193, l. 1, the following is cited from the Mahā-bh.: *Dhik dhik sūta kiṃ kṛitavān asi vatsasya me prakṛiti-durlalitasya*, where *durlalita* is ex-plained by *durvilasita*.

[2] 'Happy (those parents who), carrying (their) little-sons fondly-soli-citing-a-refuge-in-their-lap, having-buds-of-teeth-just- [scarcely, slightly] visible by their innocent [causeless, without reason] smiles, while-at-tempting-charming-prattle-in-indistinct-accents, are soiled by the dust of their (infantine) limbs !' *Ā-lakshya, ā* is here the prefix of diminution (see p. 228, n. 1). *Pranayinaḥ*=*prārthakāḥ*, S. and C. *Malinī*, the Beng. have *parushī*. This is the verse with which Chézy is enraptured : '. . . strophe incomparable, que tout père, on plutôt toute mère, ne pourra lire sans sentir battre son cœur, tant le poète a su y rendre, avec les nuances les plus délicates, l'expression vivante de l'amour maternel.'

Verse 181. VASANTA-TILAKĀ (a variety of ŚAKVARĪ). See verses 8, 27, 31, &c., 170.

तापसी ।

[a]हीदु । ण मं अअं गण्णेदि । ॥ पार्श्वमवलोकयति ॥ [b]को एत्थ इसिकुमाराणं । ॥ राज्ञानमवलोक्य ॥ [c]भहंमुह । एहि दाव । मोएहि इमिणा दुम्मोच्छहत्थग्गाहेण डिम्भलीलाए बा-ही अमाणं बालमिइंद अं ।

राजा ॥ उपगम्य । सस्मितम् ॥

अयि भो महर्षिपुत्र ।

एवमाश्रमविरुद्धवृत्तिना
संयमः किमिति जन्मनस्त्वया ।
सत्त्वसंश्रयसुखोऽपि दूष्यते
कृष्णसर्पशिशुनेव चन्दनम् ॥१८२॥

[a] भवतु । न मामयं गणयति ।   [b] कोऽत्र ऋषिकुमाराणाम् ।   [c] भद्रमुख । एहि तावत् । मोचयानेन दुर्मोचहस्तग्राहेण डिम्भलीलया बाध्यमानं बालमृगेन्द्रकम् ।

---

[1] 'O gentle sir,' lit. 'O thou with auspicious countenance.' According to the Sāhit.-d. (p. 179, l. 16) *bhadra-mukha* and *saumya* are the titles used by the inferior characters in addressing the king's son : *saumya bhadra-mukhety evam adhamais tu kumārakaḥ.* They do not seem to be so restricted, as in Act V. the Beng. MSS. make Gautamī address the king himself as *bhadra-mukha;* and K. extends the application of both terms to any *mānya*, honourable person : *Bhadra-mukheti mānyasyāmantraṇe yathoktaṃ saumya bhadra-mukhety evam mānyo rājñaḥ suto vā.*

[2] 'Release the young lion being tormented in childish play by this (boy) the-grasp-of-whose-hand-is-difficult to unloose.' Some MSS. have *maindam* or *maindaam* for *mṛigendram;* the Mackenzie, *miindam.*

[3] 'How is it that by thee, whose behaviour is opposed to (the peaceful character of) a hermitage, (thy) father's humanity [forbearance], that-delights-in-the-protection-of-the-animals, is thus outraged; like the sandal-tree by the young of the black serpent?' *Āśrama-viruddha*, cf. p. 38, l. 5. *Saṃyama=śama*, K., 'a vow to forbear hurting animals.' *Kim iti=kim-*

Verse 182. RATHODDHATĀ (a variety of TRISHṬUBH), containing eleven syllables to the Pāda or quarter-verse, each Pāda being alike.

$$- \cup - \cup \cup \cup - \cup - \cup - \parallel$$

तापसी ।

[a] भद्रमुह । एस हु अञ्चं इसिकुमारञ्ञो ।

राजा ।

आकारसदृशं चेष्टितमेवास्य कथयति । स्थानप्रत्ययाचु
वयमेवान्तर्किणः ।

॥ यथाभ्यर्थितमनुतिष्ठन्नालस्यशंमुपलभ्य । आत्मगतम् ॥

अनेन कस्यापि कुलाङ्कुरेण
स्पृष्टस्य गात्रेषु सुखं ममैवम् ।
कां निर्वृतिं चेतसि तस्य कुर्या-
द्यस्यायमङ्गात्कृतिनः प्ररू[2]ढः ॥१८३॥

[a] भद्रमुख । न खल्वयमृषिकुमारः ।

---

artham, K. ; *iti* is frequently thus joined with *kim* (compare p. 71, l. 1).
Janmanas=*janmano hetoḥ*, K.   So *prabhava*=*janma-hetu*, p. 44, l. 4,
n. 1; otherwise I should translate 'from thy birth.' The Beng. MSS. have
janmadas and *sanyamī* agreeing with it.   *Sukho*, the Mackenzie and K.
have *guṇo* (=*dharmaḥ*, K.)   *Candanam*, as to the sandal, see p. 175, n. 1.
This celebrated tree seems to have paid dearly for the fragrance of its
wood: 'The root is infested by serpents; the blossoms by bees; the
branches by monkeys; the summits by bears.   In short, there is not a
part of the sandal-tree which is not occupied by the vilest impurities'
(Hitop., Book II, verse 163).

[1] 'His behaviour, (which is) conformable to his mien, says as much
[bespeaks it, betokens it].' *Kathayati*, compare p. 224, l. 7.

[2] 'Such (being) the-thrill-of-delight in the limbs of me touched by this
scion of the family of some one (unknown to me); what bliss must he
cause in the heart of that happy-man from whose body [loins] he sprang !'
Hindū poets are fond of alluding to the thrilling effect of the touch of a
child on the limbs of its parent, and *vice versâ*.   Compare the parallel
passages in the Vikram., Act V, and the following from the Mahā-bh.,
Putra-sparśāt sukhataraḥ sparśo loke na vidyate.   *Angāt*, some MSS.,
including my own, have *ankāt*, 'from whose loins.'   *Kṛitinaḥ*=*bhā-*
gyavataḥ, 'fortunate.'   *Kṛitin* is properly 'one who has accomplished the
desire of his heart.'

Verse 183. Upajāti or Ākhyānakī (a variety of Trishṭubh). See verses 41, &c., 169.

तापसी ॥ उभौ निर्वर्ण्य ॥

[a] अच्छरिअं अच्छरिअं ।

राजा ।

आर्ये । किमिव ।

तापसी ।

[b] इमस्स बालअहृवस्स देवि संवादिणी आकिदिति विम्हा-
विदम्हि । अपरिइदस्सवि दे अप्पडिलोमो संवुत्तोत्ति ।

राजा ॥ बालमुपलालयन् ॥

न चेन्मुनिकुमारोऽयं । अथ कोऽस्य व्यपदेशः ।

तापसी ।

[c] पुरुवंसो ।

राजा ॥ आत्मगतम् ॥

कथमेकान्वयो मम । अतः खलु मदनुकारिणमेनमचभवती
मन्यते । अस्त्येतत्पौरवाणामन्ध्यं कुलव्रतम् ।

भवनेषु रसाधिकेषु पूर्वं
क्षितिरक्षार्थमुशन्ति ये निवासम् ।
नियतैकयतिव्रतानि पश्चा-
त्तरुमूलानि गृहीभवन्ति तेषाम् ॥१८४॥

॥ प्रकाशम् ॥

[a] आश्चर्यम् आश्चर्यम् । [b] अस्य बालकरूपस्य तेऽपि संवादिन्याकृतिरिति
विस्मापितास्मि । अपरिचितस्यापि तेऽप्रतिलोमः संवृत्त इति । [c] पुरुवंशः ।

---

[1] 'The speaking-resemblance of form;' 'la ressemblance parlante,'
Chézy.

[2] *Upalālayan*, 'fondling;' see p. 289, n. 2.

[3] *Vyapadeśaḥ*, 'family;' see p. 205, n. 1.

[4] 'This (custom of retiring to a hermitage) is the last family-observance
of the descendants of Puru. (They) who first of all for the sake of protecting the earth choose a residence in palaces abounding-in-all-the-

Verse 184. AUPACCHANDASIKA. See verses 77, 78.

न पुनरात्मगत्या मानुषाणामेष विषयः ।[1]

तापसी ।

[a] जह भद्मुहो भणादि । अच्छरासंबन्धेण इमस्स जणणी एत्थ देवंगुरुणो तवोववणे पसूदा ।[2]

राजा ॥ अपवार्य ॥

हन्त द्वितीयमिदमाशाजननम् । ॥ प्रकाशम् ॥ अथ सा तत्रभवती किमाख्यस्य राजर्षेः पत्नी ।

तापसी ।

[b] को तस्स धम्मदारपरिच्चाइणो णाम सङ्कीत्तिदुं चिन्तिस्सदि ।

राजा ॥ खगतम् ॥

इयं खलु कथा मामेव लक्ष्मीकरोति । यदि तावदस्य

[a] यथा भद्रमुखो भणति । अप्सरःसम्बन्धेनास्य जनन्यत्र देवगुरोस्तपोवने प्रसूता ।
[b] कस्तस्य धर्मदारपरित्यागिनो नाम सङ्कीर्तितुं चिन्तयिष्यति ।

---

pleasures-of-sense, to them [of them] the roots of trees, where the one religious vow of ascetics [i. e. control of the passions, mortification] is rigidly maintained, become a dwelling-place.' *Rasādhikeshu*, the Bengālī MSS. have *sudhāsiteshu*, 'white with stucco or chunam.' *Uśanti* (3rd pl. pres. of *vaś*, Gram. 324, 656)=*ićchanti*, S. ;=*vāńchanti*, K. *Taru-mūlāni*, so Manu enjoins that the hermit is to be *vijitendriyo dharāśayo vriksha-mūla-niketanah*, 'his passions kept in subjection, sleeping on the bare ground, dwelling at the roots of trees,' vi. 26. It seems to have been a practice in ancient India for kings when they had reigned sufficiently long, to retire from the charge of government and betake themselves to penitential exercises. They first associated the Yuva-rāja or heir-apparent with themselves, and then left him in quiet possession of the throne.

[1] 'But this (sacred) place is not (accessible) to mortals by their own means [condition].' *Vishayah*=*pradeśah*, Chézy. The Mackenzie MS. has *katham* for *na*.

[2] 'In consequence of her relationship to a nymph.' *Deva-guros*=*Kaśyapasya*.

शिशोर्मातरं नामतः पृच्छेयम् । ॥ विचिन्त्य ॥ अथवा ।
अन्यायः परदारपृच्छाव्यापारः ।[1]

तापसी ॥ प्रविश्य मृन्मयूरहस्ता ॥

[a] सव्वदमण । सउन्दलावण्णं पेक्ख ।[2]

बालः ॥ सदृष्टिक्षेपम् ॥

[b] कहिं वा मे अम्बा ।[3]

उभे ।

[c] णामसारिसेण वञ्चिदो माउवच्छलो ।

द्वितीया ।

[d] वच्छ । इमस्स मित्तिआमोरअस्स रम्मत्तणं देक्खन्ति
भणिदोसि ।

राजा ॥ आत्मगतम् ॥

किं वा शकुन्तलेत्यस्य मातुराख्या । सन्ति पुनर्नामधेय-
सादृश्यानि । अपि नाम मृगतृष्णिकेव नाममाचप्रस्तावो[4]
मे विषादाय कल्पते ।

<hr>

[a] सर्वदमन । शकुन्तलावक्त्रं प्रेक्षस्व ।   [b] कुत्र वा मे अम्बा ।   [c] नामसा-
दृश्येन वञ्चितो मातृवत्सलः ।   [d] वत्स । अस्य मृत्तिकामयूरकस्य रम्यत्वं पश्येति
भणितोऽसि ।

<hr>

[1] So reads the Mackenzie MS. The others *tarhy anāryaḥ para-dāra-
vyavahāraḥ*.

[2] *Śakunta=pakshin*, 'a bird.' By joining it with *lāvaṇyam*, the her-
mitess unconsciously pronounces Śakuntalā. *Śakuntasya pakshino lāvaṇyam. Śakunta-lāvaṇyaṃ ślesheṇa Śakuntalā-śabdaḥ uktaḥ*, Chézy.

[3] For *ambā* (the reading of the Mackenzie MS., supported by K.) some
have *ajjū* for Sanskrit *ajjukā*, and again, subsequently, *ajjuā* for *ajjukā*,
where K. has *ajjaā* for *āryakā* or *āryā*. I have everywhere followed K.
in rejecting *ajjukā*, as, according to Amara-k.-(i. 1, 7, 11) and Sāhit.-d.
(p. 179 at the end), this word, in theatrical language, is applied only to
a *veśyā* or harlot.

[4] 'Perhaps the mention of a mere name, like the mirage-of-the-desert,
is destined to (cause) me bitter-disappointment.' *Mriga-trishṇikā*, see

बालः ।

[a] अज्जए । रोञदि मे एसो भद्दमोरञ्चो । || इति क्रीडनकमादत्ते ||

प्रथमा || विलोक्य । सोद्वेगम् ||

[b] अम्हहे । रक्खाकरण्डअं से मणिबन्धे ण दीसदि ।

राजा ।

अलमलमावेगेन । नन्विदमस्य सिंहशावविमर्दात्परि-
भ्रष्टम् । || इत्यादातुमिच्छति ||

उभे ।

[c] मा खु मा खु । एदं अविलम्बिअ कहं गहिदं षेष ।

|| इति विस्मयादुरोनिहितहस्ते परस्परमवलोकयतः ||

राजा ।

किमर्थं प्रतिषिद्धाः स्मः ।

प्रथमा ।

[d] सुणादु महाराञो । एसा अबराजिदा णाम ओसही इमस्स

[a] आर्यिके । रोचते म एष भद्रमयूरकः । [b] अहो । रक्षाकरण्डकमस्य मनिबन्धे
न दृश्यते । [c] मा खलु मा खलु । एतदविलम्ब्य कथं गृहीतमनेन । [d] शृणोतु
महाराजः । एषापराजिता नामौषधिरस्य

---

p. 250, n. 1 at the end. *Nāma-mātra-prastāvo* may mean 'the occasion
of a mere name,' but the verb *pra-stu* has the sense of 'mentioning,'
'declaring.' *Kalpate*, 'is sufficient,' or simply 'becomes a cause of;' cf.
p. 191, l. 5; p. 260, l. 12.

[1] A peacock, whether living or in the form of a toy, seems to have been
a favourite plaything. So the boy in the fifth Act of the Vikramorvaśī,
yaḥ suptavān madanke tam me jātu-kalāpam preshaya śikhinam. For
āryake the Beng. have *antike.* *Antikā=bhaginī jyeshṭhā=dhātrī,* S.

[2] 'The amulet,' 'the talisman,' lit. 'the guardian casket,' 'the magical
casket.' One sense, however, of *karaṇḍaka* is 'a kind of plant' or 'herb'
(cf. next note). It was probably a kind of locket, containing some herb
with talismanic properties, worn round the waist, to serve as an amulet.
Karaṇḍaka certainly usually signifies 'a little box,' but it may possibly be
the name for the herb itself. K. explains it by *rakshā-ghuṭikā [? guṭikā],*
'a magical ball.' Some of the Beng. have *rakshā-kāṇḍo;* S. and C.,
rakshā-gaṇḍo and *rakshā-gaṇḍako.*

[3] 'This herb, called Aparājitā [unconquered, invincible], was given

ᵃजादकम्मसमए भअवदा मारीएण दिण्णा । एदं किल
मादापिदरो अप्पाणं च वज्जिअ अवरो भूमिपडिदं ण
गेण्हादि ।

राजा ।

अथ गृह्णाति ।

मध्यमा ।

ᵇतदो तं सप्पो भविअ दंसइ ।

राजा ।

भवतीभ्यां कदाचिदस्याः प्रत्यक्षीकृता विक्रिया ।

उभे ।

ᶜअणेअसो ।

राजा ॥ सहर्षम् । आत्मगतम् ॥

कथमिव सम्पूर्णमपि मे मनोरथं नाभिनन्दामि ।

॥ इति बालं परिष्वजते ॥

द्वितीया ।

ᵈसुव्वदे । एहि । इमं वुत्तन्तं णिअमव्वाबुडाए सउन्दलाए
निवेदेम्ह । ॥ इति निष्क्रान्ते ॥

बाल: ।

ᵉमुञ्च मं । जाव अब्बाए सआसं गमिस्सं ।

ᵃ जातकर्मसमये भगवता मारीचेन दत्ता । एतां किल मातापितरावात्मानं च वर्ज-
यित्वापरो भूमिपतितां न गृह्णाति । ᵇ ततस्तं सर्पो भूत्वा दशति । ᶜ अनेकश: ।
ᵈ सुव्रते । एहि । इमं वृत्तान्तं नियमव्यापृतायै शकुन्तलायै निवेदयाव: । ᵉ मुञ्च
माम् । यावदम्बायाः सकाशं गमिष्यामि ।

by his reverence Kaśyapa to this child, on the occasion of the natal
(ceremony).' As to the name *aparājitā*, compare p. 266, n. 2. The *jāta-
karman* is the fourth of the twelve Sanskāras or purificatory rites, described in Manu (ii. 27, &c.), and the first after the child's birth (cf. p. 258,
n. 2; p. 199, n. 1). It was performed by giving the child honey and
clarified butter out of a golden spoon, before separating the navel-string.

1 *Atha* here = *yadi tu*, 'supposing now,' 'but if' (cf. *atha tu*, verse 128).

राजा ।

पुत्रक । मया सहैव मातरमभिनन्दिष्यसि ।

बालः ।

[a] ममक्खु तादो दुस्सन्दो । ण तुमं ।

राजा ॥ सस्मितम् ॥

एष विवाद एव प्रत्याययति[1] ।

॥ ततः प्रविशत्येकवेणीधरा[2] शकुन्तला ॥

शकुन्तला ।

[b] विआरकालेवि पकिदिट्ठं सव्वदमणस्स ओसहिं सुणिञ्र
या मे आसा आसि अत्तणो भाअहेएसु । अहवा जह
साणुमदीए आचक्खिदं । तह सम्भावीअदि एदं ।

राजा ॥ शकुन्तलां विलोक्य ॥

अये । सेयमनभवती शकुन्तला । यैषा

वसने परिधूसरे वसाना
नियमक्षाममुखी धृतैकवेणिः[3] ।

a मम खलु तातो दुष्यन्तः । न त्वम् ।   b विकारकालेऽपि प्रकृतिस्थां सर्वदम-
नस्यौषधिं श्रुत्वा न म आशासीदात्मनो भागधेयेषु[4] । अथवा यथा सानुमत्याचक्षितम् ।
तथा सम्भाव्यत एतत् ।

---

[1] 'Even this contradiction convinces me.' *Pratyāyayati*, 'causes me to
believe,' 'me inducit ad credendum' (cf. p. 216, l. 12).

[2] *Eka-veṇī-dharā*, cf. Megha-d. verse 90, *sārayantī eka-veṇīṃ kareṇa;*
and verse 98, *abalā-veṇi-mokshotsukāni.*   The Hindū women collect their
hair into a single long braid, as a sign of mourning, when their husbands
are dead, or absent for a long period.

[3] 'Even at the time of metamorphose,' i. e. even on an occasion when it
ought to have changed its form.   As to *prakṛiti*, 'the natural form or
state,' as opposed to *vikāra*, cf. p. 71, l. 10.   *Oshadhi*, see p. 295, n. 3.

[4] 'I had no hope in my own destiny,' 'I had no trust in my fortunes.'

[5] Compare p. 262, lines 7 and 8.

अतिनिष्करुणस्य शुद्धशीला
मम दीर्घं विरहव्रतं बिभर्ति ॥१८५॥

शकुन्तला ॥ पश्चात्तापविवर्णं राजानं दृष्ट्वा ॥

[a] एक्खु अज्जउत्तो विच्च । तदो को एसो दाणिं किद-
रक्खामङ्गलं दारअं मे गत्तसंसग्गेण दूसेदि ।

बालः ॥ मातरमुपेत्य ॥

[b] अंब । को एसो पुरिसो मं पुत्तेत्ति आलिङ्गदि ।

[a] न खल्वार्यपुत्र इव । ततः क एष इदानीं कृतरक्षामङ्गलं दारकं मे गात्रसंसर्गेण
दूषयति । [b] अम्ब । क एष पुरुषो मां पुत्रेत्यालिङ्गति ।

---

[1] 'She who, wearing a pair of dark-grey vestments, having a countenance emaciated by penitential-exercises, bearing (on her head) a single
braid of hair, chaste [pure] in her behaviour, undergoes a long vow of
separation from me, excessively unmerciful.' *Vasane*, acc. du. neut. ; see
p. 158, n. 1, and cf. *vāsasī* in Mṛicchak., Act IV. It seems that men's
clothes, as well as women's, consisted of two pieces (cf. Bhaṭṭi-k. iii. 20,
manorame vastre, which in one commentary is rendered by *manoramaṃ
vastra-dvayam* and in the other by *ćeto-hāriṇī vastre*). *Pari-dhūsare*, as
the preposition *ā* is employed diminutively, so the prepositions *pari* and
sam give force and intensity, much as περί and σύν in Greek, and *per* and
con in Latin. *Pari* is even more intensive than *sam*: thus, *sam-āpti*,
'completion,' *pari-samāpti*, 'entire completion ;' *sam-pūrṇa*, 'very full,'
pari-pūrṇa, 'completely filled ;' *saṃ-śushka*, 'dried up,' *pari-śushka*,
'quite dried up ;' *ā-pāṇḍu*, 'palish,' *pari-pāṇḍu*, 'very pale ;' *pari-śrānta*,
'completely wearied,' &c. &c. *Dhṛitaika-veṇi*, see p. 297, n. 2. S'. and
C'. quote the following from Bharata: *amalāsv avadhāraṇam* [? *amalā
avadhāraṇam*, S'.] *alakānāṃ ća kalpanam anulepana-saṃskāraṃ na
kuryāt pathikāṅganā* ('a woman whose husband is absent on a journey,'
cf. p. 230, n. 1); *pāṇḍu-ćchāyā kṛiśa-tanur veṇī-yuta-śiroruhā lambālakā
dīna-veśā vibhūshaṇa-vivarjitā.*

[2] *Ārya-putra*, see p. 196, n. 4.

[3] 'Furnished with a lucky talisman,' 'protected by an auspicious
amulet.'

[4] The feminine *ambā* makes its vocative *amba*, see Gram. 108. *d.*

Verse 185. AUPAĆCHANDASIKA. See verses 77, 78, 184.

राजा ।

प्रिये । क्रौर्यमपि मे त्वयि प्रयुक्तमनुकूल परिणामं संवृत्तम् ।
यदहमिदानीं त्वया प्रत्यभिज्ञातमात्मानं पश्यामि ।

शकुन्तला ॥ आत्मगतम् ॥

[a] हिअञ्र । समस्सस समस्सस । परिच्चत्तमच्छरेण अणु-
अम्पिदम्हि देव्वेण । अज्जउत्तोक्खु एसो ।

राजा ।

प्रिये ।

स्मृतिभिन्नमोहतमसो दिट्ठ्या प्रमुखे स्थितासि मे सुमुखि ।
उपरागान्ते शशिनः समुपगता रोहिणी योगम् ॥१८६॥

शकुन्तला ।

[b] जेदु जेदु अज्जउत्तो । ॥ इत्यर्धोक्ते वाष्पकँठी विरमति ।

[a] हृदय । समाश्वसिहि समाश्वसिहि । परित्यक्तमप्सरेणानुकम्पितासि देवेन ।
आर्यपुत्रः खल्वेषः ।   [b] जयतु जयत्वार्यपुत्रः ।

---

[1] 'By-the-kindness-of-fortune, O lovely-faced-one, thou standest (once
again) before me, the darkness of whose delusion is dispelled by recollection. At the end of the eclipse, Rohiṇī has been (again) brought to a
union with the moon.' *Dishṭyā* is generally an exclamation equivalent
to 'Hail!' 'good luck!' corresponding to Shakespeare's 'Now fair befall
thee!' I have preferred to regard it here as an adverbial instr. case, 'by
the kindness of destiny,' 'fortunately,' 'happily.' *Uparāga*, the following
is the Hindū notion of eclipses :—A certain demon, which had the tail of
a dragon, was decapitated by Vishṇu at the churning of the ocean ; but,
as he had previously tasted of the Amṛita or nectar reproduced at that
time, he was thereby rendered immortal, and his head and tail, retaining
their separate existence, were transferred to the stellar sphere. The head
was called Rāhu, and became the cause of eclipses, by endeavouring, at
various times, to swallow the sun and moon. *Rohiṇī*, as to the love of
the Moon for Rohiṇī, the fourth lunar constellation, see p. 113. n. 1.

[2] Lit. 'having tears in her throat,' i. e. 'having her voice choked with

---

Verse 186. ĀRYĀ or GĀTHĀ. See verse 2.

$$\cup\,\cup\,-\mid\cup\,-\,\cup\mid\cup\,\cup\,-\parallel\;-\,-\;\mid\cup\,\cup\,-\mid\cup\,-\,\cup\mid-\,\cup\,\cup\mid\cup$$
$$\cup\,\cup\,-\mid-\,-\mid\cup\,\cup\,-\parallel\cup\,\cup\,\cup\,\cup\mid-\,-\mid\cup\mid-\,-\mid-$$

राजा ।

सुन्दरि ।

वाष्पेण प्रतिषिद्धेऽपि जयशब्दे जितं मया ।
यत्ते दृष्टमसंस्कारं पाटलोष्ठपुटं मुखम् ॥१८७॥

बालः ।

[a] अम्ब । की एसो ।

शकुन्तला ।

[b] वच्छ । दे भाग्रहेश्राइं पुच्छेहि ।

राजा ॥ शकुन्तलायाः पादयोः प्रणिपत्य ॥

सुतनु हृदयात्मत्यादेशव्यलीकमपैतु ते
किमपि मनसः सम्मोहो मे तदा बलवानभूत् ।

[a] अम्ब । क एषः ।   [b] वत्स । ते भागधेयानि पृच्छ ।

---

tears.' *Vāshpa*, not the tear itself, but the lachrymal moisture (see p. 169, n. 2) which may find its way into the throat and impede the utterance.

[1] 'Though the (utterance-of) the word "victory" be obstructed by (thy) weeping, victory-has-been-gained by me, since thy unadorned countenance, having-the-surface- [skin] -of-its-lips-pale-red, has been seen (by me).' *Jaya-śabda*, the word 'Victory!' i. e. *jayatu* or *vijayī bhava* was the regular form of saluting kings (cf. p. 65, n. 2). *Asanskāram*, so reads the Taylor MS.; the others have *asanskāra-p°*, which violates the usual cæsura. If the latter be retained, translate 'the skin of whose lips is pale red from the absence of colouring or paint.' There is no doubt that unpainted lips were a sign of mourning, but this is sufficiently implied in *pāṭaloshṭha*, and it is a question whether *sanskāra* can ever mean 'paint.' Some of the Beng., and amongst them the old MS. (Bodleian, 233), supported by S'. and C'., read *a-sanskārāl lolālakam idam mukham*, 'this countenance, having its curls hanging loosely from want of dressing.' *Oshṭha-puṭa*, 'the covering of the lip;' so *akshi-puṭa*, 'the skin covering the eye,' 'the eye-lid.' The student is reminded that in a compound, *oshṭha* optionally causes the elision of a preceding *a* (Gram. 38. *k*). The Mackenzie MS. has *pāṭaloshṭham mukham priye*.

[2] S'ankara quotes the following from Bharata : *Kākubhiḥ praṇipātaiś ća bhāgya-nindādibhis tathā, evaṃ kṛite ća narīṇām purusho 'ti-priyo bhavet.*

Verse 187. ŚLOKA or ANUSHṬUBH. See verses 5, 6, 11, 12, 26, 47, 50, 51, &c., 179.

प्रबलतमसामेवम्प्रायाः शुभेषु हि वृत्तयः
स्रजमपि शिरस्यन्धः क्षिप्तां धुनोत्यहिशङ्कया ॥१८८॥

शकुन्तला ।

[a] उट्टेदु अज्जउत्ती । णूणं मे सुच्चरिच्चप्पडिबन्धञ्चं पुराकिदं तेसु दिञ्हेसु परिणाममुहं आसि । जेण साणुक्कोसोवि अज्जउत्तो मइ विरसी संवुत्तो । ॥ राजो त्तिष्ठति ॥ [b] अह कहं अज्जउत्तेण सुमरिदो दुक्खभाई अञ्चं जणो ।

[a] उत्तिष्ठत्वार्यपुत्रः । नूनं मे सुचरितप्रतिबन्धकं पुराकृतं तेषु दिवसेषु परिणाममुख-मासीत् । येन सानुक्रोशोऽप्यार्यपुत्रो मयि विरसः संवृत्तः । [b] अय कथमार्यपुत्रेण स्मृतो दुःखभाग्ययं जनः ।

---

[1] 'O fair one ! let the unpleasant-feeling [unpleasantness] of (my) repudiation (of thee) depart from thy heart. Somehow-or-other at that time the infatuation of my mind was strong. For such, for the most part, is the behaviour of those over-whom-(the quality of)-darkness-has-the-mastery, on happy-(auspicious)-occasions. A blind man shakes off even the garland thrown on his head, suspecting it to be [with the suspicion of its being] a snake.' *Vyalīkam=apriyam*, K. ;=*vipriyam*, C. *Apaitu*, some of the Beng. MSS. have *upaitu*, which is unintelligible. *Kimapi*, i. e. *anirvačanīya-rūpam yathā syāt*, 'in a manner not to be explained,' S. *Tadā=pratyādeśa-kāle*, 'at the time of repudiation.' *Prabala-tamasām*, i. e. *prabalam ajñānam yesham te tathoktāḥ*, K. According to the Hindū philosophy there were three qualities or properties incident to the state of humanity, viz. 1. *Sattva*, 'excellence' or 'goodness' [quiescence], whence proceed truth, knowledge, purity, &c. 2. *Rajas*, 'passion' or 'foulness' [activity], which produces lust, pride, falsehood, &c., and is the cause of pain. 3. *Tamas*, 'darkness' [inertia], whence proceed ignorance, infatuation, delusion, mental blindness, &c. *Subheshu=sat-karmasu*, 'in auspicious matters,' S. *Vrittayaḥ=vyavahārāḥ*, S. *Dhunoti=nirasyati*, K. *Srajam*, see p. 272, n. 1.

[2] 'Assuredly my (evil deeds), committed in a former (birth), opposed to virtuous conduct, were in those days drawing towards (their appointed evil) issue, (seeing) that my husband, although of-a-compassionate-nature, became unfeeling towards me.' *Purā-kritam*, i. e. *janmāntara-karma*, S.

Verse 188. HARIṆĪ (a variety of ATYASHṬI). See verses 66, 99.

राजा ।

उद्धृतविषादंशल्यः कथयिष्यामि ।

मोहान्मया सुतनु पूर्वमुपेक्षितस्ते
यो वाष्पविन्दुरधरं परिबाधमानः ।
तं तावदाकुटिलपक्ष्मविलग्नमद्य
वाष्पं प्रमृज्य विगतानुशयो भवेयम् ॥१८९॥

॥ इति यथोक्तमनुतिष्ठति ॥

शकुन्तला ॥ नाममुद्रां दृष्ट्वा ॥

[a] अज्जउत्त । एदं तं अङ्गुलीअङ्गं ।

राजा ।

अस्मादङ्गुलीयोपलम्भात्खलु स्मृतिरुपलब्धा ।

[a] आर्यपुत्र । एतत्तदङ्गुलीयकम् ।

(see p. 185, n. 3 at the end). *Pariṇāma-mukham* [*pariṇatābhimukham*,
K.], 'about to issue in their appointed fruit, in their matured result,'
'ripe for an evil result.' *Pariṇāma* is 'the last stage of anything,' 'the
stage of maturity,' 'the final result :' *mukha*, like *unmukha* (lit. 'looking
towards'), has here the sense of 'tending towards,' 'being about,' 'being
on the point.'

[1] Cf. p. 272, l. 8; and *uddharen no hridaya-śalyam*, Vikram., Act I.

[2] 'O graceful lady! I should in a manner be freed from (my) remorse
by wiping off that moisture now clinging to thy slightly curved eye-lashes,
which formerly, (in the form of) a tear-drop corroding thy lip, was un-
noticed [overlooked] by me through mental-delusion.' *Pūrvam*, i. e. *pra-
tyādeśa-velāyām*. *Paribādhamānaḥ*=*pīḍayan*, Ś. *Ā-kuṭila*, cf. *ā-tāmra*,
p. 228, l. 3, and p. 298, n. 1. *Vigatānuśayo*=*apagata-paścāttāpaḥ*. For
vāshpam some of the Beng. have *kānte*, unsupported by any of the Deva-n.
MSS. The repetition of *vāshpa* seems at first unnecessary, but not if it
be borne in mind that *vāshpa* is properly 'the moisture in the eye,' and
vāshpa-vindu, 'the tear-drop when it has left the eye' (see p. 169, n. 1 in
the middle).

Verse 189. VASANTA-TILAKĀ (a variety of ŚAKVARĪ). See verses 8, 27, 31, 43, 46, 64,
74, 80, 82, 83, 91, 93, 94, 95, 100, 104, 105, 108, 123, 124, 144, 148, 152, 157, 168, 170, 181.

शकुन्तला ।

[a] विसमं किदं एेण । जं तदा अज्जउत्तस्स पच्चाभिण्णाणकाले दुल्लहं आसि ।

राजा ।

तेन ह्यृतुसमवायचिह्नं प्रतिपद्यतां लता कुसुमम्[1] ।

शकुन्तला ।

[b] ण से विस्ससामि । अज्जउत्ती एव्व एं धारेदु ।

॥ ततः प्रविशति मातलिः ॥

मातलिः ।

दिंष्ट्या[3] । धर्मपत्नीसमागमेन पुत्रमुखदर्शनेन चायु-ष्मान्वर्धते ।

राजा ।

अभूत्सम्पादितस्वादुफलो मे मनोरथः । मातले । न खलु विदितोऽयमाखण्डलेन[4] वृत्तान्तः स्यात् ।

मातलिः ॥ सस्मितम् ॥

किमीश्वराणां परोक्षम् । एत्वायुष्मान् । भगवान्मारीचस्ते

[a] विषमं कृतमनेन । यत्तदार्यपुत्रस्य प्रत्यायनकाले दुर्लभमासीत् ।   [b] नास्मै विश्वसामि । आर्यपुत्र एवैनद्धारयतु ।

---

[1] A noun formed from the causal verb explained at p. 297, n. 1.

[2] 'Therefore let the creeper receive again (its) flower, as a pledge [mark, token] of its inseparable-union with the (spring) season,' i. e. receive thou back this ring, as the beautiful twining plant receives again its blossom, in token of its reunion with the spring. *Tena hi*, with the sense of 'therefore,' occurs very frequently in dramatic composition (cf. p. 81, l. 2, p. 83, l. 4, and p. 85, l. 5). *Ritu*, see p. 228, n. 1 at the end. *Samavāya*, 'inseparable or intimate connexion.' The Bengālī MSS. have *ritu-samāgamāśansi* (the Bengālī recension, *ritu-samāgama-ćihnam*), and S. *ritu-sangama-sūćakam*.

[3] *Dishṭyā*, see p. 299, n. 1. As to *putra-mukha*, &c., see p. 223, n. 1.

[4] *Akhaṇḍala* is one of a class of epithets (such as *puran-dara, bala-bhid, giri-bhid*, &c.) applied to Indra, as breaking cities, mountains, &c., into fragments with his thunderbolt (see p. 86, n. 2).

दर्शनं वितरति ।

राजा ।

शकुन्तले । अवलम्ब्यतां पुत्रः । त्वां पुरस्कृत्य भगवन्तं द्रष्टुमिच्छामि ।

शकुन्तला ।

[a] हिरिआमि अज्जउत्तेण सह गुरुसमीबं गन्तुं ।

राजा ।

अपाचरितव्यमभ्युदयकालेषु । एह्येहि ।

|| सर्वे परिक्रामन्ति ||

|| ततः प्रविशत्यदित्या सार्धमासनस्थो मारीचः ||

मारीचः || राजानमवलोक्य ||

दाक्षायणि ।

पुत्रस्य ते रणशिरस्ययमप्रयायी
दुष्यन्त इत्यभिहितो भुवनस्य भर्ता ।
चापेन यस्य विनिवर्तितकर्म जातं
तत्कोटिमत्कुलिशमाभरणं मघोनः ||१९०||

[a] जिह्रेम्यार्यपुत्रेण सह गुरुसमीपं गन्तुम् ।

---

[1] 'Allows thee a sight (of him),' i. e. 'graciously permits thee to be presented to him,' 'vouchsafes thee an audience.'

[2] 'But on joyful [festive] occasions the (usual) practice must be observed.' The Mackenzie MS. has *gantavyam* for *ácharitavyam*.

[3] 'O Dākshāyiṇī [i. e. Aditi, see p. 284, n. 3], this is he that marches foremost at the head of thy son's [Indra's] battles, the so-called Dushyanta, the lord [protector] of the earth, through whose bow that edged thunder-bolt of Indra, having rested from its work, has become (a mere) ornament.' *Raṇa-śirasi,* cf. p. 268, l. 12, and p. 87, n. 1. *Koṭimat= sāgram=tīkshṇam. Kuliśam=vajram. Maghonaḥ,* gen. of *Maghavan,* a name of Indra, see declension in Gram. 155. *c.*

Verse 190. VASANTA-TILAKĀ (a variety of ŚAKVARĪ). See verses 8, 27, 31, 43, 46, 64, 74, 80, 82, 83, 91, 93, 94, 95, 100, 104, 105, 108, 123, 124, 144, 148, 152, 157, 168, 170, 181, 189.

अदितिः ।

^a सम्भावणीआणुभावा से आंकिदी ।[1]

मातलिः ।

आयुष्मन् । एतौ पुत्रप्रीतिपिशुनेन चक्षुषा दिवौकसां
पितरावायुष्मन्तमवलोकयतः । तावुपसर्प ।

राजा ।

मातले । एतौ

प्राहुर्द्वादशधास्थितस्य मुनयो यत्तेजसः कारणं
भर्तारं भुवनत्रयस्य सुषुवे यद्यज्ञभागेश्वरम् ।
यस्मिन्नात्मभुवः परोऽपि पुरुषश्चक्रे भवायास्पदं
द्वन्द्वं दक्षमरीचिसम्भवमिदं तत्स्रष्टुरेकान्तरम् ॥१९१॥

^a सम्भावनीयानुभावास्याकृतिः ।

---

[1] 'His dignity may be inferred from his form,' lit. 'his form has its dignity inferrible.'

[2] 'With an eye that betrays [betokens] affection for (thee as for) a son.' *Pisuna*, cf. p. 277, l. 8.

[3] 'This is that pair [Aditi and Kaśyapa], the offspring of Daksha and Marīci, one remove from the Creator [Brahmā], which (said pair) sages call the cause [origin, author, maker] of the solar-light subsisting in twelve forms [having a twelve-fold subsistence], which (pair) begot the ruler of the three worlds, the lord of the (gods who are the) sharers of (every) sacrifice, (and) in which (pair) Nārāyaṇa (or Vishṇu), he (who was) even superior to the Self-existent [Brahmā], chose [made] the site for (his) birth.' *Dvādaśa-dhā*, there are twelve Ádityas or forms of the Sun, which represent him in the several months, or, as some say, attend upon his car (see p. 279, n. 3). They are the children of Aditi and Kaśyapa, and the gods Vishṇu and Indra are reckoned among them. The other ten, according to the Vishṇu-p. (p. 234), are Dhātṛi, Aryaman, Mitra, Varuṇa, Vivasvat, Pūshan, Parjanya, Aṇśa, Bhaga, and Tvashtṛi; but the names of the Ádityas vary in the other Purāṇas. *Tejasaḥ*, i. e. *sūryātmakasya*, 'consisting of the sun,' K.; =*sūryasya*, S.; =*ādityasya*, Chézy. *Bhuvana-trayasya*, i. e. *svarga-martya-pātālasya*, S. (see p. 314, n. 2). *Yajña-bhāgeśvaram* may simply mean 'the lord of a share of (every) sacrifice;'

Verse 191. ŚĀRDŪLA-VIKRĪDITA. See verses 14, 30, 36, 39, 40, 63, 79, 85, &c., 176.

मातलिः ।

अथ किम् ।

राजा ॥ प्रणिपत्य ॥

उभाभ्यामपि वासवानुयोज्यो दुष्यन्तः प्रणमति ।

मारीचः ।

वत्स । चिरं जीव । पृथिवीं पालय ।

अदितिः ।

[a] वच्छ । अप्पडिरंही होहि ।

a वत्स । अप्रतिरथो भव ।

---

it seems, however, likely that *yajna-bhāga* is here synonymous with *kratu-bhuj*, 'a god,' though *yajna-bhāj* would be the more usual form. *Ātma-bhuvaḥ* [abl. from *ātma-bhū*] = *svayambhuvaḥ* = *brahmaṇaḥ*, K. and C. *Paraḥ* = *śreshṭhaḥ*. *Purusha* = *Vishṇu*, K.; = *Nārāyaṇa*, S. and C. *Bhavāya* = *janmane*, K.; = *avatārāya*, S. *Āspadam* = *pratishṭhām* = *sthitim*, K. and S. *Upendrāvatārasya kāraṇam uktam bhavati*, K. *Dvan-dvam* = *mithunam* = *strī-puṃsayor yugalam*. *Srashṭur* = *Brahmaṇaḥ*, K. and S. *Ekāntaram* = *ekāntaritam*, S.; *ekaḥ purusho antaraṃ vyavadhā-naṃ yasya tat tathoktam*. *Brahmaṇo Marīćiḥ, Marīćeḥ Kaśyapaḥ, Brah-maṇo Dakshaḥ, Dakshād Aditir iti ekāntaram*, K. *Ekaḥ purusho antaram antardhānaṃ yasya tad dvandvam*, Chézy. As Kaśyapa and Aditi were the grandchildren of Brahmā, they were only removed from him by Marīći and Daksha, their parents and his children (see p. 279, n. 3). Vishṇu, as Nārāyaṇa, or the Supreme Spirit (*purusha*), moved over the waters before the creation of the world, and from his navel came the lotus from which Brahmā sprang. As Vishṇu, or the Preserver, he became incarnate in various forms, and chose Kaśyapa and Aditi, from whom all human beings were descended, as his medium of incarnation or place of birth, especially in the Avatāra in which he was called 'Upendra' (or *Indrānuja, Indrā-varaja*), 'Indra's younger brother' (according to some identified with Krishṇa), and in his Vāmana or Dwarf-Avatāra (see p. 275, n. 2). *Puru-sha* is properly 'that which sleeps or abides in the body' [*puri śete*]. The worshippers of Vishṇu identify him with Nārāyaṇa and with Brahma, and name him Mahā-purusha, Purushottama, i. e. 'the Supreme Spirit,' thus exalting him above Brahmā, the Creator. Kālidāsa seems by this verse to include himself among the Vaishṇavas.

[1] *Ubhābhyām* [dat. dual], i. e. *Aditi-Mārīćābhyām*, S. *Vāsavānu-yojyaḥ* = *Indrājñākārī*, 'Indra's servant,' S. The Bengālī MSS. have *vāsava-niyojyo* (cf. p. 273, l. 3).

[2] *A-pratiratha*, 'an invincible hero;' see p. 177, l. 6, n. 1 in the middle.

शकुन्तला ।

[a] दारअसहिदा वो पादवन्दणं करेमि ।

मारीचः ।

वत्से ।

आखण्डलसमो भर्ता जयन्तप्रतिमः सुतः ।
आशीरन्या न ते योग्या पौलोम्या सदृशी भव ॥१९२॥

अदितिः ।

[b] जादे । भत्तुणो बहुमदा होहि । अवसं दीहाऊ वच्छो
उहअकुलणन्दणो होदु । उवविसह ।

॥ सर्वे प्रजापतिमभितं[2] उपविशन्ति ॥

मारीचः ॥ एकैकं निर्दिशन् ॥

दिष्ट्या शकुन्तला साध्वी सदपत्यमिदं भवान् ।
श्रद्धा वित्तं विधिश्चेति त्रितयं तत्समागतम् ॥१९३॥

[a] दारकसहिता वां पादवन्दनं करोमि । [b] जाते । भर्तुर्बहुमता भव । अवश्यं
दीर्घायुर्वत्स उभयकुलनन्दनो भवतु । उपविशत ।

---

[1] '(Thy) husband (being) like Indra, thy son resembling Jayanta
[Indra's son], no other blessing (would be) suitable to thee; mayst thou
be like Paulomī!' (see p. 272, n. 1 at the end.) As to *Ākhaṇḍala*, see
p. 303, n. 4.

[2] As to the title Prajāpati, see p. 279, n. 3.

[3] 'All hail! the virtuous S'akuntalā, (her) noble offspring, your Highness (Dushyanta)! Piety [faith], Fortune [wealth], Action; this trio is
here combined.' *Sad*, i. e. *ubhaya-kula-guṇa-sampannam*. *S'raddhā*,
being feminine, of course represents S'akuntalā; *vittam*, being neuter, her
offspring (*apatyam*), viz. Sarva-damana or Bharata; and *vidhi*, being
masculine, Dushyanta. *Vidhi*, according to C., is *veda-bodhitācaraṇa*,
'putting in practice the precepts of the Vedas;' it may, perhaps, imply
power as exhibited in action. Cf. Raghu-v. ii. 16, *babhau sā tena satām
matena śraddheva sākshād vidhinopapannā*, 'she (accompanied) by him,
who was honoured by all good men, appeared [shone forth] like Faith
visibly manifested, accompanied by action [works].'

Verses 192, 193. ŚLOKA or ANUSHṬUBH. See verses 5, 6, 11, 12, 26, 47, 50, &c., 187.

राजा ।

भगवन् । प्रागभिप्रेतसिद्धिः । पश्चाद्दर्शनम् । अतोऽपूर्वः
खलु वोऽनुग्रहः । कुतः ।

उदेति पूर्वं कुसुमं ततः फलं
घनोदयः प्राक्तदनन्तरं पयः ।
निमित्तनैमित्तिकयोरयं क्रम-
स्तव प्रसादस्य पुरस्तु सम्पदः ॥१९४॥

मातलिः ।

एवं विधातारः प्रसीदन्ति ।

राजा ।

भगवन् । इमामाज्ञाकरीं वो गान्धर्वेण विवाहविधिनोप-

---

[1] 'First (came) the accomplishment of my desires; afterwards, the sight (of thee). Hence thy favour (towards me) has indeed been un-precedented.' S'. explains thus—*Sakuntalā-prāpakam bhavad-darśanam bhavishyati iti evam mamābhipretam āsīt, tāvat prabhāvād darśana-pūr-vam nirvyūḍham. Tathā ća naimittikānantaraṃ nimittotpattir iti anu-grahasyāpūrvatvam iti bhāvaḥ*, 'my desire was that the sight of thee might lead to my recovery of S'akuntalā. But (my meeting her) was arranged through (thy) divine power, before my presentation to thee. Thus after the effect was the appearance of the cause. The meaning is, that the favour (of my seeing thee and receiving thy blessing) did not precede (the attainment of my desire), and hence that the favour was unprecedented, as the accomplishment of my wishes ought naturally to have resulted from thy blessing.' There seems to be a double meaning in *apūrvaḥ*.

[2] 'First appears the blossom, then the fruit; first the rising of clouds, afterwards the rain. This (is) the regular-course of cause and effect; but the success-of-my-wishes (came) before thy favour.' *Naimittika*, 'what is connected with the *nimitta* or is dependant on it,' 'the effect.' *Puras* = *prathamatas*, S'. *Sampadaḥ* (nom. pl.) = *abhīshta-siddhiḥ*, S'.; it is clearly meant to be synonymous with *abhipreta-siddhiḥ* just above.

[3] 'Thus (it is that) the creators of-all-beings perform favours.' *Vidhātṛi* must here be equivalent to Prajāpati (see p. 279, n. 3).

Verse 194. VAṆSA-STHAVILA (a variety of JAGATĪ). See verses 18, 22, 23, &c., 180.

यस्य कस्यचित्कालस्य बन्धुभिरानीतां स्मृतिशैथिल्यात्म-
त्यादिशन्नपराद्धोऽस्मि तच्चभवतो युष्मत्सगोचस्य कंखस्य ।
पश्चादङ्गुलीयकदर्शनाद्रूढपूर्वां तदुहितरमवगतोऽहं । तच्चि-
चमिव मे प्रतिभाति ।

यथा गजो नेति समक्षरूपे
तस्मिन्नतिक्रामति संशयः स्यात् ।
पदानि दृष्ट्वा तु भवेत्प्रतीति-
स्तथाविधो मे मनसो विकारः ॥१९५॥

मारीचः ।

वत्स । अलमात्मापराधशङ्कया । सम्मोहोऽपि त्वय्यनुप-
पन्नः । श्रूयताम् ।

राजा ।

अवहितोऽस्मि ।

मारीचः ।

यदैवापसरस्तीर्थावतरणात्प्रत्यक्षवैक्लव्यां शकुन्तलामादाय

---

[1] *Kasyačit kālasya,* i. e. *kasminščit kāle,* C.

[2] Called Kāśyapa as being of the race of Kaśyapa (see p. 22, n. 3).

[3] 'As if one were to say, "(that) is not an elephant," its form being before one's eyes, and doubt were to arise (in one's mind) on its walking past, but conviction were to take place after seeing its footsteps; of such a kind has been the change of my mind,' i. e. my mind has passed through similar transitions. Thus, as K. observes, when Dushyanta first saw S'akuntalā, he repudiated her (see p. 200, l. 2, and p. 201, l. 4); when she passed out of his presence, he began to relent and doubt (see verse 131); and when he saw the ring, he was convinced she was his wife. *Neti,* see p. 140, n. 2. *Samaksha-rūpe,* i. e. *samaksha-vidyamāna-rūpe,* C. *Padāni* =*pada-čihnāni,* C. *Vikāra*=*svarūpānyathā-bhāva,* S'. May not *saṃśayaḥ* apply to both lines? thus: 'As if there were a doubt that that is not an elephant, while he is marching along, his form obvious to the eye.'

[4] The Mackenzie MS. and my own have *aparādha;* the others, *apačāra.*

[5] 'After [in consequence of] her descent to Apsaras-tīrtha,' see p. 271,

---

Verse 195. Upajāti or Ākhyānakī. See verses 41, 107, 121, 126, 142, 156, &c., 183.

मेनका दाक्षायणीमुपगता । तदेव ध्यानादवगतोऽस्मि ।
दुर्वाससः शापादियं तपस्विनी सहधर्मचारिणी त्वया
प्रत्यादिष्टा नान्यथेति । स चायमङ्गुलीयकदर्शनावसानः ।

राजा ॥ सोच्छ्वासम् ॥

एष वचनीयान्मुक्तोऽस्मि[2] ।

शकुन्तला ॥ स्वगतम् ॥

[a] दिट्ठिआ । अकारणपच्चादेसी ण अज्जउत्तो । ण हु सत्तं[3]
अत्ताणं सुमरेमि । अहवा पत्तो मए स हि सावो विरह-
सुण्णहिअआए ण विदिदो । जदो सहीहिं सन्दिट्ठम्हि ।
भत्तुणो अङ्गुलीअअं दंसइदव्वंति ।

मारीचः ।

वत्से । चरितार्थासि[5] । सहधर्मचारिणां प्रति न त्वया मन्युः
कार्यः । पश्य ।

शापादसि प्रतिहता स्मृतिरोधरूक्षे
भर्तर्यपेततमसि प्रभुता तवैव ।

[a] दिष्ट्या । अकारणप्रत्यादेशी न आर्यपुत्रः । न खलु शप्तमात्मानं स्मरामि । अथवा
प्राप्तो मया स हि शापो विरहशून्यहृदयया[4] न विदितः । यतः सखीभ्यां सन्दिष्टास्मि ।
भर्तुरङ्गुलीयकं दर्शयितव्यमिति ।

---

n. 1, and p. 215, l. 18. According to S., *Apsaras-tīrtha=saćī-tīrtha* (see
p. 205, l. 12). Menakā was S'akuntalā's mother (see p. 44, l. 11).

[1] 'That this thy poor faithful [lawful] wife was repudiated in consequence
of the curse of Durvāsas, and on no other account, and this same (curse) has
terminated on the sight of the ring.' *Durvāsas*, see p. 137, n. 2. *Tapasvinī*
=*anukampyā*, S'. (cf. p. 246, l. 7). *Saha-dharma-ćāriṇī=pati-vratā*, S'.

[2] *Vaćanīyāt*, i. e. *sādhvī-nirākaraṇa-rūpāpavādāt*. *Vaćanīyam=vā-
ćyam*, p. 198, l. 12.

[3] The Colebrooke and Mackenzie MSS. and my own have *sattam* or
satam (=*saptam*), supported by S'. The Taylor has *saććam* (=*satyam*),
supported by K. and the Bengālī.

[4] *Sūnya-hṛidayayā*, cf. p. 137, l. 11, with n. 2.

[5] 'Thou hast gained thy object.' *Ćaritārthā=labdhārthā=kṛitārthā*.
The Mackenzie has *viditārthā*.

छाया न मूर्छति मलोपहतप्रसादे
शुद्धे तु दर्पणतले सुलभावकाशा ॥१९६॥

राजा ।

भगवन् । अर्च खलु मे वंशप्रतिष्ठा । ॥ इति बालं हस्तेन गृह्णाति ॥

मारीचः ।

तथाभाविनमेनं चक्रवर्तिनमवगच्छतु भवान् । पश्य ।

रथेनानुत्खातस्तिमितगतिना तीर्णजलधिः
पुरा सप्तद्वीपां जयति वसुधाममप्रतिरथः ।
इहायं सत्त्वानां प्रसभदमनात्सर्ववदमनः
पुनर्यास्यत्याख्यां भरत इति लोकस्य भरणात् ॥१९७॥

---

[1] 'Thou wast repulsed in consequence of the curse, (thy) husband being harsh [cruel] through the obstruction of (his) memory; (but now) indeed, on (the heart of) him freed from darkness, thy influence-is-supreme. (Even as) an image has no effect on the surface of a mirror whose brightness is tarnished with dirt, but on a clean-one easily makes impression [gains admission].' *Smriti-rodha*, the Mackenzie has *smriti-dosha*. *Apeta-tamasi*, cf. p. 301, n. 1. *Prabhutā*, K. refers to verse 73, p. 124. *Chāyā* = *prativimbam*. *Mūrchati* = *vyāpnoti*, K.; = *sphurati*, S. (see p. 201, n. 3). *Malopahata-prasāde* = *malāpagata-prasannatve*, S.; = *mālinyena nashṭā prasannatā*, K. *Sulabhāvakāsā* = *sukhena labhyaḥ praveśo yasyāḥ* = *prāptāvasthitiḥ*, S. (cf. p. 47, l. 3). S. observes that *darpaṇa-tale* answers to *bhartari*; *malopahata* to *smriti-rodha*; *chāyā* to *prabhutā*; and, we may add, *śuddhe* to *apeta-tamasi*.

[2] *Atra*, &c., i.e. *asyāṃ Śakuntalāyām, kuloddhāraka-putrotpādakatvena*, 'in this Śakuntalā, because she has given birth to a son, the upholder of my family?' K.; cf. p. 260, l. 11, and p. 124, l. 3.

[3] *Tena prakāreṇa kuloddhārakatvena bhavishyantam*, K. *Chakravartinam* = *sārvabhaumam*, 'a monarch of the whole earth,' K. (see verse 12).

[4] 'Previously (as) an-invincible-warrior, having crossed the ocean in a chariot whose motion is not (made) unsteady by uneven-ground, he will

---

Verse 196. VASANTA-TILAKĀ (a variety of ŚAKVARĪ). See verses 8, 27, 31, 43, 46, 64, 74, 80, 82, 83, 91, 93, 94, 95, 100, 104, 105, 108, 123, 124, 144, 148, 152, 157, 168, 170, 181, 189.
Verse 197. SIKHARINĪ (a variety of ATYASHṬI). See verses 9, 24, 44, 62, 112, 141.

राजा ।

भगवता कृतसंस्कारे सर्वमस्मिन्नवयमाशंसामहे ।

षदितिः ।

[a] भश्रवं । इमाए दुहिदुमयोरहसम्पत्तीए कष्षोवि दाव

[a] भगवन् । अस्या दुहितृमनोरथसम्पत्तेः कष्टोऽपि तावत्

---

subjugate the earth, consisting of seven islands. Here, from his forcible
taming of the animals, he (is called) Sarva-damana; but (then) he will
acquire the appellation Bharata, from his support of the world.' *Rathena*,
see p. 9, l. 2. *An-utkhātu°* (*nimnonnata-pradeśasyābhāvād anutkhā-
tam*, K.), so reads the Mackenzie MS., supported by K.; the others, *an-
udghāta*; cf. p. 10, l. 6, with n. 1. *Stimita*=*anishkampa*, K.;=*aprati-
bandhārtha-durgamanena*, S'. 'By this epithet it is indicated that the
chariot would have the power of going in the air' (*tena viśeshaṇena ra-
thasya ākāśagāmitvaṃ sūćitam*), K. *Sapta-dvīpām*, according to the
mythical geography of the Hindūs, the earth consisted of seven islands, or
rather insular continents, surrounded by seven seas. That inhabited by
men was called Jambu-dvīpa, and was in the centre, having in the middle
of it the sacred mountain Meru or Sumeru, inhabited by the gods. About
Jambu flowed the sea of salt-water (*lavaṇa*), which extends to the second
Dvīpa, called Plaksha, which is in its turn surrounded by a sea of sugar-
cane juice (*ikshu*). And so with the five other Dvīpas, viz. S'ālmali, Kuśa,
Krauñća, S'āka, and Pushkara, which are severally surrounded by the
seas of wine (*surā*), clarified butter (*sarpis*), curds (*dadhi*), milk (*dugdha*),
and fresh-water (*jala*), Vishṇu-p. p. 166; see Indian Wisdom, p. 419.
A-pratiratha=*a-tulyaratha*=*mahāratha*, S'. (see p. 177, n. 1 in the middle).
Iha = *asmin āśrame*, K. *Sattvānām* = *prāṇinām siṃhādīnām*, S'.; =
śarabha-siṃhādīnām, K. *Prasabha-damanāt* = *balātkāreṇa mardanāt*.
The name Bharata is derived from root *bhṛi*, 'to bear,' 'support.' Many
Indian princes were so named, but the most celebrated was this son of
Dushyanta and S'akuntalā, who so extended his empire that from him the
whole of India was called Bhārata or Bharata-varsha; and whose descendants, the sons of Dhṛita-rāshtra and Pāṇḍu, by their quarrels, formed
the subject of the Mahā-bhārata (see p. 15, n. 1).

  [1] 'We invoke all blessings on him for whom the prescribed-rites were
performed by your Holiness,' or 'we have high hopes and expectations of
him,' &c. As to *krita-saṃskāre*, see p. 258, n. 2, and p. 199, n. 1.

[a]सुदवित्यारो करीअदु । दुहिदुवच्छला मेणआ इह एव्व मं परिचरन्ती चिट्ठुइ ।

शकुन्तला ।। आत्मगतम् ।।

[b]मणोरहोक्खु मे भणिदी भअवदीए ।

मारीचः ।

तपःप्रभावात्मत्यक्षं सर्वमेव तत्रभवतः ।

राजा ।

अतः खलु ममानतिक्रुद्धो मुनिः ।

मारीचः ।

तथाप्यसौ प्रियमस्माभिः प्रष्टव्यः । कः कोऽत्र भोः ।

शिष्यः ।। प्रविश्य ।।

भगवन् । अयमस्मि ।

मारीचः ।

गालव । इदानीमेव विहायसा गत्वा मम वचनात्तत्र-
भवते कख्याय प्रियमावेद्य । यथा पुत्रवती शकुन्तला
तच्छापनिवृत्तौ स्मृतिमता दुष्यन्तेन प्रतिगृहीतेति ।

शिष्यः ।

यदाज्ञापयति भगवान् ।   ।। इति निष्क्रान्तः ।।

[a] श्रुतविस्तारः क्रियताम् । दुहितृवत्सला मेनकेहैव मां परिचरन्ती तिष्ठति ।
[b] मनोरथः खलु मे भणितो भगवत्या ।

---

[1] 'Let Kaṇva also be made acquainted with all the circumstances.' S.
has *jñāta-vistaraḥ;* the Beng. MSS., *vijñātārthaḥ.*

[2] Here, and in the insertion of *me* in the next line, I have followed the
Mackenzie MS. and my own, as I have often done, if supported by K.

[3] 'Notwithstanding, he must be questioned by us about (this) joyous-
event. Ho! there!' *S'ishyāṇām madhye ko atra tishṭhati iti arthaḥ,*
'which among my pupils is in waiting here? such is the meaning of *kaḥ,*
&c.,' S'.   Compare p. 69, l. 11; p. 263, l. 5.

मारीचः ।

वत्स । त्वमपि स्वापत्यदारसहितः सख्युराखण्डलस्य
रथमारुह्य ते राजधानीं प्रतिष्ठस्व ।

राजा ।

यदाज्ञापयति भगवान् ।

मारीचः ।

अपि च ।

तव भवतु विडौजाः प्राज्यवृष्टिः प्रजासु
त्वमपि विततयज्ञः स्वर्गिणः प्रीणयालम् ।
युगशतपरिवर्तानेवमन्योन्यकृत्यै-
र्नयतमुभयलोकानुग्रहश्लाघनीयैः ॥ १९८ ॥

राजा ।

भगवन् । यथाशक्ति श्रेयसे यतिष्ये ।

मारीचः ।

वत्स । किं ते भूयः प्रियमुपहरामि ।

---

¹ Here I have followed the Colebrooke MS. The others have *sāpatya-dāra-sahitaḥ;* the Bengālī, *sāpatya-dāraḥ.*

² 'May Indra be bountiful of (his) rain towards thy subjects! Do thou also, abundantly-dispensing [diffusing] sacrifices, gratify [satisfy] the gods [inhabitants of heaven] to the full. Thus pass (both of you) periods [revolutions] of hundreds of ages with reciprocal friendly acts, laudable on account of the favours (thus conferred) on both worlds;' i. e. you by sacrificing, and Indra by showers, confer benefits on the inhabitants of Svarga and the earth respectively. The two worlds are of course Heaven and Earth, not including the third world Pātāla (see p. 275, n. 2). *Viḍaujas* or *Viḍojas* is one of Indra's names, see p. 303, n. 4. *Prājya-vṛishṭi=pracura-varshaṇa. Vitata-yajña=vistṛita-yāga,* K. *Svarginaḥ=devān,* K. *Prīṇaya alam=alam bhāvaya,* K.; *=atyarthena santoshaya,* S. *Yuga-śata-parivartān=yugānāṃ śatāni tesham parivartanāni.*

³ K. has *śreyasi* and interprets it by *dharme.* S. has the same and explains it by *praśasta-kṛitye.*

Verse 198. MĀLINĪ or MĀNINĪ (a variety of ATI-ŚAKVARĪ). See verses 10, &c., 171.

राजा ।

अतः परमपि प्रियमस्ति । यदिह भगवान्प्रियं कर्तुमिच्छति ।
तर्हीदमस्तु भरतवाक्यम् ।

प्रवर्ततां प्रकृतिहिताय पार्थिवः
सरस्वती श्रुतिमहतां महीयताम् ।

---

[1] 'Is there any favour still greater than this? As (however) on this occasion his Holiness desires to confer a favour, then let this saying of Bharata be (fulfilled).' *Ataḥ param*, i. e. *adhikam*. *Atra praśnārthe kākur anusandheyā*, see p. 264, n. 2. The Bharata here intended must not be confounded with the young prince. He was a holy sage, the director or manager of the gods' dramas, and inventor of theatrical representations in general. He wrote a work containing precepts and rules relating to every branch of dramatic writing, which appears to have been lost, but is constantly quoted by the commentators. He seems to have superintended the exhibition of the drama called Lakshmī-svayaṃvara (composed by Sarasvatī, see p. 28, n. 1) in Indra's heaven. See Vikram., Act III, and middle of Act II, *Muninā Bharatena yaḥ prayogo bhavatīshu ashṭa-rasāśrayo nibaddhaḥ*, &c. It was not unusual to close the plays by quoting one of Bharata's verses; compare the conclusion of the Ratnāvalī. The commentator supposes that there is here an intentional ambiguity as to whether this verse is spoken in the name of the young prince or of the sage.

[2] 'Let the king exert himself for the welfare of his subjects. Let Sarasvatī be honoured among (those who are) mighty in the scriptures [lovers of literature]. Moreover, may the purple-god [S'iva], who-is-self-existent, (and) whose-Energy-is-everywhere-diffused, put an end to my future birth [deliver my soul from passing into another state of being].' *Pravartatām=prayatatām*. *Sarasvatī (=Bhāratī, K.)* is the wife of the god Brahmā. She is the goddess of speech and eloquence, patroness of the arts and sciences, and inventress of the Sanskrit language. *Sarasvatī* signifies 'flowing,' and is also applied to a river. *S'ruti-mahatām*, &c., some MSS. have *śruti-mahatī mahīyasām; K. śruta-mahatām*. According to the latter, *śruta=śāstra, mahatām=śreshṭhānām*. I see no reason why *mahatām* should not be the gen. pl. of the pres. part. regularly formed from *mah*, 'to honour.' *S'ruti-mahatām* might then mean 'lovers of literature.' *Mahīyatām=pūjyatām*, K. *Nīla-lohitaḥ*, 'blue and red;' i. e. according to K., *vāma-bhāge nīlaḥ, dakshiṇa-bhāge lohitaḥ*, 'on the

ममापि च क्षपयतु नीललोहितः
पुनर्भवं परिगतशक्तिरात्मभूः ॥१९९॥

॥ इति निष्क्रान्ताः सर्वे ॥

॥ सप्तमोऽङ्कः ॥

॥ समाप्तमिदमभिज्ञानशकुन्तलं नाम नाटकम् ॥
॥ शुभं भूयात् ॥

---

left side blue, on the right side red.' S'iva is usually represented as borne
on a bull, his colour, as well as that of the animal he rides, being white,
to denote the purity of Justice over which he presides. In his destroying
capacity, he is characterized by the quality *tamas* (see p. 301, n. 1) and
named Rudra, Kāla, &c., when his colour is said to be purple or black.
'In the beginning of the Kalpa, as Brahmā purposed to create a son, a
youth of purple complexion [blue and red, *nīla lohita*] appeared, crying
and running about [*ru, dru,* whence Rudra],' Vishṇu-p. p. 58. Some
refer this name to the colour of his throat (see p. 257, n. 2). *Parigata-
śaktiḥ; prāptā śaktiḥ Pārvatī yena sa tathoktaḥ.* Hence, S'akti=Pārvatī,
S'iva's wife. The wives of the deities were supposed to personify their
energy or active power. *Ātma-bhū,* although properly a name of Brahmā,
is applied equally to Vishṇu and S'iva by those who give the preference
to these deities. Exemption from further transmigration and absorption
into the divine Soul is the *summum bonum* of Hindū philosophy (cf.
p. 184, n. 3 at the end). Kālidāsa indulges the religious predilections of
his fellow-townsmen by beginning and ending the play with a prayer to
S'iva, who had a large temple in Ujjayinī, the city of king Vikramāditya,
and abode of the poet. Both actors and spectators would probably repeat
the prayer after the speaker and appropriate it to themselves.

Verse 199. RUĊIRĀ or PRABHĀVATĪ (a variety of ATIJAGATĪ), containing thirteen
syllables to the Pāda or quarter-verse, each Pāda being alike.

$$\cup - \cup - \mid \cup \cup \cup \cup \mid - \cup - \cup - \parallel$$

a- in *a-tas, a-tra, a-tha,* &c.
a-, before consonants, in *a-kath-ita,* &c.; *an-,* before vowels, in *an-agha,* &c.
anśa, 106[d]; °*vivartin,* 78°.
anśu, 20[b] (*hima*°); 116[b] (*gharma*°).
anśuka, 34[b]; 169[b].
ansa, 30[a]; 175[c]; du. 63[b].
a-kathita, 17, 14; 229, 11.
a-kāṇḍe, 46[a], n.
a-kāma, adj. 23[d].
a-kāraṇa, 222, 14; 247, 4.
a-kāle, 260, 1, 2.
a-krita, 51, 9 (°*satkāra*); 35[b].
a-kaitava, adj. 208, 12.
a-klishṭa, 120[a] (°*kānti*).
-*aksha* (for *akshi*), 78°; 124[c].
a-kshama, adj. 112, 4; *ā,* f. 8[d].
a-kshayya, adj. 47[b].
a-kshara, n. 53, 6; 78[b]; 144[b]; °*artha,* 184, 2.
akshi, n. 62, 2; 65, 7; (at end of a comp. -*aksha.*)
a-khaṇḍa, adj. 44[a].
a-grihīta, 230, 8 (°*artha*).
agni, 10[b]; 28[b], &c.; °*śaraṇa,* 148, 4; 189, 4.
agra, 229, 6; 190[a]; °*tas,* adv. 76, 6. 13; 212, 2; °*bhūmi,* 263, 12; °*yāyin,* 190[a]; °*hasta,* 252, 10.
anka, 74[c]; 181[c]; 66[c], &c.
ankita, 14[d]; 140, 9; 176, 7.
ankura, 228, 1; 135[a]; 230, 3.
anga, 21[b]; 277, 1; °*bhanga,* 62, 5.
anganā, 27[d] (*hariṇa*°).
anguli or °*ī,* 48, 1; 78[a]; 143[d].
angulīya, 53, 5; °*ka,* 54, 5; 233, 4.
a-ćala, adj. 175[d].
a-ćintanīya, 243, 5.
a-ćira, 6, 6 (°*pravritta*); *āt,*

99[c]; *ena,* 262, 8; °*m,* adv. 103, 2; °*bhās,* 171[b].
a-ćetana, adj. 145°.
a-jayya, adj. 162[a].
a-jasram, adv. 58[a].
a-jñātvā, ind. 107, 11.
aṭavī, 60, 2; 72, 3.
a-taṭa, 142[d] (°*prapāta*).
a-tanu, 110°.
a-tas, 27, 2; 72, 6; 125[a], &c.; °*param,* 97[d]; 315, 2.
ati-kramya, ind. 250,8; 263,11.
ati-krāmat, 195[b].
atithi, 17, 2 (°*satkāra*); 36, 2.
ati-dūra, 58, 6.
ati-nishkaruṇa, adj. 185°.
ati-parisphuṭa, adj. 115[a].
ati-pāta, m. 16, 7, 8.
ati-pinaddha, 23, 8.
ati-mātram, adv. 29, 4; 30[a].
ati-mukta, 112, 12 (°*latā*).
ati-raṇhas, adj. 5[b].
ati-rush, adj. 124[d].
ati-lola, adj. 10°.
ati-lohita, 124° (°*akshi*).
ati-vah, caus. 238, 9.
ati-śithila, 257, 10.
ati-śrama, 108°(°*apanayana*).
ati-san-dhā, pass. 99, 1, 2.
ati-sandhāna, 126° (*para*°).
ati-sandhāya, ind. 211, 7.
ati-sneha, m. 176, 11.
atīta, part. 142°.
atītya, ind. 12, 2; 148°; 274, 2.
aty-antam, adv. 27°.
aty-aya, 65[b] (*tapa*°).
aty-artham, adv. 175[b].
aty-āhita, 35, 6.
a-tra, adv. 91, 4; 311, 4, &c.; °*bhavat,* 194, 11; °*bhavatī,* 52, 11, &c.; °*antare,* 64[d].
a-tha, 1, 1; 196, 2; 81, 7; 296, 5, n.; °*kim,* 46, 7, n.; 90,11; 188,9; °*vā,* 30, 5, n.

adas, pron. 9, 8; 8[d]; 48[a]; 175[d], &c.
A-diti, f. 279, n. 3; 282, 4.
a-drishṭa, 263, 11 (°*rūpa*).
adbhuta, n. 215, 8.
adya, 4, 2; 147, 11, &c.; °*prabhriti,* 165, 7; °*api,* 30[b].
a-dhanyatā, 61, 6.
adhara, m. 21[a]; 24[c]; 77[c]; 286, 14; °*uttara,* 210, 7; °*oshṭha,* 78[a].
a-dharma, 213, 7, 8 (°*bhiru*).
adhas, adv. 104, 2; with gen. 14[a]; °*mukha,* 47, 1.
adhika, 20[c] (°*manojña*); 30[b] (*pramāṇa*°); °*taram,* 282,7.
adhi-kāra, 40, 8 (*dharma*°); 189, 7.
adhi-kṛi, pass. 8, 1.
adhi-kritya, ind. 6, 4, n.; 6, 6; 77, 3.
adhi-kship, 210, 4, 5.
adhi-kshipta, 201, 8.
adhi-gata, 42[a].
adhi-gamya, ind. 189, 8.
adhi-jya, 6[a]; 37[a]; 49[d]; 164[b].
adhi-rūḍha, 271, 2 (*ratha*°).
adhi-rohat, 274, 9.
adhi-rohin, 203, 3 (*dūra*°).
adhi-śayāna, part. 105, 1.
adhī, pass. 126[c].
adhunā, adv. 167°.
adhy-ākrānta, 48[a].
adhy-ās, 236, 8. 11.
an-agha, adj. 44[c]; 167, 3 (°*prasava*).
An-anga, 58[b]; 60[b].
an-atikramaṇīya, 68,7; 280,2.
an-atikruddha, adj. 313, 8.
an-atipātya, 187, 1.
an-atilulita, 66[c], n.
an-anurūpa, 24, 10.
an-antaram, adv. 194[b]; 5, 8.
an-anyaparāyaṇa, adj. 72[a].

aveksh, 205, 10.
avekshi-tā, 202, 5 (dharma°).
a-vyakta, 181^b.
a-vyabhićārin, adj. 237, 5, 6.
a-ryavasyat, 120^b.
a-ryāja, 18^a (°manohara).
r. aś, aśnāti, 60, 4 (pass.)
aśana, 80^d (piśita°); 265, 15.
a-śaraṇa, 124, 11; 240, 15.
a-śikshita, 123^a, 126^a.
a-śiśira, adj. 66^a.
a-śući, 113^a.
a-śūnya, adj. 75, 6; 236, 16.
a-śeshatas, adv. 158^d.
a-śoka, 284, 4 (°vṛiksha).
a-śoćanīya, 147, 10.
aśru, 65, 7; 66^b; 147^b, &c.
a-śruta, 232, 1 (°pūrva).
aśva, 17, 10.
ashṭan, 1^d.
r. as, asti, 3, 2; 5^a, &c.
a-saṃśayam, adv. 22^a; 129, 2.
a-saṃskāra, adj. 187^b.
a-saṃstuta, 34^a.
a-sakta, 46^d.
a-sat, n. 111^b; 201, 4.
a-satya, 145, 7 (°vandha).
a-sannivṛitti, f. 142^c.
a-sannihita, 136, 12.
a-sambaddha, 51, 6, n.
a-sambhāvita, 57, 11, n.
a-savarṇa, 30, 5 (°kshetra).
a-sādhudarśin, adj. 22, 11.
a-sunnidhya, n. 88, 12.
Asura, 161^a; 173^b; 274, 9.
a-sulabha, 243, 7 (°sthāna).
asūyā, 225, 3; cf. sāsūyam.
asta, 82^a (°śikhara).
astra, n. 266, 11.
asmad, 30, 1; 34, 7; 40, 8, &c.; 57, 2 (°anveshin); 93, 14; 214, 8.
a-svastha, 96, 4; 105, 11.
r. ah, 1^c; 24, 5; 27, 4, &c.
-aha (for ahan), 67, 5. 7, 8.
ahan, 158^a.
ahi, 188^d (°śankā).
aho, interj. 36^d; 95, 4; 103, 5.

ā- in ā-tāmra, &c., 134^a; 181^a. 189^c.
ā, prep. with abl. 2^a; 27^a; 169, 4; 126^a.
ā-kampita, 176, 9.
ā-karṇ, 163, 3; 182, 8.
ā-karṇya, ind. 13, 4; 185, 6.
ā-kāra, 41, 4; 291, 4.
ā-kārita, 244, 11.
ākāśa, 226, 2, &c.; e, 96, 2, &c.
ā-kīrṇa, 112^d (jana°).
ā-kuṭila, 189^c.
ā-kula, 67, 5; 99^b; °ī-kritya, ind. 65, 7; °ī-bhūta, 92, 2.

ā-kulita, 147, 8 (dhūma°).
ā-kriti, 20^d; 38, 10; 135, 2.
ā-krish, pass. 207, 7, 8.
ā-krishṭa, 9, 8; 33^b.
ā-krishya, ind. 58^c.
ā-krand, 34, 7.
Ā-khaṇḍala, 303, 14; 192^a.
ā-khyā, f. 294, 13; 197^d.
ākhyāyin, 24^b.
ā-gata, 89, 7.
āgantuka, 141, 4; °tā, 232, 1, n.
ā-gam, 2, 3, 4; 34, 3; 133, 4; 249, 8.
ā-gama, 221, 3; 223, 4; 114^a.
ā-gamana, 187, 2, 3; 222, 1.
ā-gāmin, adj. 90, 17.
ā-ghāta, 33^a (tīvra°).
ā-ćakshita, 240, 3; 297, 11.
ā-ćar, 25^b.
ā-ćarita, 144, 4.
ā-ćaritavya, 304, 8.
ā-ćāra, 62, 2; 158, 7; 105^a.
ā-ććhādin, 19^b (pariṇāha°).
ā-jīva, m. 219, 7; 223, 11.
ā-jñapta, 7, 8; 155, 4.
ā-jñapti, 90, 7 (°hara).
ā-jñā, caus. 3, 2; 10, 12, &c.
ā-jñā, 88, 6, &c.; °kari, 308, 11.
ājya, 15^b (°dhūma).
ā-tanka, m. 106, 8; 108, 5.
ā-tapa, 96, 4; 75^b; °tra, 108^d.
ā-tāmra, 134^a, n.
ātitheya, adj. 16, 8.
ātithya, n. 36, 5.
ātura, adj. 170, 9.
ātta, 110^a (°daṇḍa); °gandha, 263, 9, n.; °śastra, 269, 1, n.
-ātmaka in dāha°, 41^b.
ātman, 2^b; 17, 10; ātmā-tritīya, 13, 11; °krita, 209, 12; °gatam, 38, 4, n.; °gati, 293, 1; °jā, 42, 10; °bhū, 191^c; 199^d.
ātmīya, 77, 2.
ā-dadhāna, 80^c.
ā-dara, m. 227, 4.
ā-dā, 265, 8.
ā-dāya, ind. 95, 2; 153, 13, &c. -ādi, 44, 5; 207, 7 (evam°).
Ādityas (twelve), 305, n. 3.
ā-diś, 151, 7; caus. 161, 4.
ā-dishṭa, 142, 4; 227, 1.
ādya, adj. 1^a; 89^c.
ā-dhā, 4, 4.
ā-dhāra, 14^d (toya°).
ā-dhi, m. 98^d; °hetu, 64^b.
ānana, 31^c; 63^a; 68^a.
ā-nanda, 158, 6 (°parivāhin).
ā-nī, 238, 11; 249, 6; 172^d.
ā-nīta, 309, 1.
r. āp, āpnoti, 12^b; 16, 2.
āpagā, 172^c.
ā-paṇa, 225, 10 (śauṇḍika°).

ā-panna, 72, 2; 50^b; 122, 4; °sattva, 146, 3, 4; 199, 1.
āpta, 126^d (°vāć).
ābutta, 219, 2; 222, 4-7, &c.
ā-bharaṇa, 20, 5; 79^c, 85^d, &c.
ā-bhoga, m. 17, 14, n.
ām, interj. 100, 2.
ā-mantr, 128, 14; 165, 2, &c.
ā-marda, 178^a.
ā-mrishṭa, 166^c.
āmra, 230, 5 (°kalikā).
āyata, 57^b (°nayana).
ā-yatta, 97^d (bhāgyu°).
ā-yāta, 40, 9; 232, 12.
ā-yāsa, 120, 8; 135, 11.
ā-yāsayitṛi, 109, 2.
āyus, 91, 1; 307, 8; °mat, 9, 4, n.; 10, 6. 10; 281, 2.
ā-raṭ, 170, 9.
āraṇyaka, 57, 5; 47^b, &c.
ā-rabh, 136, 5; 230, 6.
ā-rabhya, ind. 106, 6.
ā-rambha, 227, 2 (nir-utsara°).
ārāt, 131^c.
ā-rādh, 7, 5, 6.
ā-rādhayitṛi, 125, 6.
ā-rūḍha, 176, 13; 111^d; 261, 8.
ā-ropita, 122, 10; 263, 12.
ā-ropya, ind. 236, 12; 265, 16.
ā-rohaṇa, 270, 9.
ārta, 11^b; 159^c; 263, 5.
ārti, 122, 4 (°hara).
ārdra, 20, 6 (°prishṭha).
ārya, 3, 2; 5, 2; 22^b, &c.; ā, f. 2, 3; °ka, 295, 1; °putra, 196, 11; °miśra, 7, 8, n.
ā-laksh, pass. 63^c; 138^d.
ā-lakshya, adj. 181^a, n.
ā-lapat, 38, 10 sq.
ālavāla, 22, 6 (°pūraṇa).
ā-lāpa, m. 21, 4; 39, 4.
ā-likhita, 7, 4; 248, 14.
ālikhitu-kāma, 250, 11, 12.
ā-ling, 60^b; 298, 7.
ā-lok, pass. 279, 5.
ā-loka, 9^a; 33^d.
ā-varaṇa, 75^a (stana°).
ā-vahat, 57^a.
ā-vāpa, 265, 7 (hasta°).
ā-vārya, ind. 252, 10.
ā-vid, caus. 313, 15.
āvilaya, -yati, 122^a.
āviś, 'evidently,' in °krita, 82, 10; 82^b; 85^a; °bhū, 116^b.
ā-vrij, caus. 30, 3.
ā-vritya, ind. 129, 6; 209, 10.
ā-vega, 125, 6; 139, 4; 295, 6.
ā-vedya, ind. 92, 6.
ā-śaṃs, 177^a.
ā-śank, 28^b; 242, 2.
ā-śankamāna, 202, 12.
ā-śankā, 107, 2; 15^d.
āśā, 293, 6; °bandha, 96^b.

ā-śās, 160, 1; 312, 2.
āśis, 153, 8; 159, 6; 192[b].
ātu, 71[a] (°klānta).
āścarya, 278, 4; 215, 4, &c.
ā-śrama, 13, 3; 16, 7; 48[a]; 194,11(varṇa°); °pada,16[a]; °sad, 88, 8.
ā-śraya, 181[c] (anka°).
āśrayin, 230, 11 (tad°).
ā-śri, 170, 2.
ā-śritya, ind. 7,5; 21,10; 149,3.
ā-ślishya, ind. 150, 1; 174, 12.
ā-śvas, 140, 8; 261, 3.
āśvāsin, 35[a] (darśana°).
ās, interj. 137, 4; 252, 11.
r. ās, āste, 284, 4; 202, 8.
ā-sanga, 33[b].
ā-sajyamāna, 79[c] (°īkshaṇa).
āsana, 88, 1; 153, 1 (°stha).
ā-sanna, 238, 8.
āsīna, 76, 3 (sukha°).
ā-staraṇa, 105, 1.
āspada, 191[c].
ā-sphālana, 38[a].
ā-haraṇa, 16, 6.
āhavanīya, 149, n.
ā-hāra, 60, 4
ā-hiṇḍ, 60, 2.
ā-hiṇḍat, 72, 3.
ā-hita, 37[b]; 84[a]; 106[c].
ā-huti, f. 147. 9.
ā-hṛi, 155, 5
āho, 27[d]; 130[b]; °svid, 111[c].
ā-hve, pass. 69, 15.

i- in i-tara, i-tas, &c.
r. i, eti, 101[a].
ikshu, 265, 2.
iṅgudī, 14[b], n.; 81, 3; 94[a].
i-tara, 16, 1; 130,12; 248,15.
i-tas, 2, 3; 141[a], &c.; itas— itas, 91, 3; °gata, 134, 11; °mukha, 222, 17, &c.
iti, 10, 6; 60, 1; 134, 5, &c.
iti-hāsa, 107, 9 (°nibandha).
ittham, 207,4; 209, 12; °gata, 146, 4; °bhūta, 114, 9.
idam, 8, 3; 9, 8; 10, 4; 12[a]; 20[c]; 22,11.12; 76,2; 171[a].
i-dānīm, 7, 5; 9, 8, &c.
iddha, 180[c] (°rāga).
indu, 55[ac]; 85[a] (°pāṇḍu).
indra, 107[d]; °ka, 287, 5 (mṛiga°); Indra, 284, 5.
indhana, 163[a] (°calita°).
iyat, 61, 2; 134, 6; 137, 2.
iva, adv. 7, 5; 6[b]; 239, 17, &c.
r. ish, icchati, 44, 8; 88, 6; 176, 2; 119[c] (pass.)
ishu, 39[c]; 266, 12.
ishṭa,197,9; 83[c]; °jana,64,1.
ishṭi,88,12(°vighna); 134,10; 267, 10 (°paśu-māram.)

iha,16[a]; 44[d],&c.; °stha,88,8.

īkshaṇa, 27[c]; 72[c]; 79[c].
īkshita, n. 45[a].
īdṛiś or °a, 39[d]; 86[c]; 90[d], &c.
īpsita, m. 67[d].
īrita, 26, 2 (vāta°).
Īśa, 'Siva,' 1[d].
īśvara,272,6; 168[b]; 191[h],&c.
īshat, adv. 4[a]; 248, 14.
r. īh, īhate, 122[a].

ukta,121,6(punar°); 203, 11.
ugra, 44, 11; 102, 9 (°ātapa).
ucita, 38, 2; 201, 2; 137[c], &c.
uc-caya, 43[b]; 139, 5.
uccais, adv. 141[b]; °kula, 97[a].
uc-chid, 162[c].
uc-chvasita, n. 97, 2.
uc-chvāsa, 147[b] (varṇikā°).
Ujjayinī, 316, n.
ujjhita, 42[a]; 44, 4. 7.
ujjhitvā, ind. 32, 3; 67. 4.
uṭaja, 36, 3; 57, 6; 101[b], &c.
uta, 123[b] (kim°); kim—uta, 74[ad]; 105, 11, 12.
ut-kaṇṭha, -kaṇṭhate, 178, 9.
ut-kaṇṭhā, 86[a]; 150, 3. 5; 70, 3 (ājñāpanotkaṇṭha).
ut-kaṇṭhita, 185, 7.
ut-karsha, 39[c].
ut-kīrṇa, 217, 5.
ut-kula, adj. 128[b].
ut-kshipat, 172[d].
ut-kshipya, ind. 131[d].
ut-kshepaṇa, 30[a] (ghaṭa°).
ut-kshepam, ind. 131[b] (bāhu°).
ut-khātin, adj. 10, 6.
ut-tam, 40, 4.
ut-tara, 189,9; 210, 7 (adhara°); 211, 13.
uttarīya, 256, 14.
ut-tāna, 204, 6 (°hṛidaya).
ut-tīrṇa, 156, 6; 157, 3.
ut-thā, 57, 9; 47[a].
ut-thāna, 39[a] (°yogya).
ut-thāya,ind.88,1; 107,5,&c.
ut-thita, 142, 2; 85[c]; 187, 2.
ut-pakshman, adj. 95[a].
ut-pad, caus. 79, 4; 88, 13.
utpala, 18[c] (nīla°).
ut-preksha, 95, n. 3.
ut-phula, 137, 13.
ut-sarpin, adj. 283, 8.
ut-sara, 89[c]; 232,9; 234, 4.
ut-sah, 187, 3; 241, 11.
ut-sāha, 71, 4; 72, 2; 75, 2.
utsuka,67[a]; 124, 8; 234,16.
ut-sṛijya, ind. 75[a]; 267. 1.
udaka, 36, 3; 97, 3; 157[d],&c.
ud-agra, 7[d] (°pluta-tra).
uda-dhi, 49[a] (°śyāma-siman).
ud-anta, 'news,' 226, 6.

ud-aya, 152, 7 (sūrya°); 82[c].
udara, 39[a]; 19[d]; 118, 10, &c.
udāra, adj. 205, 7; 279, 2.
ud-āhṛita, 47, 3, 4.
ud-i, 26[b]; 194[a].
ud-gata, 32, 3.
ud-gama, 15[b] (ājya-dhūma°).
ud-galita, 92[a].
ud-gāra, 219, 4 (jāla°).
ud-diś, 265, 15.
ud-diśya, ind. 122, 9; kim°, 192, 7.
ud-dishṭa, 153, 1; 214, 9.
ud-deśa,103,5; 237,3; 244,8.
ud-dhata, 8[c].
ud-dhṛita, 167[b]; 302, 2.
ud-bhinna, 248, 12.
ud-bheda, 85[d] (kisalaya°).
udbhrāntaka, 263, 1, n.
ud-yamya, ind. 13, 12; 16, 1, &c.
ud-yāna, 17[b] (°latā); 227, 5.
ud-vānta, 248, 11.
ud-vīkshya, ind. 166[b].
ud-vega, 261, 2 (viguṇa°).
ud-rejita, 78, 4.
un-nata, 95[c]; 247, 11.
un-namita, 68[a]; 78[d].
un-nidra, adj. 137[b].
un-majjat, 172[a].
un-matta, 228, 8; 254, 3, &c.
un-mādayitṛi or °ka, 46, 2, n.
un-mūlita, 174, 13.
upa-kaṇṭha, 58[c] (śravaṇa°).
upa-kārin, 114[d] (para°).
upa-kṛita, 165[a].
upa-klṛip, caus. 138, 4.
upa-gata, 26, 9; 207, 3, &c.
upa-gama, 14[c].
upa-gamya, ind. 87,9; 188, 3.
upa-ghāta, 65, 5 (gātra°).
upa-car, 97, 1.
upa-cāra, 71[b].
upa-cchandita, 207, 2.
upa-jīvin, 223, 3 (jāla°).
upatyakā, 188, 4.
upa-dishṭa, 173, n. 3.
upa-deśa, m. 37[d]; 174, 2.
upa-nata, 120[a]; 130, 8; 202, 5 (sukha°).
upa-nipātin, 237, 5.
upa-nī, 256, 10; 258, 10.
upa-nīta, 40, 2.
upa-nīya,ind. 20, 5 (with gen.)
upa-nyasta, 200, 2.
upa-nyāsa, 116, 6; 200, 4.
upa-pad, 46, 9.
upa-panna, 19, 7; 85, 12; 127[b], &c.
upa-bhoga, 85[b]; °kshama, 6, 6; 29, 2, n.
upa-mā, 208, 9 (kūpopama).
upa-mālinītīram, adv. 16, 7.

118[a], &c.; °lāghava, 213, 10; °sishya, 141[b].
gūḍha, 41[b].
gṛidhra, 222, 17 (°bali).
gṛiha, 156, 2; 79[d] (vetasa°); pl. 264, 2; °i-bhū, 184[d].
gṛihin, 86[d]; iṇī, f. 98[d]; 99[a] (°pada).
gṛihīta, 69, 9; 105[a]; 172, 7; 184, 8; 71, 1, &c.; °dhanu, 135[a].
gṛihītvā, ind. 94, 1, &c.
r. gai, gāyati, 6, 4. 7; 183, 1.
go-ghātin, 221, 5.
gotra, 43, 2; 137[d].
gopita, 115, 3 (su-manas°).
Gautama, 86, 4, &c.; ī, f. 51, 6; 97, 3, &c.; 44, 10 (°tīra).
gaurava, 61[a]; 94, 2 (rishi°).
Gaurī-guru, 149[b].
grathita, 4, 3; 180[b] (jāla°).
granthi, 19[a]; 221, 8 (°bhedaka).
r. grah, gṛihṇāti, 20, 5; 77[d]; 127[a]; 52[b]; 51, 11; 127, 6.
grahaṇa, 61, 1, 2 (vana°).
grāha, 290, 4.
grāhin, 74, 4 (vana°).
grīvā, 7[a] (°bhanga).
grīshma, 62[d]; °samaya, 6, 6.
r. glai, caus. glapayati, 70[b].

ghaṭa, 21, 6 (sechana°); 30[a].
ghana, 114[b]; 171[c]; 194[b].
gharma, 116[b] (°anśu); °ambhas, 30[c].
ghāta, 66[c] (jyā°).
r. ghush, pass. 155[b].
ghoshayitavya, 259, 14.

cha, 1[a]; 16[a]; cha—cha, 10[c][d]; 73[b]; 140[b][d].
chakita, 136[d].
chukra, 90, 4 (°raksha); °vartin, 12[b], n.; 16, 2; 214, 9, &c.; °vāka, 128, 14; ī, f. 170, 9.
chakshus, n. 6[a]; 76, 10; 161[d].
chaṭula, 137, 13 (vega°).
chatur-, 100[a] (°anta-mahī).
chatura, adj. 38, 10, n.
Chaturikā, 238, 8; 247, 7, &c.
chaturtha, 90, 17; 142, 1, &c.
chandana, 175, 1; 182[d].
chandra, 150[c]; 162[d]; °mas, 99, 1.
chapala, 15[a] (pavana°); 93, 14.
r. char, charati, 15[d]; 8c[a].
-chara, 24[b]; 38[d]; 67, 5, &c.
charaṇa, 46[a]; 74[d]; 85[b]; 49, 4 (dharma°); 178, 8 (tapas°).
charita, 101[a]; 118[b]; neut. 209, 5; 48, 3 (sat°); 169[d] (tvad°); cf. su°; °artha, 310, 12; °artha-tā, 189, 9.
chala, adj. 39[c]; 24[a] (°apānga).

chalita, 163[a] (°indhana).
chātaka, 171[a].
chāpa, 9, 2; 58[c]; 190[c].
chāpala, 209, 12; 285, 5.
chāmara, 8[b], n.
chāraṇa, 48[c], n.
-chārin, 41, 2 (dharma°); 167, 2.
chikitsitavya, 236, 5.
chikkaṇa, 81, 3.
chitta, 39[b]; °vritti, 7, 4; 64, 1.
chitra, 49[a]; 113, 2; 43[a]; 146[a], &c.; °karman, 156, 12; °gata, 154[b]; °phalaka, 238, 10, &c.; °arpita, 148[b]; °i-krita, 153[d].
chitrita, 288, 3 (varṇa°).
-chid, 9[d]; 83, 7; 239, 17.
r. chint, chintayati, 83, 7, &c.
chintanīya, 114, 2; 134, 6.
chintayat, 62, 1; 202, 10.
chintā, 141, 3; 86[b]; 138[c].
chintita, 118, 7; neut. 40, 4.
chira, 136[a]; 236, 10 (°prabodha); eṇa, 178, 3; āya, 100[a]; asya, 117[d]; °m, 137[d]; cf. a°.
chirāya, °ti, 222, 7.
chihna, 249, 2 (bhāva°); 303, 5.
China, 'China;' °anśuka, 34[b].
r. chud, caus. chodayati, 17, 10.
chumbita, 4[a]; 78[d].
chūta, 150, 8; 228, 1. 8, &c.; °manjarī, 103[b]; °sura, 140[d].
cheṭī, 228, 1; 249, 11.
chetas, n. 2[b]; 34[a]; 67, 11, &c.
ched, 16, 7; 214, 9. 10; 152[c], &c.
cheshṭamāna, 159[b].
cheshṭā, 51, 12.
cheshṭita, 111[b]; neut. 291, 4.
chyuta, 42[b]; 143[d].

chhanda-, see sva°.
chhandas, 160, 1; °maya, 148, 4.
chhanna, 208, 9 (triṇa°).
chhavi, f. 63[b].
chhāyā, 21, 10; 8c[c]; 109[d]; 108, 7; 196[c]; °druma, 91[b].
r. chhid, chhinatti, &c., 18[d].
chhinna, 15[c] ('darbhānkura).
chheda, 39[a]; 237, 2; 259, 17.
chhedin, 112, 2 (samsaya°).

-ja in ātma°, &c.
jaghana, 61[a] (°gaurava).
jaṭā, 175[c] (°maṇḍala).
jaḍa, 86[b].
r. jan, caus. janayati, 30[b]; 122, 2; 214, 10.
jana, 17[a]; 64[a], n.; ayam janaḥ, 49, 4; 144, 2; °antikam, 38, 9.
janana, 104[d] (°antara); 293, 6; ī, f. 168, 3; 262, 6, &c.
janita, 39, 4; 44, 7.
jantu, m. 104[b]; 189, 8.

janman, n. 12[a]; 126[a]; 182[b], n.; °pratishṭhā, 242, 1.
jaya, 187[a] (°śabda).
Jayanta, 166[b]; 192[a].
jala, 32[b]; 89[a]; °dhi, 197[a].
java, 8[d]; 9[d] (ratha°).
jāgaraṇa, 138[c].
jāta, 28[a]; 65[a]; 102[c]; 258, 6 (artha°); ā, f. 129, 11; 153, 3; °karman, 296, 1.
jāti, f. 218, 8; 253, 9.
jāti or svabhāvokti, 73, n. 1.
Jānuka, 221, 5.
jāyā, 258, 19.
jāla, 219, 4; 180[b]; °ka, 30[c].
r. ji, 71, 1; 85, 2; 197[b]; 65, 3.
jita, 187[a].
jīrṇa, 72, 4 (°riksha); 175[b].
r. jīv, jīvati, 68, 9; 306, 6.
jīva, 65[b]; °sarva-sva, 134[a].
jīvita, n. 10[c]; 122, 11; 266, 9; °sarva-sva, 41, 9, n.
r. jṛibh, jṛimbhate, 286, 3.
josham, adv. 202, 8.
-jña, 173, 3; 258, 4; 20[c].
r. jñā, jānāti, 13[b]; 17, 14, &c.
jñāta, 100, 2.
jñāti, 163, 5; 110[c]; 119[a].
jyā, 38[a]; 66[c]; °bandha, 40[d].
jyotis, 26[b]; 131[d]; pl. 170[b].
jyotsnā in vana°, 28, 3, &c.
r. jval, jvalati, 56[b]; 163[a].

ḍimbha, 290, 4 (°līlā).

ta- in °tas, °tra, &c.; see tad.
taṭa, 174, 13; 122[b] (°taru).
ta-tas, 9, 2; 54[b]; 23[b], n.; °tatas, 140, 2; °prabhṛiti, 110, 7.
tati, 40[c] (varāha°).
tat-tva, 24[d]; °tas, 32, 1.
ta-tra, 66, 7; 102, 10; °bhavat, 22, 11; °bhavatī, 81, 5, &c.
ta-thā, 20, 9; 13, 10, &c.; °api, 32, 1, &c.; °hi, 12, 2, &c.; °bhāvin, 311, 6; °vidha, 195[d].
tathya, 27, 4.
tad, 94[d], &c.; cf. yad; tena, 10, 7; tena hi, 10, 10; 303, 5, &c.; tat, adv. 4, 4; °api, 62[b]; °anantaram, 194[b]; °nimitta, adj. 106, 7; °maya, adj. 153[a].
ta-dā, 28, 5, &c.; cf. yadā; °prabhṛiti, 233, 6.
r. tan, tanoti, 20[b].
tanaya, 99[c]; 100[b]; ā, f. 132[a].
tanu, 1[d]; tanvī, f. 20[c]; 46[b]; °gātrī, 70[a]; °bhāva, 172[c].
tantra, 187, 4 (loka°).
tantrayitvā, ind. 107[a].
r. tap, tapati, 69[b]; 70[a].
tapa, 65[b] (°atyaya).

tapat, 116b.

tapas, 3c, 9; 54a, &c.; pl. 279, 7; 176d; °kshama, 18b; °vin, 13, 6; 21, 5; 48, 6; 150, 5, n.; °dhana, 13a; °vana, 17, 14, 15; 20, 4.

tapasya, -yati, 173b; 176d.

tapta, 60b; 247, 4 (anusaya°).

tamas, 116b; 140b; 188°, n.

taranga, 60a (Mālinī°).

tarala, 26b (prabhā°).

Tarulikā, 256, 9. 14.

taras-vin, 258, 13.

taru, 14a; 114a; °mūla, 184d.

taruṇa, 248, 13.

r. tark, °ayati, 22, 5; 248, 9.11.

tarka, 107, 14; 196, 6, &c.

-tarkin in evam°, 291, 5.

r. tarj, caus. 48, 1.

tarhi, 253, 11; yadi—°, 2, 3.

tala, 26b; 121, 2 (silā°); 30a, n.

tāḍayitvā, ind. 217, 3.

tāḍita, 40a.

tāḍyamāna, 184, 9.

tāta, 22, 4; 154, 17; 168, 4, &c.

tādrisa, 107, 10; 135, 2, &c.

tāpa, m. 91b; 62°; 65a, &c.

tāpasa, 61, 5; 94, 3 (°kanyakā); i, f. 153, 2; °vriddhā, 208, 2.

tāmra, 74d (padma°); 134a.

tāla, 74b (°vrinta).

tāvat, 2, 3; 6, 6; 17, 8.10; 158a, &c.; °—yāvat, 19, 9, 10; mā°, 203, 5.

tintiḍikā, 78, 4.

timira, n. 162d.

tiras-kariṇī, 227, 5; 266, 11.

tila, 111, 4, n. (°udaka).

tikshṇa, 254, 2 (°danda).

tīrṇa, 197a (°jaladhi).

tīrtha, 17, 3, n.; 151, 1, &c.

tīvra, adj. 109°; 33a (°āghāta).

tu, 34, 11; 78d, &c.; cf. kintu.

tura-ga, 32a; 60, 4.

turanga, 106a (yukta°).

tulya, 117° (°guṇa).

tushāra, 120° (antar°).

tūṇa, 136d (°ardha-krishṭa).

tūshṇīm, adv. 182, 8.

triṇa, 208, 9 (°channa).

tritīya, 13, 11, n. (ātmanā°).

trishita, 151a.

tejas, 41bd; 179a; 84a.

taikshṇya, n. 100, 2.

taila, 94b; 81, 3 (ingudī°).

toya, 176b; 14d (°ādhāra).

toshita, 165b (avadāna°).

tyakta, 156b.

r. tyaj, tyajati, 127a.

-tyāgin, 130b (dāra°).

-tra in ātapa°, 108d.

traya, n. 191b (bhuvana°).

trāṇa, 11b.

tri, tisṛi, f. 248, 4; °diva, 167b; °srotas, 170a; Tri-sanku, 91, 6.

tritaya, n. 193b.

tretāgni, 148, n. 1.

r. trai, trāyate, 240, 9.

tva, 5, 4; 12a, &c.; tvat-tas, 22, 4; in comp. tvad-, e. g. 169d (°carita); 164a (°mati).

tvac, 175a (sarpa°).

r. tvar, tvarate, 146, 7; 152, 2; 176, 13; caus. 26, 2.

tvarā, 229, 1.

r. dans, dasati, 296, 7.

Daksha, 191d.

dakshiṇa, 98°; eṇa, 21, 4; 165, 4.

dakshiṇa, 149, n.

daṇḍa, 110a, n.; 108d; 62, 7.

datta, 70, 3; 124, 8 (°drishṭi).

dattvā, ind. 21, 3, &c. (karṇam°).

dadat, 6a.

dadhāna, 84a.

danta, 33a; 181a; 286, 3.

damana, 197° (prasabha°).

dayamāna, 4b.

darpaṇa, 196d (°tala).

darbha, 7°; 15°, n.; 88b.

darsana, 17, 10; 21, 7; 35a; 86b.

darsanīya, 196, 7; 248, 5, &c.

darsayat, 221, 2.

darsayitarya, 310, 10.

darsita, 61, 6; 206, 4.

-darsin, 22, 11; 180, 10 (evam°).

dala, 74b; 75a (nalinī°).

dasā, 82d (°antara).

dasyu, m. 121d.

r. dah, dahati, 70a; 141d, &c.

r. dā, dadāti, 21, 6; 137°, &c.

Dākshāyaṇī, 283, 10; 304, 12.

dākshiṇya, 137°.

Dānava, 268, 7; 167b.

dāpita, 223, 13.

dāra, 293, 9; 294, 2; m. pl. 97°, n.

dāraka, 298, 5.

dāruṇa, 124a; 245, 7; 161d.

dāsya, n. 128d.

dāsyāḥ-putra, 61, 1, n.; 75, 2.

dāhātmaka, 41b.

div, 274, 9; divā, 69a; 107d; divas-pati, 269, 13.

dira, 106b; °okas, 271, 12; 169d.

divasa, m. 3b; 126, 4; 144a.

dishṭa, n. 59, 4.

dishṭyā, 186a; 112, 10; 193a.

dīkshita, 50b.

dīpa, 262, 4.

dīpaka, 87, n. 1.

dīpti-mat, 85, 11.

dīrgha, 185d; °m, adv. 259, 16; °tara, 96a; °apānga, 206, 13; °āyus, 91, 1; 307, 8.

duḥkha, n. 109, 5; 64a, &c.;

ena, 130, 12; 164, 3; °sīla, 146, 1; °uttara, 189, 9.

duḥkhita, 242, 10 (viyoga°).

dur- or dus- in °saha, 83d; °avāpa, 50, 2; °āpa, 67d; °āsada, 10, 8; °ita, n. 88c; Dur-jaya, 268, 7; °moca, 290, 4; °labha, 17a; 154, 2; °lalita, 289, 4; °vāra, 137, 13; Dur-rāsas, 137, 12; °vinīta, 34, 4; 25a; °kara, 170, 9.

Durgā-pūjā, 227, n. 1.

r. dush, caus. 298, 5; 182°.

dushṭa, 34, 4 (°madhukara).

Dushyanta, 5b; 95, 4, &c.

duhitṛi, 17, 2; 198, 7; °jana, m. 139, 13, 14.

dūyamāna, 132b.

dūra, 112, 4 (°gata); °e, 9d; °m, adv. 9, 8; °tas, 53a; °ī-krita, 17b.

dūrbā, 151, 1.

dūshita, 111a.

r. dris, pasyati, 6b; 17, 5; 16, 7; 55b, &c.; pasya, 7d; 10, 12; caus. 35, 7; 247, 8, &c.

drisya, 97°; 147b.

drishṭa, 76, 11; 238, 5; 257, 14.

drishṭi, 24a; 70, 3, &c.; °rāga, 81, 7; °vibhrama, 23d, n.

drishṭvā, ind. 35, 4; 127, 5.

deva, 44, 11; 45, 2; 70, 7, &c.; devī, 90, 17; 184, 4; pl. 90, 7; °guru, 293, 4; °tā, 85°; 136, 2; 241, 11 (pati°).

desa, 10, 8; 19a (skandha°); 39, 6; °antara, 175, 1.

Daitya, 49°.

daiva, n. 17, 3; 135, 11; 299, 6.

dosha, 127, 6; 105, 12; 262, 5.

dauvārika, 69, 12; 70, 1, &c.

Daushyanti, 100b.

dauhitra, m. 214, 10 (muni°).

dyo, f. 48°.

drashṭavya, 76, 10.

druta-padam, adv. 257, 7.

druma, 32d; 46d; 91b.

dva, 1b; 52, 8; 85, 2; 73a.

drandva, 48° (cāraṇa°); 191d.

dvaya, n. 91, 3; 55b; 82c (tejas°).

dvādasa-dhā, 191a (°sthita).

dvāra, n. 20, 11; 16b; 61b, &c.

dvi- in °ja, 123d; 160a; °dhā, 229, 12; °pa, 107d (°indra).

dvitīya, 87, 3; 88, 13 (sārathi°).

r. dvish, dveshṭi, 137a.

dvīpa, 197b (saptan°).

dvesha, 201, 2 (krita-kārya°).

dvaidha-, 'twofold,' in °ī-bhāva, 47, 4; °ī-bhū, 51a.

dhana, 81b (tapas°); 97a; Dhana-mitra, 258, 12.

nish-patat, 171[a].
ni-shyanda, 14[d].
ni-sarga, 81, 2.
nis-tamas in °*ka*, 170[c].
ni-syandin, 279, 4. 5 (*rasa*°).
ni-hantṛi, 162[b].
ni-hita, 295, 10 (*uras*°).
r. *nī*, *nayati*, 198[d]; 96, 3; 150, 3.
nīḍa, 175[c] (*śakunta*°).
nīta, 58[b]; 241, 9.
nīyamāna, 34[b].
nīla, 'blue;' °*lohita*, 199[c]; °*ut-pala*, 18[c].
Nīla-kaṇṭha, 257, n. 2.
nīvāra, 14[a]; 84, 2; 152, 7; °*bali*, 101[b].
nu, 5, 8; 43[b], &c.
nūnam, 30, 3; 37, 5; 56[a], &c.
nṛi-pa, 47[a].
netṛi, 144[d].
netra, 104, 6 (°*nirvāṇa*).
nepathya, 2, 2; e, 3, n. 2; 13, 2, &c.; °*vidhāna*, 2, 3.
nemi, 171[d]; 174[a] (*rathānga*°).
naipuṇa, 157, 2.
naimittika, 194[c] (*nimitta*°).
naiśa, adj. 162[d].
nau-vyasana, 258, 12.
ny-asta, 62[a]; 66[b] (*bhuja*°).
ny-āsa, 102[d].

pakshman, 189[c] (*ā-kuṭila*°).
pakshmala, 78[c] (°*akshī*).
panka-ja, n. 129[a]; 180[d].
pankti, 61[b].
pañcan, 135[b] (°*abhyadhika*).
Pañca-vāṇa, 99, n. 1.
paṭa, 117, 5; 209, 10 (°*anta*); °*ākshepa*, 144, 1; 230, 4.
paṭu-tva, 123[a].
paṭṭa, 105, 1 (*śilā*°); °*ka*, 239, 6.
paṭhitvā, ind. 265, 1.
r. *paṭ*, *paṭati*, 32[c]; 72, 4; 81, 3; 161[d]; caus. 122[a]; 238, 3.
patana, 7[b] (*śara*°).
pati, 16, 12; 82[a], &c.; °*devatā*, 241, 11; °*vratā*, 283, 10.
patita, 147, 9; 147[b]; 296, 2.
pattra, 18[c] (°*dhārā*); 60, 2; 96, 3 (*nalinī*°); 258, 7 (°*arūḍha*).
pattrikā, 258, 10.
pattrin, 230, 11.
patnī, 156[a] (*dharma*°); °*ka*, 258, 15 (*bahu*°); 173[b] (*sa*°).
path, 275, 1.
-*patha*, 13, 5; 14[d]; 110, 2.
pathika, 135[b].
pathin, 91[d]; 166, 3; 179, 4.
pada, 40, 1; 46[b]; 100[d]; 95[d]; 145, 7, n.; 16[a] (*āśrama*°); 68[a], &c.; °*pankti*, 61[b]; °*ban-dhana*, 116, 7; °*antara*, 34, 2. 13, &c.

padarī, 94[d]; 277, 1 (*megha*°).
padma, 176[b]; 74[d] (°*tāmra*).
panna-ga, m. 163[a].
payas, n. 21, 6; 194[b]; °*da*, 80[d]; °*dhara*, 24, 2.
para, 260, 1; 196, 9 (°*kalatra*); 191[c]; °*m*, adv. with abl. 122, 7; 157[a]; cf. *ataḥ*°; °*tā*, 241, 6; °*bhṛita*, 90[c]; *ā*, f. 123[d]; °*bhṛitikā*, 228, 8. 6; °*vat*, 81, 5; 54[a]; °*vaśa*, 49, 4; *parasparam*, 53, 6.
parakīya, 102[a]; 184, 9.
para-ma, 'best;' °*artha*, 52[b]; °*artha-tas*, 107, 11; 205, 4.
paras-tāt, adv. 46, 5, n.
parān-mukha, 144, 2; 129[b].
parā-mṛiśya, ind. 205, 8.
-*parāyaṇa*, 36[d] (*mad*°); 72[a].
parā-vṛit, 167, 8.
parā-vṛitta, 215, 12.
pari-karman, 62, 2, 3.
pari-kalpita, 43[a].
pari-kram, 26, 3, &c.
pari-kramya, ind. 20, 10, &c.
pari-kshata, 57, 16.
pari-kshipta, 104, 1 (*vetasa*°).
pari-gata, 199[d]; 269, 13.
pari-gṛihīta, 120[b] (*prathama*°).
pari-gṛihya, ind. 88, 5.
pari-graha, 22[a]; 129[b]; 132[a]; °*bahu-tva*, 73[a].
pari-grahītṛi, 102[b].
pari-gha, 49[b]; 279, 5 (*megha*°).
pari-ćaya, 156, 12; 182, 6.
pari-ćarat, 313, 2.
pari-ćārikā, 238, 8.
pari-ćita, 112[c]; cf. *a*°.
pari-ćumbya, ind. 103[b].
pari-ććhanna, 227, 5.
pari-jana, 75, 4. 7; 98[c].
pari-jñā, 227, 3.
pari-jñāta, 83, 7.
pari-ṇata, 32[c]; 130, 5.
pari-ṇaya, 203, 2; 204, 4.
pari-ṇāma, 3[b]; 299, 2; 301, 5.
pari-ṇāha, 19[b].
pari-ṇīta, 76[b]; 146, 3; 200, 12.
pari-ṇetṛi, 119[c].
pari-tas, 80[b]; 88[a].
pari-tāpa, 71[b]; 109[d].
pari-tosha, 2[a]; 159, 3.
pari-tyakta, 92[a]; 247, 4, &c.
pari-tyaj, 212, 5.
pari-tyajat, 164, 3.
pari-tyāyin, 168, 2; 293, 9.
pari-trai, 34, 3. 4. 7; 81, 2.
pari-datta, 147, 10.
pari-devin, 212, 5.
pari-dhā, 158, 2. 4.
pari-dhūsara, adj. 185[a].
pari-patana, 253, 2, 3.
pari-pā, caus. 58, 1; 164[a].

pari-pālana, 108[b].
pari-bādhamāna, 189[b].
pari-bādhā, 75[b] (°*peluva*).
pari-bhāvin, 78, 5; 137, 4.
pari-bhukta, 132, 1, 2.
pari-bhoga, 130, 11.
pari-bhrashṭa, 174, 13; 246, 3.
pari-mukta, 223, 9.
pari-mṛij, 241, 11.
pari-lagna, 58, 1 (*śākhā*°).
pari-varta, 198[c].
pari-vartin, 165, 7; 227, 5, 6.
pari-vardhita, 282, 4; °*ka*, 94[c].
pari-raha, 170[d].
pari-vāra, 63, 1.
pari-vāhin, 158, 6; 183, 7.
pari-vṛit, 177[b].
pari-vṛita, 62, 4.
pari-śrama, 37, 3; 40, 1.
pari-śrānta, 37, 5; 52, 11.
pari-shad, f. 4, 2; 6, 2.
pari-shvajamāna, 158, 6.
pari-shvajya, ind. 147, 7.
pari-shvanj, 174, 5; 176, 4, &c.
pari-samāpta, 110[d].
pari-samūpya, ind. 134, 10.
pari-haraṇīya, 93, 9.
pari-hā, pass. 5, 2; 108, 6, &c.
pari-hārya, 77, 9; 122, 2.
pari-hāsa, 47, 3; 52[b]; 240, 3.
pari-hṛi, 128, 12; 258, 4.
parīkshya, ind. 125[a].
parīta, 112[d] (*hutavaha*°).
parusha, 212, 8 (*pratyādeśa*°).
paroksha, 303, 16; 52[a].
parṇa, 172[b]; cf. *sapta*°.
pary-anta, 167, 2 (*uṭaja*°).
pary-ākula, 30[d]; 57, 5; 216, 7.
pary-āpta, 135, 14.
pary-āya, 226, 4.
pary-utsuka, 39, 6; 106, 7; 224, 12 (°*manas*); °*i-bhū*, 104[b].
pary-upāsana, 38, 2.
parvata, 279, 7.
parvan, 167[c]; °*bhāga*, 85[c].
pallava, 26, 2; 89[b]; 152[a], &c.
pallavita, 112, 12.
palvala, 40[c].
pavana, m. 15[a]; 60[b]; 91[d].
paśu, 133[b]; 159[b]; 267, 10.
paśća, 7[b] (°*ardha*).
paśćāt, adv. 34[a]; 61[a]; 245, 2, &c.; °*tāpa*, 233, 6; 234, 13.
paśyat, 29, 2.
r. *pā*, *pivati*, 89[a]; 151[b]; 60, 3.
r. *pā*, caus. *pālayati*, 306, 6.
pāṇsula, adj. 130[h].
pāṭaććara, 218, 8; 252, 12.
pāṭala, 3[a]; 187[b].
pāṇḍu, 19[d]; 61[b]; 85[a]; 115[b].
pāṇḍura, adj. 63[b]; 134[a].
pātra, 129, 7; 240, 12, &c.; cf. *prati*°; °*i-kṛita*, 121[d].

ṇa-kolāhala, 61, 1, 2 ; °grā-hin, 74, 4 ; °ćara, 67, 5 (°vṛitti) ; °jyotsnī, 28, 3 ; 29, 1, &c. ; °devatā, 85[c] ; °pushpa, 62, 4 ; °rāji, 60, 1 ; 180, 2 ; °latā, 17[b] ; °rāsa, 252, 2 ; 90[b] (°bandhu) ; °okas, 173, 2.
vanas-pati, 155, 5 ; 156, 6, 7.
r. vand, vandate, 158, 9.
vandana, 307, 2 (pāda°).
vandamāna, 205, 12 ; 246, 2.
vapus, 17[a] ; 18[a] ; 24, 10 ; 43[d], &c.
r. ram, vamati, 41[d].
vayasya, 59, 4, n. ; 65, 2 ; 68, 11, &c. ; °ka, 225, 9 (priya°) ; °bhāva, 59, 4.
vara, 30, 1 ; 49, 5 ; 159, 6 ; 117[c], &c. ; cf. svayam° ; °prārthanā, 47, 4.
varāha, 59, 5 ; 40[c] (°tatt).
-varćasa (= varćas), 238, 5 (brahman°).
-varjam, 153, 8 (Gautamī°).
varjayitvā, ind. 112, 11 ; 296, 2.
varṇa, 195, 9 (mukha°) ; 169[b] ; 118, 11 ; 181[b] (avyakta°) ; pl. 47[a] ; 112[b] ; °parićaya, 182, 6 ; °āśrama, 194, 11.
rarnikā, 147[b] (°uććhrāsa).
vartikā, 249, 6 ; 256, 4.
-vartin, 10, 8 ; 13, 5 ; cf. ćakra°.
vartman, 7[c] (kīrṇa°).
valaya, 33[b] ; 62[a] ; 102, 9 ; 66[d] (kanaka°) ; 138[b], &c.
valkala, 14[d] ; 23, 8 ; 19[b] ; 24, 10.
valmīka, 175[a].
vallabha, adj. 27[c] ; ā, f. 123, 11 (bahu-vallabha).
r. vaś, vashṭi, &c., 184[b].
vaśa in para°, 49, 4.
vaśin, 48[c] ; 129[b].
Vaśishṭha, 91, n. 3.
vasati, 48[a] ; 103[c] ; cf. saha°.
rasana, 185[a].
vasanta, 46, 2, n. (°avatāra) ; °māsa, 134[a] ; °utsava, 227, n. 1 ; 230, 5.
vasāna, part. 185[a].
vasu-dhā, 214, 18 ; 197[b] ; °tala, 26[b].
vasun-dharā, 156[d].
vasu-matī, 25[a] ; Vasu-matī, 184, 4 ; 256, 9, 10.
vastu, 4, 3.
r. vah, vahati, 1[a] ; 170[a].
-vah in srotas°, 51[b].
-vaha in ganḍa°, huta°.
vahat, 181[c].
vahni, 56[a] ; 88[d] ; 179[b].
rā, 39, 6 ; 40, 1. 6, &c. ; ka-tham°, 26[a] ; kim°, 116, 2 ; 168[a], &c. ; cf. atha°.

vākya, 68, 7 (suhṛid°) ; 315, 3.
vāć, 31[a] ; 207, 7 ; 137[c].
vāćanaka, 152, 8 (svasti°).
vāćā, 65, 2, &c. ; 288, 2 (°mātra).
vāćya, adj. 97[d] ; neut. 117[d].
vājin, m. 12, 2 ; 13, 8 ; 20, 7.
vāṭikā, 21, 4 (vṛiksha°).
vāṇa, 13, 5 ; 10[a] ; 53[a] ; 55[d], &c. ; 238, 2 (Kandarpa°) ; °asana, 62, 3.
vāta, 3[a] ; 26, 2 ; 74[a], &c.
Vātāyana, 236, 16.
-vādin, 121, 6 ; 211, 6 (satya°).
vāma, 98[d] ; 141, 2 ; 138[a] ; 149[d] ; 253, 9 ; °itara, 194, 6.
vāyu, 170[d].
vāraṇa, 252, 16.
vāri, 171[c] (°garbhodara).
vārita, 29[a] (°prasara) ; 45[c] ; 253, 7.
vāshpa, 86[b] ; 95[b] ; 189[b,d].
vāsa, 90[b] (vana°) ; 252, 2 ; cf. saha°.
vāsantika, 230, 10.
Vāsava, 306, 4 (°anuyojya).
-vāsin, 19, 9 (tapovana°) ; 122, 4 (vishaya°) ; 188, 4 ; āśra-ma°, 20, 6 ; 17[a] ; 188, 12.
-vāha in sūrtha°, 258, 12.
-vāhin in kaṇa°, 60[a].
vāhyāntaḥ-karaṇa, 276, 2.
vi-karshaṇa, 99, n. 1.
vi-kala, 62, 5 ; 157[c] (prasūti°).
vi-kāra, 38, 5. 6, n. ; 107, 11 ; 297, 9 ; 195[d].
vi-kṛi, caus. 145, 8.
vikṛiti-mat, 39[b].
vi-kṛish, pass. 161[b].
vi-klṛip, pass. 116, 4.
vi-krama, 170[c] (Hari°).
Vikramāditya, 316, n.
vi-kraya, 221, 2.
vi-kriyā, 296, 9.
vi-klava, 67, 11 ; 78[b] ; 105[d] ; 240, 14 ; 269, 8.
vi-gata, 189[d] (°anuśaya).
vi-gam, caus. 137[b].
ri-guṇa, 261, 2 (°udvega).
vi-ghaṭita, 130, 9.
vi-ghna, 13[a] ; 40, 8 ; 44, 12 ; 88, 12 ; 111[a] ; °vat, 131, 2.
vi-ćar, caus. 202, 6 ; 258, 15.
vi-ćārayat, 202, 3.
vi-ćārya, ind. 48, 6 ; 214, 3.
vi-ćintayat, 81[a].
vi-ćintya, ind. 92, 5 ; 97[a], &c.
vi-ććhitti, 169[a] (°śesha).
vi-ććhinna, 9[b].
vi-jaya, 49[d] ; 90, 6 ; 269, 1.
vi-jalpa, 240, 3 (parihāsa°).
vi-jalpita, 52[b] (parihāsa°).
vi-ji, 87, 10 ; 89, 9 ; 190, 3, &c.
vi-jñā, caus. 57, 12 ; 188, 11.

vi-jñāna, 2[a] (prayoga°).
vi-jñāpita, 139, 12.
viṭapa, 21[a] ; 32[b] ; 104, 5, &c.
vi-ḍamb, 66, 4 ; 64, 2 (pass.)
viḍāla, 266, 8.
Viḍ-aujas or Viḍ-ojas, 198[a].
vi-tata, 198[b] (°yajña).
vi-tāna, 76, 3 (°sanātha).
vi-tṛī, 194, 9 ; 304, 1.
vitta, n. 193[b].
r. vid, vetti, 81[b] ; 128[c] ; 158[d].
vidita, 54[a] ; 88, 8, &c. ; °dhar-man, 127, 5 ; °bhakti, 17, 5.
viditvā, ind. 41, 4.
vi-dūshaka, 59, 2, 3, n.
viddha, 94[b] (kuśa-sūći°).
vidyā, 147, 10 ; 126[d].
vidvas, 2[a].
vi-dhā, 1[b].
vi-dhātṛi, pl. 308, 9.
vi-dhāna, 2, 3 (nepathya°).
vi-dhi, 43[b] ; 44[d] ; 134, 4 (vi-vāha°) ; 188, 12 ; 138[a] ; 193[b], &c. ; °vat, adv. 196, 14 ; °huta, adj. 1[a].
vi-nata, 63[b] (prakāma°).
vi-naya, 29[a] ; 45[c] (°vārita) ; 127, 2.
vinā, prep. with acc. 148, 4 ; with inst. 168, 3 ; 96[a] ; 151[b].
vi-nindita, 133[a].
vi-nipāta, m. 211, 9. 11.
ri-niyoga, 156, 13 (ābharaṇa°).
vi-nivartita, 190[c] (°karman).
vi-niveśa, 147[a] (anguli°).
vi-nīta, 20, 4 (°vesha).
vi-nud, caus. 102, 7 ; 150, 5.
vi-noda, 37, 3 (pariśrama°) ; 39[d] ; °sthāna, 236, 8 ; 249, 5.
vi-nodin, 74[a] (klama°).
vindu, 89, 13 ; 248, 12 ; 189[b].
vi-panna, 258, 13.
vi-paryaya, 214, 11.
vipula-tā, 9[a].
vi-pra-kṛi, 286, 5, 6 ; 154, 8, 9.
vi-prakṛita, 98[b] ; 163[a].
vi-prakṛishṭa, 10, 7 (°antara).
vi-pralabdha, 212, 4.
vi-pra-labh, 213, 3.
vi-buddha, 139[b].
vi-budha, 176[c] (°strī).
vi-bhava, 99[b] ; 110[c] ; 227, 3.
vi-bhā, 180[b].
ri-bhāta, n. 120[c].
vibhu-tva, 43[d].
vi-bhū, caus. 29, 7 ; 141, 4 ; 143[h].
vi-bhettṛi, 168[c].
vi-bhrama, 23[d] (dṛishṭi°) ; 229, 4.
vi-marda, 295, 6.
vi-marshṭavya, 221, 6.
vi-mānita, 235, 6.
vi-mānya, 121[b].

ry-alika, 188[a] (*pratyādeśaᵒ*).
vy-avasita, 146, 2; 141[a]; 204, 3.
vy-ava-so, 18[d]; 89[a].
vy-avahārin, 258, 12; (*samudraᵒ*).
vy-avahita, 215, 2 (*sūpaᵒ*).
vy-asana, 39[d]; 258, 12 (*nauᵒ*); *ᵒudaya,* du. 82[c].
vy-ādhi, m. 236, 4.
vy-ādhunvat, 24[c], n.
vy-āpadyamāna, 13, 1.
vy-āpāra, 27[b]; 58, 7, &c.; 294, 2; cf. *yathoktaᵒ, yathoddishṭaᵒ.*
vy-āpin, 175[c] (*ansaᵒ*).
vy-āpṛita, 164[b]; 296, 16.
vy-āpya, ind. 1[b].
vyāyata-tva, 38[o], n.
vyāhārālankāra, 91, n. 3.
r. *vraj, vrajati,* 9[a].
vraṇa, 94[a] (*ᵒviropaṇa*).
vrata, 27[a]; 128[c]; 184[c]; 185[d].
rratati, 33[b].
vratin, 111[a].
vrīḍā, 156, 4; 137[d].

r. *śak, śaknoti,* 58, 6; 108, 3; 120[d]; desid. *śikshate,* 23[c].
śakuni, 61, 1 (*ᵒlubdhaka*).
śakunta, 175[c] (*ᵒnīḍa-niḍita*); *ᵒlāvaṇya,* 294, 4.
Śakuntalā, 1, 1; 4, 3; 26, 1. 5, &c.
śakta, 37[a]; 79[d].
śakti, 158[d]; 199[d]; cf. *yathāᵒ.*
śakya, 60[a]; 140, 8; 158[b]; 288, 2.
Śakra, 'Indra;' *ᵒavatāra,* 205, 12; 218, 6.
r. *śank, śankate,* 136[d].
śankā, 188[d] (*ahiᵒ*); 309, 10 (*aparādhaᵒ*); 44, 11 (*jāta-śanka*).
-śankin, 176, 11 (*pāpaᵒ*); 205, 4 (*paraparigrahaᵒ*).
Śaśi-tīrtha, 205, 12; 246, 2.
śata, 58[a]; 198[c] (*yugaᵒ*); *Śata-kratu,* 162[a]; 273, 2.
śapta, 310, 7.
śaptvā, ind. 137, 13.
r. *śabd, śabdayati,* 257, 7.
śabda, 14[c]; 44, 7 (*ujjhitaᵒ*); 48[d], &c.; *ᵒanusāra,* 285, 8.
śabdāya, -yate, 152, 3 (pass.)
r. *śam,* caus. 17, 3; 109[d].
śama, 101[a]; *ᵒpradhāna,* 41[a].
śamī, 18[d] (*ᵒlatā*); 84[b].
śayana, 107, 5; *kusumaᵒ,* 71[a]; 75[a]; *ᵒbhūmi,* 216, 7.
śayita, 147, 2 (*sukhaᵒ*).
śayitavya, 60, 5.
śayyā, 79[a]; 137[b] (*ᵒprānta*).
śara, 7[b]; 10[d]; 13, 1, &c.; *ᵒasana,* 124[d]; 161[b]; 265, 7.

śaraṇa, 159[d]; *agniᵒ,* 148, 4, &c.
śarad, 150[c] (*ᵒchandra*).
śararya, n. 161[a].
śarīra, 10[b]; 44, 4; 97, 1, &c.; *ᵒbhūta,* 226, 7.
Śarmishṭhā, 87[a].
śalabha, 32[d] (*ᵒsamūha*).
śalya, 141[d]; 302, 2 (*vishādaᵒ*).
śaśa, 'a hare;' *ᵒanka,* 70[b]; 129[a]; 113, 2 (*ᵒlekhā*).
śaśin, 83[a]; 186[b].
śaśvat, adv. 112[c].
śastra, 11[b]; 269, 1 (*āttaᵒ*).
Śākalya in *vriddhaᵒ,* 283, 9.
śākhā, 58, 1 (*kuravakaᵒ*); 46[d]; 149[c]; *ᵒbāhā,* 165, 7.
śākhin, m. 15[a].
śāṭhya, 126[a].
śānta, 16[a]; 91[d]; 100[d]; *ᵒm,* interj. 204, 9.
śānti, 97, 3 (*ᵒudaka*).
śāpa, 140, 5; 145, 8; 215, 2, &c.
Śāradvata, 193, 7, &c.
śārnga, 265, 16; *ᵒhasta,* 265, 6; *Śārnga-rava,* 161, 5; 193, 6, &c.; 160, 6 (*ᵒmiśra*).
śārdūla, 59, 5; 159[b].
śālā, 182, 4 (*sangītaᵒ*).
śālīna-tā, 82, 10.
Śālmali, 312, n.
śāva, 52[a] (*mrigaᵒ*); 295, 6.
śāśvata, 42, 9.
śāsat, 25[a].
śāsana, 222, 1. 16; 230, 11, &c.
śāsitri, 25[a]; 252, 16.
śiksh, śikshate, 23[c]; see *śak.*
śikshita, 2[b]; cf. *aᵒ.*
śikhaṇḍaka, 184, 8.
śikhara, 172[a].
śikhā, 8[b]; 14[d]; 152, 7; 4[a] (*keśara-śikha*).
śithila, 40[d]; 42[b]; 248, 11.
śithilaya, -yati, 23, 9. 11.
śiras, 130, 5; 188[d]; cf. *raṇaᵒ; ᵒdhara,* 265, 2.
śirīsha, 4[b]; 30[c]; 150[b].
śilā, 79[a]; *ᵒtala,* 76, 3; 176[o]; *ᵒpaṭṭa,* 105, 1; *ᵒpaṭṭaka,* 239, 6.
śiva, adj. 91[d]; 179, 4.
Śiva, 2, n.; 315, n. 1.
śiśira, 136[c]; 237, 2.
śiśu, 294, 1; 15[d] (*hariṇaᵒ*); 178[b] (*sinhaᵒ*); 182[d] (*sarpaᵒ*).
śishya, 95, 2, 3; 142, 2, 3, &c.
śikara, 171[d] (*ᵒklinna-nemi*).
śighram, adv. 114, 2.
śita, 107[d]; *ᵒraśmi-tva,* 55[a].
śitala, 37, 2 (*pracchāyaᵒ*); 74[a].
-śīrsha, 81, 3 (*chikkaṇaᵒ*).
śīla, 59, 4 (*mrigayāᵒ*); 146, 1 (*duḥkhaᵒ*); 185[c] (*śuddhaᵒ*).
śuka, 14[a]; *ᵒudaru,* 118, 10.

śuc, f. 99[d].
śuci, adj. 113[a]; 128[c].
śuddha, 196[d]; *ᵒśila,* 185[c]; *ᵒhṛidaya,* 145, 7; *ᵒanta,* 17[a]; 214, 11.
śubha, n. pl. 194, 8; 188[c].
śūnya, 79[d]; 266, 5; 205, 9 (*angulīyakaᵒ*); *ᵒhṛidaya,* 137, 11; 310, 9.
śūla, 224, 4.
śūlya, 60, 4 (*ᵒmānsa*).
śṛinga, 40[a]; 149[d].
śṛingāra, 41, 3 (*ᵒlajjā*).
śesha, 115, 2 (*devatāᵒ*); 157[d]; 169[a] (*vicchittiᵒ*); *Śesha,* 106[c].
śaithilya, 309, 1 (*smṛitiᵒ*).
śaila, 51[b]; 172[a].
śairala, 20[a].
śoka, 101[a]; 180, 5; *ᵒpātra,* 240, 12 (*ᵒātman*).
śocanīya, 123, 12 (*bandhu-janaᵒ*); 204, 3; 243, 7; 244, 6.
śocya, 63[c].
śoṇita, 159[a] (*ᵒarthin*).
śobhana, 218, 4.
śobhā, 19[c]; 83[b].
śobhin, 252, 9 (*pallavaᵒ*).
śoshaṇa, 63[d].
śaundika, 225, 11 (*ᵒāpaṇa*).
śyāma, 49[a]; 65[b] (*abhraᵒ*).
śyāmāka, 94[c].
śyāla, 217, 2, &c.
śrad-dhā, 193[b].
śrad-dheya, 211, 11.
śrama, 7[c]; 102, 7 (*ᵒklānta*); 108[c].
śravaṇa, 48, 3; 58[c]; *ᵒkātara-tā,* 64[d].
śrāddha, 111, n. 1.
śrānta, 107[b] (*ᵒmanas*).
śrī, 67[c]; 24, 11 (*alankāraᵒ*); 260, 1 (*Puruvansaᵒ*).
r. *śru, śriṇoti,* 21, 4 (pass.); 105, 2, &c.; desid. *śuśrūshate,* 98[a].
śruta, 47, 4; 110, 9; 233, 2; 313, 1 (*ᵒvistāra*); *ᵒvat,* 242, 1.
śruti, 96, 3; cf. *yathāᵒ; ᵒprasādana-tas,* 6, 2; *ᵒmahat,* 199[b]; *ᵒvishaya-guṇa,* 1[b].
śrutvā, ind. 188, 5; 297, 9.
śreyas, n. 260, 6; 177[b]; 314, 13; pl. 280, 2.
śreshṭhin, 258, 18.
śrotavya, 110, 9; 206, 6; 232, 6.
śrotriya, 133[b], n.
śrauta, 188, 12.
ślāghanīya, 198[d].
ślāghya, 99[a].
śvan, 222, 17.
śvā-pada, 67, 6 (*ᵒanusuraṇa*).
śvāsa, 30[b]; 138[b].

ADDITIONS TO THE INDEX.

ADDITIONS AND CORRECTIONS.

Page 34, line 7, for राञ्च रकिखदाइं read राञ्चरकिखदाइं

„ 51, „ 11, for ग्रहोतुम् read ग्रहीतुम्.

„ 60, „ 7, for कटूणि read कटूनि or rather कटुकानि

„ 66, „ 8 of notes, for *sphuṭārtham* read *sphuṭārtham*

„ 108, „ 14, for निवेदितुम् read निवेदयितुम्

„ 124, „ 4, for °रसना read °रशना

„ 147, „ 4 of notes, for -*praćchikā* read -*pṛićchikā*

„ 196, „ 6, for पडिहिदो read पडिहदो

„ 196, „ 15, for प्रतिहितो read प्रतिहतो

„ 198, „ 10, for मूर्त्तींमती read मूर्त्तिमती

„ 265, „ 2, for पच्चावणद्° read पच्छावणद्°